2

Omnibus

The Stallion
Georgina Brown

La Basquaise
Angel Strand

Healing Passion
Sylvie Ouellette

2
Omnibus

The Stallion
Georgina Brown

La Basquaise
Angel Strand

Healing Passion
Sylvie Ouellette

Doubleday Direct, Inc.

GARDEN CITY, NEW YORK

Black Lace novels are sexual fantasies.
In real life, make sure you practice safe sex.

This omnibus edition published 1995
by BCA
by arrangement with Black Lace

ISBN 1-56865-220-8

Printed in the United States of America

CONTENTS

The Stallion
Georgina Brown

Chapter One

What Ariadne told Penny was a challenge, and one she could not help but rise to.

'You'll get his backing,' Ariadne said, tossing her blonde mane whilst cupping her breast. From there, she ran her hand over her narrow waist, and down over her curving hip. As the hand caressed, her body moved to meet it, undulating appreciatively as if it really belonged to someone else. It was an alluring gesture, inviting, yet evidently self-gratifying. 'But you won't get him,' she added, almost as an afterthought.

Ariadne's eyes seemed to be avoiding her own and for a moment Penny detected an air of insincerity rather than disappointment. Ariadne hated rejection.

Penny raked her fingers through her own hair, which was dark and glossy, and a crowning compliment to the rich creaminess of her skin. At the same time, she asked herself what she'd let herself in for by signing a contract with Alistair Beaumont. The answer was easy. Showjumping cost money. Everyone sought out a wealthy backer nowadays, and he'd made her an offer she couldn't refuse. Besides that, Beaumont was handsome in that classic masculine way that silk shirts and well-cut clothes do heaps to accentuate.

There was, of course, Mark to consider. She lived with Mark, and in the heady days and weeks of early passion, had convinced herself that she would stay with him for ever. So she'd loitered in a comfortable rut until the feeling of being stultified had crept up on her. Suddenly, the urge to move on had become irresistible.

Ariadne had helped her get Alistair Beaumont's backing and she was grateful for it. This extra wager on the side added a little spice to the basic business of securing sponsorship in a very competitive sport.

Penny had known Ariadne since childhood and had once caught her giving one of her own brothers fellatio whilst her other brother pushed his immature, but responsive penis into her golden-haired cleft from behind. They knew each other well, though Ariadne consistently niggled Penny that she did not know herself well enough, that there was more in her than met the eyes.

Penny had taken little notice. She was beautiful, successful (so far), and now she had won the backing of Alistair Beaumont. In addition, Ariadne's wager had intrigued her. What was there to lose in rising to it? Besides, at the end of it, Ariadne's black stallion would be hers. Not that Ariadne would miss this most beautiful animal. Ariadne had a lot of things, in fact, that had seemed to accumulate since leaving Alistair Beaumont's stables. And that was how Penny herself had got his support – Ariadne had arranged it for her.

High breasts, blonde hair and long legs were attributes Ariadne possessed among many others. Penny did not resent that. She'd known Ariadne a long time, regarded her as beautiful, knew she was demanding and also had a particular penchant for intrigue and an abnormal appetite for men. Not that Penny could condemn that. She was very fond of them herself.

'It's a bet, then,' said Ariadne. 'If you can strike it with Alistair, you've won Daedalus – one stallion for another. If not, your horses are mine.'

Penny agreed. The very thought, that Alistair had resisted the temptations Ariadne had in plenty, intrigued her. From what her friend had told her, her benefactor only watched others making out. The very thought filled her with an obsessive determination she didn't know she had.

10

Sponsorship in showjumping was hard to come by, and when someone like Beaumont made an offer, any rider had to sit up and take notice. Horses cost money to keep, and with entry fees rising all the time, there was not one successful showjumper who didn't have the backing of a double-glazing company, a building firm or a multinational corporation.

The very first time she'd seen Beaumont, she'd liked the look of him. Power and wealth gave something extra to a man that made him more alluring. He responded to his wealth, lived up to it, moved like a cat and had eyes that darted over her body like naked flames. Like a moth, she was attracted to those flames. She'd only seen him clothed, but the body beneath the misted blue of an Armani sweater, tailored breeches and high leather boots seemed hard and well formed.

Ariadne had done a season with him. She didn't explain why it was only one season, so Penny took it that her failure to seduce Beaumont must be the reason for her not staying. Failure with regard to men was not something Ariadne took kindly to.

'Everyone rides hard, everyone plays hard, but not him,' Ariadne explained in a voice that edged on sulkiness. 'He stands, watches everything you do, as though he's looking through your clothes – that sort of thing.' She lowered her eyelids in her usual sultry way and leaned closer. 'He watches everyone else making out. He likes watching.' And she smiled in a catlike way.

And you loved it, Penny thought as she felt the hot breath from Ariadne's red lips not far from her neck. 'A voyeur? Is that what you're telling me?'

Ariadne tossed her hair and let it fall unbridled over her bare shoulder. She nodded.

'Then our wager's on? No backing out?' Ariadne asked with a catlike gleam in her eyes. 'You've seen my new stallion. All yours if you get Alistair Beaumont.'

Penny eyed her friend before answering. 'No backing out,' she said at last.

* * *

11

No backing out, she thought to herself. She had not backed out then, and she had not backed out today. Her interview with Alistair Beaumont had started off in an ordinary way; name, career to date, etc. Then he had asked her just how important it was for her to receive his backing and what she was prepared to do to get it.

'Anything,' she had replied.

He'd taken her at her word, and here she was wearing nothing but shoes, a pair of sheer chocolate-coloured stockings and a crisply frilled, but scanty, suspender belt – all, thankfully, covered by the soft opulence of a cashmere coat. Beside her walked Alistair Beaumont.

'How does it feel?' he asked in a husky, sensual voice. His steel-grey eyes did not leave the mix of shoppers and lunch-time office workers ahead and around them.

Somehow Penny didn't want to say anything. What she was doing, what was happening to her was something solitary, for her enjoyment alone. Her very breath caught slightly before release. She yearned to moan her ecstasy, but couldn't. She was in a public place, and although the thought of going public excited her, she kept her pleasure to herself though her eyes sparkled and her skin tingled. Her sex was tantalised and she relied on a rising breeze to cool the heat that burned between her legs and would not be fully quenched.

'What do you mean?' Her voice was provocative, yet hushed and as soft as the coat lining that caressed her naked body and teased her senses.

'Exactly what I said. Describe it to me.' He did not raise his voice. Still he did not look at her. 'Well?' he demanded.

'I'm trying to think,' she replied, determined to take her time, enjoy what she was experiencing despite it being at his suggestion.

She took a deep breath and thought about how she felt. Not just with regard to her nakedness beneath the swishing coat. That was only something to be relished like thick cream on coffee cake.

This was something she hadn't expected, and was incomparable to anything she'd ever done before. She liked it enough to forget that he was walking at her side. Yet she could not. Alistair was a presence, a presence much appreciated, and, judging by the looks of secretaries bustling by on their lunch-time breaks, much admired.

Ariadne had admired him, too. Ariadne had wanted him, but according to what she'd told Penny, had not got him. Why should she succeed where Ariadne had failed?

'You still haven't answered,' she heard him say.

'Erotic.' It was the first word that came to mind. How else could she describe what she was doing, what she was thinking? Delicious shivers of excitement and sensual pleasure made her nipples grow and become almost painful with their need for release. Wetness oozed from the warm lips that nestled provocatively between her silky soft thighs. 'Very erotic. Arousing!'

She stressed the words. Now it wasn't just a question of needing his sponsorship for her highly expensive sport. She had a wager to win, and what a way to win it.

So, he was a man who liked to watch. Surely something of what he watched would arouse him until he had to take her, had to give in to his own sexuality and bury his manhood deep within her inviting cleft.

Beneath the cover of her coat, her hips swayed as she tried to elicit the last ounce of sexual turn-on from the cool silk lining. She trembled, and as if taken by the chill waters of a mountain torrent, all her inhibitions seemed to flow away. Feelings and emotions she had never known seemed to bubble to the surface. Somehow she knew their identity, but also knew she had kept them hidden and had disguised her secret desires and outright fantasies with a brittle veneer of what she chose to call feminism. It had not been an honest term, she told herself, for what she was feeling now belonged solely to her, and no matter what this man might be getting from her experience, she was getting more.

'That's not a very good description,' she heard him say. 'I said describe it to me.'

There was demand in his voice now. She sensed his need to draw her own personal feelings out of her, savour

13

the sweet juice of arousal in his mind via her voice. But it wasn't his experience. It was only hers. Those new emotions told her that, those new desires would show her.

She tossed her hair, looked at him sidelong, the soft darkness of her lashes briefly alighting on her creamy cheeks. The dark-pink lips of her wide mouth smiled.

Beneath the impenetrable barrier of her coat, her nipples erected against the coolness of the silk lining, her buttocks quivering as though caressed by the fingertips of an unseen lover. Her skin shimmered with the feel of it. Her nerve ends tingled as though charged with a feather of electrical current. She buried her hands deep in her pockets and nestled her chin down into the collar.

'It's very difficult to do . . . here.' She licked her lips as her eyes flitted over the faces of the crowd. Those that did look her way she knew were only taking in her good looks – the dark hair, the dark-blue eyes – not what she was, not how she was underneath. They could only imagine her flat belly, her silky thighs, the heart-shaped tangle of dark curly hair that nestled between them hiding an awesome thirst that had need of quenching.

She wore stockings, chocolate against the milky creaminess of her skin. Her calves were taut and ankles slim above the black straps of her high-heeled shoes.

She was shapely, she was sexy and she was loving every minute of this. As she walked, she could feel the movement of the black, lace-edged suspender belt and the whispering rasp of sheer stockings as her thighs brushed one against the other. She relished the heightened sensation of vulnerability that encircled her exposed sex. There was nothing else between her and public outrage – except for her coat.

'No one can see,' he said suddenly as if reading her thoughts. 'Only you and I know what you look like beneath that coat, but only you know how it feels. Describe it to me. I want to share it with you.'

His sigh filtered into her thoughts. She licked her lips and looked at him sidelong again. She studied the crisp, dark eyebrows and the thatch of dark hair. He was

14

handsome. She had to admit that. But distant, somehow remote. His eyes stared straight ahead.

'I want to know exactly what you feel,' he said somewhat impatiently.

Impatience, she thought, was only to be expected. Alistair Beaumont was a man of influence, a man of money who was used to giving orders and used to having them obeyed.

Choosing her words carefully, she formed her answer. So much depended on them. She took a deep breath, licked her dry lips. 'Hmmm,' she murmured as the cool silk caressed her skin. 'The silk is very cool, very smooth. It's rubbing my nipples. They've grown bigger. They're stiff, almost painful. Cold air is circulating between my legs. I can feel it disturbing my pubic hair.'

Poetic, she thought, my words sound poetic. She was aroused by them as well as pleased. Funny, she thought, that no matter how cool the air, my cleft is still hot, still moist, demanding.

Her voice was husky and low. Her own words excited her. Within her body, that bud of passion that sat so secretly among lips of pink flesh was reminding her of its existence, reminding her of the effect her lurid thoughts could have on it. Fleetingly, she glanced at the other people who hurried along the pavement. She voiced what she was thinking.

'What would these people think if they knew, if they could see?'

She glanced swiftly at this man who could use his money to back her expertise, perhaps extend her sexual experience, and give her ownership of a thoroughbred stallion who had covered more than twenty mares already this year. She uttered a silent prayer that he would confirm his decision today.

Her body bristled with anticipation as draughts of cool air caressed her slim thighs, but did nothing to cool the heat that burned between her legs.

'They see nothing. They hear nothing,' she heard him say. 'Go on.'

Somehow, she knew what she had to say next, what he

15

wanted her to say. The words seemed engraved somewhere inside her along with the birth of her new desires.
Her body trembled when she answered.

'It excites me, as though I have some kind of power
over them. I am doing something that is strictly taboo,
that they would condemn me for. Yet I am doing it.
Despite them, I am doing it.'

She did not add that he, too, was one of them. Perhaps
he thought this gave him power over her, as though she
were doing it purely for his enjoyment. She wasn't. This
was for herself.

Will this one small act be enough to gain his body? she
asked herself. Had Ariadne refused to do this, yet still
got the sponsorship for her showjumping season, but not
the man to go with it? No, she told herself. Ariadne
would not have refused. There had to be more to this.

He cleared his throat, turned and smiled at her. 'That's
very good to hear, my dear. Very good indeed. I think
you might be exactly what I'm looking for.' One arm
reached out, curved around her back as he guided her
through the midday crowds towards the bank. An ordinary occurrence. Something people did every day. But
not dressed as she was. Not attired only in shiny stockings, crisp, black-lace suspender belt and a cashmere
coat.

'How else does it make you feel?'

The silk lining, that had only lightly trembled against
her bare back and taut, rounded bottom, now slid over it
from the touch of his arm. She clenched each pearlike
orb of her rear, one against the other. It was hard to
suppress the urge to thrust forward. Her legs and secret
lips parted as she extended her stride to take in the two
steps up to the door of the bank. Before very long her
love juice would begin to flow, and then . . .

He repeated his question.

She took a deep breath before answering. 'In need.' It
was an honest exclamation, but one offered in a hushed
gasp, secret and meant for nearby ears only. Briefly, she
caught sight of his smile. She returned it and knew

instantly that she had won his sponsorship for the coming competitive year, and everything else that went with it.

Eyes bright and heart beating with excitement, she watched him as he made his way forward along the roped-in queue over the dappled cream of the cold marble floor.

For his age, Alistair Beaumont was a good-looking man. Nearing late thirties, dark hair only faintly streaked with grey, and a deep cleft almost dividing the strength of his square jaw.

He was well built; not that of the over-zealous athlete or weightlifter, but a smooth firmness coupled with confidence in his own good looks, his own good body. He was of average build and average height. His status was otherwise. There was nothing average about that. His clothes cried out what he was. His shirt crisp Sea Island cotton; his jacket Highland wool in a neat, checked pattern; trousers of purposely faded green, countrified English casual, yet obviously made by some Italian fashion house.

Alistair Beaumont looked wealthy and was wealthy. He had no real need to be here today queuing with the common herd. There were more than enough people in his employ, beholden to his benevolence, to send off on the mundane errands of life.

But today, Alistair George Beaumont had an ulterior motive. Today it seemed he had put her to the test. If she was as committed to her career as she said she was, then she would do it. What would she do, he had asked her, to gain his backing? Anything, she'd told him, absolutely anything. And she'd meant it.

She'd been living with Mark a while now, and he hadn't been entirely happy about her joining the Beaumont yard. They'd ended up rowing about it. Bitterness had erupted where once there had only been deep words of undeniable lust and passion. She would be leaving him, and now he accepted that.

A fleeting self-consciousness made her raise her hand to push back the thickness of her bouncing hair, not quite brown, and not quite black, but as rich in colour as the darkest brandy. Her hands felt cold even though they had been sat in her pockets during their walk.

She looked at her long fingers. Fine, slim, but very strong when they were inside a riding glove, exercising the most energetic showjumper or three-day eventer. Yet so expert, so exciting when they were caressing the muscles and equipment of a yearning lover, wielding the crop or whip that was so important in the training of either.

Her blue eyes gleamed as she thought of the member that hand had only lately released. Mark, back there at her own stable yard waiting for her, waiting to see if she would gain what she wanted. He would be petulant, perhaps. If she was successful, he knew he would be losing her. Her time with Mark had been good, but now it was basically over. All the same, she would miss him and that rich, ripe member that reared so subtly in her hand when she squeezed his hanging balls, or playfully tweaked at the bulbous end and poked her fingernail into the weeping opening. But she had to move on. So far in her life, she had not found precisely what she was looking for.

'You're incorrigible,' he'd told her. 'Restless. Nothing's ever good enough.'

Was she? That wasn't the message she was receiving from these volcanic upheavals she was feeling inside. As yet, she didn't fully understand them. She only knew that after today, a day she'd spent sauntering half-naked through a shopping precinct in a large city, she would never be the same again.

As she watched for Beaumont's return, Penny shifted her long limbs slightly. Moistness dripped in pear-like droplets from the dark hair that nestled between her legs. Vaguely, she felt it run like quicksilver down her inner thigh and wished suddenly for a hot tongue to lick it all the way back up to her yawning opening. Once there, the tip of a hot tongue could poke inwards, lick slavishly around the satin pinkness of her vulva before entering and plugging the gap for a brief moment before something more substantial was inserted.

As she savoured her thoughts, she pivoted slightly on one heel, the soft whiteness of her inner thigh nudging gently against the thick bush of her ticklish pubes.

A bank clerk ogled her from behind the thickness of his glass screen on which was written FOREIGN EXCHANGE in big green letters. She smiled at him. He blushed and bent his head.

'All done,' said Alistair at last, sliding his cheque book into the inside pocket of his well-cut tweed jacket. He smiled as he said it. She smiled back. To those around, an ordinary enough passing of pleasantries between two good-looking people. But to her, and, she guessed, to him also, there was an undercurrent of understanding. Instinctively, she knew she had passed the test. His sponsorship was hers, her commitment was his, and her excitement at what was to come overwhelmed both.

Back at his office – with just the two of them in a room with very high windows and very thick carpets – he became suddenly withdrawn. It was as though he wanted her out of the building as quickly as possible. This was something she did not understand and was not prepared for.

Slightly peeved by his sudden lack of interest in her, she dressed slowly, turning boldly in front of the full-length windows which stretched fron gold and white ceiling to lush, blue carpet. By doing that, she knew she would better catch the light on her breasts and belly.

But Alistair had picked up a pen, and appeared to be concentrating on the sheaf of papers that came into view once he had opened the brown-leather letter folder on his desk.

His desk was big and incredibly baroque – the size of a dining table to most people, and a substantial barrier between him and her.

Only the decorations inlaid in maple and gold leaf within the pattern of the desk testified that he had any interest at all in that process which humans have abandoned themselves to since time immemorial – lovemaking.

Satyrs with outsize phalli chased blatant nymphs, their

buttocks round, and presented more for penetration than in fearful flight.

One nymph, prominently displayed in the centre panel of the huge desk, was accommodating one satyr in her mouth, whilst another she rode, his hands spread like forked twigs over her breasts, nipples gripped vicelike between finger and thumb. Another satyr came from behind, his phallus already half-hidden between the cheeks of her pear-shaped bottom.

The nymph looked strangely bloated, as though all the fluid that had, and still was, spurting into her was filling her veins, seeping in a frothy mass just beneath her skin.

Penny was stunned. Not by the leering satyrs and willing nymphs, but by Beaumont not throwing her on that plush, blue carpet and taking what she was only too willing to give.

She was deeply disappointed, but made an enormous effort not to show it. She had been so sure he had wanted her, and had been wet and ready for him.

Her disappointment stayed with her all the way back down the wide, sweeping staircase and through the green and white décor of the enormous reception hall, which was big enough to take a fair-sized orchestra.

His behaviour had confused her and given her a slight feeling of insecurity. Didn't he like her body? She couldn't believe that. Her body was good, perhaps even beautiful. Men had told her that – many men. And what was the purpose of making her walk through the streets like that? It must have aroused him, in fact, she was sure it had. His eyes betrayed his desire even though she detected no evidence of an erection behind the sharp-cut fly of his trousers.

Of course, she could have made the first move, yet somehow she had instinctively known it would not have been welcomed.

Never mind, she told herself as she swept out the wide front door and between the Palladian columns, white yet sparkling slightly pink in the late autumn sun, time is on my side. I'll be back, and I'll be successful.

Now the wager seemed even more attractive than it

had been. Now it wasn't just a case of acquiring Ariadne's prize stallion, it was also a case of massaging her own damaged ego.

On the drive home, she wound the window down. Her face was pink, her mouth dry as she fought to come to terms, to control the mix of arousal and confusion resulting from her experience with Alistair Beaumont.

She could have pulled over in a lay-by or some grassy incline on the way home, whipped off her knickers and brought off an orgasm all by herself, but she didn't. She needed a man, and Mark was back at her own stables.

The pent-up desire, the aching need, would be all the more exhilarating, all the more spurring to their mutual satisfaction. And anyway, she did have something to celebrate.

Chapter Two

'You had to do *what*?' Mark was incredulous; and, although aroused by her statement, more than a little jealous.

She avoided looking at him. She hated it when he was jealous, but no matter what rules had been laid down at the beginning of their relationship, this was the one emotion he did have difficulty dealing with.

Mark tried not to show possessiveness, tried not to let his own masculine needs dominate hers. But he was a failure at it. That was why, at times, she just had to lay down the law, remind him that he didn't own her, would never own her, and that she still had a great many things left to do in her life.

However, so far she'd mentioned nothing about her wager with Ariadne and the stallion. That, she decided, would only complicate matters. Why should she give him a false impression that her entry into that very exclusive establishment was purely to acquire the stallion?

She smiled to herself, ran her hands through her hair and openly admired her tawny reflection in the full-length bedroom mirror. She raised her arms, piling her long dark hair up on to her head. Her nipples pouted round and dark towards the mirror, her breasts lifted as if inviting willing hands to feel their softness and test their firmness.

Tonight she needed a man. Through half-closed eyes, she looked sidelong over her shoulder, and took in the effect her confession had had on Mark. Her eyes dropped to the fruitful response which was already pressing against the crotch of his jodhpurs. Too much pressure, she supposed, smiling with satisfaction as Mark unzipped.

'You heard me,' she repeated in her most alluring voice, knowing that its sound and what it was saying would make him want her, make his prick swell painfully against the hard steel of his zip. 'I walked to the bank with him clad in little more than my coat. It was arousing,' she said, lowering her voice until it was little more than a soft purr, as smooth and dark as her hair.

Lips parted and an incredulous look in his eyes, Mark got up from where he'd been sitting on the pine-ended double bed they'd often shared. His trousers were off. He stood naked, hard, his skin bronzed and hairless, each muscle standing in divisive relief from its brother.

With unbridled longing, his hot lips nuzzled against the concave space between her neck and shoulder, and his blond hair, usually tied back with a thong of black leather, fell forward so its ends brushed lightly across her breast. 'I heard you.'

The sweetness of apple shampoo, mixed with fresh sweat in his hair, filled her nostrils and loins with desire.

Eyes closed and mouth open, her hips began to move in a slow rhythm, swaying back and forth and from side to side, her buttocks sliding against his rising hardness and the crispness of his pubic curls.

His chest was warm and firm against her shoulder-blades. The slight roughness of his hands caressed her skin as they travelled round her body and cupped her breasts. His lips suckled at her shoulder.

In the mirror, she could see his eyes sliding down over the reflection of her body. He would not resist her, not like Alistair Beaumont.

Remembering Beaumont made her want to frown, but

she controlled the need to do that. Being reminded of failure was not welcome. Penny, like Ariadne, didn't like failure. It haunted her dreams, threatened her own confidence.

Tonight, she decided, she would rage with desire, devour Mark as he had never been devoured before; and he would have her in every way he could have her. She was resolute about that, very resolute.

Purring with desire, her eyes too travelled over her own body. She enjoyed the view, loved the unison between sight and senses as her hips undulated in gentle waves. In response to both, she parted her legs slightly, and her nipples rose, blushing with the dark-pink heat of deep-seated need.

I look good, she told herself, and her smile was more for her reflection than for him. I look really good, she repeated in her mind. Her eyes saw what men saw: lean ribs and waistline dividing neat, round breasts from slim hips. A nest of hair, dark as midnight, bridged the top of her thighs like a thick wedge of soft moss that entices touch, and invites plucking.

With a whispering progress, his hands slid from her breasts to her stomach, then arrowed in a deep 'V'. She sighed with pleasure as his fingers tangled in the satin softness of her pubic hair, and dipped tentatively into the rising pool of fluid.

Very gradually, a plush pinkness of velvet peered from amid the cluster of. hair. She groaned and opened her legs a little more, tilting her hips so both he and she could see her clitoris open like the head of a flower.

'I want you,' he murmured, his words drowned in the rapidity of his own breathing.

'I want you to want me,' she breathed back at him. 'I want you to want me so much, you beg me to touch you, to suck you, to take you in.'

'You're beautiful,' he stuttered, hearing her, but apprehension stunting his words and making his penis swell more and batter against the base of her spine.

'Don't you think my little bud is pretty?' she asked him, toying with his throbbing weapon as it continued to

24

beat its own tattoo against her firm behind. She tilted her hips some more, then put one foot up on a pink cushioned stool so he could see the sweet head of delight peering like a shy rabbit from a bank of spring bracken.

'Very pretty,' he murmured. 'Incredibly pretty.'

As if in a bid to capture the shy creature that blossomed so secretively, his finger ran through the mass of dark hair, then touched the rising tip of pinkness. It jumped towards him and leapt from its protective hood as if it would bite his finger. He withdrew, only to alight again with all the softness of a landing butterfly or a wandering moth.

She gasped her pleasure as one finger travelled along her welcoming slit, his other fingers rolling back the hot flesh of her labia. Each petal of her sex was outlined by his finger, its moist wetness drowning the progress of his digit before it buried itself in her opening furrow.

Her muscles clenched against it, trapping it within her, drawing it further in.

Behind her, his breathing increased as her buttocks pressed back against him. With wicked determination, she rubbed them against his probing weapon; hot, pulsating as it fleetingly explored the cleft in her buttocks from its beginning at the base of her spine to its wider point from her anus and the sparse hairs along her perineum. Upwards through the division in her bottom; downwards, through her cleft; then upwards again in dizzying succession.

No longer able to contain her delight and her ardour, she turned to face him. Her pubic mound began to beat a slow rhythm against his velvet-gloved hardness as her hips moved backwards and forwards.

'Was it that delicious?' he asked between strangled breaths. 'Walking through a crowded street with your pretty little bosoms bouncing around loose in your coat and no knickers?'

'And the breeze in my hair,' she mused, smiling mischievously up at him. 'My pubic hair!'

In obvious response, his fingers tangled in her pubic hair.

Although his white teeth flashed in a smile, she knew there was something else he wanted to ask.

She offered no relief to the curiosity he was obviously feeling. Withholding such information gave her a feeling of power. He was holding her, pressing his body tight against hers, and all the time wanting to know every detail of her interview with Alistair Beaumont.

Gradually, she sank downwards, arms and hands held high above her before she ran them from his shoulders and down over his chest.

At last, her face was level with his pride and joy. How strong it looked, how richly purple the velvet soft flesh; how vibrant and full of the force of life. The staff of life, she mused, the giver of all good things.

It pulsated with metronome perfection, its tip lightly touching her cheek, her nose, then her lips.

'So soft,' she cooed. 'So strong, yet so soft.'

As if in response to her soothing words, his glans glistened with the first pearl drop of sexual secretion. Tentatively, her tongue flicked, once, then twice, and the drop was gone, salty sweet on the tip of her tongue. His penis reared each time.

Both hands travelled over the sculpted perfection of his firm thighs, the sort of muscles that are so well formed and very hard in a man that rides horses for a living.

She could smell the warmth there, her breath disturbing the crisp hair that circled his cock and covered his balls in a sweet, dewy down so that it tickled her chin, her nose, her mouth as her tongue licked tantalisingly over his sex. Above her, he moaned.

As one hand fondled the peachy softness that hung like ripe fruit between his legs, the other grasped the rising stem. It reared with delight as her fingers wrapped protectively around it. How hot it was. How soft, how strong!

For a moment, her eyes marvelled at the contours of veins, ducts and arteries beneath the blushing purple redness. Then her mouth kissed its head, her tongue probing the opening and taking more of the salty pearl

26

drops on her tongue. Then her lips divided and sucked the first juice of his erection.

Up and down, her head moved in constant rhythm, her lips sliding downwards, retreating, opening slightly wider before travelling back towards the base. As her head moved, so did her hands. One curved around the engorged muscle, her fingertips resting on the duct that would carry his release. Her other hand gently stroked the hanging testicles, tracing the outer softness and probing the inner hardness.

Her lips sucking, kissing, she felt as if she wanted to eat it, yet at the same time, her own needs were rising, her own wetness was forming around the quivering centre of her sex.

Sensing her desires, Mark tangled his fingers in her hair and began to move her head up and down his shaft to suit himself.

When his hand released her, she kissed the rearing head one more time before she got to her feet and followed him to the blue-and-white-striped *chaise-longue* that they'd bought from some old junk shop and Penny had re-covered.

He lay back on the *chaise-longue*, his legs dropping to the ground on either side. His shoulders filled the width of the piece of furniture. At the narrowest point of his body, his penis stood to attention, strong, proud and ready for action. Briefly, he stroked it.

As she studied his erection, her own hands busied themselves. One slid between her legs, anxiously rubbing at her demanding clitoris. The other rubbed at her breasts, gently manipulating first one nipple, then the other between one finger and her thumb. It was nice, but not enough. She knew what she wanted, and from familiarity, knew he did, too.

Even before the words were out, she guessed what he was going to say.

'I'm ready,' he said. 'Ride me.'

She smiled, her eyes bright and wide as she took in the beauty of the firm mount that awaited her. His member

27

was stiff and upright, standing proud from the prostrate body to which it belonged.

Just as if she were mounting a horse, she swung her leg across his body. For a moment, she paused, suspended above him, the head of this throbbing member just reaching her and its tip touching lightly against her humid portal.

With one hand, she reached beneath her. Lightly, her fingers stroked the crown of his penis. How strong it was, how full of power standing so proud from its forest of pubic hair. It was hot, hard and full of blood and jerked appreciatively with each touch, each light caress. Pleasure purred from her own throat as she rubbed it back and forth along the length of her dividing lips. They were wet, and slippery with secretions that would coat his member like a silver sheath.

The friction of its journey from clitoris to vulva increased her breathing. She closed her eyes, relishing the experience of being over and above this man, and using his own weapon to satisfy her desires.

As her breathing quickened in her throat, she tweaked at one breast. Her head fell forward as her hand cupped her breast higher. With her own tongue, she licked at the soft flesh. She loved the feel of it, the silky gloss of her own skin. Moaning in selfish rapture, she slid slowly down to impale herself on him, her vulva sucking the man into her hot interior.

At first, her movements were slow, as her inner lips adapted to the intruder. Around its rim, her nerve endings tingled as their power increased. She clenched her buttocks, tightened her stomach knowing that he, too, would feel the constriction in her muscles. Below her he moaned, his breathing heavy and increasing in tempo as she rode him faster. Her own breath came from deep within. Her breasts leapt, almost of their own accord, as she gasped her pleasure.

Suddenly, just as if she had dug her heels into her mount to spur him on, she increased her speed, bobbing up and down as if she had urged to a trot. Only the saddle on a horse was smooth. On this mount, she was impaled, linked to the saddle, her sex divided by the intrusion of his member. Faster and faster she rode, her sex making a sucking sound as her juices increased to an orgasmic flood.

Her head was back, her eyes still closed, her mouth sagging as she sucked the air. She imagined being out riding, with the wind against her face. And all the time, impaled in place, at one with her mount.

She increased her speed and fell forward, her hands either side of his neck. Their lips sucked at each other.

As her breasts swung back and forth, his hands held them, cradling and caressing them to steady their progress; his thumbs tilted at her risen nipples.

She felt his pelvis rise towards her, felt the first threads of her orgasm racing like a mass of electric currents to concentrate around one spot. Tension pinged there, congregated like high-voltage wires waiting to explode in one almighty burst of energy.

She was barely aware of his face, of his existence. Now, he was just her mount, an aid to her own rising release. She had her own needs to satisfy.

As her release came, her voice exploded with satisfaction. She cried her orgasm to the ceiling, pinpoints of ecstasy like medals on her breasts and a violent sunburst between her thighs. With one last thrust, she felt him tremble within her, momentous at first, his throbbing diminishing until he was spent. Then they fell and collapsed into a gasping heap.

Clasped together by a light film of sweat, they lay motionless. On cue, his fingers began to feather downwards along the indentation of her spine. Her smile was hidden. She awaited the question that he had not yet asked.

'Did you go to bed with him?' He rushed the words, and she detected jealousy.

'Who?' She smiled as she said it, her mouth and her eyes hidden in her tumbling hair. There was a wicked satisfaction in keeping him in suspense. He had no right asking as far as she was concerned. He didn't own her. She was her own woman. She sensed his irritation.

'Him. Alistair thingummy.'

She smiled at his offhandedness with the name.

Half a sigh seeped from the corner of her mouth. It was hard to admit her disappointment, even to Mark.

'We didn't do anything very much.'

There was a pause. Again, she knew what he was thinking, knew what he would ask next, but offered no crumb of knowledge to free him from his query.

'Suck? Hand job?'

She raised her head. Her eyes met his. They were blue like her own, but not fringed with the same dark lashes as hers were.

His mouth was twitching a little at each corner and he was frowning slightly. Suddenly, she felt sorry for him. She was leaving him. He didn't want her to go, yet she had to. They were still friends and would remain so, but there was a world beckoning, a career in which she excelled. She had to go.

Gently, she kissed the tip of his nose. She saw his nostrils dilate and knew he could smell himself – his sex on her lips.

She smiled suggestively, but in an affectionate kind of way.

'Nothing. Nothing at all. Not even a kiss. It was all very polite. Very businesslike.'

His bottom lip dropped open. He was as surprised as she had been.

But she didn't tell him that. It was irrelevant. Her path was marked out, and she'd signed a contract. She couldn't go back on that. Besides, their relationship was at an end. Much as she enjoyed having sex with Mark, they both knew it was virtually over. They both needed new pastures.

She turned on to her back and threw her arms above her on the pillow. She stared at the ceiling for a while and prepared herself for Mark's next question which she was positive would come.

'Do you think he's queer?' he asked tentatively.

'Typical!' She laughed.

In her experience, it was the first assumption in any

30

strictly heterosexual male. Mark, she knew, would never turn down an opportunity to have sex with her or any other likely looking female and found it difficult to understand that someone else might not feel the same.

Nevertheless, she thought about it for a moment before she answered properly. On reflection, she remembered the eyes of Alistair Beaumont when she had been removing her clothes. The steely grey eyes had become brighter as each article had left her shoulders and cascaded from her limbs.

'No.' Her voice was low, almost secretive. 'No, I don't think so.'

Chapter Three

She felt no clinging affection or pangs of guilt about leaving Mark or this place where they'd lived together for nearly a year. Love had become a habit; and sex, although still enjoyable, was getting near that time where familiarity had replaced red-blooded passion.

Apprehension sapped her concentration as Gorgeous Sir Galahad, the chestnut gelding, and Flamboyant Flame, her dapple-grey mare, were loaded into the box. Soon, all three of them, her and her two horses, would be in their new home.

Excitement had coloured her preparations since early morning. No matter how Mark might feel about her going, she could not hide her enthusiasm for joining the team at Beaumont Place. Facilities were the best there, and if what Ariadne had to say was anything to go by, the social life there was pretty good, too.

Limbs stiff from an over-abundance of sex the night before reminded her that she would miss Mark's hard body covering hers, his sex nudging its way slowly into her willing body. But, she told herself, he was not irreplaceable.

All the same, Beaumont's not taking her sexually still grated on her mind. There was a niggle inside that asked whether he had not thought her good enough for his taste. It rankled and made her feel slightly insecure.

And yet, it seemed even stranger that he had not taken advantage of Ariadne. Who could fail to be knocked out by her apple-ripe breasts and available pussy? But now the wager was struck and her curiosity aroused, it didn't matter. Now, it was up to her to rise to the challenge. What kind of man was it who could watch other people enjoying sex and not indulge himself, she asked herself? It didn't matter. She would do her best. She smiled to herself as she slid the bolt into the lock of the tailboard. Pleasant thoughts came to her head.

Perhaps, she thought, his tastes had become jaded, suffused with too much of the sensuous, an item readily available to the man who could afford everything. Beaumont had a business empire that straddled the Atlantic, offices in London, Boston and New York, plus subsidiary companies in Australia, South Africa and South America. He was one of those men whose lives are dominated by their business interests. Yet still he found the time to fund the stabling, training and all the other costs incurred by those so unwise as to be immersed in the world of showjumping.

For the last time, she looked around her old stable yard where mice had chewed through the wooden stable walls, and yellow-headed weeds pushed through the cracked concrete.

Goodbye to all this, she said to herself, looking one last time at the strident growth of the elder tree that had started as a rigorous sapling and was now taking over the yard, its virile roots splintering the concrete into smaller pieces than it was already. Strange, but she'd become almost fond of it, of all it represented. It was against its trunk that she and Mark had made love the very first time, its splintery bark scratching like blunt fingernails over her naked behind.

No matter. Mark and all this were behind her now, but she still managed a little smile for the man who had made her happy, and might even do so again in the future. Mark, like any rejected male, had put on a brave face, but she couldn't tell if he was sad or merely impatient to bury his regrets and his cock into her replacement.

She turned away. Like precious stones, she folded her memories away. Her life was about to take on a whole new course, even though she had some regrets about leaving his hard body and his very satisfying prick behind her.

The tailboard was finally bolted up. The horses nickered gently, snorting as they pulled hay from the temporary nets fastened inside. They sounded to her ears as though they were urging her onwards, telling her that pastures new – where grass was more numerous than weeds – would be welcome to their tender palates.

She turned back to Mark. Their goodbye was brief, though she did detect a hint of jealousy surge momentarily.

'Never mind,' she whispered as he nibbled a last time at her ear. 'Jackie will look after you.'

Over her shoulder, green eyes looked out from a mass of bubble blonde hair and full breasts strained against a black jersey. Jackie, her understudy for the past month, she guessed was already contemplating the pleasures to come now Penny, her rival, was out of the way.

Mark patted her bottom with as much pleasure as he did his prize stallion. Penny wriggled against it, savouring the pleasure for the final time. Then he helped her up into the rattly Bedford horsebox. His hand cupped one cheek of her bottom which was tightly enclosed in her dark-blue breeches. Then his hand slid to the cleft in between as he pushed her up into the cab.

She wriggled against it and murmured with pleasure – after all, it might be some time before she got the opportunity to have some of that, though of course she had no intention of letting the grass grow under her feet.

'Hope this old crate gets us there,' she said as she turned the key.

'Last time,' he answered in an offhand, sarcastic kind of way. 'Mr Beaumont will no doubt have your new box already waiting for you with his company name emblazoned along the side. And all you have to do for it is your very best.' He smiled sardonically. Suddenly, she knew she'd have to work hard not to miss him. Either that or swiftly find her own replacement – singular or plural.

As the engine sprang into spluttering life, she took a deep breath and put on her own brave face. She smiled down at him and winked.

'I will,' she said as she thought of Ariadne and everything she had told her. She was unable to control the spreading smile that made her cheeks bunch into pink apples. 'I most certainly will.'

Foot to floor, she pulled away, eyes straight ahead. On this occasion, at this moment in time, she could not look back.

Suddenly, the seduction of Alistair Beaumont was of great importance, like going after a new trophy, a whole new wedge of prize money. A new life and new experiences beckoned. And now, she reckoned, she was ready for them.

'Alistair Beaumont, I'm coming for you,' she muttered to herself as the old horsebox rumbled out of the gate.

Built in warm, red brick at the latter half of the nineteenth century, the stable yard at Beaumont Place was entered through a curved archway surrounded by rich boughs of drooping purple wisteria.

The gravel crunched beneath the tyres as the horsebox came to a stop in the middle of the yard. Penny's eyes surveyed her new surroundings as she turned off the engine and pulled on the brake. Blank windows stared back at her. Those, she guessed, hid offices and storerooms behind their dusty façade. The other three sides were given over to loose boxes, a tack room and a hay store, numerous buildings all catering for the competitive world of equestrianism. At the far end of the enclosure was a large barn and next to it what looked like an indoor riding-school.

What a difference to her own place, she thought enviously, as her eyes took in the scene of gentlemanly opulence. There was no sign of neglect here, no sign either of lack of funding. Here, there was money. Here also, she reminded herself, was Alistair Beaumont who was both a man worth waiting for and worth having. She remembered him from that day strolling through the lunch-time crowds, that classic patrician profile set on a firm neck and shoulders that bore both responsibility and confidence with easy geniality. Just thinking of him made her moist against the crotch of her white cotton knickers. He was a handsome man, besides being a powerful one.

In the middle of the yard was a fountain; perhaps of earlier construction, from the time of the Prince Regent when the main house was built. Around it was a circular trough into which a bronze cherub peed from a green copper spout. The water tinkled like light laughter, sparkling like falling diamonds into the dark greenness of the pool.

'Nice little guy.' She smiled to herself, referring as much to the cherub itself as to the appendage he so copiously peed from. It was bigger than normally associated with classic statutary, and certainly exhibited the sort of length normally associated with an aroused adult male rather than a rotund little boy.

So involved was she in studying the rich red opulence of the stable yard and its buildings, that she did not at first notice Alistair strolling over to where she had parked. Her heart thudded and she ran her hands nervously over her slim hips. A fire ignited and simmered gently between her legs.

He looked as good as that day when she'd walked beside him through the streets with all the beauty of her body teased by the soft touch of the coat lining. His shirt looked to be silk, his pullover pure lambswool and his breeches and high brown-leather boots hand-made purely for his well-muscled frame.

But today, it wasn't just him that filled her eyes. He was not alone. A few steps behind him walked another man. He seemed with him, but slightly apart, and although Alistair still filled her eyes, they could not help but stray to this other presence, this very tall man with very blonde hair that curled in satin drifts over his naked neck. Her breath caught in her throat, and a numbness

36

stilled the flames that Alistair had ignited in her. This other man was beautiful in the same way that a woman is beautiful, or an angel, or even Michelangelo's David. His features looked almost sculpted. Angelic, she decided, was the best description. High cheekbones; high forehead beneath the luxuriant fringe of white blondness; wide mouth and profiled chin: all these gave the complete appearance of being somewhat ephemeral. His eyes were brown and seemed to look straight ahead as though they were looking beyond her, as if there must be something else more profound they were seeing rather than the red brickwork, the tangled wisteria or the yellow gravel of the stable yard.

It was strange, but even though she was still sat in the cab of the rattly old Bedford horsebox, she had the oddest urge to cover her breasts and her lower regions with her hands; as if she were naked, as if he could see her bare flesh and it was somehow lewd for him to do so. It was almost, she thought, as if she were in church and he really was a creature etched in stained glass, complete with white wings and gold halo.

The feeling passed. She swallowed her sudden breathlessness and turned her attention back to Alistair. If he had noticed her interest in the man at his side, he did not mention it. He did not introduce him either. Mature lines that enhanced his character crinkled at the side of his bright, grey eyes.

On the mild breeze, his aftershave wafted towards her, mingling tantalisingly with his most obvious maleness. Maleness was a smell she had always noticed. It was aftershave, it was sweat, it was wood smoke, damp grass, and even the faint trace of tobacco. Men had those smells, completely unlike the sweet and salty mix that women seem to have; bouquets of flowers mixed with female perspiration. Men most definitely smelt different to females, and the difference excited her.

His handshake was warm and sent shivers of expectation up and down her spine. His smile became even warmer and she thought it the sort you could drown in.

'Miss Bennet. So pleased to see you.'

She took the offered hand as she stepped down from the box. The palm was warm, the fingers firm. Just to look at him sent shivers of pleasure coursing like cold water down her spine and into the deep valley between the cheeks of her bottom. For the moment, the 'angel' was forgotten.

'Glad to be here,' she replied, breathless with enthusiasm. Her stomach was still knotted with excitement, her mind still tossing and tumbling the intrigues and stories she had heard about this place. She awaited an introduction to the tall man whose navy-blue jersey had a boat-style neckline that exposed the strength of his neck and the outline of his collar-bone. His flesh was tanned, as warm in colour as clear honey. He was not introduced. His eyes flickered over her for a moment, then stared guiltily ahead, and even though she smiled at him, he did not smile back.

The 'angel' tossed his head, throwing back the sleek blond fringe that covered his forehead. The rest alighted in soft waves around his bare neck.

Suddenly, she felt hot and her lips seemed dry. This man was something she had not foreseen. She could feel the blood pumping to her cheeks and knew they were becoming as pink as almond blossom. Lust oozed like honey in her hidden love-nest. She felt in great need.

But Alistair was speaking. With effort, she concentrated on what he was saying. After all, he was the man she had come for; the man who would pay her bills and fall to her charms if she played her cards right.

Alistair indicated the range of buildings around her, but made no obvious attempt either to introduce or bring the tall blond man into the conversation. Silently, the man walked behind them – three paces behind – like some Oriental wife or harem eunuch. It was, she thought with rising curiosity, as though he were not there as a person, only as an item, something Alistair had paid for. All the same, he was beautiful to look at in his navy sweater and his pale-blue jeans. To see him move was enough for her to imagine what might be underneath. But she listened attentively as Alistair spoke. His looks,

38

even his voice, demanded her attention. The very tone of his voice and the smell of everything expensive and masculine held her attention. This, she told herself, was a man to behold and to have. In time, she said inwardly. In the meantime, she was still curious to know the name of this blond Adonis who walked three paces behind them. Would he introduce him soon, she asked herself, and what was his job around here?

'If you'd like to unload your animals,' said Alistair in that warm timbre of his, timing his words to almost half answer her question. 'Gregory will show you your stabling. After that,' he added, gazing at Gregory with an odd look of self-satisfaction and mild amusement, 'he'll show you your own accommodation. He will also help you unwind. He's very good at that. I'm sure you'll have no trouble making yourself at home very quickly.'

A pained look followed the one of self-satisfaction on Alistair's face, but then it was gone. Penny couldn't fathom what its meaning might have been, so she didn't dwell on it. Instead, she looked at Gregory and smiled weakly.

When she turned again to Alistair, he had already half-turned his back on her. Like a schoolgirl, she felt she had been dismissed, handed over to a lesser staff member, though definitely a very beautiful one.

'I will no doubt see you this evening, Miss Bennet. At dinner,' Alistair called over his shoulder as he walked off.

'Yes. Yes. Of course ... I wish you'd call me Penny,' she said as an afterthought.

He did not turn or acknowledge her call.

'Miss Bennet!' Gregory's voice caught her unawares and caused a weakness in her most energetic muscles. His voice was melodious; a rich mix of church organ and jazz clarinet.

'If you'll come this way,' he said as he unloaded her luggage and began to walk towards the eastern side of the yard. 'The stable-lads will take care of your animals.'

At the sound of his voice, two young men, barely twenty, strode out through the wide door of the main stable block where stalls were ranged in rows down one side.

She smiled at the stable-lads. They smiled back.

She followed Gregory, taking full advantage of the opportunity to run her eyes down over his broad back and tight behind. She started at the sleek blond hair that covered his head like a page-boy in some Renaissance painting. Her observations proceeded over the thickly classical neck and the masculine shoulders that rippled beneath the jersey, straining with the weight of her luggage. His stride was long enough to suit his legs, and his thigh and calf muscles seemed to fight against the stiff cotton of his washed-out jeans as though they were trying to escape.

Her room was on the third floor in a high tower that brooded at the eastern corner of the house. It looked older than the rest, perhaps a leftover from some Civil War battle.

The steps leading up were made from stone and wound between cold matching walls. Just for a moment, she wondered about the comfort of the accommodation allotted to her. Would it too be stone, unyielding and dankly cold like some tattered poet's garret?

She needn't have bothered worrying, she told herself, as a heavy wooden door, like something out of a medieval romance, opened on a room that she immediately fell in love with.

The room was circular, the ceiling high, its beams running from the top of the walls to a central apex. It was as though the room was not a room but a giant tent.

The bed was big and old, with heavy wooden posts of barley-sugar twists at head and foot. There was a fireplace with a real fire burning, thick tapestries lining the walls, and ancient, though expensive, rugs were scattered over the polished wooden floor like some giant patchwork quilt.

There was also a mirror – massive and enclosed within a dark wooden frame of intricate carving that stretched almost from ceiling to floor.

There were plenty of cupboards, plenty of writing

space, a television and an *en-suite* bathroom. Some hotels she'd stayed in, she reflected, didn't have rooms as good as these.

'It's lovely,' she exclaimed with honesty as her bags hit the floor with a thump. 'Are all the rooms like this?' She watched him closely as she waited for him to answer. Her breathing had quickened. Was it the fault of the stairs or the study she had made of his body? He did not answer. He busied himself putting her things away; and watching him tear around her room like some manic chambermaid angered her.

So far, she'd got precious little in the way of conversation from Gregory. But it was worth trying again just to hear the rich mahogany of his voice.

'Do you ever talk?' she asked in a sudden fit of pique.

His back was to her, yet she was sure he must have heard.

'Damn you!' she yelled as he took three strides or so and disappeared into the bathroom.

Penny heard water running, then saw steam rising. It didn't take a Sherlock Holmes to realise he was running a bath.

'I didn't ask you to do that,' she called out. Either the taps were gushing too loudly, or he was deaf or just plain ignorant. Still she got no response.

'What the hell!' she exclaimed, then sighed loudly. 'OK. I'll take up the offer. I'll have a bath.'

A bath was just what she could do with, anyway. This morning had been an early start, the journey had been long, and she could do with relaxing in hot water for an hour or so. Who cares who'd turned the taps on?

'Thank you,' she cried as loudly as she could. 'It's just what I need.'

Penny approached the bathroom door, then leaned against the door surround.

'So this,' she said brightly, her eyes squinting for any reaction from him, 'is the bathroom.' He was bent over the bath, pouring something into the water from a long plastic bottle with a very interesting neck. The water eddied in pink whirls of varying degrees as a result of

41

the added essence before it formed small mounds of white bubbles.

As he didn't answer, she took the opportunity to look more fully at the bathroom. Pure white fitments with gold taps and fittings sparkled beneath deep-seated spotlights. Floor-to-ceiling mirrors covered one wall opposite the bath, where steam rose from the streaming tap.

Automatically, she undid the top two buttons of her blouse as she walked back into the bedroom, her naked breasts sensitised as the input of air caressed them. In need of clean underwear, she unzipped a bag. A hand gripped hers and stayed its action.

'I'll do that,' he said crisply. 'You have your bath.'

There it was again, that voice that made her breasts tingle and her crotch moisten with fluid anticipation. His hand, including his fingers, was cool upon her arm.

Open-mouthed, she took the opportunity to study his eyes, which looked at her with such strange intensity. This close, his face was even more beautiful, even more breathtaking. His eyebrows, she noticed, were arched and darker than his hair. His lips were sensuous and pinkly soft as though they could suck at her very soul.

His fingers released her and she felt their loss. Disinclined to argue, and having received no answers to anything she had asked, Penny sighed and slumped down on the bed. She was tired after an early start this morning and the journey itself. Why not have a bath? Why not let this man with the face of an angel and the body of an Olympian athlete wait on her?

Placing the toe of one boot against the heel of the other, she started to nudge the boot off her foot.

Without being asked, his legs straddled hers. Suddenly, she was lost in her own fantasies, her own lustful desires. There was his bottom, turned towards her face. His cheeks were rounded, the flesh tight and made of muscle rather than fat.

He tugged, his firm hands and strong arms struggling with the reluctant boots.

She let her head fall back, and allowed her hair, which had broken loose from its black velvet band, to brush the counterpane. This was luxury. How could she not let him do this? There were his buttocks, open to observation, plus his muscular haunches curving down to tight knees and well-shaped calves.

She had a sudden urge to run her hand between those fine legs, to feel for the soft scrotum that lay so secret, yet so exposed, between his parted thighs.

An ache of wanting tightened her chest as she raised her head, studied his body. Dare she touch him? Dare she feel the most private part of this man who barely spoke to her, yet was so beautiful that he was almost a work of art carved from marble?

But the moment passed.

Once one boot was off and lying in the middle of a dark red and blue carpet, the same strong grip was applied to the other.

'I'll get these cleaned,' he said, and promptly put them outside the door. Then he closed it and came back in. She hadn't expected that, but voiced no objection.

Penny rubbed her toes together. Oh well, she thought to herself, if that's the way it is . . .

With urgent fingers, she began to undo her buttons. She had an urge to catch him here, to expose her body so he had to say something, and had to stay to take her.

'I'll do that,' she heard him say.

Her own hands halted, and her mouth dropped open in surprise. This was something else she hadn't allowed for.

Now the fingers that had been so cool and long upon her arm were undoing her buttons for her.

'Please do,' she exclaimed in a breathless purr, her breasts rising suddenly higher in their endeavour to feel those cool fingers on her satin flesh.

Her senses were now flying around in wild abandonment. What would he do now? What did it matter? Whatever he wanted to do, she was game. He filled her eyes, this tall man who towered above her and had very cool fingers and a voice as warm as mulled brandy. She wanted him in any way she could.

When her blouse was open and her breasts exposed,

43

she studied his face. There was no change in his expression, no acknowledgement in the steady eyes that she was beautiful; no sign that he desired her.

It made her feel dejected somehow. As if to reassure her own self-esteem, she looked down at the two firm orbs of her breasts which thrust so invitingly towards his hands and his face. She arched her back. It made no difference. Nothing altered.

Her blouse was open, taken off her. She was naked to the waist. Her arms stayed at her side.

'Stand up,' Gregory demanded. There was no emotion in his face; no recognition that her breasts were now close to his own chest or that she was looking up at him longingly, wanting him to cup each bosom in his cool hands and to tantalise her crowning nubs with the tips of his fingers, the warmth of his lips.

She felt cheated, let down. What was wrong with her that this man ignored her most obvious invitation? Did he prefer blondes – those as Scandinavian in features as himself?

She thought of Ariadne, tall and blonde. Suddenly, she was jealous . . . least, until he spoke again.

'Put your hands on your head. I will help you off with your trousers.'

'But I can do it myself . . .' Penny began, then called herself a fool for doing so.

'Put your hands on your head,' Gregory repeated without looking at her.

Trembling slightly, Penny did as she was told. The music of his voice was irresistible. Her body wanted out of these dusty, sweaty clothes. Her body was warm. She wondered if his was, too, or whether his flesh was as cool and soothing as his hands.

Her sighs turning to pleasurable moans; Penny turned her eyes to the bathroom. Hot steam rose and curled out of the door, beckoning her to indulge; to submerge herself in its comforting heat and perfumed aroma.

Perhaps, she thought with rising excitement, he would join her. What a prospect – that sublime form squelching with her in the confines of warm water and rising suds.

44

His face was but a few inches from her now; his hands were on her waistband. Their eyes met, though his seemed strangely vacant, but still fired with an unusual intensity that turned up her toes and made butterflies dance in her belly.

'Are you taking yours off?' she asked, the hope in her voice and her eyes exceedingly obvious. She'd received no answers from him so far, so she was surprised to hear one this time.

'No.'

His reply was abrupt. His eyes held hers, then dropped as he undid her waistband then the zip of her breeches.

He didn't seem to notice her staring at him, her eyes sliding down over the broad chest, his neat ribs, his waist and then the zip of his faded denims.

She was almost surprised to see a bulge. So far, he had made such a good job of avoiding her eyes, of keeping his conversation to the barest minimum. Yet he was aroused, but seemed disinclined to do anything about it. She wondered why, but said and did nothing.

As with Alistair, she was disappointed, but determined to let this particular man see her in all her unfettered glory, without shame ... and without pity.

There was something soothing about his dextrous fingers undoing her trousers, and sliding them and her knickers down her legs. She almost swooned with joy as his hand dived between her legs to dislodge the crotch of her panties from her sweating slit. For a moment, she thought she was going to get what she so badly desired and he obviously wanted.

Desire spread in a cobweb cloud through her body and limbs once her creamy flesh, radiant with a mixture of health and sweat, was exposed. Her clothes lay discarded, like metaphors for her previous life.

She watched as he picked them up and laid them on a chair near the door in a neat pile as though they were crisply clean rather than smelling of fresh sweat and horses.

There was something annoying in seeing him give the clothes more attention than he had her. The annoyance threatened to bubble over. Even before she spoke, she knew he would hear it in her voice. But she'd had enough. She had to say something.

'Right! Now I'll take my bath.' She sounded imperious and meant to.

Tossing her head and holding herself as proudly as she could, she walked naked towards the bathroom. Perhaps now, she thought, with a pang of regret, this man would leave, or take her, or do something!

Gregory followed her into the bathroom.

Penny stopped, turned and stared at him. Again, he averted his eyes.

'Thank you. I can manage now,' she said, rolling her breasts with her hands for his and her benefit and very aware of all the other naked Pennys reflected back at her from the misted mirrors, and all the other rolled breasts and jutting nipples.

'Get in. Stand up, and I'll sponge you down.' His voice was sudden, but she was so mesmerised by its tone and quality that she felt obliged to obey.

She hesitated just for a moment. Her thoughts roller-coastered between desire and pride. Who was this man who could tell her what to do? And why didn't he just fall on her, knead her breasts in his strong hands, lay her down and press his hard phallus into her welcoming pussy? She had no answers. So she stepped into the bath and hoped for the best. She knew very well what she wanted that 'best' to be.

She began to moan with pleasure. Her skin glistened with soap bubbles as Gregory squeezed a well-lathered sponge across the round firmness of her breasts. The droplets of water and white foam tumbled like a mountain torrent down the gleaming slopes only to hang like imperfect white pearl drops from deep pink buttons.

She let her senses delight in this amazing experience. She and Mark had bathed together, but this wasn't bathing together. Like a princess, she luxuriated in the warm water and towering bubbles. Like a slave, angelic beauty and masculine strength moulded into one, he stood over her, the sponge in his right hand following the exploring fingers of the left.

With mounting ardour, she watched wide-eyed as he took off his shirt. Now! yelled her mind, Now!

But nothing happened. That was all he took off; feeling his way along the edge of the bath, he retrieved his sponge, and continued as before.

Her breath quickened as his hands explored and soaped her body. She was lost in pleasure, her throat purring and moaning in alternate spasms. Anything he wanted was his. Anything at all. She had an urge to touch the tanned, hairless skin that so tautly covered the hard, lithe body.

'Put them on top of your head,' he said. Then he stepped backwards as though he had anticipated that she would try to touch him, to run her soapy fingers over the tightness of his hard body.

'What . . . ?' she began, her words strangled by her racing breath.

'Do as you're told,' he repeated. 'Put your hands on your head. You are not allowed to touch me.'

With a moan of deep regret, she raked her eyes over the beautiful, boyish flesh that she longed to feel beneath her fingers, and cursed the heavy ache that hung like lead between her thighs. Now what could she do?

Strong urges wanted her to disobey, to run her fingers over that delicious form, the skin now glossy from the mix of steam and sweat.

Then she sighed. She would resign herself to whatever part she had to play. And if he wanted to act the part of the bath house slave, then so be it.

Tension dissipated and anxiety banished, she rested her hands one on top of the other on her head. Unsmiling, his face serious with intent, he came nearer. Now she could smell him, tangy, male and juicily desirable.

Tremors of sensation tingled throughout her body as the sponge was rolled down over her belly and in between her legs.

'Open your legs wider.'

Having no intention of missing such a golden oppor-

47

tunity, she did as she was told. The warm sponge and the diligence of his hands spread and rolled her plush nether lips until they hung with soap suds, thoroughly spread and thoroughly cleaned.

There was a pleasantness about it. Almost like satisfaction, she thought to herself – but not quite. Pink flesh much used and abused the night before felt refreshed and touched with new life.

She closed her eyes now. Better to savour that way and to fully absorb the tingling that ran over her skin and centred on her precious clit and blossoming nipples.

The hand that was not using the sponge travelled to her hip, his fingers soft and tantalising. His hand held her hip. He reached round, his fingers clasping gently at the taut flesh of one buttock.

'If you get down on all fours,' he said suddenly, 'I'll do your back.'

The request was irresistible. She got on to all fours. She wanted to do this; to feel her tension dissolve in the warmth and her sexual desire flood over her like a warm wave on a tropical beach.

The water reached her elbows. The furry mixture of sponge and soap loosed the taut muscles of her back and shoulders. She opened her eyes, closed them again and purred like a kitten. The hands travelled down over her back to her pink buttocks.

It occurred to her that Gregory did this for everyone new, and had probably done it for Ariadne. That made her jealous. Calm down, she told herself, use your self-control. Obviously this was routine, an act designed to put people at ease and promote mutual trust. And what could be better than sharing a bath? Didn't the Japanese do it anyway?

Suds circulated around her neck and dropped in white globules from her hanging breasts. She murmured with surprised delight as the squidgy softness of the sponge was pressed in between her buttocks, the soap trickling down the deep crevice and through the channel that divided her legs.

Warmth, suds and softness invaded the wet folds of

48

flesh. Her thighs opened slightly. Her head felt dizzy, her eyes closing as she revelled in the sweet decadence of doing nothing, of depending on someone else to cleanse and pamper her willing body.

She felt the long fingers, as delicate in their touch as any artist, spread her cheeks apart, expose her anus and press the sponge and its soapy issue into her puckered hole.

There was no stopping the moan of ecstasy that issued from her throat. She closed her eyes, threw discretion to the wind, and pressed her buttocks more firmly against it.

'I think you need more soap,' she heard Gregory say, his voice as melodious and beguiling as his looks.

'Whatever . . .' she replied through her moans of pleasure.

His hands ran down over her back. His fingers parted her buttocks. Something soft but basically hard was forced into her anus. She gasped, and realised the invader could only be the soap which was long and shaped more like shaving soap than toilet soap. Its effect was incredible. Her muscles gripped as it slid gently in and out. Still moaning and savouring all that was being done to her, she arched her back and pressed herself on to it. This was the best bath she'd ever had, like none she'd ever had before.

'More,' she moaned, and wished that the soap was twice the size it was; that there was something bigger to push into her pulsating vulva which cried out for attention. Her clitoris also tingled with demand, entering the scenario like a star act stepping on to centre stage.

The folds of flesh that hugged the core of her sex began to open like the petals of a lotus in bloom, droplets of dewy essence mixing with the lather as her plump labia opened in anticipation.

'All finished,' she heard him say as the soap was withdrawn. Now her moans changed to groans.

'Don't stop!' she cried out. She would have begged longer, but something in his face told her that such pleas would not be welcome.

49

'Patience,' he replied. 'I haven't quite finished yet. I have my orders.'

She wanted to ask him what orders. But her need to enjoy more of his ministrations was greater than her curiosity.

Disappointment filled her. She had a need for release, and if it wasn't for the fact that Gregory was with her and likely to do more, she would have slid her hand between her legs and tickled her tight little bud until she did come.

Quizzically, she looked over the foam that sat on her shoulder, and saw him take something down from off the wall.

Then she gasped as cold water sprayed from a hand-held shower hose washed the suds from her body. Goose-bumps dimpled her tight flesh as the soft hands directed the water over her back. Streams of cold delicacy seeped between her buttocks, and dangled in icy dribbles from her stiff nipples. She gasped, her skin tingling as the process was repeated until the shower was turned off.

'Cold water aids muscle tone.' Gregory's explanation sounded reasonable enough, but Penny did not entirely believe him, or rather she didn't want to believe him. She wanted to believe that he was enjoying this, too, that the sight of her naked form and opening sex tempted him. If it wasn't for the obvious bulge in his trousers, she would have questioned his gender. But she knew instinctively he was a man. His physique was beautiful, but decidedly masculine. And his smell was masculine. He was a man all right.

She considered his comment on muscle tone. The divide between health and sex had always been blurred. In the bath, it was sex that was on her mind, not sport.

'The soap's all gone,' he said, then switched off the cold water.

Catching her breath, she got out of the soap-filled tub and let Gregory envelop her in the softness of a thick white bath towel wrapped tightly around her by his sinewy arms.

* * *

'Delicious,' she murmured, closing her eyes and hugging the sheet to her. She was cocooned in it, glad of its warmth, of its softness, and even more glad to be so close to his body.

Wetting her lips with her languid tongue, she reached out and touched his glistening shoulder. He started, and stepped back. The look in his eyes was impossible to read. There was defiance there, and also something resembling pain or fear.

'I'm sorry . . .' she said, in a broken voice. Puzzled and disappointed, she clenched her fingers into her palm, withdrew and let the towel that so warmly enfolded her slip from her grasp.

'It's not allowed,' he said, stepping away from her like he had earlier. 'At least, not yet.'

She stared, but bit her tongue. She was new here. She had to remember that.

Her body was dry now, aglow with the warm hue of the recent bath. Her breasts pouted proudly forward as though inviting his fingers. Very slightly, she opened her legs and was immediately aware of the sweet mix of musk and highly perfumed soap.

'Don't you want me?' she asked him plaintively, running her hands down over her breasts, the flatness of her belly, the forest of soft dark hair that flowered between her thighs.

She couldn't help but frown. His expression did not change; at least not in his eyes. His jaw dropped momentarily before he answered.

'Yes,' he suddenly said in a bright way that softened the hardness of his jawline. 'I want you to lie down on the bed.' He threw the last words over his shoulder in a more casual and offhand manner.

She didn't care about that. If he wanted her on the bed, he could have her on the bed. In fact, he could have her in any way he chose. Picking up the crumpled towel, she made her way into the bedroom.

The thick green and red of the tapestry bedspread was rough against her back, and did nothing to subdue the heat of sexual desire that ran all over her body.

51

She lay her head on the crisp white linen of the pillow. Gently, she writhed her hips, rubbing one leg against the other in excited expectation.

She closed her eyes as the smell of lavender from the pillow assaulted her senses. Sensuality itself played havoc with her nerve ends.

Purrs of ecstasy escaped from her mouth as she raised one knee, then the other, so that the top of one thigh was always in contact with her aching clitoris.

Through narrowed eyes, she watched him re-enter the room and gasped with sheer lust when she saw he now wore only the briefest of coverings: nothing more than a posing pouch that hid his stem from view but nothing else.

'Why don't you take that off, too?' she asked through rushed breath.

Abruptly and without answering, he turned his back on her and became absorbed with something on the dressing-table.

She watched; licking her lips, rubbing her breasts, mesmerised by the view of his well-formed buttocks divided by the thin strip of posing pouch. She assessed the power of strong thighs and the incredibly detailed muscles in his well-honed calves.

He was totally hairless. His skin shone like soft gold in the subtle glow of the ornate lighting.

When he turned back to her, he was rubbing his hands together. Aware of the aroma of sandalwood, musk and wild flowers, she held out her arms to him, telling herself that this was the moment, this was their time.

Suspended for just a moment, she let her arms fall beside her. Although he was walking towards her, he did not look at her. His eyes seemed to stare straight over her head and her bed. What was it with this man? Was she that ugly?

'Face down,' he said suddenly, and her spirits rose.

'OK,' she smiled. 'If that's the way you want it.'

As she lay full-stretch on the bed, her eyes went to the big carved mirror that almost covered the other wall. There was a certain clarity lacking in it. The ones in the bathroom had been similar, she remembered. Then she smiled secretively. They were two-way mirrors; they had to be. Suddenly, she remembered that Alistair liked to watch. She felt like the star turn at the London Palladium. All right, if she was expected to perform, then perform she would.

With rising excitement, she awaited the soothing strokes of his probing fingers. This, she told herself, was turning out even better than she'd hoped for. Of course, there was still that tingling around her love temple that needed assuaging. But now, instinctively, she knew that this blond seraphim would bring her to full satisfaction.

The towel was folded and pushed under her hips. It was a surprisingly comfortable position. Her breasts were not crushed. Briefly, she looked over her shoulder at her bottom. It was thrust slightly upwards, round, pink and gleamingly fresh from its thorough sponging. Like softly rounded hills, she thought, before closing her eyes.

Being healthy, she decided, the blood would all be running to her head and her shoulders, the first points to be massaged.

Softly, she murmured, her senses poised for take-off, ready for her alone to take full advantage of this unexpected 'treatment'.

The fine fingers and oiled palms prodded new vitality into the tight muscles around her neck and down over her shoulder-blades. There was knowledge in them, an experience of touch that eased them to softness and coaxed her into relaxation.

Such was the exquisite rapture of the sensation that she hummed softly through closed lips in time with the sensuous sweep of his hands.

Long firm strokes ran down over the soft undulations of her firm flesh. Hands, sideways on, pressed into the long indentation of her spine. Her buttocks clenched, then relaxed as his cool palms rolled each cheek as if kneading bread. The fingers pushed gently at each knot of tightness, spreading her cheeks to either side of their joining cleft before rounding each curve and proceeding down over her thighs.

The scent of flowers and sandalwood pervaded the air with each fresh application of oil. Her hips moved against the firmness of the towel which pressed pleasurably against her soft cushion of her mons Veneris. A little harder, a little more pressure, and the thickness of the towel would be enough to bring about her climax.

But this was good enough, she thought. Most massages she had received before were from Ariadne who was good at it. She had of course returned the service, but according to her blonde and brazen friend, she was basically a no-hoper.

Her whole body trembled with pleasure as she was stroked, pressed and pummelled. The tight muscles of her thighs burned with new vitality, as the massage continued on to her calves. She was disappointed when the hands ceased. Without being asked, she turned over and her bright-blue eyes, now infused with the electric blue of excitement, surveyed the rigid form, the face that never altered, the eyes and mouth that never smiled.

Just as she had surmised, oil was being re-anointed into those experienced palms.

Speculatively, she let her gaze wander around the room; over the dark greens and dull golds of the tapestries, the dark rich wood of the furniture until they settled on the mirror which was high and wide and edged with a vibrant carving of plump grapes and plumper naiad thighs. Well-endowed satyrs chased the running naiads just as they did on Alistair's desk. For the first time, she noticed the size of the satyrs' manhoods, so large it took both hands to handle their priapic erections.

Lucky naiads, she thought to herself, and smiled knowingly at the sheet of glass. Was there someone behind the mirror at this moment in time? She guessed there was and wondered at their racing breath, their pulsing veins and their rising passion.

She stretched beneath Gregory's hands, opening her legs slightly, and smiling secretively at the mirror as she did so. How did her yawning cleft and bouquet of pubic hair look to those hidden eyes? she wondered. And how did it look to Gregory?

Would he take her now? Strangely enough, she knew the answer. There would be pleasure with this man. There would be a shattering orgasm. But there was more to him than a straightforward tumble. She also guessed he had been given strict instructions, and those that had given them were safely ensconced behind the carved mirror.

Her gaze shifted and rested on the thick tuft of pubic hair that rose so defiantly from her plump mound, like fragile trees on a far-off hill. Then it travelled to her eager nipples that blushed like crushed roses at the advent of the busy hands. Penny mewed like a kitten as the fingers pulled, pummelled and pinched. All action was welcome and invoked response. Again, she closed her eyes as tension was replaced with ecstasy.

The thumbs pressed gently against her throat, the palms and fingers circling her neck. She groaned unashamedly as they travelled downwards, pressing across her collar-bone, easing the tightness away with experienced fingers.

Nothing could stop the moistness from gathering between her legs like a hidden well, and nothing could prevent her clitoris from raising its head and pushing through the matt of dark pubic hair.

With delicious pleasure, her tongue licked slowly over her quivering lips. The probing fingers were massaging her breasts, pulling at her nubs of desire that rose so prominently from their crown of pink flesh.

Slippery with oil, the hands rolled each breast between both hands. The fingers pressed around the nipples, drawing gasps of ecstasy from Penny's throat. She raised her hips as if those sweet nubs of pink were but remote controls for the rest of her body. In response, the hands progressed down over the flatness of her belly, tracing the lines of her taut stomach muscles.

As the tight thumbs pressed against the rising mound of her sex, she wriggled her hips, aware that her seeping

juices were running towards the cleft between her buttocks and mingling there with the residue of oil.

Penny felt a charge of sensation wash over her as the
hands gently spread her thighs, then massaged in firm
downward strokes, the fingers pressurising her muscles
to let go of that last strain, that last stressed out tension.

Nothing could have prepared her for the surge of
ecstasy that swept upwards from her throbbing sex. The
hands that had massaged her thighs were now splayed
upwards over her pubic hair, the thumbs lightly playing
against her surging clitoris. A new tension gripped her, a
tension that could only be released with a sexual orgasm.
Her breathing quickened, her hands clenched beneath
her head. She wanted to open her eyes, she wanted to
close them. She wanted to see this man in action, and
watch the pliable hands taking her ever upwards to
sexual fulfilment. But yet again, she wanted to see
nothing and just to feel the exquisite sensations.

As a tumbling cascade of gratification racked her body,
she arched her back and cried out. With trembling
muscles, she sought to drain the last tremor of climax
from the knowing hands that had brought her to this
apex.

Cries of delight were lost in her hair and in the sweet
smells of the cotton pillowcase. Her hips writhed to and
fro as orgasm followed orgasm until the final wave was
spent.

Opening her eyes, and murmuring her thanks, she let
her gaze wander to the mirror. She smiled.

I wonder, she thought, whether Alistair could resist
that, whether his hands were busy masturbating his own
sex as she was brought to stupendous heights. She hoped
so. In that, there was success; and in success, there was
power.

Thoughtfully, she rubbed her hand over her own sex.
It jerked, still tingling with the residue of her climax. She
was satiated, in need of no more for the present time.

Gregory re-entered her thoughts.

'I'll rub you down.'

The statement was abrupt. No reply was awaited. The

hands that had manipulated her orgasm now rubbed her down. The towel was taken from beneath her hips and whisked briskly over her skin until it shone with honed perfection and glowed with healthy vitality.

'Rest,' he ordered, 'I'll unpack.'

Lovingly, as though she were a prize horse herself or an errant child, a coverlet of cool cotton was tucked around her. Surprisingly, she did rest. Her eyes closed, then opened. She took one last look at the mirror before she snuggled further down beneath the fresh-smelling cotton.

Sublime was the best way to describe how she felt. She felt renewed, invigorated and able to take on the best . . . yet she also felt at ease enough to fall into a peaceful sleep.

Chapter Four

The whiteness of her dress accentuated her honey-brown complexion, and the hint of gold around her neck added a richness to the simple cut and style. Her legs were bare, firm and bronze, the muscles of her calves well defined beneath the tightness of her skin.

Simplicity extended to her hair which she had left hanging in glossy waves of turbulent perfection. A rich mix of light shone through the art nouveau glass-shaded wall lights and caught it as she tossed her head. The light gave her hair extra sheen and extraordinary colour reminiscent of old port and sleek ebony.

Zest for life and new experiences shone like white-hot diamonds in the blueness of her eyes as she surveyed the finished effect in the mirror. Her breasts were high and firm, the meagre width of her waist exaggerated by the cut of her dress. Over her hips, the dress caressed rather than clung, so that when she moved, her body undulated independently of the material. Only the sound of it swishing lightly was evidence that it was there at all. And it was cool against her flesh. She wore no underwear. There was pure intimacy between the material and her skin.

Appraising her own self, her own body, she felt there was nothing she could not achieve; she could tempt or try out anything.

'Fit to conquer,' she murmured, and smiled. Her teeth were like pearls against the rich pinkness of her lips and the tawny shine of her face. With pleasure and with satisfaction, she smiled to herself, to the mirror and to whoever might be on the other side. 'I hope you like how I look as much as I do,' she purred. Then she hunched her shoulders, swayed from the waist, spread her hands and ran them down over her body. It was lurid exhibitionism, more suited to Ariadne than to her.

She eyed the mirror speculatively. Who, she wondered, was on the other side at this moment in time. A thought occurred to her and blossomed. Her smile bordered on a laugh. The face reflected from the misty glass was not just attractive, radiant with desire, but beautiful.

Carefully, so as not to crease her favourite dress, she undid the top button which was little more than a seed pearl. After that, she let the wide straps with their cool, silk lining slip down her upper arms.

Her mouth, which was as near perfect as her teeth, flashed a more obvious and wicked smile at the mirror.

'A floor show,' she cooed to the reflected brightness, pouting her lips as though addressing a potential lover. 'A taste of things to come.'

As her dress slid slightly, she cupped one breast in her hand, withdrew it from her dress and let it bide there, firmly uplifted by the rest of her bodice like a round, plump grapefruit, the areola surrounding her nipple darkly rich against the honey tone of her skin. Slowly, yet deliberately, she did the same with the other. She tossed her hair, cupped her hands beneath her precious assets and surveyed her handiwork in the mirror.

'Don't they look good like that?' she asked the mirror in her sexiest voice. 'See how firm they are, and how soft . . .' she murmured, running her fingers over the cool, silky flesh. Then she bent her head, pushed one breast up towards her lips, and licked her own flesh. She did the same with the other. She addressed the mirror again. 'And they taste so good and so soft, like melting sorbet. Wouldn't you like to taste them, too?'

The mirror did not reply. It didn't need to. She could see the effect for herself.

Her breasts were poised there – higher than they would usually be, and rounder – trapped like two plump pigeons, and their nubs dark pink like the stamens of tropical orchid. Proudly, they pointed directly ahead at the reflective glass.

They did look good. She congratulated herself and gently ran her fingers over her plush pink nubs that darkened to deep mauve as blood raced through her body.

Like a platter of plump fruit, she thought to herself speculatively, like the offering of a goddess, her breasts strapped high and blossoming. The effect pleased her. What man could resist these? she asked herself as she pointed them like loaded pistols at the mirror.

But what if it wasn't Alistair on the other side of the mirror?

It didn't matter. She would pretend he was there and that his own bodily desires, too, were racing along with his blood.

In every woman there is that longing to be the one who makes a man override his usual habits and routine existence. There is also the narcissist in each one, and Penny was no exception. She liked to look at her body, liked to see what it was capable of.

Teasingly, she rubbed the index finger of each hand over her willing nipples.

It felt good. It looked good, and a wetness began to invade her rapacious pussy. She took one hand from her breast and raised her skirt. In the mirror, her sex was reflected like a dark forest among white, although her creamy tan did subdue that contrast. She opened her legs and dipped one exploratory finger into her foaming well of juice. As she did so, she threw back her head and moaned, yet her eyes never left the mirror.

There, once she'd tilted her hips in that expert way she had mastered with experience, she could see her welcoming haven, the pink folds of satin wetness and the jewels of juice scattering among the dark hair like tiny seed pearls as she retracted her finger.

Her breathing was quick and deep; her trapped breasts quivered as they rose and fell.

Should she finish this now, or go on down to dinner and save it till later? That would be hard, of course, but then there was no knowing what encounters might arise from the dinner table, now was there?

With a sudden pang of regret, she wished she had tried harder with Gregory. If only she could have got him to lie with her, to cover her and to push his hard member through her welcoming gateway. Thinking of him suddenly made her lose interest in the mirror, and she dropped her skirt. She would save her arousal for whatever the later hours of the evening might bring.

As though they were golden orbs for occasional viewing only, she cupped her breasts again and pushed them back inside her dress. At first, she did up the undone button. Then, with a rising of her eyebrows and a careless 'So what?', she undid it again, pulled the bodice down slightly, and left her cleavage free to the world.

Nadine Beaumont and Alistair, her brother, were on the other side of the mirror. Nadine's cloud-grey eyes watched and, as her mouth was wide, so, too, was her smile.

'Well, well, my pretty pussy,' she said in her low husky voice. 'You certainly are something, aren't you?'

'She's ideal.'

Nadine turned and looked down at her brother. He was a well-made man, though of average height. Nadine was exceptionally tall.

Her generous lips twitched a little in her unfeminine yet handsome face as she looked at him. Her thoughts were hidden. They had to be. It was at times like these that she wished she could do something for him – not control his sexuality as she did now – but in that moment of release, she sometimes wished that she wasn't his sister and wasn't the woman she was.

61

'You find her attractive?' she asked with a cruel edge to her voice.

He hesitated before he nodded.

Nadine laughed just a short laugh. How well she enjoyed his discomfort. How much she enjoyed being in control. Her hand reached out to him. She patted then gripped at his crotch as though to confirm he was wearing his tight-fitting rubber underpants, the ones only *she* could release – even if he only wanted to relieve himself, she went with him.

'Then we will have to see, won't we?'

She saw him swallow, knew instinctively that his prick was hard and rising in his pants, and knew that only she could release it, and let him have what he craved.

'Ariadne was telling the truth. She said she was ideal.'

'Yes she did,' Nadine answered. At the same time, she checked the tightness of his waistband, running her hand around the tops of his thighs so she could also check that he couldn't even get a finger up to his throbbing tool to relieve his obvious suffering.

'How long do I have to wait?'

Nadine transferred her hand to his face. Her long, thin fingers stroked his cheek.

'Until I say so, my darling brother Alistair, until I say so.' She sighed, and in a motherly kind of way tucked some stray wisps of hair behind his ear. 'You know that's the way you like best, my sweet dear.'

She tried to kiss his ear. He backed away. Reflexively, she winced and consoled herself into thinking how much more delicious the torture would be later this evening. Yet again he would be just a spectator in the cabaret she had arranged for him. As always, she would be mistress of ceremonies.

Even Penny didn't know as yet that she would be performing, and from what Nadine had seen so far, it wasn't likely that their newest rider would object.

Ariadne had known. She had been well rewarded for setting Penny up and for keeping her mouth shut. But then, Ariadne had been a willing little bitch, ready for anything Nadine had thrown at her. Like all the rest. One year, and then away. That was the way it was, and that was the way Nadine intended it to stay. No morsel attained in order to entice her brother's passion was ever allowed to stay longer than a year.

Only those who have known each other since childhood really know each other well, Nadine mused. With a little more than sisterly affection, she glanced briefly at her brother before she spoke.

'She doesn't like to be told that she can't have something,' said Nadine. 'Ari said that. You know, the Barbiedoll type who you spent yourself with last time. That's good, my darling brother, very good. She's compliant, extremely sexual and very determined.'

The Adam's apple in Alistair's throat throbbed as if trying to escape. His gaze stayed on the mirror to the room beyond. It was empty now. Penny had gone, but his mind filled the void as he imagined what was to come.

Nadine watched him, saw the constriction in his throat. Just like his penis, she thought with perverse pleasure. How engorged it must be; swollen with need, yet unable to break free from its rubber prison, confined there until she decreed the time was right.

Nadine smiled to herself. How was Penny to know that Ariadne had indeed had sex with her brother? How was she also to know that – powerful man as he was, always giving orders, always having people standing in awe of him – he liked his urgings controlled ... by his sister.

He had sex when *she* wanted. The rest of the time, he wore the rubber pants and was only allowed to watch and wonder whilst Nadine imagined his rising prick, trapped and unable to do anything.

And so, his passion was saved, accrued, and when he was released ...

'We'd better be off into dinner, my dear brother,' Nadine said, stretching languidly, arms above her head so her fingertips were well on their way to the ceiling.

Suddenly, the brother grabbed hold of his sister's arm. The action took her by surprise. Eyes met eyes, and

Nadine's jaw clenched squarely as he spoke. 'You know she's going to do everything in her power to get me going, don't you? She already knows these mirrors are two-way. She'd hardly have put on that exhibition otherwise now, would she?'

Nadine's smile was undeniably cruel. She raked one black-painted fingernail down over his cheek.

'Yes, brother. Ariadne knew she would. Knew she couldn't resist the wager either. If she gets you, she also gets the stallion. Sweetly, deliciously ironic, don't you think? Two stallions all in one.'

There were chandeliers in the dining-loom, all starlike sparkle hanging from the high ceiling, which was predominantly Wedgwood blue, but with swirls of ornamental plaster picked out in crisp gold and icy white.

The windows were like the ones Penny remembered from Alistair's office, Georgian panes set in big sash windows that left little room for walls between the high ceiling and the blue and gold plush pile carpet. The curtains were gold damask with heavy tie-backs that hooked to the unusually pronounced brass phalli of flying cherubs.

The walls that were left were white, their expansive iciness relieved only with a dado rail of crisp blue and spine of gold. Large paintings also relieved the white walls. The frames were gilt, the subjects nude figures indulging in a variety of positions with more than one partner. Yet they were not piles of Titian flesh, all white and lumpy with small breasts and heavy hips. These were sleek women and well-honed and -hung men. These were today's figures, firm and supple, uninhibited in their pleasures and healthy in their bodies.

The gold, the blue, the whiteness were reflected in a myriad shades from the overhanging chandeliers and duplicated by the lead-crystal wine glasses. Some of the glasses contained red wine, dark as warm blood; others housed white wine, the liquid softly golden beneath the overhanging lights.

There were four people seated at the table: Alistair, of

course; another man introduced as Auberon Harding, a fellow rider, young and good-looking; and another man introduced as Sir Reginald Chrysling, who was older, but had worn well and had an instant, if predictable old-world charm.

'Reggie,' he corrected enthusiastically, his tongue licking over thin lips in a strong face. 'My friends call me Reggie.'

'Pleased to meet you,' she said, and smiled sweetly at him as he eased himself up from his chair in an act of old-fashioned politeness whilst she took her own seat. Old-world charm had a certain attraction about it, but even if it hadn't, Sir Reggie, although his hair was white, was a well-built man who'd obviously taken care of his body, and in his youth must have been quite something to look at. He still was now. His nose was slightly hooked, his eyebrows were dark and matched his eyes. How sensuous his lips looked when they smiled. I wonder how many other lips they have kissed in his lifetime, Penny mused, or how many breasts have been sucked to distraction between his neat white teeth.

Penny beamed at them all, for no matter who looked at her and what they said, tonight she was beautiful. Tongues confirmed what eyes already said. She radiated beauty and health, and with it, sexuality.

The other person at the table was a woman who Alistair introduced as his sister, Nadine. Vaguely, Penny remembered seeing her at Alistair's side in the VIP lounges at championship events.

The two women exchanged greetings.

Penny was immediately hypnotised and discomforted by this woman. Something in Nadine's manner and the cool look in her eyes seemed to flow out from her. Whatever the nature of this strange current, it made Penny's limbs feel weak and her sex pliant.

With world-weary eyes, Nadine gazed at her with a curiously enigmatic expression and a half-smile on one side of her mouth. 'I'm very pleased to meet you,' she said slowly, elbow on table, chin supported in right hand. 'very pleased indeed.' Her voice had a lazy buzz to it,

65

like the idle droning of bees on a summer afternoon or the faint sound of a diesel lawnmower.

It was not just Nadine's voice that was unusual. Her appearance was dramatic, if not eccentric. Her eyes were grey, her jaw strong, her cheekbones prominent. Her hair was very white and very short, just bristles over her skull. Her skin closely matched her hair. Her eyes were lined with kohl, her lids with dark-grey shadow.

Perhaps it was the shadow that fell across her face, but Penny had the distinct expression she was being undressed with alarming familiarity by someone she had never met, but who seemed to know her and her body very well.

'Another little jumper. Well I shall soon put you through your paces, my dear, you can count on that,' said Nadine. The trace of sarcasm was drowned with a sip of wine clasped in fingers whose nails were varnished black. Plush, thick lips pursed speculatively over a black cheroot. There was an exchange of looks between brother and sister that hinted at reproach.

'Quite a good one, so I hear,' Nadine added suddenly. 'You have a good body, my dear. Fit, trim; ideal for what is expected of you.' Now her smile was very wide and very warm. With the addition of more wine, her voice was deep, yet crisp as burned toffee.

'I try to excel in everything, as much as is possible,' returned Penny, unable to hide her unease that the wandering gaze inspired in her. Nadine had watched her behind one of those mirrors. She knew it instinctively. Determinedly, she declined to blush.

As she smiled at Alistair's sister, Penny took a deep breath. Her breasts struggled against the half-open bodice. It was a provocative move, one designed to suggest that she was both knowledgeable and available.

Her eyes took note of their individual reactions. Auberon merely blushed, his eyelids fluttering like frightened butterflies.

Experience and familiarity won through. Reggie licked his lips and made no attempt to stop his eyes from settling on her cleavage.

66

Alistair, she thought, looked uncomfortable. It was as though he wanted to stare at what was on offer, but didn't dare. There was an odd look in his eyes, a mix of desire and perpetual torment.

Only Nadine's gaze was steady, her lips smiling. There was absolute boldness in her look, coupled with an odd satisfaction. Her eyes narrowed through the halo of blue smoke.

Content that she had received admiration, Penny unfolded the crisp white napkin that smelt of fresh citrus and was stiff with starch.

Nadine was directly across from her. It is easy to study looks when the subject you are studying is facing you.

It was hard not to stare at Alistair's sister. Penny tried to look away, to concentrate on the meal, sip less slowly at the wine, but Nadine surprised her. It seemed quite amazing that someone with such white hair and angular features could possibly be related to Alistair.

Nadine caught her looking and raised her blonde eyebrows towards the cropped hair that shone like silver beneath the lights.

From a distance, Penny guessed, the short glossy spikes could almost be mistaken for her bare skull. Jet earrings jiggled gently in her ears when she laughed as she did now.

Sir Reggie had cracked a joke. Penny hadn't heard it, her mind too full of analysing these people, of surmising how they might fit into the overall picture of things.

So far since coming here, she'd learned little of time-table and other more sociable interactions; except for Gregory of course. But Gregory didn't talk much – not that such a minor problem as that detracted from his magnetism one little bit.

'I hope I haven't offended you,' said Sir Reggie suddenly, shattering the beauty and sheer sexuality of her thoughts as his hand landed on hers. 'I hope you don't mind being the butt of my little joke. I didn't really mean it, you know.'

'Not at all,' she said, smiling brightly and wondering if the wine she had been drinking had affected her hearing. 'I can take a joke any time.' Then she laughed. What he'd said about her in any joke was of no interest to her; besides, she hadn't heard him.

Her attention was drawn to Nadine whose hand reached over the table. Her palm rattled the glass and silverware as she brought it down heavily on the pure whiteness of the tablecloth.

'That's it, Penny darling. Take no notice of him. I'm sure you'll be an asset round here, darling girl. My brother appreciates perfection – in everything.'

'I won't,' she replied, her eyes catlike; her lips, glistening with the dark rich colour, slowly sipped her wine.

Their eyes met as Nadine straightened in her chair. For the first time, Penny could evaluate just how tall Nadine was; six foot two at least, and clad from head to toe in black, its denseness only relieved with base metal bangles and a collar that looked to be made of dull marcasite and leather and a good two inches in depth – perhaps made for a bull mastiff rather than a woman.

'No harm in that, my dears,' chirped up Sir Reginald who Alistair had explained was a fellow director and business associate in the wide and varied group first founded by Alistair's father before the Second World War. 'Perfection is to be admired, my dears . . . cosseted,' he added as his broad hand circled Penny's back. She leaned forward away from the harp-shaped back of the chair. His fingers spread downwards and slid over the roundness of her buttocks. 'All perfection,' he added with a low chuckle.

He smelt of expensive aftershave and his body appeared well looked after beneath the expensive smoothness of his black evening suit. Being of mature age, and born with privilege and rank rather than achieving it, he was the only one truly dressed for dinner.

Alistair was not casually dressed, but not formally either. His shirt was made of grey silk that matched his eyes. He wore a tie which must have cost as much as some people would pay for a whole outfit. He looked smooth, well-groomed and as expensive as the neat gold-and-diamond cufflinks that flashed at his wrists. Smooth, she thought, sure of himself, yet strangely ill at ease; and the more he looked at her, the more ill at ease he appeared to become.

Not that he was the only one who studied her. The expressions of everyone there were symptomatic of the fantasies each one was enjoying in their minds.

All eyes relished the pertness of her nipples, which were outlined like rare etchings through the thin material of her dress.

Their eyes travelled, as though they were hands, down to her waist and over the curve of her belly. Only Reggie could see any further. His eyes alighted on her lap. His breathing was quick and hot, his hand slightly sweaty upon her thigh, but pleasant.

With daring borrowed from the headiness of the wine, she opened her legs slightly, and with one hand hitched her skirt a little higher. She heard Reggie suck in his breath as her own Black Forest came shyly into view; no more than a mass of darkness between the creamy flesh of her thighs.

Sidelong, she smiled at him, saw gratitude in his eyes and was rewarded for her efforts by his fingers edging stealthily over the soft satin of her inner thigh before tangling amongst her dusky hidden hair.

His lips were wet now, flecked with spittle at each corner. He licked them dry and smiled at her. Alistair talked to Auberon in the background, Nadine adding her more tart comments.

Yet somehow their talk was nothing more than a shadow, a mime they were going through as if to put her at her ease, to let her enjoy, to indulge and to arouse. There was more yet to come.

'I raise my glass to you,' he said with gentlemanly politeness, whilst the fingers of his right hand divided her feathered lips and touched lightly on her throbbing rosebud. 'I think you are a charming young woman, a great asset to this establishment and the association.'

'Association?' she queried. Her questioning tone merely disguised the moan that had escaped from her throat along with the word. She was wet, aroused and

69

couldn't help her legs from opening wider. He took advantage of the opportunity. There was one finger now either side of her clitoris, each one folding her labia away from her innermost treasures.

He winked in a boyish way that complemented his handsome patrician features. A gold bracelet slid down his wrist as he raised his glass again.

'To you, young lady – and your association with everyone here.'

The two fingers slid towards her secret portal, dipped neatly in, retreated, then dipped again.

She was aware of her own breath quickening, her breasts rising and falling against her bodice, their curving edges peering out from the restriction of her dress like twin crescent moons. She was also aware that conversation had ceased, that she was the subject of silence and all-seeing eyes. But she didn't care. She was too far gone to care, too far along the road to a mind-shattering orgasm that she badly yearned for.

He drained his glass, she drained hers. She liked this man. Like Alistair, the power he possessed made her feel good, and secure. Now her glass was sadly empty. She lifted it and held it to the light so the wine turned pink against the lead crystal and the light from the chandeliers. As she twirled it, rainbow colours shot through each sharp cut prism of glass and threw its beam upon her face. Like people, she thought; or, at least, like the people here. White on the surface, but composed of many colours, with many facets.

'Is she very wet, Reggie darling?' Nadine asked suddenly.

Penny gasped, glanced swiftly at Alistair's sister, then back, almost in a fit of pleading, to Reggie's face.

'Very wet, Nadine darling, very wet indeed. Just a little more effort, and this little pussy will come.'

Penny was speechless, as much from her mounting orgasm as from the sudden realisation that everyone there knew exactly what they were doing, and from the sound of it, *had* done all along.

'Then bring her off, darling. Right now!'

70

Like the prisms of light that had reflected so richly from the glass, the faces of those around Penny spun in a blur of colour as two fingers of Reggie's right hand pushed further into her. Never mind that everyone was watching. She was beyond caring. In an effort to capture the full impact of his fingers, she slid slightly forward on the chair so he could invade her more fully. All the while, his fingers dived in, his thumb dancing over her clitoris in short, sharp flicks. Now he used his other hand to hold back her fleshy lips and the sleek black hair of her pubes. And then it came, flooding over her in a torrent of electric release. Her hips lifted against his hands, and crying out, she threw her head back, closing her eyes, her orgasm diminishing with each murmur of breath.

Reggie removed his hands and washed them in the bowl of water at the side of his fork. The bowl was dark blue. A slice of lemon floated on the surface. It was a relaxed and effective action, emphasising cleanliness, opulence and sensuality at one and the same time.

Tossing her hair and still breathless, Penny eyed those around the table.

'Splendid, darling!' exclaimed Nadine, cheroot gripped in her teeth and hands clapping. 'A splendid effort indeed. If you ride your horses like that, then you'll get no complaints from me.'

Auberon just smiled, and Reggie winked at her again, refilled his glass and raised it to her before sipping.

Alistair was staring at her, his mouth grim set and eyes glittering. She could see him swallowing consistently, and noticed that his lips were dry and that he seemed unable to say anything. Had he not seen enough? Or, perhaps, he had seen too much; perhaps she had blotted her copybook without meaning to.

At last, he cleared his throat. Then he spoke. 'Outstanding.'

Penny flashed her eyes as she savoured the word. That one word clarified exactly what he thought. Not the word itself: there was nothing much in that, it was ordinary, just a word. But she'd detected something else in the way he said it. Deep inside it had come into existence, yet had stuck in his throat, had grated its way to the surface so that when he *did* say it, its meaning was intensified. His voice had been as low as the depths from which it had come. She knew then that he wanted her, that in time her wager would be won.

Like liquid fire, she returned his stare with her own. When, she asked with her eyes, exactly when?

Alistair's gaze shifted, almost guiltily. From the centre of the table, he took hold of the half-empty wine bottle – one of three that sat on there – and poured into his own glass.

But other eyes watched. Other eyes surmised and made plans for these two people.

Nadine still held the key to her brother's torment. Thoughtfully, she played with the black cross that hung from her ear. It jingled playfully as she touched it. With each jingle, Penny noticed that Alistair's jaw clenched, and a nerve beneath his eye quivered.

Nadine saw her look but did not answer the question in her eyes. Nadine was taking pleasure from her brother's clenching jaw and the nerve that quivered just below his right eye. She knew what he was going through and understood how much the key, which hung behind the earring, meant to him. Only the shadow of a smile played around her mouth as she toyed with the earring and then touched the cold metal of the small key itself. Time and place was controlled by her. Nothing had changed, nothing would change. All in good time, her brother would have what he craved, and Penny would have more than she could ever have bargained for.

'More wine, Penny?'

Thoughts melted and scattered, Penny looked up into the soft, boyish face of Auberon Harding, another horse rider lucky enough to get a place under Beaumont's roof together with a wedge of his bank account.

'Yes please,' she replied. For some reason, she used her sexiest voice to answer. Perhaps it was because of the burning she felt deep inside; the need to have a male phallus inside her rather than just be played with, probed and brought off purely for the benefit of other people.

72

She smiled her thanks to Auberon Harding, the Honourable Auberon Harding to be exact, whose family were something in the meat trade and had been for generations. Perhaps they'd been high-street butchers who were suddenly landed with the privilege of supplying Queen Victoria with pork sausages. It didn't matter. Now, he was an Honourable, and he looked it. He had a look of class about him: thick lipped with a head-boy type of face and a hairstyle that sat firmly on the fence between fashion and conformity, yet flopped over his forehead. His clothes straddled the same fence. Not too formal, not too fashionable: white shirt; neat tie; neat jacket; neat, sharp-pleated trousers; polished black shoes. Everything about him was neat, correct, pleated and polished. Public school, she decided. She'd met others like him, men who found it impossible to shake off the residue of a rigid regime that had moulded them into a pre-set shape. It was as if they'd originally been made of jelly and now were cast in bronze.

He looked nice enough, but, although he surveyed her dark hair, her open expression and her gaping neckline, she was surprised and a mite disappointed when his eyes did not linger.

Fragments of conversation filtered into Penny's mind as she drank more wine, which was smooth on her tongue and mellow in her head. On top of that, the newness of everything, the excitement of it all and the experience of her dining-table orgasm had lightened her mind even more. Eager to learn and perhaps experience more, she continued to survey those at the table, her dark lashes sweeping her cheeks as her eyes flickered from one guest to another along with the conversation.

Sir Reginald fondled her knee each time he spoke to her. There was something strangely protective about his fondling, as though he were trying to put her at ease and to make her feel at home. She let him, and tried her best to let Alistair know that she was letting him. After all, there was still the wager to consider, though gradually she was becoming fascinated with this close group of people who had accepted her so easily and so completely.

For the moment, her massage with the blond angel was forgotten, though if nothing further came off tonight, she would need him again, if only to ease her aching libido with his flexible fingers, though she would of course prefer his rampant penis.

But Gregory was not here. Alistair was. She caught him looking at her once or twice. It was a guilty look, as though he was a small boy and had been caught stealing from a sweet shop. So far, she thought to herself, Alistair had disappointed her.

Adopting an air of indifference to hide that disappointment, she let her eyes study the other diners whilst her mind weighed up each one.

Sir Reggie was sweet, debonair and highly attractive. She imagined that having sex with him would be a very professional experience. During his life, he would have known many women, would have indulged most readily in every conceivable practice and with every conceivable age, colour and creed of woman. Sir Reggie had been in the army. Sir Reggie had travelled.

Auberon seemed the height of politeness, the warmth between them like one old schoolmate to another whenever he included her in his conversation. There was no strange guilt in his look like there was with Alistair. His colouring and flickering eyelids came more from shyness than guilt. Of course, she still couldn't quite work out what Alistair had to be guilty about.

Nadine was the most intense watcher. Each time Penny chanced to look in her direction, Nadine was staring back at her over the top of her wineglass, and although Alistair dominated the conversation with his talk of mergers, expansion and then the world of equestrianism, she had a distinct impression his sister might be more powerful than him.

Watching and wondering about her fellow diners ignited new excitement in Penny's loins. The actions and the scenes she envisaged each of these people in were only in her mind at present, yet she knew that what could be fantasised could also be turned into fact.

As she sipped her wine, she imagined what each man's

74

body would feel like against hers, what each sex would feel like in her as each mouth nibbled and sucked at her willing breasts.

Her eyes darted to each in turn and her mind visualised virulently before settling on Alistair. There was something about him that was simultaneously alluring and secretive. She was drawn to him, and everything Ariadne had said only added to her curiosity. Like getting to grips with a new horse, he was a challenge, a creature to be broken and ridden. Vaguely, she knew in her mind that whatever it took, she would have him.

Ariadne had told her he was a voyeur, a spectator. Then, she decided, she would give him plenty to look at. Each and every sexual encounter she had would be within his sight so he would have to take part and would be unable to resist the depths to which debauchery and her own sexuality could plumb. She drained her glass. With a smile, Auberon refilled it.

Food, wine and sparkling conversation were all in plentiful supply. As the wine poured down her throat, she began to wonder who was on offer this evening, who was there for the asking and where Alistair would be when she indulged her desire.

'Lovely meal, my dear, don't you think?' The plump-fingered hand of the errant knight squeezed her thigh, his fingers lightly touching the valley at the top of her legs.

She smiled at him, then over at Alistair. He glanced at her, almost as if he knew what was happening.

Turning to Sir Reginald, and looking into his face as though he were the lover she had always been waiting for, she opened her legs a little wider. She saw his lips get wetter, the bottom one sagging. Purposefully, she snapped her legs shut. Sir Reggie's hand retreated and his eyes flickered. He looked hurt for a moment, but only for a moment. His smile returned and he turned his face and his conversation to Alistair.

A gentle touch on her elbow made her transfer her attention to Auberon. There was a fairy lightness in his fingers, a playfulness that betrayed the strength needed

75

for the sport he so lovingly pursued. Reins were hard to hold on a plunging, rearing animal that weighed something near half a ton, and didn't she know it?

'It's nice to have you here. It really is so terribly nice.' She smiled at him and to herself. He even sounded like a head boy – one left over from some obscure and ancient public school.

And yet there was sincerity in his eyes and on his lips. She was aware of sudden silence. Conversation, which up until now had flowed almost unabated except when Penny had attracted their attention, had now ceased. Suddenly, she felt as though she were the centre of attention.

Briefly, she glanced towards Alistair. His eyes met hers before he leaned across the table and spoke to Sir Reginald. She couldn't grasp what was said. She looked from the older man to the younger, then was aware of the eyes of Alistair's sister, Nadine. They were like pale grey pools amid the heavy black make-up. And suddenly, along with everyone else, there was lust in her eyes.

Holding Nadine's gaze and tensing her back, Penny clenched her buttocks in an effort to control the familiar ache surging between her thighs. There were opportunities here, she told herself, and though her vision was blurred and her head was light, she had no intention of missing them.

'Do you think you will like it here?' Auberon asked her.

Everyone seemed to be holding their breath for her answer. All, she guessed, needed to know how her earlier sojourn with Sir Reggie had affected her opinion.

'It's nice to be here. It really is,' she said brightly. 'Am I right in thinking you've got the room below me?' She placed her hand on his thigh, felt the iron-hard muscles tense beneath her touch.

Around the table, there was a sudden exhalation of breath, as though there had been a doubt, which was now discarded.

But Penny was only half-aware now of what was

76

happening around her. She made no secret of what she was doing at the table, her smile wide, whilst her fingers flicked gently but determinedly at the awakening flesh just behind Auberon's zip-fastener. Here was a flower just waiting to be plucked, and she had just the vase to put it in, she thought cheerily.

He flushed as he nodded, and his eyes flitted briefly around the table. Other mouths smiled, other eyes sparkled as though they too were experiencing what he was experiencing. Nervously, his tongue licked at his lips. As his leg moved, his shaft jumped against his trousers.

And yet, there was a vulnerability about him, an innocence that seemed strangely irreconcilable with the determined sportsman she knew him to be. She retrieved her hand and smiled.

I wonder, she thought to herself, head supported on cupped hand whilst her other hand twirled the dark liquid in her glass, whether he's a bit of a cane man – even a bit of a gay.

'Time for bed.' Alistair got to his feet. As if it were a prescribed signal, everyone else got to theirs.

Sir Reginald coughed and yawned in disjointed unison, and Penny smiled into her wine as the shiny seat of his well-polished dinner trousers came into view.

Nadine rose in chilly black splendour like a winter's night, head and shoulders above everyone present.

She was silent, though her eyes glittered and flitted briefly from one face to another before ending up on Penny. There was no disguising the self-congratulation in her look. As though she's looking through my clothes rather than at them, thought Penny. It was as if, she reflected, weakly grasping the thought as it circled in her mind, that Nadine knew exactly what was underneath. It was then she remembered her suspicions about the mirror and also about Alistair being a man who watched, not did. There were no guesses as to who he'd be watching tonight.

'I'll be taking a stroll, if anyone wants to join me.' Sir Reginald's now bloodshot eyes searched for an offer.

No one did join him.

All the same, Penny was aware of knowing glances passing from one to the other. A curling feeling rose and fell in her stomach. Somehow she knew that no matter where she went to bed that night or what she did, someone would be watching.

Alistair bid goodnight and Nadine glared with glittering iciness at Penny and Auberon, but ignored Sir Reginald completely.

They went off in different directions, Penny holding Auberon's hand, and Sir Reginald out through the front door for his so-called walk.

Auberon and Penny went outside, too. Both wished to check on their mounts before they turned in. At least, that was what they said.

The night sky was deep indigo and scattered with stars. The air was warm, and an owl hooted from a far-off meadow.

Penny breathed deeply, threw her head back and felt the tickling of her hair against her shoulders. The cool breeze of evening lifted her skirt and wafted around her naked thighs. The muskiness of sexual secretions reached her nostrils. The memory of that orgasm tantalised the crowding nerve ends that clustered around her clitoris. Excitement re-kindled desire. There was still a need within her.

She shouldn't complain, she told herself. She'd had two superb climaxes since she'd arrived, but both had been achieved by manipulative fingers not a penetrating manhood. Yet the need to experience such a penetration was getting stronger.

Speculatively, she looked sidelong at Auberon. Perhaps, she thought to herself just a little wickedly and a little selfishly, just perhaps they could both have what they wanted – both her and the young, fresh-faced man walking beside her.

'What a beautiful night,' she murmured into her escort's ear. 'Good enough to get to know each other better.'

His smile was bashful, perhaps even vague. It irked her to see that he didn't seem particularly enthusiastic.

She eyed him again, and thought of her first impression of him. Head-boy type. And he was rather pretty in a plump and boyish kind of way. Public school, she decided, had shaped his sexual preferences. In the darkness, she grinned. Perhaps, a wicked thought said in her head, Auberon liked other things.

Gravel scrunched under their feet as they walked the path to the stables. Vague mutters born of wine and brandy drifted in the night air. Sir Reggie appeared to be wandering off towards the shining glass of the orangery.

Perhaps it was the clarity of the night air, but Penny was very aware of the odour of the man at her side, the spoor of masculine sexuality that lay in a fine film over his skin.

It was also the night air that brought the sound of other footsteps crunching on the same gravel they had walked.

Slyly, she looked back along the path. Sir Reginald had stopped in his tracks; two figures had joined him.

Beaumont is a spectator, Ariadne had said. In Penny's opinion, there were others here besides Alistair who liked to watch.

As the wine cleared from her head, it occurred to her that this could well be the first chance she would have of trying her luck with Alistair; of putting on a good enough show to at least whet his appetite.

She looked at Auberon as though she could eat him. Her fingers tangled in his. He smiled at her, a little shyly. As if, she mused, he had thoughts in his head that did not quite match hers.

Never mind, she thought, we could both get what we want tonight, or at least go some way towards it. First, she decided, she must make no secret of her intentions and her willingness to cater fully to his needs.

Lightly brushing against his hip and thigh as they walked, her fingers fondled the slight rise that pushed against his fly. His gasp hung on the air between them. He gulped and cleared his throat before he spoke.

'That's terribly nice, awfully nice in fact,' he stammered.

'Just nice?' she asked, and lent an ache of disappointment to her voice as if she were feeling just a touch insulted that her adept probings had not produced a more satisfactory response.

'Very nice,' he added on the edge of a sigh.

She moved her hand, ran it around his waist, then slid it over and between the iron-hard cheeks of his behind.

Ahhh! That's better, she said to herself as his breath and a nervous cough collided into a kind of choke.

'That's delicious!' he breathed at last, his voice one or two octaves higher than it had been.

So she was right. She smiled at the night. Tonight could finish even better than it had started.

'Is that?' she asked with sudden cruelty, her nails digging into one tight buttock.

'Terribly,' he moaned.

'And that?' she asked again as her nails dug into the other buttock.

'Awfully!' he gasped. 'Ahhh!'

'That's not good enough,' she said suddenly, thanking her intuition and enjoying the unfamiliar cruelty she brought to her voice and her clawed hand. 'I'm sure you can do better than that, boy! Don't you think so?'

Beneath her nails, his flesh trembled. Her own loins quivered in sympathy.

'I . . . I . . .' His eyes glittered, she saw a bead of sweat erupt on his brow, divide and run like melting ice towards his eyebrows.

What use did she have for his answer? She knew what he wanted, just as she knew they were being followed, and that whatever they did would be watched and enjoyed by those they had been with at dinner.

'This, I think, is what you need!' she exclaimed, her voice fierce with authority and dripping with promised discipline.

Taking careful aim, she plunged her index finger into where she judged his rectum should be.

He groaned as his cheeks tightened over her rigid finger. As much as she could, dressed as he still was in

80

his dark and well-cut evening trousers, she pressed her finger in, deeper.

They still walked towards the stables, him almost on tiptoe, her finger guiding him like some rigid and over-size puppet to where they were going.

With undisguised curiosity, she stopped in her tracks and put her other hand on his crotch. Her fingers closed over it like the petals of a flower. There it was, the fruit of her labour, hard, erect and begging for more.

So that was what he wanted.

The footsteps behind did not cease. She looked back into the darkness before walking on; she knew they were following and also what their intention was. Well, they would see everything they were coming to see ... and more.

If they expected a straightforward fuck, then they were going to be sadly disappointed on this occasion. Much as she might want it herself, she knew that Auberon's path to that end would be different from hers.

And they would be watching. She was sure of that, just as she was sure of the light scrunching of gravel she could hear from somewhere behind them.

'We'd better do something about this,' murmured Penny as she kissed his cheek and undid his flies.

His prick fell out, white, lean and topped with a foreskin like an unfolded toadstool. The moonlight caught it, giving it a ghostly appearance as they walked on. Like the cane of a blind man pointing the way, it jiggled from side to side as they walked. She enjoyed seeing that, and in order to maintain such an unusual sight, she pushed her finger as firmly as she could into the crack between his buttocks.

'I'm terribly excited you know. I can't tell you how much this means to me.'

Auberon's voice held all the excitement of a small child with worn, but well-loved toys and a new friend. It was sweet, and only made Penny more curious to know what sort of a man and how much of one he was.

'Don't mention it. I'm always willing to do a man a favour.' That at least, she realised, was the honest truth.

What a picture they must present, she thought, her finger still firmly embedded in his rectum. All the time, she could feel the cheeks tensing, then relaxing, one muscled orb moving with slow deliberation against the other. The effect was arousing to her as well as to him.

Curiosity gave wing to inflamed sensations. Already, she could feel the pertness of her clitoris pushing through the mat of satin hair that shielded it from the outside world. Soon it would demand its tribute, crave without pity for the height of ecstasy that was its due reward.

But in the meantime, she would give Auberon what he wanted, and give the approaching band of spectators exactly what they deserved.

Dark, and lit with only the light of a low moon, the stable block smelt of warm hay and the sweaty flesh of the animals it was home to. In the gloom, the beasts snickered softly and moved gently within their stables.

As his hand reached out for the light switch, she took her finger from his behind and grabbed his white wand that had almost lit their way here. She heard him gasp and, in his surprise, saw him take his hand away from the switch.

'This way,' she whispered as she used his cock to lead him into the adjacent hay store.

A round window divided into four odd-shaped panes allowed moonlight to stream through and throw a silver pool on the area she had selected to give her début performance.

She smiled to herself at the thought. Like a great celestial spotlight, outlining and accentuating everything they would be doing for their very select audience.

Beneath them, the straw was warm, its scent full of the earthiness of ripe meadows, hot summers and unbridled fertility.

'How much do you want what I am going to give you?' she asked him provocatively, one hand encompassing his hot weapon whilst the other squeezed the felt softness of his balls.

'A terrible amount!' he exclaimed. 'A truly terrible amount!'

'How much?' she asked with some sharpness.

He squealed like a pig as she squeezed his balls harder and dug her fingernails into his phallus.

'Truly! Very. Oh please . . .'

She paused, wondering for just a moment if he might faint away altogether. Tremors of mingled emotions enveloped her own mind and body. There was elation in being in control of such a situation, of having his penis so stiff, yet so vulnerable, in the palm of her hand.

She swallowed her own excitement and her own need to have him probe into her body. Auberon had definite tastes. If she was to get what she wanted, she had first to satisfy his own particular tastes.

She let his prick drop from her hands, and although she had expected her release of him to result in temporary disappointment, she certainly hadn't expected tears.

'Please . . .' he pleaded, his voice little more than a whimper. 'Please . . . anything you want you can do to me . . . anything at all.'

Now what do I do? she asked herself, her mouth slightly open, and her eyes vaguely aware of figures moving in the gloom.

Sexual innovation was part of her character so it wasn't too difficult to come up with something suitable.

'Kiss me, and I will carry on. I will give you all that you desire better than you've ever been given it before.'

Ecstasy as well as moonlight lit his face.

Then he kissed her, his lips warm and soft against hers.

But Penny was very aware that such tenderness would not be enough for him.

'Dog!' she exclaimed as she slapped his face. 'I didn't tell you to kiss me like that! You can't kiss my lips. Not those anyway!'

As he rubbed his face and stared at her wide eyed, she opened her legs and lifted her skirt. Then she peed, her golden rain hot and rising like an autumn mist from the soft straw.

A whimper escaped Auberon's throat. Even in nothing more than moonlight, she could see his eyes glittered and his cock had stiffened.

'Take your clothes off first,' she told him.

He did. With fastidious precision, he folded each item and laid it neatly to one side. She watched in silent fascination. How predictable he was, how moulded by his school-days.

Flesh quivering with delight rather than repugnance, he knelt before her and steadied himself by putting his hands on her thighs.

'Hands behind back!' she growled.

Like an exceptionally obedient dog, he obeyed.

She opened her legs a little wider and edged closer to his face. To accommodate her, he tilted his head backwards. Before long, his ears were against her thighs. His head was trapped. The lips of her sex kissed his mouth.

His tongue licked amongst the thick cluster of pubic hair before she opened her labia for him with her own fingers. With undulating movements, she moved herself over him so she could take full advantage of his heat-seeking tongue, his chin and his nose.

He sucked at her like a hungry baby, taking the last clinging drops of golden liquid into his mouth. Then his tongue worked its way over her buds and folds, prising more juice from her, but this time less salty, more sticky and resulting from desire rather than relief.

His tongue was now in her, hot, probing, like a small prick, yet strangely more pliable.

She moaned, and as she clamped his head tightly between her thighs so he could not possibly move, she let her skirt fall over him whilst she unbuttoned her bodice and let her breasts break free.

Once they were unrestricted, she rolled them in her hands, closed her eyes and felt as though she were the goddess Diana herself, bathed in moonlight and riding some creature of the night as she rocked back and forth over Auberon's open mouth and willing tongue.

Her eyes opened briefly to survey the darkness. She smiled at it. Then she took off her dress.

The moonlight streamed through the window and added an iridescent richness to the colour of her hair, an incandescent brightness to the creamy gleam of her skin.

84

She was a performer and she loved the part she was playing. The figures in the darkness were of no account. They were just spectators in the auditorium enjoying the show. But like all plays, there is a first act, then there are the second, third and fourth . . .

A pool of erotic energy was building up around her vulva and eddying with waves of rising desire to lap against her rampant clitoris. Despite Auberon's best efforts, he could not eat them.

Now, she decided, is the time for the next act.

'Enough!' she shouted, and pushed his head away.

She couldn't have pushed him that hard, yet there he lay, gasping among the straw, a film of her bodily moisture shining like silver around his lips. He looked cowed in body, yet there was an undeniable glint of liquid desire in the bright hazel of his eyes. He was playing a part and enjoying it. Well, she'd really give him something to remember, she'd really use and abuse him for all she was worth. He yearned for it, she needed her own climax, and the watchers in the shadows expected it.

'Hands and knees!' she shouted at him. 'Get on your hands and knees!'

He rolled over and did as she ordered. She walked around him, proud in her nakedness, showing herself off for those whose eyes watched from the darkness.

If Mark could see me now, she thought to herself with a lewd smile, he'd take me and take me until we were both exhausted. But Mark wasn't here. Auberon was.

Auberon had a good body, and despite her determination to play for the crowd, she admired it. With long, sweeping strokes, she smoothed her hands down his back, then smacked each cheek so that pinkness replaced the perfect whiteness. There between his thighs, his balls hung in their skin casing. She raised her foot beneath them so they sat warm and weighty, first on her toes, then on her instep. She rolled them on her foot, enjoying the warmth, enjoying the feeling of power it gave her. She heard his breath quickening, then realised her own was racing, too. In time with the rising of his desire, hers, too, rose and waited.

'Stand up,' she ordered.

Hesitantly but with obvious subservience, he got to his feet.

'Don't hurt me,' he wheedled.

Even that, she knew, was just play-acting. Of course he wanted her to hurt him. He enjoyed being hurt, enjoyed that evolution of pain that led him to that final throb of a spent member.

'I will do as I please,' she told him, and held his prick as if it were just his handle and made of something harder than normal flesh and blood.

She bound him with items of leather harness that hung on the wall. The ends she found looped up easily into iron rings that hung from a wooden beam above his head.

She stood on bales of straw to reach the iron rings, then fastened the ends of the harness back through the pieces she'd already looped around his wrists.

His arms were raised full-stretch and the tautness of his muscles outlined by a compliant moon. He hung there – like a sacrificial offering on some pagan altar – waiting for his moment, for his time of giving.

Surprisingly, she found other matching rings in the floor. She bound him to those, too, so his legs were stretched apart, thigh and calf muscles hard and unyielding beneath the softness of her hands and the tightness of the leather.

When she had finished, she stood back to survey her handiwork. She was well satisfied. He formed a near perfect 'X', his prick still proud of his body, limbs stretched to full extent, buttocks tightly clenched.

Like a preying panther, she circled him, trailing her fingers over a body that was unburdened with superfluous flesh. There was only muscle, hard, primed to perfection.

Her eyes wandered over him shining with delight, and she realised suddenly just how much those other eyes in the darkness must be shining, too.

Her body trembled in anticipation as she admired the tension that rippled his muscles and quivered in hard spasms over his taut behind.

All the time she laboured, exploring with just the tips of her fingers. The more pressure she applied and the greater the sharpness of her nails, the more his phallus grew.

'How does that feel?' she asked him. 'Now you're stretched to my liking.'

He groaned as she raked her nails over his stem, then groaned more when she squeezed his balls in her hand.

The sounds from his throat were unintelligible until she had released his balls.

'Glorious,' he murmured.

Even now, she knew he would appreciate her abusing him that little bit more until she judged him ready for her own purposes.

'That's not good enough!' she said, and took the final two pieces of harness from the hook on the wall.

These pieces were thin, almost thong-like. Briefly, she wondered what horse they were used for – a light-weight one by the looks of it. Not that it mattered. What mattered was her performance on this most auspicious night.

She tried not to look into the darkness, yet effort was needed to concentrate her eyes and her actions on Auberon alone.

With a wicked, catlike grin, she threaded the fine strips of leather through his legs, one piece at a time so that his testes were pushed towards the centre immediately behind his phallus. They bulged there, round and shiny like overblown balloons.

Auberon was in ecstasy. His head was thrown back, his eyes were closed and a series of appreciative moans escaped from his throat.

The ends of the leather she crossed over his chest, then she looped them over his shoulders so his balls and penis were bunched in one mighty mound of flesh that lunged to greater size as the man revelled in his sweet restraint. After that, she passed the end of each thong through each

87

ring – that hung like bangles behind his balls – and fastened them securely.

Observant enough in daylight to know where everything was kept, Penny took two items from the custom-built metal shelf against the wall. One was a simple riding crop, the other a lunging whip.

Now it was easy not to look into the blackness. Everything, they say, gets easier with practice, and in this case it was certainly true.

Bondage had been something that she and Mark had got up to when desires and emotions were too far beyond the normal level of tension. Even so, she had been enthralled by it, experiencing more powerful releases than straightforward sex could ever satisfy.

With professional efficiency, she cracked the whip then smiled with glee as she saw the reaction on Auberon's face. The fear of pain that flashed there she knew to be only pretence. Deep down, beneath that terrified façade, she knew his body was aching for pain, longing for the thin strip of leather that would raise redness over the taut hardness of his flesh.

Her eyes dropped to his trapped phallus. It lurched, reared with bottled-up excitement and, just for a moment, she thought he might spill his seed before she was ready for him to do so.

There was delight in her own action. Much as this man wanted her to pleasure him, she also had her own satisfaction to think about. No matter. First, she would deal with him, whip him to a trembling mass of throbbing erection. Then she would take him purely for her own pleasure.

His trembling loins shivered the very air as she walked around him. She trailed her fingers from the hard shoulder muscles and down to his round cheeks. She teased each one, tracing lines, each one terminating in the tight cleft between. Instinctively, his buttocks squeezed like they had earlier when her finger had probed at his puckered anus.

The fingers travelled on around his pelvis to his throbbing member. She saw it rear; saw it jerk as if it could take flight if set free. But it would not be set free. It was trapped pinched between two bonds of leather.

Sharply, her fingernails traced more circles around the bulbous head of his phallus. Her eyes opened wide. Never could she have believed that such exquisite pain could spur one to greater things, to a greater size. With enjoyment and without protest, she entered his world and took pleasure in the sublime pain she saw fit to endow. Amid pleasurable murmurs, she hissed through her clenched teeth as she drew her nails down over his stem. Surprised at her own reactions, she watched with interest as the veins of his neck stood in sharp relief against his skin. A moment later, he threw his head back and howled at the rafters.

This was pure delight, pure power. Thoughtfully, her fingers dipped into the slippery mixture that was brimming through the length of her labia. So far, this little act had been all his. She had given him a lot; he had given her little.

In time with her rapid breath, her breasts heaved as power mingled with sexual excitement.

Again she cracked her whip. She heard his sharp intake of breath and sensed his apprehension as he attempted to gauge her timing.

Stretching his throat again, he threw his head back and let out a yell as the fine end of the lunging whip curved over his buttocks. She saw them tense, fold one in upon the other as if he were holding something in between. She smiled. She was beginning to enjoy this, and her imagination was beginning to work overtime.

The whip rose and fell again. His cry was a rich mix of pain and delight.

Breathless, her breasts pouting to the point of ecstasy, she dropped her arm to her side, then reached out to run her hand over the quivering behind. Hot flesh trembled beneath her palm, and tight cheeks closed over the nub of her probing thumb as it dived and teased the prim ring in between. It excited her, made her stomach tighten and her clitoris rise in rapture from its sheath of dewy petals.

89

'More,' she heard him breathe. 'Give me more.'

Briefly, unable to resist the lure of the stretched torso, she ran her hand from his armpit, over his ribs, and on to his hip, then across his stomach. She clenched her fist so her fingers formed a talon. He screamed soft and low as the claw ran from navel to phallic stem, pinching at his glistening glans, before digging into the soft flesh that hung beneath.

'I'll give you more,' she growled, now unable to stop herself from entering the full spirit of the scene. 'Just wait and I'll give you more.'

The whip stung again and again across his bunched shoulders, his arched back, his round behind, the shuddering muscles of his thighs and calves.

She changed position, altered her aim so the whip fell in a long curl of leather across his heaving chest and stretched stomach, lightly kissing his jutting penis as it landed with stinging accuracy over his thighs. His knees bent slightly. Sweat glistened on the abused muscles.

But now her throat was dry and her sex soaking. Penny knew her own body well enough to know when its just desserts were due. Her aim had been strong and true, and now his flesh was glowing nicely with the searing heat of perfect pain. The sight of his throbbing weapon, leaping up and down with each new dealing of sublime ecstasy, was too much for her to bear. She had to have him. At the same time, she had to satisfy his own more specialised pleasure.

The head of the lunging whip was thick, not as thick as his penis, but thick enough. Imagination rich in original thought took over as she eyed his twitching buttocks and the handle of the whip. Her mind was made up.

'Now it's my turn. There's nothing for you to do but go along with it.'

'Whatever ... whatever you want to do to me, do!' The whimper in his voice seemed more of an entreaty than a reproach.

That to her was confirmation enough that what she

had in mind would delight him. At the same time it would get her what she wanted.

With the helpful rubbing of the handle against an odd piece of saddle soap, she slid it between the tight orbs of his behind. Slowly, she entered him. She heard him moan, wondered for a moment if she was doing right or if it would hurt him.

She glanced around to the front of his body at his jerking penis and smiled. It positively glowed in the semi-darkness, a pearl drop of moisture crowning its gleaming head. Auberon, she guessed, was in ecstasy.

With one hand holding on to the half-submerged handle that now stuck out from his anus, she brought the rest of the whip around the front with her, running its declining thickness through her fingers until she was facing him.

Her gaze dropped to his penis before returning to his face. Beneath half-closed eyes he watched her, his mouth open, jewels of sweat hanging from his nose and chin. She dropped down, poked out her tongue and transferred the pearl drop from tip of penis to tip of tongue.

She did not stop there, but continued her journey with the thin end of the whip until she was back where she started and could tie it round the portion of the handle that stuck obscenely out from between his cheeks. It would not fall out.

With the riding crop in one hand, she dragged a bale of straw in front of the restrained male. At first she knelt on it, her eyes filled with the sight of his pulsating cock, trembling as her nails followed their previous course, leaving slight indents in the purple flesh as they went. At each dig, he moaned in ecstasy and begged for more, though his moans verged on squeals of sweet pain.

She wrapped her arms around him, drawing his pelvis to her as her mouth enveloped his pulsating phallus, the soft down of his nuts caressing her chin.

As she enjoyed the sensation of her mouth drawing in then retrieving along his entire length, her hand found the half-hidden handle and began to move that back and forth in his anus.

91

Above her, he groaned and his knees sagged slightly. She felt his thighs tremble and his penis leap in her throat.

Not yet, she said to herself; not until I've had my reward.

She loosed him from her mouth, and with her foot, moved the bale of hay to one side, then rested that foot on it. Everything was in place for her to take what she wanted.

Breast meeting breast, she brought one hand round to the front, closed it around the imprisoned penis and readied it to guide it between her well-oiled lips and into her waiting vagina.

It slid in. She moved forward, then buried it to the hilt.

Delicious waves of pleasure spread upwards from where she gyrated on the rampant member. She mumbled her pleasure against his chest, apologising in a stupid sort of way for being unable to resist such a stout harbinger of satisfaction.

Unwilling to allow his member to shrink from its splendid size, one hand went back to the whip handle and began to manipulate it as before, moving it gently in and out of his anus. Just to remind him who was in charge, she flicked every so often at his bare flesh with the riding crop, her strokes getting more erratic but much more virulent as her own climax began to spread from her loins.

With one leg up on the bale of hay, it was easy to manoeuvre her clitoris so it received the full impact of his thrust against her each time she pushed on the handle of the whip, and her thrusts against him as she beat him with the crop.

As though now going into full gallop, her movements got faster. Trickles of sweat ran between her jiggling breasts from him and her, then ran off to saturate further the slippery wetness that sucked and gulped between their thighs.

'More! More! More!' Now her tongue stuck to her mouth, her arms quivering with a current of impending explosion.

Higher and higher the current of climax ascended before tumbling down in a sparkling shower of sensitive bliss.

One, two, three, four more thrusts of the whip handle, then Auberon, too, gave all he had to give. Within her, the bunched-up and heavily engorged member throbbed like an airlocked water-pipe as he cried his release to the high rafters and unsettled the roosting pigeons.

There was only a soft rustling in the darkness once they had finished and Auberon had licked the last vestige of her own secretions from her hot and well-used pussy.

Even so, she thought to herself, there is always some-one who hopes for an additional encore or who hangs around the stage door hoping for a last word or an avid leer. She wondered only briefly who it would be, and dared not hope it would be the object of her wager. All the same, she hoped she had made a good impression.

'Nice night.'

Sir Reginald had come from somewhere behind them as they left the stables.

'Splen . . . splendid,' stammered Auberon.

'Nice night for being out walking,' said Penny.

'Yes,' Sir Reggie chuckled knowingly, his dark eyes twinkling. 'Yes. Nice night for a lot of things. Very satisfactory, don't you think?' He chuckled again before wandering off along the gravel path and into the darkness.

Ears, if not eyes, tuned to the night, Penny looked into the darkness and was aware of other footfalls joining his.

Chapter Five

'*C*lear round!'
 The hollow echo of the loudspeaker announced her performance to the crowd of pink faces that thronged around the main arena.

This was Penny's first horse show since coming to Beaumont Place, and although it was only a county show of secondary merit, she'd done well and felt pleased with herself.

Hoofs thudded beneath her and clods of earth flew out behind, lifted by the animal's iron shoes. She felt the creature's muscles between her thighs, and thought as she had so many times before, just how incredible it was that she could exert her own will over such a powerful animal.

'Well done!' There was triumph in her voice and a smile on her face as she patted the sweating neck of the rangy chestnut before exiting the arena and coming to a halt.

Beaming brightly, perhaps too conceited for her own good, she nodded at Auberon as he made ready to try his round. His hand tipped politely at his hard hat. His smile was faint and he blinked a few times.

Just for a moment, she thought she saw him blush like a nubile girl and she smiled. Was he enamoured of her, or just highly appreciative of the performance she'd made him go through the night before?

She had asked him later if he had known they were being watched. He had blushed then, too, and had stammered his answer.

'Um ... Well ... possibly ... perhaps.'

He knew, she decided. He just didn't want to admit it. Did such a thing embarrass him? Obviously, it did. But she didn't feel that way. There was added excitement in performing such a delicious task when an audience was present. Just the thought of last night made her flush beneath her tight white breeches and black wool jacket.

But Auberon, sweet as he was, loved being submissive, and in all honesty, she had found the role of the dominator extremely enjoyable.

'Good round,' said the stable-lad who held her horse's head. He had dancing green eyes, copper-coloured hair and was called Stephen.

'So far so good,' she replied, her face still flushed from her ride and her breath still hurried. But she was still smiling, almost laughing. She felt good.

He helped her dismount before throwing the customary soft brown rug over her horse's steaming flanks. Her on one side of the chestnut, and him on the other, they led the horse back to the horsebox which was painted light blue with rampant gold lettering along the side.

'Well here we are,' she said appreciatively, happy to have done so well, and even more happy that this particular horsebox was like a palace compared to the rattly old Bedford she had arrived in. She still had it, of course. Gregory had parked it safely until she had need of it again. Safety, she guessed, didn't even come into it. Her old horsebox just wouldn't have matched up to the Beaumont standard, whereas this long and weighty machine had six wheels with double axles.

'I could do with a shower,' she said. She'd already loosened her white silk cravat; formal and required wear when actually jumping. Now she also undid her top button. She saw him look; had meant him to.

The ride had made her glow and her flesh hanker after

95

other things. Riding did that. Her plush sex had slid and bumped against the unyielding saddle in easy, gentle rhythm one moment, fast and furious the next.

She glanced at the young man with interest. His smile was inviting and the sprinkling of freckles over the bridge of his nose gave him a boyish, almost impish expression. His skin was creamy-white. She imagined his body being very white, as cool as milk or blue-veined like frosted ice. Like a youthful Pan, she thought, russet hair, snow-white skin and eyes the colour of a summer meadow just before sunset. Although his body was slim and not fully matured, he was poised on that threshold when the energy of youth outweighs the technique of experience. She eyed him, wondered about him, and her loins tingled.

That's not what I'm here for, she told herself. But all the same, the lad's muscles rippled like a shoal of darting fish beneath the clinging tightness of his black T-shirt. What harm was there in extending a little more than friendship and straying slightly from the path to her main objective?

His fingers curved over hers very briefly as he handed her the reins of her second mount. She thanked him.

'Need a leg-up?'

'Please.'

He looped the chestnut's reins over his arm before grasping her shin and foot and propelling her upwards to sit astride the grey which was over sixteen hands of pure muscle. His hands lingered on her foot as he assisted her to slide it into the stirrup. Through the leather of her boot she could vaguely discern the sweaty heat of his palm. There was a questioning look in the merry glint of his eyes. She knew what the question was. She also knew the answer. Perhaps later, she told herself, and returned her concentration to the job in hand refastening her button and retying her cravat.

'Have a good ride,' he said as she turned the grey's head towards the arena. He grinned as he said it and there was joy in his voice.

'I always do.'

She glanced at him; saw hope in his face and fever in his eyes. Perhaps it was the sheer bravado that she always felt when competing in equestrian events, or more likely the arousal caused by the friction of the saddle against her sex, but she returned his smile and let her tongue travel purposefully over her teeth. That, she judged, was enough to tell him that she too felt a high fever rising in her loins and would not be adverse to a mutual quenching of it.

But, for the moment, she left him and made her way back to the showjumping ring.

Nadine glanced at her as she halted her horse in the collecting ring, the place where those about to jump or those who had already jumped waited their turn or caught their breath.

Penny nodded in greeting. Nadine's eyes left her and went back to what was happening in the ring. Nadine was a professional when it was warranted. Stopwatch in hand, she noted every timing of every competitor, every movement of hand or heel as each Beaumont rider urged their animal over the obstacles.

Even her clothes today veered towards businesslike and were, so Penny thought, vaguely reminiscent of a middle-management executive. She wore a black trouser suit, crisp white blouse, black-and-white tie and black sombrero. The latter had a thick cord hanging from behind it which normally would have fastened under the chin. The familiar cheroot was gripped tightly in the corner of her mouth, and her earrings were exactly the same as they had been the day before.

Dramatic people draw curious looks, and Nadine was most definitely dramatic, even when soberly suited. Curiosity was rewarded with a cold stare. From what Penny had learned, a cold stare was stage one. Expletives ranging from purely sarcastic to downright obscene were stage two. Stage three was not for the faint-hearted, though apparently one brave journalist at some past horse show had pressed his luck, so Penny had been told. With icy-cold stare accompanied by an equally cold smile, Nadine had grabbed at his balls. His colour had drained from his face, and he'd stood on his toes, not daring to return to earth until she had let go of his family jewels. He'd scurried off clutching his groin. Nadine, he had swiftly learned, was best left alone.

There was a roar from the crowd, followed by another unemotional announcement from the loudspeaker, and people clapped. Auberon had jumped clear, too. All eyes watched as he came cantering out of the ring.

He tipped his hat as he passed her, his face flushed now more from his energetic clearing of the fences than his memories of their nights of passion.

'Good luck,' he said among his breathlessness.

Full of confidence, Penny thanked him and dug her heels into her horse's flanks. She could do no wrong today, she thought. It was almost as if she could fly.

Like a dream, the driving muscles of the grey propelled her over the first jump. With difficulty, she controlled the urges that the stable-boy with the green eyes had aroused in her. More concentration was needed to ride this animal than the chestnut. Timing of take-off was imperative and had to be gauged by the rider more so than the horse.

The hoofs thudded beneath her. Just by their sound, she could judge their pace, analyse when timing was perfect.

She gathered the reins, and with the assistance of every muscle in her body, she pushed the mare on, lower legs working incessantly to take her up and over each obstacle.

All were cleared without difficulty except the last. It loomed up high and wide before her, a triple-bar spread. Briefly, she glanced at those watching, threw a smile in Auberon's direction – then wished to God she hadn't.

Fool! Bloody fool! She cursed that smile, cursed her own conceit.

In that one split second of relaxed concentration, she'd covered too much ground. The fence loomed up, yellow-striped and large. If she did clear it, she'd be lucky. There was also the chance of landing awkwardly. Inside, she prayed. Then she narrowed her eyes.

There was no time to draw out, to pull on the reins and head off. Whatever happened, she must land safely.

A deep moan roared from the crowd and hollow echoes of falling wood crashed behind her. Her hat fell to one side, and she lost one stirrup, but she was safe and so was the horse. Softly, she swore under her breath. It was her fault. A moment's glance and she had messed up.

'Damn! Damn! Damn!' The words spilled in time with the horse's slowing gait.

As she slowed speed and came to a clumsy halt, she ran the back of her hand across her brow. Her hair clung damply to her head, but despite the fact that she had not jumped clear, she was satisfied enough to sigh and strain a smile towards Nadine.

'Diabolical!'

Nadine's mouth was as straight and unyielding as a letterbox, her eyes hard.

Effort had tired Penny. She was hot, she was tired and so far she'd done pretty well. It was only one mistake. 'But I landed safely . . .'

'Inexcusable!' said Nadine coldly. 'Horse could have been injured. You could have been injured!' The usually colourless eyes were as cold as steel.

Over the top of Nadine's head, Penny could see Auberon steadily getting redder. His mouth was opening and shutting as though he were trying to tell her something.

A flush of rebellion stirred momentarily in Penny's breast. 'But they're my horses!'

'No!' exclaimed Nadine, her fingers holding Penny's knee in a vicelike grip. 'Whilst you are here, everything is Beaumont! You will learn that!'

Penny opened her mouth meaning to deny the statement, but Nadine did not give her the chance.

'I will pass on your feelings. No doubt we will speak later about this. Punishment will be in order, I can assure you.'

Breathlessness curtailing her feelings of rebellion, Penny rose to the trot back to the shiny blue and gold

99

horsebox. It was parked in the coolest place possible, which happened to be beneath an ancient oak at the perimeter of the show ground next to a hawthorn hedge. On the other side of the hedge was an untamed meadow and copses of scattered willow, sycamore and birch.

The oak tree dappled her hot face with cool shade, though inside she was seething and oddly confused. Why was it that Nadine made her feel like a schoolgirl? And why was it that she obeyed meekly, her rush of passionate outrage buried beneath all the reasons why she should keep her cool.

Beneath the tree, her own chestnut and Auberon's other horse had been tethered. It was cooler there, and the horses plucked leisurely at the fresh green grass of the county showground and the longer more lush stuff sprouting through the fence from the field next door.

Stephen was sponging and brushing her chestnut. He was bare to the waist, his shoulder muscles rippling as his arm pushed the brush in wide, circular strokes over the horse's back and flanks.

His skin gleamed, a faint film of sweat lending greater definition to his moving flesh. She could smell him very faintly – pure testosterone, fresh and mingled with the pungent thickness of damp leather, sweating horse flesh and sweet summer grass.

Nadine's rebuke and talk of punishment were easily forgotten, and her attraction to Stephen remembered. As though he were a rare delicacy presented prior to a main course, she licked her lips. Like a hungry child, she eyed the lean torso, the fair skin and the sweep of russet hair as it caressed his naked shoulders. Her spirits were lifted, and another wetness mingled between her legs with the fresh sweat of her riding.

'Can you manage?' he asked once he'd become aware of her presence. 'I can always help you out,' he said with obvious meaning. 'You only have to ask.'

'I always can manage,' she said with a smile. 'And I never refuse a service if I can possibly avoid it.'

The smell of damp leather and sweating flanks was

strong in her nostrils as the saddle slid off the grey and into her arms.

'That's what I like to hear. A woman who can always manage.' It was no accident that his hands brushed against her breasts as he took the saddle from her.

Over the scent of leather, she could smell him better now he was closer; a lingering sensation of fresh male perspiration and the earthy closeness of warm-blooded animals.

He turned his back on her and placed the saddle in the tack area of the horsebox.

Enamoured of the day and the boy before her, Penny let her senses take over from her sensibility. Stephen was one prize that she was going to have today.

'It's a beautiful day,' she said, stretching her arms once she'd taken off her hat, jacket and cravat and undid a few more buttons than she had done before. She looked up at the sky, then over the stile to the green field and clumps of trees next door. Her desire was strong and getting stronger. This boy was good-looking: young, of course, no more than nineteen. But she needed him. Her ego needed massaging, and he seemed just the man to do it.

'Too beautiful for working,' he replied as he turned towards her.

She saw the boldness in his eyes and the front of his jeans moving as his phallus responded to what his mind was thinking and his tongue had only touched on.

'Now what else could we do on a day like this?' she asked.

His smile was knowing and the swelling in his jeans more obvious. This was no Auberon, she thought to herself. Young he might be, but he'd no doubt had his share of pussies willing to welcome his vigorous member. She glanced downwards where his rising phallus formed a curved mound as it thrust for release against his soiled jeans.

He reached out and cupped her breasts. There was desire in his eyes, and a deep hum of ecstasy escaped his lips as he bunched her breasts towards each other.

'They're so firm,' he murmured, 'so beautiful.'

'Flattery,' she told him, 'can get you anywhere.'

As her hair broke free from its net and tumbled down her back, she reached for him, touched his cheek with one hand and his neck with the other. They drew closer; both murmured unintelligible sounds of pleasure as she rubbed her body up against his. His arms wrapped around her, his hands hot against her back.

There was unfamiliar pleasure in feeling a fully-clothed body against hers, a kind of innocence as his hands travelled to press the stickiness of her blouse over the fullness of her breasts.

His lips were hot, his tongue just as experienced as she had expected. Hot skin shivered as though touched with ice beneath her searching palms as she explored each young, tight muscle.

'We can't stay here,' he said, drawing back and holding her at arms' length as though she were potentially dangerous. 'Too public. But we can go through there,' he added with a wink and a jerk of his head towards the stile and the meadow and trees beyond.

The wood of the stile was rough and dry, the grass on the other side sweet, green and cool against their hot bodies.

One pair of soiled white riding breeches and one pair of grass-stained jeans were soon lying in a single heap.

She lay beside him in the coolness of the grass, aware of the smell of wild flowers and the buzzing of insects. Her hair tumbled over her shoulders and down her back. Her eyes sparkled and her body was still except for her breathing and the slight undulations of limbs created by sexual need.

'You're beautiful,' he said, and sounded as though he meant it. Just hearing him say such things made her feel as though she were melting. Beautiful words made her feel beautiful.

'And you,' she responded, 'are quite memorable.' The words she said she meant. Her eyes drank him in from head to toe. There was a fairylike whiteness to his skin.

102

Around his mighty member, a cluster of red hair circled like a dark-gold crown.

She was filled with a strong desire to run her fingers through that feathery nest. His eyes caught hers. They were bright and they were happy. They were also excited and eager to elicit the utmost from their experience.

They kissed and caressed. Then Penny, without any urging from him, got to her feet, and walked to a tree-trunk that had fallen amidst the clump of trees. She bent over, hands resting on the broken patches of bark. Stephen followed and came up behind her. No one could see them here, not that she'd be too worried if they could.

She felt the heat of his body as he came up behind her, and trembled with delight as his hands traced down over her back and clasped her buttocks in the wideness of his palms.

He opened the cleft between her buttocks with his fingers, as though studying her tiniest orifice. She groaned appreciatively and wriggled against his fingers. She closed her eyes and in her mind she entered her own sensuous world where everything she received was more intense, more electrifying than the giver of such delights could ever imagine.

As he ran his hands down between her legs and opened the more fleshy cleft of her sex, she moaned in ecstasy. His fingers went on to draw imaginary lines around her vagina and dip briefly into her burgeoning wetness.

Then against her sex she felt the warmth of his breath as he sucked at her outer lips, her inner lips, then dipped his tongue where his fingers had been.

Wanting to miss nothing of this experience, she opened her eyes and took deep breaths of fresh air, revelling in the swishing of the leaves as the breeze took them, the buzzing of the bees and the sweet smell of summer flowers.

There was a gap in the bushes and trees in front of her. From here she could look out at the mass of people milling around in the bright sunshine. And here she was, shaded in a small copse, hands on the rough bark of a tree, bottom dappled by sunlight and pubic hair rustled

103

by a kind breeze. If this was the Garden of Eden, then she was Eve.

'Ride me,' she pleaded breathlessly, her head back, eyes closed again.

He didn't answer for a moment, as though he were thinking about it, weighing up the pros and cons of doing so. Then with a laugh in his throat, he nuzzled her neck and sucked at her ear lobe.

'You need breaking in first,' he murmured against her ear.

Then his lips had gone down over her behind until his tongue licked the shiny division between each rounded cheek.

She felt his body come up over in order to cover her. His chest was warm and hairless against her back, his lips wet and soft against her neck. His hands followed his words. They pulled at her breasts, held them almost as if he were weighing them, then let them go. His fingertips tapped lightly at their pink nipples, causing them to rear with unbridled desire.

Lost in the whirling currents of her own delight, Penny murmured, moaned and purred with each sensation. She wriggled her hips and tilted her bottom, knowing that the tousled hair of her sex would be peering out at this young man from beneath the heart-shaped perfection of her backside.

'Put it back in me,' she pleaded. 'Please. Anything. Anything at all!'

Lightly, as if in answer to her pleading, she felt the silken head of his penis kiss her fleshy lips before he pulled back.

Mewing with pleasure, she felt his fingers pull back the glowing petals of her sex again, first the outer lips, then the inner ones. Like the head of a curious snake, his finger probed further, sliding along her slippery flesh, finding the hot nub of her clitoris, and teasing it to full height, before burrowing again into the torrid humidity of her widening vagina.

His finger had been only the scout. Now the head of

his erect and readied penis followed, widening her lips as it followed the same course his finger had taken.

Pleas for more escaped her throat as the exploring penis continued to slide the whole length of her slit from nest of pubic hair to throbbing portal.

'Say please,' he demanded through his own gasping breath. 'Say please and I'll ram it home.'

'Please,' she gasped, her breath, her mind and her body lost in ragged whirls of pleasure. 'Please, please, please!'

The heat of his thighs met hers as his length of engorged flesh pushed its way into her welcoming sex. Possessed by desires that she had no control over, she writhed and pushed back on to it. Her dewy lips sucked noisily at the hard shaft as if it were draining it of all its strength.

How can it be, she asked herself, that something so hard can be at one and the same time so soft, so warm . . . and so welcome?

There was no answer. Only the fact that it was what it was and she adored its contrasts, its mix of pleasure and pain, softness and hardness.

Moans of sheer enjoyment tumbled consistently from her open throat as his balls slapped in tempo against her, his pubic hairs tickling like a mass of goose down against her silken thighs.

She wriggled on him more, determined to get the last ounce of enjoyment from the experience. Her bosoms continued to swing in time, one slapping against the other like wads of heavy silk as she moved forward with each shove of his member. All the time her throat sang to his tempo, each breath tinged with a moan and a sigh.

The warmth and hardness of his chest rested on her back as his hands sought to restrain her swinging breasts. She howled in ecstasy as his fingers squeezed her nipples, then groaned, almost pleading for her climax. His breath was like steam against her neck, and his breathing began to quicken, strangled gasps of joy like warm wind against her ear.

She sensed the immediacy of his release and began to

panic, fearful of him leaving her unsatisfied on the pinnacle of her own sexual arousal.

Perhaps he felt her sudden tension, a tightening of her vaginal muscles around his stem. Anyway, his hand travelled over her hip to her pubic hair. His finger charged through and with deft strokes, he began to manipulate the shiny wet head of passion that prodded so forcefully from her folds of flesh.

She closed her eyes, her fists clenching more tightly over the rough tree bark as ripples of orgasm spread deliciously outwards, tingling her body, flooding her mind so she barely heard his cry mingle with her own. Bodies relaxed and senses swam in floods of ecstasy before he drew himself from her.

'I much appreciate your attention to my needs,' she said softly once they were disentangled and lying on their bellies again in the sweet coolness of the meadow grass.

'I aim to please.' He reached for her, pulled her to him and hugged her to his chest. They kissed; warmth remained where a moment before there had been only the urgency to climax.

She drank in the feel, the smell of him. Then she detected another smell, then the sound of a twig snapping. She started. The faint aroma of expensive tobacco carried on the breeze.

'My, my, Stephen. You really are quite a stallion. And you, Miss Bennet, are quite a mare!' Penny, still naked except for her crumpled white blouse – which she pulled on hastily – spun round and found herself face to face with Nadine. A half-smoked cheroot hung from the corner of the tall woman's mouth.

It was difficult not to blush. But Nadine had a bold look about her. There was a sneer around her mouth. The pale grey eyes stared and made no apology for so doing.

Penny glanced over at Stephen. He was already getting dressed, though not rushing it.

Penny bent down and picked up her clothes, aware at the same time of the scent of sex upon her and the glistening droplets of her own bodily secretions that

106

clung to her nest of pubic hair. She was also aware of Nadine eyeing her naked belly and thighs. They glittered with undisguised pleasure and more than a hint of desire.

Stephen went silently, as though his service had indeed been done and there was no need for him to stay.

Nadine folded her arms across her chest. Penny reached for the rest of her clothes.

'Never mind your clothes.'

Penny froze and clutched her shirt around her. Her breeches dangled from one hand. Nervously, she glanced towards the gap in the trees.

'But there are people around. What if they should . . .'

'See you . . .?' Nadine's eyebrows arched in the manner of an old-fashioned headmistress. 'It didn't worry you just then. Why should it worry you now?' Her voice was hard; hollow, even. Her sneer only half-disturbed her face.

Penny shivered. Passion induces heat, but spent passion tends to leave one feeling cold, she thought, especially if it has been spent outdoors. Goose-bumps were erupting all over her body.

Penny held Nadine's gaze for just a moment of defiance before she remembered all that was at stake and lowered them. But the wager and her place with the Beaumont team was not the only reason Penny lowered her eyes. Just the fact that Nadine was here, that she had spoken, was enough to crush Penny's spirit and to make her feel as though her will was not her own and neither was her body. Strangely enough, the combination in her character of sensuality and the desire to please added an odd thrill to the experience. Even now, with Nadine eyeing her naked sex, she wanted to show her more, wanted her to *do* more.

'I'm getting cold,' she said at last and shivered.

Nadine ignored her comment, but seemed pleased to see her suffering.

'You do not mix professional considerations with pleasure. Never!' barked Nadine. She swung a silver-headed cane against her side as she spoke. 'Do I make myself clear?'

107

Penny bit her lip, her eyes still studying the ground, before she got up the courage to answer. 'I'm sorry, I didn't think a little lovemaking in a wood would affect my performance. After all, I had finished my round. I know I've got a place, but the presentation isn't until four . . .'

'Then you'd better get dressed.'

Penny lifted one leg to pull on her breeches.

'But first,' said Nadine suddenly, her hand gripping Penny's shoulder, 'you deserve a little punishment. Just a little tingling to remind you as you ride in the jump-off that you must concentrate. I think that would be a good idea. Don't you?'

Nadine's smile was full of teeth and stiffly held.

Penny trembled beneath Nadine's cold gaze. A rope seemed to knot in her stomach and a tingling centred in a warm spot between her legs. She knew she had no choice but to accept this punishment. Both Nadine and Penny's own yearnings required it.

Still shivering, she let her clothes drop to the ground and trembled like a flower beneath Nadine's gaze as her eyes strayed to the tangle of rich, dark pubic hair that graced the top of Penny's thighs. Nadine sucked in her breath between her teeth. She tilted her head to one side as her eyes travelled up to Penny's face then back to the clutch of curls.

'What a pretty pussy!' she said in a light and sing-song voice that hardly seemed to belong to her. 'In fact, I think it is quite the prettiest one I have ever seen.' Her eyes were half-shaded by the broad brim of her hat, but Penny knew they were devouring each nipple before sliding with intimate familiarity over each curve.

Penny glanced briefly at her own soft silky pubes gently blowing with the breeze. She didn't say anything, but a chill excitement was sending shivers of apprehension down her spine and over her skin. Nadine had power over her, and Nadine would chastise. To her own surprise, her body was responding, it was almost as though it were no longer hers, but was floating along on some never-ending stream in dreamlike fantasy. Nadine was in charge of most things at Beaumont Place. For the first time since her arrival, Penny realised that Nadine was also in charge of her.

'Lovely!' exclaimed Nadine with a sigh. 'But ripe for punishment.' With her silver-topped riding cane, Nadine pointed at the fallen tree-trunk.

Adopting meekness, head bowed and her arms still wrapped around her chest, Penny walked to the tree-trunk and placed her hands on the rough bark, bottom in the air, just as she had with Stephen. Her sex was tingling, her heart racing.

'No,' said Nadine sternly. 'Full-length along the log.'

'But it's rough,' Penny protested, looking up at Nadine as though she truly disbelieved what she was telling her. But Nadine was smiling; she knew it was rough. She would take pleasure from knowing that Penny's softness was lying on that coarse trunk. And Penny would take pleasure from it, too, enjoying the favour that was disguised as punishment, the pain that could so easily be pleasure.

Nadine's smile was faint and her eyes glittered. She said nothing. Again, she pointed at the log. Her mouth returned to the hard line it had been before.

Penny eyed the hard, dry bark before she obeyed and lay herself full-length along the trunk. Just as she had supposed, the bark was rough against her breasts and belly. There was a knot of wood where a small branch had once been. Nadine manhandled her body as though she were made of rags, until the protruding knot of wood was pressing pleasurably against Penny's pubes.

'Legs astride,' ordered Nadine in a clear, dictatorial voice.

Penny's breathing quickened as Nadine's cane tapped at each leg then pushed in between them so they divided and fell either side of the log. Now the knot of wood was pressing a very familiar spot and that spot was reacting in a very familiar way. Penny held her breath and swallowed the moan of pleasure. A pleasurable response was something she would need to hold on to, to store

109

and use to counteract the stinging burn she knew was to come.

Peering through her tangle of flying hair, Penny could see Nadine gloating with pleasure as her eyes and her silver-topped cane ran over her naked back and trembling buttocks. The breeze now blew unabated around her open cleft, which Nadine appeared to be studying with avid interest, prodding the cane against the soft lips and open portal. The cane tapped each buttock. Penny tensed. Then it tapped against her open portal, which was already moist with a new yearning.

'A very pretty pussy.' Nadine said the words as though she were purring them, delighting in pushing the cane close up against her vulva and between the cheeks of her bottom. 'But it won't get you off,' Nadine suddenly added sternly. 'You deserve punishment for fouling that jump, and punishment is what you will get. And I'm the one to give it to you. Am I right?'

Penny's own hair blew across her face. Her hands gripped the log.

'Yes,' she murmured, lacing her words with fear and impatience rather than the longing she really felt.

'Say it louder, pretty pussy,' said Nadine in a mocking voice, her cane tapping an arousing rhythm against Penny's damp sex.

'Yes!' Penny cried.

'Good,' said Nadine slowly. 'Good.' And the cane tapped her sex again before Nadine raised it and placed a stinging blow across Penny's buttocks.

Penny gasped. Her fingers gripped clawlike at the rough bark; almost as if someone had pressed a button, her nipples swelled against the rough, dry wood.

Her bottom stung and burned with the kiss of the cane. Her pelvis had pushed down with the blow. Her mons had pressed harder against the knot of wood just as Nadine had reckoned. In turn, her hidden bud had burst into bloom, sensing that another orgasm could be had.

'That was just a test,' said Nadine suddenly. 'I will give you six. You will count them. Are you ready?'

'Yes,' answered Penny, a glow of tingling delight

spreading upwards from her willing thighs, though her voice trembled, 'I'm ready.'

'Good,' Nadine purred. 'Then we shall begin.'

The air swished as the cane fell.

'One!' cried Penny as her buttocks clenched and stung beneath the blow. The knot of wood firmly kissed her secret rosebud, and her rosebud responded.

'One,' repeated Nadine.

The air swished again. Penny gasped again. Her bottom began to glow. The rough bark beneath her scratched her naked flesh.

'Two!' she cried. The smooth knot of wood delved more deeply against her brazen clitoris.

'Two,' Nadine repeated.

Again the cane flew threw the air. Now she was almost wishing for its stinging caress and for the pelvic movement that accompanied it, and pressed her more firmly against the protruding knot of the tree-trunk.

Just as she had wished, it came again. Her buttocks quivered, warmed beneath its burning touch.

'Three!' she exclaimed, and felt the fires of orgasm spreading through her loins and homing in on that very sensitive spot that was pressed so tightly to the simple tree knot.

'Three,' Nadine repeated, then ran the coldness of her long fingers over the burning flesh of Penny's reddening bottom. 'How hot your bottom is, my pretty pussy. How pink it is, and how it will tingle when you ride in the ring again. How it will remind you to concentrate. But I will take care of you. I will finish this punishment, then I will punish you again later. And then, I will soothe your burning flesh. I will rub cream into you, soothe your aching muscles and ease your tired limbs.'

The cool hand patted each buttock as if it were a pet animal, twin pink lap-dogs that quivered at the coldness of her fingers and her voice.

Penny had held her rising need in suspension and swallowed her deep murmurs of pleasure as Nadine's hands fondled her buttocks. Now, as she heard the swish of the cane again, she let it go.

111

'Four!' she cried with accompanying groans. The bark of the tree held her breasts like scaly hands. The knot of wood pushed its hard, smooth head firmly against her clitoris. Her orgasm was rising and not far off. Her bottom quivered; it was redder and warmer now, tingling as much from sexual longing as from Nadine's cane.

But Nadine had not finished. The cane fell again through the air, and Penny moaned again.

'Five.' Her voice was shaking as the first waves started, quivering through her parted labia and causing her empty vulva to shed its moist fluid so it dripped through her sex and on to the log.

The final blow of the cane would come now. She craved it, longed for its burning kiss on her behind so her pelvis would thrust one more time – just once more – before the flood of orgasm washed over her.

It came.

'Six!' she cried, and pressed herself tight against the wood knot, riding it in small sharp spurts until the last eruptions of her orgasm had melted away.

Laughing at her shameless exhibition, Nadine tapped rapidly at Penny's jerking buttocks until she lay supine. The goose-bumps had gone. A light film of sweat covered her, and Penny's hair covered her face.

The cool hands that had caressed her earlier, now caressed her again. She moaned beneath their touch, welcoming the coolness spreading over her hot buttocks, and the gentleness in Nadine's long, slim fingers.

'You enjoyed that too much, my pretty,' murmured Nadine between quick, sharp breaths. 'Much too much. I can see I will have to deal with you again; use you to everyone else's benefit so you know exactly what is expected of you. Don't you agree?'

One of Penny's tingling cheeks was gripped by long fingers and talonlike nails.

'Yes, Nadine,' said Penny.

'Say it again,' said Nadine in a cruel yet oddly affectionate way. 'Say it again and mean it.'

'Yes, Nadine. Whatever you say, Nadine. Whatever

112

you want. I'm in your hands.' Her buttocks clenched tightly in the strong hands. She almost wanted her to do it all over again, so she could enjoy once more the mix of pleasure and pain, the contrast of hot and cold, the smoothness of her own flesh against the scratching roughness of the tree bark. But the claws released her, and she let out her breath. The hand that had tortured now patted her bottom like it had before.

'Yes, pretty pussy. That is just what I wanted to hear,' Nadine purred, and she kissed one rounded buttock. 'That's exactly what I wanted to hear,' she repeated, then kissed the other, her lips soft and gently sucking on Penny's warm flesh. 'You are in my hands,' she said before sucking at the other again. 'You are most definitely in my hands.'

Chapter Six

When the horsebox returned to the stable yard at Beaumont Place, the sun was turning bright orange and the clouds were marbled with purple and gold.

In good-hearted mood, riders mucked in with stable-lads to get the horses groomed, fed and watered. Nadine supervised, barking her orders and aiming hefty whacks at the stable-lads if they gave her any backchat. Judging by their cheeky grins and laughing eyes, her actions were enjoyed rather than feared. They almost offered their bottoms for the slap of her long white hands, and rubbed up against her suggestively when she grabbed them by the drooping necks of their sweat-stained T-shirts. There seemed to be some sort of competition in progress as to who could goad her more, and who could get away it.

The stables were quiet once they'd all left.

'Stay here!' Nadine ordered in a harsh and demanding voice. 'We have unfinished business if you remember rightly.'

Penny stopped in her tracks and turned to face this imperious woman who seemed to have the ability to command at will and to cajole, persuade and manipulate.

Inside her, Penny was aware of a dark sensuality seeping from her mind and invading her body. And yet, in some strange way, she recognised it, but only vaguely, as if she had briefly touched it in the most erotic of dreams.

'Yes. I remember,' Penny said softly, her eyes meeting Nadine's before she slid the bolt across the door to the grey mare's stable. She glanced only briefly before looking down at the floor. Her cotton blouse now clung stained and damp to her bare breasts. She smelt of sex, and if it hadn't been for the savage yearnings rising in her body, she would be in her own bath or on her own bed, with Gregory running his soapy hands and sponge over her wet body or massaging her aching muscles. She sighed and shifted her weight from one curved hip to the other and waited for Nadine to make the first move as she knew she would.

Nadine grinned rather than smiled, her teeth chillingly white, and a cheroot clutched grimly in the corner of her mouth.

Despite being in a stable where combustible materials were used and stored, Nadine still smoked, ash flying and smoke curling up towards the dark wooden rafters where pigeons nested and vermin scurried. Languidly, she leaned one elbow against the stable divide, the blackness of her clothes strangely out of place among the earthy yellow ochre of the straw.

'Y . . . es,' said Nadine slowly to nothing in particular as she blew smoke in corkscrew spirals. 'Y . . . es.'

A myriad nerve ends danced between Penny's legs, yet her hands trembled as she attempted to put the grooming kit away where it belonged. If the episode on the log was anything to go by, she knew more or less what to expect, and how much the degree of discomfort was outweighed by the pleasure. For the first time, she wondered whether Ariadne had gone through the same punishments. Inwardly, she smiled. It was more than likely. She remembered her of old. Ariadne had started young, and had no boundaries when it came to experimentation.

Yes. She knew what to expect from Nadine. She also knew to some extent what to expect from Alistair. Earlier, she had discerned his look once she had left the long

115

grass and the tree-trunk behind her. With Nadine, she had returned to the box. He had been there. He'd stared at her, a wistful look in his eyes that was not entirely readable. Her eyes had met his; had sparkled enough to let him know that she'd guessed he'd watched both what she had done with Stephen and what Nadine and the tree-trunk had done to her. She didn't need a crystal ball to guess that. There was mud on his boots. There was no mud in the show field, but there *was* on the field side of the stile. Clods of mud clung to his boots. Alistair had indeed seen her punishment, her lying full-length on the log. For a moment, she had thought he was going to ask her something, even to reach out and touch her. This could be the moment, she had thought. But nothing had happened; and despite her initial elation, she had once again been disappointed.

A cloud of smoke circled Penny's head, blown there deliberately by the tall female with the gaunt face. Nadine's very wide mouth smiled and her face seemed suddenly to be full of teeth, all white and large, and flashing devilishly at her.

'I'm a very fair person,' said Nadine suddenly – as if for some reason she thought Penny might have doubted it – 'I have to be strict you see. My brother requires it of me. It's very important that everything is done in a way to suit him. He has little time to spare in his life for pleasurable pastimes, so only the very best will do, and then, only when the need is at its strongest. Everything has to be perfect. It's all a matter of self-discipline. My brother is a great believer in self-discipline.' The voice was as languorous and decadent as her pose, and dripped with the shadow of Oscar Wilde.

'I see,' replied Penny. So, she told herself, Nadine influences Alistair's life. For a moment, she wondered if there was something decidedly unhealthy in their relationship. If that was the case, then through Nadine she could actually win her wager with Ariadne. It could even be easy if those recently dormant and dark feelings that were racing through her body were anything to go by.

Nadine left where she had been leaning and came face to face with her. Penny was aware of the scent of rich tobacco as Nadine kissed her cheek.

'My brother's handsome, don't you think?'

Eyes still downcast, Penny hesitated before she nodded.

Nadine's fingers twisted in her hair which now hung tangled and slightly damp.

'He is a very rich man you know – and a very powerful man. Yet even powerful men have their weaknesses. Did you know that?'

Penny, uncertain about what reply to give, shrugged her shoulders and ran her tongue across her lips, but was disinclined to raise her eyes from the floor.

Nadine laughed close to her ear. Her submissive stance, her air of ignorance, seemed to please her no end.

'I can give him to you – if you do exactly as I say. I can arrange everything so it will suit you and suit him. What say you, my pretty pussy? Would you like me to do that for you? Would you?' Sharp fingernails traced leisurely lines over Penny's cheek. Chill thrills of excitement coursed through her veins. Her cheeks flushed in spite of herself as though she were a virgin about to lose such a state of grace for ever.

'Can you really do that?' Penny muttered, the dark feelings from within muffling the words in her throat and half-drowning the last vestiges of thought she still entertained with regard to the wager.

Nadine smiled, and a low noise issued from her throat as though she were growling or even purring. She laughed and seemed for the moment loath to answer. There was intimidation in her towering height, an icy coldness in the whiteness of her skin. The Snow Queen, thought Penny, that beautiful creature from a fairy-tale that was at one and the same time both irresistible and dangerous.

Nadine's close proximity had a strangely unnerving affect. Nadine was not touching her, and yet Penny was aware that her body was only a fraction away from her own, held there, in suspension for who knows what or

117

who knows when. Just when she thought Nadine would cross that narrow divide, the long fingers – white as snow and cold as ice – trailed provocatively over the mounds of her breasts, then slid delicately beneath the gaping front of her blouse. Fine fingertips and long fingernails played with her rising nubs, and just as she was expected to do, she groaned with pleasure, but kept her eyes on the floor.

White fingers with black varnished nails stroked the creamy flesh of Penny's breasts before they scratched, then squeezed, her nipples. A faint cry that seemed suspended between pain and pleasure escaped from her throat.

Almost with pleading, she looked up at Nadine as her breasts rose and fell against the cold white hand. A cheroot still smouldered between the first two fingers of Nadine's right hand.

'Can you do that?' Penny repeated, thinking perhaps that Nadine had forgotten she had asked a question. 'Do you have that sort of power over him?'

Smoky breath touched her lips before the cold flesh of Nadine's mouth. Then a tongue rich in the tastes of wine, tobacco and depravity locked with hers. Surges of forgotten feelings welled up into Penny's head. She remembered her sexual experiences with Ariadne. She had always put their fumbling lovemaking down to adolescent experimentation. This was a woman doing this, and now she was an adult. Her eyes studied the soft crown of hair as Nadine bent her head to kiss her throat and nibble at her ear. The head rose, and the pale-grey eyes, so blackly lined, met hers.

'I do have power over my brother, my pretty,' Nadine answered, her lips but a breath away from Penny's. 'With my help, and only with my help, you will have him handed to you on a plate.' Again, the head of shorn, white hair nuzzled against her, and the wide mouth enveloped her own. The large but fine hands held her shoulders, then fell to her breasts. 'Just do as I say, and my brother will be yours.'

Penny, whose arms hung useless at her side, sighed

118

and her nipples rose with engorged passion. Moistness spread between her legs and those dark feelings inside wrapped round her like a warm but prickly cloak.

Nadine's body was hard against hers and the smell of expensive perfume and rich tobacco made an odd and not unexciting assault on her nostrils. She moaned and closed her eyes as the kisses and caresses increased. She thought of the wager. She thought of her career. But her responses from deep within were nothing to do with either of these things. As though they had slept for a thousand years, they were shaking aside all other claims on their existence as they might thick cobwebs. They were not there for material or social gain, but to be enjoyed by her on whom they had been bestowed.

I have to do this, she told herself, the wager and her career still having some place in her mind. Then she corrected her statement. I want to do this.

There was a feeling of being on a helter-skelter as the fingers trailed onwards. To her and the dark forces she had within her, sex had the same laws as gravity. There was no way of resisting it.

She was only vaguely aware of the cheroot being thrown into the trough. It sizzled there, a last curl of smoke rising upwards like incense to an incarnate deity.

Nadine's strong arms wrapped around her, drew her closer. Penny felt surrounded by her superior height and strength, yet cosy against the hard nubs of her breasts, which were noticeably underdeveloped. She trembled in Nadine's arms, yet did not move. She waited for the orders she knew would come.

'Take your clothes off,' whispered Nadine against her ear.

Penny blinked, looked at the cool grey eyes for just a moment, then sat down on a bale of straw to pull off her boots. Her breeches followed. Then her blouse.

'What about *your* clothes? Aren't you going to get them off?' she asked Nadine.

Nadine shook her head; smiling she ran her eyes down over Penny's creamy flesh.

'All in good time, pretty,' she said, tangling the index

finger of her right hand in Penny's copious pubic curls. 'All in good time – in my time, of course.'

Strong, powerful hands pulled Penny closer before running down her back and clasping her buttocks. As Nadine bent her legs slightly, Penny felt the hard boniness of her pubic mound gyrate gently against hers, then gasped as she felt Nadine's fingers invade the deep cleft between the cheeks of her bottom.

'Don't flinch, pretty pussy. Accept it. I will do it. You will accept it.'

With the help of her new sensuality, Penny controlled her urge to cry out. All the time Nadine smiled at her, as though she were but a child or a china doll playing in imaginative games that no one else could understand.

Once the coldness of the fingers slid between her legs, Penny knew she was lost. Her breath caught in her throat. This was another woman doing this to her, another woman who would know what each reaction to her probing would be. One who had no doubt experienced the same sensations herself.

Nadine withdrew her fingers suddenly and undid her own well-cut trousers. She only wore the trousers, blouse and boots now. Her hat and jacket had already been discarded.

'Here, put your hand here.' The voice was hushed, yet firm. Penny felt her own hand being guided down into Nadine's trousers and let it be so. Her fingers slid over Nadine's flat belly. There was no spare fat. Sharp pelvic bones and silky skin without blemish passed beneath her touch. Penny stayed her hand a moment as she leaned and rubbed her head against Nadine's chest, her legs quivering like jelly.

Nadine's fingers were doing delicious things to her slippery sex. Sometimes they merely probed up beneath her outer lips and dipped into her wet vagina. Sometimes the fingers squeezed her outer lips together and the varnished nails dug into crisp pubic hair. Penny whimpered then groaned her compliance and complete surrender to those probing fingers that slid so tenderly and pinched with such precision over her valley of hot flesh.

120

She sucked in her breath as her own fingers met the shorn lips of Nadine's sex. No hair. None at all. Her flesh lean – mean, even – between her open legs.

'Surprised, my pretty pussy?' said Nadine with a smile, her hot lips drowning any response Penny might have had. Nadine was not interested in negative responses. She only wanted the more positive ones. She ate them, Penny thought to herself, drank them in as anyone else might food or drink. Silky and warm, Penny felt Nadine's labia began to slide with bodily secretions under the ministrations of her fingers. As their mouths sucked deeply and kissed deep, bruising kisses, their hands became more agitated, each imitating the movements of the other, each knowing what the other was feeling. Tentatively, Penny's hand covered one small breast. The effect was sensational. She felt its firmness tremble beneath her touch, and felt the hardening erection of the pert nipple.

Eddies of pleasure spewed upwards in greater intensity as two of Nadine's fingers played with her as the thumb and the rest created havoc among her nerve endings, stroking her inner lips and squeezing at her excited labia and jutting clitoris. Her legs trembled more. She felt as though the hand that explored between her legs was also holding her up, helping her to ride the pleasure that pulsated around her loins.

The sensations were mind-blowing, too good to keep to herself. She copied, and heard the moans of sublime ecstasy emitting in soft rushes of breath from Nadine's throat.

In complete unison, raptures of orgasm jerked their hips, which made their arms quiver with transferred sensations. Penny cried out, unable to exercise any self-control at all as her climax washed over her, her hips jerking time after time to ride the hand beneath her. Beneath her own hand, she felt the denuded lips and the soaking sex of Nadine leap in unbridled rapture as her swollen bud yielded at last to her novice fingers.

Penny sighed, then stared wide-eyed up at the strong features, as the same hands that had given her pleasure

121

clamped firmly to each side of her head. Intuition born of the dark feelings deep inside disposed her to think that pure pleasure was ended and might now be accompanied by pain.

'You're mine, Miss Bennet,' said Nadine in that low growly voice of hers. 'You belong to my brother, to the Beaumont estate. I'm a Beaumont, so you are mine. You might not think so, my little pussy-cat, but you are. And if you want my brother, you have to be mine – to do as I ask without question. Is that not so?'

Penny attempted to nod her head in the confines of Nadine's strong hands. 'Yes,' she murmured through pursed lips, which were pushed into that shape by Nadine's thumbs. 'Whatever you say, Nadine.'

A wide and leering smile cracked the granite hardness of Nadine's features. She bent her head and kissed Penny firmly on the lips with no pretence at affection or gentleness.

'I will help you have him, pussy-cat,' she said in a rushed and low whisper. 'On my terms. In my way.'

'Whatever you say, Nadine.'

There was a strange look of triumph in Nadine's eyes, and despite the satiation of her sex, Penny knew there was more to come, that Nadine could not possibly leave her feeling so satisfied. Nadine had to use, had to feel that only *she* had taken pleasure and inflicted only pain. The look of triumph turned to a glitter. The hands released her head.

'Then we will start as we mean to go on. We shall kiss on it,' growled Nadine.

Without hesitation, Penny kissed her mouth.

'I don't think you quite understand, my dear,' said Nadine. Strong hands landed on Penny's shoulders. She was pushed to her knees. With that, Nadine pulled her trousers down to her knees and lifted up her jumper.

There was her mons, her clit, and her de-nuded lips, which were white, almost silver, due to the sparse regrowth trying its best to poke through.

Penny was mesmerised and wondered momentarily whether her pubic hair, when left to grow wild, was as

122

white as the bullish crop on her head. Hairy or shorn, it was difficult to tear her eyes away, wanting instead to look up questioningly at the pale-grey eyes that eyed her with all the intent of a swaying cobra.

'Kiss,' ordered Nadine.

Penny's eyes went back to the defoliated genitals. Then she dropped to her knees, smelt the musky aroma of recent sex and saw close up the glint of silver hair follicles.

As yet, Penny could neither fully recognise nor control the dark sensuality that had risen since coming here. All she did recognise was that the buzzing current started in some hollow between her legs and grew stronger when sexual contact was ordered rather than done purely at one's own volition.

Hands caressing the smooth, silky whiteness of Nadine's thighs, she lifted her head, pursed her willing lips and kissed the pale skin of the pure white mons.

Without being seen, a fresh sprouting of hair was already rising through the flesh, its touch like very soft sandpaper against her mouth and chin.

Penny would have studied the white flesh further, but just the aroma of Nadine's sex, the tilting of her hips towards her lips, made her open her mouth and let her tongue loose to explore.

With her tongue and fingers, she prised the sticky lips apart and kissed Nadine's protruding clitoris. It was a large one and grew towards her mouth like a fledgling penis.

It didn't matter to her that Nadine was smiling as she writhed above her. How was Penny to know that she really had been set up for this, that Ariadne had primed Nadine with the details, and then offered her the wager. Ariadne had known Penny for a long time, since they were children, and she'd told Alistair and Nadine when they had explained to her exactly what they were looking for. Ariadne had personal knowledge of what Penny was capable of, what they had done together and also what each had seen the other do. All this information she had given to the Beaumonts. From what Nadine had seen and experienced so far, everything Ariadne had said had proved correct.

That in itself pleased Nadine. Still smiling and murmuring as she looked down at the tumbling dark hair that shone like a horse's mane between her legs, her mind worked out the path that she would force this girl to take. But for now she would enjoy, praise and punish until the time was right.

'Keep going, my pretty pussy,' she murmured, her fingers tangling in the dark hair. She smiled to herself, then chose her moment. Swiftly, before Penny could protest or withdraw, Nadine clamped Penny's head tightly against her sex, riding Penny's lips, nose and face with increasing vigour until, stretching her labia against Penny's clenched teeth, she let her orgasm break free.

Penny groaned against Nadine's sex. She was peeved; even angry. She was still aroused and in bad need of her own orgasm. Nadine's hands dragged her, protesting, to her feet.

'What about me? Please, you can't leave me like this,' she cried between demanding kisses that left Nadine's face smelling of the sex that still lingered on her lips.

She tried to force the tall woman's hand between her legs, but Nadine resisted.

'No.' Nadine said it with a smile – a cruel smile that indicated her enjoyment of Penny's obvious need.

'You must, you have to! You can't leave me like this!'

Penny herself felt lost, surprised at her own words and the terrible ferocity of the sexual need that made her labia ache and her clitoris tingle with expectation.

The hand that slapped Penny's face and made her fall into the straw was unseen and unexpected. So was Nadine's tying of her hands behind her back.

A new excitement weakened her limbs; her sex and behind tingled with anticipation. Her other cheek was slapped as Nadine, with very little effort, heaved her up and placed her so she was on her knees across the water trough. She gasped as her breasts dipped, then were completely submerged, in the cold water. Her head

124

rested on the rim on the other side of the trough. Her hands and arms were tied very firmly behind her back.

'I promised you more punishment, and you said you deserved it and would expect it this evening. But that is only part of it. Now for some rules,' she heard Nadine say. 'You will only have sex when I say so. If you have it elsewhere, I won't be pleased and you can expect to be punished. You will also provide it when I need it. Do you understand, pretty pussy?'

Penny had a need for more sex and another touch of burning on her behind. She just had to protest. 'But what if I . . .'

Just as she had hoped, there was a swishing of air before the fine tip of a leather crop landed on her behind, leaving her bare flesh tingling, and clenching against the sweet sting of pain. The cane of this afternoon had been kind. *This* crop had an extra sting to it; it was thin at one end, the handle bent off to the side, and was about four inches long.

'There are no buts. Do you understand what I require of you?'

But her bottom and the new sensations inside craved satisfaction. Almost as if those sensations had total control of her vocal cords, she protested again. 'I don't know that I want to . . .'

The air swished again. Her bottom quivered, and she yelped and imagined the red welt that was already running across each cheek.

Nadine's eyes were glittering, her mouth slightly open and her thick tongue running along her bottom lip, delighted with the way Penny was playing along and was willing to give a performance as Ariadne had told her she would be.

'Are you sure about that?' Nadine asked, her voice as cold and cruel as she could possibly make it.

'Yes!'

The crop landed again, and sharp heat transferred from one buttock across to the other. Nadine's aim had got both cheeks that time, and Penny's sex felt it had turned

125

to jelly. 'Then I will beat you until you do agree. Is that clear?'

Trembling with anticipation, Penny answered. 'It's perfectly clear. I don't care what you do. I don't care at all.'

Nadine could hardly control her delight. Just as Ariadne had foretold, here was a girl who had hidden depths, depths that Penny herself didn't know she had. She was everything that had been promised.

Wide mouth grinning, Nadine raised her arm again and let the crop stripe again the quivering buttocks. Three times more and Penny was whimpering.

Raising an eyebrow, Nadine stepped nearer and let the coolness of her hand run over the redness of Penny's behind. The hot flesh shivered.

'Are your breasts cold?' Nadine asked suddenly.

'Yes, they are,' Penny answered, her teeth lightly chattering, more in an effort to control her whimper than from the numbness of her erect nipples and goose-pimpled breasts which still swam in the water.

'I'll let you up from there if you agree to abide by my rules. Would you like me to do that?'

Penny lingered over her response. There was pleasure in this pain; in how it happened and how it developed.

Though her bottom burned and her breasts were cold, she didn't want it to stop; she didn't want to lose that feeling of pure envelopment of one sensation inside another.

'I have my own rules,' Penny retorted suddenly, aching for another few stings from the leather-bound crop that she knew had a silver-hooked handle.

Just as Penny had assumed, the crop resumed its course through the air and across her buttocks another six or seven times.

She cried out, wriggled against her bonds just as she was expected to. The ache between her thighs was so intense that the slightest touch would have brought her to climax. But Nadine would not do that yet. Time and patience were also part of her game. In her wide experience, she had found that anticipation inflates enjoyment both for the giver and the one who receives. The whipping ceased, and Penny could have cried.

'I will leave you to think on it now,' said Nadine with obvious pleasure, as well as authority. 'But I won't leave you without some further little reminder of me. After all, you do deserve your punishment, and at present, you are not respecting it or me as much as you should do.'

Penny began to beg her to slide her hand between her legs, to rub her clitoris until she jerked with release.

'No. Not until I say so,' Nadine replied. She began to hum merrily to herself as she slid rope around Penny's ankles and fastened them firmly to the iron rings at each side of the trough. This meant her knees, and thus her legs, were now spread wider than they had been.

Penny could hear Nadine rustling around somewhere behind her, but knew nothing about the horse collar until it was around her neck. It was a small one with jingling silver buckles and was made for a pony rather than a horse. Nadine fastened it to the anvil that sat on the side of the water trough beneath Penny's head. It was now impossible for her to move. The weight of the horse collar kept her head down and kept her breasts in the water. Her ankles were caught in the iron rings, her legs wide open, and her hands tied securely behind her back.

'That's cruel. How could you do this to me?'

Nadine's face came beside her, her breath hot against her ear and her teeth lightly nibbling at Penny's ear lobe.

'Very easily, as I am sure you are pleased to know, you rebellious little mare. But don't worry,' she said with a long smile, 'I will leave you with a little reminder that I will return.'

Her face drew away. Nadine's hands slid down her back and over her behind, fingers prising her cheeks apart, darting like sharp-nosed fishes into the puckered opening of her smallest orifice. Penny squirmed and squealed just as she was expected to. 'No,' she cried. 'You can't do that!'

'Oh yes I can, my pretty pussy. I can do exactly what I want. You told me so yourself.' Nadine laughed. Penny's buttocks burned and her sex cried out for satisfaction.

127

She was inhibited like a horse in harness. Now she was not just Nadine's pretty pussy but her little mare, restricted in the covering yard so she could not protest at the stallion's intrusion. A slimy coldness eased between the cheeks of her behind. 'What is that?' she cried. In vain she tried to move away from the sudden intrusion.

'Just saddle soap,' cooed Nadine. 'Just to help my little reminder along a bit.'

Then Penny gasped. Something hard was being pushed into her anus, something perhaps three or four inches long, narrower at its inner end than at its stem, which still seemed to be dividing her cheeks.

'Grip it tightly, my pretty pussy. We wouldn't want it to fall out, would we?'

Nadine laughed as she smacked each of Penny's hot cheeks with the flat of her hand before walking off.

'But you can't . . .' Penny began.

'I can,' Nadine retorted. 'I'll be back in ten minutes. You should be about ready by then.'

Managing to turn herself a little bit, Penny peered over her shoulder to see what object had invaded her.

With difficulty, and delight, she could see the long stiffness of the riding crop sticking up from between her cheeks like some oddly angled tail. It was the handle of the riding crop, she guessed, which was firmly embedded in the puckered hole between her taut buttocks.

The pinkness of sunset faded and the stable became darker. More than ten minutes passed. Somehow, she had half-suspected that Nadine would just leave her there to meditate on her riding faults. She closed her eyes and the effort of the day overtook her. She slept; not for long, but just long enough to know when she opened her eyes that the stable was quite a bit darker than it had been.

Horses nickered gently in their stalls. Some pawed the floor impatiently, gathering their bedding up into one gigantic heap. Others just chomped at their hay, oblivious of the delightfully tortured soul in their midst.

It might have been the rustling of straw that woke her up. There were footsteps, but she couldn't turn around

128

to see if anyone was there. Her neck was weary – the weight of the collar seemed to have increased by a ton. Her sex was still moist, perhaps more so than before.

Hands gripped her hips, and suddenly she felt warm loins against her behind.

'Who's . . .' she tried to ask and to turn round, but the horse collar was too heavy, the stable just too dark. She cried out as a penis the size of a drum major's baton entered her vagina.

'Ahhh!' she cried, as the penis and, with it, the crop handle pushed against her muscle walls. Both holes were filled, and the sensation made her aching clitoris ache a lot more.

She was trapped, in need of release, yet getting none; her senses soared inexorably higher as the penis and the crop handle pleasured both orifices but left her clitoris untouched. As she cried out that she didn't think it was fair, she felt the owner of the penis reach his climax, then heard his cry of delight.

With his final spurt, he ran his hand up her back and pushed her head into the water of the trough. When the hand released her, she gasped for breath and shook her head. She tried to look over her shoulder, but whoever had taken advantage of her situation was no longer there. Only the longing for climax still remained with her, and a faint smell of maleness clung damply on her curling hairs.

If Nadine either noticed or had contrived the coupling that had just happened, she said nothing to Penny.

'Are you ready for me now, my pretty pussy?' she asked, her voice all sweetness and honey. 'Are you willing now to follow my rules, to play my games?'

As she spoke, her long, soft fingers traced circles up and down Penny's spine before they curved around the crop and jerked it slightly so its handle jumped inside her.

'Yes, Nadine. I'm ready.' She moaned again as Nadine nudged the handle in a little further.

'You are sure of that?'

'I'm sure, Nadine. I'm sure. Please. I'm aching. Please do something.'

Nadine sighed almost regretfully, then pulled the crop from where it had been so tightly gripped. She undid the bonds as she talked, raised Penny up, then pushed her to her knees. The horse collar remained around her neck.

'Tonight,' she said, 'after dinner, you will play my first game. You will be my cabaret. Whatever and whoever is offered to you, you will take. Is that clear?'

'Yes,' Penny answered, head suitably bowed, which she felt somehow was what was expected of her. Inside, she was burning with anticipation.

'Good,' Nadine replied coldly. 'Then we're agreed on that.'

With an obvious sense of purpose, Nadine unzipped her trousers, and pulled them down slightly so her mons was yet again exposed.

Without urging, Penny kissed it.

Chapter Seven

*T*onight her outfit was darker than her hair. The top was little more than a tube against which her breasts rebelled and showed through in blatant relief.

Black trousers matched the top. They had a sash waistband that tied at one side. Once pulled, the trousers would just drop to her ankles – soft, silky and with a distinct hush.

Tonight only gold jewellery relieved her darkness. Her earrings were gold. So was her necklace and the Celtic half-bangle on her right wrist. The metal glowed against the pale cream of her skin and the darkness of her hair. Her eyes shone like two bright sapphires which were made all the more bright by the blackness of her eyelashes. She wore gold sandals with high heels that stretched her calves and caused her buttocks and bosom to thrust in opposite directions. There was no underwear between her and the soft caress of silk against her skin.

'You look glorious, my dear.' Alistair stood alone by the open door. The others had already gone in. His eyes held hers, his jaw dropping slightly as they travelled downwards over her tight bodice, her belly and thighs.

She moved slightly, pirouetting on her high heels, her hips swaying. Behind her was one of the long windows that swept from ceiling to floor. Light still filtered through, and as the material of her trousers was

131

very fine, it shone through and he could see the dark patch of hair nestling between her creamy thighs.

'How very kind of you to say so.'

He offered her his hand, though now politeness took over from appraisal. She took it anyway, and studied him as he led her into the room, left her at her chair, and went round the other side of the table to take his own.

Hair high and pulled into a pony-tail behind, it swung as Penny took her seat. Something about tonight made her feel special. This feeling could have been the result of knowing that all eyes were upon her or may have been the residue of those dark feelings deep inside that begged for acknowledgement. She looked at each of her fellow diners in turn, and they all responded individually.

Nadine winked suggestively, her usual sardonic smile gently tilting the corners of her mouth. With difficulty, she looked away.

Alistair's glances were sporadic. When she raised her eyes to meet his, he looked guiltily away. Each time Penny was aware of a look passing between him and his sister.

Auberon had a pink face tonight. Perhaps it was the wine, or maybe it was his deepest thoughts that made him blush and stammer that way. Either way, he was looking at her, blinking and taking big gulps from his very full glass. He smiled, and his eyes glittered expectantly.

Tonight felt good and so did she. The mix of smells heightened that excitement: good food; fine wine; the smell of men and her own perfume mixed with the heavy scent of huge cut blooms in blue and-white Chinese vases on the long sideboard. There was a breathless sensuality almost tangible in the air. Eyes glittered, and voices were soft and husky like a mild sea breeze blowing over coarse sand.

'A little more wine?' asked Sir Reggie, breaking into her thoughts in that gentlemanly way of his.

'Yes please,' she answered with a smile. Her pony-tail swung merrily as she turned to face him. She held up her glass and watched, almost hypnotically, as the dark-red liquid poured into the bowl of lead crystal and drowned the sparkling prisms of light thrown by the overhead chandeliers.

After some pretty healthy eating and drinking, her top wriggled down and her breasts burst upwards, round and shiny like balloons about to burst. Her nipples peered over her black top like two frightened eyes. As he poured the wine, Sir Reggie's eyes were fastened on them. His hand shook and the wine bottle trembled; some of the red liquid missed the glass and streamed over her gleaming mounds. She gasped as a large trickle disappeared down the cleft in between.

'Oh, my dear. I do apologise most sincerely. How clumsy of me. Allow me, my dear.' Sir Reggie covered her hand with his. 'I made the mess. Let me clear it up.'

Silence descended over those gathered as Sir Reggie lowered his mouth on to Penny's breasts. All eyes upon her and Sir Reggie's tongue lapping at her bosoms, Penny let herself become part of the atmosphere she had felt earlier. She purred with pleasure and felt herself and her senses blend as easily as coffee and cream. Sir Reggie's tongue licked long and ponderously as he savoured the bouquet he detected through his nose and the taste on his tongue of the unusual combination of perfume, flesh and wine.

'Allow me, my dear,' he said, as courteous as only a gentleman like him could be. 'I noticed that it dribbled down through. I insist on dealing with it.'

She nodded without speaking, her breath quickening with brazen abandon as he rolled down her bodice and let her breasts spring completely free. Then, slowly, as though enjoying every diverse taste on his tongue, he licked all over her proud orbs and down her cleavage between.

Gasps of pleasure broke from her throat. His tongue was hot and pleasantly wet. It had a certain rasp to its tissue, a bit like that of a cat.

Despite, or perhaps to spite, the watching eyes, she pushed her breasts towards his mouth, and closed her

133

eyes as his hair caressed her nipples. His tongue followed the contours of her breasts, tracing each gentle curve and valley; his tongue lapped her satin flesh, around the dark halos in which her nipples sat demanding and receiving avid attention. Tenderly, he sucked each one, rolled them on his tongue and neatly prodded with its tip.

When she opened her eyes, she looked over his head at each of the other dinner guests. Auberon was transfixed on what Sir Reggie was doing. Nadine's smile was wider than it had been.

'I think I've cleared all of it up,' said Sir Reggie at last with a smile. He brought his head up level with hers, and salaciously licked his lips. She had expected him then to handle her bosoms, to play to the crowd so to speak, seeing as she was so obviously tonight's cabaret. But he didn't. Instead, and to her surprise and disappointment, he pulled up her tube bodice, cupped a bosom in one hand and put it back in, then did the same to the other. He appeared to take great pleasure in doing this, as though they were priceless treasures that he had rescued from tarnish or destruction and was just gathering them in for further study later.

Penny took this in the spirit in which it was meant, though she had been enjoying his tongue.

'That's very kind of you,' she said, though inside her senses were screaming for more. 'I'm sorry to have put you to all that trouble.'

'No trouble at all, my dear. Always willing to do my duty.' She saw him exchange looks with Alistair. Tonight, like Sir Reggie, and even like Auberon, Alistair wore a dinner suit. Yet he didn't look quite so stiff as the others. There was something about him still slightly casual. It was the way, she thought, of the rich and confident. There was definitely a skill in looking formal whilst maintaining an air of casual indifference.

Penny felt almost triumphant when she saw Alistair eyeing her intensely, despite dark scowls from Nadine. His mouth was slightly open as though he were catching his breath. She saw him swallow. In that moment, she knew he wanted her. But what was keeping him from attempting her seduction? What barrier did he have to overcome before he could bury his manhood in her and cry his climax into her ear?

But Nadine's dark scowls seemed to get the better of him. He looked serious before he cleared his throat and began to speak.

'Nadine tells me you lost concentration this afternoon. I don't like that.' Although he was in effect chastising, his voice was even, as steady as the day he had got her to parade through the town with him. It was still gloriously deep, as if erupting from some deep fissure in the earth's crust. All the same it made her defensive, but then, of course, she felt that was what she was expected to be – something to give cause for rebuke.

'I hit the fence,' she replied hotly, her limbs already starting to tremble with apprehension. 'That's all. Four faults.' She saw Alistair raise his eyebrows. She also saw the faint nod of approval from Nadine. Obviously, she was egging him on.

The rugged features of Alistair Beaumont remained unchanged as though he were as crystal as his overhead chandeliers. In an effort to control her rising excitement, Penny looked beyond him to the windows and the reflected room and figures. It was almost as if there were two worlds, she thought; two Beaumont Places. In one of them lived real people. In the other, there were only shadows, bare reflections of the people that really existed, and those reflections were dark, muted, but could burn bright at any time just like the hidden emotions within herself.

His voice brought her back to the real room and the real people. 'So. You admit it. You lost concentration.'

'Yes.' She said it with a dismissive laugh. At her side, Sir Reginald cleared his throat and began to fidget. She glanced at him. There was a sparkle in his eyes.

'I did lose concentration – just for a moment. I smiled at Auberon,' said Penny casually. 'Perhaps I was too pleased at having cleared all the jumps, too cocksure about clearing the last one as well.'

Smiles and low chuckles seemed suddenly to surround her.

'Or even too cock-happy?' drawled Nadine, her voice as long and drawn-out as her suck on her customary cheroot.

Despite his sister's humour, Alistair's face was unchanged, but deep in his eyes, something stirred; something as dark as it was exciting. Penny caught that look. Her eyes were locked with his. She felt as though she were diving into unknown waters, waters the more sensible would steer clear of. But she would plunge into those waters headlong. In the aftermath of the release of those dark feelings within her, the sensual had come to outweigh the sensible.

A flush of defiance and trepidation lit her face as she glanced from the self-assured paleness of Nadine to the pretty shade of pink that coloured Auberon's cheeks. She knew what they wanted, knew what was expected of her. 'My sex life is my own affair,' she retorted hotly, and eyed each of her colleagues for their response.

'Not whilst you are at Beaumont Place,' said Alistair grimly. 'As I am sure my sister has told you, while you are here you become part of my team. Becoming part of my team means you give yourself up, body and soul, to this place and your sport.'

For a moment, she wondered if she'd gone too far. She didn't think so, but this was her first foray into the world of master, mistress and object of punishment. She reined in her words. 'I didn't mean to step out of line. I'm sorry if I offended anyone.'

'My sister tells me you took advantage of Stephen,' Alistair began, his eyes seeming to study the two silver pheasants that decorated the middle of the table. 'Oh,' he added, shaking his head when she tried to interrupt, 'I don't blame you. It's just that I thought a woman of your experience and intelligence would indulge in a higher level of sexual adventure than tumbling in the straw with a common stable-lad – a straightforward act of copulation.'

He watched for her reaction and kept to himself the

knowledge that he and Nadine had watched nearly everything she had done since coming here. Whilst he had watched, his cock had throbbed almost painfully against the tight rubber of his pants. But he had borne that pain, sure in the knowledge that his sex drive was becoming more powerful than that of an ordinary man. It was being conserved, saved like a bundle of electrical charges and set to explode in one almighty consummation when the moment was right.

But the antics of the dark-haired Penny had almost made him plead with his sister to release him from his strictures and have Penny right away. Nadine, thankfully, had refused. And of course, as usual, she had been right. A man of fibre does not give in to weakness. He saves his assets, acquires as much as possible until the time is ripe for a series of performances, not just one. Then what he had would be hers, and once its task was done, his prick would diminish and lie dormant, waiting until the next time.

In the heat of the opulent room, Penny felt her cheeks redden. She didn't like being thought of as unadventurous. Of course she was sophisticated enough to indulge in the more esoteric sexual scenarios. In the heat of the moment, the part she should play was forgotten. She rose to her feet, her fists slamming down on the table.

'The chance was there. I took it. What am I supposed to do here? Become a nun?'

She felt a warm hand caress the backs of her legs and knew that, inadvertently, she had made the right move and spoken the right words. She looked down into the yearning expression and strong features of Sir Reginald. What a man he must have been when he was younger, she thought momentarily. He was still something to look at even now. There was a military set to his chin, a hardness to his face and body that only rigid exercise and armed combat could possibly have moulded.

'I believe you,' Sir Reggie said, his smile stretching the dark moustache that curled over his top lip. 'I know you indulge in other things.'

137

'Yes,' snapped Nadine from the other side of the table. 'She most certainly will.'

Penny fell to silence, mouth slightly open as familiar feelings grew in the moistness of her sex. She felt hands pulling at the sash that held her trousers. They dropped with a soft hush to her ankles. Her backside was bare, and her triangle of pubic hair peered shyly over the edge of the dining table.

She tried not to moan, yet all the while her hips swayed in time to the probing of Sir Reggie's fingers. She shifted slightly and opened her legs a little wider. Where only two fingers had been, he now put his whole hand.

Leg and thigh muscles trembling, Penny rested her own hands flat upon the table in order to facilitate stronger probings. She bent forward slightly. Other eyes were upon her, glittering like hard cut diamonds. But she didn't care about them looking. As mews of delight escaped in rapid succession from her throat, she lost herself in her own yearnings, in her own dark desires.

Suddenly, there were no other people in the room. She was lost in her own delirium as though she were in a trance or taken by a high fever. All the while, the exploring fingers of Sir Reggie tangled in her hair and pushed their way through the cleft that divided her firm buttocks.

Briefly, Penny opened her eyes and saw Nadine and Alistair smiling at her. She opened her mouth to speak. Alistair spoke first.

'No need to say anything. Enjoy it. Just as we are enjoying it.'

She did not protest. Somehow she understood what they were saying. Through others' pleasure, those that watch take pleasure. Even through pain, they too witness an awesome presence of something more that goes beyond both, so that pleasure and pain become one and the same thing.

Wriggling with delight and pleased that those watching were sharing that delight with her, she felt the hand continue and felt the fingers sliding into her more easily as her sex responded to the situation.

On the other side of the table, Nadine leaned towards her brother and whispered close to his ear. Penny, her breath audible among murmurs of delight, saw Alistair smile and nod his head. Then she saw Nadine straighten up and look directly at her.

'Reggie likes what he's doing. Do you?' Nadine asked through a cloud of expelled smoke.

Penny nodded. She tried to speak, but could only gasp. Sir Reggie's fingers were plying their way through her legs, dividing the mossy hair that covered her pudendum; her pubic hair, her sex.

'Yes,' she replied at last in the hush of her breath. 'Yes, I do.'

As moans of ecstasy escaped her lips, her eyes met those of Alistair. His mouth was open, his nostrils were flared. Was he thinking, she wondered, of that day when she had been naked beneath a cashmere coat in the middle of the high street? There had only been the two of them on that particular day. Just asking herself that question was enough to bring her aching clitoris from out of its protective hood. As if pouncing on a reclusive wild animal, Sir Reggie took it between two fingers. As he squeezed it, her knees buckled slightly and deep moans erupted one after the other from her throat.

Still resting her palms on the table, she leaned a little further forward and clutched a handful of tablecloth as her fist closed over it. That way, she could steady herself so Reggie could invade her more easily. It didn't matter that there were people watching her ascend towards the delicious waves of orgasm. They were just extensions of her own delight, as much victims of their own decadence as she was.

Nadine came round to her side and placed her hand on Penny's shoulder. Falling more deeply into the abyss of her own sexuality, Penny knew that the performance had only just started.

'Your orgasm can wait a while,' Nadine said sharply. 'There are other things we wish to see before we let you have that.'

The lips that had covered hers earlier in the day now

139

whispered just a breath away from her ear. 'Remember our bargain, my sweet pussy-cat. Remember you are due punishment, and punishment can involve pleasure as well as pain. But you know that already. Go along with all that is asked of you, exactly as I told you.'

Nadine's breath was warm, and full of wine and strong smoke against her ear. Penny, still swimming upstream towards her climax, turned to look at her. She took in the square jaw and pale face of Nadine and, although she felt little more than a plaything, there was an odd security in that knowledge. For the first time in her life, she felt comfortable where she was, and with those around her.

Reminding Penny of a cat relishing a banquet of live sparrow, Nadine ran her long tongue slowly and sensually over her pale lips. In the brightness of her eyes, Penny discerned erotic imaginings, schemes and ideas. Her smile was fixed, as though it was permanently painted on her face.

In one swift movement, Nadine ran her hands down Penny's back and down to her glossy behind. They were cool on Penny's warm flesh, yet she welcomed them even when each firm cheek was cupped and parted. Penny did not need to see what she was doing. She knew – could feel – that her cheeks were open wide, and the dark puckered mouth of her most secret and smallest orifice was exposed. It made her gasp, it made her squeal. Nadine had offered a blatant invitation to Sir Reggie. Penny did not doubt that he would accept it.

Penny heard Sir Reggie's sharp intake of breath, felt his thumb prod excitedly between her cheeks and press fondly at the tightness of her anus.

'I think you need this, Reggie darling,' Penny heard Nadine purr.

As one buttock was released, Penny saw that same hand pass in front of her. The long fingers that she had come to know picked up a butter-knife, which Nadine dipped into the silver-edged butter-dish. Then the knife disappeared from Penny's view.

She wriggled her bottom, intent on experiencing

140

invasion in either of her passages. Her bodice was still around her waist, her trousers were around her ankles. Everything in between was bare. On top of that, she now knew for sure that her exposed anus was about to be smeared in butter then invaded by Sir Reggie's finger or thumb. She was tonight's star – or victim. The former, she thought. That's the way I truly feel. I'm like a performer about to give the show of my life.

The butter was cold against her anus and the butter-knife obviously blunt. She felt it being spread, then the knife was held tight against her nether mouth so a portion of it was pushed inside her.

'Push it in please Reggie, darling,' she heard Nadine say.

'Glad to, my dear ... very glad to,' answered Sir Reggie.

Penny closed her eyes and gripped the tablecloth more tightly as Sir Reggie's finger, ably assisted by the butter, entered her most secret portal. She cried out more with passion than pain. Nadine still held her cheeks firmly apart so the butter could be smeared more easily with the fingers of one hand, whilst a finger of the other hand worked its way inside her.

Penny moaned with each small thrust as the finger entered her anus up to the first joint. As the butter oiled its onward progress, his finger was soon buried up to the knuckle.

'I've got it right in her,' she heard Sir Reggie say excitedly. But his voice sounded distant to her. Whatever he was doing had transported her to another world. She was lost in her own pleasure, her legs were taut as she tilted her bottom to meet him, her vulva swirling with liquid desire.

Almost as if he were trying to staunch her sexual flow, Sir Reggie immersed his fingers in her vagina. Now she moaned more. This was too much. She was too full, both erogenous holes were plugged by his exploring fingers. Tingles of pleasure spread upwards and outwards from each exploration. She was plugged with desire, stuffed with fingers.

141

'See, Reggie,' she heard Nadine say. 'See what a lovely bottom she has. Don't you think it's the best bottom you have ever seen? See how soft the skin is, how firm the muscles, and just see how sensitive it is.'

Sharp nails scraped over Penny's skin in much the same way as Penny's own nails had scraped over Auberon's.

Penny's breath caught in her throat and she curled her fingers more tightly in the stiffness of the white, linen tablecloth.

'Beautiful,' muttered the old man. 'Simply beautiful. In fact, perfect.'

'She's wet. The little mare is very wet, isn't she, Reggie.'

Penny tensed and moaned obligingly as Nadine's fingers joined Reggie's, and dipped into the fountain of fluid that bubbled from her secret cavern. She opened her eyes along with her mouth now, and looked across the table. Now her eyes held Alistair's. What she saw, she liked. Although his face was still unaltered, his eyes sparkled with a multitude of different colours as if he were assessing what she was feeling and wondering exactly how far she would go.

Auberon appeared interested, yet somehow jealous.

He wishes it were him, thought Penny. He would like it to be him undergoing this treatment. The more scratching and whipping, the better pleased he would be.

'She's near climax,' drawled Nadine, her fingers mingling with Reggie's before rubbing excess fluid from Penny's flowing vulva and up through the cheeks of her bottom and around Reggie's plunging finger. 'Does she get that climax now,' Nadine went on, 'or do you have something else in mind, brother dear?'

Penny heard what she said, attempted to speak, but was powerless to do so. All her responses, all her actions, were being manipulated by others. They were using her as a puppeteer might pull on strings – and she was dancing to their tune.

She squealed as the talons of Nadine's graceful hands

142

tangled in her pubic hair, one fingertip running delicious rings around and over her ripening bud.

'The first lesson, sister,' answered Alistair, 'is to go gentle at first. Give her what she desires. If she is as adventurous as she says she is, she will be back for more, back for the lessons yet to come.'

Penny half-opened her eyes; through her dark lashes she saw Alistair smile briefly in Reggie's direction. Only for a moment did she wonder what the look and the words meant. Her first consideration was her mounting orgasm. It took her over, felt almost as if she were rising to the crest of a giant wave that, having reached its peak, curled over and fell crashing, splattering her jerking thighs with tingling sensations and warm secretions. She cried out. Her limbs trembled and she gasped for air and fell forward on to the table, breasts pressed against the stiff starch of the very white tablecloth.

Faces beamed around her. Sighs of satisfaction filled the air as though they had shared her orgasm, and had dipped their own fingers into the warm pool of fluid that flooded Penny's open sex.

'Kneel!' ordered Nadine, her strong hands pulling her up from the table, her fingers curling in an iron grip over her shoulders. Penny, realising that they had not yet finished with her, did as ordered. Between her legs, the last sweet aches of orgasm were flowing away. She had been absorbed in them, and therefore had not expected that more would be required of her.

Reggie, face glowing with a ruddy anticipation, moved the chair she had been sitting on so she could kneel down where she was.

Alistair came round from the other side of the table and sat in the chair she had been sitting in. Again he would do nothing but watch, she thought. Again he had disappointed her.

He had a brandy balloon in one hand in which about an inch of best Armagnac swirled. He crossed one leg over the other, sipped just once, every inch the gentleman, just waiting for the performance to begin.

Auberon got up, too, and came round. He stood like a

143

sentinel behind Alistair's chair as though in attendance on him. Both sets of eyes were glued on the kneeling Penny. Nadine stood behind her, Sir Reggie in front.

Nadine's hands stroked Penny's hair, neck and shoulders. Directly in front of Penny's face was the fly of Sir Reggie's trousers and the swelling mound immediately behind it. She froze, yet watched mesmerised as his fumbling hands tugged impatiently at his zip.

Expectantly, she swallowed hard and left her mouth completely empty. It needed no explanation to tell her what was intended. And yet she knew that more was expected than to pleasure the penis of the tall and well-made military man. The key to that more exquisite scenario was bound to be protest.

'I don't . . .'

'You will.' Nadine's fingers tangled in her hair. The roots strained in her scalp and she cried out as her head was held erect. She closed her mouth tightly. Nadine pulled her hair so her head tilted back slightly.

Unable to move her head, Penny's eyes rolled sidelong. In a bid to keep her balance and perspective, she rested her hands now on Sir Reggie's thighs which seemed to be made of iron and were covered in profuse and dark hair.

At first she continued her imitation protest and tried to draw away from the advancing member. Then she gulped and gasped for air as Nadine pinched her nose. Before her, the white length of Reggie's member approached her lips. Entranced by the sight, she freely looked it over, then opened her mouth wider. His cock was surprisingly upright and wore its mushroom dome like an imperial crown.

She closed her eyes, steeling herself for the feel of it in her mouth, the taste of it upon her tongue. Even as Sir Reggie's hands took hold of her head and guided her mouth to satisfy his needs, she wriggled in protest. Just as she had judged, his member stiffened and jerked on her lips. It danced in her mouth as her tongue traced imaginary lines over its surface, her teeth gently nibbling from its tip to its base.

144

With one of Nadine's hands still tangled in her hair, she gulped more cock into her mouth. Reggie's member gained in firmness and stature as her mouth slid up and down it, her movements controlled by his hands which remained clamped firmly to her head.

She felt Nadine's free hand slide over her shoulder, cup her breast, then pinch fondly at a nipple. The other hand left her tangled mane and did the same to the other. Now only Reggie's hands were tangled in her hair, pushing her head up and down his phallus just as he pleased. Nadine's were doing other things.

No matter how much Penny had eaten that night, there was a more insatiable hunger now prevailing through her system. She raised her own hand to touch, perhaps even to control the living organ that drove so consistently in and out of her mouth.

'No!'

Nadine's orders again. Out of the corner of her eyes, Penny saw Nadine go over to the heavy curtains that hung from the windows and then undo one of the silk-rope tie-backs.

Then Nadine's long hands grabbed both of hers, and tied them with the cool silk cords behind Penny's back.

Another gasp escaped from the mouth of the man above her. Her bondage had obviously pleased him, and the position of her restrained arms accentuated the thrust of her breasts beneath his busy penis. As Nadine lifted her breasts higher, Sir Reggie gasped again as the satin softness of her skin met the more feathered surface of his slapping balls.

'Perfect,' she heard Sir Reggie say between gasps of delight. 'Just perfect.'

Hot kisses rained on Penny's back as Nadine's fingers rolled her breasts and tweaked almost savagely their crowns of pink velvet.

Penny closed her eyes again. She didn't need to pretend that the man in her mouth was Alistair. It was enough to know that he was watching and even enjoying the experience. She certainly was. Anyway, Reggie was a handsome and dignified man. The years had been extra-

145

ordinarily kind to his sexuality and his body which was still firm, ripe and honed to a perfection only an adventurous military man could hope to attain.

She almost felt she could swallow the rampant phallus that was growing to new prominence. It was as if her tongue had a life of its own as it licked around the prickly ridge of the penis and traced the deep vein that ran from tip to stem.

Reggie's hands were still clamped on either side of her head. They tightened their grip as he continued to control her head so that her mouth moved up and down his penis at his whim. Even without being able to run her finger down the throbbing vein that ran the length of his manhood, Penny knew his time was near. His breathing had quickened, and so had the pushing backwards and forwards of her head along his length. In her mouth, the first juice of ejaculation settled like salt pearls upon her tongue.

'Mr Harding.'

Nadine's voice rang out. There was unmistakable demand in it.

This time, Penny could see nothing. Reggie's grip was too strong, his climax too near. The only view she had was straight ahead. She stared directly into Sir Reggie's pubic hair, aware that her own sex was wanting an extra release to the one it had received earlier.

As the hard shaft moved in and out of her mouth, she took a deep gulp of breath. Someone's fingers buried themselves in her sex. She realised they must belong to Auberon. Like some sort of automaton, it had been Auberon who had been summoned, and Auberon who seemed to know exactly what to do without explanation. There was no barrier to their penetration, only a new wetness of excitement flooding on top of the sticky excess from her previous orgasm. Pleasure began to ripple outwards and upwards from her centre of desire. In her mouth, she felt Reggie's penis begin to vibrate with his rising climax, and was aware of her nipples responding to Nadine's teasing fingers. Both assisted the tremulous sensations erupting around her demanding clitoris,

146

which raised its aching head towards Auberon's probing fingers.

'Is she wet?' It was Nadine's voice behind her.

'Soaking,' Auberon responded, a tremor of subdued excitement shaking the words on his tongue.

'Dirty little mare. You want it again, do you? Are you coming?'

Penny's voice was shaky, taken over by the luxurious vibrations that radiated from her engorged centre. 'Y-Yes.'

'And you, Reggie?'

'Any second.'

To Penny, it seemed as if Nadine had given a signal. The fingers massaging her sex moved with greater dexterity and speed over her clitoris. Those on her nipples pinched more avidly, and rolled her breasts with greater purpose. If her mouth had been free, she would have moaned with pleasure.

Just as she reached her own peak, with her hips jerking against the hand that pleasured her, Reggie withdrew his throbbing member from her mouth.

Splashes of warmth fell over her breasts, and the sticky whiteness was massaged into the satin skin by the same hands that had aroused her nipples to greater prominence. Above her, Reggie groaned, his hands releasing her head as his penis released his semen.

In white streams like weak icing, Reggie's come settled on her breasts. Nadine's hands rolled through it, massaging it over her until there was no whiteness left and only the stickiness sank into her skin. She massaged it right up into the tips of Penny's nipples so they glistened like spun silver.

The last tremors of climax shivered down her thighs and she sighed her satisfaction amid deep breaths and light moans of pleasure. At this moment in time, Penny felt as though she had been the centre of the universe, in this room anyway. She opened her eyes, closed them again and savoured the last tingles of delight. When she reopened them, her eyes met those of Alistair. Would he take her now? He stared, blinked self-consciously, then looked away. 'I think she's got the message,' he said, and rose to his feet.

Eyes still watching Alistair yet free of her bonds, Nadine massaged Penny's arms.

'Enough for tonight?' Nadine's question was aimed at her brother.

'Enough for tonight. But there's always tomorrow.'

Penny found it hard to drag her eyes away from Alistair. He looked so cool, and so calmly in charge of the situation. Yet there was something in his eyes that expressed torment. He was like a master of ceremonies or ringmaster. He was the boss, detailing and explaining what was to be done, yet contributing nothing to it.

Nadine's lips brushing gently against her cheek distracted her. 'Do you ache very much, my darling pussy-cat?' cooed Nadine, her voice as thick and sweet as syrup.

Penny dragged her eyes from Alistair and stared directly into his sister's eyes. She blinked, thought of herself and exactly how she *did* feel. 'Yes,' she replied, 'I do ache a little – my arms especially. At this moment in time, I'd love Gregory to give me a massage.'

Nadine positively purred with delight. The ice-cold eyes sparkled with sweet-shop anticipation.

'Gregory should be in bed by now, my pretty. He usually is. Anyway, why disturb him, pussy-cat? I'll give you a massage.'

The smile Penny gave Nadine was sweet, but not necessarily innocent.

Chapter Eight

'I want you to massage me,' Nadine said, once they were back in Penny's room, where a massive flower arrangement set on a table in the middle of the room graced the air with garden-like freshness.

She didn't wait for an answer, but just pulled off what few clothes she had on and lay out face down on the bed.

Before taking the top off the oil bottle, Penny, who was already naked, glanced at the big mirror. She had no doubt that Nadine had told Alistair something more than just goodnight.

Nadine's body was snow-white against the rich red and green of the tapestry bed cover. Her body was also very long, her feet curling over the foot of the bed and the top of her head brushing the carved headboard.

She moaned as Penny began to run and roll her hands over her body.

'My intention was to invigorate your muscles, pretty pussy, not for you to invigorate mine,' she purred, stretching as she said it, her hips rolling slightly against the roughness of the bed cover.

Penny stood statuesque and resolute, her skin glowing in the aftermath of the exacting session she had just endured. She watched her rolling behind, and the cheeks tight and small like a young boy's.

And how are you enjoying that? she thought, knowing

that Nadine was rolling her own pert clitoris against the roughness of the bedspread.

'The more pliant your muscles, the more benefit mine will receive,' Penny said sweetly.

Nadine rested her head on folded arms whilst Penny oiled her hands again. Faint murmurs of pleasure came from Nadine's mouth and were breathed into the crisp whiteness of the pillow as Penny's hands spread and pressed at the sinuous flesh.

Nadine's flesh tensed and shivered with pleasure as Penny pushed the ball of her palms into the tight muscles of her shoulders. She probed with fingers made strong by holding in check the head of plunging horses before flying over five-foot spreads or striped cross beams.

Not without selfish intent, Penny repositioned and sat astride a rounded bottom that was soft-skinned, yet hard beneath the lingering wetness and open lips of her own sex. She murmured a little as she wriggled astride the pert and rather boyish bottom. Her sex moistened and her nub of passion erected as she felt the tight cheeks bunch compulsively beneath her.

With serious precision, she worked the muscles on either side of Nadine's spine, her thumbs following each nobble of the long indentation that lay so close to the skin. She smoothed her hands upwards, the oiled flesh glistening beneath her touch, then brought them down again, the thumbs pressing in feather-like outward strokes as she progressed downwards towards the rising mounds of Nadine's behind and the forest of her own body hair.

'Delicious,' Nadine murmured, her eyes closed to add greater perception to her other senses.

Penny studied Nadine's face as she lay supine. White lashes lay barely perceptible against the paleness of high-boned cheeks. Beneath the straight patrician nose, her mouth was wide and slightly open, exposing the strong white teeth which even now clutched resolutely at a butt of a black cheroot.

Questions circled in Penny's mind. She wanted to know more about Alistair, and more about his relationship with his sister. She also wanted to know more about herself from those questions. She wanted to find out where her new and acute sexuality had come from and what had caused its release. How much more was there to discover about this place, these people and herself? Softly, she told herself, go softly.

'Was tonight a foretaste of things to come?' she asked as her fingertips deftly rubbed the nape of Nadine's neck.

'Hmmm?' murmured the wide mouth.

'Was that a yes?'

Nadine chuckled into the pillow. 'Tonight was a mere aperitif, my pretty. It gets better. The *premier cru* is still to come.' She purred her answer, like a stroked cat craving for more of what she was already receiving.

Penny paused, and grimaced as Nadine spat the cheroot butt from her mouth. Then she studied the clusters of ornamental plasterwork up on the ceiling before attempting another question. Continue the softening of the body, she reasoned, and the sharp mind will follow.

'Doesn't Alistair ever join in?'

The lashes flickered, the nostrils flared slightly. Hesitation was obvious. 'Only on special occasions – in exceptional circumstances.' The pale eyes opened and Nadine looked back at Penny over her shoulder. 'When the time is ripe,' Nadine added.

Penny slowed the massage and lowered her eyes to the white and now gleaming skin. She wondered when those special occasions would be and what the exceptional circumstances were. And when would the time be ripe and who would judge that it was so?

But she didn't ask. Not yet anyway. She altered position until she was further down Nadine's body, her legs straddling her lower thighs. Her eyes travelled over the rounded cheeks, as white as the rest of Nadine's taut flesh. The rising of her dividing cleft was marked with a solitary dimple. She leaned low over Nadine's back, her thumbs on her spine, her palms and fingers spread to encompass the narrow waist. Briefly, her nipples trailed over the naked flesh with no more than the touch of the lightest butterfly. A delicious shiver ran from her white

151

shoulders to the snowy mountains of her behind. Penny, sensing the reaction Nadine was getting from the brushing of her nipples, repeated the movement, taking her own pleasure from the brief yet tingling touch before running her hands down over the hip-bones and cupping each cheek in an oily palm, her thumbs curving over the rising flesh to the cleft between.

Nadine purred again with pleasure and wriggled her hips, her bottom rising as if inviting Penny to press harder, and to probe more deeply. Now, Penny judged, the time was ripe to ask another question.

'What are these special occasions?'

Nadine's lips curled back soundlessly from her teeth before she chuckled again into the pillow.

'Patience, my little pussy-cat, patience. I know what you're getting at.' One grey eye opened and regarded Penny above a snow-white shoulder. 'Your time will come, my pretty. Your time will come.' Her voice had become a growl. Warning ran parallel in her voice with low murmurs of pleasure.

Beneath Penny's straddled thighs and moist sex, Nadine rolled over completely, the fleshy pink crowns of her small breasts pointing obscenely skywards. 'Now, oil me some more. I want you to rub my nipples first – just to get me going.'

Her eyes opened. Penny held her gaze for just a moment, then looked down again at the pure white flesh. For all the willpower she seemed to possess at this moment in time, she might just as well have been an odalisque in some Eastern harem. It seemed as though what Nadine wanted was also what she wanted. There appeared to be no dividing line between the two. Almost by instinct, she knew what she had to do next.

Her pubic hairs brushed over Nadine's flesh as she slid up over the reclining body until she straddled her waist. She re-oiled her hands and drank in the piquant beauty of Nadine's snowy orbs, the hard nubs of dense sensitivity rising from areolae as plush as pink velvet.

Although her gaze was full of promised delights, she resisted their lure and placed her hands around Nadine's

152

neck, pressing slightly so that a look of something resembling fear entered her grey eyes. Then they relaxed, her fingers running down the sinews, over the collar-bone to the smooth skin of Nadine's shoulders.

Nadine, reassured that Penny was as compliant as she had previously judged, closed her eyes and murmured her gratitude. Her nipples visibly pouted to be included.

Unable to resist any longer, Penny closed the tips of one finger and one thumb over each. The fine ridges of the thrusting protrusions felt strangely silky beneath her touch. She felt them rise, then grow more engorged with blood and desire as her palms rested on the smooth skin.

'Harder,' breathed Nadine.

Penny clasped the nipples more tightly and pulled them upwards as high as she could until the whole of the breast seemed suspended on each glaring nub of rosy tissue. The oil made them more glossy, lending a silvery shine to the translucent skin. They looked succulent, too succulent to leave just to trembling fingers. Urged by waves of energy generated from within, Penny bent her head and took the swollen flesh into her mouth. She closed her eyes as her lips covered them, sucked hard and long and felt the nipple growing to an even greater proportion on her tongue. She sucked again and again, nibbling every so often as the fingers on the other hand continued to pull at its partner, then to tease and pinch it to respond better than it already had.

'Suck me harder,' Nadine's voice rasped through her lips. Her nails began to dig into Penny's back, then one hand pressed against her head, holding her fast against the swollen breast, forcing her to suck, nibble and bite exactly how and when Nadine wanted her to.

Penny managed to gulp air before the lean, yet uncommonly strong hands forced her lips on to the other breast. She repeated what she had already done, her mouth sucking long and hard, her teeth nipping gently, then more firmly, at the growing flesh. All the time, Penny's other hand pinched and pulled at the newly released nipple, which was now swollen and red from her oral treatment of it.

As the hand that held her relaxed, her mouth released its delicacy. She kissed between the breasts, her wet tongue and nipping teeth eliciting more cloudy exclamations from Nadine's throat.

Her head and her hands began to move again. She trailed low over the narrow waist, the flat stomach. Her own proud nipples brushed lightly over the skin as her hands massaged the lean hips.

She raised herself up slightly so her hands could come inwards, and her fingers and eyes could examine the prominence of the shorn mound of Nadine's sex. How naked it looked, the lips purely white and as smooth as silk, a stripe of pink showing like a delicate insert of glistening silk in between.

Nadine's legs widened. Hanging from amid the white fleshy lips, Penny could see the pink frills of the inner petals and the throbbing bud of Nadine's clitoris as it thrust out from its fringe of moist flesh.

Moans of pleasure accompanied the writhing of thighs, the thrusting of belly and sex before Penny's face. Beneath her fingers, Penny could feel the silkiness of Nadine's flesh together with the plump sexuality of her naked labia.

She slid her fingers further, lightly teasing the gleaming frills and the springing love bud. They looked sweet, dripping with the honey of arousal. She bent her head. Her tongue tasted the silkiness of the outer lips before dipping in between, savouring the salty sweetness of another woman on her tongue.

Nadine's murmurs of pleasure were nothing to her now. Again, her own sex was responding to stimuli, her hips rocking gently as her fingers opened the white lips of the other woman and probed more deeply, more languorously to explore the petals and undulations of Nadine's sex.

Nothing could stop her from seeking her own climax. She swivelled round so her own sex was above Nadine's face and she felt a shiver of delight course over her belly as the long, white hands gripped her buttocks before the

154

wide mouth sucked at her sex and the long tongue teased at her rearing clitoris.

Sensations of rising climax made their bodies rock in unison as their tongues dipped faster. Their teeth nipped in a sprightly fashion at each other's pink flesh, that which was usually hidden and was now so well-exposed.

Musk and sweetness spread in equal portions from the sex beneath Penny to cover her face. She plunged faster, her fingers and mouth determined not to just imitate Nadine's actions, but to surpass her.

Their bodies fell together, their hips jerking in pulsating time as the high-crested waves of a shattering climax flowed over their entwined flesh. Buttocks plunged and breasts swayed until the last eddies of delight had shivered over their sublime bodies and faded away down their lean thighs.

'You have hidden depths, pussy-cat,' said Nadine thoughtfully, as they lay together afterwards. 'I do not believe you even knew you had such depths yourself.'

Beneath the long fingers that stroked so soothingly through her mane of dark hair – and those that traced imaginary lines over her taut rear – Penny herself pondered the same things. There was no doubt that she'd always been sexual, but these new practices to which she had only lately been introduced had never been part of that sexuality. Something had triggered them off, and now, once they'd escaped, there seemed no heights to which they did not aspire. Perhaps it was the wager, she told herself, the excitement of trying to seduce a man who so far had proved elusive. She didn't know the answer, but achieving the seduction of Alistair and the winning of her wager with Ariadne might very well be it.

The hand that had stroked her hair now stroked her face. The stark grey eyes met hers, though Nadine's look was glassy and distant. 'I shall divulge a lot before your stay here is out . . . tell you things, show you things,' she said throatily. 'So will Alistair. I hope you learn well, my dear. I hope you learn very well.'

155

Penny studied the sharply defined cheek-bones and the deep set of the chilly eyes before she responded.

'I'm sure I will.'

The gaze held hers. The smile was close-lipped and thoughtful, yet at the same time full of dark knowledge.

'Any and everything, pretty pussy, any and everything.' The voice was low, and slow as poured treacle. Her kiss was warm and moist; again, Penny melted beneath the soothing hands of Alistair's sister.

Behind the mirror, Alistair watched. Gregory stood behind him, his eyes also caught by the scene.

'You just wait, you hot little bitch,' said Alistair grimly and low. 'You just wait.'

He said it almost as though he had forgotten that Gregory was there. It certainly looked that way to Gregory. Alistair's eyes were boring into the glass as though just by the heat of their desire he could make holes through it, smash it and leap through, drag Nadine off the bed and plunge his aching tool into Penny's welcoming sex.

Gregory asked himself why Alistair didn't take Penny when and where he wanted. Even though he had known her for only a short time, he certainly couldn't envisage her saying no to anything Alistair might suggest.

But he wouldn't ask Alistair why he didn't. It wasn't his place to. All he knew, as he looked at Alistair tonight, was that his jaw was clenched almost to breaking-point and his fists were balled so tight that his knuckles showed white. He couldn't believe that Alistair wasn't aroused. He certainly was. His member was rocking against the front of his faded and over tight, blue jeans, and beneath the blackness of his T-shirt, his heart flooded his body with rivers of passionate blood.

When Alistair did tear his eyes away from the mirror, Gregory could see droplets of sweat running down his forehead.

'Where's Auberon?' Alistair asked somewhat curtly.

'Saying good-night to his animals. He always does.'

Alistair nodded grimly before stalking off.

Gregory only glanced at him before looking back to the scene on the other side of the mirror.

He didn't care that Alistair was going to take his unrequited passion out an Auberon. He didn't care, because he knew Auberon enjoyed the sting of the whip and the abuse that Alistair would mete out to his naked body – indeed, he knew full well he would welcome it.

Gregory waited until Nadine rose from the bed, kissed the apparently sleeping Penny on the shoulder, then departed from the darkened room. He waited another ten minutes after the door had closed behind Alistair's sister before he saw Penny stir and smile sleepily towards the mirror. Even though she could not see him, he smiled back, went out the same door as Alistair had left by, and made his way down the steps that came out behind a thick green tapestry on the landing. Then he pushed down the handle of the door that opened into her room.

'Gregory,' she said in a soft and yielding voice, 'I've been longing for this.'

'So I noticed,' he replied in a hushed and expectant voice.

She laughed lightly, and in the dimness of the room now lit only by a few stray beams of moonlight, she watched as he removed his clothes, her legs gradually opening as the full beauty of his torso was revealed.

In the moonlight, he looked even more like a Greek god: the Apollo of legend, or Hector of Troy. His skin glistened and his muscles rippled. Proudly erect and rearing in expectation, his manhood stood but a hand-span from her face as Gregory paused and stood silently at the side of the bed.

Enthralled by its splendour, she lifted her head from her pillow, leaned on one elbow and reached out to encircle the offering he had brought her.

'It's beautiful,' she murmured. 'Good enough to eat.'

'Then eat it.'

He tangled his fingers in her hair and brought her head closer until her lips kissed his throbbing crown. It reared in ecstasy, and, as though to calm its excitement, she flicked at it enticingly with the tip of her tongue whilst her fingers held him firmly, his flesh warm and soft as crushed velvet in the palm of her hand. Of course, her actions did nothing to calm his excitement. Like a live animal, it throbbed in her hand and leapt towards her tongue.

She opened her mouth, and sucked him in until she was halfway down his mighty stem. Her hands caressed the peachy softness of his balls that hung like ripe and glorious fruit between his thighs.

'Let go,' he breathed suddenly, and to her surprise, took her hands from his member. 'Sssh!' he added. 'Just do as I say.'

She let her hands fall and lay back on the pillow.

Thick red ropes held back the green and red tapestry curtains that hung from her bed. Gregory took these; as Penny writhed with rising excitement, he wound them around her wrists then tied them to the thick barley sugar twists of the wooden uprights.

He did the same to her ankles. Now the soft moonlight lit her body. She was spread-eagled against the thick bed cover.

'Now,' he said against her ear, kissing her neck and nibbling her lobes as he did so. 'Now, don't be afraid. I am going to do everything that you need. You need only lie there and feel what I am going to do to you. It will be sheer pleasure. Is that understood?'

In the light of the moon, he saw her nod. 'Yes,' she whispered.

By the light of that same moon, she saw him smile.

'Good,' he whispered back.

From her bedside drawer he took a pair of stockings. They were black ones and, if she remembered rightly, they were trimmed at the top with black lace and red bows. But she wouldn't be wearing these, she thought to herself, not now, tied up as she was.

Raising her head from the pillow with one hand, Gregory wound one stocking around her eyes. Now she could not even see the moonlight. He tied it behind her head in a smooth and comfortable knot.

The other stocking he used around her mouth as a gag.

158

What he did to her ears, she didn't know. Perhaps they were a pair of skiing earmuffs. All she knew was that she could neither speak, nor see, nor hear. Only one sense was left to her – that of touch.

She lay in her dark and silent world, knowing that Gregory was gazing at her helpless body. In her darkness, she tried to imagine what he was seeing and feeling.

Gregory was gazing at her. He was transfixed by the helpless beauty of her offered body. Vulnerability and the softness of moonlight had made her more beautiful than he could ever have imagined. She was naked, her flesh touched with the silver of the moonlight and her sex open to anything he cared to put into it. And that, he knew, was where he scored over Nadine. He had the ultimate weapon to put into her. Nadine did not have that. Alistair did, but seemed disinclined to act.

He put Nadine and Alistair from his mind. Now, he had Penny to himself.

He ran his hands down from her shoulders and rolled her breasts in the firmness of his palms. Her back arched and her body sought to reach him.

'Patience, my beauty,' he whispered, his breath directed on her cheek. She felt that breath, but could not hear the words upon it.

His fingers rolled her nipples before he kissed them and enjoyed the small squeal of delight that broke from beyond the nylon gag.

He lay the hardness of his chest against her absolute softness. Then he raised himself up on his hands and bent his head to nibble ruthlessly at her nipples.

Beneath him, her pelvis writhed. He understood what she was after, knew the hardness of his penis was heavy against her and that her vulva was wet with desire.

'Not yet,' he murmured, even though she could not hear him.

Penny did, indeed, want his penis in her. His whole body was hot and hard against her, yet his penis was hotter. She wanted it badly, and in the dark world where only touch was left to her, the need for penetration was more greatly intensified.

159

His lips were hot as they travelled down over her body and made her back arch more severely than before. She felt them linger over her belly, and felt the wetness of his tongue dive into her navel before his journey continued. Everything was feeling; it was all touch. Her very link with the world outside her darkness was touch, and because of that, her senses were sharper and her responses more intense.

Fronds of pubic hair were sucked into his mouth along with her flesh, and she rolled her hips with pleasure as his fingers opened her outer lips then furled back the delicate flesh beneath.

Behind the closeness of her bonds, she whimpered. If she had not been gagged, she would have screamed for more.

Wetness erupted in her sex as his tongue flicked lightly over her clitoris. Her legs felt weak, and no matter what side she turned to, she could not escape his tongue, his lips or his hands. But then, she didn't want to.

Her body tingled, her sex was tantalised. Nothing remained in her mind except the sensations of this experience. In her dark, silent world, sex had taken over her mind, her being – her whole body. Nothing else existed: not the room, not the moonlight; not even Gregory. Sex had stolen her soul.

When at last it felt as though her sanity was under threat, she felt his penis enter her. But, like everything else, it filled her being as well as her sex.

Each sweet thrust made her nerves tingle and her body tremble. Slowly he thrust, then faster, then slower again. It was almost as if he were playing a tune on her body, composing a great masterpiece that could not help but be remembered.

Just the size of his penis was enough to blow her mind. She had wondered at it even before he had blindfolded her. His penis, she thought, was the one thing that bore no resemblance whatsoever to a Greek or Roman god. Like the copper statue that peed perpetually into the fountain in the courtyard, it was big and owed nothing at all to classical statuary, except perhaps its shape.

But thoughts about size, shape and what it looked like were being steadily overtaken by her imminent climax. She lifted her pelvis to meet him, the mound that enclosed her bud of passion slamming with easy precision against him.

She felt his hands cover her breasts and his fingers fondle her rising nubs and she rolled in delight. His stomach slammed hard and quick against her, and his phallus, engorged with the blood of his own passion, filled her sex like no other had filled it before.

Higher and higher her passion soared in her dark, silent world. She threw her head back, the only part of her body that could still truly move. Her teeth bit into her gag, and her pelvis heaved like a volcanic eruption to meet his.

It felt as if she could swallow him up whole inside, as though she were a very deep well around which his and her orgasm could echo till time immemorial, never-ending, always teetering on the edge of total climax.

Strongly and virulently like an explosion of dynamite, she came.

Her hips thrust again and again to meet him. She struggled against her bond, her cries of release captured in the silky smoothness of her gag.

She felt Gregory tense above her. Deep inside, she felt the throb of his release in her sex and vibrating against her flesh in gradually diminishing sensations until his orgasm was finished.

Not until he had repeated his attention twice more, and dawn had pushed morning through the window, did he untie her.

They embraced before he left, the heat of his muscles re-igniting her passion for one last, more mutual liaison before he left her.

He had been loath to stay that bit longer, a slight nervousness entering his eyes when she had first suggested it. But once her lips were on his and her hand had captured his rising stem, his will was no longer his own.

Dawn had barely broken, but Nadine, as always, was up early. Behind the mirror, she watched, grim-faced, her body still damp and naked from her early-morning shower.

'My, my,' she growled, her lips hardly parting, her teeth barely moving. She let her towel slip to the ground, and rotated one breast with her hand whilst the other folded back her shorn labia and teased her ripe bud to erection. 'But you are a disobedient little pussy, aren't you. But never mind, Nadine will do something about that. Nadine will break you in to her will.'

With that, she threw her head back and plunged her finger into her own warm depository.

Chapter Nine

Nadine was a great believer in sea water. Not that she was alone in that belief. Many in the past and present have praised its healing capacity and sworn by its ability to strengthen equine tendons as they prance and gallop through the waves.

The beach was two hours' drive away, and being that there wasn't a cloud in the sky and a warm day was forecast, lunch had been packed in generous hampers. Wine, milk, cream and butter had been safely stored in a couple of cool-boxes.

Nadine seemed inordinately full of herself prior to their departure and would probably have continued in that mood for the rest of the day if Alistair had not informed her that she was to pick Sir Reggie's daughter, Clarissa, up from the airport.

Then her brightness turned to thunder.

Taking discretion as the best part of valour, and throwing herself into grooming, polishing and helping the stable-lads, Penny noted the furrowed eyebrows and black looks and made an extra effort to keep out of her way. Auberon, perhaps by choice, did not.

It was only when Penny slipped into the dark humidity of the hay barn and heard the swish of a riding crop and the loud thwack of its contact with bare flesh, that she realised Nadine was taking out her bad mood on Auberon's bare buttocks.

She timed her footsteps to coincide with each stroke so the crunching of gravel or rustling of straw could not be heard as she crept towards the sound.

Auberon was on all fours, trousers around his ankles, and Nadine was applying red stripes to his behind with all the strength at her disposal.

Nadine's usually pale face was fire red, and her steel-grey eyes blazed with light.

Penny held still and watched a while, her own breath quickening and her hips rotating as she imagined the delicious tremors of delight that Auberon was enjoying. But Nadine knew that, too.

With a look of cruel delight in her eyes, Nadine stayed her hand.

'Roll over,' she ordered.

Auberon obeyed.

Penny covered her mouth with her hand. Her eyes opened wide as she beheld Auberon's mighty member, proudly erect, a pearl drop of semen balancing on its quivering tip.

'My, my,' she heard Nadine say. 'I see you're almost there, my dear boy.'

'Y . . . es, y . . . es,' stammered Auberon as Nadine trailed the tip of the riding crop around his upright phallus and over his ginger-haired balls.

'If I just tapped that one little opening of yours,' drawled Nadine, her voice laced with menace, 'that eyelet of passion, you'd come, wouldn't you, pretty boy?'

'Y . . . es,' stammered Auberon again. 'Y . . . es, y . . . es, I would.'

The cruelty of Nadine's sudden smile matched the look in her eyes.

'But I won't!' she growled. With that, she withdrew the crop and carried it upright across her shoulder as though it were a rifle.

The look of disappointment on Auberon's face was matched only by the sudden wilting of his erection.

Lightly touching her own twitching sex, Penny

watched in astonished disbelief as what had been hard became soft and curled in upon itself. She saw the tears in Auberon's eyes. How cruel Nadine could be when she didn't get her own way, Penny thought to herself, and how much she must have wanted to go to the beach.

From common sense and her own knowledge of Nadine, Penny suspected something special had been planned for the occasion. What that something was, she hadn't a clue, but if Nadine's treatment of Auberon was anything to go by, it must be pretty unusual and particularly special.

As she left Auberon and Nadine, she made a big effort to banish the thought that whatever plan had been scuppered today would be back another day . . . and with greater intensity.

But she forgot about Beaumont Place and Nadine once they were up in the horsebox and away.

A carefree atmosphere travelled with them to the coast. The windows were open and a warm breeze kissed her face and softly caressed her neck. Her eyes were bright, as blue as the sky, and she smelt of fresh spring flowers.

She felt cool today, shorts, T-shirt and trainers replacing the usual riding gear. Today, her long hair was plaited into a thick rope that reached just beyond her shoulder-blades.

Around her, disturbed only by the breeze, was the smell of horses and leather, and the faint, but irresistible scent of well-muscled young men.

Stephen drove, Penny sat next to him, and Auberon and a beefy stable-lad with dark hair and a cleft chin named David sat next to him.

Before they had left, Penny had watched with some curiosity as Nadine had gathered the boys to her. They'd huddled in a group for a few minutes, with Nadine's long arms around their necks, drawing them to her like a clutch of this year's ducklings.

Although her curiosity had been aroused, Penny didn't let her being left out of the head-to-head worry her. It was too nice a day for that. Whatever Nadine had instructed, obviously it didn't apply to her, so she didn't even bother to ask the boys what had been said.

Today she felt elated, and once the briny freshness of the sea breeze blew through the cab of the horsebox, all thoughts of Nadine and Beaumont Place were left behind – or they would have been, if Alistair hadn't been following them.

Alistair never travelled in the horsebox. He always followed on behind in his chauffeur-driven car, a gleaming Rolls-Royce that had a sister Bentley in the garage, plus the black Porsche that Nadine drove.

The spot on the coast they headed for was private, and belonged, like a lot of other things, to Alistair Beaumont.

Steep cliffs topped with private woods of thick gorse and virgin birch surrounded the beach. A private road ran through the trees and a high gate was locked firmly behind them.

The beach formed an almost perfect crescent of yellow sand. With the sound of tumbling waves came the sound of the horses in the box behind them, nickering with excitement once they'd detected the change of air and the fact that the box had rolled to a halt.

'It's getting hotter,' said Penny, tilting her head to look up at the blue sky overhead and the fringe of steep cliffs around them, where seagulls circled and shrieked to the bright day.

'That's why we're parked here,' said Stephen with a wink, his lithe muscles swimming invitingly beneath the whiteness of his boat-necked T-shirt. 'Shady for the horses. Never mind us mere mortals.'

Penny laughed with him and tossed her plaited tail.

'But you're going to be hot,' said Alistair, his eyes raking over her peach-coloured T-shirt and matching shorts. 'You should take it all off.'

'Yes,' said Penny in an uncharacteristically clipped manner. Alistair had taken her by surprise. There was something about him today that was different. There was no furtiveness about his wandering eyes and broad smile, no perceived barrier between her and him. What was it,

166

she asked herself, that was so different? She answered her own question: Nadine was not here.

She couldn't let this chance go. She must not; she had to take advantage of it. She pulled her T-shirt over her head. Her breasts bounced free, pink nipples responding proudly to the breezy air. Her sweat was sweet and tinged with a lightly floral spray.

As if the breeze had caught it and flung it their way, the two stable-lads stopped what they were doing; eyes glazing over and pricks pounding against their zips, they molested her breasts with their minds.

'Not a bad idea, eh, sir?' said Stephen suddenly, his eyes looking squarely at Alistair, though sidelong glances played like the breeze over Penny's firm mounds.

Alistair stared for a moment before he answered. 'No,' he said at last in a long rush of breath. 'Not a bad idea at all.'

Penny, like the stable-lads and Auberon, took everything off. Now the breeze kissed and parted her pubic hair and cooled the warmth of her rounded behind, which had sat too long on the journey to get here.

To her disappointment, Alistair did not take off his clothes, but today Alistair's eyes were fixed on her. He made no bones about it, and the barest hint of a smile played around his lips as his gaze travelled from her bouncing breasts to the glossy patch of hair that nestled between her thighs.

'What about you?' she asked him as the lads bridled up the horses.

'No!' He stepped back from her reaching hands as though they might burn him if he allowed them to touch him.

She tried to read his eyes, then dropped her gaze to his pubic area. Disappointment made her frown. How could he be so different from the others? How could he not be excited by the aspect of her bare body and thrusting breasts? It didn't seem real.

She returned her gaze to his eyes. They met hers. They were bright, and his breathing seemed tight in his chest.

He wanted her. She knew he did, and yet his phallus gave no sign of it.

Confused and feeling slightly temperamental, she turned away from him and returned the smiles Stephen and David so willingly gave her. Even Auberon was forthright in his gaze as if his inhibitions had been thrown off with his clothes.

'Do you want a leg-up?' asked David, the burly lad with the dark hair and unusual chin. The first juices of arousal wetted his palm as he placed one hand beneath her seat to get her up on the bare back of the horse.

No saddles today. They galloped the beach bareback. Alistair was left far behind them.

The horses legs splashed in the white froth of the rolling waves, their mouths straining against the confines of the bit.

Penny laughed. Stephen, David, and even Auberon, who had appeared a little distracted on the way here, laughed as the spray blew into their faces and white-winged, black-headed gulls cackled overhead.

The canter was fast, but the rhythm of its tempo was as steady as ever, the rolling slide and the horse's back warm, smooth and arousing against her naked labia.

Out of the corner of her eye, Penny could see Stephen, then David, then Auberon, their sexual members flipping from side to side across the horses' withers. Even so, she knew they were stiffening as they rode; she knew the rhythm of the ride was having the same effect on them as it was having on her.

Droplets of sea water flew into her face, clung to her hair and splattered her breasts with a brisk coolness. Her nipples burst into expectant peaks, and her exposed clitoris bumped and slid along her horse's back.

All the while she laughed as she raced Auberon on one of his mounts, Stephen on another, and David on her own chestnut. She rode her grey.

At a fast gallop, they reached the end of the beach to where unassailable rocks broke jaggedly skywards and divided their own private seascape from the more public areas beyond.

'We'd better turn round,' shouted Stephen breathlessly, his horse rearing as he reined it in.

Now Penny fastened her eyes on his unfettered penis which seemed to rear its head in time with the horse.

Just as he had suggested, they did turn round. This time, Penny did not lead the chase, but reined in at a slower pace behind. Responding to her own thoughts and fancies, she had an urge to study their gait, those taut buttocks and firm thighs bouncing up and down on the horses backs as they made their way back to the horsebox and Alistair.

It was a pleasant sight to ride behind those broad shoulders and bouncing bottoms, David's being more hairy than the other two. As they bounced upwards, she could detect the faint outline of their balls hanging like ripe money bags beneath their taut behinds. As she watched, she was aware of her own arousal, and of the heat of her sex and the liquid moistness of her folds of pink flesh.

Portable tanks of fresh water had been made ready back at the horsebox by the time she got there, and David was hanging up the last of the hay nets for the horses to pull on.

As she came to a halt, she slid down from the back of her mount and David took the reins from her.

Penny looked around for Alistair. She couldn't see him. As if in desperation, she shielded her eyes with one hand, looked up at the cliffs, then looked out to sea towards the sparkling patch where the sun danced like diamonds on the heaving surface of the sea.

'Ahoy there! Up here!'

In the shadow of a cave where the sea had eaten the cliff like a caterpillar does a cabbage leaf, Alistair stood waving his arms. Beside him, a huge flat rock had been set with crisp linen, and the sunlight that tickled at the cave mouth made the silver cutlery and lead-crystal wine glasses sparkle so much that they shielded their eyes with their hands.

'Lunch is served!' Penny heard Alistair shout. The big beefy form of his chauffeur sauntered off in the direction of the cliff road, then he and the Rolls-Royce disappeared above the prow of the cliffs. Privacy was all theirs.

'Can't wait,' said David, with one last and covetous look at Penny's crotch as though it were the delicacy of the moment. 'I'm starving.'

'Can't wait for afters,' added Stephen, glancing mischievously at David and Auberon before looking at her. A burst of sexual apprehension made her rub the inside of one thigh against her throbbing sex. Afters, she decided, was something she, too, could look forward to.

Lemon-roasted chicken, crisp salad, fresh bread rolls and yellow butter had been spread out on a low, flat rock in the middle of the cave. In a trickle of water running in mossy green bands over the rocks, stood three bottles of wine. White towels had been folded and left on top of the wicker-weave hampers in which the food and the wine had arrived, courtesy of Alistair's chauffeur.

Their bare feet having sunk into the soft warm sand, they now washed them off downstream from the lazing wine bottles, whose corks had already been removed.

'The feast is prepared,' said Alistair spreading his arms and grinning broadly. The tawny darkness of his hair was caught by the breeze and hurled across his forehead, and Penny perceived the faint aroma of fresh male sweat. A knot of delicious apprehension began to unwind in her empty stomach. It was a pleasant feeling, as though it were a ball of thick angora wool slowly being teased from its tightly bound security.

In that sudden moment when his hand brushed his hair to one side and she breathed his maleness, Alistair's eyes held hers. He smiled, and again he looked her up and down. There was a subtle ease to the way he did it, as though he had all the time in the world to focus on her breasts and nipples which the cold spray had teased to ripe prominence. Droplets of water still ran over her tingling flesh, and her breath rose quickly and excitably in her breast.

Alistair's eyes almost slid over her belly and hips before settling like a homing pigeon on the burst of pubic hair that erupted from her ripe sex. This had swollen and

170

moistened as a result of her gallop along the surf-tossed shore-line.

Visibly, she responded to his look. Her breath quickened, her flesh trembled and she ran her tongue over salt-dried lips. She couldn't believe the difference in the man now his sister wasn't around. They smiled foolishly at each other, almost as if they were love-struck teenagers allowed away from home for the first time.

But Nadine had too much power. Even here, her long arm was reaching to touch both her brother and the woman she was saving him for. Yet another tableau was about to commence, and once the food was eaten and the wine well on its way to being drunk, neither Penny nor Alistair were inclined to do anything much about it. They could only be sucked into it; become part of it, like players on a stage.

'This is like an altar,' said Stephen, once the food was eaten, the dishes packed away and the crisp white cloth folded beneath the lid of the hamper.

'Fit for a sacrifice,' exclaimed David. His eyes shone brightly, almost wickedly, as they met Stephen's and Auberon's. With obvious intent, he ran his hand over the flatness of the rock.

'Fit for a virgin sacrifice,' added Auberon, his eyes glancing swiftly towards Penny before meeting those of his colleagues.

Tentatively, Penny touched the rock. They could not know what she was feeling, that she was certain Nadine was here – in spirit if not in body. She stayed silent and prepared. Tentacles of abandonment reached up from somewhere deep and strangled any inhibitions she might still have.

'I don't know any,' said Alistair with a laugh, as he drained the last of the wine, glass in one hand, bottle in the other. Thankfully, his chauffeur, Broderick, was sat snoozing back at the wheel of his car having drunk nothing more powerful than a flask of instant coffee, so he was at liberty to indulge.

'Then we'll have to use the next best thing,' murmured David, his dark eyes fixed on Penny's bright-blue ones.

171

'An experienced woman will do.' With a sweet softness that sent shivers down her spine and caused the ball of wool in her stomach to unwind most pleasantly, he ran his fingers from Penny's shoulder to her elbow.

Her response was sparkling. Her eyes were bright and enthusiasm coloured her cheeks, making her body undulate with a rare subtlety that even she didn't know she had. The wine got the blame at first until she actually admitted to herself that in reality it was *her* who was sparkling and full of hidden depths and after-taste.

Briefly, she glanced over at Alistair, who, by virtue of his more relaxed demeanour today, was visibly more attractive, and the sight of him was extremely arousing. Abstinence was not his creed. She could see that in his eyes. And yet, where there should have been a hard lump growing and throbbing against his flies, there was nothing discernible at all. The knowledge confused and disappointed her.

She did not protest as David and Stephen helped her up on to the flat stone. Her naked flesh tingled as much from growing desire as from the coolness of the rock. It was surprisingly smooth against her back. With a sigh, she closed her eyes. Food and drink had already been digested. Now, she told herself, she was due other things.

There was silence for a moment before she realised her hands had been clasped and pulled above her head. Hands also fastened around her ankles and prised them gently apart. It was a curiously comfortable imprisonment, especially as the third pair of hands, those belonging to Auberon, massaged her proud breasts and teased her nipples to even pinker prominence.

She moaned as she opened her eyes, and told herself that today was turning out even better than she'd expected, and so what about the wager? So what about Nadine and her whispered instructions back there in the stable yard? Everything that was happening to her she was allowing to happen. Lie back, she told herself almost hypnotically, and enjoy.

'Now what game are you playing?' she asked as

172

shivers of apprehension and a fine film of sweat spread over her skin.

'One you'll enjoy,' replied Stephen whose green eyes were boyish and his white flesh still attractive even though he'd caught the redness of the sun across his broad shoulders. After his lips had kissed her forehead, his thumb and fingers gently stroked her wrist as if trying to put her at her ease. Not that she really needed that. Just remembering the sight of the male riders' naked behinds and swaying penises when they had galloped back down the beach was enough to drench her sex with spicy hot fluids. He kissed her forehead again before leaning over so his tongue could trace the contours of her ear.

'Will you play with us?' he asked, his mouth above her eyes, his eyes above her mouth.

Her breasts rose and her eyes opened wide as they met his. Of course she would play with him. Stephen had a well-formed body made even harder by the strenuous work he undertook in and around the stable yard. His hardness would feel good on her softness. And yet she wanted to tease him. 'What if I say no?' she asked capriciously, turning her head away from his exploring mouth.

'Then you'll have to pay a forfeit.' His grin was cheeky, as though he already knew what her answer would be and, what's more, welcomed it.

'First things first,' David interrupted, dark eyes dancing, dark hair falling in thick waves around his neck. 'We have to take her virginity first.'

'True,' returned Stephen. 'Mr Harding. Take her hands whilst I take her virginity.'

Penny giggled and wriggled her hips suggestively. 'What virginity?'

'What cock?' responded Stephen, who, to her surprise, waved an empty wine bottle in her face. She eyed its long tapering neck and ran her wet tongue along her dry lips. How dark it was, how cool it would feel. Her hips rose speculatively.

Obviously pleased with her reaction, Stephen's eyes

glittered before he lowered his eyes and trailed the coldness of the bottle's long neck down one side of her face then the other.

'Is this cool enough for you?' he asked, between hot breaths.

'Yes,' she sighed, her voice slow and just a little slurred; more so from excitement than the amount of wine she had consumed. As her imagination worked overtime and assessed just how the bottle neck would feel, she stared at it with mounting desire and just a tinge of apprehension. The bottle's neck was a good width as well as a good length.

Her ankles, which were gripped in David's strong hands, were spread further apart, but the cool air that blew in from the sea did nothing to subdue the heat of her sex. Like a flood of early morning dew, the honey of her arousal moistened her sex and trickled like ticklish fIngertips between her buttocks.

'Grip her tightly,' Stephen ordered Auberon.

She wanted to ask what for. She wasn't going anywhere, and anyway, Alistair was watching. Alistair was always watching.

Out of the corner of her eye, she could see him. He did nothing, either to stop this happening or to join in. All the same, she could see he was hypnotised by the unfolding scene, his eyes glazed and his square chin hanging like a half-open door. Occasionally, his tongue ran along the length of his drying lips.

But Alistair could watch if he wanted to. She was the centre of this thing, the sacrifice lying on the altar. Just the thought and the feel of it was giddily pleasant.

She moaned and arched her back, thrusting her breasts skywards as if meeting the body of an unseen lover.

With gently experienced fingers, Stephen opened her nether lips and started to insert the neck of the bottle between the petals of her yearning flesh. She gasped, her breath caught in her throat, and she felt as if she were just a mass of senses aching to enjoy and be enjoyed. Just as she had supposed, the neck was cool – very cool – and her sex was very hot.

174

'Is it in?' she heard David ask.

'The first inch,' replied Stephen, threads of excitement adding extra timbre to his voice. 'I'm just going to give her a little bit at a time.'

Penny moaned dolefully and her hips rocked in expectation. Already, that one initial inch was not enough.

'Give me more,' she begged, and lifted her pelvis away from the cold surface of the rock.

'You'll get more soon,' whispered Auberon, bending his head so his mouth was against her ear. 'Be patient.' As if to reassure her, he leaned further forward and kissed each of her breasts, his teeth gripping them gently at first before stretching them to their full extent, almost as if he were trying to swallow them. The wetness of her sex increased as her breasts strained upwards between his teeth. They seemed as unwilling to leave his mouth as *he* was to let go of her nipples.

'And now for a little more,' she heard Stephen say.

His fingers still held her outer lips and her labia apart. Another portion of the neck entered her. An inch, perhaps two.

'And more,' he repeated.

She gasped as another portion pushed its hard and cold way inside her. The muscles of her vagina gripped the intruder as if they would not release it until climax had been reached and pleasure was all hers. All the time, Auberon sucked and licked her nipples, an alternate strategy of pleasure followed by pain.

'Lovely,' she heard David say. 'Let me have a look.'

As Auberon raised his head to see what his compatriots were doing, Penny could see Stephen straighten and David lean forward between her legs to study the penetrating bottle and her penetrated sex more closely.

'Give her more,' said David breathlessly. 'Go on. Don't be mean, leaving her in limbo like that.'

Words totally failed Penny. She was lost in her own ecstasy. Whatever they did was entirely up to them. She was at their mercy, half-full, and there was so much bottle neck still to go.

175

She saw Stephen smile at David as though there was some secret between them.

'All right,' said Stephen, still smiling.

'Keep upright,' added David, his eyes now fixed on her open outer and inner lips, 'so I can see it going in.'

Penny closed her eyes and moaned louder as she felt Stephen's fingers holding her lips open and the smooth neck of the bottle being pushed in up to its neck so its shoulders pressed deliciously on her demanding clitoris and tingling nerve ends.

'Marvellous,' she heard from David, who, from his position holding her ankles, was leaning forward so he could see the invasion more clearly as it happened. 'Let me have a go now.'

Reluctantly, Stephen changed places with David. There was a slurping of juices as David thrust the neck more strongly against her hypersensitive sex glands.

She cried out, certain that her orgasm was no more than a few thrusts away and rapidly raising her hips to meet it.

David's good-natured face smiled down at her, his dark hair clinging damply around his glistening skin. 'See how kind I am to you. I won't leave you in limbo, Penny. Would you like me to really make it feel good?'

She nodded automatically.

'I thought you might.' David grinned.

Almost in defiance at her restricted limbs, she writhed on the flat stone. The feelings that were tingling her body were snaring her voice. It was trapped in her throat, and she could do nothing – nothing at all – to let it free.

Gripping the bottle with one hand, his other keeping her sex wide open, David nudged it in regular time against the dewy moistness of her flesh.

'You're soaking wet,' he said, and sounded full of wonder.

She didn't answer. She was lost in a labyrinth of her own senses, her eyes closed and her will put on hold whilst the hands held her and the bottle's neck did its work.

'That should be about enough,' said Auberon suddenly.

His voice surprised her. Even though it was him holding on to her wrists, she had almost forgotten he was there. So had Stephen and David. Above her, they both looked across her and at him, then at each other.

For the moment, they seemed to have forgotten Alistair altogether. Penny hadn't. She was intent on knowing exactly what his reactions were. Twisting herself against the restraining hands and the hard and cold intruder, Penny peered through the crook in David's arm.

Alistair was sitting on a rock, his eyes glazed, wine-glass in one hand and half-empty bottle in the other. Even from where she was, she could hear the quickness of his breathing. He was with them, but only in mind. Only his imagination was enjoying what she and the boys were experiencing. His body was still held in check: with them, wanting to be with them, yet seemingly unable to be.

The bottle was removed and Penny was helped to her feet. She began to protest. Stephen smacked her bottom in rebuke.

'Now, now. Naughty, naughty!'

'Now you have to play with us.' This was Auberon saying this, with an odd brightness in his eyes which she had never seen before. Up until now, Stephen and David had dominated the action. Now, with eyes gleaming, Auberon seemed to be taking over.

'Kneel down,' Stephen ordered. 'Mr Harding's right. It's your turn to play with us.' He grinned again, that cheeky, boyish grin that made her think whatever he had in store for her might be a lot better or a lot worse than it looked – mostly the latter.

'On this,' Auberon added, and with a consideration that she much appreciated, he placed the folded table cloth on the rough sand. Obviously, she decided, she would be kneeling for some time.

And so she knelt, supremely aware that her climax had been just a few thrusts away and that her nether lips

177

were hot, wet with juice, and just begging for the finishing line.

The three naked young men gathered around her, their bodies glistening with fresh sweat, their young muscles taut and well-formed beneath their unblemished skin.

Three erect penises were but inches from her face. They were all fine specimens, one sprouting from a nest of ginger hair, one from a fair and sparse covering, and David's standing strongly erect like a young oak from a bush of thick black hair. Between each set of thighs hung their precious sacs. How soft they looked, she thought, her eyes assessing each set and imagining which pair would feel like peaches, which like velvet and which like cream.

That for later, she told herself. For now, her eyes travelled irresistibly back to the three proud members, each one jerking with rising passion and determination. Each glans glistened, and on one a dewy pearl drop of semen sat like a precious diadem. In response, her tongue slid out from between her lips; her need to taste such beautiful weapons was urgent as her need to see them.

'Take one in your mouth,' ordered Stephen, his hand gently caressing her head as though she were a child or a pet dog. 'And one in each hand,' he added, a certain hoarseness now apparent in his voice.

Even without the benefit of a mirror, Penny knew that her eyes must be shining and her face be slightly flushed. Her eyes opened wide as she studied each one. It was as though three birthdays had all come at once. Three beautiful cocks were throbbing with anticipation, just waiting for her lips to fold around one of them and her hands to work on the others.

But this was a choice she couldn't face. She closed her eyes. 'It's hard to choose,' she said breathlessly. 'I don't want to upset anyone.'

'Soon fix that!' said Stephen. The linen towel that had earlier graced a wine bottle was bound over her eyes. It was cool, slightly damp and not unpleasant.

'This is like blind man's buff,' laughed David. 'We go

178

round you, and when you reach out and point, that's the one for your mouth. OK?'

'OK,' she replied, glad that the decision had been taken from her.

Blindfolded, it was impossible to judge who was the first she pointed at. Whose member it was, she didn't know and didn't care. His helmet sat like a rich and tasty soufflé on her tongue. She sucked at him, drew him in, then traced all round the well-defined ridge that parted crown from stem. She had a yearning to take in more; to grab his balls with one hand and his stem with another so he could not escape.

But her hands had other tasks. Other hands guided them around firm rods which she immediately proceeded to pleasure, pummel and squeeze within her warm palm and exploring fingers. Each tip was wet, each length was hard and promising.

So here she was, knelt before them, and like the goddess Kali who she'd seen on Indian icons, her mouth and hands were full, though not with a bloody tongue and a couple of snakes. Hers were full of much more pleasurable demons.

Even so, she was slightly disappointed. The first penis came fast and was closely followed by the next throbbing manhood to be placed upon her tongue.

'Enough!' she called, breathless now after two insertions and her own sex still aching with the desire aroused by the unyielding neck of the wine bottle.

'Enough?' she heard Stephen exclaim. 'Then that means a forfeit's in order. Now, work your hand on this a while.'

The blindfold was taken off her. Now she could see that the penis she held in her hand was David's. He tousled her hair as she rolled his stiffening member between her hands and kissed its dewy head. Was this the one that had been omitted? She wasn't sure, especially seeing as Auberon's member was still fully erect.

In a brief moment of panic, she wondered if Alistair was still watching. He was. She could see him there, still

179

sat on the rock, glass and bottle now completely empty. He looked mesmerised but he also looked slightly angry, as though something had been stolen or denied him. But her attention was diverted.

'I'm ready,' said David suddenly, and he lay himself out on the floor. She stared at his well-muscled body, brown and covered with dark hair on his chest, over his limbs, and thick as a forest around his upright member. His cock stood straight and proud from amid the cushion of dark, springy hair. Looking at it, the ache between her thighs increased in its intensity and her hanging labia and pert clitoris felt swollen and almost painfully heavy.

David was irresistible. She had to have him. There could, of course, also be a bonus gained from this. With hope in her heart, she wondered if this little tableau would be enough to get Alistair going, to induce him to want her.

Without being told, she straddled David's willing phallus, and held her pleasant portal just an inch from his pulsating helmet. Then, slowly and surely, she lowered herself on to its rigid length.

Pleasurable sounds poured from her throat as she drew him in. She couldn't help but close her eyes, and even when Stephen told her to bend forward she didn't open them.

Breasts jiggling, she leaned forward, palms flat on the ground. David's swollen member tightly filled her sex as she rode his rigid length. It felt as though her body was clamped to his; like two pieces of a stiff jigsaw puzzle, they were incapable of breaking apart.

'Take this.' Stephen's demand broke into her pleasant thoughts. Quickly she opened her eyes. His member was just an inch from her mouth. Obligingly, she wetted her lips, opened her mouth and took him in.

Her eyes closed again once she felt his dewy-tipped and satin-smooth penis on her tongue. In the midst of intense pleasurable delight, she felt fingers prising back the round hills of her buttocks, and stroking the steep cleft in between. There was a familiar touch of something slightly greasy and pleasantly cool being applied around her tightened sphincter. Perhaps it was butter again, the same as Nadine had used on her at dinner. Now her anus and its running cleft would be as shiny as her juicy lips, and both would be filled to capacity.

But this time it was not a thumb or a finger that entered her nether hole. It was Auberon, and he was using his penis.

Her gasp as Auberon penetrated her sphincter was silenced by Stephen pressing her head against his member. His hands manoeuvred her head to suit himself. Her mouth moved at his bidding.

Burning heat radiated from her besieged anus, though shivers of delicious expectation ran in a swift current from there to her yearning sex.

At first, only the tip of his penis entered her. She likened it to someone dipping one toe in a bath of hot water. Her muscles contracted at first and clenched the wouldbe invader in a deathlike grip as he pushed further into her body. But then, as shivers of electric delight ran through her flesh, her muscles relaxed and allowed the intruder to travel further.

Once he felt no resistance from her, Auberon pushed in a little more length.

Now she was full as she'd never been full before. A length of penis throbbed on her tongue, another throbbed inside on one side of her pelvic membrane, and another had entered her most secret orifice and was edging its way further in.

Sex and sensuality were smothering her senses and numbing her mind. She felt sex, she knew sex, she *was* sex, and wanted even more.

What picture, she asked herself, was she presenting to Alistair? But she could not see Alistair. She could only hear his rapid breathing as the three penises thrust like welcome invaders into her body.

Beneath her, David shuddered and moaned ecstatically. Behind her, Auberon mewed, his fingers holding her buttocks apart whilst he manoeuvred a further portion of his penis into her tight hole. Her legs trembled, but he held her firm, pulling her hips towards him with each thrust of his pelvis.

Above her, Stephen seemed to be humming in unison to his thrusting, though not to any tune. It reminded her of the satisfied buzzing of a contented bee on a very hot day.

Stephen held her head steady, moving it up and down his rampant stem to his own requirements. With swift, deft strokes of her flicking tongue, she followed the flood of his orgasm as it rose up the thick vein that ran up the back of his penis.

Beneath her, David's hips were slamming upwards with greater intensity, accompanied by a wet slurping from her open vagina. David, too, was nearing his climax. Behind her, Auberon yelled, his cry echoed by the wheeling seagulls, white triangles in a clear blue sky.

The intensity of her own orgasm overtook and surprised her. For the first time in her life, she had been full and her body had fully indulged itself in the experience. Her thighs shook, and as David sucked and rubbed at her swinging breasts, she slammed the last echo of orgasm from her spent and satisfied sex.

Alistair awaited the right moment. He had watched, fascinated, all afternoon as Penny had consorted and submitted to what had been planned for her. He, too, had been so naïve as to think that Nadine had been left behind them. Nadine was never left behind; she was always there beside him, no matter where he was. Penny would learn that, too. Did Penny know, he wondered, that some of her sexual liaisons were orchestrated by his sister for his benefit?

She couldn't of course. How could she? But sometimes he caught a look in her eye, a questioning curiosity, that made him think she might know that her friend Ariadne had recommended her, that Nadine was playing her like a concert violinist does a favourite instrument.

Now he could wait no longer. He had to ask her face to face even though his penis would swell unbearably against the firm restraint of his rubber underwear as his eyes wandered over her body. But he had to know. So he waited, then he followed.

In late afternoon and following a dip in the sea, Penny went behind some convenient rocks to relieve herself. He smiled at that. It seemed so contradictory. After all, she had been studied most intimately by the three men who had taken her body so completely, so why choose privacy when it came to having a pee?

He watched from the shelter of a large rock as the sand dampened beneath her. She was crouching, her buttocks towards him. She'd spread her legs. It was a delightful position, he thought, as though she'd adopted it especially for him. In that position, her cheeks were spread slightly and her anus was exposed. It was pink and running with rivulets of melted butter.

He could also see the dark, pink folds of her sex which hung rather delightfully, so he thought, beyond her outer lips.

Although he had originally had every intention of letting her finish peeing before he stepped forward, he judged that surprise sometimes yielded answers closer to the truth than considered replies could do. He stepped forward.

'Miss Bennet. I want to ask you something.'

Her plait tossed girlishly and quickly to one side as she looked over her shoulder at him. She looked startled, but stayed silent. Her liquid still flowed, and the sand got damper. Now, he judged, she couldn't stop. She was in full flow, and even though she looked surprised, she appeared unwilling or unable to cease what she was doing.

She didn't say anything and couldn't run away in her present position, so he pressed on.

'I firstly want to know if you like it at Beaumont Place.'

Rounded bottoms and parted thighs went round and round in his mind.

'Yes,' Penny answered hesitantly. How was he to know that her hand was just eliciting the last tremor of a secondary orgasm from her swollen sex bud? Her hand

183

continued, though her concentration was now somewhat distracted.

'You have no complaints?' he asked, his eyes dropping from her bright-blue eyes, and down over her back to her rounded bottom.

'No,' she murmured with a knowing smile and a twinkle in her eye as her fingers played on.

'Is there anything I can do for you?' he asked, edging closer. The huskiness of his voice intensified once it had struck him exactly what her fingers were doing.

Penny smiled. Here, she thought, somewhat selfishly, was her chance.

'As a matter of fact, there is.'

He didn't need her to outline what she wanted. Even though his prick pressed hard against its confines, he could not resist. He had to touch her, had to have her in any way he could.

His hand caressed her hair and her cheek then, once she had removed her hand from her straining clitoris, he let his own hand run down over her breasts as murmurs of ecstasy issued from his throat.

'You're so beautiful, Penny. So desirable.'

She closed her eyes and hoped, felt his hand run down over her belly and his fingers tangle in her mass of pubic hair before teasing the head of her clitoris.

As if all bodily pleasures and reliefs were associated with each other, she continued to pee into the soft, yellow sand. Alistair rubbed her clitoris, then pinched it with two fingers so that its glistening head stood more firmly upright from its surrounding petals. Then he released it, teased it, tickled it, bringing her a delicious relief to far outweigh that achieved by her emptying bladder.

As she moaned, she closed her eyes and impulsively reached for his crotch. But her hand found only empty air.

Just when she thought she had him, Alistair had moved again. She frowned, opened her eyes and got to her feet.

'Why won't you let me touch you?' she asked plaintively, and cupped her pouting breasts in the palms of

184

her hands. 'See what you can have if you want it? My breasts. Aren't they pretty? People have said so, you know. And my pussy. Look at it.' She lifted one leg and rested her foot on a two-foot-high rock. She let her breasts fall and used her fingers to pull open the lips of her sex. Pink folds of flesh blushed beneath his gaze. 'See how wet you've made my pussy. And yet you neglect it. Why is that? Please tell me.'

But Alistair could say nothing. He could only swallow hard as he stared at the pretty pink jewels she so selflessly offered him. How pretty they were, and how much would he like to get his throbbing tool into that delightful gateway.

With all the strength of purpose he possessed, he curbed the cry of anguish that lay in wait on the back of his tongue. What could he say? How could he explain? He couldn't, so he turned his back and walked swiftly away.

She stared after him. Tonight, she decided, she would console herself. Tonight before dinner, Gregory would bathe and soothe away her pains and disappointments. Tonight she would feel herself again.

Chapter Ten

*B*ehind the deceitful reflection of the ornate mirror in Penny's bedroom, Nadine watched, her eyes glittering and unblinking, her mouth an uncompromising line. On the other side of the glass, Gregory's behind rose and fell in strict tempo and his balls slapped against Penny's upturned rear. His buttocks tensed with each forward thrust, relaxing with each backward stroke. How beautiful they are, she thought to herself, how they glisten from the oil Penny applied to them earlier, and how much better they would look criss-crossed with a welter of pink and purple stripes applied by a thin crop and the hair fine end of a riding whip!

Normally Nadine would be smiling. But today had not been a good day, and although she didn't doubt that the stable-lads and Auberon had carried out her instructions, it still peeved her that she hadn't been there at the beach to oversee things herself. She'd been annoyed that her brother had ordered her to collect that damn Clarissa, and, although he seemed genuine enough about the reasons for her doing so, she hadn't been able to avoid being suspicious. She had questioned her own self-confidence, asked herself whether he was slipping from her grasp. But, she counselled herself, she would reassert her control. Dominance was irresistible. Once its sublime sensations had been tasted, tribute flowed back to the

186

dominatrix like the river to the sea. Today, its flow had merely been interrupted.

Normally, the scene now taking place on the other side of the mirror would have been orchestrated by her for her brother's delight and her own egotistical satisfaction. But it wasn't. These two were acting under their own steam now, Gregory's bathing and massaging of Penny's body automatically leading to a frenzy of energetic lovemaking that Nadine was drawn to watch, but she was indignant that she had played no part in its instigation.

Nadine was not by nature a jealous woman. Her tastes she regarded as darkly plain, her demands simple. That was as far as it went. Simple they might be, but all-consuming, too. There was a single-mindedness in her that needed those same demands to be met in her time and on her terms. At the Beaumont stable she regarded those demands a bit like rules of the house. They were there for a purpose and the purpose was all her own.

Even though the sight in front of her eyes annoyed her, she couldn't help her throat becoming a little dry and her eyes glazing over at the sight of Gregory's magnificent rump pumping away at the softness of Penny's pleasantly rounded behind.

She could see that Penny's eyes were closed and her mouth open in ecstasy. Her breasts swung in steady time with the tempo of Gregory's thrusts. She was leaning on her elbows so her nipples consistently brushed the rough weave of the tapestry bedspread. As they brushed the coarse material, her nipples reddened, and as they reddened, they grew in size.

Nadine, who stood naked in the small turret room on the other side of the mirror, could almost taste the ecstasy both were enjoying. Even her own hairless pussy ached and oozed with desire.

Hands clasping Penny's rear end tight against him, Gregory at last threw his head back, mouth wide and eyes shut. Penny was shaking her mass of dark hair in orgasmic frenzy. Both had reached their sexual nirvana.

Penny was insatiable and her appetite had sharpened

since being at Beaumont Place. She was an apt pupil and beautiful with it. Not like Clarissa, she thought to herself. Clarissa wasn't exactly plain, but neither was she pretty. She was ordinary – perhaps even boring. What a harsh word to call anyone she thought, boring. Anything – even ugly, hideous, horrendous – was better than that, she thought to herself. Poor Clarissa. And then she smiled. Clarissa was wanting and if she had anything to do with it, would get what she wanted, though she wasn't too sure whether she was really the virgin she insisted she was. Reggie, Clarissa's father, had promised her a special treat for her birthday and had implored Nadine to see it got done. So far, Clarissa, after a lot of false hopes and non-starters arranged mostly through her father's army connections, was still strangely unfulfilled. But Nadine would deal with that, or more accurately, Gregory would be used to deal with it. With mischief in her mind and satisfaction in her heart, Nadine smiled.

Increasingly obsessed with her own thoughts, Nadine lost interest in the scene on the other side of the mirror. She turned and looked at the outfit she had been planning to wear this evening. A nice choice, she thought, eyeing the black lace see-through kaftan which would have swept the floor but covered nothing. Nothing would have been worn underneath. But this, she decided, was perhaps not quite right for the evening she had in mind. Too soft and too pretty – and too exposing of her own body.

Instead, from the dark cupboard in the corner of the room, she got out a far more disciplined outfit, and one of her favourites. Once it was on, she surveyed herself in the full-length mirror that was strictly one-way only. Soft, clinging leather covered her body from head to toe. Black, of course, the collar was just a simple ring studded with metal spikes that caught the light when she moved. The collar was joined to the bodice with thongs of rolled leather, and in the bodice itself were two holes through which her nipples shyly peeped.

'Now, my little pretties,' she cooed as she rubbed each

188

one between finger and thumb, 'don't be shy. Mummy wants you to come out to play.'

Dutifully, her nipples responded and stood proud of the black leather like two pink buttons. Her eyes surveyed the rest of her outfit. The legs were slashed high to her hips. A row of studs ran across her pelvis, and silver chains ran from beneath those slashed leg openings and held her thigh-high boots in place. The boots had high spiked silver heels and matching spurs.

'Very nice. Very nice indeed,' Nadine drawled with satisfaction, then held her head thoughtfully to one side. 'Perhaps one little finishing touch,' she said. Her natural sense of drama craved the unusual. From a drawer in a unit to the side of the dark wardrobe, she took a black eye patch and a silver-topped whip.

The effect was satisfying, though vaguely sinister. Smiling with menace, she placed her palms flat on either side of the mirror and leaned towards it so her face was but two inches away from her own reflection.

'Oh, dark mistress,' she hissed slowly at the mirror, her breath misting the cold glass, 'go take your place in the scheme of things, and dance your dolls to the tune of your own desires.'

Satiated with sex and the smell of Gregory's maleness regrettably washed from her body, Penny dressed in a slim sheath with thin straps that she considered bordering on the virginal. It was low-cut, floaty and swept near the floor. Yet it clung to her curves and denied her rising breasts and curving hips nothing. Even the shape of her mons and belly was contoured by the soft blue material that a thousand silkworms must have beavered night and day to produce.

As she opened the door to her room, she glanced over her shoulder at her reflection and smiled. Her bottom, so recently pounded by Gregory's hot pubes, had a defiant and pert look about it. Like two pear halves, she thought, smothered by a layer of swirling blueberry syrup. Then she closed the door on the room and the reflection.

At dinner, she met Clarissa.

Clarissa's hair was cut short and vaguely fashionable. Her face was heart-shaped, but set slightly off-centre so that when she smiled her mouth looked a bit lop-sided and one eye gave the impression of being just a wee bit higher than the other.

Apart from her almond-shaped brown eyes, she was unremarkable. She was of average height, average looks and had poor taste when it came to clothes.

If what she had on was supposed to be suitable for evening, it certainly wasn't suitable for a girl of her age. Judging by the wide straps and elasticated waist, it might very likely have belonged to a middle-aged aunt of a particularly frumpy disposition.

Penny felt instantly sorry for her.

Even her constant wittering did little to endear her as a young girl on the threshold of life, but rather as a plain little sparrow never destined to be anything but easily forgotten.

The more Clarissa chattered, the more chance Penny got to study everyone else's reaction. Like her, it was obvious that whatever Clarissa waxed lyrical about was going over everyone's heads. They were commenting with negative words just for the sake of politeness, but apart from that, everyone seemed to be engrossed in their own thoughts.

But as her one glass of wine turned into two, then three, and then four, Clarissa's talk became looser, her inhibitions having been drowned in the warm bouquet of a decent bottle of Chardonnay.

So, thought Penny, beneath that drab plumage and Daddy's-little-girl image was a more exotic bird just ripe for the plucking. Later in the evening, she found out Nadine was thinking very much along the same lines.

It was after dinner, when Penny had removed Reggie's hot hand from her equally hot pussy, that Nadine, her face a mass of smiles, invited Penny to leave the men to themselves and go with her and Clarissa to her apartment for what she termed a 'girly chat'.

There was something oddly Victorian and out of character about Nadine's request, but Penny went along.

Once through the heavy door that divided the more prosaic aspect of Beaumont Place from the private, Clarissa was silenced and Penny herself was overcome with the sheer opulence of the brocade coverings of the corridor walls. Vivid and obviously valuable paintings in gilt frames added to the private splendour of Nadine's very own domain, and gilt wall lights fashioned into frivolous bows and ripe heads of wheat gave reflected light to heavy mirrors and gleaming brass.

Nadine's very high heels sank silently into thick runs of blue and red Persian rugs, and the cheeks of her bare bottom swung at a sharp rate from left to right as she led the way, her cohort of Penny and Clarissa marching apprehensively behind.

Nadine paused, hand on hip in front of a pair of rich mahogany double doors. Her one uncovered eye glanced from Penny to Clarissa and back again. It was obviously done for effect, and the amused smile that played around Nadine's mouth seemed directed at the former rather than the latter.

'I've a present for you, Clarissa,' said Nadine, and with an unusually sweeping flourish and a bright smile, she draped her long arm around Clarissa's meaty shoulders.

'For me, Nadine?' whispered the girl, her eyes as bright as a child at Christmas and her cheeks still flushed with wine. The more closely Nadine drew towards Clarissa, the more Clarissa recoiled, her fingers curling into the palms of her hands as though loath to touch the soft leather of Nadine's splendid outfit.

'For you, my darling Clarissa,' purred Nadine, gently pinching one of Clarissa's shiny cheeks. 'But first, you have to take your clothes off.'

'What?'

Clarissa's eyes opened wide and her cheeks took on a deeper colour than before.

Penny raised one quizzical eyebrow and waited to see just what Nadine had in store. She half-expected Clarissa to say goodbye. But Clarissa, a hint of stubbornness squaring her chin, stayed put.

'Take your clothes off, little sparrow,' Nadine went on,

191

her hands caressing the girl's cheek before she took Clarissa's chin between finger and thumb and looked deep into her eyes. 'I will help you, and Penny will take hers off, too.'

Nadine nodded at Penny. Intrigued to find out what the present was and what was behind the double doors – and knowing they wouldn't be allowed in until Nadine's orders had been obeyed – Penny let the silky dress drop from her body and fall in a silky swirl to the thickly carpeted floor.

Clarissa stared open-mouthed at her. Almost with reverence, her eyes skirted the creamy breasts and dark forest of pubic hair that was now exposed before her eyes.

'Come on, my little sparrow,' cooed Nadine as she undid the girl's bulky dress. 'We're all girls together, aren't we now?'

Clarissa couldn't answer. Her mouth seemed powerless to close. As Nadine stripped her of her frumpy dress, her eyes stayed glued on Penny's smooth skin. That is, until her own garments lay in a heavy heap on the floor.

Now Penny was amazed and Nadine looked amused. Beneath her dull exterior, Clarissa was wearing the smallest pair of red leather crotchless knickers she had ever seen. At the front they exposed a mass of dark-brown curly hair that burst forth from the opening like stuffing from a burst cushion.

Her bra was equally surprising. It was made of the same red leather as the knickers, but did nothing to keep her breasts in check. It simply held them in suspension, mere strips of wire and lace beneath heaving mounds of white virgin flesh. Dark-pink nipples and big areolae, stared menacingly forward.

'Why Clarissa,' laughed Nadine, 'what a surprise you are. And you still a virgin!'

Clarissa blushed visibly. 'I don't know what my father's told you, but I didn't say I was.'

To Penny's surprise, Nadine appeared either not to have heard what Clarissa had said or chose to ignore her.

She seemed intent that all three of them entered the double doors.

'Artificial devices will never replace the real thing, my little sweetie,' said Nadine in a very matter-of-fact way. 'I think we need to rectify that matter. Penny, take her hand. I'll take the other.'

Penny did as Nadine ordered. She took one hand, Nadine the other. It was Nadine who threw the double doors open, but it was Penny who gasped more loudly than Clarissa. There, stretched out before them, was Gregory. Around his neck was a thick leather collar studded with silver studs. From the collar hung a chain which ran across the floor and disappeared into a half-open cupboard.

Gregory's eyes met Penny's before they drank in her naked body. His penis leapt with expectation in his groin.

Sharp nails dug into Penny's arm and Nadine's mouth whispered hoarsely against her ear. 'Now, my pretty pussy, you are only here to watch, to witness.'

Penny tore her eyes from Gregory to the cool, pale ones so near to her face. She saw triumph in those eyes. She also saw a kind of revenge. She turned her eyes back to Gregory. In his face, there was no apology for responding so easily and so well to her naked body. Like Alistair, he seemed submissive before Nadine, responsive to whatever game she wished to play.

Beside her, Penny was aware of Clarissa breathing more heavily than she had been. Despite herself, she felt her own sex grow heavy as her eyes followed the subtle movements of Gregory's rising stem from its glistening glans to its firm and forested root.

'Just for you, my pretty pussy,' she heard Nadine purr, whilst her cool hands caressed the nape of Penny's neck. 'This is just for you.'

Penny was so absorbed in the lounging body of Gregory, and soothed by Nadine's long fingers, that she barely felt the chain collar fastened around her neck until Nadine yanked the trailing lead attached to it. Now she was flat against the wall, breath knocked out of her.

Nadine leaned on her, still murmuring in her ear, her

193

long fingers stroking her hot flesh. Even though her eyes were drawn to the gleaming body laid out on the thick Chinese carpet, she couldn't help but respond to Nadine's soothing hands and probing fingers. Then Nadine left her side. Penny tried to move, but her hands were as firmly fastened as her neck. She had been so absorbed with the sight of Gregory's naked body and the touch of Nadine's fingers that she hadn't felt the steel clips encircle her wrists and bind her to the wall. Now she was flat against it and unable to move.

Nadine's attention had turned to Clarissa.

Clarissa was shivering, though it wasn't necessarily from fear or apprehension. Her big breasts trembled like twin jellies against the uneasy confines of her lurid bra, and the honey of her arousal added lustre to the inside of her thighs.

'Now,' said Nadine as she curved her arm around the shivering girl's shoulder, 'Gregory is here for your delight. You may do with him as you wish. Whatever you want is yours for the asking.'

Clarissa was speechless, and although Nadine was caressing her breasts – her fingers spreading in delicious sweeping movements across one then the other – Clarissa's eyes were as fixed as Penny's had been on Gregory's upright stem.

'Anything?' Clarissa asked, her words trembling as much as her breasts.

'Anything,' murmured Nadine in reply.

Penny wanted to shout out some suggestions, but her throat had grown dry, and besides, she sensed that anything she had to suggest would not be appreciated by Nadine.

Gregory glanced almost apologetically at Penny, before responding to the tug on his neck-chain and getting to his feet. He stood before Clarissa, nakedly available.

'Feel him,' said Nadine to Clarissa, her hand tousling the girl's shorn hair before running down over her back and sliding beneath the red leather knickers.

Clarissa's lop-sided look seemed to disappear. In absorption, she had become beautiful, or at least enrap-

194

tured. Hesitantly, she reached out and touched the hardness of his smooth-skinned chest.

Penny imagined the effect of that delightful touch on both Gregory and Clarissa. She clenched her hands, buried her own fingertips in her palms as though *his* flesh was burning her rather than the short and rather plump girl who stood before him now. Yet she knew Gregory was enjoying this, and knew that he was as much caught in Nadine's web as everyone else here.

Clarissa, eyes bright and heavy breasts straining against what little held them in check, ran her hand down over Gregory's hard chest, tight ribcage and flat stomach. It came to a halt just above the golden curls that surrounded his heaving penis like a gilt halo. Her fingertips teased haltingly at the mass of soft, springy hair as though she were making a decision. Suddenly, as though such a decision had been reached, her fingers disappeared in his crinkled pubic hair before folding tentatively around his firm member.

Penny saw his eyes flicker, his mouth open slightly to accommodate a greater intake of air. His stomach visibly tightened as did her own. She was not Clarissa, and yet she *was* her. Each movement Clarissa made was hers, each touch, each feeling Penny experienced as though it was her own.

Penny almost willed Clarissa to make her next move. She wanted to feel his hand upon her breast, and her heartbeat quickened as she saw Gregory raise his hand and encompass one of Clarissa's swelling mounds. She heard Clarissa gasp, and felt as *she* was feeling. Clarissa's gasp was her gasp, Clarissa's murmur of joy – as his head bent to her breast and his mouth sucked at her nipple – belonged to her.

'Open your legs,' Nadine ordered. Clarissa obediently obliged. So did Penny.

'Go down,' Nadine ordered Gregory, pulling firmly on the chain that was attached to the collar around his neck. To Nadine and Penny's surprise, Clarissa snatched the chain from Nadine's hand. Her eyes were bright with excitement and her actions certainly not virginal.

Gregory almost fell to his knees, his mouth travelling from Clarissa's breasts and down over her stomach. His hands were clenched over her wide buttocks.

'Down to her pussy,' ordered Nadine, her hand pushing down on his head.

Both Clarissa and Penny opened their legs wider, although it was Clarissa who threw her head back in ecstasy as his tongue flicked between the hairy folds of her sex and cajoled her dormant clitoris into life.

Penny now only watched and waited, an unbearable tension hanging like droplets of lead from her own sex, her breasts rising with desire and the rushing of quickening breath. She moaned in protest that she was not a participant in this scene, only a spectator.

The soft down on Nadine's cheek rubbed against hers. Her breath and lips lightly brushed her cheek, but her voice was cruel.

'You're only here to witness, my pretty pussy,' spat Nadine, her smile half-cracking her face, and her eyes glittering with delight.

Nadine unclipped Penny from the wall, attached a fine chain to her neck collar; pulling her to her side, she ordered Penny to her knees whilst she sat herself down in a comfortable chair. Although Penny's eyes were full of the scene before her, she was also aware of Nadine reaching out, and of the lights dimming. The room was plunged into semi-darkness. Only a pool of light stayed like an amber lake in the middle of the room to illuminate the tall, blond man and the short, dark girl.

Even though they were not truly alone, the very fact that their audience was beyond the pool of light and enveloped in shadows endowed the couple with confidence.

Clarissa, and, in her wake, Penny, gasped loudly as Gregory got to his feet and bent his mouth to Clarissa's nipples and sucked first one, then the other.

As if to remind her that she played no physical part in the scenario, Penny felt a tug on her own chain. Without words, Nadine was telling her to be quiet, and she understood the reason why. Just the sound of one syllable would be enough to destroy the fragile exploration on which the two figures were embarking.

Accompanied by more intensive breathing only, Gregory pushed a yielding Clarissa back against the plush comfort of a fat sofa. He spread one leg over the back of the settee, with the other still propped on the floor. His hands ran down from her breasts until they slid inside each parted half of her crotchless pants. They hid nothing; her pubic hair and her pink inner lips were open and moist. Dutifully, and in direct response to the moistness before his eyes, Gregory circled Clarissa's sex before his finger edged into her open portal.

Penny wanted to cry out, but instead she took a deep breath, almost as though it were she who smelt the heavy musk secreted by Clarissa's willing body. She wanted to cry out again when she saw Gregory's buttocks cover the yawning gap. Under cover of darkness, her own fingers dived to the moistness of her own sex. But unseen hands, long and cool, intercepted her avid penetrations, gripped her wrists and held her tight.

'No,' whispered Nadine firmly.

So, with wet lips and staring eyes, Penny watched, yearning for the bucking behind to be above her hips, for the mangled cries of final climax to be hers and not the stocky girl with the military haircut and the lop-sided smile.

The pair lay sweating after, Gregory with his eyes closed, Clarissa with hers wide open. Not once did Penny see her look at Gregory's face. Her eyes were firmly locked on his prick which although recently used, was once again rising to prominence.

Nadine's voice echoed in the darkness.

'So you've lost your flower, my little sparrow! Now,' she said, getting to her feet and dragging Penny with her, 'now I will let you see the other ways a man may use you.'

There was a deep red hassock immediately opposite the fat sofa. Rich watermarks of heavy taffeta were picked out by the muted lights before Penny's hot flesh met the coldness of the material.

She gasped as the warmth of her breasts was cooled by the silky substance beneath her, aware of Nadine passing the chain that ran from the collar at her neck through the brass uprights of a fender which had padded velvet seats at each end and a cast-iron dog grate just beyond it. She felt her hands being hitched up behind her back and fastened with another chain to the collar around her neck. Automatically, she opened her legs slightly, wanting Gregory to leave the side of the ungrateful Clarissa and slip his rising member into her very moist passage.

Murmurs of delight caught in her throat and her hips undulated against the fingers that dipped into her cleft then ran upwards to smear the deep divide between her cheeks with the musky fluid they brought with them.

'You see,' she heard Nadine purr in that long drawn-out tone of hers. 'See how you and this man have aroused her. See how wet her pussy has become, that pretty pussy that so wants to have what *you* have had.'

Penny heard Clarissa move, wished it were Gregory, then heard the intake of breath and guessed Clarissa was responding to Nadine's invitation to inspect her damp and open nether regions.

'Will you let her have it?' she heard Clarissa say in an excited, almost reverent voice.

Nadine did not reply. Penny could visualise her smile, knew her eyes would be glittering and her teeth flashing white in her wide mouth. Instinctively, she also knew that Nadine would be shaking her head.

'Come here, my adorable angel,' she heard Nadine say.

Aroused in the knowledge that Gregory was moving towards her upended rear, Penny closed her eyes and tilted her behind just that little bit more.

'Prepare her,' she heard Nadine say. 'She's wet down here,' Nadine continued, dipping her fingers again into Penny's yearning sex. 'Transfer it to here. This is where you will penetrate.'

As Nadine's nails greased her puckered anus, Penny whimpered and writhed upon the red taffeta, her chains tinkling like fairy bells against the cold brass of the fireside fender.

Thicker fingers followed the same journey as Nadine's had travelled. Gregory's fingers dipped tentatively, then more determinedly into her willing portal.

She could not see his face, could not ascertain his responses, and yet she knew just by his breathing and the touch of his fingers that he was aroused and more than willing to fill her tightest hole.

Smears of her own fluid were spread between her buttocks, squeezed and pushed in suspended droplets into her rosebud opening. She welcomed them, clamped her halo of muscles against the intruding finger as it entered and lubricated her slim passage. Then, as it was withdrawn, she sighed and mewed with regret.

'Take her,' she heard Nadine say.

'Push it in hard,' she heard Clarissa say with rapt enthusiasm that would even, no doubt, surprise Nadine.

The warm nub of Gregory's helmet nudged gently at her wincing hole, almost as though he were asking for entry.

'*I said take her!*' she heard Nadine cry before the rushing hiss of a whip descended through the air and cracked upon Gregory's clenched behind.

As the whip landed, he burst through Penny's sphincter and parted her tightly gripping muscles.

She cried out. Nadine laughed, and Clarissa gasped.

'Pull her on to you,' Nadine said.

Gregory must have hesitated, or perhaps it was that Nadine didn't need any excuse to crease his skin yet again with the whip or crop which whispered menacingly as it cut through the air.

'Let me do it!' cried Clarissa suddenly. 'Let me whip him. I'm good at that, really I am!'

She heard Nadine laugh, felt Gregory tense against her as he pushed his prick through her tightness. His cry broke in unison with hers, but did not satisfy Clarissa.

Penny bit her lip as lash after lash sang through the air and landed on Gregory's behind. She cried out herself as the whip purposefully graced her own thighs, then slumped against the silky hassock when at last Gregory pumped his release and cried out one last and savage yell against her ear.

Penny was dragged from under Gregory before the light came on.

Outside in the corridor of thick carpets and vivid paintings, Nadine wrapped the chain tightly around her fists and pulled her close. 'No come for you, my pretty pussy. Not tonight. Just you wait. The main event will be something you'll never forget. But not tonight.'

Nadine did not allow her to dress, and the room she took her to – although round and obviously in a turret – was not her own. Terracotta walls were matched by dark and heavy silks that swept from the central point of the ceiling and ended in thick fringes around the tops of the circular walls.

There was a bed in the room of large proportions, with head- and footboards of wrought iron interspersed with gilt leaves. It was heaped with cushions covered in the same richly dark material as that draped from the ceiling.

Anticipation of what might be in store caused the leaden feeling in Penny's sex to intensify. It was further encouraged by the dull burn in her taken behind.

Nadine gagged her mouth and fastened the wristbands that she'd placed on Penny in the other room to the collar she still wore round her neck.

'Lie down on the floor at the side of the bed,' Nadine demanded.

Curious to know what was in store for her, and hoping it might alleviate the need in her loins, Penny did as ordered.

Once she was laid down, Nadine bound her ankles together with a pair of cuffs.

'Bend your knees,' she was ordered.

Penny obeyed. Her ankles were forced up behind her. A long chain ran from them, through her buttocks and up her back, and were also fastened to the collar around her neck.

Lying there, securely trussed and gagged, Penny noticed that the wrought ironwork of the head- and footboard was repeated along the side of the bed. To her

200

surprise, Nadine lifted it and secured it with a hook to the headboard. First with her hands, and then with the toe of her boot, she pushed Penny beneath the bed. Once there, Nadine replaced the ironwork. Naked, gagged and bound, she was now beneath the bed. And yet it was not a bed. Not for her. For Penny, no matter about the sprinkling of gilt leaves that decorated the wrought iron, it was to all intents and purposes a cage.

Nadine was on all fours and laughing as she viewed her through the sweeping curls and curves of the ornamental ironwork. She poked her fingers through the ironwork, and wiggled them. She made faces like people do at the zoo. Penny felt like a trapped animal, naked, bound and mute.

'No sex for you tonight, my pretty pussy,' said Nadine with a laugh. 'From your little cage you will hear that beautiful angel, Gregory, groan as he inserts his prick into that little bore Clarissa's wet vagina. You'll hear her cry out in ecstasy when his hands caress her bosom, and when he repeats with her what he did to you back there, when he fills her smallest hole with his throbbing muscle. Won't that be thrilling for you, won't that be just delightful?'

Penny opened her eyes wide and mumbled her response. But that was all it was. Just a mumble.

Nadine tutted and laughed.

'Poor little creature. Pretty pussy,' she said, reaching her hand through the ironwork and tangling her fingernail in the clutch of hair which protruded so proudly from Penny's helpless mons now her legs were bound behind her back. 'I shall think of you lying here, neatly packaged, listening to everything they do, everything they say and not being able to do anything about it. How sweet for me. How dire for you.'

Nadine kicked the ironwork and laughed again before she left the room.

How long it was before she heard the door reopen, Penny couldn't be sure. A low light was switched on. Clarissa's voice was easily recognisable, that of Gregory seemed more obscure. Yet it shouldn't be. Wasn't his

voice the most sweet she'd ever come across and the
most outstanding, rich as dark brandy?

Warm words and wet kisses preceded the dipping of
the mattress as the two bodies entwined above her. In
her mind's eye, she imagined what they were doing and
felt jealous. How hard Gregory's body would be against
that of Clarissa. How soft her buttocks were, before his
member divided them and nudged like a wary predator
into her waiting hole. Yet, to Penny's surprise, Clarissa
did not cry out.

Only once they had finished did she hear them speak
more clearly.

'You gave nothing away?' said the male voice.

'Nothing, my darling. Nothing at all.'

'Did you enjoy beating Gregory?'

'It was very good, though not as good as with you, and
I have to admit, I did rather enjoy seeing Penny have her
bottom divided by his prick. Nadine fastened her pretty
tightly whilst he did it, just like you do a mare when the
stallion's about to take her. I liked that.'

Surprised and suddenly aware that the man above her
with Clarissa was not Gregory, Penny sucked in her
breath and listened some more. She recognised that voice,
though beneath the blurred barrier of the mattress, she
couldn't quite decide who exactly it was. Yet she would.
She was sure she would.

Her breathing settled as theirs settled and they slept.
Three times further she was awakened by their resumed
sexual Olympics during the night, the springs dipping
and diving above her head together with the swish of a
whip and the cries of an anguished and bound man.

It was an odd feeling, almost as though she were part
of their action, yet no more than a residual part, a leftover thing whose attendance was not necessary to their
enjoyment.

The day had been long and the night seemed too short:
as short as the naps she managed to grab between the up
and down movements of the bed.

Clarissa and the man rose at dawn and they talked
about rolling in a wet meadow and him having his

202

buttocks thoroughly chastised with a bundle of fresh young nettles.

During their absence, Nadine released her.

With aching limbs and a lessening desire in her loins, Penny made her way back to her own bed to snatch what bit of the night was left. She slept, and although the trifling niggle in her sex reminded her that it still had not received its just desserts, she curled her fingers into her palms and saved it until the time and the man were right. Gregory or Alistair. One thing she was sure of was that the man in bed with Clarissa had not been Gregory *or* Alistair.

Chapter Eleven

*F*or wet weather, three indoor arenas were available for practice, and outside three more. Those indoors had a base of ground bark and wood chippings. The others outside had sparkling green grass and were surrounded by a barrier of tall poplars whose leaves rustled lazily in the warm breeze. This latter arena was the one Penny was using now.

Consistent practice and unyielding concentration on Penny's part had combined to result in clear rounds for both the chestnut and the grey. Penny was pleased with her performance, and her body had cooled once Nadine had suggested she remove her cotton top and take the jumps bare-breasted.

The idea had amused and pleased her. She had to admit, the rush of air cooling her sweating flesh was very welcome. On top of that, the constant tapping of her bare breasts against her rib cage seemed to aid her timing. Nadine knew her job and could tell how to get the best from her charges.

Afterwards, Penny lingered with Gregory in the coolness of the stable as, in the absence of a stable-lad, he removed the tack from her rangy chestnut.

Her head was level with his shoulder as she stood beside him, aware of the masculine scent of his lightly

204

sweating body as he reached both arms up to remove the saddle.

His muscles were obvious and inviting beneath the black of his T-shirt. Tentatively, almost as if they might melt before her very eyes, her fingertips lightly traced their hard peaks and moulded contours. As she did so, her tongue darted thirstily over her open lips. She moved closer to him and watched as the muscles in his neck tensed in response to the warmth of her breath.

He groaned as he let the saddle slide from the horse's back and into his hands. He let it slide to the floor, then cupped her face in his hands and looked down into her eyes. In response, her body moved gently against his, her bare breasts prodding, lightly skimming his hard chest muscles.

'You're incorrigible,' he said to her, and raised his eyes to heaven as if seeking help to avoid temptation. But there was nothing that could stop him falling or her catching him.

'I'm in need,' she whispered breathlessly against his ear.

'In need of what?' he responded into her hair.

'Of you.' Her hand slid down between their two bodies until it rested on the virile mound that pressed severely against the front of his faded blue jeans.

He moaned as though in pain and his breath rushed in a sudden torrent before he bent his head and kissed her. His lips were slightly salty on hers, his tongue firm and moist as it entered her mouth and met her own.

Maleness was hard, she thought to herself, and the smell of maleness was a strange mix of salt, of sweetness and the earthy aroma of a fertile field, of supple leather, of animal lust.

In unison and hand in hand, they left the stable and made their way to the most welcoming byre of all. The hay store was empty and heavy with the scent of sweet hay, and crisp yellow straw which rustled beneath their feet.

Fresh male sweat combined with the scent of sweet

hay and straw, filling her head with its earthy enticement and her sex with the honey of her desire.

Even so, just for a moment, she tensed and glanced apprehensively over her shoulder.

'Nadine's gone out,' said Gregory, loath to desist from kissing her lips and tweaking her nipples, but aware of the cause of her sudden hesitation. 'Once you'd finished jumping your round, she went off to town. Had arrangements to make, I heard her say to her brother. Something to do with some guy called Dominic.'

Penny sighed and shifted her hips. 'You can never be sure with her. She seems to appear when you least expect her.'

Gregory grinned and ruffled her hair with one hand. Silently, he nodded, a boyish understanding upturning one side of his mouth higher than the other. 'Up in the loft might be a good idea,' he murmured against her ear.

'There's no need if Nadine is out.'

His hands caught hers, stopped their progress down over his body. In that moment, it occurred to her that she should tell him about Clarissa, her lover and her imprisonment beneath the bed. But he kissed her, and in the warm abandonment of rising desire, she let it go. She'd tell him later.

'Change of scenery.' He smiled as he said it. The colour of his eyes, the fairness of his hair and the tight muscles of his lean body were too much for her to resist.

'Come on then.' She led the way, moaning with pleasure when his hands cupped the cheeks of her bottom as she ascended the stairs to the hayloft.

They took off their clothes. Silently, they stood eyeing each detail of the body they would shortly join with. He filled his eyes with her firm breasts, belly and strong legs, the clutch of downy hair that burst like a patch of exotic moss between her thighs. She eyed his satin-bright hair, melting brown eyes, strong jaw and powerful neck. Around his navel, she saw his stomach muscles tighten, each contour individually outlined, shamelessly accentuating the jerking muscle that rose beneath them from a bright halo of golden hair. Behind it, his testes hung like

206

two ripe peaches. His penis reared in abject beauty, as golden and firm as the rest of him and beckoned her fingers, mouth and the damp warm portal between her thighs.

His eyes ran over her body like seeking fingers before settling on her black diamond of pubic hair. With need flooding and hanging heavy from her labia, she shifted her legs slightly so her inner petals and its pert bud would peep from among the glistening curls.

He reached for the black band that held her hair and released it so it fell in a black cloud over her shoulders, breast and back. Then he lay her down, the darkness of her hair billowing out over the golden yellow of the straw. The straw scratched at her back, but was compensated by the pressure of his chest on hers, her breasts flattened by his weight and his passion.

She nuzzled his neck, revelling in his maleness, sliding her hands down his back so her fingernails could dig into the delicious hardness of his buttocks as they clenched to give his phallus greater driving power.

He suckled at her breasts, his mouth and tongue drawing tantalising lines of sensation around the rich redness of her nipples and quivering flesh. His mouth moved further, his tongue flicking at her skin and dipping briefly into the hollow of her navel. When his teeth nipped at her pubic hair, she groaned and closed her eyes, raising her hips and opening her legs as his tongue darted furtively into her aching valley.

There was gentleness in the probing flesh, a sweet fragility as it flicked further, only the tip running from clitoris to vagina.

As her back arched, her hips rose more. His hands dived beneath her buttocks, clasping them tightly as he held her sex against his mouth. She moaned as his teeth nipped neatly at her mound, grinding her pubic hair as though it were crispy seaweed. He nibbled her outer lips before his tongue again flicked at her thrusting bud of passion, then, like a small but sensitive penis, it entered her portal.

As if she were drowning in her own desire, her hips

writhed in his hands. Just when she thought his actions would bring her to climax, he grasped her more tightly, his thumbs digging into her hip-bones. Lifting her as though she had no weight at all, he turned her over on to her hands and knees.

Lips and tongue just as hot as before now travelled down her spine until they met the rise of her buttocks. His teeth nipped each round orb, made the flesh quiver and left pink circles on the creamy skin. She groaned, pleaded with him to do more. There was an exquisite delight in such pain, a delight she welcomed. Then his tongue took over from his teeth and began to lick between her buttocks, his hands pulling each cheek apart as his tongue travelled lower along her glossy divide.

Mewing in a rather surprised fashion, she closed her eyes as the inquisitive tongue poked tentatively at the puckered ring of her anus, its opening like a tight mauve button that pulsated among the creaminess of her pear-like behind.

His finger took the place of his tongue, pressing inwards, overcoming the initial barrier before retreating and returning the darting wetness of his tongue to explore the tightest of her bodily orifices.

Gasping into the clean straw beneath her head, she dropped to her elbows so that her backside was tilted upwards. He held the cheeks of her bottom apart as his tongue darted in and out, then sucked and licked at the puckered flesh.

She wanted him to eat her, to draw her in, chew at her most secret places as though she were some delicacy at a rich man's feast. Moaning and lost in her own hot pleasure, she raised herself from elbows to hands, unable any longer to restrain the swelling of her breast, her breath quickening as his tongue continued to explore neglected territory.

Almost with regret, he left her tightest hole and turned his attention to the fleshy lips that sucked somewhere towards his chin, their rich colour like a slash of red silk among the black satin of her pubic curls.

His tongue curled up between the glistening flesh,

diving again into her vulva, flicking in such a tantalising way over the folds of the inner lips that eddies of moaning pleasure spiralled from her throat on higher and higher octaves. She trembled at his intrusion, tingled breathlessly with the tickling pleasure of the light touch, the quickness of the action.

With one long, last flourish he took his tongue back where it had been, finally disappearing in the initial tightness of the cleft between her behind before he moved to cover her. A sigh of relief racked her body as though she had been rescued from some dire situation. She heaved a sigh, her senses dizzy from the excitement his tongue had aroused, then cooed with gratitude as his member thrust into her moist cavern.

Warm and softly downed, his balls slapped in rhythm with his ramming member, hard yet cushioned against her smooth flesh. Penny closed her eyes and moaned her appreciation behind the tumbling mane of hair that now covered her face. Her breasts swayed back and forth as he lunged, each action knocking the breath out of her. She purred with pleasure as his hands played with her breasts, cupping them, rolling them beneath his palms, his fingers tweaking and squeezing at her yielding nipples.

Partly as a signal to him to attend to her desires, and partly because she ached for her climax, she slid her hand down over her stomach and between her legs. Her fingers probed and caressed a sex that was moist, open and yearning for expression.

His hand joined hers, cupped one upon the other. As he continued to lunge into her, their fingers entwined and rode the slippery wetness of her sex, stirring its fluid heat, searing its open lips with flames of rising climax. Her sex was full of fingers, full of action. There was no way she could escape its intensity or its final rush of sensation. She cried out as a thundering crescendo of orgasm overcame her, soaking their hands and tightening the muscles in her throat as she gasped her climatic breath.

Tightly, his golden pubes crushed against her as he throbbed his essence in final surrender. She felt him jerk, felt the seepage of her own fluid cling to her pubic curls and trickle in silent streams over her inner thighs.

Collapsed in the last throes of rapid breath and shivering orgasm, only their breathing and the movement of the horses below disturbed the silence.

With her back towards him, she curled up in the welcoming curve of his body, her back against his chest, her bottom cushioned by his now soft member and its surrounding hair. His arms clasped her to him. They were both sublimely spent. But they talked. Disjointed comments were uttered softly in hushed snatches as they gradually caught their breath and dozed in the warm security of each other's body.

He told her of the night before, of Clarissa pretending to Nadine that she was rampant to have him in her bed, then closing the door on him and telling him that she wouldn't tell Nadine if he didn't. He hadn't. He'd only told Penny.

Thoughtfully, Penny ran her hands down his back and traced the welts Clarissa's hefty beating had left on his behind. He winced.

'She lay on a few extra strokes once you were gone.'

'And you let her?'

He smiled. 'It had a most engrossing effect; one you would have approved of. A most impressive erection.' Then he sighed. 'The trouble was, it didn't impress Clarissa. I thought she was going to leave me with it. I was right. She was. Then she swore me to secrecy. Would only suck me off once I'd promised to go along with her plan.' He smiled engagingly and Penny for one knew she could never have refused him.

'What *then*?' she asked, though she already knew the answer. She just wanted to hear him say it.

He grinned. 'It was a good come.' He laughed, then kissed her.

'Then I think I'd better tell you where I spent the night and who spent it with Clarissa.'

He arched his eyebrows and looked puzzled. Somehow that pleased her. It was good to unload secrets, secrets that she didn't really want to keep. So she told him everything that had happened.

'Who was it?' he asked.

Just as she was about to tell him, straw rustled and voices mumbled in the barn below.

'What was that?' She whispered it.

'What?'

She shushed him.

'Have you really made your mind up?' asked a recognisable male voice down below them.

'Yes. Most definitely. I rather think Daddy's not going to be too pleased about it, but it is my body after all, and so it is my decision.'

The female voice was firm and obviously Clarissa's.

Gregory and Penny got to their knees and slowly crawled to the edge of the hay loft. There was a gap in the wooden casing to allow hay to be thrown down below. From here they could see what was happening without being seen.

It was definitely Clarissa. Auberon was with her, just as Penny had guessed he would be.

'Your father won't be pleased.'

Clarissa's laugh was short and blunt. 'Who cares? I know what I want. And so do you.'

'He doesn't know you very well, does he?'

'No,' she replied. 'But you do, my darling. Now, just to prove you really care, get to your knees and kiss me.'

In abject submission, Auberon did that, lifted her skirt and kissed where her pubic hair peeped out from the split in her leather panties.

'Now. Let me put this on you.'

Neither Penny or Gregory had seen the cock harness before. Silently, they watched as, once Auberon had taken off his trousers, Clarissa strapped the device around his balls and phallus, pushing it forwards into one big bunch just as Penny herself had done on her first night at Beaumont Place.

Once it was in place, Clarissa took great delight in leading him around by it, his knees scraping on the straw, moans erupting from his throat, and the swish of

211

whip rending the air when he didn't react quickly enough when ordered to pull his jersey off over his head.

Penny shoved her fingers into her mouth. Her own breath was quickening at the sight of Auberon's trapped cock, which was glistening with sweat and the first pearl drops of a white, milky essence. She was aware that, beside her, Gregory too was responding to the scene.

By the time that Clarissa had Auberon still on his knees but spread-eagled to the wall, Gregory's fingers were already re-exploring Penny's body.

Auberon's head was held fast against the wall, almost smothered by Clarissa's pelvis which firmly held him there. From where they were, they could hear slurpings of Auberon's searching tongue as he pleasured Clarissa. In return, Clarissa was jerking like mad on the piece of leather that was attached to the cock bridle.

Knowing Auberon, it was not difficult to imagine what ecstasy he was feeling.

In turn, Gregory and Penny were experiencing their own.

Penny positioned herself on all fours over her beautiful angel, her lips sucking hungrily at his erect piston whilst her sex hung in delicious moistness above him. As she slid her mouth up and down his pulsating organ, his fingers, thumb and mouth teased, pressed and pulled at her flowering bud, opened her velvet folds, and dived into her welcoming vulva.

Almost in time with the ample hips that pressed so forcibly against Auberon's mouth – her own devoured – Penny's tongue whisked from tip to sturdy stem, licked a tracery of pattern and lines around the swollen circumference of his prick as her head moved up and down with total abandon.

Just like before, his tongue was in her, his lips covering the velvet frills that enclosed the heart of her sex. Gregory's fingers spread her outer lips, then tangled in the mass of black curls that crowned the seat of passion.

Always the fingers moved, willing her to greater sensations as they caressed the fine skin of her inner thighs and the satin smoothness of her behind. She lunged with greater enthusiasm on to him as his finger traced again between her cleft, ran with the juice from her seeping portal to the tightness of the smallest orifice, and – with the assistance of the warm, hot fluid – plunged in.

As his finger worked into her sacrosanct portal, Gregory's tongue continued to delight. The fingers of his other hand rammed at her wet sex, juice flowing down over his knuckles.

Visions of what she had just seen fired her imagination. Her sweet ache of passion rose from her petalled bud, flowed like lava in a hot magnum as his thumb brought her to a shuddering climax.

Sensitive to the pulsation of orgasm throbbing in her mouth, Penny opened her throat, took Gregory in further, then gulped at the hot fluid that spurted without ceasing.

Spent yet again, they listened now to the conversation below.

'Are you ready to leave now?' they heard Auberon ask.

'Yes, my darling,' Clarissa answered.

'Then we'd better be off.'

They lay undisturbed whilst they savoured the last thrills of sensation; eyes closed, energy spent.

Penny rolled over on to her stomach, the straw crisp, yet warm against her soft belly and breasts. She rested her head upon her folded arms.

'I don't think this will go down too well.'

Thoughtfully, Gregory's hand ran casually down her back.

'Not at all. Sir Reggie won't take to her going off like that, and Nadine will be furious.'

Penny sucked on a piece of fresh straw and wriggled her hips beneath the warmth of his hand. Nadine had denied her sex the night before. Nadine had thought she had devised a sublime torture for her last night. She'd be none too pleased to know that her scheme had been ineffectual, sabotaged by Sir Reggie's daughter and Auberon. Still, nothing to be done about it now. She laughed offhandedly. 'So. Nadine will think I've been a naughty girl. And you a naughty boy.'

'Then you know what happens to naughty girls!' he said with a look of sheer mischief, a look she treated casually until he grabbed hold of her, rolled her over until she was bent over a bale of straw, then landed a few well-aimed slaps on her thrusting bottom. She squealed, wriggled, but could not get free. Her behind felt as though it were on fire, the tiny hole in between already smarting from the penetrating experience it had undergone both today and yesterday.

All the same, buoyed up that such treatment proved his affection for her, she wriggled with pleasure against her casual confinement. Her breasts slapped and rubbed against the roughness of the straw with each stroke across her behind. First he struck one cheek, then the other.

The tingling of demand tantalised her erogenous zones. In amongst the pain he was dealing, there was pleasure – pleasure she would have more of.

'Enough! I've had enough!' she cried, although her mind was yelling the opposite.

'Who says so?' Gregory held his hand above her, waiting for her answer.

'I do!' she gasped with a wriggle of her bottom.

'I *don't*! Three more. All right? Do you agree?'

'Yes,' she sighed with a false whimper. Three more times the hand descended, stinging her flesh, reddening her creamy skin. Never had she been chastised in such a way as to make her enjoy her shame, enjoy being the opposite to the strong, dominant female modern society expected her to be – the one who always had to win and always had to be on top. When and where this change in her had occurred, she wasn't too sure of. She was just sure that nothing would ever be the same again, and nowhere could ever compare to Beaumont Place.

For the first time in a few days, Penny thought about the wager, the stallion and Alistair. The importance of the proposed seduction had lessened, yet somehow she knew that both that and the place she found herself in would ultimately be part of her life.

214

Now it wasn't just a case of actually winning the wager, but more one of getting to the bottom of his obvious desire for her, yet also his reluctance to take her. It had something, she knew, to do with Nadine. That was *all* she knew, however.

Nadine took a great pride in being in control. But she also gave greater insight into an individual's personal sexuality, endowing them with a more intense response to their sexual needs. As instruments of desire, Nadine knew which notes to pluck and how to pluck them.

Chapter Twelve

Neither Nadine nor Alistair were very happy about Clarissa and Auberon taking off, but seemed to accept it. That was until Penny blurted out the fact to Nadine that she'd known from the day of her imprisonment beneath the bed the couple had shared. Nadine had become frozen faced when she'd told her. Alistair was away on business, so he would not be told until later.

'He will not be amused!' snapped Nadine, venting her annoyance by lacing a whip across Penny's bottom, seeing as Auberon's was no longer available.

Penny knew better than to protest, and her wrists were tied anyway. Afterwards she enjoyed sweet compensation lying in Nadine's arms and shivering with delight as the tall woman's cool fingers soothed her burning flesh.

'My brother will not be pleased,' Nadine said against her hair. 'You have a lot to make up to him, in time. Bear that in mind. Even now his desire for you is enormous, dammed up until I judge the moment to be right; only then will he take you. He will pleasure you to distraction time and time again, and you will be breathless, saturated with sex. You must not jeopardise that.'

As the fingers stroked her hair, the image of Alistair and his mighty phallus filled Penny's mind. Now she knew for sure that Alistair did desire her – that he, the wager and the stallion would be hers. She was afraid to ask questions on what Nadine had said. It was almost as if one misplaced word would be enough to melt what she had just said to her. So she just snuggled down more securely and let her imagination run riot as to how much pleasure Alistair might subject her to.

To the Beaumont family, dining out did not mean pub restaurant, local amateur, and certainly not something hurried and served with chips. Dining out was something to be done with style and in the best place available. Tonight was no exception.

White linen and fine, clear glassware were the norm at a restaurant privately owned by a famous chef – by one as noted for his fiery temper as for his excellent cuisine.

Waiters hovered, all white jackets, slick hair and heavy French accents. Despite their eyes always being lowered, Penny saw the odd flicker, knew that beneath their dark lashes they discerned the outline of her naked body. There was little between her and them except for the clinging sheath of the red dress, a colour that flattered her glorious dark hair and creamy complexion, yet left nothing to the imagination.

Tonight her hair was fastened from crown to nape by a pearl-edged comb so it fell in crowning waves like a horse's mane. Although her dress was silky and very short, she wore thigh high boots of soft red suede. She had protested to Nadine that they weren't really suitable for dining out, but Nadine, with unfamiliar humility and barely swallowed excitement, had knelt at her feet, pulling them up her legs and kissing her knees before they disappeared from view. As it turned out, the boots were well-suited to the dress. Both were red, both soft and pleasing to the touch.

Besides Alistair, Nadine, Gregory and Sir Reggie, Penny also found herself in the company of Dominic. His features were predominantly slavic; dark almond-shaped eyes – a hint of the Oriental. His hair, too, was dark, and tied back in a pony-tail. Broad shoulders promised a physique well worth looking at, the sturdiness of his legs perceptible beneath the classy cut of his trousers.

Alistair introduced the man. 'An associate of mine, Dominic Torsky.'

Instinctively, she knew Alistair was waiting for her reaction; a change in colour of her cheeks, an extra sparkle in her eyes. Very well. She would show him. If he wanted her to suck up to this guy, she would – and some!

'Dominic,' she enthused, smiling widely. 'How nice to meet you. Alistair has told me so much about you.' She accompanied her smile with a sudden flow of very obvious body language.

She saw the two men exchange glances. Then Dominic smiled – like a cat, intent on the bird he was about to capture or consume – yet she did not flinch.

'Has he indeed?' drawled an American accent. The eyebrows rose. The mouth widened further with amusement.

He was a man, Penny discerned, who was good-looking and knew it. To suck up to him would not be difficult at all. All the same, she cast a glance at Alistair, just to see how her attitude had affected him. His eyes glittered. Apart from that, he appeared unmoved. Somehow that annoyed her. She determined to press the point a little more.

'Well, of course! Alistair is such a dear old thing. Always willing to impart friendly little asides, amusing details about his business and the people he meets from all over the world – especially from America. What part of the States are you from?'

The whole statement was a complete fabrication, but she didn't care. She wanted to goad Alistair, aimed to secure a reaction.

'La Jolla, San Diego. Not too far from the border and Tijuana.'

'Sunshine all the way, then.'

'Most of the time, honey, most of the time.' His eyes twinkled as he ran them over her body, his lips twitching around a faint smile.

Briefly, Penny glanced at Alistair. His eyes glared. His expression was unreadable.

Penny looked instead to Nadine. Nadine's glare was like fire: powerful and all-consuming. In an instant, Penny's exuberance dissolved, almost as if it had never existed. In sudden panic, her eyes fluttered around the restaurant. It was as if it had suddenly been pointed out to her that she was naked except for her flimsy dress and high boots. As her face flushed, she lowered her eyes, bent her head and studied a spot somewhere between her feet.

She stayed quiet for the rest of the evening. Though she was not invited to join the conversation, she was very often the subject of it. There were comments made about her hair, her very blue eyes and her very well-made body. To her acute embarrassment, both Nadine and Sir Reggie gave an account of the sex scenes she had been the subject of since arriving at Beaumont Place. But it was strange how her embarrassment disappeared as their words continued. There was a glowing admiration laced like toffee in their words. They spoke of using her, doing this to her, doing that; and yet, adoration and fascination danced on their tongues.

Disbelieving the compliance of someone who appeared to have a strong character, Dominic asked Nadine to prove it. Smiling, she turned her face to Penny who was looking down now at her cutlery.

'Open your legs, my pretty pussy,' said Nadine once the waiters were out of earshot. Those at the table listened. Penny did as ordered, aware that the hem of her very short dress was riding up over her thighs so her sex was completely exposed. Nadine's hand tugged it a little higher. Her nails scraped Penny's thigh.

'Lift your bottom,' Nadine ordered.

Again, Penny complied. The dress went higher, covering her bottom, but exposing her cheeks and sex to the coldness of the chair covering. There were sighs of satisfaction from those around the table. Napkins dabbed at the residue of wine that clung to smiling lips. In confirmation, Dominic came round to get a light from

219

Nadine for his cigar. Inconspicuously, he moved the tablecloth and looked down into Penny's lap. Penny felt her face redden even more as he sucked in his breath. Briefly, her eyes surveyed the restaurant beyond her own little party. No one looked their way. They looked ordinary, even conservative. Once he had looked his fill, Dominic ran his hand down her back and, without anyone seeing, lifted her skirt. He groaned very low and very appreciatively before he let her hem fall and went back to his seat.

'Beautiful,' murmured Dominic. 'And compliant.'

Am I really compliant? Penny asked herself. But she knew she was. She revelled in what was happening to her. In this tight circle, she was the centre of attention. Her sex was exposed and she was theirs for the asking. When had this happened? she again asked herself. When had she become willing to bend to the will of others, and how could such a thing endow her with a greater sense of security than she had ever known?

'She still needs breaking in,' said Nadine amid a whirl of blue smoke and in a low voice that made the others smile with glee.

'Good!' exclaimed Dominic, as a waiter refilled his glass. 'Glad to hear it!'

Even Gregory, whose eyes had avoided her for most of the evening, appeared unduly excited and more involved with the others at the table than with her.

For the briefest moment, her eyes caught those of the wine waiter. He was staring at her cleavage. She felt Nadine's hand run up her thigh and her fingers tangle in her pubic hair. She turned to look at Nadine. Though the order was unspoken, Penny knew instinctively what was required of her. She hugged herself as though she was cold. As she did so, her breasts kissed each other and bulged upwards. Her nipples peeked over the top of her dress.

The wine bottle shook in the young waiter's hand. He managed to finish pouring, but once he was gone, those around the table clapped and told Nadine, rather than her, what a success the action had been.

220

They left the warmth, dim lights and excellent service behind. Outside the night was touched with silver by the light of a glassy moon in a cloudless sky. The breeze was warm, still loyal to summer although autumn was just a month away.

Gregory had the job of driving. Alistair sat in the passenger seat beside him, Penny squeezed between Reggie and Nadine at the back, and the headlights of Dominic's hired Range Rover shone into the back window.

Street lights and buildings were soon left behind as they entered the countryside, dark blankets pierced only with the odd island of farmhouse or cottage light.

Nadine kissed her ear. Rich breath assaulted her nostrils at the same time as the long fingers circled over her bare knee and crept upwards beneath the short red dress. 'Open your legs wider, pussy-cat,' she ordered, pulling Penny's knee towards her.

Mellowed to resignation by the heady mix of old wine and soft caresses, she did as ordered. Her right knee was pulled open by Nadine's hand, her left by Reggie's. Now there was no table to hide her exposed sex.

Their hands pushed under her dress, folding it upwards so the sweet drift of her musky scent escaped to the night. Nadine's hand on the right and Reggie's on the left began to caress the soft skin of her inner thighs. The car stopped suddenly, but the caresses did not. Gregory got out of the car. Through the windscreen, she could see him unlocking a high wrought-iron gate. Stark letters on a dark sign shouted *PRIVATE. Trespassers will be prosecuted, if not shot.* They drove through. Gregory got out again and locked the gate behind them. The car began to bounce along a roughly gravelled path. At times the moon's light was intercepted by black battalions of fir and pine which stood like silent sentinels at the side of the road.

Each hand climbed higher up the soft skin of her inner thighs, which were now wide open. Hot lips mouthed at her neck and breathed moist breath against her ears. Her own arms spread along the back of the seat, and she

221

viewed via the mirror the spark of excitement in the eyes of Alistair Beaumont. Her own eyes narrowed as whispers of blissful rapture issued freely from her lips.

As their prying fingers explored her, their free hands pulled down the bodice of her strapless dress until her breasts popped forward, exposed to the night and to their sucking mouths.

Unable to control her own delighted reactions, she moaned as the two hands prodded at her flooding pussy. Nadine's four fingers held one furry lip open, Reggie's four fingers the other. Two thumbs – one long and tipped with black nail varnish, the other, thicker and cleanly blunt – were positioned either side of her straining pink button, both squeezing towards the other.

Muffling her cries into her shoulder, she threw her head back and closed her eyes. Sir Reggie and Nadine took as much delight in watching her reactions as they did in assaulting her.

'You are so wet,' cooed Nadine close to her ear before dropping once again to suckle her hardening nipples. Her lips sucked at it, her teeth held it, pulled it hard and long to the point where Penny wanted to scream. But she didn't scream. She bit her lip, held her voice and let whatever was happening to her happen without protest.

Alistair, too, was watching, and even from here she could hear the quickness of his breathing; she could almost taste just how much he wanted her.

Through half-closed eyes, she saw him turn in his seat. She felt the intensity of his gaze on her face before his eyes dropped to the two heads sucking at her breasts, which then dropped again. He gasped, almost in agony, as he stared at her pink nether lips that were held so open, her sex so exposed.

Penny felt no shame in him looking at her open sex, the glistening and reddening of her clitoris as the thumbs of Nadine and Reggie squeezed it to full prominence and coaxed it out of the protection of its folded hood. She wanted him to look, wanted to please him, arouse him. How could he not be aroused when she was being so exposed, so used?

222

Just when she thought the sucking mouths and probing thumbs would bring her to climax, the car stopped and the action ceased.

She started to pull her bodice back up over her breasts. Alistair's trembling voice stopped her.

'No. Leave your breasts exposed. It's a warm night.'

'A very warm night,' added Nadine before nibbling one last time at one of Penny's already red and stretched nipples. 'One moment,' she ordered suddenly.

From the seat beside her, Nadine brought out a collar. Even in the dimness of the car, Penny could see it was made of leather, but covered with velvet and set with what looked like diamonds, but were more likely rhinestones.

'For you, pretty pussy,' said Nadine as she kissed Penny's cheeks and fastened the collar around her neck with a strong buckle. 'And this,' she said, 'is for me.'

A chain was fastened to the collar and attached to the thick leather wrist bracelet that Nadine was wearing.

As usual Nadine's outfit was black, but strangely unprepossessing for her. Suddenly she took it off. Beneath it was something more to her style, similar to the sort of thing Roman gladiators or charioteers had worn, except that, over the metal breastplate, Nadine's nipples protruded, rouged bright red and very prominent.

'Follow me,' she said to Penny whose dress was still wound down to her waist, its hem high and showing her rounded bottom and naked sex. It was nothing much more than a red band around her middle that just happened to match the high boots she wore.

The heels of her red suede boots sank into the soft ground, but once Nadine guided her to the path, her step was sure, though somewhat artificial; a bit like a ballerina going on points for the first time.

Chain tugging at her collar, her breasts, bottom and sex exposed, Penny followed Nadine, but raised her hands to cover her breasts as Dominic's car drew in behind them.

'Uncover yourself, girl,' barked Alistair. 'Nadine!' he

223

added, turning on his sister as though she had been careless. Sudden panic registered on Nadine's face before her usual self-control returned.

'Hands on hips, my little filly!' Nadine exclaimed, and Penny wondered just for a moment why she was suddenly a 'filly' instead of the usual 'pretty pussy'. In confirmation, she felt the sting of a light riding whip across her bottom and was vaguely aware that Nadine had been wearing it at her waist. She yelped with surprise though the heat of the stroke was taken by the night breeze. But she obeyed and rested her hands on her hips. Now, what with her careful steps and her hands on her hips, she knew she was swaggering provocatively, her bottom swaying and her breasts pointing steadfastly forward, nipples raised deliciously by the night air. The night, she told herself, belonged to her no matter what might happen. And what a beautiful night it was. Crisp scents of pine, wild flowers and earthy fern acted as a natural aphrodisiac to her inborn sensuality. Silver moonlight gave sharp outlines to the nodding pines and to the figures and objects around her. It added grandeur to what was plain, magnificence to what was ordinary.

'Take your dress off,' ordered Alistair.

She hesitated, her hands hovering over her breasts and her eyes flitting between the handsome, steadfastly staring Dominic and the powerful presence of Alistair.

'Off, pretty pussy.' Nadine's hands on one side, Reggie's on the other and her dress was around her ankles, her skin translucent in the moonlight. She leaned her bottom against a tree as they pulled the dress off over her feet; the roughness of the trunk scratched her soft cheeks.

Her hands hung by her side, her fingers folding into her palms. Not wishing to ascertain her fate in their eyes, she stared down at the length of her long red boots.

She thought of Nadine not being pleased about Clarissa and Auberon; about Gregory and her. What was it she had said? You have to be broken, my pretty pussy, like a colt or a filly. Earlier, back there when they had got out of the car, she had called her a filly.

224

A pleasant thought came to her head and filled her with excitement. Tonight could be it. Tonight she might very well have Alistair. It had to be. If it wasn't tonight, then the time was not far off. Triumph was in sight.

'Let's walk.' Again, Alistair had taken control. Tonight, he was like a Roman emperor in charge of the games. Nadine, if her attitude and attire were anything to go by, was the ringmaster, the intermediary between those who entertained and him who was to be entertained.

The path through the trees was firm at first, then softer as high trees hid the moonlight. The ground gave slightly under her heels, and wisps of long grass tickled her thighs.

Under cover of darkness, unseen hands caressed her body as she walked. Even without the hands, the experience of walking naked except for a pair of high leather boots through a woodland in the night air caused havoc to her senses. Half with the sensation of fresh air over her skin, and half with the experience of walking naked among others still clothed, Penny's nipples thrust forward expectantly, and that familiar sweet ache arose between her legs. Whatever they might expect of her, she expected much of herself. Soon, her arousal would be undeniable. Her flesh quivered, and honey dew seeped from her sex and spread like silver threads through the darkness of her pubic bush.

The trees at last gave way to a circular clearing where the moon bathed the grass with its crystal glow.

Penny, her breasts rising with her breath, made a strong effort to focus her eyes as Nadine tugged her forward. The impression that she was entering an arena was very strong, and stronger when she espied what looked like fences around its perimeter. None of the fences were more than three feet high, low enough for a pony or even a human. And that, she realised, was what they were for. Not an equine jumper, but a human one.

'Very nice spot you've got here, Alistair old buddy,' she heard Dominic say. 'Nice fences. Cute little filly.'

'Here we go, my pretty pussy,' said a familiar voice

225

near her ear. 'Here's your big chance.' The words were hushed.

The men had formed a half-circle in front of her, whilst Nadine placed something over Penny's head. She started, realising it was a bridle that had been fashioned for a human head. In case of protest – of which she gave no sign – Dominic's strong hands grabbed Penny's and held them behind her as Nadine strapped the bridle over her head and pushed the metal bit between her teeth. The bridle had blinkers attached to it. She could only look straight ahead.

Dominic kissed her ear. 'Steady girl. You'll be all the better for this. All the better.'

She calmed, remembering that the sort of words he was using were not dissimilar to those she used on her own horses when she had broken them in to the showjumping ring. Anyway, just the closeness of Dominic was a kind of tranquilliser. He smelt good; the richness of cloth and his maleness combined to form a natural aphrodisiac.

Her hands were bound and fastened high behind her back, then clipped to the velvet-covered rhinestone collar which was still around her neck.

The coldness of the bit was hard upon her tongue. The blinkers had ties hanging from them in case they wished to blindfold her. These were left untied. Thankfully, she could still see most of what was going on, though she was incredibly constrained, restricted by a harness more usually used on horses.

More leather with a chain hanging down the front was fastened over her shoulders, fashioned like the outline of a normal bra but having no cups. Her breasts were pushed up and forward by its circling of leather. She gasped as it was tightened beneath her breasts so that they were held obscenely high. She gasped again as the shoulder-straps were adjusted so her breasts looked rounder and thrust out even more. She watched as Nadine's supple fingers teased at her nipples, then pulled them out so they were obscenely dominant, darkly pink in the light of the moon. The chain which hung from each

226

shoulder was left dangling. Then Nadine brought it up before Penny's eyes.

'See?' she said with delight, her usual cheroot stuck in the corner of her mouth. 'Nipple clamps.'

Penny saw. They appeared to be made of brass, like the chain. Nadine opened and closed the clamps in her fingers. They were reminiscent of bulldog clips used to grip paper together. She winced as they gripped her nipples, her cry of anguish lost in the coldness of the bit that lay so heavy on her tongue.

Something else was clipped on to the collar that encircled her neck. She couldn't see what. His eyes shining almost with reverence, she saw Gregory hand Dominic the lunging whip and knew immediately what was expected of her. In Dominic's other hand, he held the end of the lead rein that had been clipped to her collar. She would be urged to circle him, persuaded with the aid of the lunging whip. Her stomach tightened against itself and shivers of apprehension sent goosebumps over her skin.

'Walk on.' The voice was Dominic's. He stood about twelve feet away from her in the middle of the ring, a usual distance when lunging a green horse in a practice ring over jumps. The lunge whip easily reached, thick at the end where it was held in the hand and tapering to extreme thinness at the other. Its thin end tapped gently against her buttocks. It stung, and she held her breath. She walked where he directed, about ten feet in front of the first obstacle. There was no way of knowing where everyone else was, the blinkers shielded her side-view and prevented her seeing them. She could only look straight ahead and fasten her eyes upon the job in hand; the jump that came up to meet her. Now she knew how her horses felt.

'Trot.' The fine thread of the whip end laced enticingly over her behind and a cry of surprise caught in her throat. Her breasts jiggled, held tight as they were in their casing of leather.

She sprang over the first obstacle on command, the tail end of the whip assisting her concentration as it spread

227

again over her buttocks. Stumbling a little on landing, she righted herself, glad that the boots she was wearing had such a good grip.

'Higher this time,' cried Dominic. The sting of the whip was more intense. She'd received a reprimand, and although a fine film of sweat broke out over her skin, her flesh tingled in welcome. Strangely enough, she had a pride in what she was doing, what she had achieved. She, too, could jump with or without the whip, though the whip did add a certain piquancy to the achievement.

Another fence was cleared, a higher one. This time, she made no mistake, but knew it would not matter. She tensed the cheeks of her behind waiting for the inevitable, welcoming the warmth and the admiration of her compatriots with each succeeding sting on her flesh. This time, the whip stung more, but her cry was lost in the rush of air, her tongue trapped beneath the bit. Three more jumps were all cleared, yet all were accompanied by the stinging of the whip.

How red her bottom must be by now. It was warm. That, at least, she *could* feel. Would its pinkness be easily seen in the whiteness of moonlight? Probably it would. That was really, she decided, what they were applauding, what they were admiring. Not her skill on jumping the fences, but the increasing response of her creamy flesh to the stinging rebuke of the lunging whip. She was rising to the whip as though she were throwing it off and tossing its torture aside. Applause greeted her clearing of the last jump. Hands patted her red rump, as much to feel its heat as for congratulation.

'Now. Shall we try her on drive?' Murmurs of agreement greeted Dominic's suggestion. Penny tensed, her breasts starting to rise and fall more swiftly. Did they really mean what she thought they meant? To drive a horse meant to break him to harness. For that they would need a cart or chariot. But there was nothing here. Only the jumps.

'It's folded up back in Dom's car. Can someone come

228

and fetch it with me?' It was Nadine who ordered Gregory to accompany her.

Penny heard them return a few minutes later.

'Cover her eyes. Saves her worrying about the new harness.' Alistair said that. It seemed to be him who wanted her blindfolded. Initial panic was overridden by curiosity. How would it feel to be driven at his command, to be his beast of burden, his creature in harness? The closing of the blinkers over her eyes was all part of it. He was denying her knowledge, taking all as his enjoyment alone. And Nadine, as usual, was in charge of it all. It was her long, cool fingers that tied the blinkers together above Penny's nose. A leather belt was fastened around Penny's waist. She felt another piece dangling from it at the front, then hands pulling it through her legs.

'Open your legs, pretty pussy. Let's see what we've got.'

Penny obliged, aware that, despite her leather restraints, her sex was moist from the excesses of her own imagination. Her breath was sharp as some protrusion on the leather was pushed into her vagina. It felt solid and roughly the size of a medium erection. Despite crying out, she took it in. The leather thong continued to be pulled through her legs.

'Bend over, pussy-cat.'

A heavy hand on her head – it could only be male – forced her head down so her rear was up. She was highly aware of the intruder in her sex, so much so that she wriggled against it, all else forgotten.

'A little oil I think.' The voice was Reggie's and brought her back to reality. She felt the fatness of his finger rubbing oil around her anus, diving in to lubricate her more fully. She groaned as he did it, her knees bending as he pushed it in, her head pushing against the hand that held her steady.

She gasped, her head firmly held as the cheeks of her bottom were divided, the leather brought up and another protrusion – smaller than the one she enjoyed in her vagina – pushed into her rear orifice. It might not have

229

been quite as big as the other, but it was bigger than the finger that had oiled that same hole. Once both protrusions were firmly embedded in her body, then the leather strap was buckled tightly into the belt that circled her waist, her head was released and she could straighten up.

Penny groaned, and her breasts rose and fell with her quickened breathing. She could see nothing, but imagined what she looked like from the feeling her constraints gave her.

The strap that ran from her leather belt divided the fleshy lips of her sex. The muscles of her open sex and invaded anus constricted against the imitation phalli. The cheeks of her bottom were separated, made more rounded by the leather thong which she guessed was strapped tightly into the belt around her waist.

Because she could not see what they had done, her senses were heightened. Juice flowed freely around the imitation phallus, and against the back of her thighs. She was intrigued by the light touch of something wispy, like hair or feathers. The breeze blew it against her skin. With a blush that seemed to run from her head to her toes, she realised that the appendage that invaded her anus had a tail of long hair attached to it. To all intents and purposes, she was a mare, a mare to be broken.

There was movement at each side of the leather belt. She knew that the shafts of some small cart had been attached, she moved slightly, felt the rolling of wheels and the pull of something behind her – something that was attached to her.

'Keep still.' She judged the voice to be Dominic's again, and sucked through her teeth as he tapped across her belly with the whip.

'She looks a treat. Don't you think so, dear brother?' purred the dark voice of Nadine.

'So far, so good,' Penny heard him reply in a rasping way that seemed almost to crack his throat apart. He sounded entirely absorbed in what was going on; as though he were falling down a pothole and was thoroughly enjoying the experience. 'Depends on how she makes out, of course. Once Dominic's up in the driver's seat, lead her on blind. Get her used to the cart going behind her.'

This was crazy and sublime all at the same time. Here she was allowing herself to be led blindfolded and naked around this impromptu ring in the middle of the woods, harnessed like a horse to some small chariot where a driver sat, reins and whip in hand.

She felt the pressure of the reins against the bit, then a hand holding the reins next to her mouth, leading her forward.

'Walk on, pretty pussy. My brother is watching you.' The voice was low and husky and promised her much if she would only submit to what was expected of her.

Accompanied by a flick from the whip across her back, she stepped forward. The cart was light, although she was aware of there being a weight within it. She could not bend to pull it, her whole body held upright by virtue of the straps that held her to the shafts.

The strap that passed through her legs was being tightened, digging in more deeply between her pouting cheeks, and she felt the intruding rod to which the tail was attached being pushed further in. It didn't matter. The juices flowed more copiously, her legs trembling with delight in response to the mix of sensations that raced like electricity through her body.

The whip again grazed her back, the tip of it flicking across one cheek of her bottom. She gasped with the pleasurable shock, her breasts thrusting out more prominently as her back straightened.

'Walk on.'

She felt herself being guided at the order, then heard the light rumbling of the wheels behind her and felt the pressure of the weight in the light vehicle.

'Very nice little filly. Very nice indeed.' The voice had to be Reggie's.

'See how they like you, my wild little filly.' She felt one of Nadine's hands pat her bottom.

'Trot on.'

At Nadine's urging and the voice and whip of Dom-

231

inic, Penny did as required. Her breasts jiggled against their restricted suspension, and the friction of the two dildos embedded inside made her moan with delight despite her bondage. She was reaching the point of no return, the point when she would not be able to hold back her climax any longer.

As if sensing her imminent orgasm, Nadine grabbed her bridle, slowed her to a halt and spoke. 'The little mare's coming.'

'Stop. She's broken enough. Take off the blinkers.'

The sound of Alistair's voice made her tremble. Just before the blinkers were removed, she felt a trickle of sweat course down her cleavage and turn cold. Between her thighs, the fluid was hot and flowing unabated.

She wanted to walk on, to feel the false phalli grind themselves into her flesh. But for the moment, she was denied movement. Her senses were pushed to their height, yet sexual relief was denied.

Nadine moved away. The whip flicked across Penny's back, on to one buttock then another. She began to move forward, aware of the contraption coming along behind her. Why, she wondered, did tears of pain spring to her eyes when all she was feeling was pleasure, a gratefulness for not having to make any decision for herself, for being at someone else's beck and call?

'Even better, once she's completely broken. I'll try a trot next.' Without waiting for the whip or any urging from Dominic, Penny broke into a trot, congratulating herself for avoiding the whip.

'Whoa!' Dominic cried out. 'Whoa!'

The reins pulled against the bit in her mouth. Her head jerked.

'I didn't tell you to go, you stupid mare.' The whip lashed across her back three or four times, flicking also against her trussed-up arms. Then, he did the same to each pearlike cheek of her bottom. Her breath was taken away with each stroke, her eyes rolled and her body quivered.

She returned to a walk, then waited for the urging she

knew was to come. With the landing of the whip on her back then on each cheek, she broke into a trot.

The cart seemed amazingly light even at this pace and they must have cut quite a dash. Everyone began to clap with approval. Somehow, it made Penny feel quite proud. She lifted her knees higher and felt her nipples tremble beneath the grip of the nipple clamps.

'Well done, old sport,' cried Reggie. 'Well done.'

Sweating under the pulling of the reins, she came to a halt. The shaking was hard to stop, brought on as it was by the rubbing of the leather and the movement of the items that filled her vagina and her anus. When would she be allowed her orgasm? she asked herself. When?

'Well done.' Hands patted her, pinched her nipples so the clamps bit more sharply. Fingers slid down the leather thong that divided her labia and the cheeks of her behind.

'And now for your oats,' said Dominic as he came down from off the driving seat and stood beside her.

Within the shafts of the cart, she trembled with a mix of spent energy and excitement. She felt eyes upon her, though it was difficult to see who they belonged to with the blinkers still in place, even though they had now been opened. She sensed they were all waiting for Alistair to give an order. How the ache between her legs was to be cured was entirely up to him. She welcomed that. It was just another step towards impressing him, so that at some time he would have to take her, too. She wondered again whether he would take her tonight. But she'd wondered that before. Nevertheless, the prospect excited her.

'There, my pretty pussy. Not so bad, was it?'

Her eyes regarded Nadine. She tried to respond. Sounds came from her mouth, indiscernible noises fragmented by the piece of metal that still lay across her tongue. She felt her hands being untied, the shafts unfettered from the belt around her waist.

'Soaking wet,' said Nadine sliding her hand between Penny's legs as Dominic removed the belt from around her waist, and with it the one that ran between her legs

233

and intruded in her sex and anus. The bridle and breast halter were left in place.

She remembered the tree. They had passed it earlier. It was smooth like a silver birch, but larger, its lower branches devoid of leaves and bathed in moonlight. Each of Penny's wrists was strapped to its lower branches, one either side of its trunk. Straps were added to her ankles. She felt them being pulled apart and knew that once she was securely bound she formed an 'X' against the silver bark of the tree.

'Eyes.' That was all Alistair said.

Again, the blinkers were strapped together so she could see nothing. But she didn't need to. She knew what was to come, though who from she couldn't really tell.

'Well, my dear. How exposed you look now. How submissive the high and mighty rider who thought she could conquer all. But not everything can be conquered. Even I know that. Each of us has to have our own moment of humility, has to give a little of ourselves to the will of others. It's good to do that, good to depend on someone else for something, relying on their good judgement to enhance our own perceptions, our own lives.'

She knew it was Alistair. Deep inside, she knew exactly what he was talking about. The hidden woman who'd walked half-naked with him on a busy lunch-hour knew more now than she did then. She had found her real self and also found a place where that self could be fully released. Just the sound of his voice made her hips jerk forward. She pleaded for him to take her, to push his member into her sex. Even though her words were unintelligible, he took their meaning, knew what she wanted and what he would not – in fact, could not – let her have.

'Patience, my dear Miss Bennet,' he said in a soft, gentle voice that wrapped around her like a warm blanket. 'Patience. You have given me what I desire tonight. Now I will give you your reward.'

She knew he had walked away, and she heard him and the others talking. They were discussing how prominent and white her breasts looked in the moonlight, how

234

gleaming were her thighs with that glistening of sweat burnishing her skin. What a beautiful pink was that treasure in between, and how glossy was that patch of hair from where her humid sex pouted for individual attention!

Someone's breathing was suddenly close to her. Fingers pinched at the clips that still adorned her nipples. Small cries of pained ecstasy escaped from her throat and over the metal bit as they pinched some more. Hot lips kissed the hollow between her throat and shoulders. The flesh she felt against her was hot and naked. Chest hair tickled at her breasts and belly before the head of a hot thrusting penis tapped against her mound. Her mouth strained against the bit, longing to cry out in ecstasy as his penis parted her nether lips, pushing them to either side like a plough turning a furrow.

Her groan was low in her throat as she felt real flesh enter where before only a hard imitation had invaded. She tilted her hips towards him, welcoming the life-and-blood intruder filling her from entrance to womb. She rocked as he rocked, their pubes intertwined and rasping one thick nest against the other. His hands covered her breasts, pushed the clips on tighter. Her nipples responded, engorged with the blood of desire, rampant extensions of the fire that was burning between her legs. This cock, she decided, belonged to either Alistair or Dominic. It had to be, though it was difficult to tell.

She felt the loins of her intruder tense, heard the breathing climb to gasping climax. Then he was rammed tight within her. He had come, and she still had not.

She wriggled as he slid out of her. It was her only sign of protest before she felt someone else against her, someone with firm smooth thighs and a hard cock that dived into her with no preliminary explorations. His chest was held away; she felt this coupling only from the waist down.

She cried out. Excitement filled her as she felt cool fingers trail deliciously over her nipples. Confused, she frowned beneath the blinkers. The loins and thighs thrust in constant tempo back and forth against her. Her breath

235

caught in her throat, her head felt dizzy as this hardness filled her, and the tempo was strictly adhered to so her clitoris was fully rubbed and excited. This was the best so far, she told herself. It had to be Alistair.

Sensing her rising orgasm, the tempo of the lunging penis increased and the fingers pinched more determinedly at her entrapped breasts. She was beyond the point of no return and gasped in a long mutated moan against the bit as currents of release spurted like a red-hot fountain from her sex.

The body that had coupled with hers jerked in orgasm. She herself cried out again as the invading penis was rammed into her again and again with renewed force, each thrust making her shudder and resent it ever leaving. One last hard push, and it was all over. The body fell against her. The breath was sweet, a mixture of tobacco, rich food and good wine. The lips were warm and gentle, the teeth achingly familiar. Small breasts rubbed against hers.

'And how was that my pretty pussy, my broken-in little filly?'

Surprise and humiliation invaded her mind. *Nadine* had taken her in front of these people, and she had responded. Nadine wearing a false cock. How could she have been so fooled into thinking it was Alistair?

She muttered her anguish. Heard the cheers and claps from those assembled.

'She didn't know. She really didn't know,' Nadine cried, her exclamation bringing chuckles from those gathered. 'But it was good,' Nadine purred into Penny's ear before kissing the pinkness of her cheek. 'You have to admit that. And Alistair enjoyed it,' she whispered. 'He's almost there, at his height. And when I judge he's fully there . . .'

Penny stopped wriggling and instead felt elated. She was grateful for the kiss of affection. It calmed her, and the words Nadine had whispered in her ear gave rise to other thoughts and other things. Judging by what Nadine had just whispered to her, the time was coming fast when Alistair, the wager and the stallion would all be hers.

236

Chapter Thirteen

'You are almost ready, my dear brother,' said Nadine, her finger flicking at the small key that hung just behind her earring.

'And Miss Bennet?' he asked, his eyes studying the business reports on his lap as they drove down the motorway after seeing Dominic off at Heathrow.

Nadine smiled at her brother. 'I think so, I will make certain she's completely open to you. She'll need some stamina to cope. I'll have to be sure she's got that.'

'Ariadne says she has the stamina, and from what I've see so far . . .' Alistair eyed his sister almost accusingly, as though her further treatment of Penny was more for her own benefit than his.

Nadine's eyes met his at first, but did not hold him. Instead, she looked out of the car window as though the industrial fringes of London and Reading were suddenly interesting.

He smiled knowingly and turned his eyes back to the *Financial Times*. 'I won't condemn you for enjoying her body. I think she enjoys yours equally as much, even what you do to her.'

Surprised, Nadine looked back to her brother. 'Nonsense! She's putty in my hands because she's frightened of me. I am totally in control of her. Totally!'

She spat the last word as though she didn't quite

believe it herself. Alistair did not answer, but the smile that dimpled the edges of his mouth was enough to tell her that he didn't believe what she said, that *his* judgement of Penny Bennet differed from her own.

'Everything will go off as before. Once you've had her, we can send her packing.'

Alistair rustled his paper somewhat impatiently. 'Somehow,' he said, his eyes not leaving what he was reading, 'I don't think it will be the same as before. I perceive our Miss Bennet has deeper inclinations than we at first gave her credit for.'

This time it was Nadine who did not answer.

'You enjoyed it, pretty pussy. You can't deny it,' said a lounging Nadine. 'I can see it in your eyes.'

Penny stretched, smiling to herself and closing her eyes so she could relive the performance in the forest and keep her pleasure to herself. A while back before coming here she would never have dreamed of admitting that she liked being overpowered, humiliated and made to submit to those around her. Something had been awakened within her and, once roused, it was not likely to be dormant again.

She felt Nadine's teeth hard against her nipples, caught her breath as she sucked, pulling the flesh outwards, nibbling gently so the moans in her throat progressed to low yelps of pleasure.

'How can you say that?' she asked between moans of delight. 'You don't know how I felt. Only *I* know that, only *I* had that . . .'

'Pleasure? Lie back, pretty pussy,' Nadine ordered, pushing her back against the pillow. 'Lie back and remember with pleasure.'

Naked and compliant, Penny obeyed, arms stretched above her head, breasts obscenely pouting towards the ceiling. Her skin shivered with rising apprehension, her hips rose and buttocks clenched as her mind took over her senses.

Nadine's lips kissed hers, promised her pleasure, promised her Alistair. She felt the buried heat of Nadine's

238

sex brush against her as the long legs straddled her and held her clamped at the hips. The warm palms and long fingers toyed with her breasts, teased them to grow and harden. Nadine pushed Penny's breasts together so they almost formed one mass, bulging, and ripe as fresh melons. She divided them, pushed them towards Penny's face, invited her to lick them herself. With a little dexterity and bending of the neck, she did, her own skin feeling soft and silky beneath her tongue.

With the push from a gentle but firm hand, she lay back again on the pillow. Much as she wanted what Nadine was giving her, there was something else she wanted more, something she didn't have, and, because she didn't have it, she wanted. That was the trouble with being a winner; you had to be a winner in everything.

'When do I get Alistair?' she moaned through her groaning pleasure.

'When you have experienced everything. When you are completely at the whim of your own sexuality, your own blazing sensations. I must make sure you are ready for that.'

'When? How? Can't I get there faster?'

Nadine stiffened. Her hands tensed.

'You *are* impatient, my little pussy-cat. Much too impatient. You want to gallop before you've learned to trot.' It was obvious she was referring to the event in the woods, when Penny had been on the receiving end of what she usually gave out.

'But I will help you get there quicker. I will help you learn.'

She felt regret when Nadine dismounted. There was a comfort in her straddling, a warm welcome in the denuded sex that sat so sublimely, so damp and warm, against her own flat stomach.

'Sit up a moment.'

Penny did as she was told. From the bedside cabinet that was overly decorated with carved nymphs and over-endowed satyrs, Nadine took a dog collar that Penny had noticed earlier.

'Kneel on the floor,' Nadine demanded. Her body

239

already warming to anything that was about to happen, Penny knelt at the side of the bed. Nadine fastened the collar around her neck, her manner changing as much as her voice.

The leather was rough against Penny's neck, the buckle cold, yet already her sexual juices were flowing, and her stomach was tightening with rising excitement.

A willing participant, Penny held her arms high as Nadine wound a silk scarf around her back, bringing each end beneath her breasts. She took the ends up through her cleavage, dividing her breasts then tying the scarf at the nape of Penny's neck. Her breasts were parted, pushed up and outwards. The effect was not exactly unattractive. There was a pouting sensuality in it, a demand for bodily attention. Penny arched her back and, over the tightness of her collar, watched them leap to greater prominence.

'Stand up!' Nadine demanded.

Sensing there was more to come, and more she could not help but welcome, Penny did as ordered.

In the long, low chests of drawers that outmatched the bedside cabinet with the wealth of carvings and the acrobatic couplings defined, Nadine seemed to have a whole collection of silk scarves.

'Over here,' she ordered. 'Now!' she shouted as Penny threw in a hint of rebellion into the part she was about to play.

Nadine was pointing at the dressing-table stool which she had placed up against the wall. 'Straddle it,' she ordered.

Her hand flipped around Penny's head. She had started to sit down on it, legs wide apart. 'No. Not like that; I want you stood up.'

Penny did as ordered so she was stood upright, her legs either side of the width of the stool so she could not possibly close her legs. Nadine passed from one side of her to the other, tying first one of her legs to a leg of the stool with a sheer-silk scarf, then the other. The stool was fairly wide, and so were Penny's legs; her quim balanced above the seat of the stool. Fascinated by the vulner-

240

ability of her position, she ran her hands down over her belly and briefly touched the pink hood of her sex that stood to attention in the midst of her parted lips. She had a sudden need for a climax, yet also had an inkling that such a thing would not be allowed.

'Stop that. It's for *me* to touch, not you!'

Nadine's hands hit hers away, then caught them together and held them in her own.

'Hands above head,' she ordered, and Penny obeyed.

Her eyes followed Nadine as she went back to the drawer. There was a light tinkling of metal, like jewellery falling in folds, one chain upon another. Then Nadine was before her.

'More learning. More discipline,' said Nadine, her face near enough to Penny's to kiss. Surprisingly, she did not kiss her, and that made Penny disappointed. Instead, her quick fingers clipped fine chains to the collar around her neck. They felt cold yet light over her bosoms before Nadine took hold of them and threw them over Penny's shoulders so they dangled down her back.

'Lower your hands.'

Penny did so, and let her gaze sweep the floor as Nadine took them, then forced them behind her back and fastened them there, the fine ends of the chains strong and hard around her wrists.

'Very nice,' said Nadine as she stood back a while, finger on lips to admire her handiwork.

Penny was bound and secure, her hands immobile, her breasts pushed into the position Nadine wished to achieve. Her legs were permanently parted over the divide of the stool.

'What a sight you look, my pretty pussy,' she purred, her fingers pinching Penny's cheek before both hands dropped to her thrusting breasts.

'If you say so,' said Penny with a sigh.

'Silence!'

Nadine slapped Penny's face and she bit her lip. There was heat where Nadine's palm had landed. It wasn't unexpected. She now knew the way Nadine's games were played and knew her own part in them. She had to give rise, had to give excuses for abuse. Again, the question came into her head. Who was really the mistress? Her, or Nadine?

'You say nothing! Is that clear?' The hand slapped the other cheek, so that one burned, too.

'Yes . . . Yes.'

'Nothing!' said Nadine, slapping her again. 'Just nod. Or, better still, bow.'

Penny bowed, knowing full well that was what Nadine really wanted. Her breasts dangled alluringly as she did so. She fully expected Nadine to fall to temptation and cup them in her hands. Surprisingly, she didn't. So she straightened back up, longing for Nadine to get on with what she was going to do. Her excitement was already causing her sex to become more moist and making her bud of passion break free from its protective hood as it sought sexual release.

Whilst she had been bowed, Nadine had fastened another chain to the collar and attached that to the wall lamp above Penny's head. She was fixed to the spot unable to move even if she wanted to.

Nadine ran her hand from breasts, over belly to the triangle of dark fur that divided her quaking thighs. Penny gulped, mindful of controlling any sound she might make. Not that she was protesting. The only sounds threatening to escape her throat were moans of pleasure, and of surprise that she should enjoy what was happening to her so much.

'Wet, my pretty,' said Nadine as her index finger played with the cluster of fleshy petals that surrounded her yearning clitoris. 'Very wet. Very ready. No, no, no,' she cried suddenly, waving the glistening finger in front of Penny's face. 'Not yet, my pretty pussy. Not yet. Time to contemplate. Time to think, for you, not for me.' Her teeth shone white and straight, and her eyes glinted like chips of ice.

Penny tensed as Nadine moved behind her. She shivered compulsively as the long fingers ran over her expectant flesh. Her muscles clenched as she felt the glistening finger slide between her buttocks. Nadine

242

parted each cheek from the other. An illicit finger prodded at her anal bud, which tightened reflexively.

'Stand easy, my pretty pussy,' Nadine murmured. 'My pleasure is your pleasure. My wish is yours.'

She moved to Penny's side, her face and eyes close to her own. Penny looked at the pale complexion, the light eyes that seemed at times to be entirely devoid of colour.

'Now,' said Nadine, in a tone that made Penny think she had not quite finished with her bondage just yet, 'complete meditation. That's what you need. I will give it to you, and you will be thankful for it.'

Penny opened her mouth, then remembered she must be silent. She only nodded on account of the chain that fastened her to the wall-light branch behind her head.

'First,' said Nadine, with great aplomb and obvious enjoyment, 'silence.'

The scarf she tied around her mouth was of soft red silk.

'And', Nadine added, her tongue running over her lips with a relish that made Penny a little nervous, 'darkness.'

Penny attempted to protest, but her words were muffled by the scarf that gagged her mouth. Nadine tied another scarf around her eyes. Complete darkness, complete bondage; her protests were silenced. This vulnerability she was being subjected to made her tremble with apprehension. Fear was one part of it, but excitement the other.

'A little rest,' Nadine whispered into her ear. 'A time for contemplation, a few moments to think about what I will do when I come back.'

Penny wanted to ask where she was going, what she was doing. Her words were only mumbles muttered into the softness of the material. She didn't see her go, but only heard the door close softly.

She tried to move. She couldn't. Her head was held firmly against the wall light by the short chain that was attached to her collar. Her hands were between her back and the wall, her legs spread and tied either side of the stool. Her sex was wide open.

Time seemed to trickle by and her legs began to ache.

She strained her ears for footsteps, but only heard rustles from outside – night birds and the sound of the motorway traffic in the far distance. Her excitement subsided.

Her senses readjourned as she heard the door open, and felt a cold draught from the passageway outside that caressed her bare flesh and brought it back to its previous awareness. Trembling with mounting excitement, she straightened, thrust her breasts forward as if inviting a touch, however cruel or hard it might be. To have no contact, to be alone with her sexuality, was something she found hard to bear.

'Well, pussy-cat. Are you ready for more?'

Penny nodded vigorously. Her breath caught in her throat as she felt something cold being clamped over each nipple. The clamps had returned.

'How does that feel, my pretty?' said Nadine, her words purring with her tongue against her ear.

Penny mumbled into her gag. Nadine took her cue, longing for a chance to chastise any hint of rebellion in her more than willing subject. It felt as though she were exerting more pressure on to the clamps with her own fingers. Penny winced, and sweat broke out in a fine sheen over her skin as Nadine pushed two fingers inside the leather collar that circled her neck.

'No words. Just actions. Push your pelvis forward for *yes*, move it from side to side for *no*.'

Penny thrust her pelvis forward.

'Good little pussy,' said Nadine. Like she had before, she ran her hand down over Penny's dark triangle and used her fingertip to coax Penny's hiding clitoris from among its crown of flesh.

'Wet again?' Again the hands moved around to her back – tantalising her spine – and over her buttocks, that jutted at an angle from the wall by virtue of the shape of the stool.

Penny felt the finger slide down the cleft in between and wipe its wetness around her puckered orifice as if preparing it for future events.

Then there was nothing. No touch, no sound, just the slamming of the door.

244

She wriggled her hips, longed to get her thighs together, her hands free, so she could at least pleasure herself and ease the demands of her aroused sex.

It was no use. She was as firmly bound as ever, as unable to get to her inflamed sex as she had been before. Her nipples ached, reflecting the ache of her groin.

Again, time trickled by. This time her ardour did not dissipate completely; the clamps on her nipples saw to that. Like two extensions to her humid sex, they throbbed with arousal, sending messages of excitement all over her body. She trembled, her state of readiness maintained at a constant level as she awaited Nadine's return.

With a sudden surge of excitement, she heard the door open.

'I'm back.' Nadine's lips were hot and moist against her ear. Her body seemed clothed, whilst Penny's was naked.

Softly, Nadine's fingers and palms trailed beneath each thrusting breast before running down over Penny's stomach to her moist sex. Penny murmured ecstatically against her gag. It didn't matter that she couldn't see her tormentor; it was just enough to know she was there, that she had not been forgotten and left to just her fantasies.

'Just a little more exhilaration, another little toy to keep you on the boil.'

As Nadine's fingers dived into her soaking vagina, Penny gasped and thrust her hips to meet it.

'Yes, my pretty pussy,' laughed Nadine. 'Yes. You like that, don't you?'

Penny thrust her hips forward again in agreement. She didn't want another slap. She wanted an intrusion into her inner sanctum. She didn't care who gave it her as long as she got it.

Tears of frustration welled up behind the blindfold as Nadine withdrew her fingers and traced them down over Penny's back as she had before. She felt her own bodily wetness being spread around her tight orifice; her cheeks were held firmly open.

245

'Just a little toy,' murmured Nadine, the delight in her actions self-evident from her voice.

Penny's hips moved forward almost of their own accord as something wet, smooth and long was pushed into her anus. Her cheeks clenched compulsively over it, holding it securely to herself.

'That's right. Hold it in there. Enjoy its unique delight.'

Penny gasped, and found it almost impossible to relax around the foreign object. When she did, whatever was in her began to slide out. She felt Nadine's hand smack at one cheek of her behind, then the other.

'Naughty. Keep hold of it till I fix it in place.'

Penny obeyed, then felt another scarf being fastened around her waist. From that, another scarf was being drawn through her legs. Each end was tied into the belt. She gasped at its coolness and the touch of Nadine's fingers as she folded back her labia then refolded them over the scarf. With the fragile softness of the scarf, the dildo in her rectum was pushed firmly back in place, the scarf tightened so it stayed immersed in her gripping channel.

'There!' said Nadine, her hands cupping Penny's bosoms once again before she made her escape. 'How pretty you look now. What a time you will have hanging around here, contemplating the gifts I have given you.'

Penny was alone again, breasts throbbing with desire, sex soaking the scarf that ran through her legs and held the stiff intruder lodged in her nether region. She moaned against her gag and peered at the blackness of her blindfold as she awaited Nadine's return. Anything she wanted, anything at all, if only she would release this flood of orgasmic demand . . .

But Nadine bid her time. She was relishing her control, lovingly acting out each chapter of her bondage to bring Penny to the very peak of desire – to the point where she would accept anything Nadine deigned to give her.

After what seemed like an eternity, she returned.

'Are you ready for me, my pretty pussy?'

In her haste for release, Penny forgot Nadine's requirement. She nodded her head.

'No!' cried Nadine, her finger shooting between Penny's buttocks, pushing the intrusion in further. Automatically, Penny's hips thrust forward. She groaned, feeling a reflection of the reaction in her anus through the thin membrane that divided it from her aching vagina.

She heard a chair being dragged, then found herself unbound from the wall lamp and flung headlong across the chair. Her legs were still tied to the stool, her hands still bound firmly behind her back.

She felt Nadine loosen them, take them one by one and tie them to the chair legs. Her head was in the seat of the chair, her breasts free and swinging between the chair and the stool.

Coolness seemed to invade her great divide as the silk scarf that ran through her legs was removed. She felt Nadine's fingers retrieve whatever was in her anus before those same fingers removed the blindfold from her eyes.

'Look, my pretty pussy,' said Nadine. Her head resting sideways on the chair, Penny blinked. She noticed that Nadine was naked before she could take in exactly what it was Nadine wanted her to see.

She fully expected it to be whatever Nadine had inserted in her anus. But nothing could have prepared her for the monstrous appendage that Nadine was wearing so proudly and with such obvious intent.

Her eyes opened wide. She mumbled into the silk scarf that still bound her mouth.

Nadine laughed, and wiggled her hips so that the false cock swayed out in front of her. But this was no ordinary dildo. Above the main phallus was another one, slightly smaller, but not by much. It was then that Penny understood the continuous lubrication Nadine had applied to her smallest orifice and the insertion of the false penis that had been held so firmly in place by the silk scarf.

'All for you, my pretty. All for you.' Nadine's hands became entangled in her hair. She pushed down the silk scarf from Penny's mouth. Penny knew what she wanted her to do. It seemed crazy to think Nadine wanted her to suck this thing. What could it do for her? This was not a

247

real phallus. It didn't belong to a man. This was synthetic and cold. But she had no choice. Domination was Nadine's game. By using her as a man would, she would gain satisfaction from Penny's obedience.

'Get on with it. Suck my cock, hard and long as if it were real,' Nadine growled in a low gruff voice that could easily have been that of a man.

Because she hesitated, Nadine dug her fingers in her long, thick hair, thrust her bony hips forward and nudged the larger appendage into Penny's mouth. Penny took it in, gagging on its length, the taste of plastic, the smooth obscenity of it. The extra one rubbed up and down the bridge of her nose, stiff, yet fairly flexible. It was like a reminder, an example of what was in her mouth.

'Lick the end,' Nadine ordered, smiling at the sight that met her eyes, and taking a strange pleasure that she was in the position of man, lover, husband . . . or even brother!

Penny licked the end, licked the full length even down to the false balls that were harder than real ones and tasted of talcum powder.

'That one, too,' ordered Nadine, her knee bent over Penny's back as she manoeuvred the upper part of the plastic prick into Penny's open mouth.

This one was no better. Again, Penny gagged as it slid down into her throat. The lower, larger penis stroked her throat on the outside whilst the one in her mouth stroked the inner.

'Enough. I've favoured you enough,' said Nadine as she let go of Penny's hair.

Penny knew what was coming next. She opened her mouth to say something. But Nadine knew what was coming, and she would brook no protest. She'd take it all the way, have her way, and have Penny, too, in the way only a man truly can – but both orifices at the same time.

Nadine regagged her and Penny resigned herself to what was about to happen. Whatever protests or cries she made against this double intrusion would be heard by no one. And anyway, her sex was moist and needed what was coming.

She felt Nadine's naked thighs against her own. Nadine's hands gripped her hips. Both phallic heads nudged at the holes they were destined for. Penny tensed, her legs braced as she prepared for the onslaught.

Almost ready, she thought to herself as one of Nadine's hands prepared to guide the twin pricks into the holes they were destined for.

Penny moaned against her gag, then felt the anal penis break the barrier and enter as though it had every right to be there.

'I'm going to see to you good and proper,' murmured Nadine against her ear. 'I'm going to fuck you and bugger you all at the same time as you've never been done before. And you're going to love it, just love it!'

Penny didn't answer. She couldn't, but if she had been able to, she could only have agreed. But for now, her attention was absorbed by the twin penises pushing their way into her body.

The larger one met with no obstacle, and in time with the strict tempo of Nadine's movements, her hips began to move, to press back against Nadine as though inviting further invasion, more pleasurable abuse.

She braced herself more firmly, head down on the chair, legs straight and bottom up.

What a beautiful sight I must present, she thought with mounting excitement, the glossy hair of her sex spilling out beneath the silky slit of her vagina and the pink rose of her now-glossy anus.

She groaned her ecstasy as the experience progressed. Her legs trembled. Nadine's hands held her steady – one on each hip – as she pushed the sex tools in further.

Once the appendages were completely immersed, Nadine began to plunge, slowly at first, in shallow movements until she was sure that Penny's body was used to the invasion and accepted it as right. As Penny began to groan against the gag and her breasts swung faster with each pounding from Nadine's excited hips, Nadine herself began to groan and cry out as the fixings of the appendage rubbed deliciously against her own clitoris and naked labia.

Penny heard her cries and, knowing how she was enjoying this, could not help but respond. Nadine showed her no mercy once she knew she could take it. The lunging became fiercer and faster as her breathing increased until Nadine fell forward, her breasts hard and her nipples prominent against Penny's back. Now she was fully embedded, her hands sought Penny's breasts. She removed the clamps, replaced them with her own cruel fingers and squeezed her plump orbs in her palms as she pummelled away at Penny's ravaged portals.

'I've got you, Penny. I've got you. You're all mine!' cried Nadine as she thrust with all the power of a masculine orgasm.

Penny shoved back against her, her eyes closed as her own climax flowed over her body. Even as her climax shivered her limbs, she pushed backwards against the dildo that invaded her anus, and downwards on the one embedded in her vagina.

Against the silk of the scarf, she cried her delight. Wave after wave of trembling ecstasy running from anus to vagina, vagina to breast and back to anus.

Nadine thrust more aggressively, seemingly lost in another orgasm as the interior of the sex toy rubbed her own clitoris to the height of sexual expression. They were lost in their enjoyment, smothered in climax. They fell together, sticky body against sticky body, spent, exhausted and willing to sleep till morning.

Chapter Fourteen

The day had been a good day. In the horsebox on the way back from the Royal Forest Show, everyone laughed, joked or sang along to classic pop that blasted out from an independent radio station. There was cause for celebration. The Beaumont team had scored the highest points of the day, and had come away with the most trophies and the best qualifiers for the next season.

Penny was equally pleased. In her mind, she saw the look in Alistair's eyes when she had carried off the biggest prize of the day. Although she had only felt the body of the horse between her legs, in that one instant, she thought she had him.

Nadine blew a kiss from the back of the Rolls-Royce as it swerved in front of the horsebox to take both her and Alistair back to Beaumont Place ahead of them.

'Cow!' muttered Alf who lived down in the village and drove part time for the family now and again.

Alf had sandy hair and matching sandy brows. He wore a flat cap on his head that seemed to lie so heavily on his hair that it burst out from underneath it and stood out all around his head like a fringe of faded thatch.

'I take it you don't like Nadine,' said Penny, though she could see the dislike well enough on Alf's features.

'Like her?' he grumbled before spitting out of the window. 'Can't stand the bloody woman. She ain't all

251

there. She's a manip ... manip ..., makes you do things you don't want to do. There's a promise there, and a reward, she says, at the end – but when you get to the end, there's nothing there.'

'You're just jealous, Alf!' Gregory laughed nervously and glanced at Penny. He'd acted nervously – as though he'd let her down in some way – ever since the night in the forest, and even though she had whispered in his ear that she had enjoyed the experience, he still felt he was in debt to her.

'Don't worry,' she had assured him as her tongue had dipped into his ear. 'You can make it up to me.' Then she scanned her brain to think how that could be achieved.

During their sex games since she'd come to Beaumont Place, she had given into Nadine, had let her be the mistress just so she could help her get Alistair, win her wager with Ariadne and win the stallion. Now with the benefit of familiarity, Penny knew that she had all along been receiving just what she wanted. Nadine might think that she, Penny, was her slave, when in fact, the opposite was true. It seemed incredible just how well she had settled into Beaumont Place, as though she were a cork and had found just the right bottle neck to fit into.

An anxiety had arisen in her mind after it had been hinted that most riders leave after one year, that they are pleased to do so, their departure sweetened with a suitable parting gift of money, property or even horses.

She didn't particularly want to push her luck, but the anxiety she was feeling could not be ignored. When she got back, she would go straight to Nadine and ask her exactly what the position was. Deep down, she knew that no money or anything else could replace what she had felt since coming to this place. She wanted to be part of it, to stay here for much longer than a year, perhaps even for ever. She was resolute. She would speak to Nadine.

She showered first, enjoying the warm lather that trickled in pearl-like drops from the end of her nipples, ran over her belly and divided into a rush of tributaries that seeped through her mass of pubic hair and down her inner thighs.

By the time she was dressed, she smelt of Narcisse, and her skin felt like silk against the light-green linen of her dress. No underwear, of course, just the dress which was silk-lined and cool against her body.

Her legs were as bronzed and taut as ever, the calves attractively lengthening as she slipped her feet into the high-heeled sandals that shone with a greenish glint and matched her dress exceptionally well. She added a plain gold chain around her neck and let her hair hang free.

'Now . . .' she exclaimed, addressing the beautiful woman reflected back at her from the mirror, 'now to beard the lion.'

The Beaumont private rooms were in the west side of the house, unusually sumptuous, she recalled, and unusually decadent. Alistair's office was on that side – the room she had entered on that first day when he had required her to walk near-naked through the crowded streets of the town with only a coat between her and decency. A lot of water had gone under the bridge since then, and many inhibitions had been discarded on that day along with a surplus of clothes. That day, she realised, had prepared her for what was to come. It was at that time that the dark desires hidden deep inside had escaped and could never return. Beaumont Place had teased them into flower, and in Beaumont Place they must always bloom.

'Going to the party?' Gregory looked clean, but casual. His blue jeans were bright, his shirt crisp, white and contrasting sharply with the glowing healthy tan of his skin. She ran her eyes over him and felt her stomach tighten and her sex tingle. Shining bright like a new-minted coin, his hair fell like satin from his head and tonight was caught at the nape of his neck in a piece of whip-thin black leather.

'Of course,' she replied, her eyes meeting his. She wondered just how long it would take him to breach her defences and have her throwing him up against a wall and easing his stalwart member into her slippery sex.

'Mind if I walk with you?' he asked with something vaguely resembling reverence.

Her eyes met his again when she nodded. 'Yes,' she answered, 'I do.' Then she turned quickly away. She had a task in mind, and he, his body and her own sexuality could very easily get in the way of that. Best avoided, she decided with regret. The truth and her destiny beckoned, and so did Alistair Beaumont. 'I'd like to be alone if you don't mind.'

It was obvious he did mind. He looked hurt, and, in the briefest of moments, the longing that throbbed so positively through her veins almost persuaded her to change her mind.

But she set her jaw, looked straight ahead and pressed on regardless, adamant that she would achieve what she set out to do. 'I'm going to get a little fresh air.' She hesitated, instinctively knowing that the look on his face would accuse her of lying. 'I'll see you later.'

His silence made her feel guilty, but she'd made up her mind. Nadine was not an honest ride and truthful bedfellow, and that annoyed her. There was something more to this brother and sister relationship than met the eye, and she was determined to find out exactly what it was.

Her hand covered the brass handle of the wide double doors that opened on the Beaumont apartments. She was at the other end to where she had entered with Nadine and Clarissa. She levered it down; softly, without even a click, it opened.

The windows were similar, big, high and stretching from crisp, white ceiling to polished floor.

The walls were painted terracotta in dramatic contrast with the gilt-edged paintings that hung from the walls, the brocade Louis XIV furniture and the thick piled Persian carpets that sat in independent squares over the floor.

Not meaning to linger, but being unable to resist, she eyed the paintings. Rubens-like females of pert bosom and pendulous stomach cavorted with men whose over-defined muscles were mismatched with seriously inconsequential cocks.

She licked her lips as she studied the paintings. There

were other paintings that were not quite so classic in style, although what they portrayed could not be regarded as purely contemporary. In these, orgies were taking place, goat-footed satyrs thrusting enormous penises into wide-open female gates.

Most of the women appeared submissive, even frightened of what was happening to them, yet still they yielded, unable to resist the lure of the obscene, the animal and the bizarre. One painting above all others forced her to stop dead in her tracks.

There was a chariot, not dissimilar to the one she had been harnessed to in the middle of the woods. Like her, a woman was harnessed to its shafts, satyrs driving her on with leering faces and the flick of many whips.

There was an ecstatic yearning on the woman's features, as if she wanted to please, to do better than she already had.

Half-watching her, yet apparently enthralled with each other, was a couple. They looked alike. The eyes were the same, and they had the same leanness, the same grey eyes. Although they were fondling each other – the girl holding the man's penis in her hand, and he appearing to have his finger stuck somewhere up between her legs – Penny knew instinctively that these were brother and sister and they should definitely not be doing what they were doing.

Despite the high windows, the room was getting dimmer as a cloudy afternoon folded into twilight.

Penny, the heat of desire drifting slowly down her body, forced herself to walk on.

The door at the far end opened out into a corridor. Only a small window of dark-blue glass let in a subdued and tinted light. A trio of wall lights compensated for the lack of natural light, but, like the room she had left behind, the floor was covered by thick Persian and Chinese rugs.

Her feet made no sound, her heels sinking into the plush pile and rich colours of the carpets. At the faint click of what sounded like a door latch, she tried one of the doors beside her and found herself in a small room that had rows of seating like a theatre, but no screen. There was only a window; a vast sheet of glass that looked through into a room beyond it.

At first she ducked down when she saw Alistair and Nadine, until she realised that they could not see her. Engrossed in conversation, they were sat in a gangway between two rows of seats.

'Tonight, then?'

Nadine stood up suddenly and draped her long hands over her narrow hips, her face questioning. Her brother got up and began to pace up and down, hands in his pockets. He appeared thoughtful and stared mostly at his shiny black loafers and the thick red carpet of the theatre floor.

'Hmmm.'

'Well?' said Nadine with a hint of impatience.

'Yes. As long as you're sure.'

'I'm sure.'

She saw Nadine smile, a brightness in her eyes that Penny had seen so often before, but never with quite the teeth flashing smile she adopted now.

'Tell me again,' said Alistair eagerly. He reminded Penny of a small child who's been told a story or a secret and wants to hear it all over again. Excitement caught at her belly. Somehow she knew that it was her they were talking about, that the time was ripe for her wager to be won, although winning it was no longer of such great importance.

Nadine was swaying slightly on the high heels of her black patent boots, her matching skirt barely covering the tight orbs of her snow-white bottom. She sighed as if impatient at having to repeat herself.

'Completely submissive, completely in my control. She's almost ready for you. After tonight, she'll be completely pliable. There's nothing she won't do.'

'You're sure? Are you sure it's not *you* that's hooked, rather than her?'

Nadine looked childishly petulant, and a pink flush coloured her usually pale cheeks. That made Penny smile. Even if Nadine did not accept it as fact, Penny

256

knew it. And strangely enough, so also, it seemed, did Alistair.

'Of course I'm sure! You'll find out.'

'Good.' Alistair smiled, and as he did so, Nadine moved towards him like a child about to get a reward for being a good little girl.

'Are you pleased with me, Aly, darling?' Nadine asked in an oddly coquettish way.

Alistair's white teeth flashed, and suddenly Penny could see just how alike they really were; just how much one depended upon the other.

Penny remembered the couple in the painting, both standing to one side and watching the woman who had been harnessed to the chariot and the hoard of satyrs, clinging on behind, their overlarge cocks waving like baseball bats behind her.

'Beautiful stallion,' she heard Nadine mew. Then she laughed, throwing her head back and wrapping her arms around herself, though her eyes stayed fixed upon her brother's face. 'Ariadne was right. She'll do you fine. Miss Bennet will get one stallion more than she's bargained for! After that, it's on to the next one, my dear brother. There's always another one, isn't there?'

'At last,' breathed Alistair.

And Penny felt his excitement was tangible, but wondered again what had stayed this scenario up until now.

'Once you've finished with her, we'll let her go. There's always another one waiting for your money and more than willing to accommodate your other asset. I know she's been here less than a year, but she's indulged more keenly than anyone else we've had. It is long enough!' she finished crisply.

Nadine had said what she'd said with smiles. Her brother's response was less enthusiastic. There was a look in his eyes that did not match that of his sister. It was as though his plans were somewhat different from hers.

'Yes.' He hesitated. 'I suppose so. Though, somehow, I don't think a few months here will be enough for Miss

Bennet. She's a natural at what she does, my dear sister; it's like there's something deep inside driving her on.'

'She'll have to accept it!' Nadine returned.

Alistair raised his eyebrows and gazed at his sister in a calm, even forbidding way. 'She might not.'

'So what?' Nadine shrugged her shoulders and lit up a cheroot. 'There's nothing she can do about it.'

'We'll see,' said Alistair with a smile that made Penny's lips long for his kiss and her loins for his body. 'We'll see.'

So, it was true! Once Alistair had taken her, she would be out of here. But that was stupid, she told herself, absolutely stupid. How could she ever get to the top in her sport unless she had achieved some stability? But that wasn't really the reason she wanted to stay here. Other desires had been unleashed, and Beaumont Place was where she wanted to use them; and Gregory, Alistair, even Nadine, were those she wanted to use them on.

Ariadne had got her into this, and perhaps it would be Ariadne who would get her out of it.

Penny left them there with their mutual looks and their mutual plans. Suddenly, she had plans of her own.

Flushed, she slunk back into the thickly carpeted corridor that would take her back to the more public apartments in Beaumont Place.

Had she really only been here a few months? It seemed longer, as though this was a place she had known and wanted all her life. She knew beyond doubt that she didn't want to leave, and in her mind, the jumbled outlines of ad-libbed plans began to tumble into some sort of order.

She wanted to stay here. She was happy, but in order to stay here, she would have to do something drastic, and she would need help to carry out her plan. First she would phone Ariadne just to get things straight. Once she had all the facts, then she would act.

The phone rang a dozen times before Ariadne answered. She sounded breathless and Penny had the distinct feeling that her gorgeous blonde friend was not alone.

258

'It's me. Penny Bennet.'

'Penny?' If Ariadne was a friend, she certainly didn't sound it at the moment, thought Penny. But what the hell! She pressed on.

'It's about our wager. And it's about Alistair.'

Ariadne hesitated before she spoke. 'How are you getting on?'

'Too well. I get the impression I'm about to win our wager.'

'Already? My!' said Ariadne in a breathless rush. 'You certainly are a quick worker. Then the stallion is yours, darling.'

'Yes, I know that. But then again, he was from the start, wasn't he?'

There was silence on the other end of the phone.

'You know, then?' said Ariadne at last, her voice no more than a hushed whisper.

'That the stallion doesn't belong to you. That it belongs to Alistair.'

'How did you know?' asked Ariadne with surprise.

'I just guessed.'

Penny *had* only guessed. If Ariadne had been as bright as she was beautiful, she would have realised that Penny had led her into declaring the truth of the matter. But Ariadne wasn't bright and had fallen easily into the trap. Besides that, Penny was convinced that, though her mouth was speaking into the phone, other things were happening to other parts of Ariadne's body.

'It's like an aphrodisiac, you know,' Ariadne went on, her words suddenly fast and furious. 'He's a powerful man. He's got a lot of influence, a lot of energy. Nadine directs it, gets him to store it up in those cute rubber pants she makes him wear.'

'Yes,' returned Penny somewhat sharply. 'Really', and 'You're kidding', were the words on her tongue, but the quick, one word retort was enough to hide her ignorance of what Ariadne had just exposed to her.

'That's why she wears those big earrings; you know, those black-jet crucifixes and things – there's a key behind them that unlocks his pants. He can't get to his

259

delicious cock without her say so. His drive's all stored up, like a dam on a river; then when it lets go . . . Wow! Imagine if it got out. I wonder what his business associates would say if they knew,' Ariadne went on mindlessly. 'I bet he'd want to drop dead if anything got out about it.'

'No doubt,' Penny said slowly as the pros and cons of the situation ping-ponged around in her mind. 'No doubt he'd be mortified if anyone found out.'

'Devastated!' Ariadne exclaimed in a desperate hush.

Penny had known Ariadne long enough to surmise that some luscious hunk was licking or pushing his rod into her welcoming pussy at that very moment. Also from experience, she could imagine that Ariadne was dying to drop the phone from her mouth and stifle the words in her throat with something far more palatable.

Again, Penny pounced before Ariadne could think straight.

'He didn't ask you to stay?'

'No. I would have liked to, but he doesn't favour that. Anyway, I don't think Nadine's too keen on anyone being near her brother on a permanent basis – except perhaps herself. And besides, he made it worth my while. I've got my own stud farm now.'

'Mares and stallions?'

Ariadne gasped as though a thick member had found its mark in one or other of her most delectable orifices. Obviously, thought Penny, not her mouth. Ariadne laughed breathlessly into the telephone.

'Just me,' she cooed with undisguised pleasure, 'and a selection of fine . . . young . . . stallions . . .'

It seemed to Penny as though the telephone had slipped from her friend's grasp. An angry buzzing sounded against her ear.

But she had no more questions except in her head. So Alistair wore a pair of rubber pants. The picture that presented both intrigued and aroused her in the same instant. And Nadine controlled him by using those pants, stored up his sexual energy like an electricity generator does the power from the National Grid. Ariadne knew about it. Others probably did, too. But their silence had been bought, and they, unlike her, had been willing to accept whatever was offered to them. They hadn't found somewhere they wanted to stay like she had, where her desires and her need for security could complement each other.

Obviously, she had to do something about it. But what? The pants, Nadine ... then the fact – the very obvious fact – came to her that the international business community would withdraw the respect they had for Alistair if they found out about his odd home life and his peculiar underwear.

The seeds of a plan started to germinate in her head. Even without her yearning to maintain stability for her equestrian career, she would still have to do this, she'd have no yearning for other pastures than those at Beaumont Place.

Ariadne had not wished to stay here; not as much as she did anyway. Ariadne had accepted her lot, Penny would not.

Beaumont Place had brought her the kind of security and pleasure she had only dreamed of in the past. Although their use of her might have appeared to other eyes as submissive or abusive, through the pleasures and pains she had endured, she had encountered status and affection.

In Nadine's long, slim hands, there was affection. In Gregory's tying her up, so she had fully appreciated the sense of touch alone. All around her and along many roads, there was a loving desire to give her pleasure. And beneath Alistair's restraint, dictated to him by a pair of rubber pants and a dominant sister, there was an extraordinary passion aimed in her direction. All this was directed at her, and she was loath to lose it.

Knuckles white with determination, she took a deep breath and made herself a promise. With the help of Gregory, she would not lose all this. She would keep it and stay here for as long as she wanted ... even for ever.

261

Chapter Fifteen

They were in the private theatre that Penny had stumbled on earlier, only this time she was on the other side of the glass. Just as she had guessed, it was another two-sided mirror. Compulsively, she opened her eyes slightly wider as she glanced at it. Then she studied the rest of the room, the blush-red walls of washed silk, the deep rose of the thickly woven carpet, and the fact that the room had no windows, but was lit by square lanterns of Oriental origin which hung from gilded chains in each corner of the room.

In the middle of the room was a wooden frame that might have been mistaken for some kind of loom by the untutored eye. But Penny was not untutored. Much learning had gone into her time here, and although the details of how she would be tied to it might not yet be clear in her mind, she knew the frame was meant to be decorated with a human supplicant, a sacrifice to a man's stored-up sexual power.

'How delicious you look, my pretty pussy,' purred Nadine, her hair whiter, her eyes glinting like chips of hard glass.

Penny said nothing, nor did she acknowledge the lingering hand that slid down over her back and behind. Tension might be in her mind, but the light of excitement shone brightly in her eyes. Although exhilaration and a feeling of potential triumph whirled like dancing leaves in her stomach, she lowered her head in supplication and studied the deep redness of the carpet.

Penny had eaten little and drunk even less this evening. Undoubtedly, there was something in the air, and that something she knew would be the making or breaking of her.

Nadine had helped her to dress back in her room earlier, the costume chosen by her. Yet it was nothing, just a kaftan of black silk trimmed with jet and silver. It tied casually at the waist, but was not belted. Beneath it, Penny wore only her creamy skin which had been bathed, oiled and massaged by Gregory. Her hair hung in glossy waves melting in dark satisfaction with the black silk of her sheer garment.

There were just the two of them in the room now; Nadine and her.

'Is no one else expected?' Penny asked the question in a way that was both provocative and inquisitive.

· 'My brother was here earlier,' purred Nadine. 'Now it's just us, pretty pussy, just us. But he will be back.'

Nadine grinned and stretched like a loose-limbed cat. She seemed inordinately sure of herself, pleased with whatever had happened in this room earlier.

From beneath her lowered lashes, Penny saw Nadine finger a heavy jet earring, then flick at it so it jangled against the object she knew was behind it. Black earrings, black outfit and white hair. Nadine was a creature of contrasts and addicted to the dramatic. Even now her outfit was nothing more than a two-inch-wide strip of leather that started at a belt at her waist, slid between her legs and divided her boyish rear into two snowy halves.

She also wore a breastplate of silver metal between her breasts. This was supported by chains which clipped to a studded collar around her neck. Her eyes were heavily lined with kohl, and silver daggers hung from her ears.

Beside her, Penny felt strangely vulnerable, and almost innocently beautiful.

'Let me help you with this,' said Nadine, her long

fingers undoing the loose fastening at the front of Penny's long black kaftan-like covering. Once off, Nadine flung it to one side, then led her to the wooden structure just as she'd supposed she would.

Her long fingers wound leather bands firmly around each wrist. On each band was a metal ring. Nadine fastened each of these to metal clips set into the wooden frame about a foot above Penny's head. Her ankles were fastened in a similar way, beneath her. She was spread and stretched, her body forming a perfect 'X' on the custom-made frame.

Once or twice, she hesitated in what she was doing and looked at Penny a little quizzically, a half-smile playing around her broad mouth as if she couldn't quite believe just how little strength it was taking to fasten Penny in this position. Her hands were trembling.

'You are incredibly willing, my pretty pussy.' Inquisitively, she dipped one finger into Penny's wet aperture.

'My. You are ready for it, aren't you?'

Penny knew no answer was required. She didn't want to speak anyway. She wanted Alistair – more than she could ever have imagined. Furtively, she allowed her lowered eyes to look in the direction of the two-way mirror, and, as though she were playing to an unseen audience, she stretched her body and moaned in what Nadine put down to apprehension as her hips undulated.

Nadine's laugh was loud and throaty, and even more resonant once she'd fastened the now familiar bridle over Penny's head and pressed the bit between her teeth.

Penny's breasts thrust forward almost impatiently, and her skin erupted with goose-bumps as she watched Nadine roll back the bundle of red velvet on the table. A variety of whips and riding crops was suddenly exposed.

Nadine grinned at her as she pointed at each one. 'Shall I use this one?' she asked in a silly singsong voice that didn't suit her at all. 'No? Perhaps this one, then. What do you think?'

The question was ineffectual. Penny could not answer, so Nadine made the choice herself.

'This one, then!' she exclaimed at last.

264

Reflexively, Penny clenched her buttocks as Nadine trailed the tip of a bamboo-handled crop across her bare backside. She trembled again, clamped her teeth against the metal snaffle bit that lay so cold and hard upon her tongue. She looked again towards the door where she expected Alistair to enter, then back towards the vast mirror. This was a coming-together of the two men in her life, though one of them would not know that. Not wishing Nadine to see what was in her eyes, she bent her head and stared determinedly at the floor.

Nadine laughed at her own games before her face became more serious and her eyes more intense. She turned from Penny who was spread so deliciously on her wooden frame, opened the door, and brought Alistair in.

Thankfully, this time, the blinkers attached to her bridle were not tied. She could see Alistair, could see what she was getting. He entered the room as she'd never seen him before. Gone was the Gucci business suit, Egyptian cotton shirt, silk tie and hand-made leather shoes. All he wore was some strange kind of undergarment made of shiny rubber and clipped at the sides. The device covered his body in such a way that no hint of form was detectable through it. There was no evidence of him even having a penis beneath the thick covering of latex rubber that barricaded his sex and his desires from the outside world.

Yet, even though most of his flesh was exposed to her view for the first time, her gaze was transfixed by his eyes. Tonight, they sparkled and yet they were different. They glittered with a sublime heat as they ran over her body and surveyed what awaited him.

His breathing sounded rampant as though his lungs were guzzling air quicker than he could expel it.

'All for you,' cried Nadine as she unhitched the tiny key from behind her earring, unfastened the rubber pants and let his member expand to its full size.

The sight of it filled Penny's eyes, and her mouth hung open with surprise. It was a beautiful sight, throbbing there, jerking and rearing as though it were still wild and incredibly untameable. Just looking at it made her want its throbbing length within her, dividing her succulent labia, penetrating her most secret place and filling her whole being with its immense strength and power. Celibacy had engorged it with desire. Now it was free and determined, as resolute as she was to have it in her.

Only briefly did she glance at the viewing mirror. She licked her lips as she did it, as though savouring the sight of a gourmet meal.

Alistair's chest, which had a sprinkling of dark hair, looked as hard as his member. His hands were out of sight. Around his neck he wore a leather collar, and it was then she realised that his hands were tied behind his back, and possibly fixed to the collar he wore.

His body was oiled, each muscle standing in stark relief from its neighbour, his skin the colour of honey, his body hair luxuriant enough to proclaim his masculinity.

A lead rein, also of leather, was attached to the collar. Nadine picked up the trailing end of it, smiling serenely as she led him towards the naked woman who was his to do with as he pleased – or so it looked.

He looked vibrant, unequivocally male, and rampant with desire.

Penny was mesmerised; electric with a current of barely suppressed excitement as she surveyed the hard body and the harder phallus. It stood proudly before him, rearing as his eyes raked downwards over her body.

Everything he'd undergone and envisaged during the time she'd been here was in those eyes. She responded to that look, writhed in welcome on the restraints that bound her. Just by looking at him, she could envisage the feel of his skin against her skin, his flesh within hers.

Accompanied by loud breathing, Alistair lunged towards her, his head bent, lips hot on her breasts, teeth sharp on her nipples.

She yelped against the confines of the metal bit, yet at the same time arched her back so her breasts were more prominent, more thrusting towards his mouth.

'No! Not yet!'

As the riding crop laced in a series of blows across Alistair's back, he was yanked rudely from her, his head

266

jerking as Nadine pulled him away like a dog on a lead
– or a stallion.

'On your knees!' Nadine ordered.

Her brother obeyed.

'Stay there!' she snapped, not that he could do otherwise. Nadine had passed the lead rein through a link on
the wall and had left little room for him to manoeuvre.

She came to Penny's side.

'Now, my pretty pussy,' she murmured through her
big white teeth. 'Let me just get you ready for the first
part of the covering.'

Nadine adjusted the supports to which she was tied so
that they slid one inside the other towards the floor. Now
Penny was leaning forward, so far that she was forced to
go on to her knees.

Her arms were still above her, still firmly strapped to
the uprights which had now been reduced in height. Her
ankles too were still restrained, only now she was on her
knees, a deep 'V' between her legs still leaving her damp
pussy very much exposed.

'Now, my beautiful boy, come over here and do your
worst!' She said it with laughter and also with pleasure.

Nadine undid the leather from the metal ring to which
she had tied him and tugged her brother to his feet. She
brought him, his eyes still glazed and his breathing rapid,
before Penny.

Penny gasped, her eyes big with delight as his throbbing appendage leapt with anticipation before her eyes.
All the desires that had come into being after a walk
through a crowded city street now reached their full
potential. She badly wanted him. She moaned against the
restraint of the bridle and the bit, and writhed against
the bonds that held her so tightly to the frame.

How glad she was not to be blinkered. There it was
before her in all its ramrod glory; soft-skinned, yet
incredibly hard. All ten inches of it leapt with pleasure
as its soft pink crown gently kissed her lips. It was soft,
warm and begging to enter.

'Open your mouth. Take him in!' Nadine demanded.

Without hesitation, Penny obeyed. Above her, he

moaned as she tilted her head to accommodate him. Sea breezes and the tang of wind-blown sand were the flavours that assaulted her taste buds. She smelt him, the hormone of his arousal filling her nostrils and her head.

Bound as she was, the rest of her body responded. Her nipples pouted and her sex wept hot tears of desire.

Gently, slowly. Back and forth. His pelvis moved; his piston retreated, then advanced. As he moved, his forest of silky soft pubic hair muffled her breath and tickled her lips.

Nadine was now out of view. Not that Penny cared. She was lost in delight and in victory. The wager was won; yet somehow, it was no longer important. With Alistair in her mouth, her eyes slid sidelong to look towards the vast expanse of mirror that almost covered one wall. Beyond that were the rows of theatre-style seats where earlier she had overheard Nadine and Alistair talking about her.

If her mouth hadn't been so full, she would have smiled. There were other things now more important than Alistair and more important than a wager. Even acquiring Ariadne's stallion was less important now.

'Take more of him, bitch! Eat some more!'

Penny winced with pleasurable pain as the riding crop lashed one cheek and then the other. Now she knew exactly where Nadine was. Obediently she took more of Alistair's member into her mouth. Nadine was behind her and taking obvious delight in laying half a dozen whacks on each of her warming cheeks.

But the lashings were not saved for her alone.

Nadine came into view at the front now, the tight leather and metal of her outfit making more of her breasts than they really were, her naked mons strangely menacing as it curled like petals over the thin strip of leather that ran between her legs. Her face was flushed, yet her eyes were anxious. What was she seeing? Penny asked herself. Could it be that Alistair was too responsive to her mouth and her body, too carried away by a dark-haired girl whose sensuality matched, and perhaps outdid, her own?

Perhaps with passion, perhaps with fear, Nadine raised the whip and brought it across Penny's rear, then Alistair's.

'Give her more, you animal! Give her more!' Nadine snarled.

As the crop lashed his naked buttocks, Alistair shoved sharply forward.

If Penny hadn't tilted her head even more, she'd never have accommodated any more length. But she did manage it and the crown of his penis burrowed further into her throat.

The sheer imagery of it all did not escape her. She, the captive female, receiving what she was ordered to receive. He, the reined-in stallion, told to service her, to do his duty when commanded as such. His movements increased along with Nadine's lashings. He began to cry out. 'No more! No more!'

In response, Nadine stopped her lashing, which had looked beyond stopping. Her eyes were glazed, glittering with excitement. Her mouth was slightly open. This was her domain. Sex was her weapon, and power was her game.

'Silence!'

From somewhere out of Penny's vision, Nadine fetched something that clinked, and a trail of leather touched briefly on her head before she heard what it was without actually seeing it.

'There! Now you're as silent as she is! You're both bridled!' she exclaimed, and Penny knew that Alistair now had a bit in his mouth just as she did.

But then, she didn't need his words. His thrusting was stronger, and the swelling in her mouth more apparent.

He's coming, she thought to herself. No! No! He mustn't. Not yet! He mustn't! What about me? But she couldn't say that. Her mouth was full of him.

'Take it!' Nadine ordered, her hand cupping the back of Penny's head so she would not retreat from his offering.

Warm, acrid and in a sudden flood, she felt him ejaculate over the bit and into her throat.

269

Tears sprang to her eyes. How could you? she wanted to scream. The throbbing of his weapon lessened along with his cries of ecstasy, then died. How could you? she tried to murmur, but her words were just a mumble against the restraint of the metal bit.

'Never mind, my pretty pussy,' crooned Nadine as her hand ruffled Penny's hair. 'He's not finished yet, you know. He has a lot of catching up to do. This is a rare prize I've kept for you. A rare prize indeed. Now, let me prepare you for the next stage.'

The wooden uprights to which she was attached shot upwards again. Now she stood, arms above her head, legs wide open. Nadine fiddled with some ratchet arrangement on the machine near Penny's waist. Then the wood both her wrists and ankles were attached to moved to the parallel. Now she was laid out flat and a stool with a velvet padded top was slid beneath her hips. Two cushions were forced on top of that. She was arched, like a bow, her breasts falling towards her face, her thighs high and wide open. As she peered upwards between her breasts, she could see her tuft of pubic hair adorning her mons like a clump of fragile trees on a distant hill.

A fountain of desire ran rampant on the other side of that hill. She was wet for Alistair, avid for his penetration. She had no choice but to let him enter her. Yet she wanted no choice. Nadine had primed Alistair for this moment, and as Penny waited for his mighty rod to slide between her dripping lips, she understood just how he must feel.

Within Nadine's control was ultimate satisfaction. That was why, she told herself, she wanted to stay here, why she had asked Gregory to help her, and why she knew that ultimately Alistair would appreciate her staying.

With Nadine tugging him forward, Alistair stepped into the 'V' formed by her open thighs. His hands were still clasped behind his back. He didn't need them. As if his phallus knew its way by heart, it prodded briefly at her glistening labia before it nosed pleasurably into her open vagina.

She moaned with pleasure against the metal of the

bridle bit, arched her back and brought her sex up to meet his.

Already he was huge again, already he was pumping into her, filling her with his mighty muscle, the cast iron of his thighs strangely comforting against the satin softness of her inner thighs.

With each movement, his hanging balls beat a steady rhythm against her bunched behind. They were soft, they were firm, they were warm and mellow; velvet like peaches, yet hard as rubber.

No ordinary man could have performed like he had done in her mouth, then recovered so quickly to perform as he was doing now.

Alistair was indeed a powerful man, made all the more incredible by the restraints suggested by him and augmented by his loving sister.

Tremors of exhilaration ran through Penny's body with all the thunder of a mountain torrent. The extent of his erection seemed to reach every iota of nerve ending in her. She bucked beneath him, straining against the restraints of the wrist- and ankle-bands and the demeaning and curtailing bridle.

He was in her, she had him, the wager, the stallion and something more besides. Yet he wouldn't know that yet. Neither would Nadine. Only Gregory would know that, watching, waiting there on the other side of the two-way mirror.

They came together, her orgasm muffled with her lips against the restraining bit, her thighs and loins trembling until the sensations of her climax had faded to nothing more than an echo.

When Alistair's body had at last stiffened above her – his muscles screaming with tension and his tool throbbing as it unloaded its most precious cargo – she breathed a heavy sigh but did not count on her ordeal being over. If she knew Nadine that well, it would not be. If Nadine had done her job well, it most certainly had not finished yet.

Even as a smiling Nadine adjusted the ratchet again and brought Penny back to her feet, Alistair's penis,

271

which in most men would now be dormant, was already rearing its rampant head.

'And for our next trick...' said Nadine, her dark-brown husky voice bubbling with laughter as she readjusted the uprights of the frame.

Now Penny was down on her elbows at the front, her rear high behind her and exposed.

She heard a click and wondered if Gregory had been discovered, but Nadine explained its origins to her.

'I've released his hands,' she murmured, her voice grating almost with regret. 'Soon, it will be all over.'

Warm hands ran in softly caressing circles over Penny's upturned behind. She gasped as she felt twin thumbnails divide her pear-shaped bottom and run to the rose bud discretion of her anus to push and prod and judge reaction.

Lost in her own sensuality, Penny tensed against those hands that for so long had avoided her body. Rapture half-closed her eyes and made her moan and whimper against the bit. But she could do, and wanted to do nothing to halt the coming event.

'Her quim's soaking, Aly. Dip your fingers in there and make your entry easier,' she heard Nadine say.

Strong fingers poked salaciously into her soaking vagina, dipping, stirring and stroking the seeping fluid out of its deep pool and up and over her anal cleft, then entered her anus and pushed more of the sweet fluid around her tight little passage.

The head of Alistair's member nudged at her puckered opening. Penny tensed her thighs, clenched her buttocks and edged slightly forward.

Nadine, seeing her feigned reluctance, grasped her hips and held her whilst her brother penetrated.

'Are you in?' she heard Nadine ask, almost as if Penny herself wasn't there, and even if she was, the matter had nothing to do with her.

Alistair groaned in blissful reply.

His penis was still big, but, thankfully, not as big as before.

Penny groaned and moaned in alternate pangs of pain and delight as he ventured further into her most tight

272

opening. This, she knew, would be the last penetration – at least for today.

In that knowledge, she revelled in her achievement, wriggled her bottom and pushed it against him so his shaft could travel further.

With deliberate intent, she intermittently clenched and relaxed her buttock muscles so he growled with ecstasy when she held him tight, and fell silent with regret when she let him go.

The astute Nadine assessed what she was doing, judged what Penny herself wanted, and slid her hand between Penny's open thighs.

With tumbling cries of release, Penny's body jerked against Alistair's and his tensed in throbbing rapture against hers as their climax combined.

Both had got what they wanted. So, too, thought Penny to herself, had Nadine. She was still in control here at Beaumont Place, and soon Penny would see that *she* was, too.

Penny didn't wait to be summoned to Alistair's office to be told that it was time for her to go. With Gregory striding alongside her, she knocked, then barged in.

Alistair was being refitted into his rubber pants. Penny was none too sure who was the most surprised to see her; the brother or the sister.

This, she told herself, was most definitely the right time for confrontation. Both were disarmingly surprised; and even Nadine looked flustered, her mouth open and lost for words.

Without waiting for an invitation, Penny made herself comfortable in one of the leather armchairs in the room. She crossed one black-stockinged leg over the other. She did it slowly and with the optimum provocation so that at one point her bare sex flashed before the eyes of those she had come to cherish.

Yet today, they felt the aura of businesslike determination that she felt herself. She had even dressed to play this part, this very important role on which both her future and her happiness depended.

Her suit was black with white inserts across the shoulders and a white line that cinched in her waist. It was an outfit more suited to a bank manager than a showjumper. Her shoes were plain black suede and her heels high. Her hair was fastened in a bun at the nape of her neck, though its natural bounciness edged it away from appearing severe.

Gregory stood protectively behind her chair. He had a defiant look on his face and there was triumph in his eyes.

Hands clasped loosely in her lap, Penny began to speak her well-chosen and well-rehearsed words.

'As I understand it, contracts at Beaumont Place are liable to run out at short notice once a certain criteria has been filled. This is just to tell you I will not be leaving Beaumont Place. I've decided I like it here, and anyway, it's far more worthwhile in my sport to achieve stability and likeable surroundings.'

'What are you talking about?' blustered Alistair as he struggled into a pair of sharply cut black chinos.

Penny marvelled at how vulnerable Alistair appeared without the advantage of expensive suits and handmade shirts.

'Please don't get me wrong,' she started. 'I don't have any intention of ending your disciplined regime. In fact, I quite admire it,' she finished, nodding at the rubber pants which were fast disappearing behind Alistair's zip.

Now it was Alistair blushing. Although he still looked somewhat abashed, Penny had the distinct impression that he wasn't entirely disappointed that his game was not going to end on the same note as all the others.

It was Nadine whose voice rose to anger.

'What right have you to lay down what you will or will not do? How dare you even *suggest* what you want. You'll be paid well enough for what you've done, just as your friend was.'

'Yes,' returned Penny with a curt nod. 'Just as my friend was. Like her, I was not given the benefit of knowing that. I wanted somewhere where I could be free, lead my own life, follow my own career, somewhere

I could feel secure. New sensations were aroused in me. I indulged in new experiences that I am reluctant to leave behind. Now I am here, I intend to stay.'

Alistair glanced briefly at his sister before he raised his eyebrows. However, as yet, he did not smile.

Nadine still looked like thunder, though even her hard lines were beginning to break into bits.

'It's not for you to dictate!' exclaimed Nadine, her small, cold breasts quivering as she spoke.

Smiling, Penny shook her head. 'I'm staying.'

'You can't!' returned Nadine.

Alistair folded his well-formed arms across his bare, hard chest and looked from his sister to Penny in turn.

Penny took three steps towards him. In response, he came three steps nearer her. Thoughtfully, but with the barest crease of a smile on his lips, he shoved his hands into his trouser pockets. The muscles of his chest seemed to swell towards her.

'Well?' Alistair asked. 'What's the ultimatum?'

It wasn't hard to persuade him that releasing the video Gregory had taken on the other side of the two-way mirror would seriously damage his international business affairs.

At first he stared incredulously, then he laughed.

Nadine stared at him wide-eyed and open-mouthed. For once she was not smoking, which under the circumstances was just as well. In fact, it seemed to Penny that Alistair was much impressed and amused by the whole thing.

'But what about . . .?' began Nadine.

'Hush,' Alistair interrupted, patting unselfconsciously at the hidden underpants that served so well to heighten his sex drive and channel it from business to pleasure. He smiled now, stepped further forward and placed his hands on Penny's shoulders. She smiled back. Even without him saying, she knew what was to come, knew what she had achieved.

'I think Penny can cope with that; and, quite frankly, I think Penny will be quite enough to suit my needs – and yours,' he added, jerking his head towards the silent

275

Gregory who had been feeling nervous, but who now smiled. 'And you, too, my dear sister,' Alistair said over his shoulder, his teeth now flashing as whitely as hers did. 'I knew there was something different from the first time we walked through the crowded streets,' he said still smiling. 'And the first time I found her bent over the trough in the stable. I couldn't resist her then, dear sister, and I can't now. But I think I'd better mend my ways. I need to truly save myself in future. If you look in the small box on my desk there, you'll find a key – a duplicate to the one you wear behind your earring. Take it. Give it to Penny. Then, whenever she wants me, I'm hers – me alone, or me with Gregory or you. Whatever. It doesn't matter.'

Penny listened, bright-eyed, then opened her palm to accept the key that Nadine had got from the box on Alistair's desk.

'When did you get that copied?' she asked him.

'Never you mind,' he replied. 'But I think you'll agree that Penny will be a great asset to us. So, too, will Gregory.'

Frozen features melted' as the truth of his words filtered through to Nadine's brain. 'Yes!' she exclaimed with some force, her ego and self-esteem now somewhat restored. 'I think you could well be right.'

With feline suppleness, Nadine stretched, took strides to Penny's side and wrapped the length of her hand around the nape of her neck. She grinned, smiled, her eyes almond-shaped and cat-like.

'You are probably right, my darling brother,' Nadine purred in a low growling voice. 'Why would we want other pussies when we have such a pretty little one as this?'

That night, Nadine went out to the stable-lads to search for a suitable replacement for Auberon. Penny hoped she would find one. As it was, she herself was in heaven; or rather, in her room with both Alistair and Gregory. The key, or rather Alistair's duplicate, was hanging on a silver chain and snuggled between her breasts.

La Basquaise
Angel Strand

Prologue – Biarritz 1925

'*A ttention, s'il vous plaît!*' Madame Rosa had a voice that was rich, throaty and created for talking dirty. She moved like a liner coming into port, her dress floating around her in a rosy pink wash.

The salon of La Maison Rose grew quiet. There were about fifteen well-heeled men in the room attended by beautiful, semi-naked women who came to rest like butterflies on laps, on cushions, on the thread-flowers of the whorehouse chintz.

A couple of young men sitting on the soft green velvet couch exchanged a conspiratorial smile. Jean Raffoler was twenty-four and in the peak of masculine health. He had long, dark, curly hair and light brown skin. His body was big and strong under expensively cut evening clothes. He had loosened his black tie and he sat with his legs apart, confidently.

Paul Phare was in his early thirties and had a rebellious lock of sandy blond hair that wandered into his smoky green eyes. He was in his shirt sleeves, his cravat was awry and a day's growth of beard showed on his fine chin. A young woman in a chemise sat on the floor at Paul's feet, resting her head on his long, lazily crossed legs. He stroked her curly ginger hair with a tender, masculine hand.

'The moment for which you have been waiting has come,' trilled Rosa. 'My dear Baron has returned from his travels at long last, from the far-flung corners of the world, and he has brought with him some very charming erotica.'

She sailed across the room, a pair of naked young males bobbing in her wake, and stopped in front of red velvet curtains. She nodded to the boys. They clasped the curtains and drew them back. In the small room beyond stood a squat male figure carved out of opaque yellow stone. Its *pièce de résistance* was a huge, erect phallus, the head of which gleamed softly in the light from two thick, long beeswax candles.

The Baron stepped out from the shadows. He was squat too and he glowed with perspiration. His smile was accentuated by a long scar on one pale cheek and seemed to spread to his ear. He flicked his pudgy fingers at the boys and they each lit a flame from the candles. They fired a pair of silver incense burners with movements graceful as swans. The room began to fill with plumes of heady scent.

'Gentlemen,' said the Baron. 'The following performance is based on a rite over five thousand years old. This figure was found in the tomb of a queen. Around the walls of the tomb paintings depicted the dance that you are about to witness. It is re-created faithfully and lovingly for your enjoyment by a descendant of this ancient and beautiful queen.'

The boys began a soft roll on little drums as a tall, black girl, her hair cropped closely to her head, writhed out from behind the curtains. She wore nothing but charms and shells and beautiful bells. Every graceful movement she made was accompanied by the music of trinkets. From her earlobes hung huge silver hoops bearing little bells in their centres. Round her neck and clicking between her handsome breasts were hundreds of glass beads. At her waist a thousand tiny sparkling gems made a fine girdle and around her left thigh some kind of reptile had given his skin for a thong.

She shimmied, rooted to the spot like a tree in a breeze, stretching her arms up as if to the goddess of the dance. The men in the room grew still. When she could feel the whole room in her power she began to move.

Slowly she gyrated her hips, in half-moon shapes, to the drums. Her hands cut through the air like the blades of knives. She parted them at her navel and rested them on her thighs and then suddenly, she thrust her hips forward, opened her legs and showed off her best jewel. The movement was like a magician who shows off the beautiful girl he is about to saw in half. Her sex was beautiful. A mature rose. Someone in the audience growled with desire.

She turned her back on them and mounted the dais, taking some oil on her fingertips from a silver tray as she went. Slowly she oiled the head of the huge phallus. As she worked she spoke in some unknown language and her words became a strange, lilting song that twisted around the room like a rope.

The men were spellbound as she violated the statue, her body glistening with the exertion, her strong thighs rippling as her movements up and down the phallus gathered momentum. She built up to a crescendo and climaxed with a wild call that silenced the catcalls of the loutish element in the crowd, piercing everyone to the core.

Paul Phare reached for a cloak that was behind him and with one adept movement he covered himself and the girl who rose from the floor into his arms.

Jean Raffoler sat still as a bird entranced by a cobra.

But the show was not over. The Baron was announcing in his thin weedy voice that the girl would tell them a story. Hardly two minutes passed before she re-entered the room and, sitting in a big red-plush wing chair, she began:

'My people,' she said in accented French, 'believe that if a marriage is not right then it will bring misfor-

281

tune on the whole people. So the ancient ritual of the lizard is always observed. On the Day of the Marriages a very special lizard is pressed into service by each couple who wants to be married. It will take the first juices from the man's penis and take them into the woman's vagina. If the lizard refuses at any stage in the ritual it is taken as a sign that the couple must not marry. No one has ever dared go against the rule because to do so would mean living as an outcast.

'To guard against the chances of a refusal, each spring the young women who want to, go with more experienced women to the high ground where this lizard has his habitat. Once there they set about capturing and training as many as they need.

'The young women are shown how to hunt down the creatures by way of calls and beautiful songs. They beat the ground, make thunder with their fists until the lizards are drawn, compulsively, to the camp. Then the women decorate their bodies. They paint circles around each others' nipples with the juice of many different and beautiful coloured berries, till the nipples seem so huge that they almost cover the whole breast. Then they plait soft hair from female animals into their own pubic hairs and bead it so that it falls around their thighs. They make the lips of their vulvae red with the leaves of a sacred plant and paint a great area around in beautiful colours, so that the whole sex seems to reach out across their thighs. Lastly, their eyes and their lips are adorned with the brightest colours in nature and they drench themselves in the perfumes of the orange flower, jonquil and jessamine.

'At length they dance. They dance morning, noon and night; wild, sensual dances that become more and more frenzied until it seems that the camp is filled with huge nipples and whirling vaginas.

'The lizards grow mad with what they see and smell and hear and many of them die in the rush into captivity. But the dances don't end until the women are exhausted. And then they sleep where they drop. Their colours smear and run in a crazy mess and everyone revels in it.

'When enough lizards are captured we gather roots that are shaped like the male organ; mandrakes they're called in Europe. It's easy to train the lizard to lick the root because if his reward is to snuggle between the legs of a woman, this animal will do anything.

'Within seven or eight days each woman will have her own, trained lizard. She decorates him with precious stones and gems. She carves pieces out of his very thick skin and embeds her mother's own jewels that are handed down, right into it. The skin grows back to hold the gems in place. The lizards have short lives. They live while the marriage is young and produces children and then they die. We keep their skeletons and use them as charms to bring our lovers to our beds.'

'See,' said the Baron, stepping forward. He grinned as he held out his podgy palm. In the middle of it sat a tiny white skeleton. 'There were no more female children in this family and I was given it by an ancient who knew she was near to death. I paid handsomely for it.'

With the story at its end the dancer rose and, virtually unnoticed, she left the room. Virtually, but not completely. Jean rose and followed her.

Evidently he was not successful. He came back into the salon a moment later. He approached the group talking with the Baron and hovered. A butterfly, with straps falling off her rounded, peachy shoulders, came up to him and entwined her fingers lovingly in his long, curly hair. But he brushed her off gently. Finally he butted in.

'I'd like to talk to the dancer,' he said to the Baron.

The Baron performed an obsequious little bow. 'I'm sorry, monsieur, but she is mine.'

'I sincerely beg your pardon. But I really do just want to talk to her,' said Jean firmly.

The Baron touched him on the arm. 'But everything has its price, monsieur.'

283

A note of distaste crept into Jean's voice. 'Let me be clear. It is the lizard that interests me. Might I be able to buy one? A live one?'

The Baron drew in a breath between his teeth, making a hiss like a plumber. 'Well, I don't know,' he said. He stroked his chin.

'Everything has its price?' mocked Jean.

'It may be arranged,' smiled the Baron. 'Your name, monsieur. I should like to know with whom I am dealing.'

'An unusual request, monsieur, in such a place. If you want credentials, I suggest you speak to Rosa. She knows me well and knows that I have money enough.'

'No, monsieur, you don't understand. Your name would be, how shall I say, a gesture.' He grinned. 'I am very discreet.'

'Impossible. Either speak to Rosa or I'm afraid . . .' said Jean.

'Very well,' said the Baron.

When Jean returned to the green velvet couch Paul was stroking the chin of his girl.

'You have the jawline of a goddess,' Paul was saying.

'Oh, you!' she giggled. 'You bloody artists are all the same. Goddesses, mices.'

'Muses, darling, muses,' said Paul.

'Whatever they are, I'm a real woman and I want you upstairs where I can fuck you.'

Paul threw back his head and laughed. 'Sounds wonderful but you'd better not let Rosa hear that. I can't afford you.' He turned to Jean. 'Can he get it?'

Jean sneered. 'He's a cad. He tried to sell me his girl.'

But their conversation was cut short. Rosa was bearing down on them, observing Paul with open hostility. Paul rose from the couch. He was tall, slender. He picked up his cloak. He had pushed his luck by staying for the Baron's presentation. Rosa let him spend his afternoons taking photographs of the girls and didn't charge him for their time. At present he was experimenting with movement. The girls seemed to enjoy

284

themselves rolling around on the Persian rug while he captured them on film. He did it with love and, of all the people he knew, they were the only ones who seemed to believe there was something fine in what he was doing. They dreamed together that the pictures would hang in Paris galleries and capture the attention of the whole world. Besides, he always gave them proper portraits if they wanted them and some of these sold on the seafront as postcards. Perhaps Rosa resented the fact that this money all went to the girls, without a cut for her.

Jean asked him to stay, but he refused. 'I want to develop some work,' he said.

Rosa brushed the seat he had vacated before she sat on it. 'Now, Jean, tell me everything, dear,' she said.

'I want one of those lizards.'

'Well, you know the Baron's a crook, dear. I wouldn't trust him as far as I could throw him. But, as I always say, if you want something badly enough in this world, you have to take risks.'

'Rosa, come on. You know I can't get my family name mixed up in anything dubious.'

'I know, I know. What is it you have in mind? You want me to act as a go-between? For a small consideration, dear, I shall be pleased to. That will sort things out nicely, won't it? And then even if he cuts up rough I would deny any involvement on your part.'

'Thank you, Rosa!' said Jean eagerly.

'I can't guarantee your money, my love, but your reputation is safe, and that of whoever you want to share your little whim with.' Rosa's eyes twinkled and her gaze strayed to his well-formed thigh. 'Now let me send one of the girls over to soothe away your worries while I deal with the Baron. Can't have any of my gentlemen solitary now, can I?'

'Send me Annette,' said Jean, stretching his arms.

The Haberdasher's Upstairs Rooms

'Here you are, dear,' said the tiny, red-haired, haberdasher. She took a key from under the counter and gave it to Oruela Bruyere with a wistful little smile. 'You are a lovely girl, my dear. A lovely, sad girl.'

'I don't know what you mean. I'm not sad,' said Oruela. She was feeling wonderful. Every cell in her body was looking forward to the touch of love.

'Mmmm,' said the little woman, wistfully.

Oruela went up the concealed staircase that rose secretly from the midst of silks and stockings. What a funny woman, she thought. The haberdasher was the aunt of her maid, Michelle, who said she was as good as a mother. Oruela had opened up to her a bit once and ever since, the woman had seemed to pity her. It was ridiculous.

The stairs continued up past one landing and a long narrow window that looked out seawards across the rooftops opposite. She came to a halt at the very top in front of a door and put the key in the lock. The door opened into an apartment in the roof.

She dropped her green kidskin purse and a pair of driving goggles on a glass-topped side table. A small glass-fronted stove in the fireplace heated the room against the unusually chilly spring day. That was thoughtful, she thought.

Heavy velvet curtains were tied back from the face of the small window. The room was never particularly light, even in the afternoon. She turned on a single standard lamp in the corner.

She removed her green gloves and then, carefully, a cream leather hat. She had flawless olive skin and soft brown eyes. Her glossy crown of deep brown, almost black hair fell into place. It was shingled at the back and swept behind her ears. She smoothed it in the mirror. Her figure was slender and she was tall. Her stylish driving coat of pale cream raw silk was buttoned diagonally from hem to shoulder and trimmed with creamy fur. She bent down to the hem where the fur caressed her pale, stockinged legs and slipped the first button free. One by one she widened the aperture as if rehearsing a scene. Underneath, her dress was a sumptuous hand-made peach mousseline. She tossed the coat on a chair as if it were no more than a bath towel.

A single string of pearls hung at her neck and cascaded over her breast to her waist. Following the fashion, the bodice of her dress was cut to disguise the curve of her waist and it fell straight to her hips where a sash was loosely tied. Her thighs suggested themselves to the eye as long and shapely; certainly, if her calves were anything to go by, her legs were a real asset. Her shoes were creamy, with kitten heels and a satin strap at the front.

She left the mirror and walked into the bedroom. The room was windowless. The only light was from a small skylight. Its patch of blue was turning misty violet as the evening drew in. Beside the big bed was a lamp made from the carved figure of a naked, plump cupid, his hands reaching up to hold the bulb. She turned him on and the soft light that filtered through the fringed shade shed itself on the sea-green counterpane. A fire burned in the small grate. She warmed her hands by it

287

and the firelight leapt about her face and body. A secret smile danced in her eyes.

Back in the sitting-room, she took a bottle of cognac from a low cabinet next to the table. She poured herself one and, glass in hand, she nestled into the big sofa, her legs underneath her, a hint of lace peeking from under the hem of her dress. She seemed to survey the tall palm standing in a pot in the opposite corner of the room. The door of the bedroom behind her stood slightly ajar.

She was too young to marry. That was the excuse she was currently giving her guardian who acted like he was fending off suitors left, right and centre. There had been two, as far as she could gather. She found the whole business of them asking *him* ridiculous. For the moment at least the excuse seemed acceptable, but she was on shaky ground. Apart from the fact that she was pushing twenty-five and wasn't anything like too young, although she felt it, her girlfriends were marrying all around her. There was a whole rash of weddings to be attended this spring.

Her friends were very practical. Of course they would take lovers, they said. Marriage was the only freedom that a girl could get. This wasn't Paris and even though Biarritz had its fashionable visitors, a single girl just didn't have the chance to explore love. Marriage therefore was a business arrangement, best got over with so that fun could start.

The truth was that Oruela wanted something different, something more. She didn't exactly know what, but she wanted to explore life. If she married it would be for love. Her guardians' marriage was like that of two stuffed dummies. Horrible! She would have something better. Besides, she had another, secret ambition which had nothing to do with marriage. She wanted to go to Paris, to the Sorbonne.

She didn't really have an academic mind but she had a romantic one and she had a vision of herself at Henri Bergson's philosophical classes, being noticed by artists and intellectuals for her beauty and brilliance. She hadn't articulated her brilliance yet but it was there, in embryo. She had a kind of confidence in it, even if others only described her as wilful.

The sound of a key turning in the lock shook her from her reverie. In whirled Jean looking more decidedly handsome and more in love than ever.

He immediately rushed to Oruela's knees and covered her hands with kisses. She laughed and pushed his chilly outside clothes away. He jumped up and unbuttoned his overcoat, flinging it on the chair and his hat flying after it.

'Oruela, Oruela!' he moaned.

This time she made no attempt to push him away. She stroked his long glossy hair and kissed his nose.

He touched her face and sighed, he ran his finger down her neck and sighed, he cupped her lovely shoulder in his hand, sighing all the while. 'I have something for you, my darling! Something so special you will hardly believe it! I wanted you to have this as soon as I heard about it. It's taken a whole year to get!' He reached for a package wrapped in brown paper, placed it in Oruela's lap, and fixed his eyes on her face.

'How was Paris?' she asked, not quite nonchalantly.

'Paris? Open your present!'

'I shan't until you tell me at least one word about Paris,' she said.

Jean laughed. 'Paris was Paris! It was beautiful! It was busy! Open your present!'

'Did it come from Paris/'

'It came *via* Paris,' he said enigmatically.

'It's got little holes in it . . .' She began unwrapping the parcel, under Jean's adoring gaze.

The tiny, ornate silver cage that emerged contained a greenish lizard. She couldn't help but shriek. The lizard stilled itself completely, trying to merge into the grass that lined the floor of its dwelling. But the ruby embedded in its forehead, and the cluster of sapphires at its

289

neck shone and sparkled in the twin suns of the lamp and the firelight, preventing its camouflage tactics.

Jean laughed. 'Don't be frightened.' He got up and refilled her brandy glass, pouring a generous measure of the delicious amber liquid for himself.

Together they sat in the gathering twilight and he told her the story he had heard about the lizard's role in life at La Maison Rose.

Oruela found herself aroused by the thought of the women decorating their bodies, by the dancing. 'Do you mean you think we . . . What if he refuses? I haven't trained him!' she whispered, barely trusting herself to speak.

'Oruela, my darling, don't be silly. We don't need to bother with the meaning of the thing. It's an adventure. Besides, why should he? We're perfect for each other.'

'Should we . . . should we do it?' she asked again.

'Do you want to?' he asked.

She could only nod her head. Her voice was too heavy with wicked excitement to speak.

Jean kissed the rustling fabric at her breast and her skin responded to the touch of him, gradually pushing away thoughts that had no place in this moment. The silence was broken only by the crackle of the coals in the fire. The lizard moved and sent ripples into her lap.

'My darling!' crooned Jean. 'Nothing will part us, I swear,' and he raised her chin gently.

She looked at him. I could be happy with him, she thought, I could really . . .

'What do you say?' he whispered.

A wicked grin suddenly lit up her face. 'What the hell! If he refuses, he refuses! There are plenty more where you came from!'

'Minx!' cried Jean, gripping her arm.

She wriggled herself free, sending the little lizard's cage rolling on to the couch as she climbed on top of Jean. The lizard darted furiously about in his cage as she slid the delicate fabric of her dress up her thighs, showing off the tops of pale silk stockings. Jean grew

290

hard as she pushed her sex at him. He laughed, a little nervously.

She straightened her back, pushing out her breasts. They ached for kisses and the feel of his lips was heaven. His hands were strong and his touch a little rough. She pulled his hair gently as he slid her dress further up her body. Her knickers were mere wisps of silk that were tied on the inner leg with tiny ribbons. His fingers searched her sex through the fabric, rolling her swollen labia. She covered his face and hair with soft crooning kisses.

Jean rose, carrying her with him. He kicked open the bedroom door. The lamp sent wriggling shadows dancing over their bodies as they fell into the soft pillows.

'Turn over,' begged Jean. 'Let me undo your buttons.'

She rolled slowly over and lay still, sinking into the darkness as his hands discovered the lovely shape of her back, button by button, tie by tie. When she felt it bare, she raised her arse and slid out from her chrysalis and turned to him. Her bare breasts were beautiful, with lustrous dark nipples, her belly a little rounded, her dark triangle of hair waiting to be discovered.

'You're a work of art,' groaned Jean and he took her breasts once more in his mouth to suck. She loved the sight of his head bent at her breasts, his shoulders bowed at her service. A suggestion of expensive hair oil rose from his head. She wanted to see his body. She pulled at the shoulder of his shirt, reached for his waistband. 'Undress,' she said. 'Undress.' And he was forced to leave his worship of her to undress.

He hadn't an ounce of fat on him. He moved around the room, folding his clothes, like a young lion. His skin was just a touch paler than her own, the kind that goes honey-coloured in the sun. Even in his nakedness everything about him suggested wealth and the confidence that goes with it. He had just the right amount of hair on his chest. It trickled down darkly to his thick straight prick.

'Wait!' he cried and sprang out of the room. His arse was a delight to behold.

'As if I wouldn't,' she breathed.

He returned with the little silver cage and lay down next to her, resting on one elbow.

He lifted the latch.

The lizard darted out and stopped still on the counterpane. It stayed absolutely still for half a minute. Oruela watched it with a mixture of mounting apprehension and excitement.

It moved so suddenly it made her shudder.

It scampered on to his long thigh and jumped lightly from there into his lush pubic hair. It stopped, then it darted on to his cock and he groaned, falling back into the pillows helplessly. The lizard ran around his cock, up, down, across his balls. It ran into the crevice underneath and his legs fell apart. It ran under him to his arsehole and back up again. It circled his hard sex. With an effort Jean raised his head to watch.

Oruela suddenly thought, Hickory Dickory Dock, the lizard ran round his cock, and she began to giggle. But then it jumped. It was on her hand. It ran fast up her arm, over her shoulder and down across one breast, flicking its tail at her hard nipple as it went. The sensation made her serious. Her whole body tensed. The lizard ran across the smooth plain of her belly, its jewels gleaming. It dived into her soft pubic hair. She bit her fist.

The little green animal slid down into the folds of her vulva and pitter-pattered around at the opening, relaxing her, like adept fingers, gently. She began to open. She began to want it inside. She wanted it so much. Yes. She could feel the little animal begin to squeeze itself inside her.

At that precise moment Jean's fascination turned to rabid jealousy. He tore the little creature away from her and claimed her as his own. Yes, this was what she really wanted. His prick replaced the animal and he moved with a passion so complete it was

292

everything. His hair in her face, his breath on her hair. She ground against him, massaging her clitoris. There was no return from here. He was hers. The power of him made her gasp. Everything else was irrelevant. He gave one long moan as he came and she was taken along with him, into the best of all possible worlds.

Sometime later she opened her eyes and he was lying close.

She said his name.

'Let's get married,' he said, raising himself on one arm. The way his torso curved into his hip was lovely. It was perfect.

'What!' she said.

'Let's get married soon?'

'Oh!' she said.

'What does that mean?' he asked, sounding a little peeved.

She raised herself. 'I'm surprised, that's all.'

'I want you. I want you to be mine for ever,' he said, and kissed her bruised nipple.

'But I've told everyone I don't believe in it!' she said. 'Besides – don't laugh at me – but I want to go to Paris. I want to go to the Sorbonne and meet bohemians and intellectuals and go to salons and live outrageously!' There! It was out.

Jean smiled and kissed her lips lightly. 'As my wife you can do all the things you want to. Of course you'll go to Paris and meet the people I like.'

'Will I like them too?'

'Of course. And they will love you. Nothing you could do would displease me, Oruela. I love you so much.'

She reached for him and kissed his mouth, lovingly. There was a whole world in his kiss.

'Apparently, people are beginning to talk about us, did you know?' she asked after a moment.

'What? Who? How? I haven't heard anything,' said Jean.

293

'People meaning my father really. He says you won't suffer. It's me that's supposedly in the wrong.' She hadn't told Jean she was an orphan, looked after by guardians. She didn't know why.

'There isn't any wrong,' he cried. 'Oh, Oruela, what does this mean? Why are you telling me this. Is it an excuse for not getting married. Don't . . .'

'Perhaps it's an excuse *for* getting married!' she said.

'Yes. Yes. Yes!' cried Jean and leaped up as if he'd just scored a winning goal. 'Oh, my darling. Come here.' And he came back to her and before the first sex had grown cold they were making more. The stars began to peek through the patch of indigo sky in the skylight above them.

The streets outside had a touch of timelessness, the quiescence of aristocracy, of old money, even monarchy, enthroned or otherwise. On the wide, sweeping seafront the buildings of another age stood, barrack-like, pondering the great Atlantic. A stone's throw from Oruela and Jean's love-nest was one street where the houses had been turned into clinics. Each one offered a modern, specialist treatment in the galaxy of ailments that beset Biarritz's fabulously rich. Brass plaques announced the wonders of these therapies and some even had the new neon signs. About halfway up the street, above one such sign, an electric light was shining out from a first-floor window through the gaps in the shutters.

Inside this room Norbert Bruyere, Oruela's guardian, was sitting on the edge of a leather armchair in his underwear. His outer clothes hung neatly over a clothes-horse. A cup of coffee and a piece of cake stood untouched on an occasional table.

Norbert Bruyere looked tired. He stared blankly in the direction of the plain, white wall in front of him. He was a big man, yet everything seemed to droop from his bent shoulders.

294

A soft knock sounded at the door and the therapist, Dr von Streibnitz, entered. The doctor was a small, bespectacled man with lily-white hands that fluttered as he spoke.

'My dear Norbert. I'm so sorry to keep you waiting like this. Important phone call. Now. How are you feeling?'

'Not good, Helmut, not good.'

'Well, you know you always feel a little dazed after the treatment. I trust Nurse took good care of you. How long were you in the Hat?'

'An hour, as usual. But, Helmut, it isn't just that, it's my whole life. I have no energy, no zest any more. Sometimes I feel so tired.'

'Let me look at you,' said the doctor and he investigated Norbert's eyes, his ears, his throat and, with the aid of a stethoscope, his chest. 'I don't think there's much wrong with you except a touch of the spring sniffles. Change of season and all that, we're not getting any younger.' Finishing off, he washed his hands in the little sink. 'I'll give you more of the bathing salts you had this time last year. Do you the power of good. Get dressed now and come into my office for a chat.'

Norbert sluggishly did as he was told.

The pretty young nurse at her desk in the next room gave him a big smile but he didn't return it, or even appear to notice. She shrugged and went back to the study of her textbook.

'On here, my friend,' said the doctor, patting the big leather couch. 'Lie down and talk to me. What did you think of my new little nurse by the way?'

'I didn't notice.'

'Didn't notice! Norbert! Good grief, man. Didn't you notice her . . .' The doctor held his hands under imaginary breasts and juggled them.

'But that's my problem, Doctor! I've lost interest.'

'Now, Norbert, I've told you before. You came to me over a year ago in this same frame of mind and I told you that the physical treatment won't work without a change of attitude. We perked up a little bit, did't we? Now, inertia is self-destructive, you have to think positive. Do you still have that mistress of yours?'

'Well, I was exaggerating when I called her a mistress. She's an old, um, friend who does me a service. I still see her, yes, once a month or so, but I've told you what that's all about. It's not enough. I wish I were young again, Doctor. I couldn't get enough women when I was young.' A tear slid down Norbert's cheek.

'Why not get yourself a nice young whore this evening, Norbert. You've got to think positive. Think of it, old boy, a nice young bit of stuff with bouncy tits all firm and pert.' The doctor's eyes were shining. A little bit of dribble squeezed out of the corner of his mouth.

'But I can't!' whined Norbert. And he continued to whine, for nearly an hour, at the end of which he paid handsomely.

'Think positive! *Think young*, Norbert!' boomed Dr von Streibnitz as they parted at the door.

Norbert plodded down the stairs and out into the street. He turned left and left again and halted at the door of the haberdashery. The sign on the door said 'Fermé', but a light was on in the back of the shop. Norbert rapped on the door sharply.

'Why, Monsieur Bruyere, come in.' The haberdasher let him in and locked the door behind him.

'Are you well?' she said. 'You look peaky. Oh, you do look pale. Were you passing and taken ill? Oh, I'm glad you knocked.'

Norbert sat on a chair and waved her offer of water away with a dismissive, gloved hand. ' I'm perfectly all right, thank you. I want to send something to Paris.'

She smiled professionally. 'I have the very thing. Just in yesterday. Let me show you.'

'No. No,' said Norbert, heaving himself up. 'Just send it to the usual address. Tonight, you understand. It must go tonight.'

'But my girl's gone, sir. Can't it go in the morning?'

'I said *tonight!*' shouted Norbert.

'Very well,' she said between gritted teeth. She showed Norbert the door.

And with plenty of cursing, a flimsy piece of lingerie, the colour of a summer sky, was wrapped, boxed and dispatched on the night train to Paris.

Don't You Lie to Me

The sun was rising as Oruela left Biarritz the next morning in her open Peugeot. The lizard's cage was wrapped in brown paper to protect him against the chill in the early spring breeze, and the whole package was placed carefully and lovingly on the soft red leather of the front seat.

Oruela handled the car confidently. She loved driving. But she felt a little dazed this morning. Was it the right thing, to marry Jean? The glow from their night together was still with her. At the thought of his body in the firelight, her womb seemed to thud inside.

'It will get me out of the morgue,' she said to the little cage beside her. About two kilometres before the town of Bayonne she turned down a lane and brought the car to a halt in front of the immense, decorative iron gates of her home. As she sprang out of the car her coat whirled open in the breeze. She shivered as she opened the heavy gates.

Three newly built garages stood at the side of the house, which in fact looked nothing like a morgue. Its cheerful white walls and lemony green paintwork in the sunlight was very fresh. Oruela cut the engine of the car and allowed it to coast in slowly through the open doors of the first garage.

298

'We're home, *mon chéri*,' she whispered as she wriggled out of the car. The garage was cold. Oruela shivered again; she was very tired. She carefully picked up the cage. 'There,' she whispered. 'Time for sleep.'

'Where have you been?' Norbert Bruyere stood in the doorway. He was in his dressing-robe which had been fastened, hurriedly, underneath his substantial paunch. Most of his nightshirt was hanging out of the front of it. His legs were bare, right down to the crocodile-skin slippers on his long, thin feet.

Oruela didn't answer immediately. She tried to gather her thoughts in a hurry.

'Where have you been, Oruela?' repeated Norbert.

'I've been with Marie,' she blurted. 'We were tired and fell asleep. I thought it was better than driving home.'

'Now, that's not the truth, my little girl,' he menaced.

Oruela pursed her lips.

'My dear,' he said, changing his tune. And he reached out and touched her chin with his long finger.

Oruela backed away. She dropped the lizard on the seat of the car and stood there defiantly.

Norbert moved closer to her. 'Tell me the truth and I won't punish you, Oruela. Marie telephoned last night. You weren't with her.'

Oruela's teeth began to chatter. The engine-metal gave a groan as it cooled down.

Norbert gripped her wrist. His breath stirred the fur around her collar. 'You were with him, weren't you?' he urged.

'So what!' she said, looking him in the eye.

Norbert smiled. 'I love to hear that haughty tone in your voice,' he said. He moved so close that his body touched hers. 'Come on, my sweetie. Tell me all about your lover.'

And then she felt his prick against her leg, felt it move, harden a little bit. It kindled a feeling in her belly. She realised, with amazement, that the feeling was desire.

He raised his hand to her chin in a fatherly fashion and then, slowly, he let it fall to her bare neck. He traced the outline of her dress where it touched the soft skin at her breast. He smiled wistfully.

'Just tell me about him,' he said. 'Please, just tell me what he does to you!'

'No!' she said. 'No,' and she pushed past him. She stood on the gravel outside and yelled, 'Leave me alone, you dirty pig. You're supposed to act like a *father*!'

'Oh, my Oruela,' he whimpered. 'I do love you. Don't push me away. I need your comfort, let me . . .' He groped after her.

But she was out of reach. She turned towards the house.

'It's your own fault, girl,' he shouted. 'If you behave like a tart you ought to expect to be treated like one.'

She spun round. 'You hypocrite. Everyone knows you have a mistress, so why shouldn't I have a lover? Anyway, we're going to get married!'

Norbert snarled. 'Don't count on it. Your precious Jean has a hundred women as well as you!'

'I wish you'd drop dead,' she screamed. 'I wish you'd die. Right now. Right there.'

He crumpled against the sleek wing of the car as her footsteps died away.

Norbert dragged his tall, drooping frame wearily inside the house. The big sleepy mansion seemed to settle down as if, realising the day was too much to wake up to, it turned over and went back to sleep again.

But, just as the stillness began to seem complete, a figure emerged from the bushes where it had been hiding. It was a woman, moving so quietly that she barely disturbed the gravel. She was dressed from head to toe in long old-fashioned black. Her figure was slender and upright, very stiff. Her face was small and pale, her hair was raked up into a tight blonde knot at the back of her head. Her mouth was turned down at the corners, accentuating her jowls.

300

In her ill-humour Genevieve Bruyere looked older than her forty-five years and there was disturbance in her violet-blue eyes. A hint of unreality burned in their depths.

She walked in a straight line across the lawn towards a small rose tree. Its leaves were bright green and hardly unfurled. Virgin leaves. She pulled a branch close to her face and examined it for pests. Finding a tiny cluster of aphids near the shoot she enclosed it between finger and thumb and squashed it until her skin went white.

She marched to the garage to sniff around and her eye alighted on the small brown paper package on the front seat of the car. She picked it up and tore it open without hesitation. The lizard eyed her and turned sideways. He crouched, he switched his tail, he shortened it and elongated it, he hid his feet. He looked like a little green penis.

Genevieve's surprise wrote itself on her face in capitals. For one brief moment the expression made her look younger, almost better. She picked up the cage and closed the garage doors.

Upstairs Oruela locked the door of her room before she undressed and climbed into bed. She would stay in bed and she wouldn't get out again until Jean came to get her. That's what she would do.

Something was wrong with Norbert lately and now he'd gone mad. She began to cry. Dammit, he'd always been kind to her before, not like his wife. Now there was nobody except Jean. She suddenly remembered the lizard. 'You'll have to stay there. I'm sorry!' she sobbed. She pulled the covers up over her head.

She dreamt she was floating down a river with the current, a warm, pure current. Every so often a weed caressed her bare skin, its slimy tentacles slipping in between her toes or her thighs. On and on she floated, her breasts raised up out of the water to the sun and

301

the warm splashing water sprinkling droplets every-where over her skin.

Then suddenly, a change, a bed in the river and the current got faster. She was scared. But there was Daddy on the river bank and he put out his hand and grabbed her and pulled her to safety.

He was wearing a Roman toga. It flowed over his belly towards his feet. But it was all wet and Oruela was really sorry she'd made him all wet and she undressed him. She clung to him, climbing up his belly, feeling very small but her sex was huge and she wanted him. She could feel his huge hard cock right up her back. She willed him to touch her sex and at last he did. His hands pulled apart her buttocks and he lowered her onto his cock. It filled her up, there was no room for anything else and all of her emptied all over him.

When Oruela awoke her mind was full of the dream. She tried to shake herself awake but she felt strange, as if she had crossed some line and could never go back.

She rose from the bed and asked down the tube for Michelle to bring up some coffee. There was some sort of kerfuffle going on in the kitchen. She had to repeat herself. It ruffled her taut nerves. She would dress and rescue the lizard. Then she would telephone Jean and try not to go crazy in the meantime. Oruela worried about going crazy.

A minute or two later a sharp rap at the door made her jump. It wasn't Michelle's rap. Despite having already put on her knickers, her stockings and a skirt, Oruela pulled her nightdress down over them and jumped back into the bed, pulling the covers right up to her neck.

It was Genevieve, her stepmother. She put the break-fast tray on the table by the window and folded her arms.

'Can I have it on the bed. please?' asked Oruela. 'Where is Michelle?'

Genevieve ignored her and sidled to the side of the bed.

'What is it?' said Oruela.

'Your father died last night,' she said, pursing her lips.

Oruela sank into the pillows with a whimper. Her stepmother's face seemed to grow larger and larger, its sneering mouth opening wider and wider.

Genevieve sniffed.

Oruela watched her back going out of the room until it was a pinprick and then the wardrobe swelled and lumbered towards her . . .

Michelle rushed into Oruela's room and, seeing the look on her mistress's face, she ran out again and returned with smelling salts. She put them under Oruela's nose. Michelle was a lovely, sunny-looking girl with a plump peach of an arse that even the drab maid's uniform could not entirely conceal. Michelle had been in the house since she was twelve years old. They had grown up together.

Oruela pushed the smelling salts away and mumbled, 'Is he really . . .?'

'What?' said Michelle. 'What are you saying?'

'Is he really dead, Michelle?'

'Yes, he is.'

'How?'

'They don't know. Doctor Simenon says there's to be an autopsy.'

'When did he die?'

'During the night.'

'Was it a ghost then?' Oruela murmured quietly.

'What? What is it? You look funny. Come on, drink your coffee,' said Michelle, briskly.

'Michelle, something's wrong with me. Everything is moving.'

'Smell this bottle.' Michelle raised Oruela's head in the crook of her arm and held the bottle firmly under her nose.

Oruela shook her head. 'Michelle! He wasn't dead when I came home this morning!'

'What time?'

'It was dawn, about five. I was with Jean all night. My father caught me in the garage . . . . Michelle, you mustn't ever tell anyone this, but he attacked me.'

'He what?'

'He put his prick on my leg and touched me.'

'Oh, the wicked man. *Mon dieu!*' said Michelle.

'Never tell anyone, Michelle. Swear!'

'I swear!'

'I wished him dead, Michelle. I . . .'

'Well, that's natural,' said Michelle sensibly.

'There was nothing natural about my dream.' Oruela felt her own voice fading away.

'Look, don't upset yourself. You know you're a bit delicate sometimes. It was only a dream whatever it was,' said Michelle.

'Supposing I had the power to kill him! Supposing just by wishing him dead I did it! It might be possible, Michelle!' Now she was shouting.

'Sssssh! Calm down. You don't want people to hear you saying that sort of thing. Control yourself!' Michelle was having trouble being calm herself.

'Oh God, Michelle, I'm frightened. What if – '

Michelle suddenly grew angry. 'Now stop it this minute,' she said. 'Sit up. Eat your breakfast. Here.' She put the tray in front of Oruela. 'I'm going to fetch the doctor from downstairs and get him to give you something.'

Dr Simenon, the handsome young locum, followed Michelle immediately she told him what was wrong. As they ascended the stairs Genevieve came out of her drawing-room and looked stonily at them.

'Hurry, Doctor,' said Michelle. 'She needs a sedative. Her stepmother will upset her if she comes up.'

'Shock,' pronounced Dr Simenon. Oruela could hear his voice as if through a door. 'Give her this and here's another one for later. She needs rest and comfort. Rest

304

and comfort. Keep her warm and read her a book to keep her mind off things. Poor girl.' He stood up and was packing his instruments away when the door opened and Genevieve came in carrying the lizard in its cage.

'Keep that door shut please, madame. Your daughter needs warmth,' said the doctor.

'*This* is no daughter of mine!' shouted Genevieve. 'I found *this* by the side of my husband's bed today after Robert discovered him dead this morning!' Madame threw the lizard on to the bed. The little creature whirled around and around inside, out of his poor little mind.

'My little lizard!' cried Oruela. 'Oh, my baby!' and she reached for him, sending the bedclothes tumbling. All eyes registered the skirt she had on in bed.

'I wouldn't be surprised if we find out that a bite from that killed my darling husband!' wept Genevieve, tearlessly.

'Wait,' said the doctor. 'I don't remember this in the room.'

'Well, you weren't looking, were you, *Doctor*!' spat Genevieve. 'I heard her threaten him with it early this morning in the garage. She didn't know I was there. Did you!' she hissed at Oruela. 'She said she'd kill him, just because he reprimanded her for coming home at all hours!'

Oruela opened her mouth to speak. She saw Michelle trying to warn her with her eyes. She whispered, 'It's no use, Michelle! I must have done it! I did it in my sleep!'

Dr Simenon bellowed, '*Madame* Bruyere! Leave the room please. Now! I insist!'

Genevieve snorted and marched out. Oruela collapsed back on to the pillows. The sedative was taking effect. She closed her eyes. The last thing she heard was Michelle saying, 'I'm frightened, sir.'

* * *

305

Dr Simenon's calm control of the situation made Michelle feel safer. He chucked her cheek and left, closing the door behind him.

Genevieve started shouting hysterically outside and Michelle put her hands over her ears to muffle the worst of it. Then there were footsteps and the sound of the front door slamming. Downstairs Genevieve picked up the hall telephone. Michelle ran to the bedroom door.

'Mayor Derive,' Genevieve was saying. 'Hello, Jacques. No, I'm afraid I'm not very well at all. Norbert is dead. Yes, dead, and we think there has been a crime. Robert discovered him.' She paused and a slow, almost sexy smile spread on her face as she listened. 'We don't know. That stupid Doctor Simenon has been. He says there should be an autopsy. But I have discovered a poisonous lizard belonging to Oruela and when I confronted her with it she confessed . . . Yes. Will you come yourself, Jacques? . . . Oh, I see . . . but please come as soon as you can. Who shall I expect in the meantime – Peine?'

It was Michelle's turn to sneer. Hark at her turning on the soft voice for that old fat pig, the mayor. If Genevieve was capable of it, which Michelle doubted very much because Genevieve was a frigid old baggage if ever there was one, she was probably having it off with the old pig. But their sort didn't have it off. They just breathed heavily at dinner parties. She knew. She'd seen it.

She slipped quietly back into Oruela's room and looked at the sleeping form. Poor love. She hadn't had much of a happy life and it was going to get worse. This wasn't the first time she'd lost her senses. It wasn't surprising with those two as parents. There was no love in the house. A girl needed the sure ground of love.

She went to the window and pulled the curtains back into their ties. When she and Robert married their children would always be loved. It was a beautiful spring day outside. It was getting warmer. But none of it penetrated the north-facing room. Michelle shivered and turned away from the window.

It was then she noticed the little lizard again, in his cage, sitting on the bed. She went up to it and bent down. 'Look at you then,' she said. 'Cor! Look at you. You're all covered in jewels. Aren't you smart. And a little collar. You're a pet. I bet you're a pet that Jean's bought, aren't you?' She lifted the cage up to her face. 'Look at your scales. You're like a little dinosaur! You're beautiful!'

The lizard turned around slowly and squatted. It seemed drowsy. Michelle laughed. 'You're trying to show off, aren't you? I would too if I was as beautiful as you.'

And then she heard Robert's voice in the echoing downstairs hall, answering the mistress.

Oruela was sleeping soundly and Michelle needed Robert right this minute. She locked the bedroom door behind her and, putting the key in her pocket, tiptoed down the stairs.

Robert looked up and grinned when he saw her. He wasn't a particularly handsome man, but he was sexy in his way. Probably because it was mostly what he thought about. He was in great shape. His real love was sport of any kind and he kept in shape with dumbbells and barbells. Michelle frequently spent her nights watching his muscles developing.

She flew down the stairs and straight into his arms.

'You all right?' he said. 'No, you're not, are you. Come in here. It's conference time.' He opened the broom-cupboard door under the stairs and shoved her in. Inside, he lit a stub of candle, bending down to put a large rag at the base of the door so the light wouldn't show in the hall.

'We ain't been in here for a while, have we?' he said, grabbing her pussy as he stood up.

'Have you heard what's going on in this house?' said Michelle impatiently.

'I've got the gist,' he said, and grabbed her arse with his other hand.

'They're screaming blue murder!' said Michelle.

'They're all nuts,' he said. He was inching up her skirt. 'He's not cold yet and she's just told me she wants all her stuff moved out of the back room into the front where it's sunny.'

'Oh God, Robert,' whispered Michelle. 'I bet she did it!'

'Did what?'

'Killed him.'

Robert finally stopped what he was doing. 'What? Killed the old man? What makes you think any-one killed him? He died in his bloody sleep, didn't he?'

'Robert, I thought you'd got the gist. She's accused Oruela of murder and it's her all along!'

'Eh?'

'Didn't you hear all . . . Never mind. Hold me, Robert.'

He put his arms around her and squeezed her tight, kissing her hair.

'I've got to be strong. Oruela hasn't got anybody that'll stick up for her but me.'

'She can stick up for herself for once, can't she?' His hands slithered down to her arse.

'No. She's gone all hysterical, like she used to when she was a kid.'

Robert let out a sigh of contempt and held her firmly by the shoulders. 'I told you they're all mad, the lot of them. You're soft on Oruela. I know she's a nice kid and that but she's always had funny turns. Maybe, if someone did kill him, it was her.'

'Oruela's not that kind of crazy!' she insisted a little too loudly.

'Ssshh!' he said, putting his hand over her mouth.

Michelle gently took his hand away and lowered her voice. She spoke very close to his face. 'She's not mad like that, she's just delicate sometimes . . .'

Robert stroked her neck with his finger and gently circled down on to her breast. It felt like feathers. 'While you're all worried about her, what about me? I haven't got a man to serve any more, have I? I could be out of a job,' he said.

'Oh, Robert, don't be daft. She needs a man around the house.' But it was a thought. Suddenly the world was crumbling to bits. 'Here, come on, put your hand back up there. I like it.'

Robert reached down and lifted the hem of her skirt, sliding his hand into her new underwear. She felt his cool fingers pushing into her vulva and suddenly she was hornier than hell. She pushed herself on to his fingers.

He took a sharp intake of breath. 'You want it, don't you,' he said. 'You're all wet.'

'On the floor,' she heard herself say.

'Get them mats out then,' he said.

She turned her back to him to get a couple of housework mats off a shelf at the back of the long low cupboard, and as she bent down to arrange them on the floor he had her skirt right up from behind and she felt the air on her buttocks and his fingers again.

'Stay like that,' she heard him say in that low voice she loved so much and then she felt his cock pressing at her pussy.

'You got that out quick,' she said. 'Oh!' She felt herself being lifted on to it like a coat on to a hook. But it was at an uncomfortable angle and anyway she didn't want it like that. He was too quick and he hadn't got the hang of keeping her happy with his hand around the front.

'Robert!' she hissed. 'I'm going to fall over!'

He took it out of her and she breathed a sigh of relief and turned over, settling herself on the mats.

He was smiling at her. 'You needn't have worried. I can last out long enough to do that and wait for you to come, little lady.'

'Oh yeah, since when?'

309

'Since I've been teaching myself a bit of technique, that's when,' he whispered

'I'll bet you five francs one night when we're comfortable in bed. But till then you just get down here and press on this,' she said.

He lowered himself towards her. His cock was beautiful, even if it was poking out of his shirt-tails like a gangster's pistol. She giggled and reached forward to lift up the shirt and get a glimpse of the way his muscled torso flowed down into that dense mass of dark brown hair.

It was at that moment that they heard the bell and the sound of the parlour-maid running up the back passage.

Michelle held her breath. The footsteps stopped outside the cupboard door. 'Where's my damn coffee?' hissed Genevieve.

Robert very slowly took down a doorstop from the small shelf by his head and slid it silently under the rag at the base of the door.

Michelle suddenly realised she was breathing hard and tried to control it but she was panting. Her breasts were rising and falling like crazy. Robert was smiling. He touched her. She was streaming.

'Where's Robert?' asked Genevieve.

The parlour-maid replied that she didn't know.

Robert rubbed the moisture from Michelle's pussy like he was feeling silk and then he smoothed it on to his cock. It glistened in the candlelight.

'Well, find him and tell him to come here at once,' barked Genevieve.

Robert held his cock and guided it towards Michelle's sex. He slipped inside.

Robert moved inside Michelle and sucked at her ear. She caressed the soft hair on his head and kissed it. He pushed into her slowly and silently.

Genevieve trotted up the stairs.

All sound drifted away and there was only Robert and his prick thrusting in and out. Michelle suddenly

didn't care how much noise they made, she couldn't
hear anything, she could only feel. His thighs on hers,
his shirt against her breast. His head, his hair and his
cock, slowly in and out. And yet they were quiet. There
was no noise, even the slightest was willed away. He
raised his head and kissed her, long and slow and kept
his movements up. Michelle knew she felt love at that
moment and she kissed him back and lay there, still as
the earth, squeezing the walls of her vagina as hard as
she could around his cock. She held it, held it, held it
until it began like a sting inching its way to her belly
and she knew it was going to burst. It started slowly
receding into her, almost escaping; she was frightened
it would stop. It was too good. She concentrated on
squeezing again but her body had taken over and the
sting burst into a million parts that filled her and settled
her.

She gradually became aware of the sound of her own
breath. She had no idea if Robert had come or not but
he wasn't hard any more, so she assumed he must
have. The candle had gone out.

'Are you all right?' he whispered.

She managed a noise,

'Is that a yes?'

'Aha,' she said.

'You were really gone there!' he whispered.

She wished he could've said something more romantic. But he smelt nice.

He moved away and lit a match. It was horrible to
feel him go.

She felt self-conscious under even the tiny glare of
the match-flame.

'Hold this!' he hissed.

She raised herself on her elbow and took the match.
She watched him buttoning up. He smoothed his hair.

The flame touched her fingers and she blew it out.

He moved the rag from the door and reached for her
to give her a kiss as he bent down.

311

'Take these,' he whispered, giving her the matches. 'Shuffle back there while I open the door.'

She pulled his head towards her and kissed him again. His lips were delicious.

'I love you,' he said.

She shuffled back into the corner and he opened the door. 'You get yourself together. Listen out. Unless you hear me saying something then assume the coast is clear. All right?' and he was gone.

She reassembled her uniform in the dark, feeling slightly surprised that her fingers still worked. Then she stepped out into the daylight. The key! She checked her pocket. It was still there, miraculously. She climbed the stairs, a little unsteadily.

Paris in the Springtime

The same morning, in a large apartment just south of St Germain des Prés, a woman turned her attention to the luxurious box that had arrived from Biarritz a little earlier. She opened it and unwrapped the sky-blue lingerie inside. She held it up briefly then dropped it back in the box and picked up a novel and her coffee.

Euska Onaldi was in her late thirties. She had dark brown curly hair clasped haphazardly in a clip at the back of her head. She had one of those faces that is lovely overall yet not composed of typically beautiful parts. Her nose was a little too long, her dark eyes were bewitching although a little too wide apart in her broad face. Her mouth was wide, her skin was clear and healthy and, after the new fashion, it was tanned.

Euska wore a robe with huge kimono-like sleeves cuffed with black. Its shawl collar was black while the loose body was a mass of big pale pink roses and emerald green leaves on a background of cream. It fell around her comfortably without obvious fastenings. On one big foot was a flat, black satin mule. The other mule had escaped.

She read for the duration of her coffee and then, retrieving the mule, she sauntered over to the gramophone and put the needle on a record. A moment later she began to move her luxurious body in a dance around the peach and green room, her silhouette crossing the long window. She danced slowly, stretching her legs, arms, loosening her hips, dropping her shoulders, letting her long backbone slip, vertebra by vertebra, into place.

An appearance in the bedroom door interrupted her.

'You're energetic,' said Ernesto. He had a towel around his waist.

Euska smiled. 'I'm exercising! It's good for the vitality.' The tune ended. 'Sit down, I'll make some more coffee,' she said.

'Never mind that, I want some of you.' He walked up to her and encircled her waist with one powerful arm, drawing her towards him like he was picking up a slice of featherweight pastry. He kissed her neck.

Ernesto was a man of medium build and Spanish features. His jet hair was a little grey at the temples. His back was broad and well-developed, his legs handsome below the towel, his waist only a little thickened with middle age.

'Come back to bed,' he said into her ear and he slipped the robe off her shoulders.

It fell to the floor, leaving her gloriously naked. She retaliated by pulling his towel and he laughed, holding out his hand.

She allowed him to lead her back into the bedroom. He lay back on the bed, his morning erection waiting for her. She crawled on to the bed and kissed him as he began to play with her sex, first with his hand, massaging the skin around her clitoris, and then with his tongue. All the while she stroked his back, his thigh, his balls. He surfaced and kissed her breasts for a little while.

'Come to me!' she whispered.

He manoeuvred himself on top of her and fucked her as only a mature man can. Euska reflected on the nature of her lover. The concentration of a man of fifty is better tuned, she thought. Like the muscle that attaches his

314

cock to the rest of his body he has relaxed with age and become more supple. He is ready to bend and turn and enjoy positions impossible for a younger man to accomplish without pain. Ernesto was a thoroughly sensual man. Unlike some men of whatever age who leave a woman feeling as if her mind has been fucked, he concentrated with his body.

His skin was brown and softly hairy. Even on his arse he had a light covering of down and his chest was the chest of a bear. Neither was Euska a hairless adolescent and her maturity was at peace with itself. She opened seriously, her strong brown belly and thighs huge with desire, matching him in strength.

As they gathered momentum together she held his arse in her hands, feeling the muscles working. She pulled him into her, using his strength to her own advantage. He loved this. The breath escaped from him in one long moan as it ended in a glistening heap of happy flesh.

'What's this?' he asked, as she came into the living-room with more coffee. He had picked the card out of the box that Euska hadn't looked at.

'You know what it is,' she said, simply.

'He's still around then.'

'He is.'

'I don't know how you can stand him.'

She shrugged her shoulders and sat close by him.

'What is it you actually do with him?' he asked.

'Ernesto!' She sat up.

'I know, I know. But I feel I have a right to ask. After all the time we've known each other, I want to know what the bastard has that stops you coming to Brazil with me.' He poured fresh coffee into big, dark blue, gold-edged cups.

'You know what he has. He has Oruela,' said Euska.

'It's not that you enjoy him, just a little?'

Euska shook her head. 'No. Not now. I used to get a certain pleasure from it.'

315

Ernesto kissed his teeth, a sign of exasperation.

'You don't understand how sweet revenge can be, do you? You haven't got a violent bone in your body,' said Euska.

'I don't see why you stay around even for Oruela. She doesn't even know you exist, does she?'

'She hasn't been told.' Euska paused. 'But I have a feeling about her, I always have, that I must be here for her.'

'Mmm. Your instincts are usually very good.' He sounded grumpy.

'Don't be angry with me, will you?'

'I'm not angry. Not at all. But I want you with me, in Rio. We could have such a life together there. Euska, you've never even seen my house!'

'You have a girlfriend, don't you?' said Euska, matter-of-factly.

'I haven't got a damn girlfriend, as you put it. I have several in fact. They're interchangeable. None of them mean anything to me. Good grief, I'm a man! What is this, you're trying to put me off the scent. I want to know what goes on between you and your paymaster!'

'I don't mind telling you. I don't have any conscience where he's concerned. I suppose that's it in a nutshell really, the complete suspension of my conscience.'

'Come on then.'

'You'll be shocked. I treat him very badly.'

'That's what he pays you for, isn't it?' said Ernesto.

'Well, he comes once a month,' she said. 'Regular as clockwork. He hasn't missed a visit in at least ten years. He begins with little notes and love letters and then he telephones and begs to be allowed to come. I tell him some variation on I'll crush him like a piece of shit on my shoe if he comes anywhere near me.

'Then he phones again and says he's coming and I warn him not to. He sends presents, like that there. Then usually the next day he appears at the door, which I slam in his face. He rings again and I open it and say

316

he can come in if he does exactly what I say. Usually, I get him to clean the house, from top to bottom.'

Ernesto roared with laughter.

'I've got it down to a fine art. I know exactly what I want done and how, and if he doesn't do it right I make him do it again. He likes me to stand behind him and nag him, but I get bored with that these days so I tell him he can like it or lump it. But I do nag him about the kitchen floor because he never gets that right, he's such a slob.

'He always takes his clothes off and begs for more. I made him redecorate the bathroom once, just for the hell of it. But the trouble was it took days and I got so angry having him around that I beat him up.

'He loved it but it disturbed me. I made sure he paid well for that. I make him give me the money half-way through. He's so turned on he'll give me anything and of course, once I've got it, I really can't stand him so he gets all the insults he wants.

'Once he's done it all I tell him to get out of my sight and he goes. Then a week or so later the phone calls start again and the presents, and so on.'

'He must be coming soon, then, if the present arrived this morning.'

'Tomorrow, without fail.'

'What about the sex? You haven't said anything about actual sex.' Ernesto was pouting like a little boy.

'There isn't any!' said Euska smiling.

'He must do it himself?'

'He used to. I mean he never actually wanted real sex but there used to be much more physical contact. He'd cut my toenails or something and in the beginning he used to want me undressed or just in high heels, but there hasn't been anything like that for months and months. I think he's finished with the physical side of sex. I think he still needs to feel the emotions but we never touch, ever.'

'I almost feel sorry for him!' said Ernesto, hugging her close.

317

'Don't. He enjoys it,' replied Euska. She kissed his chest.

'Well, until tomorrow comes you're all mine,' said Ernesto.

'I'm all yours anyway,' said Euska, softly.

The French Policeman's Whistle

*T*he investigating officer, Alix Peine, was a tall, blond and muscular young man, handsome in a pale sort of way. His square jaw and blue eyes gave him a decidedly Germanic look, indeed his father was an Alsatian. He stood upright in his black serge uniform on the doorstep of the Bruyere house. His buttons shone, his knee-length black leather boots gleamed, his burnished silver whistle-chain glowed between his buttonhole and his pocket. It was a watch chain, in fact, a family heirloom he had adapted to give something to the stupid uniform he was forced to wear.

He thrust the absurd hat that belonged to his low rank at Robert's stomach. Robert took it with inscrutable calm and showed him into the main salon.

Its owners had never heard of fashion, Alix supposed. It had been decorated sometime around the turn of the century. Were they hard up? Were they frozen in time? Were they ostracised by society?

He only wished the explanation was something as interesting. In his heart of hearts he knew that the truth would be much more dull. This room was no more or less fashionable than any other dull bourgeois salon in this dull, bourgeois town.

He caught sight of himself in the heavily framed

319

mirror above the mantelpiece and spent some time admiring what he saw. Bayonne was not his kind of town. He was much more interested in neighbouring Biarritz and its wealthy visitors. His milieu was the casino, the night clubs. But he didn't feel he was ever going to get the chance to break into the kind of society he craved. He sighed at his near-perfect reflection.

Until the previous summer he had been a rising star in Paris social life. Alix had been a special detective. Part of his job had entailed the execution of discreet services for the rich and famous and doors had opened for him that would normally have been closed. He had haunted Bricktops, Zelli's, Le Sphinx: fashionable clubs and whorehouses far beyond the means of an ordinary policeman. Not that Alix had been entirely a playboy, his heart wasn't in it. He had also frequented more respectable enclosures like the opera and the ballet. Indeed, just before his hurried departure he had begun to smell success; mothers had cast their eyes in his direction, asking the sort of questions that pertain to marriageable daughters.

Alix planned to choose a wife wisely. He didn't want to remain a policeman all his life. He imagined himself marrying the sweet, malleable daughter of someone influential who would ease his way into politics. But there was time enough. The world was at his feet. Unfortunately, though, the world also included the wife of the commissioner, and she was mad about him.

He found a certain charm in her mountain of quivering flesh and in Paris these things were tolerated so long as they were kept discreet. In fact the commissioner was quite happy to leave the physical happiness of his wife to one of his subordinates and get on with his own peccadilloes. The bad luck was that Madame the Commissioner's wife had twin eighteen-year-old daughters whose boudoir was just along the corridor from their mother's.

One hot and sultry night, when Alix was leaving his mountainous love, he was surprised by the return of

320

the commissioner below. Not merely surprised, indeed he was almost petrified. His career flashed before him in a second; he saw the road back to his dreary little home town as clear as if it were to be trudged that very day. Coming to his senses he darted silently along the corridor and into the nearest room which of course was the daughters'.

He found them whispering together in bed. The covers were thrown back and they were naked as babes. Their twin bodies were plump and white and absolutely identical, right down to their pubes, which were as curled and silky-looking as the hair of cherubs. The arse of the one girl was exquisite and the belly and breasts of the other were classic in their beauty. What a vision! Both sides of the same coin at once!

They sat up together, their hair falling like angelic auras around their sweet shoulders. In the split second of their surprise they were still as statues, then the one nearest to Alix smiled languidly over her shoulder, while the other pulled the bedclothes up to her neck and stared.

Tearing his eyes from the lovely sight Alix dragged himself to the window and hid behind the heavy curtains. The sound of the commissioner's footsteps came closer and then died away down the hall. A door opened and closed.

Alix stayed where he was for another minute or two until he thought it was safe to leave. He mused on his discovery. Could he see himself married to one of the twins? Perhaps he could get them both to fall in love with him. Then through the heavy fabric he heard the sound of giggling.

He peeped out. Some urgent consultation was taking place between the identical girls. It seemed the one who had neglected to cover herself was trying to persuade the other to do something. The pair of them lay there, looking at him. Alix became aware of his erection at the same time as they did. How was he going to play this? He didn't feel quite sure what to do. He stood there,

321

feeling his prick heavy as stone and light as a feather all at the same time.

'What are you standing there for?' asked one of the girls. She was the more brazen one who hadn't deigned to cover herself in the first place. Something about her tone of voice compelled him to move. He left his hiding-place and approached the bed.

'Sit down,' she said. 'I am Angelique. This is Veronique. Tell us a story.'

For a moment he was surprised. He didn't have a story. He didn't have the kind of mind that thought in stories. 'I don't know any,' he said. 'I'm a man of action,' and he grinned a sly grin.

'Well, we like stories and if you don't tell us one then perhaps we will have to call Papa and then you'll have something to tell when someone asks you.'

Racking his brain quickly, Alix found something. 'I was in Bricktops earlier this week,' he said. 'They have a new show. Shall I tell you about it?'

'That will do for now,' said Angelique.

'There is a young girl and a young boy. They come on to the stage wearing animal skins, like cave people. They dance around the stage and have sex, right there on the stage.' Alix stopped.

'That's not much of a story,' said Veronique, turning to her sister. 'I don't think he has much of an imagination. Perhaps we had better call Papa.'

'No!' begged Alix. 'Please, let me please you in other ways. Have you experienced the delights of a man?'

The girls giggled. 'What have you to show us then?' said Angelique.

'This,' said Alix, opening his fly. He felt sure they'd never seen anything like it before.

'Well!' said Veronique and she reached for his swollen manhood, handling it with some expertise. She caressed it while Angelique rested back on her elbow and smiled.

Alix felt like a king. Their young bodies were just

waiting for him. Look how they admired him. 'Do you want it?' he said. 'I can give it to you both.'

'Can we use it, sister?' said Veronique.

'I think he should keep his boots on,' said Angelique.

'Oh yes, and his waistcoat,' said Veronique.

Alix felt a little bit silly but he realised he was in no position to do other than they asked. He put back on his long, shiny boots and his waistcoat. Something about being partly clothed made him feel more vulnerable than if he were completely undressed. He stood waiting.

Veronique rose and circled around him, looking him up and down critically. 'My sister needs relief,' she said. 'Lick her clitoris.'

Now this was more like it. He bent over Angelique and went to work on the pussy that offered itself to him. This was no toil. This was fantastic. He felt the other sister caressing his arse and ached for her to suck his cock. How delicious that would be. He surfaced and told her to do it.

'All in good time,' she said. 'Just get on with what you're told.'

On some unseen signal, the girls changed their positions, Angelique lay on her back and guided his cock between her breasts. Its length squeezed between them and dug into the little hollow of her neck as she pressed her breasts together. Their nipples strained towards him, two angry buttons of pink desire. Veronique, arranging herself behind her sister's head, spread her legs for him and forced his head on to her own sex.

Alix was so aroused that the first semen began to seep from him 'I'm going to come,' he whispered, 'I'm going to come!'

'Oh no you don't,' said the girls in unison. 'Not until we have.'

With a supreme effort he tore himself away and sat between them, his cock throbbing.

'You must understand, monsieur, that we are virgins

323

and we are not at liberty to lose our hymens to you. But
we are not strangers to orgasm. You will have to make
sure we get one each. Fair's fair. And then you can
have your own,' said Angelique.

'Which one first?' croaked Alix.

'Both,' said the two of them and they lay back on the
bed, legs parted in expectation.

Alix buried his face in Veronique's soft pubic hair and
worked on her with his tongue, while with his hand,
he sought its twin and massaged for all he was worth.
He came up for air and swapped but this time Angelique leapt on his arse and rode him like a horse,
working herself up on his buttocks that squashed
underneath her.

Bored with that she decided to slap him, hard. It
hurt. What's more it made a noise and it terrified him.
He stopped what he was doing. Veronique raised
herself.

'Now look what you've done. You've put her off!'
said Angelique. 'Continue what you were doing. Now!'

Alix obeyed. He couldn't feel Angelique any more
and he tried to concentrate on Veronique but the
memory of the stinging slap was on his backside and he
imagined there would be another soon.

She was watching, silently. She walked around the
room. He caught a glimpse of her out of the corner of
his eye, in one corner. Then she was gone. Where had
she gone? There she was, on the other side of the room.
He could almost see himself as she saw him, with his
boots on, the waistcoat enclosing his back, leaving his
arse and thighs exposed. Nothing like this had ever
happened to him before. He felt humiliated but incredibly turned on. He wanted her; where was she?

Suddenly, Veronique, sensing his distraction,
grabbed his hair and worked his face up and down on
her. She was coming. He could feel it. She stiffened.
His hair hurt where she pulled it. He hated the great
groan of pleasure that came from her. As soon as she
released his head he came up for air.

But before he knew it, Angelique was there. Angelique's face had nothing angelic about it: it was openly full of lust.

His cock was aching with the weight of jailed sperm. 'Touch me!' he begged Veronique. 'You've had your pleasure. Touch me.'

There was silence. In front of him another wet sex was waiting: Angelique's. She, who'd had the nerve to slap him. He raised himself. He must have her. He must give it to her. He was all cock. He got it almost there. It was just touching the opening of her delicious sex. But she grabbed it as it was about to go in and made it rub up and down on her clitoris instead. How dare she not want him! How dare these little girls refuse to give in to him! Her pubic hair was rough against him but the sensation strong and hot. She wouldn't be able to resist surely. Any minute now and he would slip it home, she wouldn't know what hit – and then he felt the shock of something cold at his arsehole.

He couldn't tell what it was but it wasn't human. It distracted him long enough for Angelique to come and then it was gone and he lay there, confused, as the girls lay back on the bed, smiling and satisfied.

They didn't give a damn. They really didn't. He was humiliated and desperate. He begged them but they merely turned over and yawned. He moved against the bed at their feet, trying to make himself come but it didn't work. So he rolled over and pumped himself. He – Alix! His sperm shot from him like champagne released from a corked bottle and he fell back on the bed, gasping.

Unfortunately he didn't hear the turning of the door handle, nor at first did he see the commissioner.

His demotion was swift as it was complete. The very next day found him on the platform at the train station in Bayonne in a hot August sun, angrily waiting for the sergeant at whose house he was to lodge. His heart was full of humiliation and revenge and for three weeks now he had fallen prey to fits of gloom. He was desperate.

But he was forming a plan. He was looking for a rich widow, no matter what she looked like or how old she was. With some money behind him he might be able to find something to do, even here. The clamour of neighbouring Biarritz beckoned him like the finger of a witch queen.

He was standing by the fireplace in the Bruyeres' front parlour, swaying slightly back and forth on the soles of his long black boots, pondering his plan, when the door opened and in came Genevieve. She had loosened her hair a little. Alix locked on to the target. The prey became the hunter.

'Monsieur Peine,' said Genevieve matter-of-factly and she seated herself in the straight-backed chair on one side of the large window.

He sat down on the couch. 'Monsieur the Mayor presents his compliments, madame, and apologises for not being here himself,' he said, all charm.

'Where is he?' said Genevieve.

'He sits on the Provincial Board of Health today, madame.'

'That's what he said on the telephone,' said Genevieve and she looked Alix up and down as if she was waiting for something.

'Madame, I understand that there has been a death?' said Alix. He fiddled with his whistle chain, curling it in his fingers and tugging at the buttonhole.

'Well, yes. My husband was found dead by his manservant at 8.30 this morning. I think you'll find the matter very simple. An autopsy will show that my husband has been poisoned by my daughter.'

Alix was fascinated by her. The way she sat demurely, her features showing barely a trace of emotion except perhaps impatience. Since his experience with the twins he found himself drawn to women who displayed even the slightest callousness. With a little business-like cluck she continued.

'She's feigning sickness upstairs in her bed. A local doctor saw her and give her a sedative. She admitted it all and then she passed out. It's all very simple!'

Alix asked to be taken first to see the corpse and second to see Oruela. Genevieve led him. She had a slim figure, he noted, and with excitement he felt *her* eyes travelling up the length of *his* legs as he bent over the body. It was unmistakable! There was an extra spring in his step as he ran downstairs to phone the coroner.

Michelle marched towards Alix as he entered Oruela's bedroom, barring his way. Oruela was lying dazed among the pillows. 'Monsieur! This is a lady's bedroom and the lady is asleep!' she said.

'I am a policeman,' said Alix, barging past her, 'and I am used to ladies' boudoirs.'

'Not this one you're not.' Michelle charged again and stood firm.

'Do stop it, girl,' sighed Genevieve. 'Get out of the way and allow this man to talk to your mistress.'

Michelle glared at Genevieve and was about to tell her she was a vicious old bag but some instinct told her to hold back. She had to be a bit clever here.

'What time did your mistress come in this morning?' asked Alix.

'I don't know, sir,' answered Michelle sulkily.

'Did you hear your mistress confess to killing Monsieur Norbert Bruyere?' he asked.

'I heard all sorts of things when she was delirious, sir, but I can't say I remember any of it.'

'Oh, this is ridiculous,' said Genevieve. 'Just wake the girl up and she'll confess.' And with a cluck of impatience, Genevieve got next to the bed and gave Oruela a shove. 'You killed your father, didn't you?' she said nicely.

Oruela roused herself. The question seemed to come from on high, booming down a tunnel of tranquillisers.

If she answered it with what they wanted to hear then perhaps this madness would stop.

'Don't answer!' she heard Michelle say. But what did Michelle know?

'Yes,' she said. 'I did.'

Alix Peine wrote something in his notebook.

'That is the poisonous animal she used,' said Genevieve, pointing to the lizard.

Alix went to the bedside table and picked up the cage. The lizard took one long look at the policeman, turned, lifted his tail and crapped. A terrible smell invaded the room. Michelle looked at Alix in disgust.

'I shall take this for examination,' said Alix and, holding the cage at arm's length, he walked out of the room.

Genevieve felt restless after the policeman had gone. She couldn't settle. Such was widowhood, she thought: a change in the routine. She made up her mind to go out and get some fresh air in the grounds, but then she spotted something shining on the sofa. It was his whistle! Fancy leaving it behind! Could it be a sign? Well, she would take good care of it for him.

She ran her fingers over the long shiny mouthpiece with its curling lip, over the bulge where the pea nestled, along the long, smooth stem, and into the slithery links of the chain. It was so deliciously cold. Cold, dead silver. She breathed on it to warm it a little and then she pulled out the neck of her dress and popped it into her shallow cleavage.

She went out into the garden and attempted her usual inspection of the budding flora but she couldn't rid herself of the image of Alix Peine's backside, his long legs. She paused in front of the tulip bed. The flowers were in full bloom. Suddenly they were a mass of dwarf red penises!

If it hadn't been for the servants, she would have run up the stairs to her bedroom. It was a dingy room, the scene of so much marital disappointment and frustration. She drew the curtains and by a chink of light she undid the bodice of her dress in order to retrieve the whistle. Just when she thought she'd got it, it slipped away again into another part of her plentiful, old-fashioned, cotton underwear. In the end she was forced to undress almost completely. All she had left on were her knickers.

She looked at herself in the full-length mirror on the wardrobe door, shyly at first, but with increasing boldness. She raised her arms above her head and twisted this way and that. Her breasts were quite long and thin, as if everything they contained was in the tips. The nipples were the palest rose colour. Her heart beat fast. She grew bolder, slipping off her knickers now and posing coyly, like the paintings of Venus in Bayonne Town Hall that were her only knowledge of female nudity. How she hated her unsightly hair there . . .

She brought the whistle between her breasts and held it by its chain, letting it drift downwards towards her tangle of pale pubic hair. Suddenly she ran and jumped on the bed and clasped the whistle to her lips, whispering to it.

'I want to make love to your owner. Do you love me? Yes, he says, I've never known a woman like you . . .'

She rolled languidly on to her back and pressed the whistle to her clitoris. There it rubbed and tickled her and made her bold. She pressed it into service further down. She lolled back in a state approaching ecstasy. After all these years, to be doing this in the afternoon! How free she felt. Wonderful!

And then, as the silver pleasure began to pump in and out, a little bit of air that had whipped up Genevieve's vagina in the excitement took its chance to escape and PEEEEEP – the whistle was blown.

329

Friday's Girls Are Full Of . . .

Over the next twenty-four hours the Bruyere mansion imploded with strange passions. Michelle and Robert fucked till they bruised. Oruela lay in a semiconscious world of half-waking dreams. Such dreams they were! A serpent slithered up the ancient bark of a tree and perfumed flowers opened like silken vaginas, dripping their golden pollen on the cool grass. A naked man – it was Jean and not Jean at the same time – tried to talk but his lips were sealed. He beckoned to her and as she went closer she saw that it was Valentino, the great lover himself, and he was hers. He held a fruit, a dark, purple fig and he peeled it and offered the ruby flesh to her lips. She sucked at the sweet juice as if her life depended on it. But as she swallowed the scene changed and she was falling, falling. Before she hit the ground she awoke, sweating, and Michelle held her against her soft breasts and murmured soothing sounds until she slept again.

But it was Genevieve, her stepmother, whose sexuality was out and all over the place. Nothing could cool either her shame over the whistle or her need. They were twin peaks of emotion between which she rushed like a crazed eagle. Movement seemed to help. She had Robert move furniture for the rest of the day and enjoyed the sight of his muscles straining under his clothes.

In the evening she sat down in the front room on a high-backed chair, shaking a cocktail of erotic images in her mind: a measure of black leather boots, shiny, slithering, enclosing shapely calves; a dash of long curving thighs . . . and a twist of pretty little jutting white arse, downy with soft hair and muscles flowing into the small of the back. She imagined how she would fling him on to the couch and he'd be helpless and then she'd lift up her severe black dress and underneath her little puss would open its little mouth and gorge itself on his helpless shank.

Her sex was so swollen and so hot that she had to touch it. She put two fingers through a little hole in her pocket and pressed the swelling. It felt so good and comforting. Little by little the rip enlarged and her hand got busier and busier and the feeling was tighter and tighter. It was lovely. She wondered what it smelled like. She shyly raised her fingers to her nose and held them there for the briefest moment. The smell was quite pleasant, she decided. Everything was pleasant.

This room had been Norbert's and it had more sun than the dingy back room he had assigned her. She felt a kind of liberation. Yes the bastard was really dead. And she could have sex with whom she liked.

Sex! Her thighs tensed of their own accord. It put a wonderful pressure in just the right place. Tense. Relax. Tense. Relax. It was a bit like riding a horse, she thought. There was absolutely no guilt either; her hands were perfectly innocent. She became hot around the waist and under her arms, her nipples scraped the fabric of her dress. She was very wet between the legs. She slid her fingers to touch herself and held on tightly as the tension built up with each squeeze of the rhythm: up and up, it was awesome! Up and up, irresistible! A shiver leapt up her back attacking her shoulders and her taste-buds at the same time. And then she fell forward and came face to face with the carpet. Well,

331

she thought to herself a moment later, that must've been an orgasm!

In the morning, when she awoke, she was still panting on the edge of a sexual precipice and she retrieved her whistle from behind the bed. This time she watched herself in the mirror, lying on the end of her huge bed, her nightdress hitched up and fanned out behind her on the coverlets like the plumage of some proud bird. The silver whistle slithered around in the moist coral-pink of her cunt; it tangled in her hair and gently stroked her pale belly.

With her elegant, pointed fingertips she tantalised her clitoris and as the need became more urgent she rubbed hard. God, it was good! Was this what you were supposed to do? She had no way of finding out. There must be a book. She lifted herself up and again looked in the mirror. There were lines on her face. It wasn't fair that she was discovering all this so late. How she hated Norbert and his brat! She went into the bathroom and had a generous pee.

She left her knickers off for lunch. That felt nice. She couldn't eat much anyway. And when she took her customary drive afterwards she wanted very much to masturbate in public in the back of the Bentley that Norbert had imported from England. But she was too scared, so she contented herself with the thigh-clenching that she had learned earlier.

Madame Radotage, the wife of the prominent industrialist, who was also driving that afternoon, felt terribly sorry for Genevieve. 'I saw her,' she told Madame Derive, the mayor's wife, over coffee. 'She was terribly abstracted. She was literally rocking back and forth with grief. How dreadful it is to be struck so young . . .'

Genevieve was so frenzied when she got back from the drive that she told Robert to delay tea twenty minutes while she freshened up. She took her refresher, for the sake of variety, in the master bathroom. The cold white tiles, the bareness of the floor, the dried soap smell of the shaving brush, the deep blue bath salts bottle, all reminded her of Norbert. She never used it while he was alive. She had her own on the dark side of the house. The eeriest feeling that he was still there took hold of her. She raised her foot up on to the rim of the green enamel, hoisted up her skirt with a laugh like a gypsy girl and began to rub her clitoris again, up and down, up and down her fleshy sex, spreading it wide and screwing her lovely long-nailed finger into its wetness.

'Dead,' she whispered. 'He's fucking dead.' The words drove into her vagina and caused her a hot pulse of agony. 'Fuck him, he's dead,' she shouted, and suddenly everything hurt. She rubbed harder and harder till it really hurt so much that she had to force herself over the hill. She came in a burst of heat and tears and unsettling laughter.

The sun was dying. It slanted off the roof of the old stables and it came softly in the window. For the briefest of moments she felt its peace and well-being. But as the sun dropped behind the roof and the room was dull, white and antiseptic again, self-disgust and fear crept into her mind with the gloom. Unnatural woman! Turned on by his death! Coming at the sound of her own voice and loving it. Somewhere in the house she heard the bang of a careless door . . . She straightened her clothing and went downstairs.

It was comforting to find the large tray waiting for her as usual in the study. She was ravenous, suddenly, and she pounced on the pastries. Robert was a good servant, she thought. She wondered what it would be like to rip off his trousers . . . and then she sat down quickly. She chewed noisily on the pastry. Then, out of the corner of her eye she saw something move . . .

Alix Peine was hovering behind the oriental screen. He was studying the lacquerwork, it seemed.

'Oh,' gurgled Genevieve.

Alix spun round. 'Madame,' he said and clicked his heels as he bowed. 'I beg your pardon. I didn't mean to alarm you.'

'Well,' spluttered Genevieve, chewing furiously. 'Mayor Derive is with your servant-girl, madame.'

'I see. Please join me in some coffee and pastries,' she squeaked, getting another cup from the sideboard.

Alix sat down on the chair closest to her couch. He took the cup she gave him and his fingers touched hers in the process. Genevieve felt tingly again, all over.

But they were interrupted by the entrance of Mayor Derive. The mayor was about sixty, well-fed and wealthy looking. 'My *dear* Genevieve,' he said, 'I'm so sorry about all this.'

'Come and sit down, Jacques,' said Genevieve, leaping up again to get a cup from the sideboard.

He sat down next to her on the couch and took a cup of coffee.

'Excuse me, I think I'll ask some more questions of the servants,' said Alix and he hastily departed.

'Where's he gone?' said Genevieve.

'He's being discreet, my dear. Now, do you have someone to look after you?' As he spoke he put his hand on her knee.

'My servants take care of me.'

'Don't you have any relatives who could come and stay with you?' Derive lifted his hand from her knee and took a sip of his coffee.

'What do I want relatives for?' said Genevieve.

'To look after you,' he said, and patted her knee again. This time he allowed his hand to remain there.

She didn't move. 'You'll look after me, won't you, Jacques?' she asked.

'Of course my dear. I'd love to. I could really make you feel special again,' he said, pushing his hand up her thigh.

She didn't stop him. She didn't actually know what to do. His breath was a bit ripe and his skin was flaky, she noticed. She really didn't want him to do it but no one had ever done this to her before and she just didn't know what to do.

334

'What will happen to Oruela now, Jacques?' she squeaked.

'Whatever you like, my dear.'

'What are the choices?'

'Do you really want to talk about it now?' he gurgled.

'Jacques, don't think me ungrateful for your help or anything but I feel a bit strange at the moment.'

'Come to bed with me, my dear. Let me comfort you.'

'Oh, Jacques!' cried Genevieve, looking deep into his eyes. 'Give me a little time.' This seemed to satisfy him for the moment and she repeated her question about Oruela.

'Well, we could have her arrested and taken to prison to await trial,' he said. 'Or you could keep her here until a trial. You look perturbed, my dear?'

'Nothing, go on,' she said.

'The third option, and I must admit it's the one I advise, is that we don't go to all the trouble of a trial at all. We put her in a nursing home for the mentally insane. All that takes is a doctor's word and your consent. We don't need to make any of it public. I only need announce that she's taken her father's death badly and gone into hospital for a rest. Unfortunately the only local facilities for the insane are attached to the House of Correction at St Trou.'

'A House of Correction!' murmured Genevieve. She wriggled in her seat. 'How long would she stay there?'

'Oh, indefinitely, my dear,' he said, putting his hand right up her skirt and in between her legs. 'Does that please you?'

'Yes,' she whispered.

'I like to please you. Don't you worry your head about anything. I'll see to that bad little bitch for you.'

'Oh, Jacques!' said Genevieve. 'Oh, Jacques! I shall always remember how you took my side against Norbert. You are so good.'

Derive nuzzled into her breasts. 'I just don't like bad bitches. I like good women, like you. Genevieve, open my fly. Come on. Touch me.'

She obeyed him. It was the first cock she'd touched in twenty years! It was a long thin one, not hard exactly, a little bendy, like a carrot fit for soup, but it was growing harder.

'Oh,' he cried. 'Your hands are like little birds. Here. Get on top of me.'

'No. No!' she cried.

'Yes! Yes!' cried the mayor and he lifted her on to his lap. He hoisted his cock right out and pushed it into her. 'There,' he said. 'We'll put that girl away. We'll make sure she gets the bad blood beaten out of her.'

He was disgusting. His breath! But it was fantastic to have a cock inside her. She was just getting used to it when it was all over.

He slapped her arse before he left and she stood there a few moments, staring at the closed door. She heard the sound of raised voices out on the driveway, but they didn't really register. A few moments later a knock seemed to come from a distance.

'Come in!' she said, recovering.

It was the parlour-maid. 'Madame,' she said. 'I thought you should know that the doctor who came yesterday, Simenon, has just tried to get in the house but Mayor Derive sent him away very firmly.'

'Good.' said Genevieve. 'What's going on upstairs?'

'Oruela is still senseless. Michelle hasn't left her side.'

'Well, it will all be over soon,' said Genevieve, smiling. 'Thank you. That will be all.'

Genevieve sat back down on the couch. Things were looking up, she thought. Another knock came at the door. 'What is it?' she called impatiently.

Alix entered looking absolutely gorgeous. She could feel Derive in her knickers and she felt quite disgusting and bold. She held her breath.

'Madame, excuse me. Did I leave my whistle here yesterday?'

Genevieve swallowed. 'No,' she said.

'Thank you, madame,' he said, sounding puzzled. He bowed again.

336

'Before you go,' said Genevieve, 'would you come again tomorrow? I might need you. No need to tell the mayor though, if you don't mind.'

Alix beamed. 'Of course, madame,' he said.

Genevieve held her composure until she heard the front door close. Then she jumped in the air and, laughing hysterically, went to the window and fixed her eyes on Alix's long legs as he walked down the drive. The great knot of the curtain tie was just at crotch height and she leaned into it. Did Alix sense she was watching him? Did he know?

Oh, how she ached for him. She pulled the knot right between her legs. Alix turned. He had almost reached the gates and he was looking right at the house. Was he watching her? Surely he was. Yes! He knew what she was doing. She knew he knew. She murmured her thoughts on to the glass as he watched her. I'm going to come, she murmured. I'm going to come while he's watching me. She pulled the knot and pushed it and . . . what a feeling of freedom she had. It was so wonderful. So outrageous.

The curtain pole relinquished its hold under the strain and the lot, pole, curtains, knots and ten years' dust, fell down about her head.

Oh, Lonesome Me . . .

Jean sat in a large golden ear, drinking coffee that was hot, Algerian and strong enough to make a dead man shit. The ear was an expensive, handmade piece of furniture by the great Steingarnele who, as yet, was little known outside a tight and wealthy circle of collectors.

Jean would have, if he could, decorated his whole room à la mode. But Jean's mother absolutely refused to have him decorate anything else in his crazy modern style. The drapes on each side of his massive bed stood like heavy brocade sentinels guarding her son, while he slept, from complete modernity. The bed itself was swathed in oceans of white silk and frills and Jean felt like a girl when he was at home. Madame Raffoler had made a gesture towards his masculinity by hanging watercolours of famous battles by a long-dead and technically accomplished painter but she insisted on relentless gilt. The bases of lamps and the legs of tables were covered in it.

Jean took all of it in his stride. She was his mother and he liked to please her.

His silken, ruby-red dressing-gown hung loosely over one long leg, leaving the other bare. It hung open at his handsome chest. It was hardly worth him wearing anything really but he had made a stab at decency for the sake of his mother.

He leaned back into the auricle and opened his mail. It contained nothing interesting and he sighed. He was horny. Slowly the bulge under the ruby silk grew until his cock popped out. And then the door opened and in whirled his sister Hélène.

Unlike her brother she saw no need to stab at convention. What had it ever done to her? Hélène was at the age of absolute rebellion. Sweet seventeen and dangerous. What did she care if the men of the household lost their minds as she crossed the landing wearing only perfume? This morning she was wearing something but only because it had just arrived in the post from her favourite Paris shop. It was a black, fine, net affair with a fur collar that covered her ears and partially concealed her chin. Its hem, at knee length, was also trimmed with fur but between these two extremities every inch of her was visible through a charming, crisscross veil, like a precious gem behind a jeweller's counter. Her hair was copper-coloured and looked unnatural. But its tastelessness was somehow utterly alluring.

'Very practical,' said Jean, leering. He leaned towards her to touch one of her precious gems.

She stuck her tongue out at him. 'Maman's angry with you,' she said.

'Why?'

'Some servant girl came to the back door earlier, asking for you. Maman thinks you should stick to your own class,' she pouted.

'I do. Resolutely!' said Jean, covering himself. 'I haven't been making love to any servant girls. What was it about?'

'I don't know, but you could find out if you want. She's been standing outside on the street ever since. Look,' replied Hélène.

They both went to the window and looked over the

wall into the street beyond the villa. Michelle stood under a tree with new leaves, looking lost.

Jean withdrew from the window and pressed the bell on the wall by the fireplace.

'She's pretty,' said Hélène. 'Pass her on when you've finished,'

Jean tutted. 'I've never been able to fathom whether your lesbianism is serious or merely a fad. There does seem to be an awful lot of it about these days.'

'What do you care what it is?' said Hélène.

'Well, I'm not sure I really want my sister to become an embarrassment to me,' he said.

Hélène laughed. 'You really are the limit,' she said. She left the room without a backward glance.

As the servant came out of the gates of the sumptuous mansion to fetch her, Michelle was thinking about Robert and how he had been the night before when he'd walked her to the train station in Bayonne to catch the milk train at 2 a.m. They both had a sense that this was the end of something. She could never go back to the house. Genevieve Bruyere had allies in some of the other servants and she would know at first light that Michelle was gone.

Michelle had been happy in that house and it was sad leaving it. But the only hope for Oruela was to rouse Jean Raffoler to storm the house and rescue her.

A shower of rain had swept inland and shed itself on the dark road as they walked along. The gnarled trunks of ancient trees loomed in their path. Strange shapes glistened as the shower ceased and the moon appeared again. None of it frightened Michelle. She felt at one with the road and the darkness. What frightened her was the mayor and what he might do.

It was this fear that drove her hand to clutch at Robert's; this fear and the violence, perhaps, of the emotion she had been witness to that left her so raw that when, as they neared the outskirts of the town, he kissed her passionately in the middle of the road she was painfully aroused. If there hadn't been only minutes before the train departed they would have made love in the glistening, dark woods.

As the servant came towards her she was imagining how it would have been . . .

'Would you like to come in, m'selle?' asked the man. 'Monsieur Raffoler has instructed me to show you to his rooms.'

Michelle brushed her skirt front. She felt a little like a tramp after spending half the night at La Negresse railway station fending off revellers coming home from a night's drinking. Gentlemen! As far as Michelle was concerned you could keep gentlemen.

As she followed the servant into the house she decided she had rich tastes. The Raffolers were one of the richest families in Biarritz and she liked what she saw.

Jean still wore the ruby-red robe but fortunately for Michelle he had put trousers on underneath it and drawn the sash tight. He stood by the tall fireplace in his suite of rooms and listened to her story. 'Good God!' he said repeatedly. It gradually dawned on Michelle that he didn't believe her.

'Are you absolutely sure about all this?' he asked, more than once. Michelle's temper was rising.

'Of course I'm sure,' she said, rising from the chair he'd shown her into. 'D'you think I'd spend the night on a railway station if I wasn't?'

Jean was watching the way her breast rose and fell with quickened anger. He'd always fancied Michelle. That arse! There weren't many of those! But her eyes were flashing and it frightened him. 'All right,' he said. 'Calm down, Michelle. Sit down.' He started to pace the carpet. 'I just find it all so terribly hard to believe. It's like the plot of some dreadful novelette. As if something cheap has suddenly imposed itself on my world . . .' He stopped in front of the window and looked out on to the grounds of his home.

This time Michelle rose and stood her ground. 'I'm sure if it's any kind of imposition, I'll go and find Dr Simenon and see if he's gentleman enough to help Oruela before it's too late. Don't you understand they may be taking her away right this very minute!' God! Oruela might think that Jean was wonderful but he was acting like a *fou*! He looked like a man all right, pacing up and down in his dressing-gown. But what was the use of him?

'She didn't tell me there was anything wrong between herself and her mother,' continued Jean.

'Oh, there was plenty,' said Michelle. 'But look, there really isn't time to go into it.'

'And the mayor colluding in a plot to take her away? He's a friend of my father's, I . . .'

Michelle walked towards the door. She would have to do something else. Just as she reached it there was a knock and a servant entered.

'Telephone, sir, for the young woman,' said the man, and he gave Michelle a wink.

She took the receiver gingerly. It was Robert. It was the first chance he had had to use the phone. Oruela had been taken away an hour ago.

This finally galvanised Jean into action and he flew off into his dressing-room. Before Michelle could drink the coffee he had ordered her, he was back.

She rose.

'No, no. Please finish it at your leisure,' he said and he was gone.

Michelle decided to write him a note telling him she would be at her Aunt Violette's haberdashery shop if he wanted her. She was sure her aunt would take her in. It wasn't as if Jean and Oruela would be using the little apartment in the roof.

Michelle was putting the note on the mantlepiece when Hélène walked in the room. Michelle looked at the young woman's extraordinary outfit and her mouth dropped open.

'Has my brother gone off and left you? Oh, how could he?' crooned Hélène.

Michelle, in complete ignorance of the idea that two women could gain pleasure from each other's bodies, did not rise to this morsel of bait nor to any others. She left the mansion a little while later having come to the conclusion that the Raffolers, like so many rich people, were a touch mad.

Jean's open DeSoto screeched to a halt outside the massive locked prison gates with their spyhole that looked out but allowed no one to look in. He parked a little way up the road. The wall around the place was at least twenty feet high and the top of it was laced with barbed wire. He ran to the doors and pounded on them with his fists.

There was a loud shout from inside. 'Oi, Oi. Stop that!'

Jean suddenly realised he would get nowhere. Thinking fast he shouted, 'It's Dr Marchand! There's an emergency.'

'All right. All right,' came the reply.

Bolts were thrown back and a small door opened in the great gates. The guard behind it was a man, five foot nothing and grossly overweight. He bowed slightly to Jean, who had drawn himself up to a height appropriate to authority.

'You'll find the reception just as you go in,' grumbled the guard.

Jean thanked heaven for the stupidity of prison guards. He considered his next move. One or two inmates sat around on benches, obviously senseless. A young nurse walked across the garden . . .

The poor woman had just finished a novel in which a visiting psychiatrist bumps into a nurse and the encounter ends in marriage. Her eyes sparked with wonder as she looked up and saw Jean, who had set himself on a collision course. Two little red spots of embarrassment appeared on her cheeks. 'Monsieur!' she murmured. 'Can I help you? You look lost!'

'I am,' said Jean, seductively. 'I'm looking for a new

patient of mine. Her name is Bruyere. She will be with your Dr . . . er . . .' He fished in his pocket.

'Dr von Streibnitz,' said the woman, 'if she's new.'

'Of course,' said Jean, bringing an old receipt out of his pocket. He tapped it and smiled.

'Shall I take you?' she offered.

'No, no,' said Jean. 'Just tell me the way.'

Following her directions he bluffed his way into the cell block and climbed the spiral staircase at one end. The spring sunshine eked its way through a long window, where two figures sat playing cards in silhouette. He stood for a moment on the landing deciding which way to go.

'Excuse me, sir, can I help you?' A small, rat-faced female guard came from nowhere and sidled up to him.

Jean turned on his smile. But something told him his luck had run out. He could feel his blood chilling in his veins. 'I'm looking for Dr von Streibnitz,' he said.

'Who are you?' asked the rat-face.

'Dr Marchand,' said Jean. 'A colleague.'

'Why are you here?' she demanded.

'I was invited to see an inmate.' Jean tried to sound offended at the questioning.

'Where's your authorisation card?'

Jean grinned like a little boy. 'Mademoiselle, I must be honest with you,' he said. 'I had one last time I was here but I couldn't find it, and as they know me on the gate they let me through.'

'I'd better check up on this,' she said.

She made a move towards the telephone on the wall just behind Jean's shoulder. He caught her off-guard with a crack on the jaw that knocked her out in one. She slid down the wall.

He heaved her weight into a recess where he sat her on a toilet and used her stockings to tie her to the cistern. He stuffed the sleeve of her cardigan into her mouth and unhooked the bunch of keys from a chain around her waist.

* * *

344

Oruela's cell was about eight doors along the third landing. Jean opened the door with the keys. A big smile lit up Oruela's whole face when she saw who it was. But Jean had a job to disguise his reaction. Her eyes were glassy, she was as pale as death. He pulled the door to behind him and closed the spyhole. He took her in his arms. She smelt strange.

'Have you come to take me home?' she whispered.

'I wish I had. To tell you the truth I don't know what I'm doing. I just had to come but I don't know how to get you out,' he said gloomily.

They both instinctively looked at the high, barred square of the window.

He stroked her hair. 'Tell me what happened. Michelle said you told everyone you'd killed your father?'

Oruela started to cry. 'I don't know what happened. I don't think I killed him . . . I know I didn't. I just wished him dead. You can't kill someone by just wishing them dead, can you, Jean?' and she clung to him.

'Of course not!' said Jean, gently stroking her hair. It was not clean. 'But why did you think you had?'

'I don't know. I got so confused. I'm still confused. What am I doing here, Jean? This is a real prison.'

'Why were you so confused? Because he died?'

'I had a bad dream.'

'I can't believe you're here because of a bad dream. None of it makes any sense.' Jean was half talking to himself. 'Michelle said your mother put the idea in your head. Why should she do that?'

'Because she hates me,' came her little voice from his chest. 'She isn't really my mother. They fostered me. It was his idea, I know that. No one's supposed to know but I found out one night when I was ten years old. I heard them arguing about it. She hates me, Jean. She hates me.'

Jean looked down into the eyes whose clear depths he had loved. 'You never told me anything about this. Why? Who are your real parents? Do you know?'

'I don't know anything about my real parents at all,' she whispered.

Jean stroked her hand, her head, her shoulders. 'I would've understood. You should have told me. I would have taken you away from home months ago if I'd known you were so unhappy.'

'Oruela reached up to kiss him. But he didn't respond. 'What am I going to do now?' she mumbled.

'I'm going to go and see the mayor. There must be some bizarre mistake.'

'He doesn't like me,' said Oruela, looking at her lap.

Jean frowned. 'Has anyone told you how long you'll be here? Is there going to be a public trial or something?'

'No one's come near me.'

The sound of a guard walking along the landing outside filtered through the door.

'I must go,' whispered Jean, and he prised himself away from her gently. 'I won't be able to help you if I get caught. I must go and start asking questions. I'll get you out of here soon, don't worry. In the meantime you'll be a strong girl?'

'Yes, Jean,' she said and she lifted up her face for a kiss. It never came.

'Take this and hide it somewhere, you might need it,' he said, taking a hundred-franc note out of his wallet. And then he was gone.

She sat holding the money for a long time, unaware that it existed. She still felt really groggy from the drugs they had administered to her. She ached for Jean. If only he were there he would kiss her and things would be all right. She tried to collect her thoughts. At least she felt a bit better now that he knew where she was. She lay back on the mattress to soothe herself with thoughts of him and suddenly remembered the money.

The obvious thing was to stuff it in her mattress. But it would be found. She could put it in her vagina. She'd read a book once with that in it. But she baulked at the idea of money that had passed through a thousand

346

hands going inside her. She settled for the mattress and lay down.

It was funny. She could picture him so vividly. There he was naked in the firelight in the room above the haberdasher's, his skin glowing and there she was, waiting on the bed with its soft sea-green counterpane. But this bed was hard. She opened her eyes and saw the pig-coloured door locking her away from the world. And then her tears came.

Eventually, when they were spent, she sat up and listened to the sounds of the prison around her. It was like being inside some animal, like Jonah in the whale, as its stomach rumbled and it clicked its teeth. Echoes of functions, small in themselves she guessed, were large and significant as they reverberated around the old building.

Someone had scratched a message on the cell door. 'C'est infernal' – this is hell.

'Hey, new girl!'

She couldn't make out where the voice came from. Perhaps she was going mad again. But she got up and listened at the door. Again it came, but from another direction.

'New girl!'

It was somewhere between a shout and a whisper. She went to the window. 'Are you calling me?'

'So you *can* speak!' came the voice.

'Where are you?'

'Next door! The wind carried my voice to you to bring you comfort.'

'Thank you,' said Oruela. The voice was accented. She couldn't place it.

'Thank the wind,' said the voice.

'What's your name?' called Oruela.

'Kim Sun,' came the reply.

'Where are you from?'

The voice laughed. 'I am from everywhere and nowhere. I am the daughter of the god whose name I bear.'

347

A lunatic. Of course. 'Oh God, what am I going to do!' howled Oruela.

'I can't tell you what he says, only that he visits us early in the morning and it's wise to turn your face to him. Keeps you healthy.'

Oruela turned away from the window and sat again on the bed. She was scared. She might go really mad. 'Oh, Jean,' she whispered, 'Hurry, hurry.'

Suddenly a loud bell began to ring. The sound of crashing gates, of shouting, of heavy footsteps rushing, filled the whole prison. A rising panic threatened to take hold of her. It must be a fire, she thought, and they'll leave me here to roast alive in this metal box. She ran to the window. 'Neighbour! Can you hear me? What do we do? What is it?'

'They're searching for your boyfriend. Somebody found out!'

How the hell did she know? thought Oruela wildly. She must have overheard. 'You mustn't tell!' she called.

'Pisht!' came the disgusted reply.

Oruela waited fearfully, repeating over and over to herself: Don't tell. Don't tell. They don't know. They don't know who he was or they wouldn't be searching everyone. She stuffed the money further into the mattress.

At last the keys penetrated her own door and three female guards entered looking grim. One of them had newly been released from the toilet and she was red with anger. She ordered Oruela up off the bed and out of the cell and then she picked up the mattress and chucked it on the floor. Another one tapped the walls.

Oruela went out of the door and stood against the wall, her legs shaking. She looked to her left at her neighbour. What a surprise! The woman was as tall as herself, taller in fact and black. Oruela couldn't take her eyes off the woman's gorgeous skin. Her magnificent cheekbones looked like they had been sculpted, her neck long and sleek, her shoulders powerful. Her hair was cropped short on an exquisitely shaped head. She even produced a smile that lingered in amazing brown, almond-shaped eyes.

'*Eyes front!*' yelled a guard.

Both women looked in front of them.

The guards found nothing and two of them came out and ordered Oruela and Kim Sun back into their cells.

The angry, rat-faced one was still in Oruela's cell. She looked Oruela up and down with undisguised heat. She fixed Oruela's eyes like a man does when he means to have a woman. She walked slowly to the door without taking her eyes away.

That look stayed with Oruela behind the locked door. So that was what a lesbian was like, she thought. They looked like she had always imagined them, like the Bolshevik women that the Russian *émigrés* in Biarritz talked about. It was true then. No man would ever want a woman like that. She'd seen women like that but had always imagined they never thought about sex. How could they? Looking like that! But now the horrible truth dawned. They did. They thought about it with women and they worked in places like this. I'm a sitting duck, she thought. And she began to shake, uncontrollably.

Some Day My Prince Will Come

*F*or a short while each evening the inmates were encouraged to mix with each other. There were only women housed on the wing. All three of the other wings of the prison were full of men.

Many of the women were in a state of decay but some were young and beautiful. Oruela came timidly out of her cell and leaned against the iron railing. She looked down on to the landing below hers. She wasn't surprised at what she saw, she was expecting it. But she was surprised at the strength with which the sight gripped her and held her in its spell.

Two women, both about her own age, were flirting together. They leaned against the wall between two cells talking. One was more slender than the other, too thin Oruela thought. Her face was sallow and unhealthy-looking. She was the one being seduced, Oruela imagined. The movements of her body, the coy little smiles, the way she laughed, everything about her was charged with an unmistakable sexual energy.

The other woman kept her distance to begin with but she moved closer until their two bodies, their faces, were very close, almost but not quite touching. It was an astonishing sight to Oruela. She wasn't sure she was enjoying being glued to it either. The thought of them together, naked, touching each other's sexes almost made her feel sick. But it was impossible not to be aroused by the sheer liberation of sexuality that was happening before her very eyes. The slender woman took the other by the hand and led her into a cell next to the staircase. They didn't even shut the door.

Oruela had to get a toothbrush. She made her way along the landing to the iron staircase and held the railings as she descended. Whether it was the after-effect of the drugs or the new culture that she had been thrown into that made her knees weak, she didn't know. As she passed the door, though, where the lesbians were making love, she looked firmly in front of her.

There were a lot of eyes on her as she went to the office of the guards to get her toothbrush. Some were friendly, some curious, some, she felt, overtly hostile. 'New girl,' they whispered and watched the movement of her hips underneath the ugly prison issue shift that passed for a dress. One thing she noticed was that the women all seemed to have adapted their own shift to make something different of it. It made her feel briefly optimistic to think that even in such appalling conditions women stamped their own individuality on their clothes.

She wasn't the only newcomer on the wing that day. The other one was getting much more attention than she was. He was the first male guard under fifty on the wing for many a month and he was a moving and vulnerable target for the heterosexual women's lust. He was about twenty, Oruela guessed. It was a wonder that such a young spawn was given the job. He had such a young face you wondered if he shaved.

The catcalls that followed him ranged from whistles to full-blown and loud descriptions of the women's fantasies. In fact it was unusual for any of the guards to patrol at the same time as the women were out of their cells *en masse*. The duty guards sat in their glass boxes like goldfish, mostly not even bothering to look out to

351

see what was going on under their noses. The young guard had been asked especially to patrol by the senior woman officer . . .

He was trying, manfully, to carry out his duties, but he was overplaying his maleness perhaps to compensate for feeling as secure as a snail underfoot. He hoisted his trousers by the belt more than was necessary. He swaggered. He ignored their jokes, he even issued a stern command or two. The response to these were raspberries and worse.

Oruela happened to be behind him as he climbed the iron staircase to her landing. He had a shapely *derrière*, she noted. She took a discreet, sidelong peek into the cell where the lesbians were but all she could see was one pair of bare feet.

She and the young guard reached the landing at virtually the same moment. The women, at the end where the staircase was, were what Oruela would have called cheap and vulgar and outside she wouldn't have given them a second thought. But in here they were compatriots and suddenly more interesting. She watched as they formed a flock and began to devour the poor young guard.

'Move along,' he said bravely as he walked through them to the very end of the landing.

'Hark! I hear a little mouse squeaking,' said a brunette. She had a disfigurement that twisted her features. It was extraordinary: she was so ugly she was exquisite. She had commanded a high price on the streets.

'What does the little mouse say?' asked another woman.

'It says move along, move along,' said the scarred woman.

'Are you going to?' asked a tiny blonde woman.

'No,' said the brunette. 'I'm going to stay here and catch a little mouse,' and she made a wild noise like a big cat.

For a split second the young guard's face showed how terrified he really was. His back was pressed against the wall and he looked as if he wished the bricks would open up and swallow him.

The scarred woman moved closer to him and he snapped out of his terror. 'What do you think you are doing?' he demanded. His tone was unsteady enough to portray his lingering anxiety.

'What do you want me to do?' she asked. 'Tell me in detail.'

At this the young man laughed, hoisted his trousers at the belt yet again and said, 'Well, ladies. If circumstances were different, I'd like you to suck my cock.'

There was silence. No one had expected it. He grinned cheekily, knowing he'd caught them off-guard. He took a couple of steps forward.

The flock of women closed ranks as one without an order. The young guard's face lost its grin. 'Now that's enough,' he said. He unhooked the truncheon from his belt and gestured with it.

The women stood their ground. 'Is this your cock?' said the scarred woman. 'It's a lovely big one. She touched it with her fingertips, lightly running them up and down the hard black surface.

'Perhaps that's what he wants sucked,' said the little blonde woman.

The brunette opened her red mouth wide, sending her disfigurement into a strange and beautiful pattern across her face. She wriggled her blood-red tongue at the tip of the black wood.

The guard was fascinated. It was plain he was no longer scared, but held, despite himself.

'I wonder if there's anything in his trousers or if he needs that big truncheon to make up for it,' someone called.

'There's more than any of you would know how to satisfy,' he said.

'He's an arrogant little mouse, isn't he?' cackled the scarred woman. 'Let's see,' and she grabbed his crotch.

His face was a mixture of astonishment, pleasure and dread all mixed up. Her hands were in his underwear.

'Help!' he squealed. It wasn't clear that he really wanted to be rescued.

'No one will come,' said the grinning brunette. 'It's a tradition. Someone has to keep a sense of tradition in this god-forsaken, modern world.'

The two main players in this game backed him into a cell and undressed him in front of a quite critical group of onlookers. He was willing, surprisingly enough. His penis stood out like a rod.

The beautiful, scarred woman pulled up her ugly prison dress to expose stately, milk-white thighs, and while the pale blonde woman held his arms, the dark woman took her pleasure from him.

Oruela peered over the shoulders of the crowd watching this symbolic deflowering and from her glimpse she decided he wasn't suffering although, surely, he must be humiliated by the calls of the women watching. They weren't vicious but they were low and lewd.

Oruela left the edge of the crowd. There was no doubt in her mind now about who ran this place.

Kim invited her for a smoke and took her into her cell. Inside there was a faded rug on the floor, some flowers in a vase, a few books. Kim lit a candle and closed the door.

Oruela took the tobacco tin she was offered and sat down on the straight-backed chair to roll herself a cigarette. It wasn't a very good one. It was too loose. But the tobacco went to her head and gave her a pleasant buzzy sensation.

'So tell me,' said Kim, lying lazily back on the bed. Her legs were long and slender and Oruela was stirred again by the other woman's beauty.

Oruela poured out the story of her arrest in a great tidal wave of relief. She only omitted the lizard, feeling nervous about that part.

Kim listened without saying much at all. She gave off a feeling of steadiness. She seemed to take everything in but nothing affected her. Not even when Oruela said she thought she was really going mad.

'Everyone's crazy in here. You can join them if you want,' she said, finally sitting up and looking at Oruela directly.

Oruela began to cry.

Kim softened. 'Look, kid. It's your choice. If you want to be a pathetic deadbeat in their hands you can. But you can also keep some of yourself and survive. Let's face it. We're all mad. It's only those of us that give up that are destroyed.' The words made sense. Oruela felt overwhelming gratitude. She wanted to hug her but she pictured herself in her imagination, going over to the bed and bending over the black woman and a new fear gripped her. Perhaps Kim was a lesbian as well. She ached to ask her. But she daren't.

Instead, she asked, 'What's your story. Why are you here?'

Kim laughed. She had a lovely set of teeth. 'Guess,' she snorted.

Oruela blushed. She felt so naïve.

Kim turned over lazily and lay on her stomach. Her arse was well-rounded and high. She didn't look Oruela in the eye. 'I trusted the wrong man,' she said.

Oruela took that to mean she liked sex with men. She was relieved in a way. But a part of her had opened to an idea that wouldn't go away. She was horny. There was no doubt about it. Sitting here in this cell in the candlelight, she ached for love.

'I was illegal,' continued Kim. 'I hadn't got my papers sorted out and I hooked up with this character who called himself a baron. We invented this story, playing on the appetite of these Europeans for anything exotic. I used to do this dance with a statue. Like this.' She knelt up on the bed, making a thrusting movement with her hips. 'And I went round the brothels telling stories about a far-away erotic culture. It was all made up but they were good stories. We made a lot of money. But just my luck we had an African king in one of our

355

audiences and he made a fuss. Called it an insult and there was this terrible scene. My so-called baron played innocent. He made out I'd duped him and the whole thing was my fault. I was arrested for fraud. I couldn't believe how seriously they took it. Kurt, the baron, had gone too far though. He imported some lizards from Africa and got this taxidermist to embed stones in their skin so they were like the ones I talked about in my story. They were still alive, just, and he sold them for a small fortune. But I never felt right about that. The taxidermist turned up as a witness against me in court –'

'Oh, stop!' cried Oruela, 'stop.'

'Oh, I'm sorry. You're feeling wobbly and I'm going on,' said Kim.

'Owww,' cried Oruela. But it wasn't only tears. It was laughter.

'Hey, don't have hysterics on me,' said Kim Sun.

Oruela took some deep breaths and told her of her own experience with the lizard.

'Whoops!' said Kim.

Later, back in her cell, Oruela sifted through the tangle of her thoughts and stumbled on a kernel of truth about herself. She was going to give up giving up. Kim was right. You had a choice. She'd given up once too often and now she was in hell.

In the midst of these thoughts, a sound began next door. A strange, rhythmic sound, not quite singing, not quite speaking. A chant. She got up and stood by the window. The sky was beautiful. The sun was at last going down and the heavens were blushing. Soon there would be stars. The strange chant got slower as the sun dropped. The sound wound its way into her senses and stirred her.

The attraction to Kim had disappeared as they had talked further. It was as if the intimacy of friendship had filled the desperate need. What if it appeared again? The chant soothed her, like a mother's song. Now she lusted after the sky, after the stars. This was the kind of madness she could handle! She felt like dancing and began to move. The prison bars ceased to exist.

Suddenly a harsh voice rang out: 'Shut up, No. 7!'

Oruela lay down on her bed and watched the sky darken. Presently a new moon appeared.

The next morning was Sunday and it was shower time. She longed for a shower. She grabbed her soap and towel and rushed along the landing as soon as the doors were unlocked.

Women of all shapes and sizes stood naked in the steam under the hot jets of water pouring out from the walls. Steel poles that had once had shower curtains attached to them loomed in the light that filtered through the window and swirled with the mist. Oruela undressed and made her way to a vacant jet.

Some of the women turned to look at her. She felt their gazing eyes touch her and was thankful for the water that washed everything away. She closed her eyes.

Suddenly, she felt a hand on her bottom. She opened her eyes and saw a tiny, blonde girl grinning next to her.

'How dare you!' shouted Oruela.

Kim appeared from nowhere. 'You can handle yourself then!' she said.

'It looks as if I'll have to,' said Oruela.

Then at the end of the room a shout went up. 'La Grande Prix des Derrières!' and all at once there was a line of women forming at the wall by the door. They sat on the tiled floor with their feet on the wall. Women shouted their bets to each other.

'Stand back!' said Kim.

Oruela flattened herself against the wall as someone shouted: 'On your marks! Get set! Go!'

The racers pushed off from the wall with a yell and went skidding up the length of the floor on their bums, crashing into heaps of laughing flesh at the other end. The onlookers whooped and clapped.

Someone shouted, 'New girl! New girl!' and before

she could even think of protesting, Kim Sun had grabbed Oruela and she was on the floor waiting to push off.

'On your marks! Get set! Go!'

Oruela gave one almighty push against the wall with her strong thighs and she was off, yelling with the best of them, as the bump, bump, bump of the grouting thudded under her bum. She saw the steel pole coming up behind her and grabbed it. She spun round twice and hurtled off diagonally, crashing into a group of onlookers and laughing so much she thought she'd die.

'A stylist!' shouted Kim, coasting towards her. 'We could be a formation team!' Someone else took up the idea and someone else, until there were about six women sailing round the shower room on their arses, some with one leg in the air, Oruela with her arms up like a ballerina. All of them cracking up with laughter.

Inevitably the whistle blew and their game was stopped. Kim Sun and Oruela walked back to their cells dripping.

'Do you play cards?' said Kim.

'A little,' said Oruela.

'We usually have a game on Sundays, in the evenings.'

After breakfast everyone was called for church.

'No, thanks,' said Oruela bravely to the rat-faced guard. The last thing she felt she needed was the droning of a miserable priest. She was surprised, though, when everyone else seemed to go. She spent the hour alternately worrying and steeling herself should the rat-face come back and attack her. But nothing so predictable happened.

The evening's card game was in Kim Sun's cell. Three of them sat around on the floor. The third woman was about twenty, white, with luxurious rich brown hair. She had been a whore since she was thirteen. Her name was Marthe. She seemed to know everything there was to know about sex.

'Everyone wants to sleep with their father,' she told

Oruela. 'Even if they don't know it. Fathers are our first loves. But, naturally, societies build up rules about these things to protect their survival. Some of us are open enough to see through the rules, that's all. We wouldn't necessarily do it, but we admit it's possible. The fact is, that sexuality is a wild and roving animal. It doesn't move along straight paths.'

'I just wish I could be wild enough to make the first move,' said Kim Sun. 'Coming back from church today I got forgotten and I was locked in the ante-room with the fellow who fetches and carries for the priest down there. We stood there like dummies. I've been thinking about it ever since. We must have been there for ten minutes and I'm sure he had a hard-on. You could feel the sexual tension. But he didn't make a move. It's ridiculous. Me! I can dance in front of a whole room full of men but when it comes down to the real thing I just can't say it. I like a man to take *me*. Kurt was good for that. He was revolting but it used to turn me on when he ordered me to do things. It was that tone of voice he had. Commanding. Saying things like "Spread your legs, baby." Oh God I miss him.'

Marthe gestured with her finger to her temple. 'Mad as a hatter,' she said.

Oruela giggled.

'I don't have any problems with that,' said Marthe. 'I used to have one after the other like that. I had a different one each day. I had a couple of servants just to wash them first.'

It was Kim's turn to make the finger at her temple.

'And I'll have you know I'm going to have another one very soon,' continued Marthe.

'What? How? Who?' cried Kim Sun.

'Well, I found out that if you get married in here, you get a honeymoon.'

'No!' cried Kim. 'How long?'

'Forty-eight hours,' said Marthe smugly.

'Oh, think of it,' moaned Kim Sun.

'Exactly,' said Marthe. 'I've put the word out I'm

interested. I expect I shall be interviewing them next Sunday in church.'

'Nice and proper,' said Kim, sweetly.

Marthe laughed.

'We'll have a hen-night for you,' said Oruela, at last feeling able to offer something to the conversation.

'Yeah!' said Kim. 'What a great idea,' and she beamed at Oruela.

The conversation was interrupted at this point by the arrival of another woman who wanted to play cards. She was a short white girl with sandy, curly hair, rather heavy of feature and very curvy. She came in and they were half-way through a hand when Kim and Marthe were called out by the rat-faced guard. When they were gone, the girl suddenly took off her shift and sat there in only her pants.

'Whew!' she said. 'Freedom.

Oruela felt the atmosphere change, as if they had suddenly begun to gamble with real money. The girl's breasts were magnificent.

'I can't understand how I put on so much weight on the meagre amount of food they give us,' said the girl, pinching her own belly.

Oruela looked at the girl's belly and breasts and felt an overpowering urge to touch. The tits really made her feel horny. Horrified, she rolled a cigarette from Kim's pouch. It was only a minute or two before the others came back but it seemed like an hour. Oruela played on, smoking resolutely until the bell rang for lock-up. The naked girl clothed herself again, gave Oruela a big, friendly smile and was gone.

Back in her cell Oruela repeated to herself, 'Sexuality is a wild and roving thing.' There was no need to worry, she told herself. Everything was OK. But she felt like crying.

'Psst,' came the voice from the window.

'Yes?' she called, shakily.

'You must go to church next week,' said Kim.

'That's all I need!' said Oruela, ruefully.

'The men are there!' said Kim.

'Men?' said Oruela.

'The inmates from the other wings,' said Kim.

'Hmph!' said Oruela and got down from the window. As if she could ever be interested in men again. She was probably a lesbian. That much was blatantly clear.

But Monday morning brought her a surprise.

She heard the jangle of keys at her door after breakfast and her stomach muscles tightened, a wall closing against intrusion. A male guard stood outside the door. He told her to come with him.

'What for?' she asked assertively.

'Doctor,' he barked. 'Get a move on.'

She prayed she wouldn't be interrogated and fixed a cooperative smile on her face. On the ground floor she was told to sit on a bench outside a cell. The guard disappeared into another door opposite and shut it behind him, leaving her alone in the cavernous pig-coloured space.

At least, she thought she was alone. And then she sensed a movement in the shadows. She turned around. It was a man. He emerged from the gloom backwards, sweeping. His back was broad and long and his arse was firm. Something about his movements was fascinating, even just sweeping.

He didn't seem to have noticed her. He was about six feet away before he turned. He made a brief, flickering but penetrating study of her body.

The look thrilled her to the bone. She found herself smoothing her hair, straightening her back to push her breasts out. Her eyelashes fluttered of their own accord and she looked right back at him. His body was truly magnificent. His shoulders and chest were massive under his striped prison shirt. The kind of shoulders that a woman would want to crush her cheek against when they were on top of her.

His face was not exactly handsome but it was rugged. He had the most sex-filled deep blue eyes she had ever encountered. His nose was magnificently hooked, like

361

an eagle. His dark hair curled into his neck. His shirt was only slightly open and the sight of his throat with his big Adam's apple intrigued her. What was his story, she wondered, looking again at his wonderful eyes. At that moment their eyes met. She looked at him steadily, thinking of sex.

Seeing his freedom, at least in her brown eyes, he smiled. It was an inmate's smile, so discreet as to be almost unnoticeable except to the person it was intended for. To Oruela it had the strength of an embrace.

Before she could formulate the word hello, the doctor's door opened and the man went back to his sweeping. It didn't suit him, sweeping, thought Oruela. He looked like a prince.

The doctor stood behind his desk not looking at her. He was searching through a pile of files on his desk. The nurse next to him pointed at one. He opened it and looked up, straight into Oruela's eyes.

Von Streibnitz appeared exactly the same as he did in his private practice. It would be gratifying to think that in this place he looked evil, but he didn't. Perhaps because it was Monday morning and the procession of lunatics had not yet eaten away at his calm, he was smiling, he was kindly. He bade her sit down.

'I'm glad we didn't have to inject you. I like my patients to be compos mentis if at all possible. Now, do you understand why you are here?'

'No,' said Oruela.

'Well, we have to find out the truth, because the truth is the best way. You're in here because you confessed to the police that you murdered your father.' Again he looked at her intensely. He was, in fact, trying to see a resemblance between her and her father. 'Did you kill your father?'

'No,' said Oruela. 'I was confused. I confessed because I thought I would be taken care of if I admitted it. I wished him dead because he attacked me. But I didn't kill him.'

362

'Aha,' said von Streibnitz. 'Very good. He attacked you. Yes.' He looked again at her file and then beamed at her. 'Tell me, what do you think? Is it right for a woman to have sex outside marriage?'

'I don't see the harm in it,' said Oruela.

'Have you had sex?'

'Do I have to answer that? It doesn't seem to me that it's any of your business,' she said.

Von Streibnitz merely smiled. 'Come with me,' he said. He opened the door and led her into the next cell. A guard in a white coat stood next to a surgical couch. Von Streibnitz opened a box on wheels and pulled out a huge hat-shaped contraption on runners. Oruela's bowels began to curdle.

'What is it? I don't need any electricity! I'm perfectly willing to stay here and cause no trouble to anyone at all,' she pleaded.

'It's not electricity. Look, there are no wires. This is a purely natural therapy, just to make you feel better. It's very exciting. You will benefit from the most advanced science known to man. Inside these compartments at the temple, see, we put curative crystals that come from the deepest recesses of mother earth. All you will experience is a deep feeling of peace, of oneness with nature.' He spoke down to her, like a father.

'I don't want it.'

The warder took hold of her arm and told her to lie down on the couch.

She didn't feel a mite different afterwards except for twinges around her head where the pressure pads had been. Back in her cell she massaged her temples and when the coast was, as far as she could tell, clear, she whistled out of the window to Kim.

She had heard of the hat. 'How do you feel?' she said.

'Absolutely no different,' said Oruela. 'It's nothing. I just lay there for twenty minutes and then he came back and asked me something about the modern woman.'

363

'Like what exactly?'

'Did I think the modern woman was somehow freer than her sisters down the ages? Something like that.'

'What did you say?'

'I said I wasn't sure. I guessed he was asking me the same question as he'd asked before, really.'

'Good girl!' said Kim. There came a strange noise. Oruela suddenly realised Kim was giggling.

'What are you laughing at? What if it brainwashes me?'

'Don't be a fool. Nothing can do that if you don't let it. You don't feel any different you said. Just fake it.'

'Oh, thank you, Doctor, I'm cured! I shall be chaste and virtuous from now on,' said Oruela in a silly voice. She suddenly laughed. She could do it too!

The pair of them were veritably snorting with laughter by the time the guard's footsteps came heavily down the corridor. Both of them leapt down from their windows.

The danger passed and Oruela went to the window again.

'I saw a gorgeous man,' she shouted softly.

'Oh yeah?' came a sceptical whisper on the wind.

'The cleaner down there.'

'Don't know him,' said Kim.

Oruela described him.

'Hang on a minute, that sounds like Cas,' said Kim. 'He's a bit of a bastard. Watch him.'

Oruela was more excited than she cared to admit. She was curious but pride stopped her asking further. Kim supplied the information without prompting.

'He had an affair with a woman along here so I heard. He kept telling her she was stupid all the time and then he dropped her. He just didn't show up one night. She really liked him and he just dumped her for no reason. The man is a goat. There was silence from the window for a moment. 'Mind you,' continued Kim. 'I know her and she is a bit stupid.'

'Wait a minute. You say they had an affair? What do

you mean? In here?' said Oruela. 'Marthe has to get married to do it.'

'Cas can pull strings,' said Kim.

'How?' asked Oruela.

'I don't know,' came the reply.

But Oruela had the feeling she might know more than she let on.

Alterations on a Theme

'Monsieur Raffoler!' trilled Madame Rosa. 'You're early today. Come in. Come in.'

The smell of washing soap hung in the air at La Maison Rose. It mingled with the cooking smells from a noisy lunch in progress in the back kitchen.

'Rosa, I want to see Annette,' said Jean.

Rosa squirmed. 'Annette is not available today, my dear monsieur. Let Diane see to your pleasure. She is very good.'

'OK. OK,' said Jean impatiently.

Rosa screeched kitchenwards, 'Diane!'

Through the half-open kitchen door Jean caught a glimpse of the girls in various states of morning undress. There were a round dozen of them, all Europeans. None of them wore make-up. Scrubbed faces shone and hair went every which way. They were charming in the raw. Their talk was of local politics and men. From among them the only redhead rose and came out into the hallway, closing the door behind her.

Diane led Jean up the pink and red stairway to the boudoir at the top. Inside the room the bed was on the floor with shimmering drapes hanging from a pole above it, desert-tent style. There were masses of cushions, a single lamp and on the dark red walls a number

366

of drawings from a work of Persian erotica showing couples pleasuring each other in extraordinary positions.

Jean's movements were weary. He took off his jacket and shoes and flopped on to the pillows on the bed. Diane slipped off her camisole and knickers and joined him. She undid his shirt, button by button. She opened his trousers, sliding them off with the merest effort. There was a mountain in his underwear, a warm delicious, fertile mountain. She set it free. Jean closed his eyes as her hands enclosed him. In the darkness of his closed lids he felt both her hands but then he felt a third and he opened his eyes. There was Annette too. She was as graceful as a gazelle. Her body was boyish and she had small, honey-tipped breasts. The hair on her sex was little more than a wisp of straw, the same colour as her long, flowing hair.

For a moment Jean thought he was going to get a duo. But Annette shooed Diane away and set up her base camp at the foot of his mountain in a flurry of thighs.

She spread the lips of her sex and, taking his cock in her other hand, she pushed him inside her.

Jean cupped her arse in his hands as she moved up and down on him. He raised himself. The muscles of his stomach rippled as he caressed her thighs on the soft inner part that was stretched across him like a bridge to the next world.

She kept her hands on her own thighs, at the back, as if she was proud of her balancing. She made Jean wonder, briefly, what was going through this gentle whore's mind. But then she drove her clitoris into his belly and she fell forward on to him, her hands caressing his chest, his neck, her lips kissing every bit of his body they could reach.

This was why he liked her. She gave herself to him, unlike the others who did an expert professional job and indulged his every whim but saved their orgasms for someone else.

He sat up and took her with him. He seized her face in his hands and kissed her passionately, desperately. Her thighs slid around his back and squeezed him close.

'Annette,' he breathed her name. 'Annette.' His cry was full of pain.

Annette held him close, resting in the pleasure of being full of him. Oh, she was on dangerous ground. So dangerous she felt his pain and it stirred her. She began moving on him again and he responded with a thrust so powerful it jerked her body backwards. She let herself fall and lay stretched out before him, her sex enclosing his, the rest of her dreaming her private dream.

Jean climbed on top of her, pressing her slenderness into the bed. She was so tiny, underneath him, like a fragile child. His senses overpowered him and he drove into her hard again and again until she laughed with pleasure.

When it was over she lay in his arms until the sound of his breathing changed. He slept and she lay quietly, naked and alone, enclosed in his arms. Her eyes began to glisten with tears.

He slept for about half an hour. During that time Annette barely moved. When he began to stir she watched him come awake.

'I suppose I had better go,' he said, coming around. 'Where's my shirt?'

'Before you go, I have to tell you something,' she said.

'What?' he said.

'I've stumbled on some information that might help you and your . . . your girlfriend.'

'My girlfriend?'

'Oruela Bruyere,' she said.

'You mean my ex-girlfriend,' said Jean. 'I'm not . . . I can't consider her my girlfriend any longer. She lied to me, she's locked up and . . . I'm not interested.'

'That's because that old git Mayor Derive told you

what a whore she is. I wouldn't take his word for anything, he's such a creep.'

Just at that moment the door opened and someone coughed politely. Annette spun round with fear in her eyes.

'It's me,' whispered Paul.

Jean grinned. 'Come in, old boy.'

As Paul entered the room Jean began dressing but Annette made no attempt to cover herself. Paul looked at her body lovingly.

'Rosa's looking for you, Annette. She's in a bit of a temper,' said Paul.

'Christ,' said Annette. 'If she catches me here . . . Look, you two, I overheard Mayor Derive's cronies talking yesterday. They were talking about your friend Oruela.'

'Who were these men?' asked Paul, quick as a flash.

'Armand Pierreplat and Gaston Everard,' said Annette. The pair were known in Biarritz. One was a judge, the other the coroner.

'What were they saying?' asked Paul.

'I didn't catch everything but they seemed to be worried in case Jean caused a fuss. They were cursing Norbert Bruyere for being so softhearted. I didn't really understand it. I just listened. Rosa was trying to keep them sensible. She said that it was all in their imaginations and that the mayor had spoken to Jean so they should just sit tight and keep it to themselves.'

'Rosa was there?' Paul fired the question at her.

'Rosa knows them all from years ago.'

'I suppose she does,' said Paul.

'You haven't heard everything yet though. Earlier this morning a woman I've never seen before comes to visit Rosa and the old girl went white as a sheet when she walked in the kitchen. She hurried her off and I thought, it's the same business. So I listened at the door of Rosa's room where they were having their talk. They started having an argument. This woman was saying things like: "What do you expect me to do? How can I let that bastard get away with it all over again?" And then suddenly Rosa rushed out of the room and bloody caught me! She's banned me from seeing Jean now.'

'Who was the woman, did you find out?' asked Paul.

'She had a Basque name. Rosa kept repeating it. "No Euska, no, Euska," she kept saying. She was really beautiful, the woman.'

'I wonder who she can be?' said Paul, looking at Jean. Jean had dressed himself during the conversation. 'Frankly,' he said, 'I really don't care. I don't want to know any of this. I'm trying to get over Oruela. I thought I was going to marry that girl and she's let me down. I really don't care.'

The three of them stood there momentarily in silence.

'But surely this information changes things, Jean,' said Paul. Then the door opened wide. Rosa stood before them.

'Go upstairs and pack your things, Annette. I warned you, and now you must go.' Her voice was soft but deadly. *Now!*'

'Oh come on, Rosa,' said Paul.

'Don't open your mouth, you leech. You get out too.'

'Don't call me a leech,' said Paul. 'You make your living out of other women's bodies, you're no one to talk.' His eyes were smouldering dangerously.

'If I just had shit like you to deal with I wouldn't make a living, would I!' shouted Rosa.

'I'll meet you outside,' said Paul, calmly, to Annette. He looked at Jean, a question in his eyes. But it was obvious that his friend was uncomfortable. He wasn't going to say anything at all. 'What's going on, Rosa,' continued Paul in a softer tone. 'What's the big secret? What does Oruela know? What has Derive got to be so scared of? Who was the woman who came here this morning looking for Oruela?'

The effect of his relentless questions on Rosa was marked. She seemed to crumble into an old woman. Her face sagged. 'Don't push me,' she said. 'I won't tell you anything.' She looked at Jean, who was staring at the carpet. 'I don't want anyone else hurt,' she said, 'so I won't discuss this conversation. But equally, I won't tell you anything either. Get Oruela out if you can. She's done nothing, poor child. But take the advice of an old whore who's been in this town, girl and woman for fifty years. There are people too powerful to mess with.' Her pale eyes seemed to wrestle with some unseen ghost.

'Are they frightening you into silence, Rosa?' said Paul.

'Just get out of here and take this bloody lovesick chit with you.' She turned to leave. 'And she's had her wages,' she said at the door.

'What do you make of that?' said Paul in wonder.

'She said Oruela's done nothing,' said Jean.

Paul looked at his friend hopefully.

'In fact, the whole tragic affair is causing me to feel quite unwell,' Jean continued, his eyes fixed on some distant horizon. 'I can't fathom this at all.' With that, he took his hands out of his pockets, picked up his hat, and went to the door. He left without saying anything more.

Annette watched him go and then began to cry.

'Come here,' said Paul, taking her in his arms gently. 'Don't worry. Get your things. You can come and stay with me until we figure this out.'

He went alone down the stairs. Rosa stood in the doorway of the salon. When she saw him coming she closed the door quietly in his face.

Outside, the fresh Atlantic wind rushed at Paul's face, soothing him. He walked right into it, as far as the promenade railing. A few early visitors walked on the beach. He was so angry he could have wrenched the railings from their concrete moorings and thrown them into the swelling sea.

So it had come to a head. Jean would never know the effect his turncoat behaviour towards Oruela had on his best friend. How could Jean believe that Oruela, the lovely girl he'd snatched up the minute Paul had pointed her out that night in the casino, was the monster that Mayor Derive had told them she was? The vitriol that Derive had poured on her when they went to see him was revolting. Paul had almost laughed in his face. That corrupt, no-good bastard who'd made his money selling cardboard shoes to the army during the war. As a rookie press photographer Paul had been sent to take photographs of the men at the front and he'd seen how they were dying as much from rotten equipment and bad food as enemy fire.

How could Jean believe it? When Oruela had chosen Jean, Paul had continued the relationship with Renée Salmacis that was still tearing him apart. Renée was hardly ever in Biarritz. She was a racing driver and she went all over the country. Their problems, she told him, stemmed from the fact that she was successful and he wasn't. Perhaps there was a spark of truth in it. A girl like Oruela went for Jean because they were of the same background.

But Oruela had been fooled by Jean. She thought he was a bohemian because he wore long hair and bought art in Paris. True, he was rich and he could do anything he wanted to whereas he, Paul, had nothing to show for years of stubborn addiction to his art.

And Renée was fundamentally wrong about their own affair. They fought because she was immature and attention-grabbing. They fought all the time and when they weren't fighting they were fucking. And there was his weakness. He loved to make love, and he loved to make love with someone he knew well. Even if he could have afforded it he couldn't have had any satisfaction out of making love to whores, not as a substitute for the real thing. He kept an ideal in his heart. The woman he would love for ever would be his best friend.

And what about poor Oruela now? Whatever she had come from it made her different. The one mistake she'd made with Jean had been not to tell him about her background before this happened. Jean didn't trust her any more. He'd retreated into his bourgeois fantasies about the evil nature of people from the wrong side of the tracks. He no longer cared. What a waste.

Paul looked out to sea and suddenly he knew he was going to do something. I'm from the wrong damn side of the tracks too, as far as these people are concerned, he thought. And I know how it feels. I don't know what I'm going to do but I will do something. Damn Jean. Damn the lot of them.

Annette was coming along the promenade, clutching a small cardboard suitcase in one hand. She kept close to the railing as if she was scared that the wind might blow her away.

'Come on,' he said, taking the suitcase from her. 'Let's go home and get drunk.'

Paul and Annette weren't the only ones to get drunk that afternoon. Genevieve had discovered the drinks cabinet and the effect was liberating. The words seemed to tumble out of her mouth like little things with a life of their own.

'Robert,' she asked, as he was moving furniture yet again. 'Would you make love to me?'

Robert stood up straight and said, 'Would I get extra wages for that, Madame?'

She thought she would die of embarrassment. 'Get out of my sight,' she screamed. When he was gone she slumped down on the sofa and cried. But the tears didn't last long. Oh, there was no need for tears she told herself. She was free! Robert was replaceable. Nothing could ever be as bad as it had been. Not now. Not now that dreadful brat Oruela was locked up and gone for ever. She pulled herself together and ran up the stairs and knocked on Robert's door.

'Come in,' he said.

She went in. He was packing his suitcase. He stopped when he saw who it was. In his hand was a photograph of Michelle. Genevieve had always suspected they were lovers. She felt an urge to be nasty but she held herself in check.

'I've come to apologise, Robert,' she said meekly. 'Don't go. I need you.'

Robert's chest was so broad and manly she found it irresistible, almost, especially as it was puffed up with pride. 'I am a servant, Madame,' he said.

'Oh look, I know, Robert. It was a momentary lapse. What I mean is, will you stay and be my servant? I need . . . I need some stability in this house, everything has changed so quickly.'

Her words seemed to affect him immediately. A look of pity crossed his face and he lowered his eyes.

'I'll give you an increase in wages,' she said.

'Then I'll stay, at least until things are more settled,' he said.

'Oh, thank you,' she said.

'I might remind you that you haven't done the accounts with cook for over a week, madame,' he said.

Genevieve sighed. What a bore. But she smiled, left him and rang for Cook. Within minutes the woman came to her sitting room and bored her even more with niggling little amounts of this and that. Genevieve found herself wondering, as the woman's ample bosom rose and fell, who Cook had sex with and what she looked like when she was doing it. Did she knead her man as she kneaded dough. No. Cook, she thought, would ride her lover like a horse, her breasts bouncing around, her great hips bearing down.

Thank God the accounts were soon finished. Alone again, Genevieve went to the drinks cabinet once more and poured herself a generous amount of Norbert's twenty-year-old whisky that he had sent especially from Scotland. The fire hit her loins and made her want to dance. Oh, how she and Alix, the lovely policeman, would dance. She jumped up and waltzed around the study with her invisible lover. She could feel his hands searching for her breasts, taking them in his mouth, sucking. And then her fantasies took another turn. He was begging her, 'Please, please'. She flopped down on the couch and passed out in a heap.

374

Literary Classics

*T*he next thing the prison authorities decided was that Oruela needed work to improve her. She wasn't the only one. Kim worked in the kitchen and wanted Oruela to try and get a job there. But as luck would have it, when the allocation came up, she got the library. So she began a new career.

Any woman who worked outside the wing where she might come into contact with men, was ordered to wear dungarees and a shirt – men's uniform, in other words. Oruela pulled on the shape-concealing baggy blue trousers and tucked in the shirt. She fastened the waistband with the big brown leather belt that came with the set. She had no mirror but imagined herself to look like a farm labourer. In fact there was something quite appealing about her slender frame swathed in all those clothes. No amount of disguise could hide the fact that she was a beautiful young woman. There was a certain androgynous quality about her now that was not displeasing.

The library was a small, dingy building. Its contents had been donated by a wealthy philanthropist for the improvement of the minds of the poor.

'There's bugger all left,' said the librarian guard, a fat hairy man who smoked stinking, cheap tobacco in a worn pipe. 'They use the pages as toilet paper, ignorant bastards.' Behind the guard stood his assistant, a one-eyed old inmate called, she found out later, Pierre. Pierre's job was to take the book trolley over to solitary confinement and the condemned cells.

The guard turned and spat over his shoulder. 'Where's the bloody coffee, that's what I want to know.'

Pierre shrugged his shoulders and shook his head and finally raised his one eye to heaven in a secret gesture to Oruela.

As the days passed, she found out why. The coffee was never on time and Gerard, the guard, said exactly the same thing every morning. The work was mainly humping books here and there according to where they were supposed to be and sometimes a whim would overtake Gerard and there would be a reorganisation. Apart from that, in between the hours when inmates were allowed to visit, there was plenty of time to pass among the dingy shelves and delve into the treasures she found there. Strange that she should have to come to this place to realise an ambition to read but here she was and she made the most of it. She moved, sylph-like in her boy's clothes, her mind a sponge, soaking up everything. She was almost content.

Two days a week she had to go to see the doctor and have her treatment in the hat. Every time she went the tall man with the hooked nose was there, sweeping the same piece of floor, over and over again. She was dying to find out if he was the cruel Cas that Kim thought.

One day, as soon as the guard who had escorted her went into the little office, he rested his broom against the wall and walked over to her quickly. He stood in front of her, a towering giant. For the briefest of moments she was scared.

'May I sit down?' he asked. His French was heavily accented and as he spoke his body seemed to beg her.

It was such a small gesture but it was beautiful, so

polite, so different from the crudeness she was coming to believe was normal. It turned her on. She felt the cream ooze into her knickers.

She nodded.

He sat his great body next to her, not too close, but she could feel him all the same.

'What's your name?' he asked.

She told him.

'That's very pretty,' he said. 'Is it Spanish?'

'Basque,' she replied.

'Aha!' he said, nodding sympathetically. 'Have you noticed how so many of us are political prisoners?'

It wasn't easy to concentrate on what he was saying. As he'd sat down she thought she'd seen a patch of skin on his hip, where the side opening of his work dungarees was not properly fastened. If she had, perhaps he had no underwear on. She could think of nothing else, but she dare not glance again. He held her in his gaze.

'Can I come and talk to you tomorrow?' he asked.

'Yes,' she said.

Immediately he had his answer he got up and walked back to his broom, taking it up again just as the nurse came out of von Streibnitz's office to call her in. It was uncanny. How had he timed it so perfectly? Oruela looked at the nurse as if she had come from Mars.

The next time she visited the doctor he was there and the same routine was repeated. This time as he sat, asking her questions and admiring her with his eyes as she talked – yes, she could talk at last – the strap of his dungarees slipped off one shoulder. Her eyes travelled over the expanse of muscle that was as good as bare to her heightened senses. Under his shirt his body moved. She could feel the heat of it. Looking at the fallen bib that had left his shirt bare and under that his chest, Oruela could only think of how it would be if she pulled it. She could hear it almost . . . rrrip! Underneath would be his underpants and in them . . . She adored the look of his skin. How would it be on his . . .

377

'Your mind is wandering,' he said. 'You're not listening to me.'

She apologised, searching her lust-drenched mind for something to say. With a smile that hovered on his red lips, he rose and was gone, just like before, with perfect timing. The doctor came out just as he took up his broom.

His name was Caspar, he told her eventually. He was Russian. 'Rossian,' he pronounced it, proudly. He was being held illegally. The bourgeois French were traitors and hypocrites and a conspiracy was afoot. One day the story would come out and the truth would shock many people. They held him for the killing of a Bolshevik pig.

Oruela never asked him if he had actually killed the man. It didn't seem the right thing to do. Besides, she had other things on her mind. That night she cut off the legs of her standard issue cotton bloomers and hemmed the edges the way Kim had done hers. She ended up with a pair of short wide-legged knickers that left her thighs air to breath. Even if she looked like a boy on the outside, she thought, she could feel womanly underneath . . .

The next time she saw him, he told her she was lovely and she felt lovely. He took two pieces of chocolate out of his pocket.

'Here,' he said. 'One's for you.'

'How did you get this?' she asked in wonder.

He looked at her with his deep blue eyes and they told her that in this place this gesture was equivalent to flying to Russia and back in a day to get her the best caviar in the world. He raised a finger to his magnificent nose and tapped it. Then he bit into the chocolate.

'You'd better eat yours,' he said, licking his lips.

She couldn't, her mouth was dry. She wanted him to bite her skin. He knew it. He smiled, taking her chocolate and breaking off a small piece. He fed it to her, touching her lips with his long, slender fingers.

* * *

So she worked in the library and thought of him. Other inmates came in and weren't oblivious to her charms by any means. They flirted with her like mad, men and women both. Pierre told her that the use of the library seemed to have risen considerably and word must be getting round. But none of them had the panache of Caspar. They all managed to get caught talking to her in the aisles.

Then one day Gerard the guard opened the doors and a queue shuffled in as usual. The daylight outside was white that day. The clouds were high and blanketing and the light hurt the eyes. All the same, the silhouette was unmistakable. The last one. Tall, black against the sky. She recognised him instantly. She felt him. He could pull strings all right, deep down in the secret recesses of her soul.

He made straight for her. His face was inscrutable but his eyes were hers and hers alone. She felt as if everyone around her must feel the sexual tension between them. But no. Gerard the guard was grumbling away at the hapless line in front of him as usual.

'Can you explain the system to me?' said Caspar. 'I want the literature section. I haven't been here before.'

One or two of the inmates noticed something. But they moved aside for him, without complaining.

Oruela came out from behind the counter, her knees trembling, and told him to follow her. They found an aisle that was deserted.

'I've found you,' he whispered. 'Now I can see you every day,' and he moved towards her and touched her face gently.

'Be careful!' she whispered.

'I know what I'm doing,' he replied. 'The secret is to do it right under their noses.'

She knew he was going to kiss her. She wanted it so much. He bent his head towards her and brushed her cheek with his lips. He smelled her hair. It was the desperate drinking of a man in the desert and it was

379

fast. There was no time for romance. It was his senses drinking her. She'd touched the boy in him and she felt it for the first time, the soft needing-her boy under the man carved of history and the rough stone of life. It was almost as if he'd come right there. She wanted to feel it but it was forbidden.

Every day that she wasn't at the doctor's he came to the library. She began searching for a nook, a cupboard, anywhere where they might slip beyond the public domain and be together. He had pressed his body against hers and she had felt the contours of it, the bulk of him in her arms.

Words became caresses. They talked to each other in whispers about the world, about the books they read and each word was loaded with passion. He taught her how to read one book following another so that her education had some direction and she didn't flounder. So he had her mind and her soul. Only her body was not yet his. One day, he promised, it would be.

Meanwhile, especially on Sundays, when everything closed down and she was stuck on the wing, she wondered why she hadn't heard from Jean. Not only Jean was silent. There was no news from the outside world at all. Not that she wanted to be free now without Caspar. But, as the hours ticked by and the gossamer thread that bound her to him dissolved, she lay on her bed in the belly of the whale, listening to the sounds around her and the boredom was excruciating. When evening came she could concentrate on her reading, which had become a habit. But the days were only punctuated by mealtimes.

The wing was a hothouse for whatever atmosphere was breeding that day. It seemed as if everyone was affected one way or another, by everyone else's mood. One Sunday, when she'd been there about three weeks, there was tension. Women were snappy with each other. Something was brewing. Kim appeared behind her in the lunch queue and whispered. 'Watch with eyes out of the back of your head.'

'What's going on?' asked Oruela.

'Watch those two,' said Kim. She nodded to a couple of big women further along and then she was gone.

Oruela missed Kim. Her work in the library and Kim's work in the kitchen kept them on different timetables and their intimacy had lapsed. There was only Sunday evenings and there was always, more often than not, a crowd playing cards.

Just as she was thinking this the queue suddenly erupted. Oruela was thrown back into the person behind her by the force of the disturbance.

The two women that Kim had pointed out were glaring at each other about two feet apart. Women were scattering. Oruela backed against a wall and from where she stood she could see that the shorter-haired of the two had pulled a knife. It gleamed with the fear of a hundred pairs of watching eyes. The other woman in the fight watched it closely.

Hovering like a wasp around the women was the small blonde who had grabbed Oruela's arse that first day in the shower. It was clear. She was the cause.

'Do it!' she screamed. 'Do it, Marielle.'

Marielle jabbed the knife point at the other woman. And then from nowhere there was a flash of body and Kim was there. She kicked Marielle's hand hard and the knife flew out of it. Marielle looked as if she would turn on Kim, but the intended victim saw her chance and she went for her assailant.

Marielle defended herself and the two women locked in combat. Oruela watched in fascination. They were like two rutting stags. Great grunts came from them as their arms gripped each other's and they wrestled each other to the ground. There was no pretence, it was life and death. Their shapeless prison dresses rode up on their thighs. Strong feet kicked and necks twisted in impossible ways.

After her valiant attack to stop bloodshed, Kim stood

381

back panting and watched intently, as did the whole wing. Thirty big burly guards swarmed in from different directions and pulled the women apart. One was kept on the ground, her head crushed to the floor in a mass of damp hair, her face twisted in pain. The other was frog-marched away first, screaming.

The whole wing was affected afterwards with a strange sense of the erotic. The way violence touched on a sexual nerve, the way fear twisted itself into the women's souls and made them jumpy. It was too much for everyone. They clubbed together and talked it to death.

Kim was treated like a brave warrior. Women showered her with praise and she walked tall, her face disturbed, back to her cell.

Next door, Oruela heard the chant begin. She wanted it to relax her but she was too filled with her own violence. She wanted to hit the damn walls. She cursed the damn cell and the damn daily routine. She cursed Jean and Michelle and everyone who had left her here to suffer. She was on the point of tears.

But then suddenly she saw the pad of prison-issue writing paper and she knew she had to get something down on paper.

Dear Michelle, she began. She wanted to write *Help me! help me!* on the page over and over but she couldn't. So she sat, listening to the sun chant for a while, staring at the square of moonless sky.

Dear Michelle, she began to write, I sit here thinking of nothing but sex. It has been so long since I felt the satisfaction of pleasuring a man sexually. You know what I mean, when they're surprised because you're ravenous. I have such fantasies about Jean and about a man I have met in here. In my fantasy, Michelle, I am no longer in this dreadful place. I am at a party at one of my friends' houses in Bayonne, it's Lauren's party I think. It's summer and the night is warm and glowing with stars. It's just like it used to be on her terrace with the torches burning in the trees. Beyond the garden is black as ink. I am with Jean and we have danced and danced, our bodies are tingling with the dance, small drops of perspiration trickle down my back. I know he wants me and I want him so badly that I cannot wait. I suggest to him that we walk away from the crowd into the dark garden. He is hesitant because our parents are in the ballroom but I manage to persuade him and we slip away. The darkness gathers on us until it's almost impossible to see our hands in front of us.

The night is drenched in the perfume of flowers and as soon as we can, we stop. He is still nervous, he wants to go further into the darkness so I allow him to lead me on. We come to the topiary garden and I pull him into a hedge made into the shape of a satyr. I pull at his clothes and he at mine. He has chilly hands and they touch my flesh like ice. He lifts me into him with my legs around his waist, my dress rustling against his clothes he takes me standing up.

He lifts me up and down on him, the cheeks of my arse spread wide apart and I am pushing into him; the hedge is springy and supports us. It prickles my arms as I cling to him.

And then I notice someone walking through the maze. It's just his head. His face is white in the darkness. I will him to see us and he turns. It is Caspar.

He is making his way towards us. Jean is unaware of him. Only I see him. He turns the last corner of the maze and comes to stand on the small lawn just beyond our statue, where I can see him. He is dressed in a flowing white shirt which he unbuttons and pulls out of his trousers. I'm still fucking Jean. His cock inside me is filling me up.

Caspar unbuttons his trousers and takes them off. He is naked from the waist down and he pulls up his flowing shirt to show me his body. He is performing for me. He starts to urinate on the ground. In the dark the only sound is of his golden stream hitting the floor.

I've never seen anything like this and it makes me

forget Jean. All I know of him is his cock and where I bang against his belly in the night.

Caspar goes to lay down on the stone bench. He lifts his shirt again and poses for me, like a model.

Then suddenly Jean gets wind of what is going on. He is angry but when he sees Caspar he is drawn to him himself. We both go to Caspar who comes up to meet us. Jean is behind me and Caspar in front. They sandwich me between their two cocks. I can feel both of them.

This time I climb on to Caspar and take him with Jean's body warm at my back.

Then we are on the floor and Caspar and Jean touch each other's pricks while I watch. They kiss each other and pump each other's sex.

Rescue Me

S he went down to the doctor on Monday morning and waited as usual outside his office. But Caspar wasn't there. She spent the usual amount of time in the hat and as she lay on the wheeled couch she wondered where he was. She came out expecting to see him but he wasn't there.

The next day she went to work in the library and she was like a cat on hot bricks waiting for him but still he didn't come.

In the evening she whispered her agony out of the window to Kim.

'I'll put some feelers out,' said Kim.

Three almost intolerable days went by before Kim was able to find out the truth. Caspar had been taken to solitary confinement.

'What for?' asked Oruela out of the window.

'I wouldn't trouble about that,' said Kim mysteriously.

Oruela didn't. She had only one thought in her mind. To get to his cell. She began forming her plan.

All she would have to do was convince Gerard that she could do a good service if she swapped jobs with the old man. The next morning she asked old Pierre what he thought. She put it to him that she could save his old bones if she did it.

'You wouldn't be safe,' he said. 'I couldn't let you do it.'

'Oh, I'd be as safe as houses, all those guards around. Nothing would happen to me. Let me come with you.'

So they approached Gerard together. At first he was suspicious.

'So you finally got someone to believe your stories, did you, old man?' he sneered at Pierre.

Pierre didn't contradict him. He didn't say a word about how it was Oruela's idea. 'It wouldn't take such a long time. I'm sure she'd be back well before the lunch bell.'

'You'll have to show her the ropes,' said Gerard. 'She won't last!'

That evening in her cell, Oruela could barely breathe with excitement. She daren't even say anything to Kim during their nightly whisper, in case of being over-heard. So the anticipation was hers alone. Her heart beat like a drum in the silent night. She put her trousers under her mattress to iron out the creases and slept fitfully.

The next morning she paid particular attention to her hair, to her nails. Gerard was in a bad mood because coffee arrived late as usual and they were late starting. They trundled the trolley out of the library and across the courtyard to the men's segregation block and rang the bell. There were three guards in the control room. The one that came to open the door was a giant, blond. Tattooed on his neck was the word 'Maman' like a scar.

'Haven't got authorisation for two of you,' he said, looking at Oruela suspiciously. 'Can't allow you in.'

Oruela thought quickly. 'Well, I can't stand out here on my own. I'm not authorised to move freely, only with Pierre.'

The guard snarled. 'That's not my problem,' he said, and he shoved the gate closed.

'Might I suggest,' said Pierre, with whining humility, 'that you telephone the library. It must be an oversight. Guard Gerard at the library was going to telephone you

386

but the coffee arrived late and I expect it slipped his mind.'

'It's not for you to imagine what goes on in an officer's mind, you old lunatic.'

'I wouldn't presume,' said Pierre, he was wringing his hands in supplication.

The blond guard relented. 'Wait there.'

'You'll have to learn to lick their boots, my dear,' Pierre said, when the guard had gone. 'They think a lot of themselves, these ones here. It's a prison within a prison, you see. Rules of its own, it has.'

'Thank you,' said Oruela politely. She suspected she would do anything to get the man she wanted, who was buried within.

The guard returned and began opening the gate.

As they stepped into the doorway Oruela smelled for the first time the warm, human body smell that characterised the place. It wasn't pleasant. But neither was it totally unpleasant. It smelled like bedrooms in the morning. Human odours mixed with the inevitable prison cleaning fluid, an eggy smell.

There was only one landing and all the cell doors were shut. An energy filled the place. It was danger. Strange danger. As if the men enclosed in the steel cells were so huge that only this method could keep them small. They were dangerous beyond the normal run of damaged and impulsive men and women serving their time on the other wings. Captured danger. The dark side of humanity. But here they were tamed, kept behind thick steel. The doors were pig-pink as usual, but they had an extra bar on them that had to be lifted.

The guard asked for the first name on the list and, reading it, went to open the cell. The door opened inward. Oruela got the shakes. What would she find in there, what raging beast?

'Library visit,' said the guard, and stood back to let them in.

The man inside arose as a sick patient arises from a hospital bed, sluggishly, as if living with his own

387

dreams, his own excavations, day and night, as if his self was his cell and it moved with him.

'Hello, Pierre,' he said. Then he saw Oruela.

He jumped up and threw a towel over a bucket in the corner and then sat down on the bed again. Pierre perched on the other end of the steel cot and Oruela made for the small chair that the man gestured to.

Pierre introduced her and the man held out his hand. Oruela looked into his eyes and saw something she hadn't expected to see. It wasn't lust, not sexual at all. It was gratitude. She felt acutely embarrassed.

They passed a few words.

They continued on down the wing, repeating the same process. Each door was locked behind them as they left. And Oruela began to feel the atmosphere changing in the place. A stir. It was as if the very walls spoke: 'Beauty is here. Beauty is here, even here, in the midst of all this warped humanity. There's hope.' Oruela carried the thrill of it in her body.

'What's the next name on the list?' said the guard, looking at it.

His words hit Oruela like a stone falling from her throat to her womb. 'Alexandrovich.' She had been expecting it but it still did it to her. Her feelings almost burst. It had been days.

Caspar sat, cowed, on the bed, in much the same attitude as any of the others they had visited. But there were his long legs, his broad shoulders, just as lovely as ever.

His eyes registered the joy he felt and his face broke into a great smile that, luckily, the guard didn't see. Pierre saw it though and quick as a flash the perceptive old man gave her the book, *Le Rouge et le Noir* by Stendhal, and asked if he could leave his helper to have a few words with the 'aristocrat'. The guard was of an age with Cas. He looked at him.

'He's no trouble,' he said.

The two men walked out of the cell leaving the door open wide.

'You're so good to see,' said Cas and he held out both hands as he leaned forward. She held out her hands to him and he took them, enclosing them. It was wonderful to touch him.

'I'm sorry you had to come to this disgusting place but I'm so glad . . .' he said.

'What are you doing here? What happened? I was so . . .' She couldn't speak.

'It's a mistake,' he said. 'I'll be out of here soon,' and he got up and pushed the cell door to so that it was almost closed. If she was not mistaken the bulge in his denims had grown. She did so ache to see it. It felt like another presence as he walked back and sat on the bed. Huge and powerful. The creases around the bulk of it were etched like rays from a warm sun. She could smell his sex. He moved with less agility than before, yet this spot was alive. Her entire soul went into her sex. It felt happy like a fruit waiting to be taken and eaten.

And so they were alone. They crammed a real conversation into five minutes and he laughed, saying he was going to get even more reading done. Then suddenly he held up his finger to stop her talking.

Perhaps he could hear something she couldn't distinguish.

'Stand up,' he whispered. 'Go to the door.'

She did as she was told, without question. She stood facing the tiny glass window, about three inches square. She could see the landing. He rose and stood next to her, very close.

The closeness of him was almost intolerable. She yearned for him to take her in his arms. She turned to look at him. He held his fingers to his lips and then put his fingers to her lips. A kiss that was not a kiss. But a kiss none the less. 'Keep look-out,' he said.

Then she felt his hand at her waist. She felt his strong hand push between her belt and her belly. She felt his fingers at the top of her knickers, then his palm on her pubic hair. Then his searching fingers at her sex, drenched in its moisture. His forearm, flat against her

389

belly, shoving down further, his fingers reaching, searching and yes, inside.

She reached for the bulge in his trousers and held it, just as the guard and Pierre came into view in the glass. They were about six feet away. Caspar wrenched his hand out of her pants and put both hands in his pockets. She spun around and assumed a stance natural to casual conversation. The first thing that came into her head was:

'Well, yes, but I think the Mercedes is a much easier car to drive . . .'

A glint of laughter shone in his eyes but he seemed to have lost the power of speech. She knew if the others came in with him like that they'd be able to smell something was up.

'Well, goodbye then,' she said and opened the door just as the guard came to the other side of it.

'Oh,' she said, surprised.

It wasn't easy to hold a conversation with Pierre on the way back across the courtyard. Her sex seemed to be yelling 'I've been touched! I've been touched!' in her pants.

All she could say was yes, she liked the job very much and thought she could do it.

And so it was hers. She became known as the library girl and all the men looked forward to the visit. Even von Streibnitz got to hear of the 'stimulating effects', as he said, that she was having on the solitary male population. She told him that literature was certainly improving their minds and rehabilitating even the most hardened criminals. He bought it. In fact the service became so popular that another woman was assigned to help her. A nun. And so Oruela and the nun went demurely twice a week.

Oruela managed to get Kim to steal some elastic from the workshop and made herself a hook and eye out of some lead wine tops that she purloined from the kitchen waste bins. This made Cas's explorations into her pants a great deal easier.

She gradually increased her time with him from five to ten, to fifteen minutes, leaving the nun to perform her mission with most of the other chaps. Despite the lack of time, Caspar somehow managed to observe the delicacies of courtship. Everything was just fast.

'How are you today?' he would ask and she always had the time to tell him. She learned to express herself exactly and succinctly.

But when words could say no more, they would stand by the door and he would ease his forearm into the elastic. He would press his prick into the softness of her arse, not urgently, just gently, while he worked on her sex with his hands.

She would lean back on him, stretching her belly a little, pushing her sex forward and he would work with his hand. At first she was scared to let herself come and then one day he whispered 'Trust me' and she closed her eyes to the jailers and let him keep watch, over her shoulder. She closed her eyes and concentrated on the sensation and let herself be taken away. In the dark the rub, rub of his fingertips, gently now, harder, massaging, compelling, took her to the brink of a precipice and held her there, terrified, in agony. Then came the ecstasy. She felt herself going and he felt her too and whispered, 'Go, my sweet, go,' and she went. He held her up as her body absorbed the first wave of release, and the second, the third and the soft aftershocks.

He still held her tight, kissing her neck. It was too much to bear, not kissing him back and she turned and pulled him down under the glass panel and kissed him full on the mouth. It was so brief it hurt.

The next time she entered the cell he wasted no time. Immediately he took her to one side of the door and kissed her again, drinking her in through his lips, throwing caution to the wind and just kissing, kissing, kissing. She decided it was his turn this time and at last

391

she reached down and undid his zip. His sex wasn't immediately hard. It was substantial enough though and warm and gorgeous. At last she had it in her hands after all this time. And as she handled it, it became hard, gradually, and wet at the tip.

He leaned back against the wall and she kept a look-out through the glass window. She moved her hand up and down, up and down, caressing his cock, smoothing its moisture over him and down, lubricating her hand.

He was helpless. His trousers pushed down off his hips and he crashed against the wall as if a tidal wave had washed him there. His eyes were closed, his mouth open in an 'O'.

'Come, Cas,' she breathed, 'come,' and she felt him responding. She went to him, and, lifting her shirt, she pressed his shaft against her belly. He opened his eyes, reached for her breast and gave a low groan. She felt his sperm shoot at her belly, his cock pumping in her hand and she held him.

Still she kept one eye on the little window.

The next day she went to the uniform issue hatch and persuaded the inmate working there to give her a much bigger shirt. She took it back to her cell and tried it on. Perfect. It covered her bottom and thighs. Then she took her trousers and undid the crotch seam. The wound in them was about six inches in all. She tried them on, leaving off her knickers. She opened her legs and *voila*! The fabric split to reveal her sex, easy to get to, displayed in all its glory. She undressed and folded the set neatly.

For some reason, the next time she visited, the nun told her to spend the whole time with Caspar and she would do the rest. Oruela didn't question it, nor the fact that the guard was gentle with Cas as he opened the door.

She sat down with him in the cell. She sat opposite him on the little chair and he asked her how she was.

392

She told him, thinking all the while of the split in her trousers. They talked for quite some time. And then he said, touching her chin, 'You're so beautiful.'

'Well,' she replied, 'this beautiful woman has got something very beautiful to show you.' Her own voice excited her. He cocked his head on one side, wondering.

Slowly she uncrossed her legs and pulled the fabric apart at her thighs. He caught his breath as he looked at her sex. He looked right into it, studying. She reached for his bowed head and stroked the curls at his neck. Then he put his fingers inside her and jabbed in and out.

'We must do it,' she said. 'Come and sit on this chair and I'll sit on top of you.'

'They'll see us,' said Caspar. 'Here, bring the chair up to the door.'

He sat with his back to the door and pulled his prick out. It was hard, standing there in the folds of his clothes at the crotch.

As she lowered herself on to him she could feel his clothes on her inner thigh. But oh, his cock was so wonderful. She clasped her legs together around the chair and pushed on to him. He held her arse and helped her up and down. It was fantastic. She suddenly thought of where they were and began to laugh. Her body felt so wonderful as he gripped her waist, his big hands almost reaching right round her. She kissed his head and lifted his face up to look at it. She smiled at his eyes and he responded. They laughed together. The feeling of fucking in this mad place while the guards walked up and down outside, while all the locks and bolts in this world tried to pin the wings of sex and hold it, was wonderful. Yes they had done it. Yes. Yes. Yes.

She came like she had never come before, while his cock throbbed inside her with his own orgasm.

It was even delicious afterwards to sit and smile and

come down. They sat apart again, very properly, each wordless for a while. And then he said something she would always remember afterwards. He said, 'Whatever you do, Oruela, be true to yourself. You're a wonderful woman. You're beautiful inside and out.'

The Anonymous Benefactor

*T*he next day, Kim whispered across the food counter, 'They took Caspar last night,'

Oruela felt her legs go numb. She looked at Kim. Her friend's face was deadly serious.

'Why?' asked Oruela. But the queue was pressing behind her and there was no time for further conversation.

Oruela ate her breakfast still in a state of hope. They had probably taken him to another part of the prison, she thought. But as the eggs hit her stomach she knew it was impossible. The idea that she would never see him again was too hard to bear. She waited resolutely.

When it was time for work, instead of going to the queue for the gate, Oruela went along the landing to Kim's cell.

'Where have they taken him? she asked.

'Back to Russia,' said Kim, 'They've traded him for someone from the other side, a Frenchman the Bolsheviks were holding in one of their prisons for trying to stir up counter-revolutionary sentiment.'

Oruela's knees went completely. She sank on to the small chair.

'Don't go to work,' said Kim. 'I'll look after you. Just sit there and when I bring the guard, act it up a bit.'

Oruela didn't have to. She was feeling the old strangeness again. She didn't say a word to anyone as the guard and Kim helped her to bed.

'If she doesn't get any better, I'll have her taken to hospital,' said the guard.

'Let me bring her some hot tisane,' said Kim.

The guard agreed.

Kim wasn't long. The tisane smelt of blackcurrants. It also had a liberal quantity of cognac in it.

She slept for a while after that but when she awoke the reality hit her again like a hammer blow to the head. It was actual physical pain. Kim was there again, with lunch and another, miraculous tisane. Oruela drunk it and stared at the blank wall.

Kim reached across the bed and took her in her arms gently. 'I need to see some tears at this point, otherwise I'll be worried,' she said.

It was all Oruela needed. She let out a wail of total grief that turned into huge racking sobs that went on and on. Kim stayed with her until they were ebbing and then she left, to cook dinner.

Come evening Oruela felt less pain but she was still shaky. The thought of poor Caspar made her weep again. His own people would surely execute him. She felt the touch of his death. His last words to her came back. No! He was still alive now, surely. There hadn't been time to get him back to Russia.

He was out there, somewhere, in some lonely train carriage, only enemies for company. She would remain beautiful for him. She got out of bed, changed her clothes, putting on the drab black prison skirt and blouse. She took up her brush and ran it through her hair.

There was tons of hair on the brush! The sight of it shocked her. She felt her head. There was still plenty there.

She needed company. Her cell door was open and the sky was dark outside. She reckoned it to be about 9 in the evening. She crept out, feeling like a new chicken just out of the egg, and went along to Kim's cell.

There was no one in it. Then she noticed that the rug on Kim's floor was missing. A sword of sheer terror stabbed her heart. Not Kim too!! But no. Her other things were there. She backed out of the cell. Something else was strange. The place seemed empty. Then she realised what it was. There were no guards about. She made her way along the landing to Marthe's cell. That was empty too. The little wind chime that Marthe had made from bits of tin tinkled on a breeze that came in through the open window.

And then she heard another sound. The sound of soft laughter. It was coming from the communal room at the end of the landing. This was a tatty dump that no one ever went in. But someone was in there tonight. She crept slowly along the landing to the door.

The sight that met her eyes was fantastic. The room was lit with candles. It was full of women. They were laughing, lounging around on rugs, even cushions. It was luxurious, almost another world. She opened the door and all eyes turned her way. There was a strange sweet smell in the room. The air was heavy with smoke. A group of women in the corner passed a hookah between them.

'Oruela! Oh, I'm so glad!' Marthe raised her luxurious body from the group and, stepping over the legs outstretched on the floor, she came towards her.

Of course! It was the hen night! Marthe was dressed in a real dress. It was beautiful, a black silky affair, beaded and tied at the hip with a jet scarf. Around her forehead was a black headband and she had a feather poked in the side of it. Earrings made of heavy silver adorned her ears and her lips were red as strawberries. Her eyes were cloudy, the pupils dilated, giving her a sleepy look.

'Here, have a glass of wine,' she said, gently leading Oruela to one corner of the room where a low table held

397

several opened bottles and glasses. She poured a glass of the blood-coloured wine and handed it to her.

'There's hashish too,' she said, her eyes twinkling. 'I bet you've never smoked hashish.'

'No, I haven't,' said Oruela. She wasn't sure she wanted to.

'Come with me,' said Marthe.

Oruela followed her to the other corner of the room, stepping over the lounging women like Marthe did. Their bare legs gleamed in the candlelight.

Marthe beckoned to her to sit in the circle of women who were passing the hookah. Oruela sat next to a big-thighed black woman whom she recognised as one of Kim's co-workers in the kitchen. The woman smiled at her and adjusted her sitting position.

The hookah was coming round the circle and was passed to the black woman who settled it in front of her and took the mouthpiece between her lips. She drew on it, taking a big hit and withdrawing the mouthpiece. Her eyes closed as she held her breath, taking the smoke down deep into her lungs. She took three hits and passed it on to Oruela.

Oruela looked across at Marthe, who had fallen into conversation. Perhaps it would make her feel better. She copied what she'd seen the woman next to her do. She raised the metal mouthpiece to her lips and drew. Her heart began to beat faster as the perfumed smoke hit her lungs and a spot in the middle of her forehead seemed to open like a window. At the same time she began to feel everything. Her fingertips glowed. She could feel the muscles in her shoulders loosen and relax. Within, her bowel began to feel anxious and then relax soon after. But the main sensation was between her kneeling thighs. Her sex began to swell.

The old fear of her attraction to other female bodies surfaced at the same time.

'Take another hit,' whispered Marthe, just as Oruela was about to pass the thing on in alarm.

It worked. The fear gradually dissipated. So what?

Sexuality is a wild, untameable thing, she said to herself. She could feel the thigh of the woman beside her resting on her own. One long warm sliver of thigh. But she didn't move. It was human. It was nice.

There were conversations going on either side of her, intimate conversations. She didn't feel as if she had the resources to interrupt or join. So she relaxed into a sitting position, her legs tucked to the side of her.

It disturbed the woman on her left. She turned. She was a large-boned, blonde creature. Her smile was threatening but brief. Oruela caved in on herself, on her own thoughts. The introspection seemed to last a long time, whereas in reality it was probably brief.

She thought of Caspar, not with fear for his safety or with pain at the loss of him, but how he was. How they were together, that last time, laughing their heads off in joy at getting away with what they were doing. She was so proud of herself!

Was this the woman who went mad because the policeman came and accused her of murdering her father? No, it was not. Damn them all. She had come a long way. She would always hold Caspar, and Kim and Marthe in her heart. They'd changed her. They'd set her free. One day she would be out of here, too. She would be truly free and then there'd be no stopping her.

And then it hit her. The letter. She'd sent it to Michelle. Good God! Von Streibnitz would have her in the hat for ever if he read it. But he must have read it by now if he was going to and nothing had changed. Perhaps she'd got away with that too.

She wondered what Michelle would think of it. Perhaps Michelle would think she was a bit mad. But it wasn't a mad woman that wrote that letter, it was a free one. Oruela smiled to herself.

Here was the hooka again. Its body was made of glass that bulged at the bottom. It was passed on a wooden base. Inside there was a long black shaft that air bubbled out from into the water. The long pipe slithered like a snake.

She took a deep hit, just as the door opened behind her. She saw through the smoke the way Marthe smiled with delight. She passed the hookah and turned round.

There was Kim, closing the door behind her. She was wearing dancing clothes. A long, flowing skirt fell from her bare hips. It was held up by a scarf, knotted at the side. Her midriff was bare. Bare and shapely, deep brown and beautiful. Covering her breasts was another scarf. Her neck was bare and her slender, beautifully rounded head moved like a black swan's.

Her ears, her wrists and her ankles were decked in bracelets that clicked as she moved.

A space parted for her, like the Red Sea parting for the Jews of Israel, and Marthe leapt to the gramophone in the corner of the room and cranked it up.

Marthe put the needle-head on the spinning disc and the sounds of a trumpet with a mute wound around the room. Slow, lazy notes as if through a fog.

Kim began to move to the tune, gyrating her hips on a single vertical plane. Up and down went her hips, her navel a dark centre of her body, mysteriously still.

She began to move her bare feet, treading a circle close to the women at the edges of her designated dance floor. Strong steps, proud and firm, marking the boundaries. Women shuffled back against the walls. Kim's feet beat on the carpet in time to the music.

She lifted her skirt, showing off her legs, long and thin calves, pale heels.

With the circle beat out to her satisfaction she moved into the centre of the rug again and gyrated her hips in half-moons, raising and lowering her arms alternately, caressing the air. Then the music changed and she brought them together over her head and sliced them through the air into the centre of her bare stomach.

She changed the position of her legs. Bending one knee, she rocked her hips. She held her ankles above the higher hip. They seemed to say 'look at this'. One long thigh moving up and down as a woman's thigh moves up and down when her man is between her legs.

In the dimness of the room the dance churned the women's senses. Someone began to clap. Others took up the rhythm. Oruela found her palms clapping out encouragement to the dance. The music in the background came to a stop and the needle took up the rhythm as it rasped on the centre of the record. Oruela longed to sing but she was inhibited. And then someone came to her rescue. A girl on the other side of the room began the song. It was wordless, some kind of peasant tune that Oruela knew in the deep recesses of her unconscious. Others took it up and Oruela heard her own voice joining in, weaving around the others, now with, now against.

The power that seemed to generate in the room was intense, as if the breath of a great, strong-thighed goddess had blown in from the south. The excitement charged the air.

Someone began to beat on an improvised drum giving a deep bass undertone to the symphony of sound that mingled with the darkness of the room and the heat of the women's bodies.

On Kim danced, whirling and shimmying, swooping to the ground and up again, swaying. She seemed lost on the wave of sound. Her eyes closed and she raised her skirt further up her thighs. Her gleaming bare skin flashed around the room. She shook her shoulders so that her breasts moved voluptuously under the flimsy scarf. She shook and shook and stepped backwards and forwards. The scarf began to inch its way down until her breasts were bare. The scarf cascaded to her hips and rustled there, spinning around her like gossamer cloud.

And then the woman singing the lead in the song began to slow it. The rest of the room followed her like a flock of birds follows its leader, without any obvious signal. Kim began to slow. People's voices dropped

401

away. And then it was just the lone singer and the drum, thudding.

Kim stilled her body gradually. The song ceased. The drum beat quickened and grew softer at the same time and Kim sank into a sultry heap, raising her head. It settled gracefully on her neck. The drum stopped and she lowered her eyes.

The applause was deafening. Women thundered their appreciation and Kim sat, smiling, her breasts heaving with the exertion.

Marthe got up and wound up the gramophone again, putting on the other side of the record. Women began their own dances and Kim crawled across the room to where Oruela sat, flopping against a cushion by the wall.

'That,' said Oruela, her words seeming to have a resonance, 'was fantastic.'

'Pass the smoke,' said Kim. 'I'm dying for a hit.'

Marthe refilled the bowl quickly and gave it to her friend with a smile. 'Thank you,' she whispered.

Soon after the dance, couples began to disappear off into other, private worlds. The sight made Oruela a little nervous but she was easily distracted. There was a group of five women in her corner of the room. Herself, Kim, Marthe and two other white older women of about forty or so. They sat on either side of Marthe and the talk was of men, of marriage and sex.

One of them had been a prostitute and she told Marthe stories, of nights in Paris under the glow of street lamps. Of men who nuzzled her breasts and pulled out their cocks before she'd got her skirt up so the push of it on her thigh felt like an attack. She liked the men who wanted her to wear clothing of some description while they fucked her. She liked, especially, something around her waist, tightening, or her ankles.

She liked to be bound. The feeling of being tied to the bed with her stockings, hand and foot, helpless was, she said, such a stimulant that she would come almost immediately. And she liked to watch the men come for her. She wanted to scream, get into the fear, terrify herself so that the coming would be intensified.

Oruela listened with mounting lust. She wanted to experience that. Then the other woman began to tell her stories. She told of working in the fields one day alongside a big labourer from outside her village, how the sun beating down on their bodies had warmed them until their blood boiled. She had finished a basket of strawberries and had taken it to the edge of the field where the baskets were stacked and empty ones waited to be filled. The stackers had driven away loaded full and there was no one else there. She had bent down to pick up an empty basket when she felt him behind her. He wrenched up her long, thick working skirt and felt her sex, just like that. She was wet and she wanted him. She spread her legs and he took her hips in his hands and held her tight as he slid his cock inside her and fucked her.

'I never could figure out how he did that,' she giggled. 'I was thinking: Look! No hands. But it was wonderful. It was over in a few minutes and I didn't even come. But I went back to work with renewed strength. We worked together all day and at the end of it he took up his bundle, collected his money and with a nod he was gone.'

Kim Sun had laid back on some pillows in the corner and seemed to be sleeping. The sight of her suggested sleep to Oruela's hashish-laden brain and she grabbed a blanket and some of the cushions lying around on the floor and settled herself. But then Marthe said, 'Loving a woman is a different experience,' and all Oruela's senses came awake. She opened her eyes a crack as one of the other women said, 'We ought to give you a perfect send-off you know.' And as she spoke she caressed Marthe's shoulder.

'I've never loved a woman,' whispered Marthe.

'Well, you should then,' said the third woman. 'Just once, before you become a respectable married woman.'

Marthe turned from one to the other, silently, and each of them smiled mysteriously.

'Me first,' said one and she gently kissed Marthe's cheek and her hair. She took her breast in her hand and fondled it.

The other one gently pushed Marthe down so they were lying among the rugs and went to Marthe's feet and stroked her legs. Slowly, as Marthe was being kissed at one end, the woman slid her hands to the hem of her dress and pushed it up. The other woman pushed down the top over Marthe's shoulders, exposing her.

Together they pulled the dress right away from the body of the bride-to-be. She lay naked, warm, living, theirs. Her legs flopped. Her sex, cherry red and swollen, glistened. Her triangle of wet hair spread luxuriously over her belly.

They kissed and they caressed the pale body. The bride's legs opened wider. They attended to her from the direction of four hands, here and there, every crevice delved, stimulated, every dark secret spot touched, invaded by a womanly need.

The bride responded with an arching of the back, her sex pushing on to her attendant's fingers, her strong arms supporting her body on its elbows, her luxurious hair falling to the rug in a cascade.

Then it was sixfold. Two mouths joined four hands in their work. Sex lips pushed. The gash in the face said 'Yeah.' Red, soft sex met a tongue, tastebuds crashed. Strawberry mouth travelled to a nipple and sucked it till it was wet and passed on to another and made the skin wet there too. A blonde head nuzzled at one pair of breasts, snuggling, crooning and then moved to another pair. Breasts pressed together like crescent moons.

The three bodies rolled and the pace quickened. Three full arses rose and fell, one in a face, one in the air, one sunk to the floor. Their hair was wet all over, their faces gleamed with sweat.

Three sexes were touched with white fingers, with lips again. But it was the bride who got most of the attention. The bride's sex had one of the finest nights of its life.

'She's going to make it. Look at her!' said one of her attendants.

The other one grinned. 'There's no way she's going to be a faithful wife now she's discovered this.'

The bride merely moaned.

'I always wanted to be a bridesmaid,'said the first woman.

The bride's legs closed together and she went rigid. Suddenly she collapsed and rolled and writhed as her orgasm was complete.

The bridesmaids had their own pleasure over the murmuring body of the satiated bride and then they slept, one enfolding the other's back with her arm in a gentle gesture of possession.

Oruela was fried! She was the only one left awake, as far as she knew. When she was sure that the others were asleep she rose and went to the door, intending to go back to her own bed and relieve herself of the wave of sex that had taken her over as she watched the other women.

The door was locked. She stepped back over the sleeping women and lay back among the cushions. Did she dare do it here? Not in public surely.

But her question was answered for her.

She felt the hand on her thigh, moving upward slowly and she almost cried out. She opened her eyes a crack but all she could see through her lashes was a covered body down by her thighs moving closer. She shut her eyes again and pressed against the fingers that massaged her sex.

Then they disappeared and she was left in agony for what seemed like an age before the mouth touched her. Oruela slid her hands under the blanket and felt the soft head of hair that moved between her legs. The tongue circled her clitoris again and again. It drove into her, hard and wet. Oruela pushed herself on to it, taking it inside her as her orgasm came.

* * *

For a few days, inevitably, she looked about her, trying to figure out who it could have been. At the wedding, she saw the little blonde wasp looking at her. When Oruela stared at her, she smiled secretively. But even that didn't faze Oruela. So what? She was hardening off.

And then, one morning, the letter came. It was on her bed when she came home at lunchtime from the library. It was from Michelle.

'Dear Oruela,' it began. '*Mon dieu!* Although I'm not sure I should write his name in the same breath as what I'm thinking. Your letter was terrific. It's started off all kinds of thoughts with me. Robert's wondering what's hit him. But I'll tell you about that later. There's news. Good and bad.

'I've had a job to stop Paul Phare, you know, Jean's mate, tearing the letter out of my hand. He's been fantastic. I haven't seen hide nor hair of Jean bloody Raffoler and I'm not sure I should tell you this in a letter but I don't think that man's worth a light compared to Paul. Paul says he's in a state of shock and you can't rely on him doing anything. Jean I mean. But I reckon you can rely on Paul. He's going to do some detective work. There's something very funny gone on. I mean we all know that but even funnier than we thought.

'Paul says he's going to come and see you sometime soon. So you can look forward to that. He is a nice man. I would've come myself but you have to get papers and that and, to tell you the truth, Oruela, I'm scared. That Paris policeman came and questioned me at Aunt Violette's (I had to leave the house to go and try and get Jean to do something the night before you were taken away). I was scared they were going to make me an accomplice and put me in there. But that's dropped, it looks like, and Paul said I should write whatever I want to you and he would bribe someone to get the letter in. I just hope it works. Anyway, don't worry, Oruela. Robert sends you his love too.

'So I must tell you what I did with him the other

night. We went down on the beach. He said he had to pee. It was that imaginary bloke in your letter that did it. The one that peed. It's got me really excited about that kind of thing. I made him let me hold his prick while he peed at the sea. It goes a long way, you know. I pointed it, like it was mine and it was all warm and lovely.

'I was so horny with it that I got him to make love to me right there on the beach in the dark with the waves crashing around our ears and not giving a damn about who was in the shadows.

'Well, I'd better sign off now before I wet my own knickers writing it! I'll seal this tight and send it with lots of love. Keep hoping, my love. We're doing our best.'

Oh, how it did Oruela's heart good to read that. She gobbled down her lunch with real hunger and lay down on the bed for a rest with a smile on her face.

Why she could still feel so happy if Jean had deserted her, as Michelle seemed to be saying, she didn't know. Perhaps she'd always known he might. It really just seemed expected, somehow. Had she grown immune in this place? Or had Caspar cured her of some wound for ever?

And then her thoughts turned to Paul Phare. How wonderful of him to find the motivation to help her. Why?

The thought hit her right in the womb. That time when the three of them had met. She remembered it and remembered that initially it had been Paul that she'd been attracted to. What had changed? Jean had come to her first and flirted. She'd known he was flirting and hadn't taken him entirely seriously. She'd been funny and he liked her sense of humour. He'd asked her out.

It had begun from there. But now she saw again something that she'd forgotten. She saw Paul at that first meeting, over Jean's shoulder, brooding, glancing

407

their way. She saw him walking away to talk to someone else and coming back later, looking somehow more
closed, smaller than he'd been a half hour before. She
could hardly remember him after that. It dawned on
her why. There had been something unmistakably
there, but it had fled in the competition that he'd lost.

Dare she think that? It gave her a future if she did.
That was something she couldn't think about. She
wrenched her mind back to the sensual, to the brooding
looks, to the first time she saw him and scuppered her
sensible intentions. He was there. She could feel him.
And for the first time in weeks she felt safe.

Summertime (and the Living Is Easy)

'There aren't many professions,' said Paul, 'where you are likely to ask another man if you can borrow his naked girlfriend.'

Paul and Robert, Michelle's lover, were taking a morning walk along the sands. The heat of the early summer sun had not yet begun to burn. The sea was blue and glistening and the sand was cool beneath their bare feet. Robert picked up a flat stone and skimmed it across the waves.

'I like the way she's changing,' said Robert. It was an understatement. He loved her new sexual adventurousness. He agreed to Paul's suggestion.

The idea had grown organically out of a theme that Paul had been working with for some time. There was an Englishwoman, Daisy, who lived in one of the cluster of cottages surrounding Paul's house on the harbour front in old Biarritz. She was the wife of Bertrand, a fisherman. Bertrand was also a hashish smuggler in a small way. Out at sea, beyond the prying eyes of the law he would take on board enough of the North African medicinal herb to keep his friends going.

It was a woman who ran the trade. She lived as a pirate outside the national waters of all countries. Several attempts had been made to catch her but she was as skilful a sailor as a smuggler and she eluded the Customs every time.

Bertrand went aboard once in a while to buy his hashish. She dealt opium and cocaine too but these didn't interest him. He heard stories of opium-induced dreams that went on for days and sex that broke all taboos.

Daisy would often come over to Paul's and they would smoke together from Paul's Moroccan hookah. Sometimes she would pose for him and they had been working on what was known as an oriental theme.

Daisy was the very essence of an English type of woman: all peaches and cream and pale brown hair. Her body was pear-shaped and petite. So far, she had not posed naked but with the arrival of Annette the scenes began to get more exotic.

Annette's knowledge of sexuality gave them ideas. Annette knew how men were turned on. She knew the species, man and boy. She knew the simple things that drove them wild and the way these fancies grew into obsessions as they became older. Men, she told them, do not let themselves be inhibited with a whore the way they do with women in front of whom they have to be fathers and suitors and sons.

She knew what turned women on too. She had lived in a stew of sex for most of her adolescence. She had a pale unhealthy pallor, as if her body, never seeing the light of day, was a china doll for the boys to play with in the darkened, over-furnished rooms of La Maison Rose. It gave her body a photographic value that Paul was quick to take advantage of before the fresh air and relaxation made her glow like an ordinary young woman.

She discovered a hidden talent for prop-making. They raided, wholesale, the ideas of the Orientalist painters of a generation before and pooled their collections of objects and fabrics from around the world. What they didn't have, Annette began to make and in her hands, ordinary fabric became mysterious curtains and exotic

410

sarongs. Scarves became turbans and veils. Feathers collected from the beach became fans. She made a fabulous snake from papier mâché and painted it and even changed the dustbin lid into a believable warrior's shield.

Michelle came by one morning and watched them setting up for a series Paul called 'The Odalisque'. The couch was draped with fabric and set by the window so that the light fell softly on it like the light of a dream. The snake was placed at the foot of the couch on the floor in the shadows. Daisy dressed herself as a harem guard and stood in the shadows at the back on a plinth, her figure veiled in mystery. Annette undressed and settled herself on the couch, fixing a velvet choker around her neck as she settled naked in the soft fabric.

Michelle sat spellbound and eventually plucked up courage to ask if she could join in but Paul insisted they ask Robert first.

And so it began in earnest. Michelle raided Aunt Violette's haberdashery shop for ribbons and braid and they spent a whole day together tying the beautiful strands to the body of one woman, then another, while Paul snapped away.

They chose dark ribbons for Annette, purple and black, saturnine colours to bring out her deathly pallor. They tied them to her wrists, to her ankles, to her hair. On the back of one leg she had a fine set of bruises left over from the roughness of the whorehouse. The purple and yellow injury was dressed up by the other women in a ribbon either side. They put an open yellow orchid in the cheeks of her arse and called it 'Aphrodite'.

Daisy they dressed in green ribbons like a hunter in the long grass. They found a knife and made a sheath that hung between her breasts.

Michelle they dressed in red and pink, with a turban around her head and a veil covering all of her face but her eyes. She wore red ribbons at her ankles and her wrists. She wore red lipstick on her lips and on her sex and did wonderful bendy dances, stretching now to the

411

ground, now for the ceiling, leaping about with the freedom of it all and the drive of libido.

Paul encouraged them to do what they wanted to. His only input into the scenes at this point was to get the light how he wanted it, or to get them into the light that was available. He enjoyed the way the women took control of the ideas given the chance. The photographs took on an unusual, female interpretation of old ideas. Their burgeoning creativity stirred him. It was a kind of intellectual lust, he was so used to photographing women. Not that the naked flesh that filled his transformed studio day after day didn't have its effect in more physical ways but he was all too aware that these Three Fates were on loan to him. Daisy and Michelle were other men's women and Annette was too vulnerable to be seduced. He knew he wouldn't want to continue an affair with her and so he didn't start one. It cost him a lot of sexual frustration but he channelled all his energy into his work.

Daisy got it into her head that she wanted to be photographed naked, emerging from a net of freshly caught, silvery, flapping fish. The problem was getting the fish. Bertrand put his foot down. He wasn't going to have a catch wasted on a photograph. No. Definitely not.

Daisy took him home. The next day he not only brought the fish but was transformed by the women into Neptune. He refused to pose completely naked so Annette went and collected some fresh seaweed and he had it draped over his genitals and falling from his thighs. The studio smelled of the sea for days afterwards and Nefi, the cat, went into spasms of ecstasy. Annette scrubbed the place until it shone like a new pin.

Paul had an idea that Robert would be easier to get to pose naked so he searched his library for tales of famous kings of antiquity who were known for their luxurious tastes, and left the rest to Michelle. Robert was coy at first but the chance to show off the body that he had

412

worked on for so long was eventually irresistible. The studio became a king's lair.

The women directed his poses, setting him here and there on cushions, on rugs. Gradually he became less self-conscious, more inclined to let his loincloth slip and reveal . . .

The photographs were phenomenal. Strange, almost breathing, erotic scenes covered the workbench in Paul's darkroom. They emerged mysteriously from the developing fluids in the small hours of the morning and the next day the women would look at them with him and start on new ideas.

Paul began to put something very small into each picture to indicate only to the most observant connoisseur that what they saw was an illusion. Shoes were his favourite. Poking out, barely visible from under a curtain in a perfectly re-created harem scene would be a modern shoe. Even the Three Fates didn't notice it until one night when Annette and Paul were on their own, poring over a new batch, she spotted it.

'Do you know,' she said, 'that there are drawings of shoes that they used to wear in the Middle Ages? They were like this.' And she proceeded to sit on the floor and draw a slipper. The toe was a long, erect phallus.

This began a whole new series of photographs of Annette drawing the things she had heard of during her days as a whore. Annette always naked, Annette surrounded by drawings of phalluses.

Paul's lens closed in on her face concentrating hard on her drawings that grew more beautiful as the days went by. His self-control was being stretched to the limit.

The days grew into weeks and the summer grew hotter. The studio seethed with heat and languor. The very walls seemed to sweat with sex. Paul padded around in bare feet, his beard growing for days before he had a shave. He wore a sleeveless vest and trousers that he rolled up when he went down to the sea and walked by the water when the day grew cool enough.

Annette made a huge fan and Robert would be employed as a slave to fan them. They were drifting into a demi-monde where nothing was quite what it seemed. Their sexual imaginations seemed inexhaustible.

One morning the Three Fates decided to dispense with props and form a naked ring on the floor, their bodies completely unadorned, their hands clasping each other's ankles. They stretched, their backs arched.

Paul was snapping busily, the fabric of his trousers stretched across his arse as he almost did the splits to get the shot. They heard a screech of brakes as a fast car pulled up outside. The door opened and a slender youth blew in. Daisy's lazy smile changed into a look of alarm. But Michelle and Annette, unaware of who the youth was, merely blinked.

Renée wore a yellow silk shirt and tie with plus-fours and silken brown stockings. On her feet were men's brogues. There was nothing to suggest she was anything other than a slender young man in a driving hat and goggles. Her yellow-green eyes surveyed the ring of naked women and travelled around the walls where Annette's drawings hung with their abundant interpretations of sex. The very air was heavy with erotic dreams.

There was mayhem. The Three Fates scattered, pulling on their clothes as Renée embarked on a spree of destruction. Paul's camera went flying and he caught it just in time to save it. But this infuriated Renée even more and she managed to tear two of Annette's drawings from the wall and rip down a flimsy curtain before Paul finally wrestled her to the ground.

She lay under him, her face close to his, a mask of anger, silent, hating, dangerous.

'It's not what you think,' he whispered. 'Calm yourself.' And he kissed her bloodless lips, kissed her temples, kissed the little red spots of anger on her pale cheeks. Tears began to form in her eyes.

'You bastard,' she said. 'You bastard.'

414

He kissed her again and felt her stiff, slender body begin to yield little by little. She kissed him back, her tears wet on his face.

The feeling of her body close to his made Paul into that strange male creature who is both putty in a woman's hands and master at the same time. Nothing would stop him from ,fucking her after all this time apart, even if she'd wanted to stop him, which she didn't.

He released her and pulled her shirt out of her trousers, pushing it over her nipples. Her breasts were a mere softness of the ribcage, hardly there at all. He adored them. He bit playfully at her nipples, licked them until they stood up.

But what he really wanted was in her trousers. Her belly was concave, her waistband loose on her. He undid her fly buttons and pulled her trousers and knickers down to her knees. There she was revealed. The uniqueness of her that was both awesomely beautiful and her ugly shame at the same time.

Paul pressed his lips to her enlarged clitoris and sucked.

Some hermaphrodites were born with huge penises; she ought to think herself lucky, the doctors had told her. But Renée knew she was anything but lucky. They told her a lot of women would be grateful never to have to menstruate. Renée didn't believe a word of it. She felt like a girl but her body stared back at her from the mirror, a mockery of those feelings. She just didn't know what she was. The real humiliation had been when her first lover, a boy of her own age, had been sick when she took off her knickers. He had left her naked, full of sex and ashamed, her overgrown clitoris sticking out of her pubic hair like some horrible half-grown thing.

It had been years before she allowed herself to be so vulnerable in the presence of another man.

Paul had adored her totally at first. He prized her uniqueness. He fed her a diet of undiluted love and she had blossomed with confidence. Her whole life had been affected. She realised her ambition to race cars and she became better and better at it. The speed satisfied her soul as nothing else.

And now? She had wanted him to be a slave to her all her life but he could never be that. She didn't understand his free-ranging soul. She grew jealous of his every move as their affair settled. He wasn't quite as enthralled as he had been at first. How could he hope to make her believe that he was hers alone when he spent his time with other, naked, normal women? She hated him now.

He dragged his tongue up her belly, to her breasts, to her mouth and manoeuvred his body to take her completely. She hit his big strong arms with her useless fists. She hated him. She wanted to hurt him.

Then he was inside her and she loved him again because he made her into a woman.

Her deformity crushed into the pit of his belly and gave her its gift of orgasm that left her almost unconscious underneath him.

Cheek to Cheek

With Renée back, the Three Fates laid low and Paul gradually brought her round to some kind of sanity. She had come home to train for the great August race held every year in the mountains in Spain. This was the first year she had been accepted, albeit in the guise of a man, for entry into the big-engine race. She would race against kings. She and her little team of two mechanics would take on the best in Europe. She knew she wouldn't win but she would compete. She made a fine sportsman and none of them even suspected that she was a woman.

The training kept her busy and Paul moved Annette out into one of the empty cottages without Renée even realising she'd been living there.

It was at this point that Michelle began to agitate for some more action to help Oruela. The hunt for the truth had been halted by the sudden, suspicious death of Dr Simenon.

The doctor's car had been found in a gully after mysteriously skidding off a mountain road in the middle of the night. There had been no obvious reason for the crash and it had scared Paul and Michelle. Their attempts to follow up Annette's lead on the coroner and the judge had been thwarted by closed doors and two of the mayor's henchmen had stopped Paul in the street one night as he was coming home from dinner at a friend's and warned him. It had seemed not only sensible, but a matter of life and death to lie low. Their wild burst of creativity had followed this warning and had restored them to life. But now it was time. It was no longer possible to put things off.

Through Bertrand's contacts they got letters smuggled in to Oruela, asking her to tell them everything she could think of that might involve the mayor. She had letters smuggled back to Paul by the same route but there was nothing she could think of to help him. Jean continued to refuse to answer Paul's calls.

Paul felt a sense of frustration that seemed to settle like a blanket of cloud over him. Even sex didn't lift it. He hated injustice and at the moment he wasn't sure which he hated most, the mayor's corrupted system or Jean's faint heart.

He was drinking a good deal of cognac, he realised, as if he was blaming himself. His common sense prevailed. He could do nothing. He made an effort not to drink so much and the discipline he imposed on himself gave him back his dignity.

One evening he came home from the market where he had bought some *saucisson* and Robert and Michelle were waiting for him. They sat on the wooden bench that stood outside his house under the low, shuttered window. He observed them for some few minutes before they saw him. They were talking close together, ignoring the world around them. The rythmic crash of the waves on the golden beach went unnoticed and unheard as they reached for the landscape of each other. They looked up, startled as two wild rabbits, when he said 'Hello.'

'We were waiting for you,' chirped Michelle. 'Robert's got an idea.' She looked at Robert with adoration as he spoke.

'There's a strongbox in Genevieve Bruyere's bedroom,' began Robert as Paul sat down on the warm bench next to them and put his shopping on the floor. 'She keeps her private papers in there. I've discovered how to open it without a key. I think you ought to come out to the house and have a look. There are a lot of official-looking documents in there. They don't make much sense to me but you'll be able to tell if they could give us a lead or something.'

Paul felt excited for the first time in days. 'When shall I come?' he asked.

'Tomorrow?' said Robert. 'She goes out driving a lot these days in the afternoons with that Alsatian policeman.' Robert scoffed. 'What a peasant that man is! I could throttle him with my bare hands. She can't even see that all he's after is her money. Still, what do I care?'

'You don't care at all,' crooned Michelle. 'Don't let him make you angry. You won't have to stay there very much longer. A job will come up, I'm sure.'

'Tomorrow's good for me,' said Paul. 'I don't have any plans. Right, now come and have some dinner with me, you two. I've just bought some of the most delicious *saucisson* in the whole of France.'

But Michelle and Robert made their excuses. Aunt Violette was cooking. Paul smiled to himself as they left and he opened his front door. Nefi appeared from nowhere and rubbed her lithe little body against his legs. He bent down and picked her up. He held her close to his chest with one hand and spoke to her in soft tones. 'Why do they make me feel so lonely, Nefi?' he asked her. 'Why am I so sad?' The cat purred loudly and pushed her head against his cheek as if to tell him that she loved him truly.

He ate a lonely dinner and gave Nefi Renée's share of the *saucisson* when she didn't put in an appearance. It was very late when she finally did show and she stormed out again when she discovered there was nothing to eat, announcing her intention to eat at her friend's café. Paul was asleep when she returned and got into bed. He had only the vaguest memory of her climbing in beside him when he awoke the following morning.

He left her in the dark, crumpled bed and closed the door quietly. Within the hour he was on the train for Bayonne.

The train clattered through the bright morning with its load of shoppers, business and tradespeople. Paul studied their faces. Which of them was really happy, he wondered? It was hard to tell. The mundane journey etched itself into their features. But what hidden depths of passion, of anything, were these façades concealing? The only two animated people on the train were a pair of matrons in the next bank of seats. They were different. They gossiped with relish, their lips glossy with glee, their eyes shining with salacious imaginings as they discussed people they were careful to identify only by initial. Paul wondered what the affairs they pored over were doing to their organs. Surely they were bursting with sex, he thought. They were such handsome, ripe women.

The train squealed to a halt at Bayonne and emptied itself with a gasp on to the platform. Robert was waiting beyond the smart ticket-office out in the sunshine. He leaned gracefully on the family Bentley with its top down. Robert wore a very handsome black chauffeur's uniform.

'You must be hot,' said Paul.

Robert made it clear that he was with an exasperated click of the tongue against the teeth. 'She won't have me drive this in anything else,' he said.

'How am I going to avoid being spotted?' asked Paul.

'It's all right,' said Robert, as he opened the back door and stood back for Paul to get in. 'She's gone out in the Citroën with the peasant again. They've gone in the other direction.'

Paul would rather have sat up front but there were no seats next to Robert's wheel. The leather of the passenger seats in the back was warm from the sun. Robert steered the car through the narrow streets and out of town towards the villa. The breeze refreshed Paul and modified the strength of the sun on his face. As they drew closer to the gates of the villa the trees were denser, overhanging the car, and then very suddenly the cool shade opened and the dazzle of the midday sun glinting off the lemon and white façade of the villa was too much for the eyes.

They drove slowly up the driveway and came to a halt outside the house.

'We had better not waste too much time,' said Robert. 'Her behaviour is unpredictable. I'll take you straight upstairs. But I'll put some coffee on for afterwards. Would you like some?'

Paul could have murdered a cup of coffee. He followed Robert up the surprisingly narrow stairway to the master bedroom. It surprised him. The room was sombre, not at all what he had imagined.

'She's going to decorate it she says,' said Robert. 'What she means is she's going to ask me to do it. She's a real skinflint sometimes.' He walked across the room to a wooden linen box by the window. He opened it and inside was a strongbox. He pulled it out and closing the linen box sat the metal one on top of it. Then he picked the lock with his butler's knife and said, 'There you are. I'll make that coffee.'

Paul made himself comfortable on the window seat. The pile of papers was mostly old financial documents, nothing that really leapt out as suspicious. But then he found Oruela's adoption certificate and along with it, her original birth certificate bearing the name of her mother. He had brought his Leica. He put the two papers on the window seat in the light and focused. He clicked the shutter at the same time as Robert burst into the room behind him shouting 'They're coming, look!'

Two figures were running hand in hand with gay abandon across the back lawn towards the house.

'Quite a girl, ain't she!' said Robert. 'Look at her. They're going to come straight up here, I bet you.'

421

Two minutes earlier and he could have escaped. 'Damn,' said Paul.

'We'll never get you out in time,' cried Robert. 'I know. Wait in here. Look.' He turned the key of Henri Bruyere's bathroom. 'She never uses it. I'll lock you in and take the key.'

So Paul sat on the edge of the bath and twiddled the strap of his Leica. He heard a lot of giggles, put the camera down and covered his ears. But nothing could block out the scream that a moment later, echoed round the whole house. He completely resisted the temptation to spy through the keyhole – for about thirty seconds.

Genevieve was pinned to the big wooden bedhead by Alix like a great drawing pin. His trousers were round his calves and his boots were still on. Both participants were wailing their way towards a very fast climax.

The temptation to take a photograph through the keyhole was overwhelming. Would it work? Paul uncovered his Leica and tried to focus. It might, he decided. He pressed the shutter button and it was all over.

In the peace Paul felt rather ashamed of himself. He straightened up and looked around. The bathroom smelt of disuse. A dried facecloth hung on the sink. The sun's rays fell in through the high window on to the edge of the bath. A blue chemist's bottle glowed on the side. Its label, half-turned, read '-*blende*'. In its neglect the once elegant bathroom had a touch of pathos about it that appealed to Paul's aesthetic sense.

He wound the film on under the muffling effect of his jacket and focused. The noise of the shutter seemed to echo round the bathroom like a thunderclap. He cursed under his breath and his heart raced as he bent down to the keyhole again. Alix and Genevieve were talking. Paul put his ear to the hole.

'Darling, this is more than just sex to me,' said Alix. 'It's on a higher, spiritual plane.'

'Oh, Alix,' she replied. 'We are as one!'

Paul breathed a sigh of relief. He amused himself for

a little while, taking photographs of the bathroom. Then he went back to the keyhole. Alix was smearing Genevieve's pussy with *confiture*. Oh dear, they would need the bathroom next.

He climbed into the bath and assessed his chances of getting out of the high window. They were not good. It would have to be a last resort. An hour ticked by very, very slowly. In the end he drifted into a kind of sleep, leaning on the side of the bath.

He was woken by the sound of another scream. This one curdled his blood. He was drawn to the keyhole again like a moth to a flame.

This time it was Alix screaming and Paul could see why. Still in his boots he was tied to the bed while Genevieve wielded a silver chain. It was a tiny instrument of torture, but torture it was. Alix's backside was red raw where she'd whipped him with it. The policeman begged for mercy but Genevieve's violet eyes had a fixed stare. She licked her lips and brought the chain down on to the pained flesh again.

Paul was really convinced he was about to witness a murder. The whole thing became clear to him. Genevieve had killed her unsuspecting husband in a bizarre sex game and blamed it on her daughter. But he was halfway out of the window, almost tearing his stomach on the catch, when he realised that the couple in the bedroom were laughing together. He eased himself back into the bath and went to the keyhole again. They were cuddled together on the bed, happy as lovebirds in a nest.

'Oh, Alix. I've never done anything like this before. All those wasted years. Oh, Alix, I feel alive,' breathed Genevieve. 'Let's do it again.'

'No, sweetest,' said Alix. 'Your lover needs some refreshment. Let's go downstairs and eat.'

Thank heaven, breathed Paul. It took another twenty minutes for Robert to unlock him.

* * *

Paul had heard of the English vice, naturally, among the girls at La Maison Rose. He'd heard of it in detail in fact. Especially tales of the rich Englishmen who came to Biarritz and paid handsomely for their humiliation. Some of the girls liked to do it, others didn't. But it didn't matter what they liked or what they didn't like. It had to be part of a whore's repertoire.

It had shocked him though, to see Madame Bruyere, naked, her pale wisp of straw at her sex, wielding the weapon. He'd never heard of a respectable bourgeois matron doing it. But then who ever heard what respectable bourgeois matrons got up to in their bedrooms? Paul steered clear of married women as lovers. He'd only slept with one and that was when he was an inexperienced boy. She had been a dark, Spanish temptress, a woman with a reputation, whose husband was a hotel-keeper with a heart condition. As a boy, Paul used to watch her doing the laundry of the small hotel in the open back-yard. He'd sat in the branches of a walnut tree watching her move as she carried the heavy baskets to and from the back of the building in the hot sun, her face glistening with perspiration, the sleeveless bodice of her dress revealing the dark hair under her arms, her heavy breasts moving in the thin material, all day. He would go home and dream of her at night.

The day she'd caught him watching her he'd almost died of embarrassment but he had not lost the stiffness in his pants! She made him help her like a little child but she knew he was ready to be a man and after days of their bodies brushing in the steamy laundry room she stopped him one afternoon, in his tracks, and suggested his shirt needed a wash. He peeled off his rough shirt and saw her eyes light up at the gorgeous boy's body underneath. He hadn't even started shaving but he was graceful and the promise of what he was to become was there in all its appeal.

She taught him, that day, how to please a woman. She felt it her duty, she told him, to let him know about a particular spot that needs to be loved if a woman is to respond to a man. A whole treasure trove opened up to him before his very eyes.

She had a voluptuous body. Its curves, its softness, drowned him in the first delights of sex and once he'd started there was no stopping him. He couldn't get enough. Every minute of the day he was dying for love of her.

It was a rude awakening to find that she had another lover. It wasn't even her husband. It was a goatherd, a rough and ugly man that he'd always disliked. A man who got drunk whenever he came down with his goats from the beautiful Basque mountains and raised hell in the village where they lived.

One day he caught them together. His darling and this oaf in the same pile of laundry where she'd whispered sweet words to him only hours before. She was thoroughly enjoying herself. She liked it from behind with the goatherd. Paul crushed the little bouquet of wild flowers that he'd picked for her under his feet.

As he walked along the lane to the town of Bayonne, a man now, he remembered her and smiled.

The other thing he thought about was the name on the birth certificate that he had taken a photograph of. Euska Onaldi. Oruela's mother was the same woman Annette had talked of. She was here somewhere. What was she, some poor girl that had had her baby snatched?

It was pure instinct that drew him towards the graveyard. There was half an hour to wait before the train back to Biarritz. The town of Bayonne was busy with early evening shoppers. The churchyard was cool and quiet. The distinctive round, Basque gravestones of the older graves stood under the trees in the shade.

At the very edge of this community of the dead he saw a woman standing at a newer grave and before he admitted it rationally, he knew in his gut that he had found Euska Onaldi.

He kept back, leaning against a tall tree, peeping round it every so often to watch her. She seemed to be having a conversation with the occupant of the grave. It crossed his mind that she might be mad by now. But madness didn't fit with the picture Annette had drawn of the beautiful woman who had visited La Maison Rose.

In due course she left the graveside and began walking towards where he hid. He sidled round the tree. She passed by, about two feet away, without noticing him. He could have touched her if he had just stretched out his hand. He wanted to.

She was dressed from head to toe in a pale shimmering grey. Even her face was obscured by a fine grey veil falling from a small soft hat on her head. He caught a glimpse of dark eyes under the veil. Her arms were bare and he surveyed them with a connoisseur's eye, judging her age more or less accurately. She walked with elegant sensuality and as she passed by he surveyed her fine, broad shoulders and long back with admiration.

As she reached the gate of the churchyard she turned and caught him. She held his gaze for a moment and then a sliver of amusement lit up her face before she turned again and was gone.

He started to follow her but as he reached the gate all he saw was her *derrière* disappearing into the back of a sleek black Hispano-Suiza. Her small, podgy chauffeur closed the door and walked round to the driver's door. Something about the man's movements told Paul he was homosexual. As the car pulled away Euska turned around and glanced at him through the window.

She was wondering what strange desires led the handsome young man to lean against trees in the churchyard and watch. He didn't look at all weird. In fact she had been rather flattered when she saw how fine-looking he was. It amused her to think that at over forty she could still attract those kind of glances. In younger days she might have got into her car and left the door open to see if he would climb in. But nowadays she wanted only one man.

426

With Henri dead she was free to join Ernesto in Rio. All she had to do was free Oruela. It was not an easy task but she was looking up old acquaintances one by one and calling in favours. Ernesto had insisted that his own chauffeur, Raoul, drive her down in his car to Biarritz on her dangerous mission. He would have come himself but he was too tied up with business in Paris.

Euska liked Raoul. He was a terrible queen. They talked girl talk and she told him where to find what he desired in the small private clubs of Biarritz.

The car sped along the road from Bayonne to Biarritz and her hotel on the Grande Plage. As she watched the people going about their business her thoughts turned again to the handsome young man in the graveyard. Perhaps he had wanted something else. The look from those gorgeous smoky green eyes stayed with her. Perhaps she would run into him again.

Paul arrived home to find Renée in a bad mood. She had returned the studio to its usual state. In other words, it was no longer a studio, it was a sitting-room. When she was in town she insisted. It was one of the things that irritated Paul and made him angry with himself. Why on earth did he put up with it? He poured himself a glass of country wine from the flagon he kept in the larder and while he was feeding Nefi he resolved to have it out with Renée.

She slung her magazine on the floor and glared at him as she walked into the studio.

'I want to talk to you, Renée . . .' he began.

'There's a letter from Paris,' she said. 'You've sold some pictures.'

'You opened my letter?' he said, taking it.

She merely reclined again, and lit a cigarette.

He looked at the letter. He had indeed sold some pictures. It was from a dealer that he'd sent the very first set of prints of 'The Odalisque'. The dealer had sent a money order for a sum that he could live on for

427

at least three months! The joy of actually selling some work flooded through him.

'We're going to celebrate!' he said. 'Get your dancing shoes on, Renée.'

Even Renée was infected by his joyous mood and she smiled. She rose to go upstairs as he picked up the telephone and dialled Aunt Violette's.

As soon as he asked for Michelle, Renée jumped. She was on him, claws out, scratching at his face, tearing the phone away from him, screaming. He had to cut his call.

'You're supposed to be taking me out to celebrate! And you phone another woman! You bastard!' she screamed.

'Renée,' he said firmly. 'I'm not going to phone one woman, I'm going to phone three and a couple of men too. These are the people who made these photographs with me. Of course I'm going to invite them to celebrate with us.'

'No. No. No!' screamed Renée. 'I won't have it!'

Paul suddenly snapped. He'd had enough. Perhaps it was the image of Genevieve spanking Alix that did it. He'd certainly never done it before. He took her over his knee, reached for a slipper he saw poking out from under the couch and holding her firmly he gave her real solid spanking until she cried.

It didn't turn him on at all. It certainly quietened her though. He stopped and let her go. She stood up, a changed person.

'Go upstairs, wash your face, get dressed and be down here, ready to go out, with as many people as I choose to invite, in half an hour,' he said and she trotted off, meek as a kitten.

She re-appeared when he'd made his phone calls, in a beautiful black evening dress, her little velvet purse clasped demurely to her tummy.

As he dressed he thought about it. It was amusing to see Renée change like that. It was disturbing though. He was willing to try anything once but he wasn't the kind of man to get addicted to sexual violence. His whole being strained away from it. The women he enjoyed were beyond all that. He liked mature sex, real fucking. He liked his women naked. The thought of the trappings of sado-masochism just made him want to laugh. Poor Renée. When he was loving with her she just got in a bad mood. He understood why. The profound unhappiness that she carried around with her could, perhaps, only be relieved by violence. But it wasn't going to come from him.

He gave his hair a casual brush and walked downstairs without looking in the mirror. He wore his clothes like a second skin.

What a night they all had on the promise of money from the Paris dealer. They danced to the black American jazz band at the casino until dawn. They drank champagne and ate exquisite food. They toasted success and talked over new projects.

Annette looked stunning in her evening clothes and had a selection of beaux virtually kissing the ground she walked on. Michelle and Robert ogled the rich and famous and had the time of their lives. Renée behaved herself so well that Paul remembered the good times. He held her close as they danced and tasted the bittersweet love on her pale lips.

None of them noticed, among the comings and goings in the luxurious club, that Euska and Raoul sat in a darkened booth at the back. None of them saw her make enquiries of the waiter as to who they were, or saw her leave as the clock struck three.

They tumbled out of the club with the other bright young things as dawn was breaking and bundles of early morning newspapers were being delivered into shop doorways.

They were too tired and too happy to bother looking at the glaring headlines.

429

Put Your Foot Down, Baby
(and Turn My Wheels)

'CASPAR ALEXANDROVICH SHOT BY THE BOLSHEVIKS IN MOSCOW' glared the headline from the copy of the daily newspaper that came to the prison library. It was mighty strange for Oruela, having such an intimate connection with a man who was not only an international *cause célèbre* but most definitely dead. It brought her strange dreams and sleepless nights. The only way she could sleep was if she masturbated herself as thoughts of him skittered through her imagination.

During the day she was attracted to even the ugliest of the inmates who came into the library. She began to masturbate at night over them. In her dreams she would take all of them, two or more at a time. Desperate for the feeling of something inside, she stole a carrot from the kitchen and inserted it into her sex while she rubbed at her clitoris. She had the most violent orgasms.

She went to church and imagined everyone took off their clothes and bodies heaved in the pews.

Then one Sunday evening, when she was playing cards with Kim, Marthe came into the cell and, with a smug grin on her handsome face she said, 'I've discovered something.'

'Don't tell me,' said Kim, chucking a card into the

430

centre of the improvised table. 'You're going to get divorced and married again.'

'No,' said Marthe, still smugly smiling her smile.

'Come on then, Marthe,' said Oruela. 'Tell us.'

'Well,' said Marthe, 'I've found a way to spy on the men's shower.'

Kim and Oruela's four eyes lit up. 'How?' they chorused.

'Well,' said Marthe, 'you know that air vent next to the library building? You know how it has steam coming from it sometimes. Well, that's where the steam comes from. All we have to do is loosen the cover and crawl up the shaft.'

'You silly cow,' said Kim. 'We'll be cooked!'

'No, we won't. Most of the heat goes out of the window. It's only a trickle that comes out through the vent.'

'I wouldn't like to chance it,' said Kim.

'I already have,' said Marthe.

'You did?' they wondered.

'I did,' said Marthe. She wasn't just smug now, she was positively gloating. 'Boy, there are some honeys incarcerated in this place. Real peaches. There was this one with a body like a god. A real muscular type. You know what I mean? He strode in and took the jet right under my eyes . . .' She stopped.

'Go on!' cried the other two.

'No,' said Marthe. 'I'll spoil it for you. You'll have to come with me to experience it.'

And so they were hooked. The next day saw them up at the crack of dawn like model prisoners and out in the yard in dungarees. All three now had passes to walk freely within the inner compound. Oruela kept watch while the other two unhitched the grating. They crawled into the darkness one after the other and replaced it. Marthe led the way in the dark. They turned a bend and climbed up a metal ladder fixed to the wall. At the top it opened out and some light came from another grille. Below them was the empty men's shower room.

431

They didn't have long to wait. No sooner had they settled themselves to watch, their faces virtually pressed up against the grating, than an inmate walked in wearing only a towel around his waist. He was an Algerian, the same who worked in the church. He took off the towel, revealing his slender hips and his sleepy genitals. The three watching women sighed. He took a jet on the opposite side of the room so they could only really see the back of him. His arse was tight and paler than the rest of him. He turned on the water and it gushed over his body. Soon another inmate came in and another and another until the shower was filled with them. All shapes and sizes wandered sleepily to the jets and turned on the water. The water made their bodies shine. Rivulets of liquid covered their skin and ran through the hair on their chests down to their loins. Over their backs, it ran down arses of all kinds. It was noisy enough in the shower for the muffled groans of the three women to go unheard.

'Look at that,' whispered Marthe. 'That's him.'

'Christ,' groaned Kim.

Through the steam walked Marthe's honey. He really was something. His bulk was a delectable sight. His chest and shoulders were smooth and hairless with a slight film of steam glistening on his skin. His hair was long, to his shoulders, and beginning to curl damply. He stood right in front of them, a little below their grating and whipped off his towel. He was well endowed.

He turned on the stream as other men were leaving the room, and a look of pleasure spread across his face as he turned it upwards towards the jet and, unknowingly, towards the watching women.

'Oh yes,' groaned Kim. 'Oh baby, yes.'

Marthe signalled her to keep it down. With less men in the room Kim's groan was more audible. But the unsuspecting man below them carried on regardless. He turned under the spraying jet of water, round and back again and then he reached for the soap.

432

The foam slithered across his skin and dripped off him on to the floor. He soaped his hair and rinsed it. He soaped his underarms, his delicious chest, his belly and the water poured and poured. Then he soaped his cock. As he handled it it grew some.

Suddenly Kim went crazy. She began undoing her clothes.

'What are you doing?' hissed Marthe.

'I'm going in,' said Kim. And she began unhooking the grate. The man below them heard something. He left the washing of his cock and looked up. His face was a picture as out of the wall above his head came Kim, naked as the day she was born but all woman.

'Come here, big boy,' she said. 'I want you now.'

He didn't take any persuading. He didn't have a chance. She almost threw him against the wall. She climbed on to him without another word. He supported her arse as she fucked him under the streaming jet of water, their two bodies merging in the steam in one great, glorious celebration.

Oruela and Marthe nearly fell out of the hole in the wall with watching.

On and on it went, the two of them rutting like mad up against the tiled wall.

When at last it was over, Kim climbed off him and they stood for a moment smiling at each other. 'Help me back up,' she said, and he gave her a leg up. Oruela and Marthe pulled her in.

He hadn't expected to see the other two and he looked as if he couldn't believe his eyes. Oruela gave him a little wave and Marthe gave him the thumbs up. Then they refixed the grate. Kim pulled on her clothes and they crawled back down. Her skin was still steaming as she came out into the courtyard. They replaced the grating and walked back to the women's wing, Kim trailing wafts of steam like some glorious fiery demon.

As they waited for the guard to open the gate to let them in Marthe said, 'You bastard.' Kim merely smiled weakly back. After a minute she said, 'I'm sorry, Marthe. I just couldn't help it.'

Marthe grinned.

Paul had got permission to visit Oruela through sheer luck. Now the day had come he stood in front of the mirror worrying over whether his shirt was the right colour. Renée watched him from the bed. Her submissive mood had begun to crack over the past few days and they were becoming fractious with each other.

'What are you so fussy about?' she barked at him.

He knew damn well why he was so fussy this morning. It was the thought of seeing Oruela. If ever there had been any doubt it was gone now. He didn't answer Renée. He just looked over his shoulder. Her short brown hair was all tousled and she was reaching for a cigarette. She seemed so fragile; her ribs showed through her skin.

'Drive me out to St Trou,' he said.

'Is that an order?' she replied, her yellow eyes searching his.

'Yes.' he said, with all the command he could manage. Why not, he thought. The train journey would be deadly.

'OK,' she said, and she smiled.

While he was waiting for her to get ready he went into the darkroom and looked at the photographs he had tried to develop the night before. They were the ones on the film that he'd taken in Bruyere's bathroom. Every single one of them was fogged. He couldn't understand it.

He rummaged in a drawer and took out some photographs of a smiling family. His sister Marguerite lived nearby St Trou and he was going to deliver them to her.

'What do you think?' cried Renée, behind him. She stood in the open doorway of the darkroom in breeches of silky mustard, a soft jacket like a Battenberg cake and a vanilla shirt and tie. She clicked the heels of her tan suede brogues and saluted.

'We're visiting a prison, for Christ's sake!' he replied, ungallantly.

She looked at him questioningly.

He knew he wasn't playing the game correctly. He was thinking of other things. 'Get dressed more soberly,' he said. 'And bring me some coffee.'

'Get it yourself,' she said and flung off her jacket.

An hour later he stood waiting in the yard at the garage in the Avenue de la Marne while she went with the attendant to one of the small, green garages. The attendant drove the car out of its stable and handed Renée the keys. It was a Panhard-Lavassor, low and dark green with white-walled tyres. The spokes glinted in the sunshine.

'Jump in!' called Renée.

But Paul had seen something. The gleaming black Hispano-Suiza had just drawn up. Raoul jumped out and unscrewed the petrol cap.

Renée flung the keys into the front seat of the car and asked him if he was going to stand there all day.

'Look,' he said, nodding at the Hispano-Suiza.

'Beautiful,' she replied. 'It's the H6. Van Buren Body and four wheel brakes. It's got an 18½-litre engine, you know. They weather the castings on those machine for two and a half years.'

'The chauffeur,' said Paul. 'It's the same car that was outside the graveyard in Bayonne.' But he was talking to the air. Renée had gravitated towards the Hispano-Suiza.

Paul watched Raoul's face soften as his gaze fluttered over Renée. He obviously took her to be a beautiful youth and Paul knew he'd been right about the chauffeur's sexual orientation.

He walked over to join them. Raoul gave Paul a queen bitch's dagger of a look and announced that he was late and had to go.

435

The road out of town twisted alongside the valley of the Nive. Beyond Bayonne the forest began, a green corridor winding into the foothills of the mountains. The new young leaves sparkled over their heads like stained glass. They turned off after about an hour, at Paul's request, and ordered coffee sitting outside a village bar.

Renée was fed up with listening to Paul's speculation about the chauffeur and Oruela and God knows what else. 'This is so pretty here,' she said, changing the subject. 'I feel I belong here in the Basque country. I'm not a native like you but I've adopted it.'

Paul shrugged. 'It's all very well romanticising it,' he said. 'It's beautiful and I'm glad this is where I came from, but I'd go mad in the country. It's nothing but sheep and gossip.'

'You're a fine one to talk,' she replied. 'All this snooping around and playing detective. You're like an old woman who twitches her curtains and gossips about what's going on next door.'

Paul slammed his cup down in his saucer. 'Are you serious?' he said. 'What do you mean? This is important. And while we're about it, let's have less of this old business. I'm only thirty-three. I know that's ancient to you at your tender young age of twenty-two but I'm not old. I only feel it with you sometimes because you're so bloody childish. And you're not the giddy young thing you pretend to be all the time. If you were more serious and stopped acting like a two-year-old . . .'

'I'm deadly serious,' she said. 'About my racing. But about you, well, I don't know. Why should I be? Where have you got these last ten years? What have you achieved?'

'I'm selling pictures, Renée, you can't bring that old knife out of its sheath,' he growled.

'Probably a one-off,' she said, nastily.

They sat in silence. He looked across at her. She was looking away. He hated her at that moment and at the

436

same time, to his chagrin, he wanted her. Christ, this absurd game was getting to him.

They paid the bill and got back into the car in silence. The car began to climb towards St Trou. As they drove alongside the denser forest she sped up, skidding round the bends in the treacherous mountain road. The beeches flashed by, stretching away from the road like silvery columns in some fantastic outdoor cathedral.

Suddenly she drove towards the edge of the road and brought the car to a stop. The roof of leaves above their heads was made of green and gold. The sunlight barely penetrated the gloom. She was breathing quickly.

For a second or two he thought she was going to drive on but then she said, 'Come on, come on and get me.' And she cut the engine and was out of the car like a flash.

Paul sat watching her as she ran in and out of the silvery trunks like Pan. The keys were still in the ignition. He was tempted to move over into the driving seat and leave her. But he couldn't. His heart wouldn't let him. He leapt out of the car and went after her.

She was fast but he was faster. He caught her by the sleeve as she darted round a tree. She screamed and twisted her arms in his grip and escaped. It must have burned her arm. His hand stung. He watched her run deeper into the forest, deeper into her own fantasies.

He had a flash of inspiration. 'Forfeit the jacket!' he cried. 'I caught you!' His voice echoed throughout the forest.

She turned, hesitated and then took off her jacket and dropped it on the ground.

Paul took advantage of her pause and sprang after her again but she ran like the wind. Deeper and deeper into the forest they ran. He came to a small clearing and suddenly she was nowhere to be seen. His heart beat fast. He could see for miles in the solemn darkness around him but she had disappeared. He turned around and saw a flash of rust-coloured trousers behind a silver trunk. Then she ran off again.

437

He decided to change his tack. Let her run herself into the ground, he thought, and he sat down against a tree trunk and waited.

When she realised he wasn't chasing her any more she started coming back towards the clearing, tree by tree, until she was very close.

'Don't you want to play?' she called.

Paul pretended to pant heavily. 'Too much smoking,' he said.

She looked disappointed. 'Don't stop,' she wailed. 'I like it.'

He stayed where he was, silently, looking at her out of the corner of his eye. She came closer and closer until she was standing right next to him. He looked up at her slender legs. She crouched beside him.

'Gotcha!' he growled and he held her fast.

Her scream pierced the silent forest and echoed back at them. 'Oh, you tricked me!' she cried. 'That's not fair!'

'Take off your clothes,' he said. 'Now!'

Her eyelids drooped and she whispered, 'Yes. Oh yes.' Her fingers flew to her collar but he sprang at her like a tiger and wrenched her trousers down and pulled them off. He spread her legs. The leaves of the forest floor crackled under her.

'Raise your arms,' he told her.

As she dropped her arms back above her head on the leaves, a look of fear flickered in her eyes. He clasped her wrists in one broad hand and clung to them as he forced his cock into her warm and wet sex.

The feeling that he hated her guts was so strong in him that he said it. She squirmed under him as he fucked against her hard little knot of a clitoris, as the warmth of her cunt enclosed him and drenched his cock. He covered her breasts with his body and bit into her long, white neck, his teeth scraping up towards her ear. His tongue tasted the waxiness. He kissed her face but she turned it away from his lips.

Their rhythm began to slow. She lay under him like a dead thing, barely responding. He pulled away.

'Turn over,' he demanded.

She rolled over on to her belly and lay there, her arse moving from one side to the other. He slid his arm under her belly and lifted her up on to all fours. He parted the cheeks of her arse and for a moment he stroked her magnificent sex from her clitoris to her arsehole. His strokes grew rougher and she began to drip. Her glistening cunt swelled as he massaged it. And then he manoeuvred his cock into her and, driving it home he fucked her until she collapsed underneath him and he shot his load. He didn't give a shit whether she'd come or not and he rolled off her like a lout and lay spread-eagled on the forest floor.

He lay there until he felt her roll over on to his right hand and push herself into his hand. He cupped it and raised himself and slid one finger of his left hand into her arsehole the way he knew she liked it. She writhed like one of Daisy's fishes on the leafy carpet and then went stiff as a board for a moment. And then her release came in a great shudder. They lay for a while, the leaves rustling all around them and then Paul dressed himself, washed his hands in a mountain stream and walked back to the car to wait for her.

They arrived at the prison about half an hour later. They were a little crumpled and the guard on the gate eyed them suspiciously, refusing to let them drive through until he had telephoned the management. They stood outside while they waited like strangers, a little embarrassed, kicking their heels.

Eventually the man opened the small gate and beckoned Paul. 'Only you.' he said.

'Well,' said Renée. 'I don't suppose it would've mattered what I wore.'

But Paul didn't hear her. He had stepped over the threshold and was gone.

Inside, the grounds were dotted with the casualties

of life. Their subdued demeanour chilled Paul to the bone. In his mind he had a picture of a happy, laughing Oruela. But what would he find?

He was waiting in the dim, wood-pannelled reception when a black woman appeared from behind the stairs and meandered past him, looking him up and down. He thought he recognized her and wracked his brains. She smiled slyly at him as she passed him and went out into the courtyard.

He had no time to think about her further because Dr von Streibnitz came hopping down the stairs. He came towards Paul with one outstretched hand. The other fluttered in the air like a butterfly as he introduced himself. 'It is most unusual, Monsieur Phare to see – what is it you said you were? – a relative?'

Paul had to reply to the doctor's back as the man had started to lead the way back upstairs to his office. Paul tried to sound authoritative as he said, yes, he was her uncle.

The doctor grinned. 'I wish more people would take the trouble to visit these poor souls,' he said.

Paul entered the office and took the chair the doctor offered him.

'We shall effect a cure, you know. No need to worry about that,' said the doctor.

'Exactly what for?' asked Paul. 'What is your diagnosis?'

'Well,' said the doctor, 'I don't diagnose in the accepted sense of the word. Let's just say . . . well, a woman as promiscuous as your niece has been is probably capable of anything, even murder. Mind you, on the other hand, she's been a model patient since she's been here. No trouble at all. She's as chaste as a nun.'

Paul fought down a rising tide of disgust. 'Is she going to be charged with any crime?' he asked.

The doctor sniffed. 'I am not at liberty to discuss the legal procedure of this case,' he said. 'My job is to observe my patient. At present all I know is that

Mademoiselle Bruyere is here because her mother thought it the best thing for her. It is for the police to decide if and how they proceed further.'

Paul was beginning to find this tiresome. He was more than eager to see Oruela. He was almost on the edge of his seat.

'I say,' continued the doctor. 'Would you like to see my latest invention for curing the mind, Monsieur Phare? I'd appreciate the opportunity to show a man of culture. As I said before we don't get many visitors here, you know. People don't care – '

Paul broke in. 'I'd be pleased to,' he said. 'After I've seen Oruela.'

'Of course,' said the doctor. 'Excuse me just one moment.'

Alone in the doctor's book-lined office, Paul couldn't sit still. He went to the window. The row of cell windows in the next block squinted at him like caged eyes and a feeling of anguish grew in Paul's chest like a wave. He almost dreaded seeing her. What would this place have done to her?

When the call came for Oruela to come down she was still fiddling with her hair. She tugged at it with her brush in front of the old piece of tin that she used as a mirror. She was terrified of seeing Paul. She felt like an awkward teenager again. What would he make of her now? She'd been like this ever since the letter had arrived announcing his visit and Kim had been relentless in her teasing.

She had decided to wear her men's trousers. They were stitched back up at the crotch and they looked well on her but she hated them. She had pulled the belt so tight that it almost strangled her waist but at least she had a waist. Her shirt was freshly ironed but there was nothing she could do to make it more feminine. She was convinced she looked disgusting.

But there was no time to do anything more about it. She descended the iron stairs saying to herself that this was all stupid, that he probably didn't really fancy her at all. It was just some story Michelle had cooked up to make her feel better.

By the time she reached the gate it was the truth. And then, as she stepped out into the sunshine she suddenly thought of Caspar and the last time she'd seen him. She thought of the love they'd made and it gave her heart. It was as if his ghost was there, a friendly ghost, by her side, telling her that anything was possible.

The doctor greeted her at the doorway of the main building and she followed him up the stairs. She felt confident now. Whatever would be, would be.

The doctor opened the door of his office and there stood Paul, by the window. Her soul opened like a flower.

They stood looking at each other for a moment or two, unable to say anything and then the doctor discreetly disappeared and Paul smiled.

She sat down and he took a chair and sat opposite her at a short distance. The light was behind him. He seemed so fresh and clean and normal.

'How are you?' he asked. 'You look much better than anyone else in here.'

'Oh, thank you,' she said. 'It's nice to hear that. We haven't got any proper mirrors in here.'

She liked the way he sat at a distance. She would've died if he'd reached for her hand or shown any passion at that moment. Part of her wanted him to but she also wanted to study him a bit. She liked what she saw. There was a kind of dignity about him that was more appealing than anyone she'd ever met. She liked his clothes too, the way he sat easily on the chair. Her sex began to flutter in her knickers. She crossed one long leg over the other and swung it as she accepted the cigarette he offered her.

Paul watched her take a drag and blow the smoke slowly out. He studied every inch of her face and recognised beyond all shadow of a doubt that he was in

442

love with this woman. His nervousness left him. She was easy to talk to. She thought clearly and she talked to his deeper self. He longed to touch her, to express his love physically but he could wait.

Eventually he told her that he thought he'd seen her real mother. She wanted to know every detail.

'Can I approach her for you?' he asked.

'Oh yes,' she said. 'Find out for me. My God, it would mean so much to me to know I had someone of my own.'

'You have me,' he said.

She smiled. She sat up straight, slowly easing back her fine shoulders. The curve of her breasts under the shirt swelled and he glanced quickly at them, appreciatively.

She caught the look and felt herself blushing like an idiot, but she knew in that instant that if she got free she would be his lover. The possibility of sex seemed to hang in the warm afternoon air between them.

They rose from their chairs, when the doctor returned, in unison and Oruela smiled again at Paul, through a sudden unstoppable film of tears. He took her hands in his and pressed them to his lips without another word.

When the door had closed behind her the doctor perked up. 'So, would you like to see my invention?'

'OK,' said Paul gruffly.

The grimness of the locked gates and the old buildings they passed through depressed Paul thoroughly and he marvelled privately at Oruela's strength.

'In here,' said von Streibnitz. He pulled a blind down over the barred window in the therapy room and unlocked a big cupboard with a key from the bunch that was always on a chain at his hip. With a great smile he wheeled out the hat.

'Here it is.' he said.

It reminded Paul of the iron mask in the Dumas novel and he fought down an impulse to laugh.

'It's a revolution and I tell you it works,' enthused von Streibnitz. 'It works on your little friend; she still comes here once a week, and she is most definitely changed by it. I question her and she gives me much better, more sane answers.

'Look, you see these little doors?' He opened and shut one or two compartments at different parts of the hat. 'The radium chloride goes in here.'

'Radium chloride?' asked Paul.

'Mmm. Isn't it exciting? The whole thing is made of aluminium. The metal acts as a filter. Some use of high doses of radium has caused burning, you see. I read all the papers written by the Institute in Paris, you know. They have been using it very successfully. It's capable of curing anything – papillomata, epithelial tumours, even syphilitic ulcers. Why shouldn't it cure the mind as well? Eh?' Von Streibnitz gurgled. 'It's going to be the answer to all of humanity's ills, you know. It comes from deep within the earth where the balance of things is as perfect as nature intended it. Now, these little chambers inside correspond with the parts of the brain that cause mental illness, this one is for murderous impulses, this is schizophrenia, you see it overlaps, and this one at the back is for overly developed sexual impulses, especially in women. It's a combination of sciences, a partnership, if you will, between phrenology and the Streibnitz method!'

The only thing that Paul could remember about radium was that it was astronomically expensive. He said so.

'Ah yes. It took a group of charitable American ladies a year to raise enough money to buy Madame Curie a gramme to work on. But I,' the doctor looked around as if checking that no one else was in the room, 'I have a *patron* and of course I use very very small doses, because the brain is very subtle. Then my private customers pay the proper price, so I'm able to give one or two patients here their treatment free. I believe in socialism, you see.'

444

Paul opened one of the compartments and closed it and wished he could get away. He was all churned up inside.

'Now don't go spreading the news about,' said the doctor. 'I don't want anyone picking up on my idea just yet. When my paper is written it will cause a revolution. I'm working on it now. Your friend is part of my research. You may depend on it that I am going to cure her and become famous for it.'

Take Me to the River

*L*ater that night Oruela, Kim and Marthe went on a raiding party to the kitchens. Their midnight feast was not solely food. Since the discovery of the shower room vent they had got more and more daring in their exploits. They could usually bribe one of the guards to let them out and almost every night they were out somewhere doing something they shouldn't.

The honey from the shower room had become a kind of pet. He couldn't believe his luck. By this time Marthe had had him too. Tonight it was Oruela's turn. They were going to raid the larder for the best food that the guards kept for themselves and he was going to meet them later.

But when it came to it she no longer wanted him. She gorged herself on a delicious breast of roast duck and told Marthe and Kim that she'd keep watch if they wanted him. They didn't have to be told twice.

Oruela sat against the bars of the gate, watching the night sky and dreaming gloriously romantic daydreams of Paul while her two friends had their fun with the hunk behind the warm ovens.

A few miles away Paul, Renée, Paul's sister Marguerita and her husband sat outside the restaurant in the village square. Paul's niece and nephew ran around on the cobblestones having an adventure. He watched them and remembered doing the same things with Marguerita.

His anguish was slowly dissipating under the canopy of the stars. The after-dinner cognac helped, and the warmth of being with his sister and talking about nothing and everything. He'd been in trouble when he left the prison. A feeling of sadness had hit him like a thunderbolt right in the solar plexus as he walked out of the gate and over to Renée's car.

Renée, surprisingly, was well-behaved. He was grateful. Eventually, Marguerita announced that the kids should be in bed.

'I'd like to sit a little while longer,' said Paul. 'You go back, Renée, if you like.' They were staying the night at the farmhouse.

'No,' said Renée. 'I'll stay.'

'I'll leave the back door on the latch,' said Michel, Marguerita's husband.

Renée and Paul watched them round up the kids in the pool of light in the square that gleamed from the porch of the hotel opposite. And then there was silence.

Renée looked at him. 'I know when I'm licked,' she said.

'What do you mean?' he asked.

'Just that I know you're in love with this girl Oruela and I have no hold on you any more.' Her voice broke as she spoke and tears glistened in her strange yellow eyes.

'Oh, Renée,' he said, reaching across the table for her hand.

'Don't,' she said softly. 'Don't pretend.'

'I won't,' he said. 'But – ' He was interrupted by the sound of a car. It was the Hispano-Suiza. It pulled into the pool of light and stopped.

'Oh, great!' said Renée as Paul's attention was lost.

'I promised Oruela I would speak to her,' said Paul.

Euska got out of the car on the hotel side and walked

up the steps of the entrance. Raoul got back into the car and the car started to pull away.

'I know!' said Renée. 'I'll talk to the chauffeur. That'll help you, won't it? I'll do something for you. Then you'll love me again, won't you?'

Before Paul could stop her she was up from the table in a flash and flying across the square. As the car sped up she ran nimbly alongside it and jumped on to the running board.

Paul was furious! He paid the bill and rushed out into the street.

Raoul noticed Renée as he looked into his mirror to turn into the hotel garage. Renée was glad he played it cool and didn't jump out shouting at her. All he did was stop in the yard and climb out to look at her.

She hadn't a clue what to say. So she smiled her most beguiling smile. He laughed. She jumped down from the running board standing tense, ready to fly.

'Don't run away,' said Raoul. 'Don't be scared. What a funny little thing you are. Get in the car, come on. I have to drive it in there. We can talk.'

Renée felt terror in every pore of her skin. But he sounded nice. She opened the passenger door at the front and climbed in. The car smelled of leather and polish.

'You take good care of the car,' said Renée. 'I would too, it's beautiful.'

'Well, I like cars. I take care of my boss's car in Brazil.' He drove it smoothly into the garage and switched off the engine. 'I mean that's what I do, take care of cars,' he said and turned to look at her.

'You're from Brazil?' she asked.

'What do you care where I'm from or where I'm going? The moment is now,' he said, turning off the lights.

'Come for a walk with me,' she said, in the darkness, before he made his move. 'By the river, I love the wetness down there, the smell of it.'

Raoul started fumbling around under the dash. 'Wait in the yard,' he said.

He wasn't long. He came waddling out and took her by the hand. 'Can I have a little kiss?' he said and put his lips to hers.

She kissed him lightly and looked into his face. He was really very nice-looking, kind. 'Do you have a dark side?' she asked.

He laughed. 'I've got whatever side you want,' he said softly.

Wait till you find out what I've got, thought Renée. They reached the gate that led down to the riverside. The sound of the water rushing over the precipice was too loud for them to talk. Renée took him by the hand and led him along the path past it. But he pulled her back at the noisiest point and began to kiss her.

It really was lovely with the water roaring beside them but she manoeuvred him away. She had to talk, to tell him what to expect if he touched her sex, which he would. She stopped him and pulled him on, along the path.

Meanwhile Paul was having kittens. By the time he got to the garage it was all dark. He called softly but there was no answer. He walked back to the hotel. There were a few people in the bar, all local men. He recognised one he had known years ago and dropped into a surreal conversation. The man was really pleased to see him, but Paul said he was looking for his friend and left.

'City dweller,' said the men in the bar, to each other, sagely.

He went back to the garage. Nothing. Surely Renée wouldn't have gone somewhere with the man if she had sensed danger, would she? He walked up the main street, eyes peeled, looking into the dark shadows and crevices. He turned and came back down the other side. She could, of course, be back at the restaurant by now and not know where he was. She'd go to Marguerita's

449

probably. There was only one more street in the town. He walked up it and down again. He went back to the restaurant. She wasn't there and they were closing. No. They hadn't seen her. He went round the square once more. Surely she wouldn't have allowed herself to be taken down any of the lanes.

And then he stopped in his tracks. He was doing it again, wasn't he! The pull of her particular madness had sucked him in. Damn her! He hurried back to the hotel and asked for Euska Onaldi at the desk. The clerk phoned up to her room; who wanted her? Paul told the clerk his name and received permission to go up . . .

'Oh, it's wild! Oh, you wonderful little freak! Oh my God, you've got both. OH MY GOD!' squealed Raoul.

Things had progressed.

Renée was so relieved he wasn't angry that she almost cried. They were leaning in the crevice of a rock.

'So what are you? I mean you, really, in here?' He pointed to his heart.

'I'm a woman,' she said. 'I think.'

'Oh, and you can be, can't you. Oh, you lucky devil,' he said.

But he had lost his erection. Renée began to cry.

'Oh, love. Oh, sweet thing. Don't take any notice. I like men. That's all. Don't be . . . Oh, I'm sorry.' He put his chubby arms around her. 'Come here.'

'I've only ever met one man who isn't revolted by me and I've grown to hate him,' said Renée. 'The affair's worn out. He kind of ignores my difference. He worshipped it at first but now it's . . . oh, I don't know. He's not, well, ideal.'

'Well, no one's ideal, darling,' said Raoul. 'I mean all that love and marriage. How many happy couples can you count on one hand?'

'I wish you could have made love to me,' she blubbered.

'Oh dear, you're hurting, aren't you?' said Raoul. 'You're lovable. Someone will love you.'

450

He was certain he could introduce her to some people in Paris who would really appreciate her and he had heard of a Greek island (the name escaped him) where hermaphrodites were worshipped as the ultimate human being.

'Well,' said Renée, 'worship would be nice!'

Paul knocked on the door of the room on the second floor. He heard her footsteps on the tiled floor.

Euska opened the door and smiled warmly. 'Come in,' she said. She was dressed in a long orange gown. The colour against her skin and her dark lustrous hair gave the impression of southern fire. Around her neck was a heavy, gold necklace with a topaz at her breast. 'I'm going to order something to drink, would you like to join me?'

He said he would and he wandered out on to the balcony as she telephoned room service. Below, in the square, the brightly coloured umbrellas of the restaurant swayed a little in a breeze. The trees rustled and the gas lamps sprinkled their light on the cobblestones.

'Would you like to sit out here?' she asked. 'It's lovely, isn't it?'

'Wherever you please,' he replied.

'I'm sure you'd like to smoke,' she said. 'I'll just get my wrap.'

He did indeed want to smoke. He took an American cigarette out of his packet and tapped the end on the railing of the balcony before he lit it.

She reappeared, wearing a black shawl and sat in one of the cane chairs. 'Well,' she said.

'You're Oruela's mother?' he asked, still standing.

'I am,' she replied, with a slight frown. 'And what are you to her?'

'I don't know yet,' he replied. 'I only have hopes.'

A big smile lit up her face. 'A suitor?'

'We're talking as if she were in the next room,' said Paul.

They were interrupted by the waiter at this point and

451

they waited until a bottle of cognac had been set down and two drinks poured.

Paul watched her as she picked up her glass. The resemblance to Oruela was most definitely there, and if Oruela aged like this then he knew he would never tire of her. Metaphors of ripe fruit came to his mind but they were inadequate. There was something strong, an excellence about this woman, that was most desirable.

'I saw her today,' he said.

'What is she like?' asked Euska.

'She's strong and beautiful,' said Paul. 'She's magniticent, considering what she's been through.' He paused. 'What exactly has she been through? Do you know any more than I do?'

Euska was obviously delighted to hear him praise Oruela. Her face shone. 'My guess is that Jacques Derive has colluded with Genevieve Bruyere to have her incarcerated.'

'That's self-evident,' said Paul. 'But why? And more to the point how do we bring them to justice and get her out?'

'The answer to the second part of your question is easier to say than the first part. I know why, but . . . well, let's say I'd rather tell the story to Oruela herself first. That's why I'm here. I am going to the prison tomorrow to see her and introduce myself.'

'I've told her that I think you are here,' said Paul.

'Yes, good. I was worried about that. I didn't want to give her too much of a shock, – ' said Euska. She seemed nervous.

Paul warmed to her. 'You said the second part . . .?'

'Yes. It's simple. Jacques Derive thinks I'm dead. I am going to give him a shock. I'm going to simply go to his office and tell him that if he doesn't release Oruela I am going to spread my story all over France. That's why Oruela has to know first, in case he calls my bluff. I don't think he will though. I've been to see some of the other people involved and at least one of them is on my side and will corroborate my story.'

452

'He's a dangerous man,' said Paul. 'I think he's killed one man already and I was warned off in a pretty ugly fashion.'

'I know. I know. I won't say I'm not nervous. But if he did harm me in any way he'd be dead.'

'Would you like me to come with you?' said Paul.

'It'll be too late for us all if you're dead.'

'You would come?' asked Euska, smiling. 'It could put you in danger, too!'

'I don't do things by halves,' said Paul.

Renée was awake, sitting up in the big old iron bed when Paul finally arrived home, quite drunk and very happy. She was in a strange, skittish mood. Neither of them could sleep although they hardly spoke. And then, in the darkness, she wriggled her arse into his groin and enclosed his prick. He immediately became rock hard.

She manoeuvred him inside her from behind and settled on to him. He closed his eyes and thought of Oruela as Renée's warm sex enclosed him. He reached around her smooth skin for her strange and wonderful malformation and cupped it in his hand. He took some of the juices that flooded from her and lubricated it. It hardened and Paul held it tighter.

Suddenly she said: 'This is goodbye, Paul.' She said it to the darkness, into the pillows. He couldn't hear her.

He stopped fucking her. 'What did you say?'

'I said this is goodbye.'

Paul felt his freedom being born in his gut. It hurt him and excited him at the same time. He pushed her down into the bed so that she lay underneath him and he rose on top of her like a Titan, the strength of him bearing down on her now, fucking her one last time, thighs on thighs, belly on her buttocks, madly. He hated her because she couldn't live up to him and he loved her because she was weak.

Unforgettable

Oruela began to cry before she reached the end of the document that Euska had left her. Von Streibnitz had allowed only a brief visit.

'Try to forgive me,' her mother had said as they parted. Her very own mother! This is what Euska had written:

'I grew up on the Calecon estate near Navarre. My father managed the estate for Anton Calecon and I spent my girlhood as free as a bird among the vines and the animals.

'When I was fourteen my father died and Anton made a promise to him to look after me. Anton loved me in a fatherly way. Women did not attract him. His taste for boys was his weakness. He used to travel to certain private clubs in Biarritz to indulge his tastes.

'When I was sixteen I fell in love with a boy from Navarre and one evening we were caught making love in the barn.

'Soon after that Anton and Madame Jaretière, the housekeeper, concocted a plan to show me another side of life. Anton needed a camouflage to indulge his developing tastes. It wasn't exciting enough for him to go always to the private clubs; he liked to court danger in society. He dreamed of a real man who would see

454

him by chance across a crowded room and fall in love. A man with whom he would have the courage to declare his love to the world.

'He never found it, poor Anton, but it was a romantic dream that he had and the mere chance that it could be realised excited him.

'He bought me gowns and jewellery and we went to the casino, to the opera, to the races. It certainly did show me what the world had to offer but I loved my Navarre boy. I continued to see him and eventually I became pregnant.

'While it was still unnoticeable I decided not to tell anyone. I continued going out with Anton and he treated me well.

'Then one night, Anton thought he had found his man. This man was part of a gambling party that had continued long after the casino had closed, upstairs in one of the suites. The party included Jacques Derive, Rosa – his mistress at the time – Norbert Bruyere, Armand Pierreplat the judge and Everard, who is now the coroner. They were all young hell-raisers in those days and when they gambled they were completely outrageous.

'I never knew who Anton's man was but I remember his face. He was an ordinary-looking man but he had lovely eyes. I found out later by chance that he was a Greek and that he went mad and died in the arms of a Hungarian countess after an overdose of opium. I have no reason to suspect that he knew what havoc he caused that night.

'Anton was taken by a total madness. He gambled everything, just to impress his Greek god. But when the last chips were down and the fate of the whole of the Calecon estate was laid on the turn of a card, his man merely yawned and left.

'The cards were turned. Anton had lost. He was out of the game and it dawned on me that all my dear friends on the estate were going to be homeless. Then

455

Jacques Derive and Norbert Bruyère whispered to each other.

'"Anton," said Norbert, "you have one more chance."

'Anton looked up. He was coming back to his senses and realising what he had done. He was as white as a sheet.

'"The girl," said Norbert, looking at me.

'I urged Anton to agree to it, on the condition that the old servants on the estate would be looked after for the rest of their lives if we lost. Anton put this to the other men and they agreed.

'When Anton lost again I was sad but not desolate. I thought I would be taken somewhere and I would escape and be with Lauren, my lover . . .

'But that was not what these men had in mind. Henri was drunk. He staggered up to me and shoved me against the wall. He tore my clothes and they all laughed. All except Anton who tried to help me. But it was no use. They beat him up and called him names and threw him out.

'Norbert dragged me into the bedroom next door and, thinking my life was at stake, I allowed him to have me.

'He left me crying on the bed. Then in came Derive, then Pierreplat. By the time Everard was shoved into the room by the others, all laughing and jeering, I was in such a state that he took pity on me. He didn't touch me. He tucked me up in the bed and called Rosa.

'She came in and sat down and that's when we heard the shot. I didn't know Anton had a gun and I wish he'd had the sense to threaten those bastards with it. The police came and I don't know how the affair was kept quiet.

'I spent the next few days with Rosa at the apartment Derive kept for her. We didn't see any of them. They didn't come near us. Rosa was kind, but the future looked bleak. I couldn't think of facing Lauren. I felt as if I'd betrayed him. I never saw him again, ever. I heard he was killed in the war but for me he was dead long before that.

'Norbert eventually paid us a call. He was a strange mixture of remorse and threat. When he saw my bruises I thought he was going to cry and he begged my forgiveness. But then he said that if I ever opened my mouth about what had happened I would die. With some prompting from Rosa, he agreed to rent me an apartment. It was the only way for me to stay off the streets at the time.

'So I became his mistress. It was the only way to survive. And I wasn't his mistress in the usual sense. I never made love to him again. He taught me that there are some men in the world who take their pleasure from pain. I gave him plenty of what he wanted and I later made my fortune practising the English vice. I only had a small number of clients but they paid me well.

'This was a long time after I had given you away, Oruela. You were born in Paris. Hearing I was pregnant Derive put pressure on Norbert to get me out of Biarritz. I was lonely and frightened in Paris. There was only the visit from Norbert every fortnight and his demands. You were young and you would sleep through it in the small bedroom. But I feared for you. I didn't want you to grow up in that tawdry life.

'Norbert's marriage to Genevieve had been barren and he thought he could place the blame on her now. He was sure you were his child. Some fantasy led him to believe that I was a virgin before he raped me. I didn't disabuse him of the idea. I couldn't. I feared being put out on the street.

'When he first suggested he take you and adopt you and bring you up as his own, I resisted the idea with all my heart. But gradually he persuaded me with the practicalities of it. You would have a stable, normal upbringing, he said, with the best education that money could buy and all the things a young girl could want.

'The reality was different but I thought I was doing the best thing. I never stopped loving you and I was Henri's friend until the day he died because I could never break the link with you. If anything happens to me I urge you to contact Ernesto Medejar, at Villa Carioca, Rio de Janerio. He is my dearest friend and will vouch for the truth of my words.

'During this past year, Norbert's health has been failing and he has paid a king's ransom to some bogus doctor to cure him. I believe he had nothing left. I suspect he was trying to blackmail Jacques Derive with the events of long ago and I suspect he was killed because of these blackmail attempts. I cannot prove this but I am going to try the same thing, with a different motive. Should I die in the attempt, a copy of this document will be in safe hands and someone will contact you.'

By the time Oruela read this, of course, she also knew that Paul was involved and that Euska felt safer. Nevertheless the ruthless mayor was dangerous and the tension gripped her like a torturer's rack. Her body felt like ice.

Kim advised her to come on their nightly adventure as usual, especially as tonight the honey was bringing a friend and it was definitely Oruela's turn. The thought of anyone other than Paul still revolted Oruela but she knew she needed distraction.

The five of them met in von Streibnitz's well-upholstered office in the main building. Getting in here past the guards was the latest dare they'd set themselves. It went off without a hitch. The two men were waiting for them. They had already undressed down to their shorts.

The second man was another strong-looking beauty. He looked a bit nervous though, as if he wasn't sure what was expected of him.

Marthe locked the door behind them.

'Our friend is tense,' said Kim. 'She needs relaxing.'

The honey looked at Oruela with obvious lust. He was longing to get his hands on her.

'No, really!' said Oruela. 'I, er . . .'

'We'll give you a massage if you're tense, won't we, Alphonse?'

His mate looked Oruela up and down. 'Sure,' he said.

Oruela had a delicious feeling deep in her womb. She knew if they massaged her she'd want more, but she didn't want to know for certain that it would happen. 'Well,' she said. 'Just a massage then.'

'On the couch then, young lady,' said the honey. 'I'll need your clothes off if I am to make a thorough examination.'

A shiver went down Oruela's spine. She began unbuttoning her shirt.

'Here,' said Alphonse. 'Let me help you.'

She sat on the psychiatrist's couch and allowed him to undo her buttons all the way down. Kim and Marthe were busy picking the lock of the booze cupboard.

He pulled her shirt out of her pants and slid it off her shoulders. She was naked underneath and both men, she could tell, liked the look of her breasts.

She undid her belt and slid her trousers down and off. Then she lay on her belly and closed her eyes.

Someone's hands, big strong hands, massaged her back, at the shoulders first, then down her spine vertebra by vertebra until he reached the elastic at the top of her knickers. Then his hands made a great sweeping motion over both her hips and up and held her waist gently before smoothing up her ribcage, just brushing the curve of her breasts as they went. Down her spine again went his palms and up the same way, again and again and again.

The other man began on her legs. He had some kind of oil on his hands that made them soft and he massaged her feet with it, lifting each leg up and bending her knee so that he could get a good rub going on first one calf, then the other, first one shin, then the other. Then he bent her toes about and massaged around and in between each one.

It was heaven. They were so good at it that there was no threat in it. She began to relax and really give herself over into their hands.

Each time the hands on her back touched the elastic

459

of her knicker waistband she felt more and more that she wanted him, the next time, to touch her arse.

The second pair of hands let her lower legs down gently on to the soft leather couch and then started on her thighs. Up and down he massaged, both thighs at the same time and with each stroke upwards she felt as if her thighs were parting little by little, and her sex was opening. And then, instead of rubbing down her thighs, his fingers travelled up a little bit higher on to the cheeks of her arse. Now, each time, they went higher, massaging her glutes and her knickers were pushed up so that the fabric was tight against her sex and each time he squeezed her arse her clitoris got a tug.

The other man – she looked up and saw it was the honey – started on her arms. He massaged her shoulders in their sockets and then stretched her arms out in front of her, rubbing them, loosening them. She felt as if she was flying, her torso was stretched, her breasts cupped in the soft leather.

'Turn over,' said Alphonse, at her heels. She eased herself over and he pulled down her drawers in one decisive act.

She lay before them totally naked. Honey began to massage her torso, avoiding her breasts at first, like a professional. But Alphonse was more daring. He slid his hands right up her legs, touched her triangle of hair and, bringing his hands to rest on her belly, he bent his head down and kissed her right on her clitoris. It was a light kiss, testing the water. Her eyes were full of the beauty of his shoulders, his arms, big and strong.

He parted her thighs and slowly massaged them with both hands, up and down like before. Honey's hands circled her breasts once and then stopped, caressed her ribs and then went back to her breasts, massaging them firmly. It felt so good, so very very good.

She wanted sex. She wanted Alphonse. There was something about the slight perfume of his skin that she liked. She liked his hungry mouth too and the curiosity of his blue eyes. And then he moved his body closer to her and she felt the hardness of his sex through his shorts. It pushed at her thigh. He couldn't help it. He was so turned on by her and what could she do, now, if he decided to fuck her? Nothing. Her sex was wide open.

She saw him issue a silent command to the other man to get lost – just with his eyes. Then there were just the two of them. He climbed on to the couch and held her.

The weight of his body was energising after all this time without a man. He buried his face in her shoulder and struggled with his shorts. She felt his cock spring out and it was so warm and friendly and he was so dying for her. She let her legs fall right apart, and he entered her with a 'Mmmm' and kissed her. No sooner was he inside her than she felt herself on the brink of coming. She was so excited to be in the hands of a complete stranger. And in his hands she was, so completely. His belly was hard like a board. She wrapped her legs round his waist. Her arse pressed into the soft leather.

'I love you,' he said.

She heard him and knew he had to say it. Her lips were close to his ear and she licked it.

'I love you. I love you,' he repeated and she felt him coming and let herself go . . .

They lay together in bliss afterwards.

'Thank you, little girl, you're a peach,' he said. Then he kissed her nose.

There was, thankfully, no sign of the others. Oruela and Alphonse got dressed and he kissed her again and again, little pecks in between each piece of clothing that he put on.

He was acting as if he expected that this would happen again. But Oruela didn't want him for a regular lover. The anonymity of it had turned her on. He seemed sweet but she didn't want him any more. She thought she had better tell him.

'This was a one-off,' she said.

461

He looked at her suspiciously.

'It was unique. It can never be repeated, it was so fantastic,' she said diplomatically.

'We'll see about that, little lady,' he said.

'We'd better find the others,' said Oruela.

They looked for them in the adjoining office. There they were, drunk as skunks, arguing politics in loud whispers.

'Don't look at me!' said Kim. 'He started it.'

The man they called honey was looking decidedly gloomy. He glowered at Oruela.

'We'd better get out of here,' said Oruela.

They tiptoed to the door and along the hallway to the stairs where they split up. Alphonse gave Oruela's arse a healthy slap as they parted, which for some reason shocked her much more than the sex . . .

Euska and Paul ascended the steps of the town hall just as the great clock struck twelve. The door at the top opened and Jean and his father Etienne stepped out into the sunlight. Etienne was more handsome than his son. The hard edges of youth had disappeared from him but he had the same irresistable air. He was solid, a rock of a man. He spotted Euska instantly.

'Hello, Paul. Haven't seen you lately,' said Etienne. He was looking at Euska.

'Let me introduce you to Euska Onaldi. Euska, this is Etienne and Jean Raffoler.'

'My pleasure,' said Etienne.

'Father, I'm going to be late,' said Jean and he ran away.

Etienne passed the time of day and then followed his son.

'Who were they?' asked Euska.

'Jean might have been your son-in-law,' said Paul.

'Better tell me later,' said Euska.

They had reached the door and Jacques Derive was in the ornate entrance hall, talking to some other politicians. Paul opened the door for her and she sashayed into the dim interior. The look on Jacques Derive's face was a framable picture.

Euska went straight up to Derive and stood inches away from him, not making a sound. The look on the mayor's face showed that he recognised his nemesis in the form of this beautiful woman he had thought long dead. The whites of his eyes flashed.

Paul watched from a discreet distance as planned, but Euska's voice was loud enough for him to hear.

'We have a long delayed appointment,' she said to the stricken mayor.

He nodded, fixing a smile on his face and excusing himself from the rest of the politicians, most of whom were busy looking Euska up and down. But then Paul saw the mayor's eyes flicker a signal across the room. Paul followed the direction of it and saw a flashily dressed man move quickly across the floor towards Euska's back.

Euska seemed to sense danger. She turned and saw the gangster. 'Why not hear what I have to say?' she said to Derive. 'Better you, than the whole of France.'

The gangster hovered as Derive said something to Euska that Paul couldn't hear. Immediately she beckoned him and Paul steeled himself to walk over to the group. The look that Derive gave him was venomous.

'You had better come up to my office,' said the mayor.

As they ascended the great ornate staircase, Paul suddenly saw their strange party as some absurd ceremonial procession. He looked across at the gangster. The man's eyes were blank and deadly.

Once in the office, Derive sat down behind the huge leather-topped desk and lit a cigar. He didn't offer Euska a seat but she took one, calmly. 'I will get straight to the point,' she said. 'Either you release Oruela or I will send the full story of what happened to me at your hands to the newspapers.'

Derive leaned back in the mayoral chair. 'I don't think anyone would be even slightly interested in a story that old, much less believe it. We were all just youngsters at the time, having fun the way youngsters do. I've held office in this town now for a long time. People won't believe their mayor was ever a criminal, if that's what you are trying to say.'

'Interesting,' said Euska. 'I haven't told you yet how I would describe you. But criminal will do. And you are obviously out of touch. Do you surround yourself with sycophants, or has no one told you how unpopular some of your policies are? This new road, for example. Everyone knows you've given the contract to your friends. It's a perfect time for the newspapers to run something from your past. It will put the last nail in your coffin.'

'That's outrageous!' said Derive. 'The newspapers in this town would never stoop . . .'

'Oh I wouldn't bother with the small papers, she interrupted. I assume you've either got them in your pocket or under your thumb. But the national papers, now they would. . .'

'You'd have difficulty finding anyone to corroborate your story. The big papers wouldn't dare to run such a story unless you could back it up. I don't think they'll readily take the word of a – '

Euska cut in. 'I have witnesses,' she said. 'I've spent the last few days talking to them. Everard was never happy about it, you know that. Even Pierreplat has been nervous since you killed Norbert and locked my daughter away in a prison for life. Anyone would be revolted by what you have done except you. *You are despicable!'*

Derive pulled one cauliflower ear and his eyes narrowed, as if the two were connected by some mechanism. 'I didn't kill Bruyere. Your daughter did. Her blood is bad. St Trou is the only place for her!'

'It's not her blood that is bad,' shouted Euska. 'It's yours. She has none of you in her. Her father was a boy from Navarre. I was pregnant when you all raped me!' she spat.

Paul felt anger and pity in his breast as he listened to

464

her words. He had guessed it was something like this although she still hadn't told him. But to hear it spoken was a shock.

'You filthy bitch,' said Derive. 'You filthy, lying bitch.'

'That's enough' barked Paul as he stepped forward.

The gangster moved forward at the same time, ready to fight. Paul glared at him.

Derive ignored them both. 'You made poor Bruyere believe that she was his child. I knew all along she wasn't. She has the mark of the devil on her.'

'He believed what his guilty conscience wanted to believe,' said Euska. 'And you are forgetting something. I was an unwilling participant that night. It was you. You Bruyere and Pierreplat that were the devils. Don't you dare twist it around. You are the filth! *J'accuse!*'

Paul could see her hands shaking in her lap and he knew that it cost her all her strength to face the man who had stolen her life. But she had won. Derive was squirming.

'Give the order for her release, now,' said Euska. 'Give it because you know that what you did was wrong.'

Derive sneered.

'Failing that,' she continued, 'give it because the whole story is in document form and is held by my lawyer, and if I don't telegraph him tonight telling him I am safe and all is well, he will contact a certain national paper whose editor is my friend . . .'

Derive was silent for what seemed like an age. Then he picked up the telephone. 'Von Streibnitz,' he said into the receiver, 'I want you to release the Bruyere girl. Yes that's right. New evidence has come to light. New evidence. Release her. Don't question my judgement, man. As mayor, I am also chief of police. Release her. Very well then. Tomorrow morning.' Derive replaced the receiver.

Once they were outside in the hallway, Euska and Paul walked quickly towards the top of the stairs. Only as they descended into the ordinary day to day bustle of the foyer did they turn to each other and smile.

The next morning Marthe came to say goodbye. She was dressed in her own clothes. She looked lovely in the red dress. She seemed happy. When she'd gone Oruela and Kim went along to the shower together.

'You know, I don't even know what she did,' said Oruela.

'She shot a man, killed him,' replied Kim.

'*Crime Passionnel*?' asked Oruela.

'I doubt it,' said Kim. 'She'll probably be executed.'

'What? She's not going free?' cried Oruela.

'No. She's going for trial.'

'Oh God!' cried Oruela and she ran back to the end of the landing. She was in time to see Marthe being taken out through the gates. She called her name. Marthe kept on walking.

Oruela went back into her cell and sat dazed. Kim came back from her shower and stuck her head in. 'Why didn't you tell me?' said Oruela.

'It wasn't my business to tell you,' said Kim, simply. There were tiny droplets of water on her shoulders still.

'It's going to be boring round here without you two,' said Kim.

'We don't know that I'm going yet,' said Oruela.

'It's only a matter of time.'

'I'll come and see you,' said Oruela.

'Don't,' said Kim. 'It'll drive me mad.'

'Write to me then. I'll write back,' said Oruela.

'Give me an address then,' said Kim. Oruela wrote down the address where she sent letters for Paul. It was his home he told her, but she'd never seen it. She longed to.

Oruela knew something was going on when she wasn't called for work, but she didn't dare hope that this was really it. She went and had her shower. More of her hair snaked down the plughole. It really was getting alarmingly thin in places. What if she was going bald with the worry? She had heard of such things. It made her feel sick.

It wasn't until the middle of the morning that the news came. She was going home, they said. She didn't contradict them, but in her heart she knew she wasn't going home to the house where she had grown up, ever. She was starting a new life.

She had no clothes! Her only personal clothing was the nightdress they'd brought her into the prison in. And then her cell door opened and a guard threw in a package.

'Your people sent this,' he said.

Oruela opened the brown wrapping paper. It was a dress. It was green silk. She pressed it to her cheek. It was so long since she'd felt the touch of silk. As she dropped it over her head and the fabric settled next to her skin she felt good.

The guards came for her and led her downstairs. She stopped by the serving hatch where Kim was bringing warm plates on to the counter.

'I'm going,' she said.

Kim put the plates down and came round to hug her. 'Nice,' she said. 'Nice dress.'

'Look me up when you get out,' said Oruela.

Kim nodded.

They hadn't allowed Euska's car to drive into the prison that day. Raoul sat in the front seat while Paul paced up and down by the gate and Euska sat on a shooting stick under a tree. The flies buzzed around. Paul felt he wouldn't believe it until they had her in the car and they were driving back to Biarritz.

On the other side of the gates Oruela fought down the impulse to run and walked slowly and calmly across the courtyard. Von Streibnitz shook her hand in a fatherly fashion and told her to be a good girl. She didn't reply.

She kept on walking and didn't look back. She held

the thought of Kim tight in her heart as she went up to
the guard at the gate and showed him her pass. He
opened the door for her and she stepped out into the
lane.

Let's Face the Music – and Dance

E rnesto was at the Miramar when they arrived.
'Better late than never,' said Euska and she gave him a kiss.

It gave Oruela pleasure to see the woman who was her mother reach up to her lover and kiss him.

They all ate a delicious lunch in the luxurious suite, overlooking the sea. The sounds of holiday-makers drifted up from the beach and the promenade on the hot and heavy late August air.

'I'd like to give you a party,' said Ernesto. 'But I expect you'll want to wait a while.'

'I'll be fine soon,' said Oruela and her gaze strayed to Paul. It would be their party. He knew it too. His eyes said so. They would dance and afterwards . . .

'Where would you like it to be?'

'At the casino,' replied Oruela.

The way Paul grinned was boyish and she loved it. He was delighted that she'd chosen the place where they had first set eyes on each other, she knew. This time they would do it right. He sought to cover his delight by talking to Euska. He obviously didn't want to let her know it all, not right away. She admired that. It was exciting to be almost certain, but not quite.

469

'Ernesto, I want to do some shopping. Come with me,' said Euska, rising from the table.

'I ought to come too,' said Oruela. 'I must get some clothes.'

Euska frowned at her. 'Don't you think you should rest?' she said. 'I'm sure Paul will stay with you if you don't want to be alone.' And she looked at Paul with wide, innocent eyes as if the thought of leaving them alone together had just occurred to her.

Not for the first time Paul found himself on the point of sexual arousal at the thoughts that were going through his mind. Ernesto had gone to the bathroom and there he was, alone with the two most delightful women he knew, and they were mother and daughter. Two dark-haired, dark-eyed playful beauties. He was aware of every movement they made: the way Euska picked grapes from the fruit bowl, not using the pearl-handled shears, the way Oruela's eyes seemed rimmed with red as if the world outside prison was too bright . . . These details he watched and because he had knowledge of them that the women hadn't themselves he knew he had power.

And yet he was rendered totally powerless by them, helpless and awash in his desire, his soul bumping against the hard fact that he daren't express his thoughts and his hardening sex pressing against the buttons of his underwear.

'Well, I'll get ready,' said Euska, seeing that Oruela was not going to stay behind.

When they were alone Oruela went out on to the balcony and looked down at the people below. Paul joined her.

'She's angling to leave us alone.' said Oruela.

'I'm glad I have your mother's approval,' replied Paul, leaning with his back on the railing.

He looked good enough to get close to but Oruela held back. 'Strange to think I have a mother after all this time,' she said.

'How do you feel about that?' asked Paul.

She could have melted. She could have touched him just then. Green eyes, square jaw, blond hair and a brain too. How did she feel? She felt like taking his hand and putting it to her breast. She felt like nuzzling in his neck, opening the buttons of his shirt and seeing, feeling his stomach. She felt like undoing the leather belt and feeling the warmth inside his trousers. It was so strong, her attraction, it was hard not to act upon in some accidental way. Her gaze dropped involuntarily to his shirt collar. She loved the way it was loose at his neck.

'I have mixed feelings,' she said. 'I don't quite know what to think.'

'I'm sure it will come right,' he said. 'Just give it time.' He turned around and looked out to sea. 'Your mother is a great woman.'

Oruela felt a sudden quick flame of indignation. Something about the way he said it. Did he think of Euska as a lover? But the indignation turned to amusement just as quick as it raised its head. Doubtless her own sexual adventures had done her good. So what? She liked a man with broad-ranging tastes. Just so long as he didn't act on them.

'When can I next see you?' he asked, cutting into her thoughts.

'Tomorrow?' she suggested.

'Dinner?' he replied. 'Just us two?'

'*Pourquoi pas?*' she said, shrugging her shoulders as if she didn't care.

The afternoon was spent in the *haute couture* houses of Biarritz. Big fans in the ceiling turned lazily, merely stirring the air as the bony mannequins paraded before them in the latest designs. Euska ordered Oruela more than a dozen outfits. But when Ernesto got bored and went off to have a beer Oruela confessed that she needed something ready-to-wear in the meantime and something special for the following evening with Paul.

They went to Oruela's favourite little shop where she

471

bought a deep blue cocktail dress off the peg and some linen trousers.

'Trousers!' wailed Euska.

Oruela jumped on her firmly. Euska wouldn't dare comment again.

'I know,' said Euska, as they came out of the shop. 'Let's go to the Turkish baths.'

The sight of her mother's body unwrapping itself was extraordinary. Deep feelings stirred in Oruela that confused her. Euska's breasts were the fuller. They rested heavily on her ribs. Her posture was good and so she looked well for her age. Oruela peeped at her furtively. She looked at her dark and lustrous triangle and the thought that she came out of there sent shivers into the very fibre of her being.

In the steam room she lay on one of the benches, higher than Euska, still drawn to watch her mother's body as she talked of how Oruela could live in her apartment in Paris if she wanted. She found it difficult to answer her. She wanted to say that she didn't know what she would do. It depended on Paul but she felt too vulnerable to pour out her heart.

In the pool afterwards they swam and Euska complimented her on her body. They swam lazily. Oruela floated on her back, letting the water wash over her. There was a great glass roof to the indoor pool. The sun baked their skin and made the water warm.

Euska's body cut through the water, droplets glistening on her fine brown skin as she paused and trod the water. Suddenly she called 'Race you!' and they swam fast and strong up and down the pool. The exercise cleared Oruela's mind and she felt better. They dived and played like a couple of dolphins.

Paul came for her the next evening and drove her along the coast in Renée's open-topped Panhard-Lavassor all the way down south to St Jean de Luz where they chose a small fish restaurant overlooking the sea. The sounds of the plates clattering in the kitchen mingled with the talk of the other diners. They ordered champagne cocktails to start with and the bubbly went straight to Oruela's head.

'How's it going with Euska?' he asked, as they sat down to their crabs' claws.

'It's difficult to talk about what I really want to talk about with her,' said Oruela. 'Have you read her story?'

'No,' said Paul. 'I think you're supposed to give it to me.'

'She was a whore,' said Oruela. It was difficult to say it out loud. She felt like she'd dropped a bomb into the middle of paradise.

Paul merely smiled. 'Does it make you feel uncomfortable being the daughter of a whore?' he asked her.

'Well, it's not every day you discover that your mother was a dominatrix!' she replied.

'A dominatrix? Was she Norbert Bruyere's mistress by any chance?' he asked.

'Yes,' said Oruela. She felt on edge, as if everything she said was a matter of life and death. But he was smiling again.

'That's irony for you,' he said.

'Why?'

'I got the impression that Genevieve and Norbert Bruyere never had any kind of sex.'

'They didn't,' said Oruela. 'How did you know that?'

Paul told her about being locked in the bathroom and the policeman being whipped raw with his own whistle-chain.

'It makes you wonder though,' said Oruela when they finally stopped laughing, 'how those two lived together for all those years and never discovered each other. I wouldn't live like that for all the security in the world. I would want to explore love with the man I . . .' She trailed off and attacked her last claw.

'Do you imagine yourself wanting to tie a man up and whip him?' asked Paul. He was pulling the flesh out of a claw with a tiny silver fork.

'No,' said Oruela, sucking on the meat. 'I've seen

473

enough punishment to last me a lifetime. I hate the thought of narrowing everything down to such a trickle. In prison, the whores used to talk about how certain men wanted a procedure to be followed and never diverted from. Only this way would they get their pleasure every time. I hate the idea! It's like the only path to the child within, to the human being who is free and sensual and alive, is down a tiny crack in the rock underneath which they're buried. There are footholds that have to be followed: pain, fear, belittling – horrible.

'Myself I want mature sensations. I want to feel all the different colours, sounds of love. I want breadth and depth, the smells and tastes that are waiting, unknown, to be discovered.'

Paul was looking at her, she realised, the way a man looks when he is utterly smitten.

After dinner they walked along the seashore for about half a mile under the craggy rocks, the darkness enveloping their bodies, the sound of the sea on the shore a lilting music behind their conversation. They talked about everything under the crescent moon. He told her about the photographs he'd sold and she listened with excitement as he described their content. But there was no hurry. She felt as if all she had to do was wait. And she must wait. He must come to her. He would come, she knew, eventually.

They climbed down on to the dark beach and walked barefoot for quite a way before he asked if she was tired. She was, but she wanted the night to last for ever.

As they turned she found him watching her again, looking into her face and this time she gazed back, lazily, at his lips.

They were soft and full as they met hers. He held her tight in his arms, her breasts pressed against his chest. Her hands felt his back, under his thin shirt. It felt good, well-formed.

They kissed for a long time, tasting each other's skin, caressing each other's hair, lightly touching each other's

474

body with their hands. They were absurdly proper. He didn't touch her breast, she didn't grab his arse. It felt right like that. She had never felt so purely romantic before.

Eventually they drew apart and they walked back along the beach without saying very much. They held hands.

Then he said. 'I have nothing very much to offer you, Oruela, in the way of material things.'

She held her breath. It sounded like he was leading up to something else. It was too soon. She almost said 'Don't!' But luckily she didn't. He wasn't that simple. He continued: 'But I might have more of a chance to make money in Paris. I should have gone there a long time ago but I got stuck like the needle of a record. If you were there . . .' He paused.

'Oh, it would be wonderful!' cried Oruela, forgetting herself.

'It would,' he said, grinning.

The next day Michelle came to visit. Oruela noticed a change in her friend. She was more self-assured. She carried herself better, her posture, usually a little hunched, had improved and she walked tall, carrying her high breasts with a sexual confidence.

She was never going back into service. Robert had been offered a job in a garage and they were going to get married. It was everything she wanted. Their sex life was fantastic and she thanked Oruela for setting her free with the letter.

'I've discovered that when I reach a climax if I let myself pee at the same time, the strength of my orgasm is intensified. If I just let myself empty completely my body feels wholly alive. I like to be on top of Robert and do it all over his belly. He really loves it, although the first time it happened we were in bed and we had to sleep on the floor. Now we do it in the open air wherever we can find a secluded place. I was always frightened that I would do it before but now I'm no longer frightened and I know he wants me to, everything is better. Everything. A trust has grown through that simple thing.'

Oruela listened closely, her own sense of excitement rising. The room was shady and cool. The electric fan droned on. She told Michelle about Caspar, about the anonymous sex with the woman at the hen night, about Alphonse.

Michelle told Oruela about when they had posed for Paul's photographs, about the freedom she had begun to feel.

'That's what it's all about,' said Oruela. 'That's what life is. It's stepping out and doing what you want to do. It's seeking experience for its own sake. I wish you were coming to Paris. Paul might come to Paris as well.'

'I'd bet my life on it,' said Michelle, smiling. 'He's besotted. You're lucky. He's a lovely man.'

'Did you ever . . .?' Oruela stopped.

'Did I ever what? Have sex with him? No I didn't, none of us did. He never made a move. It was all art to him. I used to wonder sometimes what it would be like.' Michelle stole a glance at Oruela's face. 'You don't mind me saying that, do you?'

'No. I don't think so,' said Oruela. 'I expect I'll have to get used to the fact that he makes his living that way.'

'Renée didn't like it,' said Michelle, and she told her about the day the photographs stopped.

Oruela fought with her feelings. 'How much of a hold do you think Renée still has on him?' she asked.

'None. Annette told me they have broken up for good,' said Michelle.

But even as they spoke, Renée was sitting in the big, old armchair by the open shutters in Paul's studio telling him what had happened.

She had run into Raoul again at the garage on the Avenue de la Marne and invited him to the track. He was thrilled to go. He was fascinated by the atmosphere and the paraphernalia of the big teams. They had their own caravans for the mechanics and prepared food on the spot. 'It's like the circus!' whispered Raoul gleefully.

It was nice to have someone around who paid attention to everything she did with a kind of awe.

'Oh, well I never, there's someone I know,' said Raoul, waving over the fence. 'It's Victoire! I must go and say hello. Excuse me, darling.'

Renée watched him. He met a tawny-haired young man at the fence and waved to her to come over. She left the mechanic to his job.

'Here, this is Renée, my special friend. Renée, this is Victoire, the little devil. He's playing the gigolo to the rich woman.'

Renée gulped.

'Oh, look, isn't she sweet, she's shocked,' said Victoire. 'Don't be, love. It's a living. Do you know the countess, dear?'

'No, but I've met her driver and of course I've seen the team at races,' said Renée.

'Oh, you *must* come and meet her, she's such a sweet,' said Victoire, giggling. 'She's such a naughty sweetie.'

'Renée's embarrassment was growing. It wasn't the done thing to climb the fence and introduce yourself. She had her dignity as a fellow team leader to consider.

But the countess herself saved the day. Seeing her boy chattering away, something drove her over. Renée wondered if it was jealousy. The countess was a thin but handsome woman of about forty-five. She was dressed for the terrain in flat shoes and a green dress that reached her calves.

Introductions were made and the countess enquired how the two boys knew each other. Victoire said they'd been at school together. The countess smiled sweetly at Renée. Renée, of course, was dressed in her boy's clothing and the countess obviously thought she was of that sex. She complimented her on her driving.

'Do come and have champagne with us,' she drawled.

As they walked across the grass Raoul whispered that he wasn't schoolfriends at all with Victoire, that Victoire was an *habitué* of the Biarritz night clubs and quite a brilliant dancer, and he'd only met him last week.

Renée's sense of dread was heightened by this remark. 'How long has he been her gigolo?' she asked.

'Oh, ages,' said Raoul. 'At least a month.'

Under a candy-striped awning a flock of young men and women, fashionably dressed, not a sign of grease on any of them, laughed too loudly and sized up the newcomers in a flicker of drawn steel. This was the party crowd, explained Victoire. They all lived off the countess one way or another. Judging by the attention Renée herself was receiving, she guessed that most of the men were homosexual. How on earth did they please the countess?

'But *you'll* be a star when she finds out what you've got, dearie,' said Victoire.

Renée felt like she'd been struck a blow in the face. 'Raoul told you?'

'Don't be shy, darling. We're all a little freaky, you know.' Victoire smiled kindly at her.

'Well, *don't* tell anyone else. Just *don't*. My career will be ruined if you do, understand?'

'Oh dear. I think it's too late.'

At a distance, Raoul was in conference with the countess.

Renée took her courage in her hands and marched over. 'Forgive me, Countess, but I hope Raoul isn't boring you with silly stories.'

'My lips are sealed, my dear,' the countess crooned. 'He thinks you're wonderful, you know.'

'Please don't tell anyone else these lies, Raoul,' said Renée. 'My career is at stake.'

Raoul looked embarrassed.

'Run along and leave me alone with Renée,' said the countess. 'Come and sit in the shade, my dear. We'll leave this crowd of ghouls and talk.'

What choice had she, now her secret was out? She

478

followed the countess to a little table parked by the side of the caravan. They sat down and a servant brought them cakes and more champagne.

'Would you drive for me?' said the countess.

'I prefer to be independent,' said Renée.

'I understand that, but do you have the money to keep going?'

'I . . . I have enough,' said Renée.

'Couldn't you do with more?' said the countess, a smile playing on her bright lips.

'Undoubtedly.'

'Well, I could give it to you.'

Renée's heart was pounding. 'In return for what?' she asked.

'Your affection.'

'Really?' said Renée sarcastically.

The countess's eyes travelled over Renée's face, her tiny breasts and her legs. It gave Renée the feeling she was standing in the line of a falling tree.

'I have the heart of a woman, madame,' said Renée, deliberately using a lesser title.

The countess winced. Renée felt a little sorry. She hadn't meant to be unkind.

'You have everything I want,' said the countess simply.

In truth Renée was sorely tempted, not by the woman, but by the chance to drive with money behind her. But the thought of becoming one of the crowd of dependants didn't appeal either. She would rather walk off now into poverty and obscurity.

But she sat still. 'I'd be happy to be your friend, Countess.'

The countess seemed amused. 'How näive you are and how very, very charming.'

Renée rose to leave.

The countess stood up and looked her in the eye. 'Why not leave it to chance? Race my best driver. Cars of your choice. If you win I will back you for three years. That will be enough to get you famous and have

479

car manufacturers falling over themselves to back you. You'll be independent and probably very wealthy. If you lose, you'll drive for me for the same length of time. There, how can you refuse, you're a sportswoman?'

Renée stared at the gleaming cars in the paddock. Pierre Suliman, the countess's driver, was there, working and as greasy as the rest. A man who loved racing, passionately. A man respected worldwide.

'I might agree,' she said slowly. 'On one condition.'

'Oh?'

'That if I lose you treat me with respect, you don't consign me to that crowd . . .' She nodded to the candy-striped tent.

'Oh, don't be silly. I don't know who half of them are, they change every race. They amuse me, so I pay their bills. My drivers are a completely different thing.'

'How do those people amuse you?' asked Renée. Her voice came out a little wobbly.

'I'll tell you if you agree to my wager.'

'I agree,' said Renée.

'That's the spirit!'

As they walked back towards the candy stripes, the countess said, 'They do whatever I ask, you know, anything for a crust of bread, poor loves. The naked wrestling can be rather fun. If you lose I'll give them to you as a consolation prize! Oh, look at you, your eyes are as wide as saucers!' the countess cackled.

Renée's knees were a bit weak as she walked back to her own car with Raoul. They got into the Panhard-Lavassor and she drove out of the compound.

'Well! I'm absolutely dying to know!' said Raoul.

She told him. 'But don't tell anyone else!' she said.

'Look,' yelped Raoul. 'My lips are like a buttoned fly!'

'She doesn't care about your friend, you know,' said Renée, thinking it only fair to tell him.

'Of course she doesn't. God, you have led a sheltered life, haven't you. He doesn't care about her either.'

480

Renée put her foot right down on the gas and Raoul screamed with delight.

She told the story in a diluted form. Paul was disturbed. He wasn't angry. In his love for Oruela he felt he had left Renée far behind. But he worried about her now, like a father.

'When is this race to be? Don't you have enough to worry about with the big-engine race only two weeks away?' he asked.

'Oh, I knew you'd disapprove,' she said. 'I don't know why I bother telling you things.'

'I'm not disapproving, I'm just worried,' he retorted.

'You're a liar!' she said, raising her voice. 'You just don't want me to get on in my career. You're jealous.'

'That's absurd,' he said, and he threw the coffee spoon in the sink. It clattered on the crockery that had sat there all day and Nefi turned and looked sleepily from the pool of sunshine that she was basking in on the kitchen windowsill.

Renée picked up her coffee from the counter and sipped it. She looked up at Paul. Her yellowish eyes gleamed. She had him and she knew it. It was the only way she knew anything about him now, when he showed signs of disturbance. She craved his violence and she would make him violent even though she hated him and didn't want him at all. She had meant it when she bowed out in favour of Oruela but now she wanted to sleep with him again. She missed him.

'That's right,' she said. 'Call me absurd, insult me. It stimulates you to do that, doesn't it? Go on! Admit it!'

Should he, he wondered. There was a part of him that responded. Even now, as he looked at her angry little face, the temptation to reach out and soothe her, to pin down her wild ego, was tempting. He was even beginning to get hard.

But then she said, 'You only care about yourself, you do.'

He knew she was wrong. 'I've cared too much about

you,' he said. 'Far too much. You wear your difference like an open wound. You use it as an excuse to abuse those who love you.' His tone was deadly. Renée began to cry.

He ignored her. He went and opened the front door and sat on a cane chair outside. The afternoon was waking up again after siesta. A woman he knew nodded to him as she passed by with her shopping bag. It was all pleasantly normal. But as he raised his coffee to his lips he heard Renée's crying get louder and louder. He'd never heard her cry like that before. It sounded as if her heart was breaking. He went back into the house and shut the door. He went to her and put his arms around her.

Her closeness suffocated his reason. She clung to him moaning his name over and over again. He stroked her hair, he held her as he had held her a hundred times before. He tried to soothe her, to make her whole. Her fingers searched his clothes and reached between his legs and before he knew it they were naked on the couch in the dark cool of the studio and he wanted to fuck her.

He took her hands in his grip and held them fast. She pushed on to him with such strength that the struggle took over. It was all he could do to hold her. It excited him so much. She moved on top of him like a woman possessed, her deformity sliding into his belly. He watched as it worked its magic and its spell drew him in. He was hers once more, she was whole. But he was empty.

The following morning Paul's telephone rang. Renée had just left, threatening to come back later, after training. He picked up the phone and heard Oruela saying: 'We've arranged the party for Saturday evening, just a few of us. I would like to ask your friends, Annette and the people that helped us get the letters through. I was thinking of taking a walk. I thought I might drop by and see you . . .'

482

But he knew he couldn't face it. He made an excuse and put the phone down, after promising to ask their friends himself and saying yes, he would love to come, he looked forward to it.

Saturday was two days away; by then surely he could free himself of Renée for good.

Oruela felt as if he'd slapped her face. She instinctively knew it was an excuse. With her feathers ruffled she sat pondering. Had she fooled herself over this man? The clerk at the reception desk told her someone wanted to speak to her. She waited a moment while the phone was transferred. It was Jean! He'd heard she was out, he said. Would she like to come over to his house for a swim?

And so, on the rebound, she said yes.

He was waiting for her in the lobby, looking gorgeous in linen trousers, a pale cream silk shirt, a straw boater. His eyes fluttered over her body as she walked towards him.

It was strange, walking with him through the busy streets. He acted with exaggerated politeness; every time the holiday-makers barred their way he led her, considerately, through. The crowd thinned as they walked up the slight incline that led to his villa.

'I owe you an apology,' he said, when they were alone in the street.

What she thought was, you bet your life you do. What she said was, 'What happened?'

'I don't really know,' he said. 'I got sucked in by the stories I was told about you.'

Oruela looked sidelong at him and saw a cloud of shame in his eyes.

When they reached the villa, a servant showed her where to change. It dawned on her as the woman opened the little cabin door by the pool that she didn't have a swimming costume.

The exit from the house to the pool was hung with pale cream muslin curtains that shimmered in the breeze. Over the top of the wooden door of the cabin she saw Jean's form as if through a mist. The curtains parted for him as he stepped out into the sun. He wore a striped bathing suit with thin straps that followed the contours of his muscles. The bulge at his crotch was well-defined by the jersey fabric.

Oruela slipped on the wrap that hung on a hook and stepped out. The blue and white tiles under her feet were cool.

'You're not swimming?' he asked.

'Not yet,' she said.

He pulled a chair out from under one of the tables for her and they sat down and ordered drinks from the waiting servant. 'Bucks fizz,' he said.

'Why did you ask me over here today?' she asked, as the servant walked away.

'Well,' he said, 'the pool is new, I thought you'd like it. I have all my friends over.'

'Are we to be friends then?' she asked. 'After what has happened?'

'Oruela,' he said. He looked sincere. 'I can't ask you to forgive me, because I'm not sure I wouldn't do the same thing again. Perhaps we can't be friends but I wanted you to enjoy this.' He swept his hand over the luxurious pool. 'I know what a terrible time you've had and I just wanted to share it with you.'

Oruela felt her toes itching with anger. He sounded so calm, sitting on his wealth like a fat chicken on an egg. The servant brought the drinks with fresh flowers in the glasses and then left them. The pool was still, like glass. She sipped her drink. 'Are we alone in the house?'

'Yes.' he said. 'Hélène's in Cap Ferrat and my parents have taken a trip to America.' He looked at her.

She stood up, let the robe slip off her shoulders and dived into the pool. Her naked body shot through the water, white and slender.

Jean practically fell over himself in the rush to join her and they swam leisurely. Eventually she rolled over on to her back and floated, her breasts bobbing in the sun-sprinkled water, the dark hair between her legs floating like a drowning animal.

It was too much for him. He swam over to her and held her around the waist. She kept her eyes closed. He felt like a stranger as he pulled her close to him in the warm water. She felt the hardness between his legs and pressing at her buttocks as he pulled her to the side. They reached the steps and emerged from the water, glistening. He held her and kissed her breasts. He picked her up and carried her through the curtains into the conservatory. He laid her down on the couch and stood up to peel off his soaking wet costume. Still she kept her eyes closed. She heard the flutter of the breeze outside and felt his wet body close over her own, felt his kisses on her damp skin. Her hands felt his dripping hair, and slid down the well-remembered back to the protuberance of his fine buttocks. In her chest, something opened, a door into her soul. There was nothingness inside. Nothing at all. His head disappeared from her grip and he kissed her white belly. Further down went his face into her wet pubic hair, seeking her clitoris and finding it. His tongue circled it, sucked it. Familiarity seeped in through the door that had opened. She took his head in her hands and moved herself against it, her sex open, her thighs stretched apart. She pushed and pushed. He sounded like a pig at the trough, greedy for her, greedy as hell. He took the whole of her sex into his mouth and gobbled at her. She felt the swell of her climax approaching and pushed down on to his tongue as she had pushed down on to the anonymous female head in the hashish-thick room that night, and a great wave of laughter welled up inside her. He was nothing more than a tongue. Nothing. Nothing. She felt him move his body as if to come up and get ready to slide into her but she held him there, made him suck her until she came in a great physical relief that bolted through her and relaxed her.

Realising she'd come he looked at her and smiled.

485

'There hasn't been anyone else, has there?' he said. His voice had a note of triumph in it.

She smiled at him lazily and he raised his head to kiss her. 'Oruela, I knew you'd still be mine,' he said as he came close to try and kiss her.

She averted her head, swung one leg over his body and stood up. She said nothing as she glanced over her shoulder and then she walked out through the wafting curtains, her legs feeling a little shaky underneath her.

He was still kneeling at the couch, kneeling at nothing. 'Don't leave me like this! Look at me!' he called. He was holding his penis in his hand. It was stiff and red.

Oruela walked away.

He came to the cabin door, slobbering something about how he understood and he knew she'd make it up to him next time.

She dressed herself and came out. He was still naked, his cock had gone down a bit but it perked up as soon as he saw her.

'Darling,' he said.

She went to him and gave him a little peck on the cheek. 'Oh, touch me,' he moaned, 'touch me.'

'Just stand there,' she whispered. 'Let your arms drop to your sides. Just stand.'

He did as he was told. It was shady on this side of the pool. His upturned face was dark and at the point of no return. She held his cock, massaged it. She could feel him responding. She held his cock, pushed it. She put her other hand on his chest and pushed him hard. He fell backwards into the water. She got a good look at his amazed face as he fell, still loaded. The surface of the water broke on his back.

He phoned her solidly for two days after that. He sent flowers, he made a nuisance of himself in reception but she felt things were resolved enough for her and she ignored him.

By Saturday though, Paul still hadn't been in touch

and she was beginning to feel that perhaps she would be going to Paris the following week without hope of seeing him again.

Euska told her not to worry about it. She had heard about Renée through Raoul and she told Oruela everything she knew. Oruela felt as if she now shared the knife-edge that Paul was on. She had to wait for him to jump her way towards a new life, and if he didn't then she had to believe he wasn't worth it.

She spent the afternoon writing her agonised thoughts to Kim and regretting she'd let Jean anywhere near her body. When it came to the evening Ernesto poured her a stiff drink.

She had come to like Ernesto more and more. It was impossible not to appreciate his mature sexuality. It was in his every movement, in his eyes. He appreciated her too. When she came out of her room in the evening gown he complimented her with just the right amount of enthusiasm.

She did look marvellous. Her black dress was floor length, very simple. It followed the contours of her figure without being too tight; a slight train that fell from her thighs at the back in folds gave the suggestion of an exotic creature just come from the sea to live on land. The dress stopped at her breasts in a classic neckline. Her broad milky shoulders were displayed to perfection and her hair, which had stopped thinning, shone glossily.

Euska came out of the bedroom. She was also in black. Her dress was clasped on one shoulder with a huge, single diamond and it fell in folds, the shape of a finely wrought J, down and across her full breasts. It clung to her waist and slithered over her belly down to the floor.

'I'm the luckiest man in the world!' exclaimed Ernesto, picking up his dinner jacket.

Euska was staring hard at her daughter's bare neck. She went back into the bedroom and came out again

487

with a diamond-drop necklace. 'I want you to have this,' she said, fixing the clasp round Oruela's neck.

'Thank you,' said Oruela. But in truth she felt uncomfortable. It was such a personal present. It was as if Euska had hung herself round her neck. But when Oruela looked into the mirror over the fireplace, she saw how nice it looked: how simple and fabulously expensive and she decided she rather liked it.

'It was the first piece of jewellery I bought when I had enough money of my own,' said Euska.

Oruela went to her mother and kissed her on the cheek. Euska held her fondly for the merest moment but it was too long for Oruela. The moment was supposed to be beautiful but it didn't feel it. Having a new mother was all very complicated.

'Let's go then,' said Oruela.

'But where's Paul?' whispered Ernesto to Euska as Oruela went to the door.

She told him to ssshh and followed her daughter.

Heads turned as they stepped out of the elevator into the palm-lined foyer. As they crossed it the revolving doors spun and in whirled Paul, in a heated state, his tie askew.

Oruela certainly admired her mother's presence of mind. Euska immediately took his arm and told him he was her date, leaving Ernesto and Oruela to follow. Paul looked over his shoulder not once but twice on the short walk through the balmy streets to the casino but Oruela kept firmly to her conversation with Ernesto.

Annette had brought a date and so they sat boy, girl, boy, girl once the introductions were over, around the best table the casino had to offer. There was great excitement because the show was from America. A new show, on a try-out before Paris – *La Revue Negre* with Josephine Baker.

Oruela took to both Diane and Annette immediately, especially Annette, whose delicate beauty was blooming again. The seating prevented her from talking to Paul but as the meal was eaten and the wine drunk their infrequent eye contact grew more. As soon as they finished the show began.

First came the chorus girls, their long legs flashing in the dance, their barely covered breasts swaying under feathers and beads. The men too, with their superb physiques. The music was like nothing anyone had heard before, with drumbeats that stole into the heart and opened it. A table of elderly diners got up and walked out. Michelle, who had moved next to Oruela, kept exclaiming, 'Look at that!' Oruela felt warmer and warmer as the dancers whirled now far, now close to their table on the edge of the dance floor.

Then on came the star. She had the longest legs anyone had ever seen and her bottom was high. Her breasts were bare and high too. She leapt into the centre of the stage and began her incredibly elastic dance, her legs bending in impossible ways, her arms floating freely. She wore high-heeled white shoes with thick anklets, thick bracelets at her wrists and ropes of white beads that flew and bounced off her breasts as she bent and flung her extraordinary body around. All the time she smiled, her broad white-toothed smile that flashed in the glinting stage lights. Her dark-rimmed eyes smiled too and the kiss curl in the middle of her forehead gleamed black and damp on her coffee-coloured skin. She placed her hands crosswise on her knees and pulled them back and forth. It was the most riveting display of dance that had ever pounded the boards of the casino floor and she looked as if she enjoyed every moment of it. She stomped around, wiggling her tail-feathers, lifting her legs and shaking her barely covered sex. This was a different sensuality. This was life and joy and raw passion.

It roared through Oruela's veins, through every cell in her body. It made her want to dance too. She joined in with a passion as the audience thundered its approval and the delightful dancer bowed gracefully to her admirers.

The white band and singer that came on afterwards

felt a bit like an anticlimax but as soon as the first note sounded and the singer began to croon her song, Paul was on his feet asking Oruela to dance.

Not yet crowded, there was room on the dance floor for them to move and he surprised her. He was a graceful dancer, leading her expertly.

'Wasn't she wonderful?' he said.

Oruela replied, 'Yes.'

'Oruela,' he said. 'I haven't been to see you because I've had some unfinished business to take care of.'

'Me too,' she said, looking over his shoulder.

They stopped speaking, with words at least, and let their bodies speak, let their bodies sing to the music. They moved easily together. Oruela felt at peace with him. There was no need to talk. She felt the movement of his shoulder beneath his jacket and it spoke of his body. She became acutely aware of his hand that held hers as they danced and gradually the dance floor became more crowded and they closed the gap between their bodies.

She lost track of the number of dances they'd danced. She lost track of everything except the music and the feel of him. He had her hand close to his breast now. Her cheek brushed his chin, his lips close to her ear and, lower, her belly close to his. Closer still as they moved to the delicious tune, she felt the curve of his hip touch her lower down, her thighs on his. They moved together in perfect harmony, each movement of his sparking off a tenderness of her flesh under her clothes.

His lips brushed her neck and he held her closer. Her sex rested on his thigh now; it came alive as she swayed her body close to his, now touching, now not, tantalising her, building a cocoon of love around her that made her invisible to the other dancers. She closed her eyes and floated in it, feeling his sex at her own hip, not hard but swelling. The rhythm of the dance took her on to it and then away. The rhythm had first his sex then hers, brushing against a hip bone. She felt sex in her

490

fingertips, in the cleft between her shoulder blades, in her buttocks.

'Let's go upstairs,' he said as the music sped up and became a rag. So they went up to the gambling lounge and he put money on the number she chose and won. Then they left the table and went out on to the balcony. Biarritz was below them, twinkling in the indigo night.

'Do you think they'll miss us?' he asked.

'I don't mind even if they do,' she said. 'I like your friends.'

'I wish I could take them all to Paris with me,' he said.

Her heart leapt. 'So you're definitely coming?'

'Oh yes,' he said and he took her hand and led her into the shadows where they couldn't be seen from the room. He drew her to him. His lips were close to hers. 'I want to be where you are,' he said simply.

The relief was overwhelming. She raised her lips to his and they were met with a kiss that touched her everywhere she could feel.

Anything Goes

*T*hree days later she boarded the train for Paris with Euska, leaving Ernesto and Paul on the platform. It was torture to tear herself away from him. With every moment of waiting for him the desire grew more intense. She seemed to exist in the same cocoon of love that he had woven round her on the dance floor, immune to everything. The bother of packing, of leaving, of arrangements, existed outside. She was immune to everything except his next touch. As the train pulled out she sank into the cloth seat feeling the wrench deep inside.

The train was a fast one but every turn of the iron wheels seemed like an hour further away from him. Finally Euska brought up the subject, and Oruela poured out her heart.

'A man like that is always worth waiting for,' said Euska. 'Ernesto didn't touch me for three months. I thought I'd go mad! But he wanted to be sure we could be friends. Now he's my greatest friend in the world and the sex is still wonderful.'

'What if it's not that? What if he's just not much interested in sex? Michelle said he didn't make a pass at any of the models when they were working on those pictures.'

Euska was too busy laughing to hear most of that. 'You must be joking. If I'm any judge of men, that one is as sensual a man as you could hope to find. He's serious though.'

And with that Oruela had to be satisfied. A few hours later the train pulled into the station in Paris and the great city consumed her thoughts.

They stepped down into the crowds as the steam hissed from the tired locomotive. Porters dodged this way and that through the crowds. Their baggage was coming in the car with Ernesto who had to make a stop in La Rochelle on business. So they had the luxury of walking out into the wide boulevard free of concerns.

Euska was tired so they took a taxi and Oruela rode with her gaze glued beyond the windows, watching the hustle and bustle of the streets. The number of beautiful women made her feel a little insecure. They all seemed so certain of where they were going. Her lack of sophistication overwhelmed her and she became gloomy.

Euska's apartment building was swish from the outside and no disappointment inside either. The peaceful modern vestibule was manned by a young handsome attendant who had difficulty taking his eyes off Oruela's legs and backside as she walked in. She felt him looking and it cheered her. If he was sufficiently impressed when there were fashion-plates wandering up and down on the street outside his window every day then things weren't as bad as they seemed.

Euska took her out to dinner to La Coupole in Montparnasse and they talked about the people they saw. She learned from her mother's knowledge of Parisian life.

The next morning she lost no time. After breakfast she looked at the street map and excitement filled her to overflowing as she realised that they were living on the very edge of everything she wanted to see and do. She dressed in her trousers and a silk vest and flew out of the apartment building: the nice young porter stared after her in wonder.

Instead of taking the Boulevard St Germain, with its fashionable shops, she walked south along the pretty Rue Mabillon and at St Sulpice she turned towards the Place de L'Odeon and her Mecca. Almost every street name she saw brought some historical fact to her mind. The sad death of the English poet Oscar Wilde, Beach's bookshop 'Shakespeare & Company' on Rue de L'Odeon where James Joyce's *Ulysses* had been launched upon an unsuspecting world. Then suddenly she was on Boulevard St Michel, the Boule Miche as it was known to the students who flocked around the Sorbonne.

The cafés were only just waking up. Sleepy waiters in long aprons brushed soapy water in the morning sunshine. And then along the street came a man dressed in purple and yellow, sporting a lustrous moustache and a lobster on a leash. Oruela's mouth dropped open and then she closed it quickly and tried to be sophisticated. After all, this was Paris.

She crossed the road and walked into the Place Sorbonne almost on tiptoe. Students, up early, hurried along the streets towards the great building and she followed their direction. It led her into the foyer of the university which was crowded with people all talking and shouting. On the walls great boards announced the subject and place of the morning lectures. She crept to the wall, keeping out of the way of the jostling crowd, aware of their bodies. One or two young men smiled at her and she smiled shyly back. She looked up at the boards towering above her head.

L'historie de la revolution. Socialisme et change en Europe. La nouvelle francaise 1812–1889. La nouvelle anglaise. Les philosophies anciennes. La philosophie–Henri Bergson. If her mind had had a sex of its own it would have been creaming her eyes.

Suddenly a sharp bell rang once and galvanised the crowds. Within a minute she was alone in the echoing hall. She felt silly. How would she ever become part of this great institution? There didn't seem to be anywhere to go to ask about enrolment. She stood there, against the wall, staring blankly at her stupid little shoulder bag that swung against her legs.

'Are you lost?' said a voice.

She looked up. An old man stood there. He was dressed in a black suit, a cravat at his throat. He carried a couple of books and a sheaf of notes.

'What lecture are you due in? Perhaps I can show you the way,' he said, kindly.

'No. Thank you,' said Oruela, excusing herself. She headed for the glass doors.

'Wait,' he said. And he took her gently by the arm. 'Don't run away. You shouldn't be frightened, you know. This is a friendly place. Are you a student?'

'No,' she said, eaten up with shame.

'But you would like to be, is that it?'

She managed a smile. 'Yes, but . . .'

'Knowledge is here for the taking, my dear. Come. What subject interests you?' he said.

'Philosophy,' she said.

'Which particular philosophy?' he asked. 'We have a variety. It's like a shop, look.' He gestured with a broad sweep of the hand to the lectures on the board.

'I would really like to hear Henri Bergson,' she said, still shy. 'I used to dream of it when I was in pris–' she stopped, horrified.

'Were you going to say prison?'

'Look,' said Oruela, 'I really don't think . . .'

'On the contrary,' said the man, 'I expect you have thought a lot. Come. I will get you into the lecture. And we will talk more, afterwards, about your dreams, n'est-ce pas?'

He hurried up the stairs and she followed him, like a virgin walking to a strange crowded bedroom where all her half-formed desires would blossom.

Other students turned to look at them as he settled her in a seat at the back of the stepped auditorium and

495

made her promise that she would not run away afterwards.

Then he trotted down the steps to the applause of the room and took up his position at the lectern.

Oruela spent the next hour listening to the great man in a kind of trance that lived each word he spoke as he spoke it. Bergson was the great irrationalist. In his vision, the great force of life struggled to break a way through inert matter and the universe was a clash between these two vital forces. Life organised itself according to need, unknowing beforehand but driven by want and satisfied only by action. Life, for Bergson, was creative, like the work of an artist.

Yes, yes, yes! cried Oruela's soul and that wasn't all. She fidgeted in her seat, feeling hot between her legs, as if God himself had taken her by the hand and led her into his den . . .

The signs were not lost on a young male student sitting in the next row. His eyes travelled over her body and her hair. He scribbled on a piece of paper. When the lecture was over he thrust it in her hand and rushed off into the crowd. She opened it. It said 'Venus lives!' It would have been rather amusing but for the fact that he waited for her at the bottom of the stairs and clung to her like a leech. She stamped solidly on his foot and went off in search of Monsieur Bergson.

The old gentleman wanted to hear her story and listened attentively. He decided there and then that she should be enrolled at the university. He cut a swathe through the tedious bureaucracy and got her a date to sit the entrance exam. Then he took her to a café and introduced her to some young gentlemen who were his best students, and left.

The café was in the heart of the Latin Quarter and was crowded with students eating their lunch. Her companions were rather morose but she took it that they were thinking great thoughts. The women seemed sexless. They wore shapeless clothes that hid their bodies completely and thick stockings even though it was still hot outside in the September streets.

On another table was a much more colourful group of people, Americans. They spoke in a slow lazy drawl and although Oruela's English was not that good she picked up a few words here and there. They were talking about sex.

They seemed to radiate sex. The women's eyes were hidden mysteriously in the shadows that fell from the cloche hats pulled low down on their foreheads; the men, hatless, made big gestures. Other people joined the group, a black couple, an oriental man in dark glasses, a dissolute and hungry-looking man in a faded, crumpled suit. They changed their language to French. A woman with bare arms and a deep, sensual voice complained about a famous painter who was taking advantage of the women that flocked around him. He made them race, naked, across the floor of his studio and the first one to grasp a thorny rose that he dangled in front of them won him. Then he drew her with distended misshapen muscles, with her sex where her eyes should be, grotesque forms that jolted the mind.

The others derided her, even the other women. Sex, the subconscious, the passions and the gross realities were the stuff of art, they said.

The conversation was hypnotic, it drew Oruela in. She wanted to be turned inside out. Her excited mind longed for the complementary stab of sex, with all its physical and emotional openings.

Her studious companions left to return to their lectures and she sat alone, self-consciously, listening to the gossip and ideas of the artists at the next table. Then she left and wandered the streets, hoping to be picked up.

In the days that followed she seemed to split into two people. On the one hand she was Oruela with her new friend and mother. They went to Maxims for cocktails and saw *tout Paris*. She met politicians, sportsmen, film

497

stars and talked small talk. Underneath this Oruela was another, powerful creature who roamed the streets on her own. The animal that passed by the apache bars and longed to go in, who walked quickly along the low-life streets absorbing the forbidden atmosphere but too timid to step over the line into this *demi-monde*.

Then she failed the entrance exam to the Sorbonne. The test was cloaked in the tricks of academia and she had answered the questions too simply. She didn't find this out till much later. She thought she had done well and so the letter was a shock. That day, out on the streets, she stepped into the half-light.

The man who showed her the way was a young apache. His face was etched with the violence of his life. He approached her on the street from behind and spoke crudely, in a low voice, of what he would like to do to her. She knew, from the moment he approached her, that she wanted him, but she played a game with him. It was as if she were enacting a grotesque carica-ture of the broader give and take of sexual dynamics. She made a half-hearted attempt to walk on but he was relentless. They were passing a bar and he invited her in.

It was dark and almost deserted inside. One or two other Arabs were drinking at the tables and a woman wearing too much make-up sat at the bar, her skirt was split at the thigh and her blouse was stretched over big breasts. No one stirred when they entered. The barman served them drinks. The liquor was strong and slightly sweet. Her apache grinned at her as he led her to a dark corner.

His clothes were tight on his body and as they drank more of the liquor she became absorbed by the way his torso moved, by his smooth brown hand that clasped hers across the table. Everything was drowned but his touch. She remembered dancing with Paul at the casino; the drink gave her the illusion that she was experiencing something similar.

Eventually he led her out of the bar, along the street

and up some iron stairs at the side of a bakery to a grimy room without much light. The windows were open and the sound of a family arguing in one of the rooms off the courtyard at the back accompanied his love-making. He kissed her violently. His body was taut as if tensed for flight. As he broke off his kiss and fondled her breasts she saw, over his shoulder, a murky fish tank with big, black fish slumbering in the water. She thought of Paul as the apache undressed her and she closed her eyes and tried to pretend . . .

The physical sensations overtook the fantasy. He threw off his clothes and pulled her to the small cot that was his bed. The sheets smelled evil. There were no preliminaries. He stabbed her sex with his cock, leaving her to warm to him as he moved inside her. Her heart and soul never opened to him but her sex did. The delicious knowledge that this was a stranger, that this was the one and only time, gave her feelings an impetus. She opened her legs wider and wider, stretching her thighs. Then he pushed her knees up to her shoulders, so that her knees were forced into his shoulders and her sex protruded between her thighs. He fucked her hard. She felt him deep inside her, so deep there were stirrings of pain. It frightened her and she tried to move her legs but he held her fast. Her fear made her aware of where she was and made her stronger. She got her way. Her legs were wide again, she could push her clitoris towards him. But he had no idea of what she needed. He was bent solely on his own climax and she realised that she was not going to have an orgasm, that she didn't even want one with him. She gave up trying and lay there soft and pliant as a pillow.

The experience cured her. She almost thanked him. He said he had to be somewhere afterwards and left her alone in the room, telling her to slam the door as she left. She doubted that the room was even his own. She dressed and listened to the sounds in the courtyard at the back of the building. Just as she was about to turn

499

from the window she saw a man sitting on the fire-escape across the way, on a floor higher. He was staring straight down at her. He was sketching and she realised with horror that he could see right into the room.

She left the room and ran down the fire-escape quickly and out, between the buildings into the street, turning to look over her shoulder once only before escaping.

That evening, to cheer her up, Euska suggested they go to the opening of a new show by some fashionable artists. Euska and Ernesto were always receiving invitations but they rarely went. Ernesto got bored too easily.

Euska was aware that Oruela was disappointed about the entrance exam and pining for Paul who had not written or telephoned at all in two weeks. She knew nothing of the afternoon's adventures in the seedy room.

Oruela spotted him as soon as they walked into the gallery. He was studying one of the paintings. Her heart jumped. It was the man she'd seen sketching on the fire-escape earlier. Every instinct told her to avoid him and she excused herself, deserting Euska, and went to the back of the gallery and tried to look at the work. But the place was too small, the drink was flowing and everyone talked to everyone else. She found herself in a group that included him. He gave no sign of recognition until chance stood them next to each other.

'My guess is that you have afternoons free,' he said. 'Would you consider sitting for me?'

So she began a stint as an artist's model. It was one of the happiest times of her life. It brought her back from the edge of disillusionment like a lifeboat brings back a survivor from a wreck. He brought her back. He was the opposite to what she expected of an artist. He was calm, quite rational, he had a quick intelligence that stimulated her and she trusted him. Once more she had found someone who would help her grow.

He didn't seem to want sex with her. He painted her

500

naked but he tasted her body only with his eyes. He touched her only with his brush. He had a wife in the country who adored him and he went home to their houseboat at weekends. He was only in Paris temporarily. His name was Albert.

They became good friends and in the evenings they went out to the cafés and bars. Oruela began to meet other interesting people. Everyone she met was talking about sex or doing it with whoever they chose or were addicted to. She heard stories and wondered. But her own sex drive had retreated into the safety of merely being looked at and appreciated.

One man she met was a brilliant linguist and academic. He lived with his mother who cooked for him and kept him comfortable. He was unable to make love to a woman and he couldn't with boys. He had an ingrown testicle that was such an embarrassment to him that it had twisted him. He was like a spider. He wove webs with words. He distorted stories that people confided in him until they became sordid and cheap. No one trusted him and it had made him bitter. He sat in his room translating scientific papers into all the known languages of the world but he couldn't speak the language of love. Oruela felt enormous pity for him.

There was another man who had a young wife who constantly slept with other men. He was desperate. People laughed at him and told him he should slap her. But he was kind and gentle. He'd been duped into keeping her but he held up his part of the bargain until it got too much and he took to drinking, and when he drank he cried bitterly. Oruela comforted him too.

These men were on the edge of a brilliant group of people, writers, artists and academics. Everybody told Oruela she should take the entrance exam again if she really wanted to but she wasn't sure now. Other artists asked her to pose and she became something of a favourite with them. Then a young, experimental film-maker asked her to be in a film.

She was instantly addicted to it. It was such fun.

501

There was an energy about the people who made films that was unlike anything else. In one she appeared in a cage, wearing a mask, with only flowers to clothe her. In another she was a hat stand that came alive.

Albert complained that she was no longer around to model for him and that she was not using her fine mind but she ignored him and drifted away from him. He was soon to leave Paris and return to his houseboat. But what he was saying was true. She was drifting, but she was not free. Paul had been silent for weeks and she was learning that she didn't have to be locked up to be in a kind of prison. Her new acquaintances provided her with a daily carnival of colour, excitement, stimulation that lasted briefly. Once again she felt drawn to have some deeper experience. She found herself thinking about the apache.

This time she slept with a writer who had a domineering wife. He and Oruela escaped together one afternoon to a cheap hotel and locked the door against the world. He was very gentle, almost passive. He seemed overwhelmed that, as he said, such a beautiful woman would want to make love to him. He had a deformity of the spine which made him self-conscious and he was ugly. But as he warmed to her he was a good lover. He spent an age at her breasts, sucking, crooning. He touched every part of her body with light fingertips, he made the fine hair on her arms stand on end because he made love to her arms as much as her breasts. He touched her body for so long that when he eventually got to her sex, she was streaming with anticipation. He fucked her for an hour, never coming himself, but giving her orgasm after orgasm until the shocks were deep inside her, momentous shiftings like the movements of continents, that merely tremor on the surface.

They took a break and he ran out to the shops to buy wine with her money. When he came back they drank the dark red liquid together and she begged to be allowed to make him come in whatever way he wanted.

'Do you mean that?' he asked.

'Of course,; she replied. She was so full of sex, so dreamy that she meant it.

'Get dressed then,' he said. 'We're going out in public.'

He told her to leave off her underwear and she stuffed it into the paper bag that had held the wine. They walked out into the street and took a tram to the *Exposition*. Tourists still flocked to the pavilions where the decorative arts of twenty-one countries were on display. The crowds were ordinary people, families, soldiers on leave, a few businessmen.

They went into the Bon Marché pavilion and spent a while moving though the crowds, looking at the sumptuous and imaginative Art Deco displays of furniture, clothes and interiors and touching each other surreptitiously.

One display was of an executive suite from America. The huge black wooden desk stood on chrome-plated semi-circles. The lamp was made of aluminium. Oruela found out this detail because they went up close to the display and hovered until there was no one looking. Then quickly he pulled her behind the scarlet curtains that formed the backdrop to the display. They were in a small space next to the wall, so small that one step backwards and their bodies would be visible to the world under a skin of scarlet.

'Here,' he said. 'Lift up your dress.'

She lifted up her dress as she was asked and he unbuttoned his trousers. The sounds of the tourists outside their curtained world continued as he took her against the wall. His climax came quickly, almost as soon as he penetrated her and moved in the swollen walls of her sex. She felt like a vessel but shé was happy to be one this time. He had satisfied her so well already.

They saw each other every day for a week. They ran over Paris. He had a whole list of places that appealed to him. They were always just out of the public gaze. There was always the chance of getting caught. There

503

was a nook behind the museum at the Palais de Lux-
embourg, a shrubbery within sight of the Arc de
Triomphe, an alleyway just off the Quais. They spent
hours and hours together touching, stroking, cajoling
each other's bodies into heightened life and then they
rushed out and fucked like dogs in the street.

Their adventures were stopped by his wife who
discovered them at the hotel. He apologised fifty times
as she led him away and Oruela waved goodbye. She
had grown philosophical. It didn't matter. She could
find another lover.

But there had been no word from Paul for weeks and
as she sat up in bed in the cheap hotel she had the
uncomfortable realisation that she could no longer fool
herself. She got dressed quickly and sat by the window
facing on to the street, watching the writer and his wife
arguing as they walked down the street. At least they
had each other. There was no getting away from it; Paul
had deserted her. She hated him at that moment. She
hated him for being such a coward as to leave her
without telling her. He might have written even if it
was only to say that he had changed his mind. In the
moment of hating him she also knew that this was a
point of no return. Her heart was closing to him and
with it, all her other feelings. It was a dreadful release.
It made her cry. Everything was one big mess.

Life Could Be a Dream

Jacques Derive jumped up from the mayoral seat in the council chamber and fled out of the door. The members of the roads committee looked at each other in perplexity and debated what to do in his sudden absence.

Meanwhile, in his office, Derive was pouring himself a stiff drink. He grasped the glass with a shaking hand and slung the liquid down his throat in one go. It made no difference. The fiend was still there, hovering in the shadows, he knew it.

Ever since that hell's bitch, Euska Onaldi, had risen from the dead and come to see him, he had been seeing things. He saw them out of the corner of his eye, creatures like little black cats underfoot. It kept happening and the delirium tremors were getting worse. He had begun to see things everywhere. Before tonight's meeting he had seen what looked like a bat hanging from the highest bookshelf in his office. They regularly sat under his chair, whispering and tugging at his socks. But this evening was the first time they had followed him into the council chamber.

He knew she'd cursed him. She was a devil in woman's form. He'd been loath to tell anyone, but now they were coming out in public he knew he must. She had cast her spell on him. She had forced him into a moment of doubt that he, Jacques Derive, had been in the wrong, and once that spell had entered his soul he was doomed unless he could get help. He remembered how the jewel around her hag's neck had flashed in his eyes that afternoon, blinding him to the truth. That was when she must have bewitched him.

He made his excuses to the deputy mayor and left the building. He climbed into the back of his limousine and instructed the driver to take him to a church in one of the poorer neighbourhoods behind the railway station. The priest at St Jude's was well known for being a successful exorcist.

But as the car rolled down the street, Derive suddenly realised a devil had smuggled itself into the upholstery. It was sitting in the corner grinning and ready to leap at him.

He shouted at the driver to stop. 'I'll walk,' he said. 'Take the car home and disinfect it immediately.'

The chauffeur scowled and drove off. Derive pressed on towards St Jude's. The clock above the railway station struck two into the still, hot night as he passed by. At the back of the station he needed to relieve himself and he squeezed in between a bush and a wall and unbuttoned his fly. There was one in his trousers! It flapped its wings and flew at his throat. He screamed and grappled with it until he flung it off and dashed it to the ground.

Gasping, he continued his journey. He turned up the long dark narrow street that led to St Jude's. In the distance the solitary spire of the big church rose into the inky sky. The area was more than just poor. It was Biarritz's most dubious quarter. Its population was mostly transient. This was where unlucky gamblers holed up, waiting for their luck to change. The only natives of the place were the commonest of streetwalkers who plied their trade in the shadows.

A blousy redhead stepped towards him but, seeing who he was, stepped back and snarled. Once he had passed she gave a low whistle. Derive was well known. More than once, during an election campaign, he had made the lives of the women who depended on the street trade a misery, locking them up and having them beaten just so he could gain the votes of the respectable hypocrites in Biarritz society.

In response to the whistle, eyes peered at him with hatred. Women, usually inviting, seethed with anger. As he passed, the local people came out of their doorways and watched. They sensed something was wrong; that he was weak. They laughed at him. One or two began to follow his stumbling tracks up the street.

He could hear them, their soft devil footfalls. He knew it was the devils following. They were almost silent, but he could just hear them. He knew he daren't look back lest they turn him to salt, but it was hard not to. They had him in their power. He willed himself to concentrate on the dark shape of the church in front of him but the power of the devils was too strong. They forced him to look back. They forced him. He turned.

He was so surprised when he saw the grinning women behind him that he tripped. He fell backwards and there was one almighty crack as his skull hit a sharp stone protruding from the kerb.

One of the two women took her chance and reached inside Derive's thin, linen jacket, even as he lay dying, to rob him of his wallet.

'How much is in it?' asked her friend.

'Only ten francs.'

'Pig,' she said, and gave him a kick in the ribs.

The pair disappeared into the shadows and the street was once again quiet and still as Derive's life blood seeped slowly into the gutter.

His death dominated the news for several days. Murder was suspected and almost every resident of the St Jude's district was questioned. No one came forward. No one was caught.

Alix Peine was not directly involved with the murder

investigation team but he had his own ideas and tried to tell his superiors that they were on the wrong track. No one wanted to listen to him. He would prove them wrong. Alix had had feelers out for a long time. He was always on the look-out for anything that might serve to give his career a boost. He knew that Oruela had been freed through the machinations of a mysterious woman. A few notes in an hotel clerk's hand and he knew who the woman was. It was as plain as the buttons on his uniform to Alix that, not content with being free, Oruela, and probably her mother too, had murdered the poor mayor.

On the strength of this, he immediately moved into Genevieve's house to protect her. They decided on separate rooms, for the sake of the servants, but their evenings were spent in the twin pursuits of detective work and debauchery. Genevieve had invented a new game that he loved. Just thinking about it now, as he sat by the window in the station house, looking out onto the street, made his cock grow stiff.

He left the office early and rushed to Bayonne with anticipation in his heart and his loins. Genevieve was waiting for him, as she had been for the past three evenings, with a bottle of cognac on a silver tray on the coffee table, ready to pour him a drink after work. He didn't immediately go and see her, however. He passed by the door of the salon without so much as an acknowledgement. He went straight up to his room and changed into something more comfortable. While he was changing he thought about her. She was always more appreciative of him when he kept her waiting. She was so pliable in that state. He enjoyed being the master of the house when she was like that. As the evening wore on, though, the balance would change subtly. She would become mistress and he would be putty in her hands.

Eventually he came down that evening in his smoking jacket and his patent leather slippers and sat down next to her on the couch. Even before he had sipped the drink that she handed him lovingly, he was elaborating on his plan for tricking Oruela, once they found her, into confessing to the mayor's murder.

Genevieve held up her hand. 'Be quiet,' she said. 'Stop. There is something you have to know, my dear Alix, before you proceed with this plan. Oruela didn't murder her father. She wouldn't hurt a fly. I found that lizard on the seat of her car and I lied about finding it next to Norbert's bed because I wanted the little brat off my hands.'

Alix was struck dumb by this. The words wouldn't come out. What was there to say? What he did know though, was that his cock was stiffening even as he sat there gaping at her. She had such a marvellous neck. Her head, as she spoke, was held high. She had such a firm chin. He was truly at her mercy now. He wanted to bury his face in that neck. He reached for her. 'You're so vicious. I love you madly,' he said as he brushed her skin with his lips. 'Tell me. Did you kill him?'

'Oh good God, no,' said Genevieve. 'He died of his own accord, I suspect. He was always being ill and vomiting. I used to hear him. It was absolutely disgusting.'

Alix drew back. The thought of Norbert Bruyere vomiting had destroyed the mood somewhat. He took a sip of his drink.

'Do you want to play doggy now?' she said, suddenly. She held her head high again. Her lips were a little pursed.

'Oh yes,' he groaned. It was his favourite game. They played it only when she allowed it.

'Go upstairs then,' she said, 'and get prepared. I will join you.'

Alix ran up the stairs two by two and threw off all his clothes. He rummaged in her wardrobe and found the mink that he was to wear to be her dog. The feel of it was heaven to him. The lining was cool on his skin. He slipped it on and crouched down on all fours waiting for her.

509

'Fetch your leash,' she told him, when she entered the room.

He crawled off into the wardrobe and expertly fished out the leash with his teeth.

She put it round his neck and led him around the room threatening him with the direst punishments if he was a bad dog. The things she would do were too tantalising to resist, so he bit her leg and she immmediately put her threats into action. She beat him severely with the leash until he cried for her to stop.

'Undress too!' he pleaded.

Eventually she gave in and undressed and pretended to be a doggy too. He liked to sniff her and she did the same to him until they were both so excited he mounted her, just like a dog and took her. She howled fit to bring the house down.

After dinner in the dining room, when the servants had withdrawn, he reached for her hand, and said, 'We have to get married soon. The waiting is driving me to distraction. When will it be the proper time?'

Genevieve smiled at him. 'It happens that I am going to see my lawyer tomorrow. The final accounts are ready. This time tomorrow I will know exactly how I stand. Once I have control of Norbert's money, then, my darling, of course I will marry you and make a politician out of you.'

Alix was overcome with emotion. 'With Derive dead, there is bound to be room for new blood in the town hall. We will go far together, my dearest one.'

'Yes, my sweet,' she said and she took a morsel of pudding between her two fingers and popped it in his mouth.

The next day at the office Alix told the sergeant to make his own damn coffee. The sergeant replied that he would be out of a job if he didn't do what he was told and Alix laughed at him. The police station was just over the road from the lawyer's office and he saw

510

Genevieve going in just minutes after the coffee incident. She looked delightful. She wore her floatiest of floaty black dresses. Just thinking about what that respectable looking woman got up to under her big iron bed at home gave Alix a stiff cock in his trousers.

Inside the lawyer's office, though, things were grim. He came straight to the point. He told Genevieve that Norbert's accounts were in such a bad state once they were finally unravelled, that everything would have to be sold to pay off his creditors. There was nothing left. Not a sou.

'What about the house?' asked Genevieve. Her voice was little more than a frightened whisper.

'It must be sold,' said the lawyer. 'I suggest that as a matter of urgency, you get in touch with your family. I will hold off the sale of the house for as long as possible but I'm afraid eventually the creditors will have to be paid.'

Genevieve composed herself before she left. She crossed the street and made straight for Alix's office. The sergeant was rude and nearly made her burst out crying but she kept hold of herself as she sat on the wooden bench and waited. Eventually, Alix came out and led her into an office that looked out on the street. It was one he shared with another man, he told her, the other man was out at lunch.

Genevieve plucked up her courage and told him what had just happened. He was very sympathetic. He was marvellous, in fact. He took her in his arms while she had her little weep and told her everything would be all right.

Then he made sure she was comfortable in the car and told her to rest during the afternoon and not to worry.

'I'll have your cognac waiting for you at – ' she began.

'Oh, don't go to the trouble, my dear,' he said. 'I have an engagement this evening. I won't be back until late.'

511

Genevieve went home and spent some time going through her jewellery box. There were a couple of expensive pieces and she must be sure they didn't fall into the hands of creditors. That done she tried to fill in the hours until he came home, but it was hard. There was so little to do. Then it got dark, the clocked ticked on and he still didn't come. Eventually she went to bed and fell into a restless sleep.

Alix, meanwhile, was at La Maison Rose with the sergeant who he had offered to treat him to the services of a whore for being so bad tempered earlier that day. The sergeant had accepted his apology and they were having a great time. But even as he had his hand up the skirt of a pretty little whore, Alix was pondering his next move. He'd spent the earlier part of the evening with the widow Derive. She was so charmed that a young man like him should take the trouble to visit an old woman like herself that she gave him plenty to drink and listened as he told her the story of his life. She dimpled when he chided her for saying she was old. Why, fifty wasn't old, not for a woman as handsome as the widow Derive . . .

All in the Game

*A*nnette had been very busy. She was training to be
a croupier at the casino. Her plan was to travel
once she was good at it, to work the transatlantic liners.
She had been so busy that she hadn't seen much of
Paul at all, apart from saying hello in the afternoons as
she rushed off to work. Nevertheless she had noticed
how sad he looked and she had made an effort to invite
him over to eat. As soon as he arrived, while she was
still preparing the meal, he spilled out his heart.
Annette listened and then she rounded on him.

'You're a fool,' she said. 'I can't believe you can be
such a fool!'

'Hold on,' he said, a little peeved. 'Just hold on. I'm
not really such a fool. She's gone off to Paris to have
the time of her life. If she wanted to include me she
would have written. She would have told me about all
the exciting things she's been doing! I think it's pretty
damn obvious by now that she's just too busy to think
of us down here, of me. I can understand it. This place
holds terrible memories for her. She's probably put it all
behind her.'

'Rubbish,' said Annette. 'You'll get nowhere sitting
on your fine *derrière* understanding, my friend. I think
that twisted little fiend has eaten away at your brains.

513

Hasn't it occurred to you that Oruela will be expecting to hear from you?'

Paul drained his wine glass and grinned a rueful grin. There was an element of truth in Annette's prognosis that Renée could twist his mind. He didn't like the idea but it could be true. She had pressured him not to go to Paris until the outcome of the race with the countess's driver was known. 'Renée needs me,' he said. 'She's in above her head.'

'I'd watch her drown and say good riddance,' said Annette. She detested Renée.

'She hasn't changed my mind. I still love Oruela,' said Paul.

'Well, for goodness' sake tell her then. Write to her and explain your duty or whatever you call it. Otherwise you'll lose her. I warn you.'

And with that they closed the subject and ate dinner. That night Paul went home and wrote. He wrote eight pages. He explained exactly what was happening, the whole of it. All he left out was that Renée was still sleeping in his bed. But it was there, between the lines for anyone with insight to guess at. He knew Oruela had that insight. But he was making his own gamble – with his hopes and dreams, his love as the stake. He rose early the following morning and posted it in the box at the end of the road.

At first, when Renée had asked Paul to stay, she was telling the truth that she was in over her head. At first she needed an escort to be seen with. The countess kept her promise. She showed Renée, and Paul, what her entourage did for their keep. When they arrived at the first 'party' in her luxurious, specially furnished hotel suite, the young men and women whom Renée had first seen at the racetrack were already semi-naked.

The theme was 'Rome'. Paul and Renée were unaware of this when they were asked and there were other guests in ordinary evening dress. It was only the countess's employees who were in Roman attire, show-

514

ing off their fine limbs, a breast here, a flash of hip there.

There was a meal for twenty or so people, the ones dressed in their own clothes. A whole pig was carved in the room and served by the young slaves. There was an abundance of wine, of fruit served Roman style. It all quite appealed to Paul's sense of theatre.

But there was an undercurrent of abuse. The way the countess ordered the slaves about, the way, as the guests got more and more drunk, they too ordered the slaves to do certain things . . . It was getting out of hand. Paul wanted to leave.

But Renée insisted they stay. After the dinner was over the slaves had mostly been undressed. Some still wore a belt or a sash or anklets. The guests had taken to pulling them by these pieces of bodily decoration. One middle-aged man was being given fellatio under the tablecloth.

The countess clapped her hands and the slaves rearranged the furniture so that the guests could sit on chairs around the perimeter of the room and the centre was a mass of cushions. The gorgeous young people arranged themselves on the cushions and the orgy began in earnest. The carpet became a mass of naked bodies, clawing and sucking, rising and falling with sex and sweat. The other guests were invited to join in if they wished. The young slaves came and encouraged them to do so. They draped themselves over portly middle-aged men and women. Two young men stripped a perfumed matron of her evening clothes, her corsets, and plunged into her rolls of flesh with glee.

The countess merely watched. So did Renée and Paul. And the countess watched them.

Later, when they got home, Renée and Paul had savage sex. Her pale skin glistened in the moonlight that filtered through the unshuttered window and her taut little body writhed under him with an urgency that was irresistible. She called him a hypocrite the next day

515

when he said he didn't want to go to any more of the parties.

'You were just as turned on as anyone,' she sneered.

'Of course I was,' he said. 'How could anyone not be? But I didn't like the abuse of power.'

'You're stupid,' she said. 'It isn't an abuse. It's their job. It's what she pays them for. If it wasn't for her, those talentless fools wouldn't have enough money to eat. She told me, she finds them virtually in the gutter.'

'Exactly,' said Paul. 'And that's where you'll end up if you get more involved with this absurd set of people.'

'They're not a "set" as you call them. They are nothing. It's the countess that creates it all, pays for it all. She's just amusing herself. She could walk away from them at the drop of a hat. She told me so herself. You're just jealous.'

That little discussion ended predictably, with Renée slamming out of the house. She told the countess about it and the countess agreed, to a point. She didn't think Paul was jealous, just full of bourgeois inhibitions.

Renée knew she wanted more. She felt sultry all the time she was with the countess, knowing she could have anything she wanted because the countess had the money and the set-up to order anything. The countess encouraged Renée to try out being a master. She presented her with a couple of young boys one day and told her they were hers. Renée ordered them to wrestle and she and the countess watched as their firm naked bodies gripped and pulled and mauled at each other. Renée liked being a master; it was the other side of the coin from being spanked and it was just as captivating.

The countess had a special thing she liked. She called it a private ceremony, but she had about five or six of the young slaves with her when she did it. She wanted Renée to join in. Renée dithered a bit and tantalised her by not agreeing immediately. Renée was well aware that much of her power over the countess was dependent on her not giving away too much too soon.

516

'I might agree,' she told her, 'if it doesn't involve me undressing. I'm very shy of anyone seeing my body.'

'No,' said the countess. 'It's only me that undresses, me and the slaves. All I would ask you to do is touch me when I shout for it, with this.' And she unwrapped the silk scarf from around her neck. 'Please, Renée, say you'll do it. I must do it. Even if you don't want to. I must. It's a compulsion. It's time.'

Renée couldn't resist finding out what it was and so she agreed. The slaves entered the room and undressed the countess down to her garters and stockings, which they left on her. She had a fine body for a woman in her forties, if a little too skinny in places. The slaves helped her arrange herself on the couch where she proceeded to masturbate. The slaves stared at her intently, as, presumably, instructed before.

'I like to be watched,' said the countess. 'When I tell you, you must tickle my skin with the scarf here,' and she raised her legs and touched her squashed buttocks.

She closed her eyes and rubbed herself harder and harder. Suddenly she shouted 'Now!' and Renée draped the scarf lightly at the place where she had been asked to. The countess's body convulsed. Tears streamed from her eyes as she orgasmed.

Every night at first Renée went home to Paul and cuddled up to him in bed and he put his arm around her and held her. Almost every night she whispered long into the darkness, 'Don't leave me. Don't leave me. You keep me sane. Your body is the world I must keep touching. Your hands are the ties that keep me here. I would be lost. I would be lost without you . . .'

After a while she no longer whispered these things. She merely clung to him. And then after another little while, she stopped coming home every night. The race was drawing near, she told Paul, and she trained every day and camped out by the track in a tent the countess had provided for her. She came back sometimes and she cuddled up to him silently. They no longer argued at all.

517

It was the day of the race that Paul posted his letter to Oruela. Renée had asked him to be there for the start at eleven.

Renée woke early and tried to shake off the grogginess of the champagne of the night before. She had escaped making love with the countess by a whisper. In the fireglow the air had been heavy with desire. The countess had dismissed her retinue and they were left alone. Renée felt the power she had and revelled in it. She knew she must win today to avoid losing that power. She was nervous.

She ate breakfast and went across to the car. The mechanic was under the bonnet.

'Everything all right?' she asked. She suddenly had a sense of how mad this was, how unequal. The countess and her circus were all out, milling around Pierre's car. Here was she, just herself and her mechanic. Where was Paul? It was 10.45 and he had promised to be here. She felt so terribly alone.

But there he was, walking across the field. He seemed so ordinary to her. He was an embarrassment. Why hadn't he brought any of his friends with him to give her moral support?

'Jump in,' said the mechanic.

Her nerves were so taut she sprang into the car like a cat. Paul stood next to the car.

'Gas,' called the mechanic.

She put her foot down. The engine roared.

'Right,' said the mechanic. 'She's as good as she can be,' and he lowered the bonnet, twisting the silver catch shut and giving it a little pat.

Renée slipped on her hat and goggles and adjusted them. She glanced over towards the countess. Paul wished her luck. The mechanic ran with the car out of the paddock and on to the track.

She took the car round once, coasting, listening to the engine, feeling it, becoming part of it. One twitch of her toe and this magnificent machine would respond as if it was an extension of herself. She coasted to the start grid and did some regular breathing.

He was coasting now, too, the countess's driver. She didn't think of him as a person, although she knew damn well who he was. She thought of him as a mythical beast, half-man, half-car, her sexual opposite . . . This was going to be fun. A surge of excitement went through her. The flags were waving. He drew alongside. The leader car came on the track. They would follow it round once and then the race would begin. There were twelve laps.

It began and the leader car slowly picked up speed. They were half way round, coming up to the start line.

Her foot went down hard as the leader disappeared. Hard but smooth so that the engine appreciated it. She knew how to control this car. She knew what it liked. She took the lead and a glow of satisfaction descended on her. It shouldn't be too hard to hold on to a lead for twelve laps; all she had to do was prevent him from overtaking. She had the prime position and she knew it. She set the pace lower than full speed.

He made his first attempt to take her on a bend. She felt him coming up on her flank, but she had the reserve power to pull away and block his chances. He went down in her estimation. Fancy trying it on a bend!

They settled like a needle on a record player, into a groove, for the next four laps. Then he tried again, this time on a straight. He pulled alongside her, glanced at her and grinned. She ignored him and pulled ahead, but this time, instead of hanging back, he was right on her tail, forcing her to go faster than she wanted to. Her adrenalin pumped. It was impossible! He couldn't do it! It was a bluff. She steeled her nerves and raised her gas toe very very slightly.

He hadn't expected it, obviously, because she felt the terrifying brush of rubber on her tail. The steering wheel wobbled. She held on tight but did not increase her speed forcing him to drop back before the bend.

Now they had a race! She was prepared for anything!

On the sixth he tried the same trick again but she was prepared for him this time and she fought him off with panache. Ha! Let him sweat! She took the seventh and eighth with nerves of steel. Then, on the ninth, he came right up close again, right on her tail, bumper to bumper. She felt a moment of disbelief. Surely he wouldn't continue. She had to go flat out this time. He seemed determined to force her off the road! They raced the tenth at full speed.

On the eleventh lap, on the straight, he pulled alongside her. She put the throttle down full but the bend was too near! She had to slow or die. He took her, the bastard!

She caught up with him again on the penultimate straight. But the next bend was now in sight. A moment of doubt seized her. She couldn't do it! She didn't have the skill to take him on the bend so she sat on his tail as they hurtled round it, reserving all her energy for the final straight.

As they hammered into it she pulled out and floored the throttle. She got alongside, inching forward, inching. The finish line was in sight. She willed the car to go faster. She pushed and pushed, concentrating with all her resources.

The car responded. She was even surprised herself when she crossed the finish line just feet in front of him. The two cars coasted off the track and came to a halt. Pierre Suliman jumped out of his car and came over to congratulate her. The countess was there too. Renée stripped off her goggles and her hat and climbed out of the car.

'Congratulations,' said the countess.

Renée went to her and hugged her. She felt the woman's body thrill at her touch. Renée gave her a long, outrageous kiss on the lips and then they walked, arms around each other, to the big tent where champagne corks were already popping.

Paul stood at the trackside. It surprised him that she didn't even give him a backwards glance. He considered

520

going into the tent, just to say goodbye, but then he thought better of it. He left her car where it was and thumbed a lift back to Biarritz.

Back in Paris Paul's letter sat in the Onaldi pigeonhole along with the rest of the mail. Euska and Oruela had gone to the country. They had taken a small cottage near Albert's houseboat and were enjoying the ease and beauty of the clear autumn days. The river slunk like a gleaming snake through the plain, reflecting the sun. Small patches of orange and gold appeared daily on the trees, heralding winter. Morning mists rose from the land and hovered, fruits began to drop.

When they had been there for a couple of days Euska announced that she was planning to sail to Rio with Ernesto. He wanted to get married at sea.

A deep indefinable anger took hold of Oruela. She became irritated with every little thing. They bitched about household tasks, about what to do for the day. Eventually Euska asked her to come out with what was really bothering her.

'I feel deserted,' said Oruela. 'I feel deserted by everyone. First Paul, now you. What am I going to do with my life?'

One of the crowd in Paris had suggested she have analysis, that she go to Vienna. She didn't want to. She had always imagined Vienna to be a cold, soulless place. But she didn't know what to do. Paris was not turning out as she had hoped.

'Come to Rio,' said Euska. 'At least for the winter. You can decide what you want to do after that.'

'I don't think I want to,' said Oruela. 'I want my own life.'

'Why don't you write to Paul?' said Euska one afternoon as they were walking along the river towards the houseboat. 'Why don't you ask him what is going on? My instincts tell me there's a reason for all this. I suspect he's trapped in something that his honour won't let him desert.'

521

So Oruela tried to write, but each time she wrote a few sentences she ended up in tears. It was pathetic. Her pride wouldn't let her ask the kind of questions she wanted to ask, not of Paul, not even of Euska. Why have you deserted me? Why? The wound inflicted by Euska was an old, old one. She dreamed of a misshapen child sucking at the breasts of a wolf. The wolf changed into a man, the man was Norbert Bruyere. She woke up covered in sweat.

The local men watched her as she walked the countryside, like cows watch, turning from their business to stare impassively and chew. They had time on their hands. The harvest work was over. In the village bar they played chess and a young man offered to teach her.

He was very young, too young to leave home and go to Paris. He was a farmer's son but he was a poet, he told her. He wrote in cramped handwriting. He had pale skin with a fine down on his chin and around his eyes was the palest mauve. He was slender and fit and his movements were graceful, a touch feminine.

He explained the pieces to her in human terms. The king, he said, was stolid. Seemingly powerful, he was in reality very vulnerable whereas the queen was emancipated and bold. She had licence to roam wherever she wanted to. The power was largely hers. He reserved his pity for the pawns, the mass of humanity allowed to advance only to get them playing the game and then restricted. The bishop, tricky like any cleric, attacked from an angle and the knight, the impetuous gallant, could jump to the lady's rescue. The rook he described last; the rook he said was decisive, an officer in the royal guard, making his decisions and going straight to the heart of the matter.

As he finished explaining he looked straight at Oruela, took her hand and made her move a pawn.

Oruela played her first game intently, unaware of his quick little *double entendres* except on the periphery of

522

her consciousness. He didn't let her win. He showed her her mistakes and advised her to learn by them.

She was amazed at his wisdom. For such a young man, a boy really, his intellect was so acute. She played on regardless, thinking of him as sexless, his beauty yet unripe. He was precocious, nothing more. But every day spent in the misty autumnal countryside took her more and more into a dreamlike state, a sultry, full mood. As they played in the evening in the quiet café getting used to each other, she began to notice him and wonder if he had ever tasted the rich fruits of a woman's body. She began to respond to his little jokes, to his cleverness, less as a mere companion, more as an older woman.

One evening it grew cold and the proprietor of the café lit a fire. It roared in the grate and was too hot. Oruela took off her jacket and as she turned back to the table she caught him looking at her bare arms. She felt protective towards him, naturally, because she was older. That evening he told her about his frustration living under his parents' wing, of his dreams. She began to muse on the fantasy of taking him under her wing, taking him to Paris. He would, she thought, become a real friend to her. He would be so grateful to her he would never leave her side. She didn't examine her fantasies. They gave her pleasure.

He walked her home each night if Euska wasn't in the café, back to the cottage where a light would be burning in the darkness. They would draw closer and see that Euska was reading. Oruela opened up to him on these walks, told him about the unusual relationship with her mother, the frustrations that she still felt. Her admissions made her feel that they had common ground, that they were equal in a way more profound than mere years. Their friendship stepped outside the boundaries of the evening's games. He defied his father and took time off from the autumn work of the farm to walk with her. He taught her to perfect her techniques in horse-riding. They galloped through the lanes and

523

across the fields. One day they went deep into the woods. The horses' hooves thundered through the sweet-smelling forest as they raced along the track. There was tension in her knees and thighs as she stood in the stirrups; the body of the mare she rode was warm with exertion underneath her. She was hot herself.

Lauren beat her, as usual. She chided him as they led the sweating horses to drink at the river.

'You should let me win something!' she said, laughing. 'You're better at everything than I am!'

He told her off. 'Women need to strive to be better than men. If they are going to have real power in the modern world they need to be pushed to the limit by men like myself who believe in their power.'

As he spoke she knew that there was one area of human experience that she knew much more of than he, one thing that she could teach. Something he needed.

She walked away from him, back in among the trees where no eyes could see them. She walked slowly. He caught up with her. When she came to a glade she stopped and lifted her face to the misty sun above. He stood in front of her, looking at her. 'You're so beautiful,' he said. She looked into his eyes. He came close and touched her face with his fingertips. Their lips were close. She waited. His kiss was long and wet and explorative. His tongue searched for hers.

His fine brown hair at his neck was soft and young, his shoulders and back were firm and slender. She slid her hands into the warmth between his jacket and shirt and held him lightly. She was excited by his inexperienced desperation. When he kissed her neck, pausing on her Adam's apple, tickling it, she bent back her head and exulted in her maturity and power. His hands unbuttoned her waistcoat and her blouse with terrible urgency and he fed at her breasts like a baby.

His hands were less certain as they touched her hips' roundness. They fluttered down to her thighs and she imagined he had never touched a woman there before.

But he raised the hem of her soft woollen skirt forcefully and grasped her soft thighs in between her garters and her knickers strongly, pushing his still clothed hips into her sex.

'Let's see what you're made of, little boy,' she said, unbuttoning the rough woollen cloth at his fly.

He glowered at her and looked down to see his own stiff sex emerge from its shelter. 'What do you think? Will it satisfy you?'

It was huge! She was secretly amazed at the size of it. Her whole body was amazed; alarm bells, tiny ones, rang in her mind, in her womb.

'Suck it,' he commanded, pushing her shoulders down.

'No,' she said. 'I want it here,' and she held it and pushed her own sex towards it. In truth she thought it would choke her if she took it into her mouth.

They searched for a soft, leafy spot under the trees and lay down. He pulled off his trousers and kneeled between her legs. He spread the rosy folds of her sex with a strange precision that echoed in his young face as the twisting of his cherry-red lips. His lashes shadowed the pale mauve of his eyes. He opened her sex so wide she felt the cool air chill the inner folds. She felt tight at the same time, she anticipated pain.

Then he was in, a little at first, pushing against the resistance of her panicking vaginal walls. And then the soft walls relaxed, opened and she took him all. The surprise of finding that her sex could stretch to give him a home was delightful. He moved with a frantic passion, undiluted passion. She held his downy young arse in her hands and marvelled at the firmness of it, the way the muscles moved. She opened, curled her legs over his calves, stretched her body to push her clitoris against the board that was his belly.

She had expected him to come quickly but he seemed to be in no hurry so she relaxed, she opened yet more, felt him deep inside her, pushed against him and had her orgasm as he had only just begun to emit the

525

sounds of endings. With his final thrust he tore into her, like someone leaping over a cliff. Then he was quiet and he quickly rolled off her.

She lay alone, looking up at the sky between the leaves for a moment or two, then she felt his hand on her arm, stroking it like a little puppy wanting attention. She looked at him, his eyelashes sweeping his pale skin. She reached for him and took him in her arms.

They rode back slowly. He chattered nervously about all kinds of things. She wanted to ask was that his first time but he chattered and chattered.

The next time they played chess he was more damning in his criticism. He was sarcastic and hurt her feelings. She told him and he apologised. She felt as if he were acting like a woman who has lost her mystery to a seducer. It didn't endear him to her, it irritated her. She made an excuse for the following evening and went out to dinner in a nearby town with Euska. They went to a small theatre and laughed at the farce that was playing.

The next time she saw him she told him about the farce and he laughed at her for going to see something so unfashionable. She was really a bourgeois at heart, he said. She was happy with the mediocre.

Oruela felt hurt but she was still insecure. The failure that she felt she'd made of Paris so far had left her unsure. She imagined her clever little chess player was right. Her tastes were perhaps, dubious, unrefined as yet. Her doubts made her want his instruction and her body remembered his, how easily she had reached a climax with him. They stole into a barn on the way home and he took her in the hay.

Euska began to talk about going to Paris. Ernesto would be there soon. She had a lot to organise. They would be flying to London first. The liner they had chosen sailed from Southampton. Everything would be a rush.

Oruela thought there was something else that Euska

526

wasn't saying. Her little chess player had taught her to watch every move the other player made very carefully.

'I might stay here a while,' said Oruela casually.

'No!' said Euska, betraying herself.

'I'm going out for a walk,' said Oruela haughtily.

Euska rose to her feet. 'Oruela, please stay. We need to talk to each other. I thought that being here in the country we would be thrown together and we would have to. I have spoken to Albert about this. He agrees with me. It's no use – '

'What do you mean speaking to my friend about me?' shouted Oruela.

'Why shouldn't I?' said Euska, calmly. 'We both care about you.'

'I resent it,' said Oruela.

'I think Albert resents the fact that you've hardly seen him at all since we've been here.'

Oruela walked out of the cottage and Euska kicked herself for not keeping to the point. Her motherhood was lying heavily on her shoulders. It wasn't easy picking up the threads. The threads that had been broken so many years before. She didn't for one minute disapprove of Oruela's sexual experimentation but she observed that whatever was going on, of which she knew very little, was not making her daughter happy. She cursed Paul Phare, she cursed her own naïvety in thinking that Oruela, free of the Bruyeres and of the disastrous consequences of her own fateful decision, would find the path to a sense of herself an easy one.

Oruela walked to the village and found her little chess player in the café. He drank more these days, she noticed. He used not to drink during the day. When he saw her a slow smile spread across his face. He was playing a game with one of the old men and he went back to it.

Sitting, watching them and thinking, Oruela knew she didn't want this life at all, out here in the country. When the game finished she asked him to come to a

527

corner and talk. As he stood up from the table he was swaying.

She told him quietly that she was leaving, that their affair was over.

'No it's not,' he said, grabbing her arm roughly. 'No it's not. Not while I have life in my body.'

His words, the way his slow stare rested on her, chilled her to the bone. 'I'm sorry,' she said. She got up and walked out.

'No you don't!' he shouted.

Heads turned. He ran up the street after her, shouting, 'I love you. I love you. Don't leave me.'

She walked quickly and broke into a run but he was faster than her and fleet of foot. He caught up easily and held her arm again, tightly. He spoke loudly. A woman cleaning her doorstep stopped and stared at them.

Conscious of the attention they were drawing Oruela told him to keep his voice down.

'I won't!' he cried. 'I want the whole world to hear how much I love you!' His grip on her arm was hurting her. She pulled away but he held her tight. 'It's not over,' he said. 'Understand? It's not over.'

She struggled with him and eventually broke free. She walked quickly back towards the cottage. He kept up with her. 'You can't just use me and then go back to your comfortable life in Paris. You can't.' Over and over he said the same thing until she began to cry, even as she hurried along. His voice felt like torture. She ran into the cottage only to find it deserted. He followed her in and kept on talking. She became afraid he would force himself on her but he didn't, he just kept talking in that same voice, accusing her. Then he left, slamming the door after him.

The tears that flowed from her came from a deep well of sadness. She cried and she cried and she cried. Euska came back and found her still weeping.

The following morning dawned bright and they packed quickly and took a taxi to the station. Oruela looked over her shoulder frequently to see if he was following them, but the train drew in and they got on without bother.

Only when it was drawing out did she see him running alongside it swiftly, running, running, just running. She knew it was a threat, a gesture, no more, just to torment her.

That same evening the slop cart went as usual to the prison in St Trou. The driver parked the funny little three-wheeler under the kitchen chute and called at the kitchen door. The chef opened it and let him in.

The darkness of the compound was broken only by the single lamp burning at the porchway of the reception. The rooftops stood black against the deep night sky.

Kim caught her breath and waited behind a big chimney-stack until she heard the gate below locking up again. Then she ran at a crouch to the edge of the roof of the cell-block and looked down. The kitchen roof was a drop of about ten feet. She sprang into the air.

The roof hit her feet and she went into a roll, coming to a stop at the edge. She crawled along to the drain-pipe. Testing it first and finding it firm she swung her leg down on to the brick and carefully began to climb down. She dropped the last couple of feet into the slop car and flattened herself on the floor. She waited.

The sound of the mechanism of the chute door opening at the other end broke the quiet. She heard the men's voices as they lifted the bin. She heard the slop sliding down and the next moment she was buried under a huge mound of stinking pigswill.

The cart drove out of the gate and down the small country road towards the farm. As it reached a bend a figure leapt out of the back and stood gulping the air for a second or two. She stumbled into the wooded bank and dropped down into the river.

* * *

529

Paul had been to an old friend's house for a wonderful dinner. He was saying farewell to people he knew. His letter hadn't been answered but he had decided he was going to Paris anyway. A collector had bought more of his photographs, so he had plenty to live on and he had been reading about the new films that were being made in Paris. The dealer said he would introduce him to some people. Paul was unhappy that he hadn't heard from Oruela but he thought that perhaps if he was there and they should happen to run into each other he could at least explain and renew their friendship. He had new strength, new purpose. Whatever the future held, it was his and he could only try . . .

He was too drunk to find his key easily and he fumbled around on the doorstep looking for it. When he did locate it he muttered to it because it wouldn't go in the lock. Finally it went in and he turned it. He was about to step into the hallway when he felt a pair of hands on his back and he was pushed roughly inside.

In the darkness he fell against the wall and swore. He could hear her breathing hard. 'Damn it, Renée!' he cried.

'Please don't be frightened,' said an unfamiliar voice in the darkness. 'I didn't mean to hurt you.'

Paul sobered up immediately and punched the light switch. Kim stood there, filthy and blinking in the electric light. He looked her up and down and was not impressed. 'Who are you?' What do you want?' he demanded.

'I'm Oruela's friend. She gave me your address and I thought I might be able to trust you. I've escaped.'

The sense that this girl's whole life depended on his next words touched Paul's compassion. 'It's OK,' he said.

'I'm sorry I pushed you. I didn't want to have this conversation on the road,' she said.

Paul had a flash of recognition. 'Are you the dancer?' he asked.

'Yes,' she replied.

'Well,' he said. 'You'd better have a hot bath!'

She staggered, the relief and tiredness hitting her all at once. He took her arm and showed her upstairs. The water was not very hot but it was warm and when he had found her something to put on he tottered downstairs and brewed some coffee. He took it, on a tray, to the armchair by the window, closed the shutters and fell asleep.

Kim got half a tubful out of the geyser and washed the accumulated grime of the forest from her body. Her skin was scratched and torn in places and discoloured with bruises. She applied some of the witch hazel she found in the bathroom cabinet and wrapped herself in Paul's second-best dressing-gown. She padded down the stairs to find him still asleep.

She decided to drink the coffee without waking him up. It was delightful but it made her realise how hungry she was. She looked about in the kitchen for something to eat. There was bread but not much. She hesitated.

'Eat it!' said Paul behind her, yawning.

She turned to him with a grateful smile and he realised with a start that, without the dirt, she was gorgeous. He suddenly got very nervous and fled up to bed.

Kim's night's sleep was so sweet and so comfortable that it was really late when she got up. Something wonderful was cooking downstairs. She wrapped his dressing-gown round her and followed her nose. Paul had made fresh brioche. They ate it with butter and *confiture* and drank coffee. Kim filled in the details of her escape.

'How on earth could you hold your breath for so long?' he asked.

'I used to do it as a kid,' she said. 'In Martinique. We used to dive for coins and jewels that fell from the rich people's boats. We became a legend. The children that do it now are famous in America and tourists come especially to see them and throw them coins for luck.'

She had stolen a bicycle and rode all the way. She

531

planned to escape France, she told him, exactly the way she had entered it, by stowing away at La Rochelle on a ship. It would be easy enough if she could find one with a Caribbean crew who would help her. The hard part would be getting to La Rochelle.

'I'm too visible to travel in the open, even if I had the money to do it.' She paused and looked him straight in the eye. 'I don't plan to inconvenience you more than necessary. I shall be gone tonight. I just needed a rest.'

'Oh, don't go!' said Paul. 'I mean not before you want to. I'll be going in a week or so but you can stay here.'

'Thank you, I'd like to stay a little while,' she said 'But they may come looking for me.'

'I doubt if they'll come here,' he said. 'And I think I know a hiding place in an emergency.'

He led her upstairs to the darkroom. 'Under here,' he said and he removed a board from the underside of the developing tank. The space was small but she was slender enough. 'Try it,' he said.

He held the board while she wrapped herself around the U-bend like a handsome snake. His eyes lit up at the sight of her lithe legs. He repositioned the hardboard and pushed it back in place. But it wouldn't quite go.

'Wait,' she muffled from behind the board.

He stepped back as she rolled out from among the cobwebs lightly and stripped herself of the robe. She was entirely naked underneath and unselfconscious.

His gaze struck her like a wave strikes a beach. She tried not to think about it as she wrapped herself around the pipe again. This time the board fitted back nicely. She could be safely hidden.

Paul repeated that it was very unlikely they would come. In fact he repeated everything he'd already said twice more and went on about all kinds of rubbish, physically maintaining as much distance from her as the small darkroom would allow. He stood holding the board like an advertisement for a department store and looked stolidly at her feet. They were long and flat, the skin irresistibly paler on their underside.

She pulled on the robe and belted it and stood looking around her as he replaced the board.

'Alternatively,' he said, once she was dressed and they were back down in the studio. 'You could come to Paris. It would be easy enough to disappear in a large city. I'm sure Oruela would love to see you, if she's still there.'

'How is she?' asked Kim. 'I haven't heard from her in a while, a long while, in fact. I'm not very good at letter-writing I'm afraid. I suppose she got fed up of writing and not getting a reply.'

Paul was stroking Nefi, who had come to see what was going on. 'I don't know how she is. I haven't heard anything at all.'

'Since when?' asked Kim.

'Since she went to Paris. Oh, I know I should have written to her earlier, but I wrote a fortnight ago and she hasn't replied,' he said sadly.

'It doesn't make any sense,' said Kim, almost to herself.

Just then there was a knock at the door and Kim flew upstairs to her hiding-place. It was Daisy and Annette with some fish for Nefi and a little something for the human spirit. Paul made an excuse and left them in the studio while he went to tell Kim it was all right to come downstairs if she wanted to. 'They're safe,' he said, 'but I haven't said you're here.'

Kim decided there was no harm in it, if they could be trusted. There might be advantage in knowing a few more people, in case she decided to stick with her original plan and not go to Paris.

Daisy took to Kim immediately. Her forthright way of approaching things was easy to like. And Annette remembered her dancing.

'Still no word?' said Annette.

Paul shook his head.

'There's a telephone here, isn't there?' asked Kim.

533

Paul nodded.

'It's a relatively new invention, Paul,' said Daisy, 'but you pick it up like this, see and you dial the number . . .'

'Look,' said Paul, 'I want Oruela to make her own decision, can you understand that? Anyway, I need some air. I'm going for a walk. Come on, Nefi.' Nefi trotted like an obedient dog out of the front door with him.

The three women exchanged looks as he left, expressing varying degrees of impatience. Men!

'In a way I can understand it,' said Daisy. 'She does have to make her own decision now. He's written to her.'

'Trust an Englishwoman to say that,' said Annette. 'Fair play and cricket, what? I wonder how you lot across the water ever get together.'

'What do you think I'm doing here?' said Daisy with a dirty grin.

'A man who lets you make your own decisions and isn't trying to mould you all the time is a rare thing,' said Kim. 'Worth having I reckon.'

'True,' said the other two sagely.

All I Want

Oruela arrived back in Paris feeling beaten and exhausted. She trudged up the stairs leaving Euska to collect the post, and opened the door of the apartment. As she walked into her mother's living-room it suddenly dawned on her how much she hated this place. It represented a life she had missed, one that could never be replaced. She made a decision. She would move out. She would find work. Anything to shrug off the awful sense of loss she felt in these rooms.

'There's a letter for you,' said Euska, as she came in. 'From Biarritz.'

Oruela went to her own room and opened the envelope. She curled herself up in the chair by the window to read it. It stirred mixed feelings within her. When she saw his name on the last page, which naturally she looked at first, her heart leapt and she willed it to be good news. But as she read, she grew angry and upset. If her own charms, if the love that she'd thought they had, weren't enough to pull him away from his sense of responsibility to a dead love affair, what was she supposed to do? What use was there in waiting? Only a nice girl would wait and she didn't feel nice. She felt betrayed.

She tossed the letter on the coffee table and left it

there. Over dinner that night she told Euska that she was going to find her own apartment and go back to modelling to pay the rent.

Euska agreed it was a good idea. 'But you don't have to get a job,' she said. 'I can give you an allowance. Let me, it will give you time to make a decision about what you really want to do.'

It wasn't easy to resist. Why work when you can be kept? Oruela rose early the next morning to go apartment-hunting.

The nice young porter stopped her on the way out. There was another letter. When she saw Paul's writing on the envelope she felt happier. It was a good sign. She put it in the deep pocket of her coat.

She called at a place that was advertised in the newspaper and didn't like it. She read the letter over coffee at her favourite café.

He told her about the result of the race, about Kim, and said he was arriving in Paris on a date about a week away. He hoped, he said, that he could visit her.

A smug little smile crossed over Oruela's face as she replaced the letter in the envelope and drank the remainder of her coffee. Yes, she thought. You can visit. But you are going to have to work very hard if you want anything more.

When she got back to the apartment she took out the first letter again and read it with new eyes. She could hear his voice as she read the words, see his face. It was all genuine, she could see that now, as her anger was softened by her growing sense of power. He really had stuck it out with Renée until the bitter end, until he could walk away honourably. A man like that, one who would always be there, standing in the shadows while his woman made her own mistakes, although hopefully not too many, a man who would let you live your own life . . . could be marriageable.

She emerged from a pleasant little daydream about ten minutes later and clapped her hands on her head. She knew she was hooked. Steady on, she told herself.

You'd better not let yourself be reeled in without a good struggle.

The afternoon post brought yet another letter, this time from Kim, who was worried in case Oruela had left Paris and wouldn't be there when they arrived. She felt bad about asking, she said, but she was hoping to stay with Oruela. She needed somewhere where she could lay low for a while. She had given up the idea of sailing back to the Caribbean straight away because the next boat with a Caribbean crew was not due to leave for another six weeks. With Paul coming to Paris she felt her chances were better if she accepted his offer of a lift.

Oruela put it to Euska who was more than happy to give Kim shelter. She also suggested that she invite Paul until he could find somewhere to rent. Oruela didn't think it was a good idea.

'How am I going to appear distant if he's staying here?' she asked her mother with exasperation.

'There'll be too many people around for you to be alone,' she said with a smile. 'And just think what it will do to him to be in such close proximity and unable to touch. You can't give him a completely cold shoulder now, can you? It's ideal really, for your purposes.'

So later that afternoon Oruela picked up the telephone and dialled Paul's number.

'Hello,' he grunted.

'It's Oruela,' she said.

'Oruela,' he cried, his voice leaping to life. 'Oh, thank God. I was beginning to think you had left Paris.'

'Well,' she said, wickedly, 'Euska's asked me to go to Rio with them.'

'And what have you decided?' he asked.

'Well, there are things to consider . . .' she said, trying desperately not to lie outright.

'I'm sure you'll come to the right decision,' he said.

God, he was a cool customer, she was thinking. But he was saying something else. 'When is she going? When do you have to decide by?'

'She's going in two weeks,' said Oruela.

'We'll be there before that,' he said. 'We'll be there next week . . .'

There was a brief silence between them. She wanted to hear him beg her to stay but even as she wanted it she knew a man like him would never do that.

'Euska's invited you both to stay here,' she said.

'Oh, that's really nice of her. Thank her from me,' he said.

There was another momentary silence.

'Well,' he said. 'See you next week then.'

'Yes,' she said.

'Kim wants to speak to you,' he said. 'I'll say goodbye.'

Kim came on the line and asked her to tell Euska she would be grateful for ever. She dropped her voice.

'And I want to hear what you've been up to. In detail,' she said. 'If there are any broken-hearted men in your wake tell them I'll soothe them . . .'

Oruela put the phone down and sat staring blankly into space. Euska came back into the room a moment later with a pile of clothes to go to charity.

'What's the matter?' she said, putting the bundle on a chair.

'I feel bad,' said Oruela. 'I told him you'd asked me to go to Rio and let him think I hadn't made a decision about it. I virtually lied to him. I don't want to start out by lying to him.'

Euska dropped the bundle on a chair and sat down next to Oruela on the couch. 'If it makes you feel any better,' she said, 'I don't think what you did was really wrong. I suppose it puts us in a bit of an odd situation because we'll all have to play along with it, but it's just a little mistake. Ernesto doesn't know. It's only you and I and I'll play along.'

'I thought I was so clever,' said Oruela. 'But I was stupid.'

'No, you weren't. You had your first taste of power and you made a very small mistake.'

'I don't feel comfortable with power,' said Oruela. 'I'm no good at it.'

'What's the alternative?' said Euska. 'You left it in his hands when we came here and it didn't work because he didn't write to you until it was almost too late. Do you want to live like that?'

'No. But I want a marraige that isn't about power,' said Oruela.

'*Ma chérie*,' said Euska, 'if it's a marriage you want then you had better keep the power in your own hands. Only a woman who has it knows how delightful it is to relinquish it in the right place at the right time. Women who let men have control are fools. Men don't know their ABC when it comes to love.'

'But how can you respect a man that you have such power over?' said Oruela.

'You already love him, don't you. You already respect and admire him? You won't lose that unless you lose respect for yourself. Besides I don't expect he'll be easy to rule. You won't tire of him quickly.'

Oruela felt thoroughly confused. She picked up her apartment-hunting without enthusiasm. But it was when she saw the third place, early in the evening, that the confusion cleared. It was lovely. It really was. It had a glass roof at the back. It was a storey higher than the other buildings around it and so it looked down on the world. The glass roof sloped to the floor and had a little door in it that led out on to a flat balcony. It was just perfect.

But she kept looking at it through Paul's eyes. How he would love the light. How he could change that room into a darkroom. How that would be their bedroom and she would have her desk in the corner there . . .

She wanted him. She wanted to live with him and wake up in the morning in his arms. She wanted to make love to him under the stars as they shone through the roof.

'I'll take it,' she said to the landlady.

'Good,' said the woman. 'I think you will be happy here.'

Euska approved of her decisiveness and they formed a plan. Oruela wouldn't move in. She would stay until Euska had gone and then would move in with Paul. She would pretend to have just found it. If he didn't want to live with her and make love to her under the stars then she would move in and find somebody else who would. Oruela had made up her mind. She knew what she wanted.

Ernesto came home the following morning and caught her humming the wedding tune.

'Is there news I should know?' he asked.

'No,' she said, giving him a hug.

'All will be revealed,' said Euska, taking her turn.

'I'm going out to buy a dress,' said Oruela. 'Back for lunch.' And she closed the door behind her.

When Euska and Ernesto were alone he asked, 'What kind of dress? Is there a second wedding in the offing?'

'You'll know what happens when the times comes,' she said.

'Hmmmm,' he said. He came close to her and held her hands. He edged them round the back of her body and held them there. 'You know what is going to happen to you right now, don't you?'

She smiled. 'Show me,' she said.

And he edged her backwards into their bedroom and closed the door behind him.

Oruela spent her allowance for the week on a beautiful cashmere dress that felt like a dream and clung to her shoulders and breasts like a second skin. It fell straight to her hips and the skirt was cut on the bias so that it drifted round her thighs and swayed when she walked.

She bought some new lingerie, some silk and lace camisoles and soft, handmade knickers with delicate little ribbons. She bought beautiful lace garters and fine silk stockings. She even bought chocolates, dark, bitter-sweet little nuggets of pure heaven.

That night she went out with her friends from the café to the Bal Negre and watched the African men dance with the society girls around the floor, gradually loosening them up. The men gave everything to the dance, to the women, while their white men sat and talked with each other at the tables, seemingly and perhaps genuinely unperturbed. Why should they be? They owned the goods. There were a few African women too, not as many as men but to Oruela's eyes they seemed to be setting the pace. The jazz singer was a black woman with a huge voice, an American. Her voice hit the womb and opened love out into a three-dimensional flower of many shades and depths.

'What are you thinking?' asked a middle-aged poet who was next to her at the table.

'About love,' she said.

'Do you need love?' he asked her.

'Of course,' she said.

'Let me show you love tonight,' he said. 'Have you ever made love to a mature man like me?'

She was tempted, sorely tempted. There was something quite fascinating about his looks. He had penetrating grey eyes.

'Not tonight,' she said.

'When?' he asked.

'I'll let you know if I decide,' she said, and turned back to the music.

The days stalked by. The city grew crisp and chillier. The boxes belonging to Euska piled up in the big hallway of the apartment one by one.

Part of Oruela thought over the things that had happened since she'd come to Paris and resented Paul again for making her wait. She looked up the middle-aged poet and visited him.

It was a strange afternoon. He didn't leap on her. He sensed, perhaps, that she wasn't really looking for sex.

They smoked hashish together instead and talked about love. His views were not dissimilar to Euska's. Women, he said, know much more about the way people work – in general, he said. 'Some don't, of course, and some men do.' He drifted off into his own thoughts.

Oruela pulled out Baudelaire from the bookshelf and read poems that made her senses expand. 'Borrow it,' he told her. 'Bring it back another day.' She read it for days afterwards and then started writing herself. Her lines seemed childish to her and she threw them away.

It was raining on the day that Paul and Kim were due to arrive. She felt jumpy from the minute she got up. They were driving through the night to try to avoid Kim being spotted. At last, about ten, she saw a car draw up, the rain streaming off its flanks. She saw Paul get out and turn up the collar of his raincoat. She saw the familiar form of him, his hair, his shoulders. Her heart sang and her womb thudded.

Kim didn't wait for him to help her out of the car. She climbed out and stretched. She saw Paul place his hand on her back and guide her into the building. Something about the body language made a shaft of unease cross Oruela's mind.

Oruela flew into the bedroom and slipped on the dress. She looked stunning. It wasn't just the dress. Her skin glowed, her eyes were lively, her mouth was very kissable.

Ernesto opened the door and in they came. Kim ran to her and hugged her first and Paul kissed Euska on the cheek and shook Ernesto's hand. Then he walked into the living-room where she and Kim were. If Oruela had been in any doubt about what her true feelings were, she would have been relieved of it by the fact that the mere sight of him made her sex dance inside like some genie who needs a rub to get out.

He came over.

'Hello,' he said.

'Hello,' she said.

And they stood there for what seemed like an age,

542

just looking at each other. It wasn't an age. It was only a couple of seconds. The maid asked him for his coat and it broke the spell.

She was aware, as she moved about the apartment, showing him his room, ordering coffee and sitting on the couch with her legs curled under her, that he didn't take his eyes off her.

Euska noticed it too and made sure that either she or Ernesto or Kim were with them the whole time.

'What's going on?' said Ernesto quietly in the bedroom. 'Don't you want me to continue helping you with your packing?'

'This is more important,' said Euska, and she pushed him back towards the living-room.

That night when they were tucked up in bed, Oruela told Kim about her plan to stay and move into the little apartment with Paul. 'You can stay here as long as you like,' she said. 'Euska and Ernesto will be back in the spring next year.'

'Thanks,' said Kim. 'It'll give me some time. I don't think you'll have any trouble getting what you want. I really don't. He's really serious about you.'

'But it has to be right. I don't want to have to wait again like I did before. It has to be right this time. I want it my way.'

Kim grinned. 'Good for you,' she said.

It crossed Oruela's mind to ask Kim if anything had happened between the two of them. But she thought better of it.

Paul lay in his bed on the other side of the wall wondering. He might be in love but he wasn't stupid. He saw through Euska's manoeuvrings as clear as through a sheet of glass. He guessed it was some mild punishment for his silence for all those weeks. Every woman he knew thought he had been wrong and he knew they were right really, deep down. He considered the facts. If she was seriously displeased then she wouldn't have had him to stay, would she? Given that

543

he was sleeping in the very next room – the thought of it gave him an erection – he sensed it was a matter of waiting. He hoped it wouldn't be too long.

The next few days were an intense mixture of happiness and frustration for them both. There really was no chance to be alone in the apartment. There was the continual hustle and bustle of preparations. Once and once only they had some time alone and only because they met on the street. She had bought a table for the new apartment and had gone there to see it delivered. He had been to meet some film people.

'Come and have a drink with me,' he said. 'We've hardly had a chance to talk since I arrived. I like talking with you.'

They went to Le Dôme and drank beer. They talked about the misunderstandings and he promised never to be so stupid again. It was disarming.

'Have you made a decision about Rio?' he asked, when their second beer arrived.

She couldn't lie to him. 'I'm not going,' she said.

The smile that spread across his face was worth it. He beamed! She rested her elbow on the table and smiled back at him.

'Come here,' he said, and he kissed her lightly on the lips.

They walked back to the apartment together along the crowded, lively streets. 'The whole world is here,' he said. 'This is the place to be. I know it. If people like us are going to make a success of what we do, this is the time and place to do it.'

'I can take the entrance exam again if I want to,' she said.

'Do it,' he said. 'You've nothing to lose.'

That night they all went to a club. Kim was feeling brave and fed up of being inside when life was going by out in the city. So they chanced it. She didn't stand out. People from all over the world had gravitated to Paris and the excitement it offered.

544

If anything, Paul looked more hungry for Oruela. He watched her movements with his smoky green eyes as she and Kim were talking. Oruela caught him and when their eyes met he gave her a look that started her juices flowing.

The following day, though, it all stopped. Ernesto came across the article in the newspaper in the morning. In an American clock factory a group of women workers had been dreadfully poisoned and they had discovered the cause was the radium-based paint that they were using to paint the luminous clock faces. There were terrible predictions of deformed children, a slow death. The news provided an answer to the cause of Norbert Bruyere's death, but it also struck terror into their hearts.

Ernesto rang his doctor immediately and he told them he would meet Oruela at the Institute right away. Paul and Euska went with her and tests were done while they waited in the hall. The results would take three days. Ernesto and Euska put off their plans to spend a day or two in London before sailing. Everyone wondered if Euska would sail at all.

She continued packing. Everyone tried to act as normally as possible but it was difficult. There wasn't one of them that wasn't scared stiff.

They went back three days later. They all went. No one wanted to be left alone. Everything seemed fine, the doctor told them. The initial tests had all proved completely negative. They would monitor Oruela over the next few months but she seemed to have escaped harm because the doses she had been exposed to were so tiny.

It was the last day before Euska and Ernesto were due to sail and the rest of the afternoon belonged to Euska and Oruela. They both knew that it was right to say goodbye to each other, at least temporarily at this point. There would be time to reflect before they saw each other again. Having agreed this they spent a lovely afternoon together.

The same afternoon Kim had a revolution all on her own and went out and got a job in the chorus at Le Sphinx. Not only that, she met a black American trumpet player, a man as big as a house, she said. She was convinced he was the man of her dreams. She was to start that very night and she went off early to the club.

The other four decided to go to the club for Euska and Ernesto's farewell.

'And my return,' said Oruela. 'I feel like I've come back from the dead.'

Over cocktails the men went into a conspiratorial huddle. Euska had plenty of people to say goodbye to at La Coupole and everyone wished her *bon voyage* but Oruela wanted to know what was going on.

'We were talking about the idea of you and I flying to England with them to say goodbye,' said Paul.

'Oh yes!' said Oruela. 'I'd love to fly. Can we?'

'I don't see why not,' said Ernesto. 'I've hired our own plane.'

Kim looked delicious in her satin and feathers costume. She did little except bend and sway in the background with thirty other beauties. She joined them at their table after the show. But she wasn't staying. Things, it seemed, had progressed.

'I sort of ambushed him in the wings,' she told Oruela. 'The sparks were really flying and he's asked me out drinking. So don't expect me home . . .'

'We're going to England,' said Oruela.

'You and Paul?'

'Yes.'

'Marvellous,' said Kim. 'Have a good time.'

'You too,' said Oruela.

And then they both had the same thought at once. 'We'll give them one each for Marthe,' said Kim.

'I'll drink to that,' said Oruela.

Kim arrived home just after dawn, as the taxi that was coming to take them to the airfield was chugging up the street. She managed to let Oruela know in no uncertain terms that she was in love and wouldn't miss them a bit.

It was essential to wrap up well, even for the short hop over the water but even under her furs Oruela, sitting close by Paul in the plane, could feel a different tension. As soon as her mother was out of the way, things, she sensed, would warm up considerably.

They both enjoyed their first time flying and Oruela found herself thinking along very practical lines about how they had a lot in common as far as tastes went. Would they like each other in bed though? It was strange, for once, to be thinking so calmly about it but there was so much at stake. If they did like each other this could easily last a long, long time. It wasn't only air turbulence that gave her stomach little jolts.

The coastline of England appeared below, breaking the monotony of the grey sea and soon after, their descent began. Oruela gripped Paul's hands as the wheels of the tiny plane hit the tarmac and they sped along the ground at incredibly high speed. She opened her eyes to see him laughing at her. But there was no malice in it. She guessed he'd been a bit nervous too.

Having spent more time in Paris than planned, they were driving straight to the port. The liner was waiting in dock to sail on the afternoon tide. It was an American ship, the Atlantic Queen and it was 40,000 tons of pure luxury. They all went on board and made their way through the hustle and bustle of wealthy travellers, old and young, of porters, of stewards who were courteous to the passengers and barked at each other. Their uniforms, Oruela noted, were very dashing. But real wonder was reserved for the quarters that were to be Euska and Ernesto's home for the crossing. Everything was sumptuous. Floor to ceiling windows looked out on to the dockside where a band was assembling to play farewell. They ordered brandy to warm themselves up and peeled off their flying clothes for a tour of the ship.

547

The staterooms were magnificent, great high ceilings lavishly decorated with chandeliers, with filigree screens. The staircases were wrought iron. Elegant women glided up and down speaking in the American drawl that sounded so exotic to Oruela's ears. She noticed, too, how they looked hungrily at Paul and how he seemed completely oblivious to their attention.

The minutes ticked inexorably by and soon they had turned into an hour and the sailors were giving the call that all on board who were not sailing were to make their way ashore. Oruela and Paul were almost the last to leave. Euska and Oruela hugged for a long time.

'Be happy,' said Euska.

'You too,' said Oruela.

Then finally they were saying goodbye. Paul and Oruela walked down the gangplank on to the dock and waited in the chilly, damp air, huddled together as Euska and Ernesto did the same on deck.

The sailors threw ropes and as the ship began to move the band on the shore played a lucky song. There were tears and waving of hankerchiefs and the great floating hotel moved slowly out into the sea. Paul and Oruela stayed long after most people had left, watching the big white stern sail off. He held her close.

Eventually she turned around and looked up at him. He was hers now. She kissed his cold nose.

The car was waiting to take them back to the airport.

'It doesn't seem right,' she said as they settled in the back, 'to come to England for the first time and stay for only a few hours.'

'Would you like to stay, go to London perhaps?'

'Could we?'

'*Porquoi pas?*' he said. 'Why not?'

The city was misty when they arrived. It was after five and as they drove across Waterloo Bridge in the taxi crowds of bowler-hatted commuters streamed towards the railway station. The back of the cab had become cosy and warm. It felt like their world now, to do with as they wished.

'Have you got any ideas about where you'd like to stay?' said Paul.

'Ernesto stays at the Savoy when he's in London,' said Oruela. 'He has an account.'

'Do you want to stay there?' said Paul.

'No,' she said. 'I want to stay somewhere we've discovered ourselves. I want to get away from their influence. I don't want to follow in their footsteps any more.'

Paul smiled. 'I agree,' he said. 'What about Bloomsbury? I've heard about Bloomsbury.'

'Yes,' she said.

He was just about to tell the taxi-driver to go to Bloomsbury when he stopped.

'I've just realised something,' he said. 'You're not wearing a wedding ring.'

'Oh,' she said.

The taxi driver looked over his shoulder. 'Pardon me for eavesdropping, guv'nor,' he said, 'but there's a jewellers' in the Strand here. I happen to know because the wife and I bought her a wedding ring there, sir, and it brought me luck, I can tell you. She's as good a wife as any man could wish for.'

Oruela got the gist of this and began to giggle. They stopped at the place he suggested and paid him. He gave Paul directions to Bloomsbury and Oruela looked around her. The street seemed to be full of the sights she'd always associated with London: big red buses, men in caps selling newspapers to men in bowler hats, a theatre across the street had its lights on and its doors open waiting for the audience to arrive. She drank it all in. She had a delicious sense of being alone with Paul, a sense of adventure.

They went into the shop and spent ages choosing. It wasn't easy. How real was it? Would they ever really get married and, if so, would they keep this one? These were questions they couldn't even think of discussing.

549

Not there, not in the shop, with the obsequious shop assistant doing his best to please.

Eventually they saw one that they both liked. It was plain but it wasn't too cheap. The assistant put it in a box and Paul paid for it.

Outside in the glow of the doorway he took it out of its wrapping and took her left hand. 'I now pronounce you my wife,' he said. 'It's a bit of a risk really, I don't even know if you are any good in bed.'

Her mouth dropped open. 'You!' she said, and then she stopped and fixed him with a look. There was fire in her eyes. 'Heel,' she said, and pointed to her ankle.

For a moment he looked utterly perplexed and then a look of wonder spread across his face as he realised that she was putting him in his place. He reached out his hand, offering it to her. She took it and they walked out into the street.

The woman on the hotel desk was obviously suspicious but being foreign helped. They weren't questioned too closely. Paul's English was pretty good, although he had had most of his conversation practice with Daisy and so produced a fine cockney vowel or two which seemed to offend the woman's nose.

At last they closed the door of their room behind her and burst out laughing. The fire crackled in the grate. The room was cosy. There was a big iron bed with a lace cover and a window that looked out on to the street below. Outside the lamplights gleamed in the mist and the almost bare branches of the trees in the square below threw shadows across the pavement. It had grown quiet in the street in the hour before the city livened up again with nightlife.

Paul took off his coat and came close behind her as she stood by the window.

'Hungry?' he asked. 'Would you like to find somewhere to eat?'

'Not particularly,' she said, her voice was a little unsteady. She certainly wasn't going to say exactly what she did want.

550

He didn't need to ask. As he enclosed her in his arms her body became warm with life.

He helped her off with her coat and threw it on the chair with his own. She stood in her dress, the fine cashmere with its high neck. The soft material hugged her.

'That's a lovely dress,' he said. But he didn't mean that at all and she knew what he meant, because of the way he looked through the material and wanted what was underneath. His eye touched her, made her aware of her nipples becoming hard.

What was it about him that she liked so much, she asked herself silently. He took her by the small of her back and drew her close, bending his head down to meet and snare her eyes in a tender, rude question that could only be answered by an equal. She felt a smile curling on her lips, a faint smile shining in her eyes, its light betraying shadows of a deep feminine fear and desire. She drew her head back a little and looked at his lovely face, his lashes, his fine, straight nose with one or two freckles. This was all hers! This man, this soul, this person, wanting her as much as she wanted him.

Then she looked at his lips and she was captured. They were soft, sensual lips that kissed gently at first, tasting her, and then his hand slid up her back between her shoulder blades and drew her very, very close. She touched his neck, curled her fingers into the hair at the back and as his kiss became stronger, more urgent, she drank him in.

He drew away first and closed the curtains against the last of the outside world, then he took off his jacket and she watched his fine shoulders and his strong arms emerge in the shirt sleeves and touched the crisp fabric. Her fingers were so sensitive that the warm urgency of his body seemed to flow into her through their tips. She ran her hands up to his shoulders and round and down on to the silk back of his waistcoat. He touched the knot of his tie and she stopped him with her hands, taking the task away from him. She loosened the red knot and opened the collar. She pulled the tie apart as he unbuttoned his waistcoat and then she started on his shirt buttons.

Slowly she undid them to the waist and then she pulled out the shirt from his waistband and he gasped with the sensation of the fabric sliding across his skin. He slipped off his shirt and stood before her naked to the waist. The bulge in his trousers was evident.

He was really lovely and the sight made her wet between her thighs. He had a small amount of hair on his chest and the way his shoulders fanned out from his pectorals was fascinating, but Oruela didn't have that long to feast her eyes because he wanted her close and he took her body in his arms. He reached for the fastening at the back of her dress and slipped it undone and then he peeled the dress down from her shoulders. It dropped to the floor and, as if he were manoeuvring one of his models into a pose, he gently took her by the shoulders and sat her on the edge of the bed while he removed his trousers with one quick movement.

His arse was in perfect proportion with the rest of his body and his legs were long and Oruela almost purred out loud like a pussy-cat who has got her cream. But there wasn't long to look.

Quickly, he joined her on the bed and his strong hands enclosed her; strong, confident hands holding her ribs, feeling the curve of her waist as he shifted up her silky camisole, bringing his palm around to her belly and reaching upwards to the softness of her breasts where he paused . . . He stroked the outline with his fingers, mapping the unknown with the care of a renaissance painter, making her skin come alive with colour, light, electricity and sound.

Mouth. She wanted his mouth on them now. She wriggled herself out of the silk and lace and gave her breasts to his lips. He kissed and sucked their heaviness in his mouth, wetting the skin, licking the whole of one and then the whole of the other. She stretched her arms back lazily and gave herself up to the sensation of his

552

lick, lick, lick, warm and wet. He took her nipples between his fingers and rolled them, he pulled a little, stretching the sensation out so that it became sharper, so that shocks crackled among her ribs and earthed in her hips, and then he massaged her breasts strongly, sending the blood tumbling in her skin and making her feel as if she'd never had her breasts loved till now. She rotated her shoulder and pushed one breast deep into his hungry mouth so that the white crescent squashed into his face and he snorkled. When he stopped momentarily to take some air the shock of the air left her skin bereaved.

He kissed her belly and she screamed with tenderness. She took his shoulder and pushed him on to his back. His hands encircled her waist as he fell into the softness of the big cotton- and lace-covered mattress. She stretched her torso and put her breasts again in his mouth each in turn and he sucked until she was satisfied and gave him her lips to kiss instead.

He rolled her on to her side and ran his hands down to the waistband of her knickers. He slipped his hand inside, on her hip, and pulled the fabric away. When she was bare he stroked the rounded softness of her arse.

'You're beautiful,' he said and she felt it. She kissed him, kissed his mouth, his chest.

His head was at her belly again, his mouth at her groin, first one side then the other, kissing her, eating her and then he kissed her hair there and pulled it gently with his teeth. His bite became stronger. He took the bulky, hair-covered flesh and squeezed it between his teeth until she screamed again because it was so strange the way it pulled the rest of her sex, the way it pulled the buried heart of her desire into the jaws of a certain and painless death.

Then he left her there, like that, open and dying while he divested himself of his underwear. She opened her eyes and glimpsed his cock standing straight and heavy in the curls of his body hair, but it was only a glimpse because he was with her again quickly, his body between her legs, his hands opening her thighs, stroking the soft skin at the top, moving to her sex and massaging round and around the heart of it, rolling the sensitive flesh in his fingers and sliding in. His thumb enticed her clitoris while another finger massaged inside until she was desperate to have his cock inside her and she raised one leg, spreading her sex wide so that he had no choice.

As he raised himself, she waited for the moment of truth with her whole body rigid inside, tense. There it was pushing, entering, the shiny pulsing sex of him, piercing the tenseness and making her love flow over him, bringing her the first peace. His whole body covered hers, she clung, burying her face in his neck and shoulders, pushing her hips to meet his and taking all his sex inside her.

The delight of having what she had been wanting for so long gave her an immediate charge, purely physical, that made her feel as if her body had jumped into a different existence. She was overwhelmed by a sense of being at one with him. He kissed her face, her ears, every bit of her that he could, and he whispered her name and held her tight.

She wanted to say his name but she couldn't form the word. Her spine was undulating, her belly touched his, her breasts slid against his chest. She kissed his waist with her inner thighs. She grasped her man by the shoulders and she printed herself on his pelvic bone.

And then the good stuff started. The heat and the sweat and the muscles working hard, the aquaplaning breasts and Queen cunt doing what she's best at, hot and heavy and lush. The first thud of her climax jumped at him like a tiger taking the plunge, its stripes rippling as it surprised its prey and rolled with it until it was conquered.

Who conquered? Who was defeated? She first, then him, filling her heart as he filled her sex and collapsed, spent.

They lay together for a long time, entwined, kissing, until they felt time ticking away in the room on the mantelpiece and looked at the clock.

'I'm starving,' she admitted and so they dressed, which was difficult because they couldn't stop kissing each other's skin as it was hiding itself from sight.

They found a chop-house that had stayed open late and ate lamb and peas and grilled tomatoes that tasted to Oruela as if they had just fallen from the plant that bore them. They had a discussion about the paying of the bill and decided that, because Paul wanted to, he should pay this time but they would share their expenses so that questions of money would never be an issue. They both knew that they were speaking about the future and that it was going to be their own personal struggle.

They each thought about it on the walk back to the hotel holding hands. Then Paul spotted a tavern and they went in and drank ale from big heavy glasses and studied the occupants of the room, who were few and absorbed by their beer or their books. The drink made them mellow and they left like spirits, without disturbing the timeless drinking of the men. As they walked lazily back to the hotel in the sweet darkness they talked about the future. He was excited about film-making, she about studying. But overall they were excited about each other. They didn't dare say so. Not yet.

As she lay beside him on the edge of sleep, she felt truly wonderful and she dreamed of great palatial doors opening and opening into infinity.

They both woke early, excited even subconsciously by each other's presence. She opened her legs and wrapped them around him and they made love in the chilly dawn. Afterwards he stroked her body as she drifted back into a half-sleep. Beneath his fingers her skin became known, became his as the minutes ticked by on the big old clock. At eight-fifteen exactly, when she was sleeping, purring softly, the clock ran out of spring. It stopped ticking and he lay listening to her breathing, to the faint sounds of the city going to work outside, imagining that they had stepped outside of time. He kissed her awake. He took her mouth and drank, he took her breasts and sucked, he kissed her belly and her hair and he buried his head, his lips in her salty cave, and she came awake at the point of no return.

She pushed him on his back and she straddled him. She enclosed him with a single slide and she rode him until her orgasm came like a horsewoman from the apocalypse. She fell off him and rolled and he rested back on the pillows, doomed. He knew it and he loved it. Briefly they lost consciousness of each other.

They were awoken by a knock on the door. A man's voice outside asked them did they want breakfast in bed and Paul, coming to first, covered Oruela's precious body with a sheet. He looked around the room. It was in complete turmoil. 'Yes,' he called. 'Hold on a moment.' He put on his shorts and went to the door. An ancient waiter, bent in the middle, stood there with a heavy tray. 'Let me take it,' said Paul.

'It's all right, sir,' he said. 'I'll bring it in.' And he did. He didn't bat an eyelid at the state of the room.

Oruela sat up, pulling up the coverlet, as he came back in and closed the door. She looked charming, all full of love and morning sex. He poured out two cups of tea and put one on the bedside table for her before climbing back into the warmth of the bed beside her. They sipped the hot brew.

Later they dressed and went to the British Museum where they marvelled at the Egyptian gods and goddesses in the quiet, still rooms, where they gazed at manuscripts written and drawn hundreds and hundreds of years before and where, on the staircase, when no one was looking, they kissed softly and quickly and held hands.

In the afternoon they went to a department store in

556

Oxford Street and bought underwear and a small suitcase. He sat a bit primly in the women's department, fiddling with his hat on his knees as the assistant showed her a selection. She brought him over a beautiful set of fine broderie anglaise underwear and asked if he liked it. He blushed crimson, making her laugh.

Then they went back to the hotel and he let her know who was boss.

After two days in London in a cocoon of love and sex they grew tired of tourist sites and made a crackly telephone call home to Daisy who squealed a lot and gave them her mum's address in the East End.

It was as they walked through the dark, narrow streets with the railway bridges overhead that Oruela became scared of something unknown. Paul held her close and told her that any murderous fiend had better watch out because she was his and he loved her and would let no one touch her.

It tripped off his tongue easily, the little phrase that meant so much. It had all seemed so natural and easy but now she knew she was scared. She became obsessed with doubts that it couldn't last. She kept quiet about it though and shook off the doubts in the parlour of Daisy's mum's little terraced house that was filled with family and furniture.

Later that night in bed, Paul sensed she was troubled but he didn't ask her what was wrong. He held her close, wrapping her skin in love and kissed away the phantoms. He held her close until she relaxed and turned to him and reached for his sex.

But the spell had been broken and she wanted to say goodbye to London and the little hotel where they had first made love and leave her doubts behind. He was good at sensing her moods. He agreed that they should go back to Paris. The day they left dawned bright and clear. The ferry boat was only half full of travellers. They sat wrapped up on deck and watched the white cliffs disappear.

On the train between Calais and Paris, as the twilight descended, he brought up a subject that had been on his mind since they left England

'I want you to live with me,' he said. 'I want to find somewhere where we can be together all the time.'

Oruela's whole body felt his words. She exulted. Her smile gave him the reply he wanted, even before she spoke. 'When we came back from the countryside I looked at a place that I liked,' she said.

'Let's see if it's still vacant then. Tomorrow,' he said.

They arrived back in time to go to dinner at the club where Kim worked and they told her the news. To Oruela's surprise Kim's reaction was understated, even a bit subdued. Oruela hustled her off to the powder-room.

'What's the matter?' Aren't you pleased for me?' she said.

'Yes,' said Kim. 'But I don't know about moving in with men. Every woman I know who has done it says they take you for granted in the end.'

'But that's a long way down the road,' said Oruela. 'Besides, I think I can keep him interested.' And she smiled a lewd smile. 'Anyway, what's made you so cynical? How's Earl?'

Kim grunted.

'What's the matter?' asked Oruela.

'He gives me the best loving I've ever had in my life and he's talking about marrying me and taking me off to America.'

'But that's lovely!' squealed Oruela.

'What do I want to marry the first man I've had since you-know-where for?' Kim wailed. 'I don't want to get wafted out of existence on some pink cloud of romance and I don't want to go to America.'

'You don't love him then?' asked Oruela.

'That's the problem. I think I might. I'm falling, I really am. Seriously. And I'll end up with kids and washing. I'm not doing it. I don't want to be anyone's slave and you'd better watch it too.'

The thought of laundry stirred Oruela up somewhat and two militants exited the powder-room.

'What do you think about housework?' said Oruela, when Kim had gone backstage.

'Housework?' said Paul. 'What do you mean?'

'Do you think women should do it?'

He smiled. 'I think we should get a maid,' he said.

Oruela had to go through some silly pretences in order to keep up the illusion that she hadn't yet rented the place. It meant telephoning no one, popping out to 'pick up the key' early while he was still in his pyjamas. But it was worth it. Knowing something he didn't made her feel more secure, more certain of her own strength.

He loved the apartment as much as she did and then she had to stop him wanting to sign the lease. 'I'll do it,' she said. 'It's my first home of my own. I want to.' And he accepted that without so much as a whisper.

They moved in. They put the bed next to the sloping glass roof. They filled up the cracks that let in the cold. They stored plenty of wood for the stove. They made the place sunny even when the sky was grey, with flowers and fabrics and lots and lots of love.

As they got to know each other better their fucking became deeper, closer to the bone, her orgasms became bigger, longer lasting. They made love in the bed under the stars, and against the sink with her arse squashed against the cold enamel. They went back to the bed and they spent whole days naked together with the stove blazing out heat to warm them.

Her body felt good all the time. People complimented her on her appearance. Often, if she happened to be alone, in a café, the men passing by would turn and look at her with hungry looks. She barely noticed.

* * *

Kim persuaded Earl to stay in Paris. It was the centre of things, she argued. Everyone was there. Everything was happening. She didn't want to go to America and have to sit in seperate bars from white people. There were no 'No Coloureds' signs in Paris to kill your spirits. The whole city was alive and exciting. He was convinced. He had plenty of work. The Parisians loved his music.

He took Kim and Oruela and Paul to a club where the musicians went to jam sometimes. The small, basement room was crowded with people from all over the world. Oruela and Kim talked quietly about the variety of men. All shapes and sizes, all colours, all shades of sexuality. The two women whispered their fantasies to each other. Nice though, they agreed, to have someone to go home with.

Paul was about as good as a man could be when it came to the domestic arrangements. But Oruela ended up barefoot and pregnant.

He took photographs of her as she swelled and they made love so that the infant would feel good. It wasn't all bliss. The labour was sheer pain but the newly born baby, all wet and slippery, mewling on her thighs. That was something.

Healing Passion
Sylvie Ouellette

Chapter One

*T*en toes were mischievously staring at Judith, almost begging to be pinched, peeping out of the rectangular hole in the mint-coloured sheet like a family of tiny, stumpy puppets. They looked so out of place; her eyes were always coming back to those silent characters, her attention constantly diverted.

On the whole the feet looked rather anonymous; quite rugged but distinctly female, their wrinkled skin tinted a dark yellow by the iodine-based disinfecting lotion. But only the toes seemed to be in a laughing mood this morning.

At the other end of the operating table the patient's face was hidden behind yet another pale green screen, held up by a contraption hanging from the ceiling. The rest of the body was entirely covered under a sterilised sheet, the legs propped up in preparation for the surgery.

From where she was standing Judith could just see the top of the head of Edouard Laurin, the hypnotist sitting next to the patient's head. However, she could hear his voice fill up the room; warm, calming, haunting.

'Your feet no longer belong to you,' he said slowly in a heavy French accent, each word forever echoing in the room. 'We have borrowed them and in a few minutes we will give them back to you, all nice and new.'

Judith couldn't contain a nervous giggle. This was her first day at work and already she was overwhelmed by the unusual nature of the Dorchester Clinic, which offered state of the art cosmetic surgery and treatment to its select, wealthy clientele, in addition to a comfortable stay in a modern, luxurious building overlooking Holland Park.

Today, Lady Austin, rich widow of the late Lord Austin, the shipping magnate, was about to have her feet re-shaped. The woman was a regular patient, having visited the Clinic no less than eight times in the past five years, first to have a face-lift, then a tummy tuck. This had been followed by a long series of various repairs, according to her whims, on a body which would otherwise reveal its real age and probably betray almost five decades of over-indulgence.

This time she had claimed to no longer like the sight of her feet, complaining that she found them very unfashionable as she walked on the sandy beaches of some remote exotic island or strolling along the deck on the yacht of a rich friend.

Judith thought that they simply showed the result of years of torture from endless shopping sprees. Rich feet made to be pampered. No wonder the toes were in such a happy mood.

The cost of the operation and hospital stay would probably be more than the annual salary of the staff who would be looking after this wealthy patient, but that was always the case with the clients of the Dorchester Clinic. Here, money could buy them a new, lovely body, made to order.

The set-up of the operating theatre was impressive to Judith. All the equipment was top of the range, brand new and shining. The sweet smell of honeysuckle filled the air, a nice change from the strong smell of disinfectant that usually floated throughout the corridors of other clinics.

Smooth music was escaping from a loudspeaker, concealed somewhere in the ceiling. The soft orange tint of

564

the ceramic tiles both on the floor and on the walls gave the room a subdued, quiet look, which was pleasantly different from the standard dark green found in older institutions.

The atmosphere was warm and comfortable and, if she closed her eyes even for just a second, Judith could almost believe this was a room at an expensive beauty salon, not a hospital.

It was only a month since she had graduated from nursing school, and she was lucky to have been hired right away. Most of her classmates had applied for the vacancy and had reacted jealously when Judith had been offered the position.

A prestigious clinic, and a matching salary. Not bad for a first job. On top of that everyone here was charming, young and good looking. It seemed as though the Clinic's staff advertised how the clients could expect to look like if they came here. Judith had been told her pretty face and her attractive figure had been a key element in obtaining the job. Nevertheless, she had been hired on a three-month contract and had to prove she was a competent nurse.

Today, for the first time, she would assist on a procedure where the patient was not anaesthetised but hypnotised. As Lady Austin was being put under, Judith somehow felt Edouard's voice transport her as well. She was finding it difficult to concentrate on setting up the instruments in preparation for the surgery.

The tinkling sound of the metal seemed louder than usual, although it couldn't quite bury the words that were still coming to her ears, the way Edouard slowly pronounced each word, the R's rolling like a cascade in his throat.

'You shall remain in this state, relaxed and comfortable until I tell you otherwise,' he continued. Judith breathed a sigh of relief. Lady Austin was now in a trance, but thankfully she was herself still wide awake.

'I think we are ready, Nurse Stanton.' She was startled when he spoke again, this time in a more lively tone. It took Judith a few seconds to realise he was now talking to her.

Peering in his direction, she saw a smiling face appear over the pale green screen, topped by a matching green surgeon's hat. Two blue eyes were looking at her, eyes so pale, so washed out they seemed unreal, like the eyes of ancient porcelain dolls. Edouard wasn't much older than her but the unusual tint of his eyes gave him a certain authoritative look.

Judith felt herself blush, ridiculously, like a teenager under the gaze of a handsome teacher. She dropped a scalpel and the noise it made as it hit the ceramic floor brought her back to reality.

'The Doctors should be here in just a minute . . .' The remainder of her sentence was lost in a ruffle of noise as the operating team entered the room.

Like a magical ballet three people, all gowned, coiffed and masked in matching green, proceeded around the table and its patient, speaking only a few words, their movements precise and decisive, like robots.

As the powerful lamps were switched on above the operating table, the rest of the large operating theatre disappeared in the dark, the strong light swallowing the whole of the room, save for the patient and the attending staff. Almost simultaneously the music that had been creating such a comfortable atmosphere seemed to die as well, leaving only silence to accompany this darkness.

Judith came forward to join the team and took her place to the right of Doctor Robert Harvey, the chief surgeon. He turned to face her. She couldn't see his mouth behind his mask but his laughing eyes told her he was smiling.

'You're the new nurse . . . Miss Stanton, right? Welcome to the Dorchester Clinic. I hope you enjoy working with us.' His voice was warm and low, his tone velvety, making him sound like a radio announcer on the late-night programme.

His proximity was disturbing. His dark and piercing eyes watched as her trembling fingers tied her mask

566

behind her neck. Judith looked away, unable to stand his gaze without blushing.

'Are we ready?' he asked around. Everyone nodded. 'Let's start then.'

Two other doctors on the opposite side of the operating table, a man and a woman, were assisting him. Judith didn't recognise them but they also acknowledged her presence and silently smiled at her with their eyes. Smiled and stared. Intensely.

Judith suddenly felt uneasy under their gaze. Not so long ago she had faced a series of examiners who wanted to probe her knowledge, forcing her brain to recapture and spit out everything she had learned in nursing school. Those grilling sessions had been difficult but she had passed the final tests with flying colours.

Today, however, the questions in the surgeons' eyes were of a different nature. She had no answer for them, unable to make out what they wanted of her, only that their powerful glare was overwhelming. It was as if they were seeking to get at her very soul; they didn't care for what she knew but rather they wanted to find out who she was. It soon became intolerable and she swallowed a nervous sob.

The atmosphere grew heavy as she looked at them in turn. Was this their way of showing their authority? A new nurse against three experienced surgeons, what did they expect from her? Dressed identically they almost looked threatening; a uniform colour from head to toe, completely concealed, anonymous. Time stood still for a while and so did Judith.

When Doctor Harvey held out his hand in her direction, it took her a few seconds to realise it was his way of asking for the scalpel. The surgeons' eyes were still on her, Harvey's as black as marble beads, the assistants' a matching pair of emeralds. Once she reacted, however, they looked down towards the task at hand and they seemed to forget all about her.

Almost instantly she ceased to be the object of their curiosity. Their hold on her, the spell, was broken. As if they had extracted what they wanted out of her, even if she couldn't make out what it was, they were silently dismissing her.

For the next four hours Judith lived a dream, like a spectator to the operation rather than a participant. Occasionally the surgeons glanced at her, but only briefly, and when they did she could read their silent questions.

She replied swiftly and exactly to each of their demands by handing them the instruments they required. Meanwhile the surgeons worked their art on yet another pair of feet, transforming the rough, tired extremities into delicate jewels any fashion model could envy.

All the while only Edouard's voice would break the clicking sound of the instruments, always soothing and haunting, as it kept the patient under the spell and cast its relaxing effect all around the room.

Now and again she had to wipe the surgeons' foreheads, keeping her eyes on the procedure to anticipate their demands. Her concentration was extreme and she was so busy that it was all over before she knew it.

When instructed by Edouard, Lady Austin began humming an old folk song. This was his way of gradually guiding her out of the trance. During the surgery the patient hadn't uttered a word, oblivious to what was going on in the room.

Judith helped Edouard push the operating table and the patient out of the theatre and into the recovery room. The doors closed behind him and the patient but her work wasn't over, she still had to set the instruments aside for the cleaning staff. She turned around and walked back into the large room. The powerful lamps had been switched off and the room looked just as cosy as before. It even seemed larger, now that the table had been pushed away.

The doctors were exchanging comments following the operation, and paid no attention to her, unlike before the surgery. The smacking sound of latex covered their words as they all pulled off their gloves. In unison, they also took off their hats and masks.

At that moment Judith recognised one of the assistants as Doctor Elizabeth Mason, a loud, feisty brunette she had met at her job interview. Doctor Mason had been very friendly that day, but why hadn't she spoken to Judith at all during the operation? A single word of encouragement could have made a big difference. And although she had remained silent during the whole time the surgery had lasted – as if her mouth was gagged by her surgical mask – her loud voice was now making up for lost time. Pearls of laughter bounced around the room, amplified by the emptiness and the ceramic walls. But even then she didn't have a single word for the new nurse.

The other assistant was a young blond man Judith hadn't been introduced to, but she knew he was Doctor Tom Rogers, one of the orthopaedic surgeons. He looked boyish, almost frail and delicate in his manners. He seemed nice enough, but not very manly, to say the least. His high-pitched, whining voice was very irritating. His sandy hair was wispy like a baby's, straight and squarely cut all in one length just above his ears. A good-looking boy, in a cute sort of way. Nothing to get excited about. Probably a spoilt brat; a mummy's boy.

The two assistants kept chatting together, making their way out of the room. Only Doctor Harvey stayed behind. Judith's heart began to pound when she realised she was alone with him and he was still staring at her, his smile now plainly visible.

All was silence in the operating theatre once the assistants had gone. There was no way Judith could avoid him now. She felt uneasy but somewhat flattered by the way he looked at her; no longer threatening, rather amused, almost friendly. Immediately she felt herself blush again.

This was stupid, what was so embarrassing about being alone with a man? But there was more to it than that, obviously. Without his mask and hat, Robert

Harvey was incredibly handsome. Although he was barely in his thirties, he was already a prestigious surgeon. Tall and dark, he vaguely reminded Judith of those actors cast as doctors on television, so good-looking they're almost unreal. Yet in real life anyone half as decent-looking had failed to materialise once she started nursing school.

He hoisted himself on a high stool and grabbed a piece of slim, clear rubber tubing from the table next to him, slowly studying its length and twisting it with his fingers.

'You work fast,' he commented simply, his voice echoing in the empty room.

Judith didn't reply, unable to find anything to say. Her hands began to shake as she placed each instrument in a basin of green disinfectant solution. Just as when he had first entered the room and looked at her so intensely, the effect he had on her was surprising and quite difficult to manage. Thankfully she had been able to control her hands during the surgery, when it really mattered.

Never taking his eyes off her, Doctor Harvey continued toying with the plastic tubing, slowly wrapping the long piece around his fingers several times before tying it in knots, using only his fingertips.

Judith watched the play of fingers intensely, mesmerised by the sight of his hands and the way they moved. Curiously, the effect was similar to the sound of Edouard's hypnotising voice, or perhaps even more powerful.

During the operation those hands had looked unreal through the latex gloves; like expert and strong tools. Now she could see them for what they really were. The long, slim fingers appeared smooth and caressing, just like the man's voice.

And as she felt his eyes on her, two hot rays surveying her body, Judith suddenly wished, foolishly, that his hands could follow the path of his gaze. To feel his fingers twitching over her bare skin the way they were toying with the rubber tubing would no doubt be extremely enjoyable . . .

570

She had to force herself to look elsewhere, to take her eyes away from the captivating sight. Her feet were like lead by now but she found the strength to move around, desperately trying to look casual as he kept watching her every move. She turned around, gathered the soiled linen into a heap and dropped it into the basket by the door.

His eyes followed her and were now fixed on her breasts. Judith could feel the weight of his stare. The surgery had been demanding and Judith had felt very hot. Half-moons of sweat had collected under her breasts and were now emphasising their plump roundness. And that's exactly what he was looking at.

Her nipples grew hard despite herself, brushing against the rough, starched cotton of the green gown she was wearing and making her blush further. If he kept looking at her like this for much longer, there was no way he wouldn't notice the effect he had on her.

Then he spoke, but by now Judith was so troubled she couldn't hear words, only the melody of his voice. She looked up, the fire of her embarrassment throbbing on her cheeks. He smiled again. 'Are you always this quiet?'

'N ... no ...' she managed to reply as she turned around, unable to stand this sweet torture any longer. She was angry with herself for reacting this way, yet she was also flattered to have him look at her like this.

She wasn't used to being the subject of so much attention, especially from a man like him. Up until now all the doctors she had worked with, even the most competent, couldn't remember so much as her name.

'So, I'll ask that you be assigned to my team whenever I'm operating,' he concluded. 'I'm sure we'll work well together.'

Judith wasn't quite sure what to make of that, hearing the words but not really understanding their meaning. Did he want her on his team because she was competent, or was it simply because he wanted the opportunity to disrobe her with his glare as often as possible?

Without a word he let himself slide from the stool, in a silent, feline motion. Still without a word he walked away, glancing over his shoulder and smiling at her one more time before disappearing.

Chapter Two

*E*verything was quiet as Judith glided down the long corridor of the sixth floor, the thick carpet cushioning her steps, her white uniform reduced to a faint shadow in the dimness of the night lights.

She passed a series of pale, solid oak doors, all identical, all numbered in sequence regardless of whether they were patients' rooms or just utility closets. Of course, there were no wards at the Dorchester Clinic, only private rooms.

But in the corridor each door was identical to the next. This was somewhat disconcerting and confusing, and Judith couldn't help feeling lost. If only there were signs to indicate what could be found on the other side of these doors.

In other clinics only the patients' rooms where numbered and there were always signs to differentiate the bathrooms; the treatment rooms had very large doors and the closets narrow ones. And in most places the doors to the patients' rooms and the wards were always kept open.

Curiously, at the Dorchester Clinic, the doors all looked the same, numbered from one to thirty on each of the six floors, and they were all kept closed, making the place look just like a hotel and ensuring maximum privacy for

573

the patients. But whilst this added to their comfort, it didn't make things easy for the staff. Only in time would Judith manage to figure out behind which doors the patients' rooms were.

As she made her way to the end of the corridor the silence seemed to increase, the sounds swallowed before they were even born. She looked down and saw that her feet had become two white stains on the dark carpet. That was something else she had never seen before: this was probably the only clinic in the world to have carpeting in the corridors . . .

She stopped by the last door on the right and consulted the chart once again, making sure she was at the right place, then entered the room. Her shoes made a faint squeaky sound as she walked across the hardwood floor to the bed at the far end of the room.

The only source of light was a tiny halogen lamp above the headboard, casting a vaguely greenish glow. Lady Austin was laying comfortably, as if she were in her own bed. Only the bulk of the bandages around her feet looked out of place, the rough bundle a stark contrast to the ivory silk night gown she was wearing.

Judith had to take her patient's blood pressure one more time before going home. Her first day at work had turned out to last longer than she had expected and her back was getting sore, her feet tired. However, in just a few minutes she would finally be allowed to leave.

Lady Austin stirred from her slumber, looked up at the nurse and smiled, still groggy from the medication she had been given.

Judith reached into one of the drawers of the wall unit and took out the leather cuff. She secured it around the naked arm and set the stethoscope in the groove of the woman's elbow. The cuff swelled gently as Judith pressed the pump and the sound in her ears isolated her for a minute. She felt rather than heard a presence behind her. In the circle of light around the bed Doctor Harvey appeared, his white coat cutting a large patch out of the

574

darkness. Obviously, he had also come to check on his patient.

Judith's heart started to beat faster as she recalled their brief conversation in the operating theatre that morning, although now it seemed like years ago. Looking back, he had been very friendly with her, nothing more. It had lasted just a few minutes, yet she had been glued to the floor the whole time as she had felt him examining her. Was it only her imagination, or had he really been trying to guess the contours of her body under her pale green gown?

She couldn't figure it out. Perhaps it was all because of his voice, so sensuous, seductive, that in Judith's mind it had turned small-talk into a flirtatious chat.

Again tonight, as he addressed Lady Austin, he spoke in a low voice which was both captivating and warm. No doubt he was trying to make Lady Austin feel she was more than just another pair of feet to him.

'The bandages should be coming off in a couple of days,' he told her as he came to stand just behind Judith. 'So if everything is in order you'll be able to go home by Friday.'

Once again Judith was so troubled by the sound of his voice that she ceased to understand him. She only knew that she didn't want him to stop talking.

She hadn't seen him at all after the surgery, although she had kept an eye out for him. For a couple of hours after coming out of the operating theatre she had imagined him around every corner, her heart pounding fast whenever she saw a vaguely familiar silhouette across a crowded corridor. And every time she had been mistaken and disappointed – until now. Now he really was there, just a few inches away from her.

Standing between him and the bed, she couldn't dare turn around and look at him, nor even merely divert her eyes in his direction. But what was *he* looking at, peering over her shoulder? Did he come to make sure she took good care of her patient? Or was his visit simply aimed at comforting Lady Austin to help her relax before going to sleep?

He had come in and talked to the patient. Now it seemed he had nothing else to say, and Lady Austin had closed her eyes and was gradually going back to sleep. So what was he still doing here?

Judith grew confused and nervous, unable to read the result of the blood pressure on the tiny meter. She had to pump up the cuff again, clumsily. At that moment she was taken by surprise, almost shocked, when his hands gently lifted her dress. First she felt the faint caress of his fingertips, slowly pulling up her white uniform until her buttocks were exposed, clad in tiny cotton panties.

A wave swept her and she desperately tried to hold in the nervous sob of joy that rose in her throat. Listening to the swishing sound of the blood flow in the stethoscope, somehow she felt it was her own blood she could hear racing through her veins.

She didn't need to look at his face to know that there could be no doubt about his intentions. The only problem was that her own mind was in no condition to function clearly.

She couldn't gather the strength to turn around and look at him. His hands were slowly studying the swell of her behind, like a blind man feeling the dark world around him. Already her skin was replying like an echo to the pulsating warmth of his touch.

Deep within herself, sensations long forgotten surfaced: the first time a boy had lifted her dress, the first hand she had felt caressing her behind. She hadn't been touched in such a long time it seemed ... But what was she to do? Should she encourage his behaviour, and possibly have to deal with something bolder, or would it be best to tactfully ask him to stop?

Then his fingers found their way inside her panties, ever so easily, as if they belonged there. The same fingers she had marvelled at earlier that day were now teasing the smooth skin of her buttocks, their touch light as a feather. She could never ask him to stop now . . . Her legs began to tremble in excitement.

'I think we should let Lady Austin sleep now, Doctor,' she managed to whisper. Her hands still trembling, she undid the blood pressure cuff and rolled it up in a bundle before putting it back in the drawer, along with the stethoscope.

'Quite right, nurse,' Doctor Harvey replied in her ear, the warmth of his breath caressing her neck as he slowly pulled his hands out of her panties. 'However, I would like to discuss her chart, if you have a minute.'

'Of course,' said Judith, glancing at her watch. 'I was just about to go home but if you need to speak to me I can spare a moment.' The timing was perfect and she saw it as a good omen, though she was wondering what he really wanted to discuss, if indeed he wanted to talk at all.

She couldn't erase from her mind the way he had looked at her in the operating theatre, and how he had now caressed her so intimately. Surely he would want more than just a friendly chat this time around? There could be no doubt about his intentions. Judith knew she probably wouldn't have the strength to refuse his invitation.

He didn't turn around as they walked out of the room, stepping back into the semi-darkness of the corridor. Instead of turning left and making his way back to the brightly lit nurses' station, he opened the door to the stairwell and started to walk down several flights of steps.

Judith was just a few paces behind him, obediently following his white silhouette all the way down to the basement and then to the door marked 'Doctors' Lounge.' She didn't know what to expect and didn't dare to hope.

'They're all gone at this hour,' Harvey said, opening the door. 'We won't be disturbed.'

Judith hesitated a moment as he ushered her in. The only light came from the open door which revealed the entrance to the doctors' lounge to look like a posh sitting

577

room, with leather furniture, glass tables, cushions everywhere and a large bookcase alongside the far wall. Beyond that it got darker, and it was almost impossible to tell how big the room actually was.

Doctor Harvey stood tall behind Judith, gently pushing her inside, his hands on her shoulders.

'What exactly did you want to discuss with me?' she asked, without turning around. She was excited yet afraid to be discovered in a place where nurses were not allowed to set foot.

'Well, for one, I don't like the way you take your patients' blood pressure. I think you need a quick refresher course.'

Without turning on the lights, he led her to a leather couch at the back of the lounge where he made her sit. Once the door closed behind them the cloudy light filtering through the frosted glass enabled her to make out his profile in the shadow as he sat next to her.

'First, you need good equipment,' he said, taking out a stethoscope from the pocket of his white coat. With his other hand, using only his fingertips, he started to slowly undo the series of buttons at the front of Judith's uniform, stopping half-way down her belly.

Judith felt the cool air of the room flow inside her dress as her skin was gradually exposed, her nipples reacting to the difference of temperature and also in excitement. The doctor was just about to examine her . . .

He placed the flat piece of the stethoscope between her breasts and she was startled by the cold contact. She shivered nervously.

Of course, she knew this 'refresher course' was just a farce and would probably lead to something outside her nurse's duties. At any other time she might have tried to stop him, but tonight it seemed she was no longer in control of her own body. She was also intrigued by the way she had responded to his blatant invitation and so wilfully followed him. Her own desire both amazed and scared her at the same time.

The memory of his eyes on her body had stayed with

her all day, and only served to enhance the desire to be near him again. She felt powerfully attracted to him and although in some remote part of her mind something was telling her this wasn't professional at all, at this moment her body was more than willing to do whatever he would ask of her.

Already she could feel the fire of arousal building up between her legs. So far she had only ever been with men her own age. And although he wasn't much older than her, Doctor Harvey was already a prestigious surgeon. He was her superior, but nevertheless utterly irresistible. She had never been attracted to a man this way before – after all she had only met him that morning – but tonight she was most eager to yield to his charm.

He placed one hand on her lower back whilst the other held the stethoscope gently on her chest. His face was just a few inches from hers; he looked even more handsome in the dark. In a blurry shadow she could see the fine hair of his eyebrows, his thin nose, his dark lips.

Her heart was pounding fast and hard, and Doctor Harvey could certainly hear it. There was no need for words to disclose her arousal, her body spoke loud enough. She felt her face flush and the heat spread down along her neck to her abdomen, then all the way down between her thighs.

After a while he dropped the stethoscope but not his hand and looked at her with an amused smile. Slowly he reached inside her dress, his fingertips gently stroking her breasts through the white lace of her bra.

Judith closed her eyes and let out a faint sigh. His touch was like fire. She felt him coming closer and gently nibble at the corner of her mouth whilst increasing the pressure of his fingers over her erect nipples, sending delicious waves directly to her loins. His lips at the corner of her mouth were smooth and full, and just as warm as his fingers.

Memories of her teenage years came back to her as she placed one hand on his thigh and clumsily slipped the other inside his white coat, caressing his muscular back

579

with trembling fingers. She felt a bit silly, not really knowing what to do. There was always a risk of somebody entering the room, but she didn't want to leave. His tongue was now on her chin, gradually working its way down. Its wet warmth left a cool trace on her skin, only enhancing the fire that now raged inside her. She knew she had to do something in reply, but what? Surely he would expect more from her than to just remain passive to his caress. Yet as she made a move to unbutton his shirt he stopped her.

'Don't forget I am the teacher tonight, nurse.'

She didn't reply, giving up. Maybe he didn't want her to do anything after all. Perhaps it would be best to just let him take the lead. It was much better this way.

Slowly pushing her down until her back came to rest on the couch, he gently seized her ankles and lifted her legs, bringing them behind him as he sat on the edge of the seat. Then he slipped both his hands inside her dress and began massaging her skin, caressing her breasts, teasing her nipples.

Judith turned her head sideways, pressing her burning cheek against the cool leather. His touch was increasingly warm on her sensitive skin. Those hands again . . . She could see them in her mind as well as feel them on her body. Tonight they were operating another kind of magic, something that wouldn't require any fancy instruments, but that would heal in its own, special fashion.

The pins holding her hair up slipped and her straw-coloured mane spilled onto the dark leather. Her own image appeared behind her closed eyelids: a white, virginal figure just waiting to be taken.

She could feel the heat of his body through the thin cotton of her uniform as he gently bent over her, his abdomen pressing against her thighs, and immediately longed to get rid of this cumbersome obstacle. As if reading her mind he brought his hands up, slipping the dress from her shoulders, and his fingertips undid the hook holding her bra fastened at the front.

Her generous breasts jutted out, nipples erect and

580

pointing to the ceiling, finally freed from the restraint that had held them prisoner. The cool air in the room was not enough to calm the heat of their excitement. And at this moment Judith desperately wanted to feel his naked skin on hers.

'Excuse me, Doctor,' she ventured timidly, 'but could I just unbutton your shirt?'

He laughed softly, surprised by the childish tone of her voice. After all, she was just a new recruit. A competent nurse no doubt, but only fresh out of school.

'Don't move,' he said. 'I'll take care of that myself.'

Standing up, he took his white coat off and threw it over a chair. His shirt followed. The stethoscope had mysteriously disappeared.

The room was dark but Judith's eyes were quickly getting accustomed to it. At least she could see his broad chest, covered with dark, tight curls. This sight doubled her excitement. All her previous boyfriends had been bare-chested, and the thought of losing herself in this velvet carpet suddenly fuelled her desire for the man.

Instead of sitting down again he kneeled on the floor, next to the couch. Instinctively, Judith lifted her hips and in a swift move he pulled down her dress, then gently took off her bra, throwing it aside nonchalantly.

Finally his head came down on her chest and his tongue started dancing on her breasts, at first gently but gradually increasing its eagerness, worrying her nipples. His hands continued to flutter over her body, one on her belly and the other on her thighs.

Judith thought she was going to faint with excitement. She spread her legs slightly, instinctively. Her vulva was so wet that her dew was quickly spilling between her buttocks and the leather of the couch. It felt warm and wet, and its sweet smell gently floated to her flaring nostrils.

All her senses were ablaze. She let out another sigh, slightly louder. She knew this was a dangerous game, anybody could enter the room. However her uniform was now on the floor, she had lost sight of her bra, and

581

her panties were soaked with her warm dew. She didn't really want to leave, at least not just yet.

'This is wild,' she thought. She had never felt this good, not even that time behind the barn with Jon, last spring when she had gone back home during half-term break. She smiled in the dark. Jon was just a boy in comparison, just a naughty boy. He knew nothing of a woman's needs. Doctor Harvey, on the other hand . . .

He let out a loud sigh as he got up, looking at her almost naked on the couch; her legs apart, her breasts heaving with every breath, her long blond hair spread over the contrasting brown leather. He bent down slowly, his slim fingers catching the elastic band of her panties and pulling them down.

He was impressive, towering above her, half-naked, his eyes sparkling in the darkness of the room. There was a distinct bulge in his trousers, his organ pushing to get out and meet her.

Judith felt warm and wanted to bask in this warmth, like a lazy kitten on a carpet. She closed her eyes and caressed her breasts with her fingertips, her hands toying with her own nipples for a while, pleasantly surprised by their engorged size, then slowly sliding down on her belly until they came resting on the inside of her thighs.

She looked up at Harvey and smiled. She had never caressed herself in front of a man before. Yet tonight she felt boldly comfortable, she knew he was turned on by the sight of her hands fluttering over her own body. He just stared at her for a moment, the same amused smile still on his lips, until she extended her arms up towards him, arching her back.

He made her stand and then sit in a swivelling arm-chair, a few feet away from the couch. This time the leather felt ice-cold on her bare skin and she shivered. However, the sweat of her body quickly formed a thin film between her skin and the soft leather, and she could feel her body slip every time she moved, the motion enhanced by the rocking of the chair. She felt hot, very

582

hot, the surface of her skin now alight with the fire of her excitement.

Harvey knelt in front of her. They were closer to the door this time, she could see him better. And she liked the sight of him as he gently parted her legs with his hands and caressed the soft skin of her inner thighs.

Inserting his middle finger in her wet vagina, he slowly caressed the inside wall in a circular motion. 'You are very relaxed,' he commented. 'That's very good. Very good.' His voice had become a mere whisper.

Judith could feel his warm breath on her vulva, sensing his mouth was just a few inches away. She wanted him to kiss her there, to seize his head and direct it towards her flesh, but she didn't dare ask him. Instead, she parted her legs as wide as she could, hoping he would soon reply to her silent invitation.

'You have a nice, clean smell,' he said as his mouth drew close. 'I like nice, clean girls.' His sentence barely finished, his tongue started probing her intricate folds. At the moment he touched her Judith jerked her hips in a spasm of surprise and joy.

Then his tongue went deep inside her as his thumb flickered on her clitoris, his hand gently cupping her curly mound. The sensation was exhilarating, his mouth and hands now concentrating their caresses around this most sensitive area of her body. She liked the way his tongue felt especially, soft and wet and moving about sensually, discovering her slowly, methodically. She knew it wouldn't be long before she would climax right there against his mouth. Already she could only muffle the sounds of pleasure that were coming out of her mouth in a mix of cries and sobs.

His thumb let go of her stiff bud and he lifted her thighs onto his shoulders, pressing his face against her fragrant bush, now licking her with long, gusty laps, grunting noisily as he relished her wetness.

By now Judith had ceased to think, letting her body react instead. Crossing her legs behind his head, she pushed her knees together, forcing his tongue to probe deeper and deeper.

Her behind was now bathed in a mix of his saliva and her lovejuices, her body making slurping sounds as it moved on the chair, slipping and sliding, rocking back and forth and sideways, like a frail boat caught in the storm of their arousal.

Suddenly, she felt an irresistible urge to point her toes, contracting all the muscles in her legs, her calves quickly growing rock-hard, aching under the strain. The wave of the orgasm rose from her knees, crept up along her legs and rapidly reached deep inside her pelvis. She clenched her hands and her fingernails ripped the thin leather of the armrests.

She let out a loud moan as she climaxed, throwing her head back, out of breath and exhausted. Now she felt nothing but utter delight, no longer concerned that somebody could walk in on them. It seemed her pleasure had taken the whole of her body and her mind into another dimension. She didn't feel like she was sitting on a leather chair anymore, but rather floating above it, her skin no longer in contact with anything. In a haze, a blur, she saw Harvey getting up. The smile had disappeared from his lips, but in his eyes now shone a new light, the fire of lust. Unmistakably, his own desire hadn't been appeased; he wasn't done with her yet.

With a fluid movement of the wrists, he undid his belt and dropped his trousers, suddenly standing completely naked in front of her. He stood still for a minute and she admired his tanned skin, his hairy chest. His erect member was so stiff its tip almost reached his navel and the purple head was glistening in the dimness of the room.

As though in a dream, Judith reached out, grabbed the shaft with both hands and squeezed it gently. It was like an iron rod enveloped in a thin layer of soft fabric, the skin fluid and moving under her fingers, the core stiff and unyielding. For a moment she felt him throb in her hands, its velvety hardness radiating warmth and softness.

But almost immediately he seized her wrists, laughing, and forced her to let go. Then he pulled her arms up, as if he didn't want her to touch him but wanted her to remain passive under his domination. Bracing himself on the back of the chair, he raised his knees onto the armrests, then lifted his pelvis to her face and brought her hands down to his buttocks before thrusting his organ into her mouth.

At first its size almost gagged her, yet holding him in her mouth gave her a sensation of power, as if his pleasure now depended on her. Already she could feel a throbbing vein on her tongue as the head began sliding back and forth, along the roof of her mouth, compact and rounded like a small cushion. It was soft and warm, and a few drops of warm fluid escaped from the tiny slitted mouth, tasting sweetly new and pleasant, a bit salty.

She simply let him move in and out of her mouth and let her fingers run all over his bottom. By now she was reacting instinctively, gently scratching his bottom with her fingernails whilst in her mouth her tongue tentatively caressed the ridge of his glans.

'You are new to this,' he remarked. But already I can tell you have potential.' In reply she slipped one of her hands under his balls, hesitantly discovering and caressing them with her fingertips. They were small and firm, like two marble beads tightly held up in his sac which was covered with soft, silky hair.

Against her nose his flat stomach brushed repeatedly and she liked his aroma, a clean, musky scent that was also new, her brain unable to associate this manly perfume to anything she had ever smelled before.

In her mouth his plum seemed to grow bigger, tiny drops of fluid now freely flowing out of the slit-like tip. She found it most arousing to get him to react to the caress of her tongue and began sucking at him eagerly. She brought both her hands to take hold of his shaft and this time he didn't try to stop her.

He was right, she had never done this before. She was supposed to be a nice girl and in the small village she came from, nice girls saved themselves for their husbands. The thought almost made her laugh. None of the boys she knew would ever ask their wife to do something like this!

She was amazed to discover the extent to which she could have a man's pleasure at her mercy. Grabbing his shaft tightly, she began to suck the swollen head forcefully, feeling a strange hunger within her, compelling her to suck on further as her breath grew shallow. She felt powerful, holding his cock in her mouth, stiff and velvety. As it throbbed on her tongue she felt another rush of warmth between her legs; she was ready for more.

So was Harvey. Breathing fast, he let go of the back of the chair to stroke her hair, moaning loudly from the pleasant embrace of her eager mouth. She could feel him pulsating on her tongue, whilst she sucked and licked the purple head, somehow wishing she could swallow it completely. As she reached out to caress his balls again she realised they were now withdrawing inside him and wondered if he was about to climax. The thought of receiving his seed in her mouth was both exciting and frightening.

But then he suddenly withdrew. For Judith this was totally unexpected, and somewhat disappointing for she was anxious to discover more of him and to find out whether her mouth could bring him to the peak of pleasure. For a minute she thought she might have done something wrong but his smile reassured her.

'You learn quickly,' he commented, laboriously getting off the chair. 'You deserve top marks for enthusiasm.'

Again he stood naked before her. With her eyes she caressed his muscular figure, his flat stomach, his narrow hips, his firm thighs. He was indeed very attractive and probably the best teacher any woman could wish for. And right now he was with her. She longed to feel him inside her, she wanted to be taken by a man who knew what he was doing, not by some post-pubescent stable boy.

He went down on his knees and grabbed her hips, pulling her towards him. Very slowly, he entered her. Still slower, he began thrusting back and forth. Judith found these unhurried thrusts most pleasurable, so different from the quick, jerky stabs she had endured with her inexperienced boyfriends in the past. She moaned gently as she felt him fill her repeatedly.

'I won't come until you do,' Harvey said. It sounded like a promise.

'It shouldn't be very long,' she admitted.

Already she could feel the surge of another orgasm building up inside her, his hardness rekindling the reaction his mouth had triggered earlier. He slipped his wrists under her legs, the backs of her thighs slipping down along his forearms to comfortably nestle in the groove of his elbows.

His motion then started to gain momentum, accompanied once again by the swaying movement of the chair. Her climax came back very rapidly and suddenly, almost violently. She couldn't help the cry that came out of her mouth, she didn't care if the whole world could hear.

'Totally uninhibited,' he whispered, almost to himself 'It's nice to see a woman enjoying herself to the limit.' His thrust grew fast and powerful. He bent forward and grabbed her breast in his mouth. His suction was strong and he briefly took the nipple between his teeth. Judith screamed again, enjoying the slightly painful sensation. Then he let go with a groan and threw his head back, his mouth wide open. Cries were coming out of his throat in tandem with every jab of his member; stronger, louder, echoing through the room.

An ultimate sob came out as he climaxed and he fell on top of her, lifeless, as if his pleasure had taken all of his energy away. For a while his head rested on her breasts, his breath gently brushing her nipple as it came out from both his mouth and his nose.

His hair had the sweet smell of summer. Judith ran her fingers down his cheek and kissed his forehead.

'Thank you,' she whispered.

He slowly looked up at her and smiled. 'The pleasure was all mine, nurse.'

He remained motionless whilst the fire within Judith's body slowly subsided. She was exhausted, but happy. She could have stayed like this forever, holding his warm body in her arms silently. But after only a few seconds he got up and staggered towards the bathroom.

'I think I need a shower,' he said drowsily, looking at her over his shoulder. 'I hope we shall have the opportunity to work together again soon. Once again, welcome to the Dorchester Clinic.' He disappeared behind the door. Soon she could hear the sound of the water running in the shower.

She got up and picked her clothes off the floor, her legs now barely supporting her. Her first day at the Clinic had been a revelation, in more ways than one. It was nothing like the places she had been sent to during her training years.

But as her brain began functioning again she realised that what had just happened was beyond belief. She was amazed at her own reaction, how easily she had let him seduce her. But how could she have refused?

She looked around, suddenly worried. This was not professional at all, especially on her very first day at work! If anybody had walked in on them she could have lost her job. She couldn't let herself fall prey to a doctor, no matter how good looking he was. She couldn't take such a chance.

She sat down again, her flesh still warm from his touch, her body weak from the pleasure that had just rocked her. This would be the first, and the last time. It would have to be.

Chapter Three

*J*udith opened her sports bag and pulled her towel out. Still panting from her jogging session, she felt relaxed and alive, ready to start her second day at work. She was also pleased with herself and how she had managed to find her way through the busy streets of south-west London.

The nurses' locker room was deserted in the early morning. Judith's locker was in the middle of the last row, quite far from the main door but close to the sitting room. It was one of about 60 tall metal boxes, all painted pink, all bearing a golden sign with the occupant's name.

Sitting on the wooden bench, she peeled off her damp T-shirt and leggings and placed them in a plastic bag. It was a good idea to run to work. She could take a shower before starting her shift, washing away the dirt that collected on her skin as she ran through Hammersmith. Arriving early also meant she would have time to recover from the strain of the five-mile run.

She slowly walked around the corner and entered the shower room. The white ceramic tile floor was cool and refreshing under her aching feet. This was one large, communal room, not individual stalls like she was used to at her health club. But this morning Judith had the whole place to herself and could choose any of the nine showers alongside the far wall. She picked one some- where in the middle and turned the tiny tap.

The water came out of the shower head in a powerful jet, immediately drenching her from head to toe, massaging her sore legs, calming the fire that still throbbed on her cheeks. She dribbled a small puddle of shampoo into the palm of her hand and combed it through her wet hair, working it into a rich lather. Its papaya fragrance was also refreshing and soothing, the thick foam sliding down like white fat snakes along her neck and over her breasts, gathering at the bushy mound at the base of her abdomen.

Her fingers followed, covered with soap, as she slowly reached down between her legs, letting her fingertips lovingly slide against the soft, sinewy folds of her vulva. In a fraction of a second, her clitoris responded stiffly, rearing its tiny head under the soapy caress.

Judith sighed. In her mind the images of the previous evening were emerging once again, images that had haunted her sleep through the night. Despite the guilt she felt after he left, she now longed for Harvey to come back and again take her to the ultimate peak of pleasure. Given a chance, she would not remain passive next time . . . If there was a next time.

In her mind she had everything worked out. It would be just perfect if they could meet outside working hours so nobody would find out about it. But this was very risky, they would have to be very discreet.

That also meant they would be having an affair! Her, Judith Stanton, nursing school graduate, having an affair with Doctor Robert Harvey, the prestigious surgeon! Unbelievable!

Yet she knew he might have many lovers among the staff. She wasn't stupid enough to think she was the only nurse ever to have been taken to the doctors' lounge. But she would gladly share him if in return he could keep her satisfied.

Would he want her again? He seemed pleased with

her the previous night, but was it due solely to the thrill of a new conquest?

She tenderly traced the path his tongue had followed on her silken flesh, inserting two fingers inside her vagina, stroking her clitoris with her thumb. Her pussy contracted and readily sucked at her fingers, her body gently yielding to the arousal that had been kept constant within her since the previous night.

He seemed just right for her, instinctively knowing how to pleasure her, how to make her body react in ways she had never even suspected. But then there was the danger of being discovered. Could she risk her job for a few minutes of pleasure, however intense it might be?

This was a difficult decision. She would have to fight her desire if ever he came near her again whilst on duty. At the same time she could still feel him inside her, and would be prepared to do anything to be in his arms again. Such a contradiction. She didn't need that; she hated facing dilemmas.

Right now, however, there was nothing she could do about it, but let her mind wander and the recollection increase her excitement.

Her fingertips began dancing on her vulva with a life of their own. Already their pace was quickening, and Judith reached deep inside her, stroking the very centre of her bushy treasure as she felt her climax approaching.

'I bet she's thinking about Harvey!' an unexpected voice clamoured behind her.

Judith turned around suddenly, surprised to realise she was not alone in the nurses' locker room after all.

The shower room was steamy from the hot water gushing out of the wall, but she could clearly see two white silhouettes, two of her colleagues staring at her naughtily.

Her right hand was still clutched to her vulva, fingers engulfed in the throbbing tunnel, whilst her other hand was paused on her swollen breasts. She suddenly felt ashamed and turned around to face the wall again, quickly bringing both hands to her head and pretending to be washing her hair. How long had they been standing there? What had they seen?

'Nice addition to our staff,' the girl behind her continued in a loud voice. 'I wonder if she's had her initiation yet...'

The other nurse burst out laughing. 'From what I heard she's already had Harvey, which is not a bad start for a first day.' They both laughed hoarsely, almost grunting.

Judith didn't reply, desperately wanting them to go away, to leave her alone. She was also upset about their talk. Who were they? And how did they know about her and Doctor Harvey? She continued to rinse her hair, hoping they would soon disappear.

But instead she heard them giggling again as they approached her. A small hand grabbed the tap and turned it to increase the flow of hot water. Judith suddenly felt trapped and turned around to leave but the taller girl pushed her against the wall. Her mind raced furiously and now that they were closer she remembered them from the previous morning.

Tania and Jo, two nurses on the night shift; they were probably finishing work at this hour. Right now they seemed to be enjoying themselves tremendously, holding Judith against the wet ceramic wall, preventing her from going anywhere.

'What do you want?' she asked, becoming suddenly annoyed with their behaviour and a bit frightened. 'Let me go.'

The other two kept on giggling, still pinning her against the wall. Tania was dark and beautiful, with long, straight jet-black hair and piercing eyes. Tall and slim, she held Judith's arm in a grip of iron, her slim fingers clenched around Judith's soft skin.

'Let you go?' she said sarcastically. 'But my dear, we've only just met. It would be a bit rude not to offer to get to know you better at this point. Right, Jo?'

Jo was shorter, pale, blond and voluptuous. Very pretty, but she looked a bit artificial, probably because of

592

all the make-up she wore. The two women were night and day, yet both seemed cruel, each in her own way.

Judith wished for them to disappear or at least let go of her. The hot water coming from the shower nozzle was creating a lot of steam and their uniforms were getting splashed. Surely they wouldn't want to remain here much longer. But they seemed to take pleasure out of tormenting poor Judith. Obviously they knew exactly what to do to annoy her.

'So what did you think of Harvey?' Jo began. 'Isn't he something else? Did you like to feel his hands on you? I know I do ... Did you like him caressing your breasts?' She slowly ran her fingers around Judith's breasts, cupping them in turn, teasing the nipples which reacted like traitors by jutting out.

'Good,' Tania said, staring down at the swelling globes. 'I see we can get something out of you, my pretty. We were really looking forward to welcoming you, in our own special way.' She kissed Judith on the cheek, forcefully, almost violently, her thin lips quickly working their way down until they reached her mouth.

Meanwhile Jo kept teasing Judith's breasts, caressing them gently, almost lovingly, her fingertips delicately playing with the droplets of water that were still pearling on the white skin.

Judith was petrified. The women were caressing her against her will, but surprisingly she couldn't help being aroused by their behaviour. Never in her life had she felt the caress of a woman's touch, although she suspected it would not be very different than being touched by a man. And somehow her anger was offset by her curiosity.

'You have wonderful breasts, my love,' Jo whispered in her ear. 'Would you let us taste them? Your nipples look delicious. Let's see how much they can take.' She reached up to grab the shower head and redirect the flow of the shower onto Judith's nipples. The water fell like a boiling rain of needles, pinching and bouncing off her chest. Judith gasped under the sweet torture. Tania and Jo laughed again.

'Do you think we'll get to her eventually?' Tania asked before taking a hold of Judith's mouth and invading it with her tongue. Jo continued whispering in her victim's ear.

'Nice tongue, isn't it? Don't you like the way it possesses you with its pleasant roughness? Don't you wish you could feel that tongue elsewhere on your body?' She continued caressing Judith's breasts for a moment. 'Here? I know you'd like it.' Her hand swiftly slid down Judith's belly until the fingers disappeared under the bushy mound. 'Or here? She is a good licker, she knows exactly what to do to make you come quickly. Or slowly, if that's what you prefer. Today, however, you are in no position to tell us what you like. We're in charge.'

Judith couldn't reply. Her knees now buckling under her, rapidly growing weak. Tania's mouth was glued to hers, caressing Judith's lips with her tongue in a snake-like movement. Jo kept talking the whole time in Judith's ear, only slightly louder than the noise of the splashing water.

'How often did Harvey make you come? Did he lick you first before he took you with his delightful rod, or was it the other way around? I can't begin to tell you how often I've climaxed under his tongue. He's so skilful . . . But you know, Tania here is just as good, if not better . . .'

Both women reached down simultaneously and their fingers assaulted Judith's throbbing vulva, stretching the wet tunnel to the limit, creating a painful but pleasurable sensation as they slowly moved around inside, discovering the softness of the smooth prison walls. Judith felt herself yielding under their touch.

She was aroused despite her anger, reacting to the caresses of her tormentors beyond reason. She couldn't figure out whether it was solely due to their touch or because of the images that were forming in her head as she listened to Jo's litany. Perhaps it was a combination of both, compounded by her memories of the previous night.

Tania was very strong and domineering, her mouth still in control of the new recruit. 'Let her suck your tongue,' Jo advised in a sultry voice. 'Then you can better imagine what it will be like when she starts to lick your gorgeous clitoris . . .' At this point Judith realised she was actually replying to the tall girl's kisses, their tongues twirling around each other, their lips sealed in a passionate embrace. Her anger was quickly vanishing, giving her mounting arousal even more room to flow.

By now she was held up only through the strength of the girls pinning her to the wall. She was still somewhat incensed, but she was also close to climax. This combination of anger and arousal was something she had never felt before and the latter was quickly increasing as a result.

She couldn't decide whether she loved or hated it, nor if she wanted them to stop or continue. Her breath became laborious, her heart pounding furiously as her legs became weaker and weaker.

They let her go slightly and she slid down along the wall until she came to sit on the tiled floor. The water now fell just a few inches away, but not on her body, which was a relief. Jo knelt behind her, hoisting her head and wet tresses onto her lap, grabbing both breasts in a tight grip, holding her so that she couldn't escape. But by now Judith was beyond thinking of escaping. Although she couldn't approve of their cavalier approach, her excitement was such that she had to yield to their attack despite herself

Jo bent forward until she came to take Judith nipples in her mouth. 'They are so big, so luscious,' she said. She stopped talking only briefly to give them a quick, slurpy suck. Meanwhile Tania was kneeling between Judith's legs, her mouth quickly aiming for the stiff bud that was eagerly expecting its reward.

'Wait,' Jo said. 'Have a taste of these first.' Tania smiled wickedly and approached her target. Her fingers, long and slim, quickly surrounded the heavy breasts whilst

595

she pinched a nipple between her lips. The feeling was so strong that Judith couldn't help cry out in pain.

'Don't you like it?' Jo asked. 'It's a most marvellous pair of lips. When I tell her she'll begin to lick and suck your clit like you've never been sucked before. Believe me, not a man on this planet can tease a woman the way she does. That's why she got her job here, by the way.'

The two women were now working on her breasts, hunched over her like hungry vultures. Judith couldn't move, either because they were restraining her with their bodies, or more probably because she was simply hoping they would soon fulfil their promise to make her achieve her climax.

Tania's mouth was swiftly grazing on her nipples, alternating between the two erect peaks, fast and furious. Ever so often her teeth would brush them as well, sending a bolt of pleasure and pain through Judith's abdomen, all the way down to between her legs, all the while still increasing her arousal.

Jo was using only her tongue, caressing the whole of the breasts with long, deliberately slow licks. Every so often Judith would feel their cheeks brush against her tender skin, so much softer and more pleasant than a man's rough skin. Even their hands were more gentle despite the way they were caressing her. At this moment she realised that perhaps a woman would know better how to pleasure another woman . . .

Judith began to sob, more in pleasure than in outrage now. Her tormentors were skilful, but she was still somewhat concerned about the power they seemed to hold over her.

'Now,' Jo ordered, before bending down to take hold of Judith's nipples once more.

And Tania went down, her mouth switching targets, going from Judith's breasts to her vulva in a flash. Immediately her thin lips grabbed the swollen clitoris like a steel clamp, making it react and become even stiffer.

Judith screamed. The sensation was intense and painful, like a bite, but it also sent a simultaneous wave of pleasure through her whole body, making her tremble uncontrollably. A second later, Tania released her grip completely. Judith was somewhat relieved, but her body was terribly disappointed. She moaned loudly. Jo burst out laughing.

'What did you think of that?' she asked loudly. 'Didn't I tell you she was good? Now would you like her to make you come? Would you?'

Judith started crying. She was exhausted, she needed release, she wanted her attackers to pleasure her yet she was too ashamed of her desires to ask them.

'That's enough!' another voice shouted.

Tania and Jo looked up suddenly. Judith continued crying. At the entrance of the shower room stood Mrs Cox, the Clinic's nursing supervisor, a woman in her late thirties, quite tall and curvaceous, with dark wavy hair. Extremely beautiful, she looked like a movie star from the 1940s, her skin pale and her lips a luscious red. But despite her classic beauty, she was also stern and very strict.

Although she generally spoke in a low voice, her words were almost always orders, as they were right now. Judith had heard from a colleague that despite this severe attitude the woman was nonetheless respected and even liked by all the nursing staff. However this morning she seemed most angry at what was going on.

Their uniforms soaking, Tania and Jo stood up sheepishly. Laying motionless on the ceramic tiles, the water bouncing off the floor just a few inches from her shoulder, Judith looked at them through her tears. Both women looked like lustful vampires, two vague silhouettes lost in a cloud of steam, their erect nipples nevertheless clearly visible through the wet fabric of their uniforms. For a split second, Judith couldn't help feeling attracted by the sight of their swollen breasts. If only Mrs Cox hadn't come in, she might have been given the opportunity to caress them as well . . .

'You both know the procedure regarding new members of staff,' Mrs Cox told the two girls. 'I do hope you can restrain yourselves in the future. Meet me in my office before you come on duty this evening. Now go.' The two dripping figures disappeared outside the steamy room.

Judith stood up slowly, slightly relieved, but her body still aroused and angry at not having obtained release. Mrs Cox walked towards her and turned off the flow of water.

'I'm sorry about this,' she said dryly. 'I hope they didn't hurt you. They will be punished, if that's any consolation to you.'

Judith continued sobbing, more in frustration than in relief

'Did you come?' Mrs Cox asked still in the same tone. Judith looked up in amazement. Why was she asking her that? The question was direct, matter-of-fact, but so out of place that Judith lost her speech for a moment. However, the tone of voice commanded a reply

'N . . . n . . . o,' she stammered.

Mrs Cox walked to her with determination and quickly slipped her arm around the nurse's naked waist, holding her tightly, her other hand sliding down between Judith's legs.

Judith was too surprised to say anything. The woman's touch was not too gentle, a bit forceful, but pleasant. Already she could feel her arousal mounting again. Quickly, the expert fingertips teased the swollen clitoris into madness, rapidly sliding back and forth on the wet vulva, once again transforming Judith into a wanton puppet.

She slipped her arms around the woman's neck and shyly nestled her head in its curve. Her pleasure grew, increasing powerfully until it burst within her, and was finally allowed to overflow. Her climax was long and strong, like a tidal wave. Judith moaned softly as her head fell on Mrs Cox's shoulder, her tears quickly absorbed by the thin fabric of the supervisor's uniform.

'There,' Mrs Cox said as she released her embrace

around the naked waist. 'Now get to work, you have patients to attend to.' She turned around and disappeared, leaving a fulfilled, but very puzzled Judith alone in the locker room.

Chapter Four

Judith's arms were so weak she was barely able to lift her raincoat to hang it on the rack. Leaning against the wall, she took her shoes off without untying the shoelaces, prying each one off with the other foot, too tired to bend over.

She kicked them away in a remote corner and each banged the wall with a thump. They bounced back in different directions, her left shoe disappearing under the telephone table whilst the right one found its niche behind the umbrella bin.

She looked at them and sighed. Brand new shoes, but they wouldn't last long if she didn't take better care of them. Not to worry, now that she had a job she could afford a new pair every month. Besides, this pair wasn't of the greatest quality, to say the least. The thick leather didn't want to yield and adapt to the shape of her feet, making her heels sore after just a few hours.

Under her sore feet the carpet of the entrance hall was much softer and she wriggled her toes a couple of times. That felt better, but what she needed most right now was simply to put her feet up.

Walking to her room, she mechanically undid the clip that held her hair up and her blond mane fell all over her shoulders in a cascade of pale curls, bouncing around her neck, free at last. That was also quite a relief, she hated having to tie her hair up.

For some strange reason her handbag was heavier than when she had left that morning. She had taken it up the three flights of stairs to the flat half-dragging, half-carrying it. Tomorrow morning before leaving for work she would have to go through it and take out all the useless stuff that constantly found its way in there.

As she passed the door to the kitchen she noticed there was somebody in there. Already she knew it wasn't Brenda, her flatmate, but probably one of the many boyfriends that constantly streamed through the flat, in one day, out the next. Judith glanced in furtively, not really wanting to meet this one.

The man was half-hidden behind the open door of the refrigerator, his head tilted back as he drank milk straight from the bottle. A stream of thin, pale drops trickled down along his neck and his bare chest. He didn't seem to notice her. Judith made a mental note to take her coffee black the next morning and kept walking.

She turned her head slightly and took one last look as she opened her bedroom door, only to see him right before he disappeared inside Brenda's room. Only then did she realise he was completely naked. All she saw was his back, broad and muscular, and a tight pair of buttocks, round and firm. No-one she knew; obviously a new guy on Brenda's list.

She entered her own bedroom and sighed as she shut the door behind her, throwing her bag in a corner before collapsing face down on the bed. Another hard day at work, only half-way through the week, and she was already exhausted.

Hours of walking through corridors, meeting staff, getting to know the set up, in addition to helping out in the operating theatre. Hopefully it would get better once she knew everybody and where everything was.

She slowly turned onto her back and laboriously stood up. As she flicked the switch of the lamp on her bedside table the faint light cast a blue glow around the small room. With a tired sigh she started to unbutton her uniform, the white cotton amazingly still crisp under her fingertips. She would have to buy more of these when she went shopping for shoes.

The rules of the clinic stipulated all the nurses had to be dressed in white from head to toe, even their underwear, but they didn't have to wear the traditional cap. Apparently it looked more professional yet less medical; just like in America, the realm of cosmetic surgery. In fact, many of the clinic's guidelines were modelled on American institutions, to give the patients an impression of Hollywoodesque glamour and to make the nursing staff look more like beauticians.

Judith stared at her half-naked reflection in the mirror as her dress fell to the floor. She barely recognised herself, but was quite pleased with the image she presented.

Her bra was brand new, a thin lacy garment with a metal wire, and fastened between her breasts, pushing them up and emphasising their perkiness, letting the brown circles of her nipples shyly show through. She was wearing matching panties, deliciously soft and lacy as well and revealing, ever so slightly, the small mound of her blond curls. Her suspender belt completed the outfit and held up sheer white stockings, although she wasn't required to wear stockings if she didn't want to. Nevertheless, Judith had tried wearing them for the first time today and definitely felt prettier that way. White suited her, something she never would have thought, considering the milkiness of her bare skin.

Suddenly she didn't want to undress any further; she wanted to simply look at that pretty girl who stared back in the mirror. Was this the girl Robert Harvey had caressed just a few evenings ago? The same girl who had been submitted to sweet torture in the shower room the previous morning? Judith now felt different, somehow she even looked different . . .

Again today she had been rather uncomfortable at work. Everyone she had been introduced to had stared at her perhaps a little longer than was really necessary, their eyes travelling up and down and quickly sizing her from head to toe, seemingly studying her body with a barely disguised interest.

Maybe this was just her imagination running wild. She had to admit everyone had been very friendly and welcoming, even if at times it had puzzled her. Perhaps they seemed too friendly. That scared her, yet excited her at the same time.

She had started her new job in a most unusual fashion, her sensuality being awakened and even challenged at the very outset. Now she was thinking clearly, she could see the situation for what it really was. What had happened with Robert Harvey, and then with Tania and Jo, was just a coincidence. They were probably the kind of people who enjoyed sex and got a kick out of impressing the new nurses. All she had to do in future was avoid them. But would she have the strength?

Tania and Jo were not really a problem, unless she had to work a night shift. That would come sooner or later, but she would deal with it in due time. Robert Harvey was another story. She hadn't seen him at all today, but she was bound to work with him again sooner or later. What then? Would he try seducing her again? Hopefully, yes . . . Or not . . . She didn't know anymore.

As for Mrs Cox, there was nothing to worry about. The supervisor had probably simply sensed her need to be pleasured that morning in the shower room. She had given the young nurse the release she needed, that was all. Yet Judith couldn't shake the weird feeling that had seized her and still lingered as a result. The woman had been so cold, almost clinical, in the way she had pleasured her. It was almost as if it was part of her job. Strangely, Judith somehow longed to experience this again, as if the woman's rough caresses had only left her yearning for more.

She looked in the mirror one more time. She realised she was very attractive, but also quite inexperienced when it came to physical pleasure. Even as a teenager, the few young men she had gone out with were almost

603

scared of touching her, afraid of rejection. Those who did were out to get her like a trophy, interested solely in their own pleasure, never hers.

She needed a man, a real one, like Harvey. Or did she? Her body yearned to be taken to the heights of pleasure, to experience new sensations, to discover fulfilment. Her flesh was aching to know how much there was to take.

Across the hall sounds were coming from Brenda's room, the same, familiar sounds Judith could hear almost every night: moans and grunts. She sighed. Brenda was insatiable, having in her bed one man after the other, unable to spend even one night on her own it seemed. Judith was somewhat annoyed about that. Yet at times she couldn't help but feel aroused by the loud love-making. It got to the point where she couldn't figure out whether she was fed up with Brenda's loud cries, or if she was simply jealous of always being alone.

She lay back on the bed and closed her eyes, imagining she was the one being taken right now. The warmth of her man's body enveloped her in a comforting embrace, like a fluffy cloud. Involuntarily she began to writhe on the duvet, her arousal coming alive within her, her fingers gradually initiating their dance on her warm skin.

And in her mind he appeared, tall, beautiful, powerful. An imaginary lover, incredibly handsome, wanting nothing but to pleasure her, a slave to her desires. As usual he didn't have a face, or rather he had many looks. Sometimes dark, sometimes fair, always perfect in his male beauty. Of course, his muscles were taut and his skin warm and soft. But most of all he was hers, and hers alone, only one of the many men who had visited her like this, as she lay alone in her bed.

Laughter rose in Brenda's room. Whatever they were up to, they seemed to be enjoying themselves. Suddenly Judith was no longer annoyed or upset: now she understood. She realised that she and Brenda indeed had something in common, they were sisters in their quest for fulfilment.

604

Judith was now guiding her invisible lover's hands over her lace-covered breasts, pressing him to caress them gently, to softly toy with her nipples, making him graze them with his fingernails, worrying them until they became so stiff they practically pierced the delicate fabric. Her nipples were so much more sensitive when being teased through the lace . . .

Next she showed him how to caress the underside of her breasts, having him cup them gently but without ever ceasing his ministrations on the erect peaks. His touch on her was exquisite, as always, and she moaned gently through pursed lips.

Her vulva replied readily and immediately she brought his hand down to briefly feel her wetness. She didn't let him slide his hands under her panties, not just yet. He had to touch her through the fabric first. Just like her nipples, her tiny shaft wanted to be teased indirectly, gently scratched into submission.

She moaned and pressed her legs together, the tender skin above the edge of her white stockings pushing against his fingers, squeezing his hand into a soft embrace, holding him prisoner. His thumb kept moving nonetheless, at first lightly discovering her warmth, but quickly growing insistent on her swollen clitoris, rubbing it forcefully along its length, crushing her still-clothed flesh. He caught the whole of her soaked pussy with his hand, pushing at her entrance through the gusset of her panties, his fingertips desperately trying to pierce through and directly touch her wetness. His palm kept massaging her mound, grinding down on it, stopping only short of her throbbing clitoris.

His face now lightly rested on her chest, his tongue gliding inside the cup of her bra, laboriously pushing the fabric down to uncover an engorged nipple. First he took it between his pursed lips and pinched it delicately, deliciously toying with it until it grew long and firm. Then he gently seized it with his teeth, letting their sharp edge lightly graze its stiffness whilst his tongue hovered over it like a butterfly.

605

Judith grunted, echoing the sounds coming from Brenda's room. She opened her eyes and stared at the ceiling for a moment, suddenly wondering what it would be like to press her naked body against the rough and cold stucco surface, to feel each prickly bump softly scrape against the warm skin of her breasts, her hips, even the moist folds of her vulva : . . Yet at the same time she felt much more comfortable laying on the thick duvet, her body enveloped in warmth and softness. And, of course, that was the way it should be; no-one would ever think of using something rough to generate pain in order to achieve pleasure.

After a while she lifted her head and looked at her reflection in the mirror once again. Of course, she was alone. As usual, her imaginary lover had disappeared from the moment she had opened her eyes. All she could see was a wanton creature laying half-naked over a thick duvet, one breast uncovered, a stiff nipple caught between her pink nails, the other hand hidden between her legs.

In the blue light of the lamp her skin looked even whiter and perfectly silky, the smooth curve of her thighs amazingly pleasing. The more she looked in the mirror, the more she became aroused by the sight of her own image, as if she was watching another woman, beautifully sexy. So that's what they had seen, those who had so casually approached and caressed her . . .

She sat up and squarely faced the mirror, her stockinged feet landing flat on the floor. As she undid the clasp that held her bra fastened at the front, her breasts jutted out, round and swollen, pushing the lacy fabric away, revealing stiff nipples pointing up and protruding proudly. She wriggled her shoulders lasciviously, watching the straps gently glide down along her arms until they encircled her wrists. She was surprised by how warm such a slim piece of elastic could feel, knowing that this warmth could only have been imparted by her own burning skin.

Then she swiftly tossed her head forward, her blond

locks landing right on top of her swollen breasts. She grabbed them with both hands and pushed them together, rubbing and enveloping them with her hair, pinching her nipples between her thumb and forefinger though the silken strands.

Her hair felt coarse on her tender skin, but she rather enjoyed the slightly prickly sensation. She caressed her breasts with her hair in a slow kneading motion, all the while watching herself in the mirror. Her skin grew hot in her hands, and that warmth radiated through her body, following a delicious path right down to her throbbing pussy.

Her parted legs revealed a soaked patch at the crotch. The flimsy fabric wasn't thick enough to stop the flow of her dew as her arousal kept mounting. She briefly let go of her breasts to unfasten her stockings so she could pull her panties down, suddenly wanting to see her own wet bush.

Her fingers fumbled impatiently as she undid each of the clasps. She didn't even bother taking her suspender belt or her stockings off. Her hips jerked up and she pulled her soaked panties down, revealing the golden hairs of her mound now dark and curly with wetness, clinging together and adorned with pearly drops of her own moisture. Her stiff clitoris stood out, swollen and glistening like the rest of her dark pink folds. She licked her lips nervously.

If only she really had a man with her . . . She would make him kneel in front of her right now, his hands tied behind his back, and bid him to lick at her folds endlessly. He would be her slave, he would have to do anything she would ask, or else . . .

She reached down and gently brushed her clitoris with the tip of her middle finger. It was hard as steel, smooth and slick. Her own touch made her tremble, as if her fingers were charged with electricity. She closed her eyes again and imagined her finger was her lover's tongue. She knew he would soon grunt with desire for her fragrant bush, licking it in long strokes, wanting to taste

607

all of her. His tongue would then find its way deep within her, discovering her silken tunnel, losing itself in its throbbing warmth.

Judith looked up again, watching her fingers disappear inside her, her flesh sucking them in greedily. She could almost see her stiff bud contracting under the strength of her rising climax.

She wanted to watch herself come, but the wave of pleasure that began to shake her made that difficult; she was almost forced to close her eyes, yet she managed to keep watching, a voyeur to her own climax, and her pleasure was even more intense. She saw the muscles in her legs tensing rapidly, her knees shaking under the strain. Only when she saw her wet vulva contract forcefully under her fingertips did she allow herself to let go, collapsing on the bed in a soft thump as her pleasure swept through her.

Turning onto her side she pulled a corner of the duvet over her midriff. She didn't have the strength to take her stockings off, that could wait. Her body was still reeling from the wave that had just shaken her, leaving her completely drained. Even sliding under the duvet seemed like too much of an effort right now.

Across the hall, she heard Brenda yell with pleasure. Her lips twitched in a faint smile as she fell into a dreamless slumber.

Chapter Five

Mike Randall. Judith couldn't believe her eyes. The Olympic athlete turned movie star was lying just a few inches from her, his left leg in an enormous plaster cast from the ankle to the hip. She put the chart down on the bedside table and looked at him more closely before pulling the blanket over him.

He was gorgeous. Still sedated, his breath was regular, with occasional sighs coming out from between his parted, luscious lips. His right leg was slightly bent, the thigh firm and covered in fine golden hairs, the calf perfectly sculpted.

Nothing but the thin straps of a black G-string around his hips held up the distended pouch that muzzled his genitals. Fine pubic hair, strands of silk, escaped from under the hem. His abdomen was flat and ridged like a washing board, emphasising the square definition of his chest. The body was uniformly tanned, taut and inviting.

Images flashed though Judith's head: the Olympic Games, three years ago. His muscular body crossing the finish line triumphantly; his maleness blatantly encased in the tight, dark blue lycra running shorts, finishing first in the 400 metre hurdle race, the sweat of his effort glistening on his arms and chest.

Upon his return home he had been plagued by hordes

of women hysterically throwing themselves at him, some of them completely naked, stupidly claiming they wanted to have his baby. He was everyone's idol, his smile could have melted a statue. Afterwards he had become a popular movie star, unashamed of filming steamy bed scenes, showing off his firm flesh, flexing his muscles, often stealing the show from his female partners, the glamorous actresses who would have waived their fees just to be his partner in bed, albeit for the benefit of a camera.

And now he was asleep, almost naked, right in front of Judith. She had been assigned as his nurse for today, to help him recover from the surgery, his leg having been repaired following a motorbike accident. The surgeons would make sure there would be no scarring, for it could jeopardise his career. As his nurse, Judith would make sure he wanted for nothing.

She checked the orders on his chart and took his blood pressure. He had a manly aroma about him which was musky and inviting. It was probably one of those upmarket men's colognes he had advertised on television. As she set the stethoscope on the pulse point, she let her fingertips slightly caress the hard muscles of his biceps, tracing the edge of the groove at the junction of his elbow.

He opened his eyes slightly and looked up at her. 'Hi,' he whispered with a sleepy smile. His famous smile, rich and inviting. Judith felt a sudden rush of warmth invade her.

'Hi,' she replied, returning his smile.

He looked at her hand, still paused on his arm.

'I like your touch. Will you take good care of me?'

'Of course.'

'Promise?'

'Promise.'

He closed his eyes and tilted his head the other way. Judith dropped the stethoscope but her fingers continued their journey for a while, feeling the curve of his biceps, the rounded shoulder, then stopping at the base of his neck. His skin was warm and soft as velvet.

His regular breathing told her he was sleeping again. Sweet temptation grew. The medication he had been given was very strong, chances are he wouldn't remember any of this when he woke up, or at most he would think it was all a dream. What harm would there be in letting her hand wander?

Judith became more daring and cautiously slipped her hand under the thin blanket, following the sliding path of his bare chest. He didn't even twitch.

His skin was supple over the hard muscle, the nipple large, readily contracting under her touch. She lightly caressed him with the palm of her hand, letting his warmth radiate up her wrist. Her fingertips followed the underside of his pectoral muscle, the ridge deep and hard, and then switched to caress the other one. On that side his nipple was already hard, yet seemed to pucker further still under her fingertips.

She kept her eyes on him the whole time, looking out for signs that he was coming out of his slumber, but she was happy not to see any indication that he could feel what she was doing. Her heart was pounding fast and she bit her lip nervously. This was dangerous, he could wake up at any moment.

Not being able to see what she was touching was also a strong incentive to keep going, but it made her feel very naughty to caress his sleeping body without his knowledge.

Yet this was an opportunity too good to pass on. Already her fingertips had resumed their journey down his abdomen, bobbing up and down along the peaks and valleys of his finely ridged stomach. She stopped when she felt the beginning of a long line of silky hairs she knew would lead down to the thick bush right above his genitals.

This was getting a little too far, she thought. She began pulling out her hand, caressing him just as slowly on the

611

way back. At that moment she realised she wanted him. Such a body.

She sighed. He probably had enough women to deal with, what would he want with her? Besides, right now he was her patient, it wouldn't be right to think of him in any other terms. With regret, she turned around and left the room to attend to her other patients.

'I'm sorry to hear you are leaving tomorrow,' came the voice behind the peach-coloured curtain.

Judith had silently stepped in the room, but stopped when she recognised Edouard Laurin's heavy accent. Lady Austin's bed was hidden behind the drape, yet the light coming from the window was casting the patient's and Edouard's shadows on it. From where she stood, Judith could see them like a Chinese puppet theatre: two silhouettes, one lying on the bed, propped up by pillows, the other standing next to it.

She had to check up on Lady Austin, apply some medicated lotion to her feet and give her another dose of painkillers. Yet the fact that they had pulled the curtain told her they might not want to be disturbed. She hesitated a moment. Should she let them know she was in the room with them or just quietly make her way out? Would her squeaky shoes betray her presence?

'I'm sorry I didn't get to see more of you,' Lady Austin said in a childish tone. 'I remember last time I was here, you couldn't get enough of me.'

'My dear,' he replied, 'believe me when I say I am just as sorry as you are. But you are not leaving just yet and I am here now, n'est-ce pas?'

Judith was just about to turn around and leave discretely, but froze in her steps when she saw him bending down to kiss the woman. She was astonished, yet there could be no doubt about what was going on behind the curtain. She distinctly saw their tongues coming out of their mouths to touch in a sensuous caress, their lips never quite coming into contact. At the same time his hands pulled down the blanket, and then ran across Lady

612

Austin's chest. Judith was mesmerised by the sight of it all, it looked so unreal.

'Undress for me,' Lady Austin whined again, sounding like a spoilt child.

Judith watched as his shadow stood up again and he started to quickly undress. First he took off what Judith concluded must have been his white coat which he wore even though he wasn't a doctor. With a swift move of the wrist he then managed to get rid of his tie and started to unbutton his shirt.

Simultaneously Judith also saw her patient pulling up her gown above her head. The woman's breasts, reshaped or false as they might have been, pointed up perkily, like a teenager's, her nipples stiff and eager.

A second later Édouard dropped his trousers. The shadow of his naked body was very impressive; his erect cock standing up, a long and thick rod. The image on the curtain were so clear that Judith could make out the ridge of the head, an enormous, swollen plum.

She ran her tongue across her dry lips. Although she had seen him quite often in the operating theatre, she had never realised what a nice body he had. His shoulders were broad and square, his buttocks rounded and pert. His shaft seemed powerful, pointing towards the ceiling, animated with a life of its own.

And as she watched, Judith's vulva came alive as well, exuding a warm, honey-like dew, suddenly hungry to feel Édouard's length enter and fill it. She felt like a voyeur, watching two faceless, naked bodies. She didn't know what to do, torn between the temptation to stay and be a witness to their coupling – the need to follow orders and attend to her patient – and her wish to simply do the decent thing and leave them alone.

Her thoughts were interrupted when she felt a presence behind her. Mrs Cox had also entered the room.

Silently, she took a hold of Judith's arm and swiftly led her out of the room whilst sighs and moans began to rise from behind the curtain. The nurse followed without a word, horribly ashamed.

They stopped in the corridor just a couple of feet from the door. How long had Mrs Cox been there? Did she realise Judith had been watching the couple? If she did, this could only mean trouble.

'You are very likely to be a witness to scenes like this,' Mrs Cox told the blushing nurse. 'Never intervene unless you are invited to do so. After you've been here a few weeks, you will have a different perspective on such situations. In the meantime, just go about your duties and come back to your patient in a few minutes.'

She turned around and walked back towards the nurses' station. Judith's heart was pounding, the supervisor's words still echoing in her head. Luckily, the corridor was deserted and hopefully nobody would ever find out that Judith Stanton, the new nurse, was a voyeur.

She was on the verge of tears. She hadn't meant for this to happen, it was just a case of being in the wrong place at the wrong time. Surely they couldn't fire her for that? Yet at the same time she had taken some kind of wicked pleasure out of watching them . . .

Things were happening too fast. Everywhere around her there seemed to be wantonness beyond control. Somehow Judith felt left out, she wanted to be part of this whirl of passion, her body was aching to experience new sensations, to merge with all these gorgeous, desirable sources of pleasure. Doctor Harvey, Tania and Jo, Edouard, and even Mrs Cox. The effect they had on her was overwhelming. She was being teased in a cruel way, like a child left looking at a window full of toys but never being allowed to play with them.

She briefly ran her hand across her chest, feeling her nipples hardening under her uniform. She could also feel her panties soaked with her warm dew, like they had been so often since she had started to work at the Clinic, just a few days ago.

This was too much to take. She had been in a perpetual state of arousal, but only seldom been satisfied. Right now she craved the touch of another body. Her desire was so powerful it was sending shivers down her spine. She leant against the wall, her mind numb.

Suddenly Edouard appeared in front of her, a broad smile on his face. '*Ma chère*,' he crooned, 'were you in there watching us? That would be naughty...' He quickly looked around; they were alone in the corridor. Coming closer, he raised his hand and casually stroked Judith's breasts, feeling their heavy weight in turn, gently tweaking the erect nipples through her uniform. She sobbed and shuddered, unable to resist his touch, unwilling to push him away.

'I see you enjoyed it,' he continued in a whisper, his accent getting heavier, sexier. 'I wish we could spend more time together, but right now I have to visit other patients.' His right hand continued stroking her breasts whilst his left hand quickly snaked its way under her dress and inside her panties, never stopping its search until the fingers finally lost themselves inside her wet, gaping vulva.

His smile got even broader. 'I can smell your desire,' he continued, his face now just a few inches from hers. 'Soon, *mon amour*, very soon...' He let his lips lightly brush her cheek, then suddenly let go of her and quickly walked away, leaving her even more puzzled.

As he disappeared around the corner, Judith leant back against the wall, as if awakening from a dream, wondering if all this had really just happened or if her mind was going crazy with lust.

Lady Austin was sitting upright in her bed, noisily nibbling on chocolates. The thin blanket covering her chest was tucked underneath her armpits.

'Would you like one?' she said with her mouth full as she pushed the box towards Judith. 'They're Belgian, the finest. I find the Continentals are such refined people. In any case, they make lovely chocolates.' The tip of her pink tongue slightly came out of her mouth to lick her finger.

Still shaking from her encounter in the corridor, Judith

615

pushed the medication trolley aside and lifted the blanket to have a look at her patient's feet. Tiny red lines betrayed the fact that there had been surgery, however they would disappear in just a few weeks. Already the feet looked younger; the skin seemed soft and plump, and the blue veins had disappeared.

'Aren't they adorable?' Lady Austin asked, wriggling her toes. 'I know a boutique in Madrid where they make lovely sandals. I think I'll drop by sometime next week.'

Spreading the feet thickly with medicated lotion, Judith carefully massaged the skin, making sure the heavy cream penetrated even between the toes. Lady Austin lay back and let out a sigh.

'What a nice touch you have,' she commented softly. 'I wish you had been here a few years ago when I had my breasts done.'

She pulled down the blanket and uncovered her bare breasts. Judith was startled by their sight. They looked even better than the shadow she had observed on the curtain just a few moments earlier. Firm and round, the two globes were pale and milky, the nipples dark and puckered, pointing at the ceiling, proud and sophisticated.

'Just like they were when I was twenty,' Lady Austin continued. 'They're all mine, you know. I refused to have implants. Just make them look good, I asked. Doctor Harvey works wonders on me. He's quite expensive, but worth every penny.'

Judith's fingers continued finding their way between the patient's toes, clumsily, almost mechanically, for she wasn't paying attention to what she was doing anymore. Now she couldn't keep her eyes off those breasts, inviting, compelling. Never before had she been so disturbed just looking at a woman's chest.

Lady Austin was slowly caressing them, as if she wanted to make sure they were real. 'I told him to pretend he was a sculptor, and to make them as he liked, something he would be attracted to.' She looked up at Judith and winked.

616

'It worked.' she confided. 'He can't keep his hands off them when I come here now.' She paused to stare at her nurse's hands.

'Would you like to touch them?' she asked in a childish tone. 'Please?' Her voice was the same that had been talking to Edouard earlier, as if issuing some form of invitation. 'I'd like you to touch them. I know you'd like it . . .'

'I don't think this would be very proper, Lady Austin,' Judith said in a trembling voice. She could almost picture Edouard's hands on them. No wonder he couldn't resist their sight. Judith was tempted to touch them as well, just to see what it would be like to feel the nipples contract under her fingertips, but could she ever bring herself to willingly fondle another woman's breasts? A woman who was her patient? 'Not very proper,' she repeated. 'After all, you are my patient . . .'

'What does it matter,' the woman whined. 'Wouldn't you like to join me in bed? Edouard was here just a few minutes ago. His caresses were exquisite, but right now I want a woman with me.'

Judith didn't reply. Now there was no doubt Edouard had ended up in bed with his patient. In fact, she could still smell him on the blankets. Not only was that highly unethical but now Lady Austin wanted Judith to join her in bed as well! How strange. How tempting.

She looked at the breasts once again. Judith couldn't understand this new attraction and arousal she felt by the sight of a woman's body. She licked her dry lips as a wild image flashed through her head. She saw herself reaching out towards the firm mounds. Somehow she could feel their fluid weight in the palm of her hands. She closed her eyes and willed the thought away. There was no way she could let herself do that, she had to fight it.

She flipped the blanket back over the woman's feet and quickly pushed her trolley out of the room, almost running away from temptation.

* * *

617

'We hope to see you again soon,' Mrs Cox said with a smile.

'So do I,' Lady Austin replied. 'I have enjoyed my stay like never before. Your staff have been most pleasant, as usual, especially the new nurse. She has such a sweet, innocent look about her, although she seems bit a hesitant when it comes to dispensing special care . . .'

'We can assure you this will change when you come back. She has only just joined our staff. We hope to make her one of our best nurses.'

The chauffeur closed the door and got in the car. Mrs Cox stood silently as she watched the dark Bentley drive down the tree-lined street before disappearing around the corner.

She had mixed feelings about Judith. She fondly remembered their moment together in the shower room, but masturbating girls was not her style. Although she found the young nurse's innocent look most attractive, the plans she had for her would surely change all that. With a shrug, she turned around and went back inside.

Chapter Six

*T*he lecture hall was buzzing with the noise from several simultaneous conversations. Judith entered hesitantly through a door at the back and quickly picked the nearest empty chair, in the last row. She sank into the deep seat, almost out of breath, her heart still pounding.

She was nearing the end of her shift – and the end of her second week – and she was so tired it was hard to believe she could still walk. Yet she practically had to run through the corridors, desperately looking for directions. It would have looked rather bad had she arrived late, but she had made it with just a few minutes to spare.

The meeting was just about to begin. A few latecomers were still arriving, red-faced and puffing, quickly finding chairs amongst the two hundred or so people who were already seated. These sessions were held on the last Friday of each month and attendance was mandatory. Only one nurse remained at each station and would be given a transcript of the discussion.

Her colleagues had been rather vague about the usual content of these meetings, so Judith didn't know what to expect, although she suspected they were probably on the whole rather boring.

Yet the atmosphere was charged with electricity,

people laughing and waving at each other from across the room, giddy and excited like a bunch of school children. The front row seats were occupied by people dressed in street clothes, members of staff who were off duty but had to attend the lecture anyway, colourful dots in the sea of white uniforms. The rest of the staff seemed segregated, doctors on the right hand side, nurses in the middle, kitchen and cleaning staff on the left.

A tall man walked to the lectern and started shuffling a bunch of papers.

Judith recognised Doctor Alan Marshall, founder and Director of the Clinic. He was a handsome man of about fifty and was therefore quite a bit older than the rest of the staff. Standing tall and proud, he looked very distinguished but somewhat snobbish; like a businessman rather than a doctor. His tanned face offered a sharp contrast to the silver threads of his hair. Judith still remembered the first thought to cross her mind when she had been introduced to him: he was the man with the expensive haircut.

His lips were dark and thin, seemingly unable to smile; his jaw square, stern and unforgiving; his nose perfectly shaped. The white coat he was wearing didn't suit him, he would look better in dark clothes. In fact, a dark aura seemed to follow him, making him look attractively calm, yet sending disturbing vibrations, giving the impression of imminent threat. On the whole, he seemed an utterly cold man, with the cruel beauty of a vampire.

Judith cast her gaze around the room, looking for familiar faces. From where she sat she could only see the back of their heads but she recognised the brown locks of Elizabeth Mason's thick mane, alongside Doctor Rogers's pale head. These two were almost always together, inseparable, like a kid brother endlessly following his older sister.

Robert Harvey was sitting at the far end of the front row, engaged in a deep conversation with another surgeon whom Judith didn't know. The seat he had taken was at a diagonal extreme from where she was sitting, away from her body but still very close in her mind. After all, it was only a few evenings ago that they had shared that moment in the Doctors' Lounge. Yet somehow it seemed like a lifetime already. Her hopes of being with him again were quickly evaporating, but without any bad feelings or regrets.

Her heart jumped in her chest when she noticed Tania and Jo sitting a few seats apart in the front row. Perhaps she still hadn't recovered, or come to terms with the unusual treatment they had put her through. Their faces haunted her every time she stepped into the shower room, wondering if they would ever come back, in some sort of frightened anticipation. But today they were just two women sitting in a large crowd, anonymous and completely harmless. At that moment Judith remembered she was scheduled to work a few night shifts the week after next. That would mean working with them. Could she cope with that?

They would have to do their rounds together, strolling along the dark corridors or doing the inventories in the isolated stock rooms. She would be at their mercy, in more ways than one. The thought of having to spend even one night working with either one of them also conjured up fear and, curiously, sweet expectation.

Doctor Marshall coughed and silence fell across the room. He began talking and everyone kept still, drinking in each of his words as if they were Gospel. Judith was rather surprised to see the effect he had on his audience, for what he had to say was in fact rather insignificant.

There was an update following several complaints about the lack of parking space around the clinic, announcements about the new fire drills and emergency evacuation procedures, and a brief discussion on possible plans to extend one of the wings and take on more patients. Utterly boring.

'We had only one addition to our staff this month,' Doctor Marshall continued, 'in case you haven't already met her . . .' He paused briefly and looked around the

621

room several times. 'Miss Stanton,' he called out, 'could you please stand so that everyone can see you?'

Judith suddenly felt her face flush. She had to stand up and show off in front of all these people, one of the things she hated most. She sank in her seat even further, hoping in vain that everyone would conclude she wasn't in the audience.

But already some of her colleagues had spotted her and were gesturing to her to stand up. In the second row Mrs Cox stood up and turned around, staring straight at her above the audience, silently ordering her to do as she was told. Judith lowered her eyes in embarrassment and slowly stood up.

Murmurs of appreciation travelled around the room, and she felt like some piece of art on display. 'There you are,' Doctor Marshall announced. 'Please let us welcome you to our clinic. We hope you enjoy working with us.'

Judith wanted to disappear a thousand miles away. She could feel their eyes on her, and this time it wasn't just her imagination. She looked up and stared at the audience briefly. Most faces stared back, some curious, others indifferent.

Far away in the corner Robert Harvey looked at her and winked. Judith suddenly felt better, realising he had not forgotten her after all. Tania and Jo were already looking elsewhere, completely uninterested. She sat back, her heart still pounding. The rest of Doctor Marshall's speech became utterly insignificant to her, and, no longer paying attention, she didn't try to understand what he meant.

'Because Miss Stanton has not finished her probationary period with us,' he continued, 'I shall not discuss in detail the issue of our Special Care Programme, which she doesn't know about yet, but I shall only say it is going very well and as usual we have received very good comments.'

There followed a short question period but Judith was no longer listening; her ears were still throbbing with the rush of blood that had flowed to her face and was only now slowly returning to her shaking limbs.

It hadn't been so bad after all. Everyone had looked at her with various degrees of interest, but once Doctor Marshall had resumed talking they had seemed to forget all about her instantly.

The talk ended shortly after and Judith quickly made her way out of the lecture hall, not wanting to talk to anybody. She couldn't wait to get home.

'Step on, step off,' the voice yelled at the front of the class. 'And on, and off.'

The music was loud but entertaining. In the over-heated room, sweating bodies moved in unison, stepping on and off their square plastic boxes, their arms rhythmically rising above their heads in a complicated pattern.

In the back row, Judith was trying to concentrate on the choreography. Her thighs and buttocks were on fire. Her lips were dry and droplets of sweat left a burning sensation on her cheeks as they rolled down her face. Another fifteen minutes before cooling down. If she concentrated on breathing deeply, she knew she could keep up with the rest of the class.

As usual, her leotard was rather uncomfortable, the strip between her legs constantly moving back and forth, a most delicious torture on her swollen folds. As she kept moving the pressure seemed only to increase, and so did her arousal.

'Oh no . . . Not now,' she thought to herself, 'not again.' She had to resist. Unless she kept her mind on what her feet were doing, she knew she would have an orgasm again. The timing couldn't be worse. She remembered the last time she had climaxed during the aerobics workout. Luckily, everyone else in the class was huffing and puffing in loud, moaning sounds. With any chance nobody guessed the real reason behind her sighs.

Again today everything was against her, from the tight, rounded buttocks of the man in front of her, to the obvious, large nipples of the aerobics instructor. Some of her classmates were not wearing much, which didn't help either. Everywhere she looked the muscular, sweaty

623

bodies were arousing her senses, coupled with the brushing touch of her leotard on her stiff clitoris.

'OK,' the voice yelled again. 'Cool down.'

The tempo of the music changed and Judith collapsed to the floor, legs wide apart, stretching the muscles inside her legs. She was relieved it was finally over, but her flesh was protesting. Too bad, she thought.

Some people were already rushing out of the room, not taking the time to stretch and cool down. This was the moment Judith liked best, feeling her limbs graciously lengthening as her heartbeat slowly returned to normal, the sweat of her effort gently trickling down her back, soothingly cool and tickling.

Turning her torso sideways to stretch the side of her ribcage, she noticed the man who was sitting on the floor next to her. Slim and blond, his body was toned and well-defined, chiselled but without the bulk of muscles that usually attracted her. He looked almost aristocratic, his movements slow and elegant. Catching her eye, he blushed and turned his head the other way.

Judith was somewhat puzzled at first, but realised the reason for his uneasiness when she glanced down between his legs. He wore tight lycra running shorts, the kind that leave nothing to the imagination. And judging by the stiff, erect cock that distended the elastic fabric, his imagination had also been running wild during the aerobics session. His legs were extended remarkably wide, like a ballet dancer, and his genitals practically rested on the floor, as if the fabric of his shorts couldn't hold them up.

So Judith wasn't the only one who got aroused during exercise. The thought both comforted and intrigued her. She was slightly amused and decided to wickedly make the most of the situation. Extending her arms behind her back, she pulled hard, stretching the muscles in her chest and hoping he would notice the way her breasts were thus emphasised.

He stared at her with a bewildered look. Her heart pounding, she issued a silent invitation by demurely

624

licking her lips, looking at him through half-shut eyes. He finally smiled and she saw his cock throb slightly through his shorts. Encouraged by this reply, her movements became exaggerated and deliberately slow. She knew he was watching her intensely now and, curiously, at this moment she liked nothing better than showing off.

Quickly glancing around the classroom, she noticed quite a few people had already left. In fact, only she and her handsome neighbour were still on the floor, stretching and subtly examining each other. The others were standing by the door, chatting and paying absolutely no attention to Judith and her companion.

The music was now softer, relaxing, but her mind began working frantically. She closed her eyes for a minute and quickly assessed the situation. Just a few inches from her was a man with a gorgeous body, a man who was obviously enthralled by the sight of her, and for the past few days she had herself been in a near-constant state of arousal. Right now there was a handsome body within her reach, a body which no doubt wanted her as well. Would she dare make the most of it?

Thinking fast, she assumed it was up to her to make the first move. Would he respond to her invitation? The anticipation sent a shiver through her abdomen; there was no way of knowing if he would want anything to do with her, but she had to find out.

The last few people were coming out of the equipment room, having replaced the plastic boxes where they belonged. Yet they seemed in no hurry to leave the gym. Judith knew she had to do something before her prey escaped, but what? There was no way she could do anything until everybody had left.

The instructor was standing near the audio system, sorting out her tapes. She finally turned off the music, took the tape out and waved at Judith before making her way out of the room. Soon after, the last few people who had been waiting by the door followed her out. By now there were just a couple of women still in the equipment room, but they were probably about to come out any minute.

In a mental gamble Judith decided it was stupid to wait any longer and got up slowly, gathering her towel, her water bottle, her plastic box. Without looking behind her, she slowly walked towards the equipment room, letting the last person out before going in. With any luck he would join her soon enough, if indeed he was interested. Otherwise, she would just leave it at that.

Just as she was hoping, he came up behind her almost immediately and she felt the warmth of his breath on her neck. His body exuded a sweet aroma, musky and attractive despite the effort he had just put into the work-out. She reached out to put her box on top of the others. His arm brushed hers, warm and smooth, as he stepped forward to help her. Now the game was afoot, and there would be no looking back.

Without turning around, her heart pounding with excitement, she extended her hand behind her until she came to lightly touch his cock with her fingertips. At the same time, she heard the main door of the gym close shut. They were alone now.

She felt him hard as steel in her hand, and still getting harder. Immediately she wanted him inside her. She closed her eyes and tilted her head back. In a brief flash she saw herself being taken, impaled on this delightful shaft. Somehow she could already feel his thick phallus stretching her, she knew his thrusts would be powerful and strong. She wanted him *now*.

Still standing behind her, he got bigger in her hands. She felt his fingers on her body, finding their way to her breasts, quickly zeroing in on her erect nipples, kneading the soft mounds in a rough, frenetic caress. She turned around and grabbed his mouth in hers, roughly, releasing the fury of her arousal. The taste of sweat was still on his lips, salty and bitter.

Grabbing hold of her hips he swiftly hoisted her onto a stack of floor mattresses as if she had been feather-light. She marvelled at his strength as she quickly fondled and surveyed the hard muscles of his shoulders and upper back.

Raising both his hands to her cleavage, he ripped her leotard apart without hesitation and she screamed gleefully, her excitement rapidly increasing as her breasts were exposed. For a second he stared at her naked breasts, as if mesmerised by their sight then lowered his head to take them in his mouth. He was rough with them, his mouth travelling incessantly between the stiff nipples, sucking them violently and even grazing at them with his teeth.

But Judith liked each of his love-bites, and found his rough treatment even more arousing. In reply she dug her fingernails into his skin, letting out a loud moan of painful pleasure.

Their sweaty bodies melted onto each other, his enormous cock pushing forcefully against her clothed vulva. His arms around her waist held her tight, his hands pulling down the back of her leotard and kneading her sweaty skin.

She buried her face into his wet hair, pleasantly surprised by its spicy scent. She liked the way their moist bodies brushed each other in a raw friction. Soon, hopefully, they would be naked and she could feel all of him.

Already his hands were fretting over her crotch, unable to get at her flesh. Under her leotard she was wearing a pair of exercise shorts, which came up to her waist. He had to fight the fabric to get to her pussy, at first trying to pull down the shorts from under the leotard but to no avail, thus becoming more and more impatient. Next, he fitfully tried to get at it by running his hand up her leg underneath the shorts but his success was still limited.

All the while he kept caressing her breasts with his mouth, forcefully, grunting like an animal between each sucking bite, his hands desperately trying to find a way to get to her flesh. Their coupling was noisy and almost violent. Judith was already moaning with pleasure, the strap of her leotard between her legs digging deep into her vulva, squeezing her clitoris in exquisite torture as

627

she wrapped her legs around her new lover's waist. With a sigh of impatience, he let go of her breasts for a moment and quickly glanced around the room.

She felt a cold chill run down her spine when she saw him reach for a large pair of scissors on the shelf behind her and immediately tried to push him away in a panic.

'What are you doing?' she screamed in anger. Suddenly worried, she tried to make him let go of her, but he was stronger and no match for her tiny arms. Because his hips were pressed against her there was no way she could reach his groin and hit him there, and her fingernails digging in his skin only seemed to excite him even more. His face buried between her breasts made it impossible for her to slap him. All she could do was pound his muscular back with her tiny fists, still trying to push him away.

But his arms around her waist held her tighter, preventing her from escaping. They struggled for a minute, she wanting to get off and him not willing to let her go. The pile of mattresses upon which she sat collapsed under her and she fell to the floor, taking him down with her.

She ended up on her back, with him on top of her, his legs straddling her naked chest, the bulge of his erection just a few inches from her mouth. He seized both her wrists in one hand and pinned her arms against the floor up above her head. She felt trapped, yet amazingly excited.

'What's the matter, love?' he said with an amused, lustful look in his eyes. 'Don't you trust me?'

'I don't even know you!' she screamed. And suddenly, the reality of what she was doing hit her: she was just about to have sex with a complete stranger, in the equipment room of a health club. The thought seemed preposterous, but very arousing at the same time. For the longest time it had been a fantasy of hers to be taken by a complete stranger, almost by force, by someone she had never met before and would perhaps never see again.

On either side of her chest his tanned, hairy thighs

offered a stark contrast to the fluid softness of her breasts. Her globes were falling on either side of her chest under the pull of gravity. They lightly brushed against the rough skin of his knees, which touched her armpits. She could already see faint, pink marks on them, her skin delicately throbbing in reply to his rugged caresses.

Putting the scissors aside, he took her breasts in his free hand and tortured them skilfully, worrying her nipples until she moaned with desire despite herself.

'Let me do it my way...' his tone became softer, yet still slightly threatening. 'I promise you won't regret it.' Slowly he let go of her wrists and she stopped trying to fight him off.

Once again she was torn between anger and pleasure. Of course, she wanted him, but what exactly did he want to do with her? Once again, it was up to her to decide.

In reply she quickly pulled his shorts down and eased his member out. She marvelled at the sight of the thick shaft, never before had she seen one so big. The purplish head was enormous and luscious. This suddenly eased her last worries and she took him in her mouth, quickly running her tongue along the slit of the swollen plum.

She tasted him only briefly as he almost immediately pulled out and pushed her breasts together, using them to envelop his cock, slowly gliding back and forth inside the soft cleavage. With each of his thrusts the swollen head found its way inside Judith's mouth, her lips quickly closing around it in a strong suction before releasing it again. Tiny drops of clear fluid seeped at the mouth and she felt his buttocks contract on her stomach. She increased the strength of her suction, now wishing to make him lose control and abandon himself in her mouth. But instead he pulled away even further to escape this burning embrace.

'Not yet,' he said as he moved down along her belly.

Kneeling between her parted legs, he took tke gusset of her leotard and pushed it to one side, contemplating the large, wet patch her vulva had cast on the pale blue

fabric of her shorts. Judith remained motionless, paralysed by arousing anticipation.

Pinching the fabric delicately between his index and
forefinger, he took the scissors and made a small cut in
the shorts, then inserted the lower blade in the small
hole.

Judith shuddered as she felt him at work. Very slowly,
he cut the hole bigger, moving the scissors around
expertly, as Judith writhed with pleasure under the icy
assault. She was no longer angry, reassured that he
wouldn't hurt her, almost amused by his resourcefulness.

Putting the scissors aside once more, he inserted his
fingers inside the opening and tore it to make it bigger.
As she glanced down Judith could see her wet, curly
bush appearing out of the hole, encasing the red, swollen
lips glistening with the dew that was drenching them.

Bending down, he caught the whole of her throbbing
pussy in his mouth. She moaned under the invasion as
his tongue foraged around, quickly discovering each of
the intricacies of her vulva. She grabbed both her breasts
and caressed them roughly, duplicating the treatment
she had just received from his mouth.

With each of her breaths she let out a sigh, feeling the
wave of an oncoming orgasm quickly building up inside
her.

'Fuck me,' she whined, surprising even herself. 'Fuck
me now!'

He responded without hesitation and impaled her
guickly, thrusting forcefully as she contracted the
muscles of her pelvis under him. Just as she had imagined, she could now feel him stretching her to the limit,
in a perfect, almost painful but pleasant fit.

Although she was pleased to hold his thickness inside
her, it still wasn't enough for her. She wanted to come.
She wanted to come now. Sliding her hand between their
bodies she began to tease her clitoris herself, rubbing its
shaft up and down, pressing on it with her fingertips. He
pushed up from the inside, squeezing the swollen flesh
only tighter between her fingers and his hardness. She

wasn't used to being touched so intensely, but this made her response even more violent. Her climax was sudden and powerful, and she let out a loud sob. Meanwhile the stranger inside her continued his in-and-out motion, clearly amused by the wanton creature that writhed underneath him.

'How often ... do you go for ... strangers ... in gymnasiums?' he asked laboriously between each of his thrusts. She was amused that he wanted to carry on a conversation at this point, but felt happy to answer his question.

'Believe it or not,' she replied slowly, 'it's my first time.'

'You are ... incredibly ... beautiful,' he managed to say. 'I can tell ... you were made ... for pleasure.' She didn't reply this time. More than a compliment, this was a revelation about herself, something she had never thought about before.

She felt her arousal mounting again as he continued to impale her. Back home she had had a few physical encounters with occasional boyfriends, but never had she felt this urge to be pleasured over and over again, her body alight with a passion she couldn't seem to quell.

The change had seemed to start the moment she had started working at the Clinic. From that day she had begun to feel constantly aroused, always yearning to give and receive pleasure. Even now, the gorgeous cock in her vagina would soon make her reach her peak once again. This was the moment she liked best, as she felt the fire grow out of control before the explosion. She moaned.

He withdrew and turned around to take her in his mouth again. She moved onto her side, towards the luscious phallus that appeared in front of her, stiff and glistening with her juices. She tasted her own dew as she took him in her mouth, caressing him with her tongue, hungrily sucking the swollen head as if it were a ripe fruit.

His mouth on her vulva was like a spider, slowly rediscovering her, this time only just brushing her swollen folds with the tip of his tongue. His hands ripped her shorts completely, freeing her rounded bottom and surveying it roughly, groping and kneading her smooth skin.

She bent her knees and crossed her legs up behind his neck, holding him prisoner, forcing him to delve harder into her wet pussy. Soon after she felt a hard, pinching blow on her buttocks and she immediately sensed she was being hit with a metallic object. Without looking up she also realised there was now somebody else in the equipment room, standing just a few inches from them. Somebody who was watching them closely.

'Do you like sucking the little wanton, Jimmy? Do you like her sucking you?' a voice croaked.

'Jimmy' didn't reply. If indeed it was his name, Judith knew he wouldn't let go of her pussy to talk to this newcomer. She tested him by lowering her legs and releasing his head. She was proven right as he kept on licking her.

The notion of having a spectator aroused her even more and increased her eagerness. She grabbed Jimmy's thick shaft and roughly squeezed it with both hands, working on it frantically in an up and down motion, holding the swollen head fast in her mouth.

She recognised the clicking sound of metal from what probably was a set of keys. In a slow movement of the wrist, their lone spectator was using it to hit her behind methodically, at first merely brushing her tender skin, but steadily increasing the freguency and the force of each blow.

The keys were cold and rough, their serrated edge sending needles of excitement through her buttocks, like mild electrical shocks. Gradually, she felt Jimmy's mouth moving away and the keys getting closer and closer to her aching bud.

Jimmy pulled away completely and turned her onto her back, holding her legs apart. Looking up, she recognised Bert, an aerobics instructor. He was also wearing running shorts and sporting an enormous erection. However the look in his eyes was only mildly appreciative and he didn't seem tempted to touch her.

She remained motionless as he kneeled between her legs and smiled wickedly. Without a word he began swinging the heavy set of keys in a triangular path, nonchalantly, from one thigh to the next, then on to her engorged vulva.

'I don't care much for pussy,' he finally said in an arrogant tone, 'but I can't resist the sight of a pretty woman such as yourself. If you'd be kind enough to suck my friend Jimmy off, I promise I'll make you come.'

Panting with desire, Judith was too weak say anything; her mind numb but her body very much alive and yearning for more stimulation. Jimmy was now kneeling next to her, kneading her heavy breasts, pinching her nipples forcefully. She quickly grabbed hold of his shaft once again and greedily sucked him into her mouth.

At the same time the keys hit her bud directly, sending a shock wave of pleasure through her belly. She moaned.

'You like it rough, don't you?' Bert asked in a low voice before lowering his hand again.

Judith moaned louder in reply to each stroke. Never before had her tender folds been treated so roughly. Yet the pain quickly gave rise to pleasure, growing more and more intense with each blow, the sensation so powerful she thought she was going to faint with excitement.

He encircled her swollen vulva with his thumb and forefinger, holding it into a wet, musky bundle, making her stiff clitoris stick out, throbbing and glistening. Dropping the keys, he slapped her flesh with his bare hand. At first it was just a series of friendly taps, but he kept teasing her treasure expertly, each slap sending waves of pleasure that quickly merged into a strong, mind-blowing orgasm.

All the while, she kept on torturing Jimmy, echoing the treatment she was receiving despite herself, often letting her teeth graze the purplish head, sucking him so hard he was also moaning in pleasure and in pain. He reached his climax as she did, spilling his honey inside her mouth. She received him with a loud moan, her pleasure enhanced by the taste of his seed on her lips.

Judith was too weak to get up, and slightly dizzy. She lay on her belly, her moist skin stuck to the floor mattress, a witness to the heat of the passion that had transported her some time earlier. Reaching out in front of her, she grabbed the shapeless bundle of her torn leotard and cut up shorts and brought it to her face. They were soaked with her sweat, fragrant with the animal smell of her excitement. Turning onto her back, she blinked as the light coming from the ceiling assaulted her sleepy eyes.

Jimmy and Bert were gone. She couldn't remember when or why they had left, but the treatment they had given her body was unforgettable. Her vulva was still aching, swollen and occasionally throbbing. Her bottom and her breasts showed large, red marks; her skin was raised and still burning. She didn't feel any pain, but her whole body was now numb. She didn't care, she was fulfilled.

Lying completely naked on her back, in the equipment room of a health club, she could hardly recognise herself now; a wanton creature, willing to submit to strangers, keen to be violated, albeit in the most delightful way.

What else lay ahead for her? She didn't feel any shame, only amazement at what she had just done, and the overwhelming desire to do it all over again and again. Her whole body had become a slave to pleasure, and somehow she was wickedly happy about that. She wanted to explore all possibilities, yearning to learn more, yet she wasn't sure how to.

It had all happened so suddenly, so recently. Was this just a phase she was going through? Somehow she didn't think so, and she also felt her job had a strong influence on her lustful behaviour.

In a brief flash she remembered Mrs Cox, and how the supervisor had released her in the shower room. The woman had been very straightforward that time, asking her bluntly if she had come, as if it had been of the utmost importance.

Her vulva clenched violently at the recollection, her dew once again oozing out of her. She had to go and see her superior again. Deep within her was this powerful feeling that there was some sort of connection between the Dorchester Clinic and the unexpected awakening of her senses. She had to find out why her body had become so lustful, and somehow she knew that Mrs Cox had the answer.

Chapter Seven

Judith wanted to take her gown off. Never before had she felt so constricted, so uncomfortable, and the atmosphere in the operating theatre was warmer than usual this morning. She had dressed in a hurry, not realising that the mint-coloured garments stacked in the sterilisation cupboard were all of different sizes and she had picked one that was too small for her. Now the seam under her armpits was digging into her skin and the fabric was crushing her breasts, chafing her sensitive nipples. But it was too late to go back and change, she had work to do.

On the operating table, the naked girl smiled at her sleepily. 'You look nice in green,' she mumbled. 'Just like in the films . . .'

Judith smiled at the patient and pushed the girl's left breast up to put the stethoscope underneath it. The smooth skin fell back under the fluid weight of the breast and gently touched her fingers. Simultaneously, she noticed the coffee-coloured nipple contract and felt a tingling sensation tease at her crotch.

Lisa Baxter was twenty years old, a hip and modern girl, with skin soft as velvet. Three months earlier her father had died and left her a generous inheritance. Like any other girl of her generation, Lisa had everything figured out: now that daddy was no more, there was no reason why she shouldn't have that nose job she had been wanting for so long, even though she was probably the only person on the planet who thought her nose was anything but pretty.

Just a few years younger than Judith, her body had the fresh look of youth with round, perky breasts, a slim, inviting waist and a soft, pale mound of curls which most probably hid a lovely clitoris. Her hair was hidden under a pink cap but a few straight strands the colour of straw stuck out behind her right ear. Her skin tone was even, tanned to a pale brown but without any marks from a bathing costume.

This was a girl who probably liked to lie in the sun covered only with lotion, Judith thought. She felt tempted to run her hands all over that smooth skin, glancing at the brown nipple again and suddenly longing to take it in her mouth, to discover its smoky taste.

She pulled the stethoscope from underneath the girl's breast and placed it higher up on her chest, half-way between the two globes. Lowering her wrist, she let the cuff of her gown gently brush against the girl's breast without realising it. Once she saw what she had done, however, she felt herself blush and nervously pulled her hand away.

Lisa closed her eyes and sighed, and Judith was startled by this reaction, then realised it was probably more from the effect of the sedative she had received than from the caress of Judith's cuff.

Replacing the stethoscope in the pocket of her gown, Judith let her eyes wander some more over the naked figure. She imagined her own body was probably not much different from this one, albeit paler and milky. But did her skin look just as soft and inviting? The only way to find out would be to reach out and touch . . .

She shut her eyes for a second, ashamed at the images that were now forming in her head. Not again . . . Why was she feeling like this? Her own desire scared her now. How could she ever be attracted to another woman?

Why was it that every inch of exposed skin sent her mind racing and her flesh come alive? Would she ever be able to chase these thoughts and feelings away? What was happening to her? She had to fight it.

She took a deep breath and looked at Lisa again. Reluctantly, she pulled the thick, mint-coloured sheet on top of the lovely body, then turned to Doctor Wilson, the anaesthetist.

'She's comfortable, you may begin,' she said.

The rubber mask came to cover the pretty face. 'Take a long, deep breath,' he said to the girl.

Doctor Wilson was a man of a few words and soft manners. Like the rest of the staff, he was also terribly attractive. But right now Judith could only think of the nude body she had just covered. She had seen lots of naked, beautiful women before, but she had never felt attracted like this. This wasn't like her, something had happened to her. She was different now, and she had to find out why.

'Did you like it?' asked Mrs Cox. 'Do you wish I hadn't shown up to rescue you from them?'

'I don't know,' Judith replied slowly, carefully weighing each word. 'At first I was angry with them. But then I couldn't help feeling attracted.'

'Attracted by what?'

Judith blushed and stared at the floor. 'When they got up,' she continued hesitantly, 'I could see their nipples through their uniform . . .'

Silence fell. She sat still in the leather chair, her feet flat on the floor, her heart pounding with embarrassment and anticipation. Mrs Cox kept pacing in front of her. Every time she came near, Judith felt tempted to reach out and touch her bare arm, on the underside, right below the hem of the short sleeve, right where the pale skin looked baby-soft.

She had come hoping to find a listening ear. Instead, Mrs Cox was rather cold, almost cruel, as she forced

Judith to reveal more, to relive every moment of the past couple of weeks, recounting every lustful detail.

'Do you like the sight of erect nipples?' the woman continued.

'I never really thought about it until I came to work here,' she confessed, 'but now it seems I always have naked bodies on my mind.' She paused for a few seconds, trying to make some sense out of the mess of thoughts in her mind. 'You see, it all started when I came to work in this clinic. Since then I have been having these thought all the time . . .' her voice broke.

Mrs Cox stopped pacing just a few inches from her and looked down at her intensely. 'What kind of thoughts?' Her voice was a hoarse whisper.

Judith wrung her hands nervously. 'Thoughts of others . . .' she muttered.

'Could you be a little more specific?' Mrs Cox said as she bent down towards a blushing Judith, putting her hands on the armrests.

'There was Lady Austin.' Judith began, lowering her head.

'What about her?'

'She asked me to touch her breasts . . .'

'Did you?'

Judith couldn't reply. Her heart kept pounding against her chest, her face flushed as she recalled her patient's invitation, feeling the heat rapidly spilling down her neck.

'Did you touch them?' Mrs Cox repeated louder.

'No,' Judith whispered, almost to herself.

Mrs Cox began pacing again. 'How were her nipples? Describe them to me.'

Judith closed her eyes and took a deep breath. Their sight rose in her mind, and she remembered how she had been surprisingly aroused.

'They were dark and puckered.' She stopped, unable to say more, her throat tightening under the heat of the fire that blazed within her. Mrs Cox didn't say anything, as if expecting Judith to tell her more, her silence pressing for a reply.

'I could almost imagine them becoming harder under my fingertips, stiff and pointing,' she managed to say in a whisper.

'Did it arouse you, or were you already aroused?'

'I don't remember . . .'

'I don't believe you. You had been watching her with Edouard, surely your pussy must have been soaked.'

Judith looked up in dismay, once again stunned by the casual tone of the supervisor's voice as she spoke such words. It seemed she was almost doing it on purpose, either to shock or to excite the embarrassed nurse.

'Would you have liked to suck them?'

'No,' Judith protested.

'What about Lisa Baxter? What do you think of her?'

'She's very pretty . . .' Judith began.

'Isn't she?' Mrs Cox continued, her tone suddenly turning sarcastic. 'Very nice body. Does she turn you on?'

'I don't know.'

'Of course you do, she has skin just like velvet. Wouldn't you like to wrap your body around hers, to feel her young, warm flesh on yours?'

'Maybe . . .' Judith hesitated.

'Imagine, for a minute, that you are in bed with her. What would you do to her? Suck her nipples? Lick her clit? Would you like her to do the same to you?'

Judith couldn't reply. The conversation was having a powerful effect on her, making her arousal bloom as she recalled the moment she had touched the girl before her operation, how indeed she would have liked to caress the youthful flesh. Sensing her confusion, Mrs Cox insisted.

'Would you like her to suck your nipples? What about your clit? Do you want her to lick your pussy, to suck your clit? Tell me Judy, are you wet yet?' She paused and bent down again, her face just a few inches from

Judith's. Her voice became low and sultry. 'Would you like *me* to suck you?'

Judith couldn't stand to look at her. Yes, she did, she wanted the woman to pleasure her, to torture her flesh into submission, like she had done in the shower room. Only she would never dare ask her.

'Since you're not replying I can only assume you don't want me to,' Mrs Cox said dryly. 'But we're not finished. I want to hear what else you have to say. You told me you were aroused by women now, but do you still like men?'

'Yes,' Judith replied softly.

'Then tell me about the last time you were fucked,' she said, sitting down behind the desk. 'I want to hear every detail.'

The equipment room at the gym, two days ago. Judith tried to describe the scene but only succeeded to blush further.

'I had it with a man at the gym, a man I had never seen before,' she confessed, twisting in her seat, feeling her vulva contract deliciously as she remembered her encounter with Jimmy and Bert.

'And?'

'That's it.'

'That's all?'

'Well, what else can I tell you?' She was on the verge of tears, she couldn't stand this much longer. Mrs Cox was obviously waiting to hear more, but Judith didn't know how to.

'I'm afraid it's not good enough,' Mrs Cox said. 'You came here asking me to help you but so far I have failed to understand where the problem lies. You're holding back, and I can't let you out of this room until you have told me everything. At this point I have no choice but to ask you to take your clothes off.'

Judith stared at her in disbelief. Take her clothes off, right here in the office?

'You heard me,' Mrs Cox insisted. 'Get up and undress for me. That will make things much easier for both of us.'

641

Her whole body swept by a hot wave, Judith got up slowly, looking the woman in the face, and began to unbutton her uniform. Her hands were strangely steady as they worked their way down. The dress glided off her shoulders and fell to the floor with a soft thump. She kicked it away with her foot, shivering nervously as the cool air from the ventilation system assaulted her bare skin.

Across the desk, Mrs Cox licked her lips nervously. The young nurse now stood in her underwear, her nipples erect and pushing at the lace of her bra, her panties heavy with the warm dew that was soaking them.

Still hesitant but deliberately slow, Judith clutched her fingers around the clasp of the bra between her breasts.

'Now talk to me,' Mrs Cox ordered in a commanding tone.

'I didn't know him,' Judith began as she unhooked her bra. 'He was lovely and I could tell he was turned on . . .'

'What made you think that? Be specific.'

'I could see his penis hard under his shorts.'

'Did he have a big cock? Describe it.'

'It was quite long and thick, very thick,' she continued, pulling her panties down. She closed her eyes, unable to look at her superior, lest the woman would notice the desire in her eyes. 'I wanted to feel him inside me, stretching me.'

'That's much better,' Mrs Cox told a naked Judith as the wet panties fell to the floor. 'You have to say it out loud, I want to hear it all and so do you.'

Encouraged and aroused, Judith described the encounter in greater detail, telling how rough Jimmy's mouth had been with her breasts, what he had done with the scissors, what Bert had done with the keys. Mrs Cox started fidgeting in her chair at the mention of the rough treatment, the scissors and the keys.

'Did it excite you to feel cold metal on your skin?' she asked, standing up and slowly walking towards Judith.

'Yes,' Judith admitted. 'I have to admit I liked it.' She

watched the woman come forward and stop just a few paces in front of her. The shape of erect nipples now showed through the uniform, and Judith realised she had succeeded in arousing the woman.

Yet there was something unusual about those breasts, as if both nipples had an unusually distorted shape. There was no doubt that they were erect and pushing against the fabric of the woman's bra and uniform. However, it was impossible to figure out their shape; the fabric was too thick. Flat, rounded shapes were strongly visible, but that was all, unfortunately. There was no way to guess what the colour of those nipples was either.

Judith was intrigued and desperately wishing the woman would now take her clothes off as well.

'Are you aroused now?' Mrs Cox asked, suddenly walking away.

'Yes,' Judith confessed in a whisper.

'Then sit down and spread your legs,' she ordered, 'I want to see your pussy.'

Judith did as she was told, ready to do anything in the hope of having the woman come back towards her. She spread her legs wide, her hands gliding along the inside of her legs until her fingertips came to grab and gently pull apart the swollen love-lips.

Already she could feel her dew escaping and quickly gathering between her buttocks and the chair. Its sweet scent also rose, unmistakably. She looked at Mrs Cox and smiled demurely, hoping to see some kind of favourable reaction on her part. But the lack of response disappointed her. It was worse than Judith could have imagined; Mrs Cox stood back even further, and walked back to the chair behind her desk.

'I'm not too sure where your problem lies,' the woman advised, 'so I'll need a second opinion.' With a steady hand she pressed a button on the corner of her desk and, before Judith could ask what exactly she had in mind, a door opened behind the young nurse.

Turning her head slightly, Judith felt her blood freeze in her veins as she recognised Doctor Marshall, the

Director of the Clinic, entering the room. Her clothes were on the floor, quite a few feet away from her. She instinctively crossed her legs and covered her breasts with her hands.

'Don't be such a baby, Judith!' Mrs Cox snapped. 'Doctor Marshall has seen thousands of naked women in his career. Spread your legs this instant, he will want to examine you.'

Putting both hands flat on her desk, Mrs Cox turned to the man as he came to stand in front of Judith and began talking about the young nurse as if she wasn't there.

'What we have here is a young healthy female with an overactive libido,' she explained. 'I have not been able to establish whether there is something wrong with her or if indeed she is normal. I was hoping you could shed some light on the subject.'

'That can be quite tricky,' he acknowledged. 'You are right Mrs Cox. But I'll need to know more.'

He stood tall in front of Judith and briefly glanced at her with a look of disdain, his lips slightly twisted at the corners. His eyes looked down but he didn't lower his face. In fact, his nose seemed to turn up even further. Under the bright light coming from the ceiling his silver hair shone strangely, almost metallic. His blue eyes had a similar gleam, indifferent, even hostile.

Judith felt his icy glare survey her body and she couldn't help the shiver that shook her.

'Her nipples are hard,' he coldly stated after a while. 'Is she aroused?'

'Perpetually, it seems,' Mrs Cox advised. 'She claims to be constantly disturbed by thoughts of naked bodies and she is attracted to both men and women at this stage.'

'Is that so?' he said sarcastically. 'That doesn't tell us much, though.' He finally looked at Judith's face. 'Spread your legs, nurse,' he ordered. 'Let's see what kind of pussy you have.'

Judith slightly parted her legs and felt a sob rise in her throat. Now there were two pairs of eyes examining her. Although she wasn't too concerned about showing off in

644

front of Mrs Cox anymore, it was all very different now that Doctor Marshall was here.

She saw him lick his lips at the very moment her pussy appeared. Obviously, he wasn't insensitive either, and the thought gave Judith some comfort. After all, he was a man, just like any other.

He leant on the edge of the desk and bent forward slightly, staring at Judith's wet bush. With a sharp slap on the inside of her thigh he forced her to spread her legs wider, all the while still examining her with eyes of steel, clinically. After a moment he turned to Mrs Cox and nodded silently.

The supervisor turned to Judith. 'You need release now,' she advised. 'Let's see you masturbate.'

Whereas up until now Judith had been embarrassed, she now felt utterly mortified and yet somewhat disappointed as well. What they were asking her to do wouldn't have been so bad if their attitude hadn't been so clinical. But Mrs Cox was right, she needed release; her flesh was aching to be pleasured.

Only she would have liked Mrs Cox to do that herself, of course, and she hadn't counted on anybody else being there with them. However, both Mrs Cox and Doctor Marshall were staring at her in such a way that she knew she had no option but to obey.

Her hand hesitantly snaked up along her thigh and two fingers gradually disappeared inside her throbbing tunnel whilst her thumb began flickering over her clitoris. Despite the charged atmosphere in the room the effect was almost immediate. The reaction of her body erased her concerns from her mind and in a matter of seconds she was on the verge of reaching her peak. Tilting her head back, she moaned gently.

It seemed ages since she had last given herself pleasure, for recently she had realised this was in no way comparable to having somebody else do it to her. Yet having her superiors watching her was a novelty, a wonderful and exciting experience. If she obeyed, maybe she would get a reward.

As her arousal mounted she became more daring, eager to reach her climax. She rubbed her clitoris hard and fast, already feeling pleasure build up inside her. Once she got to this point, she usually liked to come quickly, unable to hold out any longer. Today was no exception.

She gave a wailing scream as she climaxed, totally unconcerned, but rather pleased with having an audience. Panting but happy, she opened her eyes and demurely smiled at Mrs Cox and Doctor Marshall. What would they ask of her next?

'Thank you,' Doctor Marshall said, suddenly walking towards the door. 'I don't think your problem is very serious and I'm sure there's nothing to worry about. I'm afraid that's all the time I have for you.'

Mrs Cox reached down, picked up Judith's discarded clothes from the floor and practically threw them at her.

'Now I need you to take Major Johnson to Physiotherapy,' she said dryly. 'He has an appointment at two o'clock. You should hurry or else he'll be late.' She followed Doctor Marshall out of the office, closing the door behind her.

Judith was left all alone, still rocked by the vanishing strength of her orgasm. She stood up slowly and began to dress. Once again she was baffled. They were dismissing her! Having just spent an hour discussing her most intimate moments, undressing for them and even masturbating in front of them, was that all the effect it had?!

She had achieved absolutely nothing by coming here today. None of her questions had been answered. If anything it made everything even more complicated. Instead of finding out why her body craved constant pleasure, or at least how to control her urges, she had fallen into some kind of trap by yielding to her arousal once again.

And what about Mrs Cox and Doctor Marshall? For a while Judith had thought she had managed to arouse her supervisor, but things had not turned out the way she had planned, to say the least. In fact, it was quite the opposite.

The situation was most upsetting, and left Judith more puzzled than ever, even angry at herself and her superiors. This was the first time she had been rejected like this, and it wasn't for lack of trying. Initially she had come to Mrs Cox's office just to talk, but the woman's behaviour had led her to think she actually desired the young nurse.

However, it seemed Mrs Cox had a powerful sense of restraint. She could have kept Judith in there after Doctor Marshall had left, and possibly continued their conversation, maybe even touched her. There was no doubt the woman was aroused, but obviously not enough to engage in anything more than a useless, cruel interrogation.

And although Judith had never thought she would eventually need the woman to hold her again, the fact that Mrs Cox seemed unimpressed only fuelled the young nurse's peculiar hunger to try seducing her superior.

She felt wicked, confused by this sudden desire to get the woman to pleasure her, by the need to play some kind of game, a game she had never even played with men. Yet she didn't want to fight her impulses anymore.

Just like the other day, in the gym, when she had foolishly set out to seduce Jimmy, she knew that if she could get Mrs Cox, the result could only mean intense pleasure, in ways she couldn't even imagine. She could already feel it. It would be her way of turning the tables on her superior, a revenge on what had taken place just now.

There had to be a way of getting to the woman, to tempt her enough that she wouldn't be able to resist coming close to the young nurse and caress the waiting flesh. Judith felt resolute that someday she would find a way to get to her, only on Judith's own terms.

All she had to do was to find a way to break through Mrs Cox's defences, to offer herself in such a way that the woman wouldn't be able to resist.

Chapter Eight

*T*he wheelchair purred softly as it rolled along the corridor. Major Johnson was sitting comfortably in the leather seat, content to be driven by such a lovely nurse. The dashing young army officer had injured his knee during a manoeuvre and now needed some physiotherapy following the surgery.

Steering the chair around the corner Judith stared down his neck, through the large opening of his T-shirt, examining the sinewy line of his shoulders. Ever since she had been a little girl she had been impressed by strong, taut bodies, attracted by the smooth skin that usually tightly wrapped the hard muscles. When her femininity had blossomed, the men who had begun appearing in her fantasies were always superb machines, strong and fit.

The man in the wheelchair was just like them, but he was no fantasy. He was close enough to touch. Her hands clenched around the handles of the wheelchair, her knuckles rapidly turning white as she backed up into the lift. The doors closed and she reached down to lock the wheels.

Being alone with him in such an enclosed space suddenly made Judith feel powerful. After the unusual session in Mrs Cox's office just a few moments earlier, she needed to be in charge for a change; she wanted to call the shots. And right now Major Johnson would be a perfect victim. Too bad she had to keep her hands on the handles of the wheelchair, his skin seemed to be calling at her to touch it.

Judith let her imagination drift for a moment, wondering what would happen if she were daring enough to slip her hand under his T-shirt, to awake in his body a desire for her, to impose her will on him, to get him to do whatever she would ask.

Standing silently behind the wheelchair, she looked at him from above. Slowly she reached forward to push the button on the panel next to the door, and moved back almost immediately when she noticed she had been pressing her body against his back for a moment. For a fraction of a second, she had felt the heat of his skin against her abdomen. She hadn't done it on purpose, but now she was glad she had.

But this was a stupid, silly little game. How dare she touch a patient like this? Major Johnson didn't seem to mind however; he didn't make any effort to move away from her.

Judith was almost surprised he had not reacted to such a close contact. Or had he only slightly noticed her belly pushing at his back, her breasts brushing the back of his head? If he had, there surely was no sign to betray his reaction. Judith was annoyed. How can a man not react? Wasn't she tempting enough for him?

She let her gaze travel down the front of his body, studying him. The sleeves of his T-shirt were too long, covering his biceps completely. In fact, the whole shirt was too large, not revealing much except for the base of his neck and a bit of his shoulders. Judith was somewhat disappointed, she would have liked to see all of him.

His legs were completely hidden under khaki cotton trousers, the left leg supported in a horizontal position, the large bulge of his bandaged knee stretching the fabric. There was no way of knowing what his legs looked like, but Judith could safely assume the thighs were muscular and well-defined. Was the skin tanned or pale? Bare and smooth, or covered with hair? Would she ever get to find out?

In front of them the doors of the lift were an unpolished metal surface, reflecting only vague shadows. But the three walls of the lift were dark, tinted mirrors, and by turning her head slightly Judith could see the man's profile repeated endlessly, subsiding into oblivion.

The Major stared right in front of him, not caring much for the mirrors. The lift stopped with a faint jerk and the doors opened onto the main corridor of the basement. Judith was lost in her thoughts and her contemplation of him and took a few seconds to realise it was time to get out. The Major turned his head towards her slightly, as if wondering why she still hadn't moved.

'Don't you know where we're going?' he asked. 'I can navigate if you like.'

She bent down to release the break on the wheels. 'I'm not too sure,' she lied, pushing the chair forward. 'I've never been down here before.'

'Right behind that corner,' he pointed as they came out of the lift. She pushed him along slowly, this time standing as close to his back as possible, her knees rubbing through the leather back of the wheelchair, gently hitting his buttocks in turn, her breasts mere inches behind his head. She was playing some sort of childish game, as if she wanted to prompt some reaction out of him. But still he didn't seem to notice her proximity, or at least didn't mind.

They passed the frosted glass door of the doctor's lounge and Judith couldn't help the tremor that shook her body, remembering that night, not too long ago, when she had been invited to visit this lair.

'Doctors' Lounge,' the Major read aloud. 'Have you ever been in there? I heard that in every hospital it's the most interesting place.'

Judith laughed, trying to sound casual. 'I wouldn't know, I only started to work here last week.'

'Young, pretty, and inexperienced. What a lucky man I am.'

Judith didn't reply, although she was wondering what he meant by that. She expected him to say more but he kept quiet until they arrived at the physiotherapy department.

'In we go,' he said cheerfully as he pushed the door open using his good leg. The sound of rustling fabric welcomed them and a man wearing a white nylon track suit appeared, gesturing for them to come forward into the adjoining treatment room.

'Desmond, old chap!' Major Johnson said joyfully. 'It's such a pleasure to see you again. Look at the pretty lady who drove me here.' He turned his head and looked at Judith.

But Judith wasn't looking at the Major anymore. The sight of Desmond had frozen her brain in stupor. She pushed the wheelchair close to the massage table, but without entirely realising what she was doing. Her brain had ceased to function the moment Desmond had appeared.

She thought she recognised him, she had seen him before, in a dream or another life. His skin was dark as the night, his head completely bald, a shining ball so black it reflected a slightly blue veneer.

She had seen him a thousand times yet today she was looking at him for the first time. He was that pirate from the south seas, the genie from the lamp, the dark slave of Roman legends. He was every man in one.

The word "impressive" wasn't strong enough to describe him. Desmond was tall, very tall; and big, very big. His broad shoulders and narrow hips made him look more like a sculpture then a man. The fact that he wore white only enhanced the darkness of his skin. He looked at Judith as well, vaguely puzzled by her stare, and smiled.

Two rows of teeth shone like a thousand tiny lights, like white snow in the bright sunshine, accompanied by

651

the faintly yellow gleam of a single gold tooth towards the back of his mouth.

Judith smiled in return, still hesitant. He looked almost unreal, a devilish figure, both threatening and beckoning at the same time. He took off his nylon jacket to reveal a white polo shirt, the stretched fabric clinging to every curve of his chest, mounds and valleys of dark, tight flesh, ripples of black velvet.

Bending forward, he helped the Major out of the wheelchair. The Major slipped his arms around the thick, dark neck and Desmond practically lifted him off his feet, almost carrying him in his arms onto the narrow table. There was nothing Judith could do but stand there and watch.

The Major was dwarfed by Desmond's impressive size, holding on to him like a small child. Judith watched as Desmond silently pulled down the Major's trousers, his big hands carefully slipping them over the bandaged knee.

Just as she had imagined, the Major's legs were quite a sight, muscular and tanned. But compared to Desmond he almost looked like a little boy. Even the way he smiled suddenly seemed demure, as if he were in admiration, yet afraid of the big, black man.

But despite his size Desmond was not frightening. His movements were slow and caressing, his big hands handling the patient's limbs as if they were made of delicate crystal. He undid the pins that held the bandage fastened and slowly unrolled the long piece of elastic fabric. Without a word he examined the injured knee, his thick finger gently tracing the path of the pink scar, slipping his other hand under the joint to support it.

The Major looked at him and smiled, and then shyly removed his T-shirt. Only then did Judith realise he was completely naked, and almost turned away in surprise and embarrassment.

In her mind a question rose: if the Major was here to exercise his knee, why was he completely naked? This didn't make any sense. She looked at him again. By now he lay on his back, eyes closed, whilst Desmond finished unwrapping the knee. The contrast of the black man's hands on the Major's paler flesh was mesmerising.

But even more impressive was the sight of the Major's phallus, slowly coming out of its slumber and gradually growing turgid, as if awakening under the touch of the therapist. The glistening head slowly appeared from under the foreskin; the shaft was getting thicker and faintly twitching.

It all became very clear to Judith: Major Johnson was the kind of man who liked to be touched by another man. Now she knew why he had been so eager to get to the physiotherapy room. No wonder he had remained unmoved by her touch!

Once again she looked at the black hands. Desmond was massaging the thigh thoroughly, his fingers digging deep in the muscle, kneading it in preparation for the exercises. He then moved down to the calf, repeating the treatment, warming the flesh that had been kept idle after the surgery.

And all the while the Major grew stiffer, clearly aroused by Desmond's touch, unconcerned – or glad? – that Judith was watching them. Desmond didn't pay any attention to her either, as if she had become invisible. But she was there with them, watching closely, her hands once again clenched on the handles of the wheelchair, her knuckles whitening under the tension, betraying her excitement.

For a moment she could almost feel Desmond's hands on her as well. She, too, would get aroused by his touch. The thought was so vivid in her mind she felt her vulva contract, screaming its desire to be touched by the large fingers.

Judith had to let go of the wheelchair as a cramp set in her wrist. She remembered how she had felt watching Edouard with Lady Austin, the previous week. Once again she was witness to a most arousing, if unusual, scene. And this time Desmond and the Major knew she was right there with them. But still they didn't seem to care.

She forced herself to look elsewhere, unable to stand the increasing pounding of her heart. The scene that was taking place just a few paces away from her was most impressive. She wanted to watch, yet she was afraid to. Her eyes travelled around the room, looking at the long row of jars and pots on the shelves but without really seeing them.

After a moment she closed her eyes, but couldn't remember what she had just looked at; she couldn't concentrate on anything. The only sight that rose in her mind was the man on the table being massaged, caressed even, by the black man, and how he was visibly enjoying every moment of it.

She tilted her head back and forced herself to look at the ceiling. To her amazement the flat, white surface she had expected to see – a ceiling just like any other – failed to materialise.

Instead there were rows upon rows of sturdy metal tracts, from which bundles of thick chains hung. At the end of each chain leather cuffs of different sizes were attached. For a fraction of a second her surprise was such that she almost forgot what was going on in front of her, but she heard the Major groaning and the sound brought her back to reality.

By the time she looked down Desmond had lifted the injured leg in his arms, and the Major's phallus had attained respectable proportions. The contact shared by the therapist and his patient seemed to be getting more and more intimate. The sight made Judith uneasy.

Suddenly she felt the room becoming hot, almost suffocating, the air squeezed out of her lungs with every crushing beat of her heart. Yet she quickly realised it could only be her imagination.

She couldn't stand to watch them, she had to get out of there; get out before she fainted with excitement. Reacting instinctively, she quickly opened the door to the

654

next room and set out to explore it as a way of escaping Desmond and the Major.

She turned on the light as she entered, closed the door behind her and breathed a sigh of relief. Now she was alone. All she had to do was to find a way to spend her time until they were finished. The image of the Major's stiff cock was still imbedded in her mind. But there was no reason for him to be naked in there, no reason whatsoever. And Desmond hadn't seemed the least bit surprised. What exactly were they up to?

She was tempted to go back and continue watching them. Yet she couldn't bring herself to open the door again, not just yet. Her reaction angered her. Why was it that wherever she looked she seemed to be constantly surrounded by naked bodies? And why was it so disturbing, so frightening, so arousing? And why did it have to be her patients?

She forced the thought out of her mind and looked around her. This was another similar treatment room, slightly smaller, with a massage table in the middle and shelves loaded with lotions and ointments. Only in this room the chains that hung from the ceiling were not tied up in bundles but hung freely, bringing the leather cuffs just a few feet from the floor.

Judith walked amongst the chains as if in a forest, pushing them aside with the back of her hand as she crossed the room. The metal felt cold and unforgiving against her skin, the thick links bright and solid. Looking up to the ceiling once more, she realised the chains seemed to be fixed in a certain pattern, yet she failed to understand their purpose.

This wasn't the first physiotherapy room she had ever seen, but never before had she noticed such an elaborate system. As she turned around, the side of her face met one of the leather cuffs and she let out a small cry, slightly startled by the contact.

She laughed nervously, her nerves on edge, kicking herself for being so stupid. She seized the cuff between her fingers to examine it more closely. The leather was soft and pliable, the buckle slightly worn. As she pulled on it she realised the chain was in fact hanging from a pulley, so that its length was adjustable.

Toying with the buckle, she managed to secure the cuff around her wrist and tugged on the loose part of the chain, pulling her arm up. Although the chain was cold, the leather around her wrist felt warm and almost comfortable. She pulled back and forth a few times, forcing her arm to go up and down, playing with the chain like a child discovering a new toy.

The noises it made distracted her for a while, until she seemed to hear an echo to the metallic clinking. She stopped.

But the echo continued. As she turned her head towards the door, she realised the sounds were actually coming from the next room and she immediately understood the chains and pulleys were being used in there, most probably by Desmond.

Her heart began to pound again. What on earth could they be up to? She licked her dry lips. Would she dare peep? She freed her wrist and slowly walked to the door, pressing her ear against it.

The noises had stopped but only to be replaced by sighs and groans. And that only served to increase Judith's curiosity and rekindle her arousal. Once again, in her mind she saw Desmond's dark skin spreading itself over Major Johnson's paler flesh. The lovely dick appeared as well, throbbing in reply to the therapist's touch.

What had gone on after she had left the room was a mystery, but Judith was convinced the chains had been used, probably the cuffs as well. But could it all be a coincidence? There was only one way to find out, she would have to ask.

She turned around one more time and cast her eyes around the room. There were no windows, there was no other door and no way out. She suddenly got scared, she needed to get out, but she was also afraid of what she would now see on the other side of the door.

The best of two evils. Her curiosity won over her fear and she decided to go back to Desmond and the Major. Her heart still pounding, her eyes closed, she mentally prepared herself for the worst and forcefully opened the door. She took a deep breath and opened her eyes.

To her amazement, Desmond was gently helping the Major back into the wheelchair, fully clothed. Both men looked up at her and smiled.

'Enjoying your visit?' the Major asked cheerfully.

'Er . . . Yes,' she replied.

'Time to head back now,' he continued in the same tone. 'Can I hitch a ride home with you, Miss?'

Judith slowly walked forward, as if finally awaking from a dream, her steps still hesitant. She looked around again. Nothing had changed, except for a jar of cream that had been taken off the shelf and now lay open on a small side-table. Its contents exuded a faintly sweet fragrance that mixed with another scent which hung around the room, the latter one vaguely familiar, not unpleasant but rather acrid.

Her eyes were diverted towards the ceiling. All the chains were neatly tied up in bundles, there was no way of knowing whether any had been let loose recently.

The Major followed her gaze and smiled. 'What are you looking at?'

'The chains . . .' She cleared her throat. 'What are those chains for?' Her tone suddenly grew strong, she wanted to know and was no longer afraid to ask.

Desmond didn't reply but Judith noticed a slight twitch at the corner of his mouth.

'What are the chains for?' she insisted.

Still not a word from Desmond. In fact, Judith realised at that moment she had not heard him speak a single word since she had arrived.

Major Johnson laughed loudly. 'As they say in the Army,' he stated in a judicial tone, 'that's for us to know and for you to find out . . . Can we go now?'

Chapter Nine

*I*t took Judith a few minutes to remember where she
was. Her body seemed to be floating, snugly wrapped
in warm cotton. Yet gradually her mind began to come
round out of the comfortable embrace of slumber and her
thoughts began to focus on reality.

She finally opened her eyes and looked at the alarm
clock. Her sleepy brain concluded she had been sleeping
for almost fourteen hours. Raising her arms above her
head she stretched with a yawn, then lasciviously twisted
her hips this way and that a few times. A day off, at last,
and nothing to do but sleep.

Noises from the street were finally reaching her ears.
She could hear the lorries complaining at the street
corner, the cries from the children coming out of school.
It was the middle of the afternoon yet it was as dark as
the early evening.

As her mind slowly emerged from its slumber she also
recognised the noise of the rain hitting the roof above her
head. A dark and wet day, a day to spend in bed.

She rolled onto her stomach and grabbed her pillow
with both arms, parting her legs on either side of it,
pressing her naked hips against its soft roundness. Her
bare breasts rubbed against it sensually, digging into the
warmth she had herself imparted.

She didn't often sleep naked, in fact she hadn't done that in years. But now it seemed her body couldn't stand any obstacle anymore, her skin needed to be free. Her nipples grew stiffer under the caress of the soft fabric, pushing at the down on the other side.

This wasn't like her she had changed. Her feet used to automatically hit the floor a second after her eyes opened, and she could have slept just as well if her bed had been a wooden bunk. But now she liked to lay under the duvet for hours, simply enjoying the feeling of her bare skin lightly brushing against the downy fabric, to cuddle her enormous pillow and wrap her legs around it, her hips gently thrusting against the soft cotton.

Every morning and every night, her naked body could now find the sweet, comforting caresses it seemed to constantly crave. When had it all begun? Always the same reply sprung to mind: when she had started to work at the clinic. Before that her body was almost a non-entity, something that simply asked to be fed, washed, and exercised.

Now her body, more than food or sleep, needed to be pleasured above all; to be pleasured time and time again. And the pleasure she could give herself wasn't sufficient anymore. She needed the touch of another body, of warm flesh against hers. She needed to feel it, to taste it even, like an overwhelming hunger she couldn't seem to appease. The change had been subtle yet sudden, she couldn't remember exactly when or how it had happened.

Outside the house the rain pipe was leaking again. Judith could hear fat drops escaping and hitting the windowsill just a couple of feet from her bed. Their rhythm was regular and hypnotising.

This curiously reminded her of the first morning at work, in the operating theatre, when Edouard's voice had cast such a strong effect on her. Had she been hypnotised as well?

That recollection jerked her thoughts and she abruptly sat up in her bed, throwing her pillow aside. She suddenly realised what had happened to her. Now she understood. The realisation sent her heart pounding and her mind working fast. Of course, it had to be, it made so much sense! Why hadn't she thought about it before?

The more she thought about it, the clearer it became. If, from the moment she had started to work at the clinic, her sensuality had so violently awoken, it could only be for one reason: she had been hypnotised. There was no other explanation.

She grabbed her head with both hands and forced herself to remember more, to put all the details together. It had all started that morning, in the operating theatre. As Lady Austin was being put under, she had been hypnotised as well. It was all very possible, a master could make her do anything he would want, even make her forget she was in a trance . . . It was preposterous, yet so simple.

So that's how it had happened. Edouard had hypnotised her. He had suggested that her body would now always be in a state of arousal, couldn't be without physical contact, or something like that.

He must have devised a way to trigger her senses. He had probably told her about something specific that would make her react without even realising it. Then right afterwards everything would go back to the way it was before; only a few minutes spent recovering and then it was back to work, as if nothing had ever happened. That would also explain why she had never felt this desire to just linger at leisure after having climaxed. This way she would go back to her duties as quickly as possible!

Everything made sense now. She had been set up, programmed . . . By Edouard . . . But was anybody else aware of this? Robert Harvey? Of course . . . He had been the first to 'test' her. The fact that she was unable to resist his advances was the proof She hadn't seen him much since then, only in passing really, but that could be because of their conflicting schedules. Besides, it was

660

only a few weeks ago, he would surely try to seduce her, to 'test' her again.

Who else? Tania and Jo? Less likely. On the other hand, maybe they were hypnotised themselves? Maybe all the nursing staff was programmed this way, so that they were unable to resist the sight of a naked body.

Lady Austin? That was doubtful. Or maybe not, she could be in on this with Edouard. After all, they were lovers . . . Or was she hypnotised as well?

This was still confusing, yet the pieces of the puzzle were starting to neatly fit together. Judith threw her blankets aside, jumped to her feet and almost ran naked to the bathroom. The thoughts racing through her mind were making her frantic, she needed to think clearly.

She turned the taps but didn't wait for the water to get warm. She hopped in the shower right away, presenting her face to the cool stream, hoping to wash away all traces of sleepiness and restore some thinking power to her brain.

The water hit her face hard and she shuddered in surprise. But she needed that to help clear her head. The water trickled down her face, assaulting her puffy eyes and she forced herself to put some order to her thoughts.

So far she had established there was a strong possibility the people with whom she had been in contact with at work could have been either hypnotised, or they were aware that Judith was under a spell and had taken advantage of the situation.

She had managed to determine the status of Robert Harvey, Tania and Jo, and Lady Austin, not to mention Edouard himself. Of course, Edouard was at the root of all this . . . But what about the others?

Mrs Cox? Now, that was a little more tricky. Looking back, however, it was possible the supervisor knew that Judith was in a trance, and although she was aware of the situation, she didn't agree with it but might not have a say in the matter.

That would explain her behaviour: the supervisor knows the young nurse is always aroused despite herself, so she does her best to help her by providing release when Judith needs it most. After all, it's part of her job to look after the nursing staff. Hence the reason for what she did in the shower room, and why she had asked all those questions in her office!

Doctor Marshall? Surely he knew what was going on, possibly he was at the heart of it all as Director of the Clinic. He could be the one who decides which members of staff get hypnotised, and Mrs Cox is in charge of making sure things don't get out of hand.

Desmond? He knows something, but he could be some kind of puppet, like the others. That was only a supposition though, for Judith had no proof something had actually taken place between him and Major Johnson.

What about those guys at the gym? Coincidence? They could have been 'planted' there to test her ... There was always a chance the Directors of the Clinic might want to monitor her activities just to be sure she was still under their spell.

So there it was, it all fell into place! There was definitely something fishy going on at this clinic, and now she knew what it was. But what about the patients?

Were they also hypnotised and submitted to the whims of the doctors? If so, that was not only highly unethical, it was also illegal. She would have to get proof and go to the police.

But how could she? She would need to get out of the trance first. Yet the fact that she had been able to piece this all together was proof that her mind could fight their suggestions, and that she was strong enough to go against it.

She had no option at this point but to confront Edouard, tell him she knew what he was up to and that the game was over. If she could avoid his eyes, and pay no attention to his voice, she wouldn't fall prey again. She would have to be strong. She knew she could do it, and she still had forty-eight hours to prepare herself.

* * *

He laughed so loud Judith could almost feel the floor shaking under her feet. She sat in front of him in the leather chair, motionless, determined to fight him every step of the way, but she had never expected this reaction from him.

He stood up and walked to the cabinet just a few feet from his desk, took a tissue out of the box and wiped the tears hanging at the corner of his eyes. His face was red from laughing, drops of sweat pearled on his forehead.

'Hypnotise you?' he repeated for the seventh time, almost choking. '*Ma chère*, what an imagination you have!'

The laughter resumed, louder than before. At some point he had to brace himself on the corner of the bookcase, his knees slightly giving under him.

Judith was becoming quite impatient. She had been expecting him to deny her accusations, but not like this. She waited until he calmed down and continued the speech she had rehearsed in her mind so many times over the past couple of days.

'I told you I know everything. It's no use denying it. And I know Mrs Cox does not agree with this. So unless you take everybody out of their trance I will ask for her help and together we will go to the police.'

'Mrs Cox?' he burst out laughing again. 'The police? This is really too much . . .' And he continued to laugh, always louder.

Judith bit her lip and lowered her head. His reaction was throwing her off balance and she was worried he might actually be trying to turn the tables on her. But she knew she could beat him. All she had to do was to remain true to her convictions and keep fighting.

After a while his face gradually returned to its normal colour and his laughter slowly subsided. He looked at Judith again and she held his gaze despite the dangers she knew she faced by looking at him. But he didn't scare her, not anymore.

'You realise these are serious accusations?' he asked, coming back to sit behind his desk.

'I know. But I also know what you are doing is unethical and illegal, so I am asking you to stop now.'

'Did you talk to anybody about this? Any expert on hypnotism?'

'Yes, I did. That's how I was able to find out what you were up to.' She was only bluffing, of course, but at this point she didn't have any choice.

She had been expecting him to deny everything angrily, even to rant and rave. But he had the opposite reaction and that completely destroyed her plans, so now she had to improvise.

'You're lying,' he said, suddenly recovering his seriousness.

As he spoke Judith felt she was quickly losing ground. She had to think fast, to come up with strong arguments and show him she knew what she was talking about. Yet in her mind everything was getting confused again and she was starting to panic instead.

He got up and walked to the front of his desk, standing just a few inches from her. At this point she should have looked up at him – at least that's what she had planned to do – but she didn't have the nerve to.

'If you really had consulted an expert,' he continued, clearly enunciating each word, 'you would have learned that what you are accusing me of is absolutely impossible. Even the greatest masters of hypnotism cannot suggest to a person the things you mentioned. Even in a trance, you cannot make people do what they wouldn't do when they are wide awake. And you cannot put a suggestion in a person's mind that would remain long after he has been taken out of the trance.'

Judith sensed he was perhaps expecting her to look up at this point but she didn't dare. The other morning, when this idea had germinated in her head, everything had seemed so logical. Now she wasn't so sure anymore. And she realised how stupid it would all look if indeed she were wrong.

She closed her eyes, keeping her head down, feeling as if her life were drained out of her with each successive beat of her heart. Her determination was vanishing quickly, only to be replaced by an overwhelming feeling of embarrassment.

He was right, of course; his explanation made perfect sense. She had heard that before, and more than once. But she couldn't go back now.

However, the more she tried to think, the more extravagant her theory appeared; and she had this image of a house of cards on the verge of collapse as each of his words shook the fragile foundations.

On top of it all, there was no doubt she was making a fool of herself. In an ultimate attempt to turn things to her advantage she decided to play her last card.

'Then how can you explain what's been happening to me these past few weeks?' she asked defiantly. She looked up at him as she spoke, despite knowing that her eyes would probably betray her embarrassment. But she had nothing to lose at this point.

He looked down at her tenderly, his pale eyes still alight with an amused sparkle. 'There is only one word to explain this,' he said softly. 'It's called "life".' He bent down and took her hands in his. 'Just look at yourself, Judith. You are young and beautiful, how can people not be attracted to you?'

He bent down and delicately seized her hands. Surprised, she didn't protest and obeyed his silent invitation to stand up. Slowly, he led her to the back of his office, all the while still smiling.

She didn't know what he had in mind but didn't have the mental strength to fight him and risk making the situation worse than it already was for her.

He gently guided her towards the far wall where she came to face a large mirror. She didn't speak, still taken aback by the logic of his argument, surprised by his behaviour, and stared at her reflection.

'Do you see what I see?' he asked softly, standing behind her, his face above hers in the mirror. 'I see a sweet, healthy young lady, perhaps still a bit innocent. She has grown up in a small village and now she comes to work in a big city. Almost immediately she is surrounded by people who are attractive, but who also have much more experience in sexual matters. Naturally she is overwhelmed . . .'

He stood tall behind her, his hands resting on her shoulders, his touch ever so light. Looking at her in the mirror, his pale eyes travelled up and down her body, a tender smile resting at the corner of his lips.

'I see a young body that has just begun to experience pleasure and is eager to find out more. Believe me, Judith, there isn't anything anybody can force you to do without your consent. All that has happened to you is completely normal. Maybe it seems extreme because it is all happening so fast, but that is just a coincidence.'

His hands on her shoulders closed into a soft but firm grip. Still he kept looking at her in the mirror.

Judith didn't know what to think anymore. He was making sense, of course. Or was he simply trying to turn things around?

'You might think that I am trying to hypnotise you right now,' he said as if reading her mind, 'but I cannot put you in a trance unless you agree to it. I have no control over your mind unless you let me.'

Once again this was something she had heard before. At this moment she realised how foolish she had been. The thought almost made her laugh. There was no 'hypnotic' conspiracy, of course. It was just her imagination running wild. And there was nothing wrong with the desire she was feeling, nothing at all. Edouard was right.

'Look at yourself,' he continued. 'Not a man on this planet could resist you. Tell me honestly, Judith, is it really such a bad thing?'

His hands then slid off her shoulders, down the length of her arms. She could feel him close behind her, and still getting closer, almost pulling her body towards him. She could also smell him, a rich, clean aroma that was a bit reminiscent of a forest after the rain.

'I can prove it to you,' he said. 'Will you let me?'

She nodded. He let go of her arms and gently encircled her waist with his left arm. His right hand glided up the side of her ribcage and gently brushed her right breast. In the mirror she saw her nipple grow stiff and peak through the fabric of her uniform. She shuddered.

'You see? This is just your body responding. I have no control over your mind. Everything you do, it's because you want to.'

He was right. There was no-one to blame for what had happened to her, it was just a natural reaction. At that moment she felt an enormous weight lift from her shoulders. All she had to do was to accept that her impulses were nothing to be afraid of, and in fact something she had to deal with and gain pleasure from.

She leaned back and practically fell into his arms. Why fight it? If her body wanted to be pleasured, so be it. She felt his cheek brush hers and closed her eyes, immediately abandoning herself. It was futile to look for any sort of explanation. She was young and beautiful, and sweet pleasure was within her grasp.

His lips gently took hold of her earlobe and began to suck on it. The wet and smooth caress translated into a warm wave that extended all the way down her abdomen, once again triggering that familiar feeling at the junction of her legs.

'Take everything life has to offer, Judith. It is there for you, make the most of it.'

She tilted her head back on his shoulder, listening to the calm tone of his voice. Was he hypnotising her right now? She didn't care anymore. All she knew was that she wanted to find comfort in his words, and pleasure in his arms. That was real; she was not imagining it.

His hands made her turn around and face him, encircling her tiny waist with both arms. He smiled sweetly.

'Tell me to stop and I will,' he whispered, his face just a moment away from hers. 'You are in control, always.' He bent down further and caught hold of her ear again, this time gently pushing his tongue inside it, sending shivers down her spine.

'No,' she heard herself say. 'Don't stop, not now.' She wanted him. She hadn't been able to chase from her mind the image of his shadow on the curtain in Lady Austin's room. She remembered the sight of his erect cock and now she wanted to see more than a simple shadow.

He began undressing her as she stood motionless. His fingers worked fast, undoing all the buttons of her uniform before pushing it off her shoulders.

Judith didn't try to help him, content to just enjoy the smooth caress of the fabric as it slowly fell to the floor, brushing her skin on its way down. He used his hands only to shed her clothes, all the while caressing her solely with his tongue.

She felt it, soft and wet, licking the side of her neck, gliding down towards her breasts and quickly finding its way inside the cups of her bra as he dropped to his knees. It seemed to be animated with a life of its own, snaking around her stiff nipples in turn, bathing them in a warm moistness, increasing the excitement she was already feeling.

The hook of her bra gave without any resistance under his fingers and the cups immediately glided aside as his tongue pushed them away. Her breasts peaked up, finally freed, swelling with the heat of her arousal, causing Judith to moan loudly as they were assaulted by the cool air of the room.

As his tongue surveyed every contour of her breasts it left a wet trace behind, cooling the heat that throbbed on her skin, creating delicious shivers along its length. She could hear him breathe loudly as he tasted her skin, sighing occasionally as if he were getting just as much pleasure from this as she was.

Every contour of each milky globe was soon bathed in this wet warmth. He flicked her nipples with the precise tip of his tongue time and time again, and sucked on them between each long lick until they became engorged. Judith felt her vulva contract violently in reply, her pussy rapidly getting wet with her own dew.

He continued discovering her with his mouth, tasting

every inch of her abdomen, his head pushing her arms up to gain access to her armpits, then slowly licking down the underside of her arm, all the way to the palm of her hand, stopping only to briefly suck on her fingertips.

His tongue then foraged inside her belly button for a moment, his nosed pressed against her belly, before moving on to the other arm.

All the while he kept his hands off her. From the time his fingers had eased her panties down, they seemed to no longer serve any purpose. He needed only his tongue to caress her.

And soon she felt him on her hips. By then he was down on all fours, slowly crawling around her as she stood still, worshipping her with his mouth. Her eyes remained closed, her mind went numb. All she could feel was this hot wetness gradually covering her, slowly, deliciously, inch by inch.

His tongue bathed the whole swell of her behind before slowly sliding down between her buttocks. Judith moaned loudly as its tip briefly pushed at the puckered rose of her anus. The sensation was overwhelming and she suddenly felt her knees become weak under her.

But a second later she felt his hands push her feet apart as he came to kneel in front of her. His tongue licked at her ankles and traced a sinewy path up her calves, stopping briefly behind her knees to suck at her tender skin, before continuing until it came to taste the softness of her inner thighs.

By then her legs were parted wide, and Judith had to put her hands on his head for support. She heard him grunt as the pointy tip of his tongue brushed her stiff clitoris, but only for a split second, before moving back down her thighs.

Then his hands got to work, taking each foot and pushing it back one after the other, forcing her to step backwards in a silent tango until she came to rest against the wall. At the same time he crawled forward, his tongue never losing contact with her skin.

Only once her back rested against the wall did he cease to caress her so methodically. Instead, he reached up and grabbed her buttocks in his hands, pulling them apart forcefully. His tongue immediately darted at her vulva, assaulting it with all his might.

Judith moaned loudly, surprised by the change in him. In a fraction of a second he had turned into a ravenous madman, suddenly losing control, licking and sucking as if he wanted to swallow all of her, roughly penetrating her vagina with his tongue, occasionally grazing at her clitoris with his teeth.

His mouth opened wide and practically grabbed the whole of her pussy in a tight suction; it was most deliciously painful. Judith screamed with pleasure, her cries of joy echoed by the grunting noises he made as he relished her.

She looked down at him and was almost surprised to see he hadn't even shed his clothes. He was half-kneeling, half crawling on the floor, his hands clinging to her behind, his fingertips pushing at the entrance of her anus.

His mouth was still devouring her swollen vulva, and getting more and more impatient, his tongue sliding deep inside her and then back out again, his lips nibbling and sucking at her clitoris endlessly.

Judith felt her sweaty back sticking to the wall behind her, her skin glued to its cool surface. She slid down inch by inch, her arousal so intense that her legs no longer supported her. The whole of her weight practically rested on Edouard's mouth and she dug her fingers in his hair, pressing his face towards her vulva.

She felt him choke against her flesh, gasping for air as he continued his assault on her pussy. His nose dug deep into her curly mound and she could feel his warm breath brushing her skin as it managed to find a way out despite the close contact.

He grunted loudly and Judith realised he was actually talking, in French, but she couldn't make out his words. Then he turned to her clitoris once more, sucked it into his mouth and closed his lips around it in a tight grip.

670

Judith started to pant, feeling her climax finally approaching, yet not wanting to peak just yet. She wanted to feel his mouth on her still; she wanted his tongue to possess her, to fill her completely. But she couldn't fight the wave of pleasure that rose up her thighs, grasped her vulva and made her scream in a loud moan of pleasure.

Tears pearled at the corners of her eyes as her orgasm exploded within her. At the same time she felt Edouard slowly getting up, his tongue tracing a path up her belly, his face soaked with her warm juices, sliding wetly against her skin.

He pressed his clothed body against her, pinning her to the wall as he finally stood on his feet. She nestled her face against his chest and slid her arms around his waist, under his white coat.

She was a weak, naked puppet in his arms, her energies completely spent. But he was not finished with her, not just yet. Her mind was numb and she felt him move as in a dream, barely realising he had unzipped his trousers and eased out his erect phallus.

He bent his knees and used them to force her legs apart, presenting the purple tip of his cock to the entrance of her vagina. Slipping his hands under her armpits to support her, he impaled her forcefully, thrusting upwards, lifting her off the ground simultaneously.

Judith awoke from her torpor as his successive jabs rekindled her arousal. His hips jerked up violently and she felt herself lifted off the floor each time under the strength of his assault.

The rough fabric of his trousers grazed at the soft skin of her thigh, and the metal buckle of his belt dug into her tender skin, enhancing the heat that enveloped the whole of her pelvis.

She moaned as she held on to him, feeling his member thrusting into her repeatedly, her body crushed against the wall. He pushed her up laboriously, heavily panting under the effort, groaning with every jerk.

As she repeatedly slid up and down his thick shaft to the

hilt, Judith felt her vulva stretch and her bottom hit his engorged balls. Her pleasure returned, growing more intense with each of his jabs. They screamed in unison, both swept by a simultaneous orgasm. Her vulva clenched as it milked his seed and she felt him throb within her.

He dropped to his knees and she followed him, collapsing on the rough carpet. He lay her down and almost immediately zipped up his trousers.

Judith remained motionless, feeling her life draining from within her, the whole surface of her skin now so sensitive it throbbed slightly. She opened her eyes sleepily and looked at him.

Édouard was sitting on the floor next to her, once again fully clothed. Not a hair on his head had been displaced, his neck tie was perfectly done and there wasn't a single crease in his shirt.

In contrast, Judith lay completely naked, her skin red and hot, her hair undone and spilling all over the carpet, her limbs weak. A distinct, sweet smell hung in the room, a smell Judith was by now only too familiar with; the smell of pleasure.

Her vulva was still occasionally shaken by mild contractions; after-shocks of the earthquake that had just devastated her. She slowly brought her hands to her breasts and caressed them lightly.

Édouard smiled and bent down to deposit a gentle kiss on her lips, his tongue briefly toying with hers.

'You taste wonderful, *ma chérie*,' he said in a whisper.

Judith felt wonderful as well, now that she knew she didn't have to be afraid of her desires, but could enjoy them instead. She laughed out loud, suddenly realising the unusual sight they offered: she, lying naked, her body still shaking from pleasure; he, casually sitting on the floor, looking just like nothing had happened.

She turned onto her stomach, the rough carpet scratching her sensitive skin, and soon she felt his tongue on her again, this time slowly discovering her back, tracing the curve of her armpits and each of the rounded bumps of her spine.

Thinking back to her mood when she had first entered the office, she couldn't help laughing again, and she heard him laugh in reply. There were still questions left unanswered in her head – a lot of questions, in fact – but it didn't really matter right now.

There would always be time to find out more later.

Chapter Ten

*T*he attendant took her aside and looked around before bending down to speak in her ear.

'You've got to save my life,' he whined. 'It's almost midnight and I'm supposed to be off now, I really can't stay a minute more. I was called to help on the third floor and it took longer than I had thought so I fell behind in my list of tasks. All that's left to do is to help the guy in room 627 with his bath. I know it's not part of your duties, but if you have a minute could you take care of that? He says he doesn't mind waiting. Everybody else is asleep in their bed, so you shouldn't be too busy. Please?'

Judith looked around as well. They were alone by the side of the nursing station, the other nurse who was assigned to work the night shift with Judith was nowhere to be seen.

She hesitated for a moment, knowing that when the attendants weren't finished with their tasks at the end of their shifts they were expected to stay and work overtime. The nurses had more important things to do.

She looked at him and was surprised by how young he looked and decided he was rather cute. Then she glanced down again to read his name on the tag pinned to his breast pocket.

674

'Listen, Ray,' she began, 'you know that nurses are not supposed to do the attendants' work...'

'I know,' he interrupted her impatiently, 'but my friends are waiting for me outside. We're off to this party and it's late already. I would have been finished by now if it hadn't been for that problem on the third floor... The guy in 627 is very cool, he won't say anything, I'm sure. Please?'

Judith hesitated, looking at him and trying to decide whether she should let him off. Yet he seemed sincere and there would be no harm in helping him out. She knew he was about the same age as her yet he looked much younger; his cheeks seemed as soft as a baby's. His eyes were a pale brown, almost amber, and she thought, curiously, that his hair was just about the same colour.

He looked sweet and his voice sounded slightly worried, with a tinge of desperation. She felt her heart melt. He was right, there was hardly anything to do before her first round at one o'clock, and room 627 was one of hers. Besides, if anybody found out about it the blame would be on Ray who left without finishing his tasks, not her.

'Where is the patient now?' she asked.

Ray smiled, knowing he was winning. 'I just put him in the tub, he's soaking now. All you need to do is to scrub his back and then help him out of there. He's got a bad leg but other than that he's fine. He's in an island tub and he's on some kind of muscle relaxant. Desquel, I think. He shouldn't give you a hard time.'

Already he was pulling away, smiling at Judith. He winked before turning around. 'Thanks!' he whispered. 'I'll make it up to you.'

Judith went back to her station and sifted through the order sheets. The team who had just finished on the evening shift had left nothing to be done. All the medication had been distributed, the observation charts filled, the patients tucked up, except, of course, for the patient in room 627.

PATIENT WAS PUT IN THE BATH TUB AT 23:50, the

last nurse had written and put her initials in the next column.

Judith checked her watch and took out her pen. PATIENT WAS TAKEN OUT OF THE BATH TUB AT 00:30. She put her initials. That would give her about 20 minutes to get him out of there.

The island tub Ray had mentioned was the kind installed in the middle of the bathroom, on a small pedestal, high enough and far away from the walls so that the nursing staff could go all around it to help the patient, making things much easier for everyone. This would only take a few minutes, yet Judith didn't want to rush the patient.

The other nurse assigned to the station was checking on her own patients, rooms 600 to 615. Room 627 was the last one at the other end of the corridor, so chances were nobody would come and check up on Judith for a little while.

She re-arranged the papers on the desk and looked around quickly before heading down the corridor in a fast, silent pace. She had been assigned to this floor just last week, during the day shift, but she couldn't remember who was in 627 anymore. Besides, it wasn't unusual for patients to request a change after a couple of days, if a better room became available. This particular room was at the very corner of the building and had windows on two sides, offering a better view than the other rooms, and therefore making it quite popular with many patients.

When Judith entered all the lights were out, even the tiny lamp above the head board. A pale triangle of light painted the wooden floor at the far end. It came from the bathroom door, which was only slightly ajar and let faint splashing sounds escape. The lights in there had not been turned on to their full power and she concluded that the patient probably wanted to relax in semi-darkness. After all, it was after midnight already.

She walked over to the bathroom and glanced in. Just as Ray had told her, the patient was in an island tub, his back to the door. A thin cloud of steam was rising from the water and all she could see of the patient was his broad shoulders and the back of his head. She didn't recognise him and concluded it must be a new patient. She knocked gently on the bathroom door, not wanting to startle him, and slowly entered.

'I'm coming to help you out of there . . .' she began. She swallowed the rest of her sentence when the patient turned his head up and smiled at her.

'Very nice of you,' he replied with a smile. It was Mike Randall, laying in the bath tub with water up to his waist, covered only with a small towel over his loins. His left leg was still in a cast, covered in a plastic film and held up a few inches above the bath tub by a thick rubber strap to prevent it from touching the water.

He looked comfortable, his arms dangling on either side of the tub, his upper back propped up by a rubber pillow. Judith slowly came forward, fascinated by the sight of his near-naked body, enthralled by the way his tanned skin contrasted against the whiteness of the enamel.

Mike was wide awake tonight and did not seem to remember her.

'I was just about done,' he said. 'Just relaxing now. Can you do my back?' He leaned forward and handed Judith a large blue sponge.

Without a word Judith grabbed the sponge and plunged it into the warm water, gently brushing the side of his ribcage with her wrist in the process. The moist heat of the steam rising from the water almost choked her for a minute, forcing her to breathe deeply.

As her hand hit the water she felt the heat rise up her arm and instantly radiate through her body. She didn't know whether it came from the water or his body. Slightly blushing, she looked at him. He looked at her, still smiling. He leant further to give her better access to his back, his chest now practically resting on his cast.

The fragrance of the soap assaulted her nostrils, a refined, distinct smell that hung in the room and which she would most probably associate with him from now on. She gently rubbed his back, working up and down along the length of his spine and then across the width of his shoulders. She let her hand disappear under the waterline, pressing the sponge all the way down until her fingers came to hit the bottom of the tub, where she could feel the cleft of his buttocks.

He laughed softly. 'You are very daring,' he said. 'We've only just met!'

'No, you're wrong,' she replied. 'I was with you when you came out of surgery.'

'That was you? I thought I had been dreaming about angels . . .'

He let out a sigh of satisfaction as she slowly squeezed the sponge over his shoulders, making the water trickle to rinse off the soap. His voice grew soft as he continued talking to her, in that flirtatious tone she had heard him use in one of his films.

However, she wasn't really paying attention to his words. Still holding the sponge in a light grip she traced the line of his muscles with her fingertips. She was fascinated by the way his wet skin felt, and somehow hoped she could drop the sponge and simply let her hands run over it.

A few days ago she had taken advantage of his sedated state to caress his chest. Now she was pretending to wash him to continue her discovery of his body. She brushed his shoulder, lost in her thoughts, desperately wishing that the sponge could miraculously vanish . . .

His hand came up suddenly and seized her wrist. She let out a small cry and dropped the sponge, which splashed soapy water around as it fell back in the tub.

Still holding her hand he leant back and brought her wet fingers to his lips. 'Now I remember you,' he said before kissing them gently. 'You're the nurse with the nice touch. I thought you only existed in my dreams . . .'

Judith started to tremble as she felt his lips nibbling at her fingers. Once again she marvelled at the sight of his naked chest, the taut muscles, the tight skin now glisten-

678

ing and bringing even more definition to the ripples of his flat stomach.

Her eyes wandered down and paused over the small towel which barely covered his genitals. His leg held high caused the towel to strain and run up his thigh. If he tried moving his other leg at all there would be a strong possibility that his maleness would be revealed in its entirety.

She couldn't stop looking at the slight bump in the middle of the towel, and wondering what lay underneath. He followed her gaze.

'Good old Desquel,' he laughed softly. 'Always available when it's not really needed.'

At first Judith couldn't understand what he was talking about but then she remembered the attendant had mentioned the patient was still on that medication. Desquel was popular in surgery, a powerful, non-addictive pain-killer but with a slightly inconvenient side-effect: certain men were unable to achieve an erection whilst they were taking it. Obviously, Mike had also been told about this possibility.

So that's what Ray had meant when he said the patient wouldn't give her any problems. Somehow Judith felt relieved, knowing Mike wouldn't feel at all tempted to make a pass at her under these conditions. Therefore she could easily resist temptation. But suddenly she noticed a twitch in the fabric and the towel began to rise above the water line.

'But then again,' Mike continued, 'they stopped giving it to me a couple of days ago . . .'

Judith pretended not to notice anything and pulled her hand away from his to quickly reach down and pull the plug out. The water spiralled down the drain with a gurgling sound and she turned around to grab a large towel, throwing it across her shoulder.

Despite her efforts to keep calm, a storm was now raging within her. She had to help him out of the tub, dry him off and then help him to bed. That meant close contact with his naked body and his glistening skin. Just

679

standing near him was enough to feel the heat of his body, compounded by the lingering warmth of the bath water.

How would she react to the moist touch of his arm around her shoulders? Perhaps she would also have to slip her own arm around his waist. She would most probably be tempted to touch more of him . . . Would she be able to restrain herself? Now she wished she hadn't let Ray go. That was all his fault; she shouldn't have agreed to this. If only she had known, she could have avoided finding herself in such a compromising position.

On the other hand, she was probably nothing to a man like Mike Randall. He most probably saw her as a nurse just like any other; one of those horrible women who like nothing better than to stick needles in people's behinds and force them to swallow all sorts of foul-tasting medications.

Yet his behaviour was quite revealing; the way he had kissed her fingers, and then blatantly directed her attention to his aroused genitals. She might have to fight off his advances, and this would require enormous strength from her, both physically and mentally.

He waited for the water to drain completely then braced himself with his arms on either side of the tub. Bending his good leg underneath him, he raised himself up until he came to rest his buttocks on the edge of the bath tub. Judith helped him by unhooking his cast from its support, slowly lowering his leg until his foot touched the floor.

He now sat astride the side of the tub, the towel around his waist soaked and dripping, threatening to come loose as the bulge of his erection kept straining the fabric, continually sending trickles of water down his thighs.

Judith came to him and held him whilst he swung his right leg out of the tub. Her arms were too short to encircle him completely and she felt his wet skin slipping under her fingers. She let him lean against the tub and handed him the towel whilst she went searching for his bathrobe. So far, so good, she thought. The worst part was over, and on the whole it had gone quite well. She had felt a vague fluttering in her loins as she watched him get out of the tub, and saw his muscles playing under his skin. But at this moment she figured all she had to do was to cover his body. Then at least her attention wouldn't be diverted by the sight of his bare flesh.

She found his robe hanging on the inside of the bathroom door and took it to him. When she turned around, however, she saw him pulling at the wet towel impatiently, tossing it back in the tub in a wet bundle.

She froze in surprise for a second as she saw his turgid phallus pointing in her direction and looked up at him, rather puzzled.

'The towel was dripping,' he explained in a childish tone. 'I can't get my cast wet, can I? I can't bend down with that cast, could you please dry my leg?'

He handed her the towel with a smile. Judith licked her lips nervously and sensed her breath becoming shallow in excitement. Now he stood completely naked in front of her, except for the cast. He was asking her to touch him, to bend down in front of him and pat his leg dry.

She knew that by doing what he asked she would have to bring her face just a few inches from his erect member, which was still getting bigger. She felt her crotch grow wet at the thought of getting this close to his luscious body, and having to run her hands all over his muscular leg, albeit through the thickness of the bath towel. She had to think fast to find a way to avoid this contact or else she would not be able to resist this sweet temptation.

Stirred by a flash of inspiration she stepped forward and almost forced him to put the bathrobe on, even fastening it for him at the waist. He let her cover him without uttering a word, an amused smile on his lips, perfectly aware of her confusion.

The robe came down to mid-thigh and Judith was somewhat relieved. She could still see his phallus pointing through the cloth but the rest of his body was almost completely hidden, making it less compromising for her if she had to offer her shoulder as a support.

She bent down briefly to pat him dry, starting with his foot and working her way up his calf, stopping slightly above the knee. But although she tried to look casual and professional, all the while she sensed her breath quickening. She felt his muscles hard under her fingers, and almost wished she could touch him directly. But even more disturbing was the motion of his hips as she knelt in front of him.

She could feel his erection brush the side of her head repeatedly, as if he was doing it on purpose, and she desperately tried to retain her composure, not to move her head away too quickly, pretending she hadn't noticed anything. As his hips swayed next to her face she thought she heard him moan but quickly willed the impression away.

All her efforts seemed in vain. If he hadn't moved his hips so suggestively on purpose, then her imagination was once again getting the best of her. What if he really tried to make a pass at her? Would she be able to refuse him? There were hundreds of women out there who would probably want nothing better . . .

Once she stood up he threw his arm around her, supporting himself on her shoulders and they got out of the bathroom to laboriously make their way to his bed. He moved forward in short hops, his left leg trailing behind, pressing his body against hers to keep his balance. The knot of his bathrobe belt came loose and as the robe fell open his cock slowly appeared, gradually getting harder with each step he took.

The bathroom door slowly closed behind them, and soon Judith found herself trying to guide her patient in the dark. The only light came from the lamppost outside the window, which cast a pale blue light on the bed. They approached it inch by inch, his body now heavy on her shoulder.

She could feel the moist heat of his body through the

682

cloth of his robe. Because of the way he held on to her, she had no choice but to bend forward slightly, keeping her head down, thus watching his thick shaft bob up and down, the purplish head slowly emerging from beneath his foreskin, gradually coming alive.

Her own arousal began to mount as well, as she watched the glistening plum jump towards her lips time and time again, almost begging to be kissed. In the light of the lamppost she thought she could see a fine drop pearling from the tiny mouth. By the time they reached the bed his bathrobe was completely opened, and his member stood fully erect. Judith helped him climb into bed and lifted his cast up to lay it next to the other leg.

Although the trek from the bathroom had gone rather well, he seemed relieved to finally reach his bed and lay down quietly, his bathrobe spread underneath him, his taut body once again revealed. Judith took one last look at him. Outside the room the wind blew through the branches of a nearby tree and the light from the lamppost cast their moving shadows all over his smooth skin.

The effect was surreal and captivating. He just lay there, still smiling, his eyes half-shut. Judith knew she had to leave. Not only was she afraid she wouldn't be able to fight the temptation to run her hands all over this gorgeous body for much longer, but she had been away from the nursing station for quite a while now and her colleague might start looking for her at any minute.

She turned around to leave but at the very last moment she felt his fingers grabbing hold of her arm and she was gently pulled back towards the bed.

'Do you remember your promise?' he asked in a whisper, his eyes still half-shut and staring at the ceiling.

'What promise?'

'That morning, when I came out of surgery, I asked you if you would take good care of me, and you promised you would . . .'

Judith didn't reply. Obviously he remembered more about that day than she would have expected. But exactly how much?

'I remember your hand caressing my chest,' he said as if reading her mind. 'I felt your touch soft and warm . . .'

Judith remembered as well, of course, but was that his way of asking her to do it again? She looked down to his engorged phallus and saw it twitch slightly in the blue light.

'You promised,' he repeated, 'you can't leave me like this now . . .'

Of course she couldn't, but she had to. She was so confused, remembering how warm and soft his skin felt in the palm of her hand, how she had wanted him that day. Yet she knew perfectly well that he was a patient, and that she had to go back to her desk immediately.

He loosened his grip on her but his fingers continued to caress her arm. She felt a tingling sensation at the surface of her skin and let out a faint sob. Only then did she notice a large mirror on the wall by the foot of the bed. She looked up and stared at their reflections, a tiny white figure standing next to this gorgeous, naked flesh.

'You want me, I know you do,' Mike continued. 'Besides, aren't you supposed to do everything your patients ask you?'

'I . . . don't know,' she stammered. 'This wouldn't be right. You are my patient . . .'

'You must be new here, then. I heard it's a policy of this Clinic to offer special care to clients who ask for it. That means giving them everything they ask for . . .'

Judith was disappointed by this sad excuse, thinking it was indeed a strange way of trying to get to her. Yet at the same time she wished it was true, so she could let herself yield to the force of her desire. She began to tremble and immediately sensed his fingers growing insistent on her skin, travelling up and down along the length of her arm, the bone of his wrist brushing the peak of her erect nipple each time.

He must have felt the confusion within her, for his tone grew even softer and his invitation more open. 'I want you, Judith. I want you to undress for me, to show me that gorgeous body of yours. I am hot for you, wouldn't you want to feel my skin against yours?' He reached up and gently seized her neck in his fingers, slowly pulling her head down towards his.

She didn't offer any resistance as her lips came to meet his and she felt his tongue invade her mouth, its softness sending a shiver from her breasts to her loins. She had to put her hand on the bed to stop herself from falling on top of him, but he anticipated her move, grabbed her wrist and brought her hand to his chest instead. She slowly bent her elbow until she came to gently rest against him, pressing her chest against his, once again letting the heat of his body radiate through her.

He let go of her mouth after a brief moment and pulled his head back slightly. 'Undress for me, I want to see all of you.' His voice was still soft but his tone was more authoritative. In the darkness she saw his eyes sparkle, and read his desire. He wanted her.

She hesitated a moment, but suddenly realised how good it would be to feel her bare skin on his, if only for a moment. There was no doubt in her mind that it wasn't right, mainly because he was her patient. But if no-one ever found out about it, what harm would there be? Besides, when she had been hired to work at the Dorchester Clinic, there was absolutely no mention on her contract of what to do in such a situation . . .

Closing her eyes, she also realised she was now trying to find excuses, however futile they may be, to justify this desire that was still growing within her. She also knew it was useless; she was vanquished.

She stood back and undressed quickly, her fingers trembling but precise. Her dress fell to the floor and her bra and panties followed right after. She couldn't fight her desire any longer, it was pointless. Right now he wanted her, and she wanted him. All she had to worry about was that somebody might see them.

Standing completely naked, she quickly drew the curtain around the bed, making sure that if someone entered the room they would think the patient asleep. The bed was now contained in a small space formed by the

685

window on one side, the curtain on the other, a blank wall at the head of the bed and the wall with the large mirror at the other end.

She took some sort of wicked pleasure out of walking around naked in the blue light, knowing his eyes were studying her every move. Coming over to the other side of the bed, by the window, she climbed and knelt on the bed.

She watched her own shadow rise on the curtain and felt her arousal bloom. All she needed to do was to turn her head slightly and she could also watch herself in the mirror, she could see her now-naked body bending down to worship his.

By now her excitement was such that she practically fell on top of him, covering his chest with hers, pressing her swollen breasts against his hot skin, straddling his right leg with hers.

She knew he couldn't move because of his cast, and the thought of being in control of the situation excited her even more. She grabbed his mouth within hers forcefully, now wanting to taste all of him, her hips thrusting up and down rhythmically, grinding her wet pussy onto his hard thigh.

He couldn't do anything but yield to this passionate embrace, and he gently caressed the side of her hips as they melted onto his thigh, letting his fingertips wander over the swell of her bottom, his nails grazing at her delicate skin, just stopping short of her swollen love-lips.

Judith groaned with every breath, now slightly pulling away from him, her hands sliding between her body and his, caressing both his chest and her own breasts simultaneously.

She kissed, licked and suck his mouth, his jaw, his neck, his chest. She heard herself gasping and moaning loudly, no longer in control of her own breathing, as she writhed on top of him.

From the moment she had climbed onto the bed she had been given a certain power over him; he was at her mercy. If she wanted to get off and go back to her station, leaving him alone and frustrated, she could do just that. Even if she chose to stay, because he couldn't move unassisted, she was in charge of both her own pleasure and his.

She sat up on his thigh and let her own weight crush her wet vulva against him, her hips never ceasing their thrusting motion. He reached up and grabbed her breasts, feeling their fluid weight in turn, letting his fingertips gently worry her erect nipples. She sighed.

This was better than she could ever have imagined. Of course he was at her mercy, but it was also up to her to satisfy him. 'Ask me anything,' she announced in a whisper.

'Sit on my face,' came the reply.

She smiled and looked at him. She hadn't expected that. Rather, she would have thought he would ask her to pleasure him first. Changing position, she slowly crawled along his chest and turned around to straddle his face. He reached up, grabbed her hips and eased them down gently until her moistness met his mouth.

His tongue on her flesh was a revelation. Judith felt herself melt onto him, his lips studying her methodically, his tongue reaching deep inside her. Her hips resumed their dance, using his mouth as a soft surface against which to grind.

His hands kept surveying her thighs, his fingernails gently scratching at her soft skin, sending tingling, hot waves all the way up to her pussy.

Judith looked up and was almost surprised to see herself in the mirror on the opposite wall. She saw his body, hard and tense, lying on the white sheet, brushed by the blue light, the shadows of the branches playing against the curves of his muscles. His stiff prick stood up against his belly, twitching sporadically.

But most impressive was the sight of her own body, straddling his face, writhing incessantly. She didn't recognise herself, not tonight. It was another woman she saw tilting her head sideways, her eyes half-shut, her face betraying the storm of pleasure that ravaged her.

She watched the woman bring her hands up to caress her own breasts, as her face began to contract in repeated spasms of pleasure, the eyes barely able to remain open, the mouth frozen in successive oh's and ah's.

Her gaze came back to the statuesque body that lay underneath hers, and to the stiff cock that still remained untouched but now craved its reward. She bent down and grasped it delicately, gently pulling the foreskin back to completely expose the swollen plum. At first she bathed it in long licks, from the base of the shaft all the way to the tip of the head, inserting the tip of her tongue at the entrance of the tiny mouth, feeling her man's hips jerk smoothly every time.

Her hair fell forward and covered his hips. At the same time she took him in her mouth, completely, to the hilt, and began sucking gently. She heard him moan under her and his mouth grew impatient on her vulva.

In reply she lowered her hips even more, almost choking him, now grinding her pussy forcefully against his face. Yet she didn't increase the intensity of her ministrations of him. He had to earn his reward. He had to make her come first.

She let go of him for a while, sitting up again in order to concentrate on the wave of pleasure that was being born deep inside her at this very moment. Once again she looked up in the mirror. She wanted to see herself come.

She smiled at her reflection. Yes, it was her. How beautiful she looked on the verge of her climax, her hips now swaying rhythmically, her hands clasped on her breasts, kneading them furiously, her fingers pinching her engorged nipples.

She opened her mouth to scream her joy but no sound came out. Instead, her whole body arched under the strength of her pleasure and she leapt forward in an ultimate spasm, falling against the hard rock of his flat stomach.

Her vulva lay half-way down his chest, her thighs now straddling his shoulders. He inserted his finger in the gaping entrance which lay just a few inches from his chin. The moist flesh sucked at it readily, in successive spasms, as Judith's body shook under the intensity of her climax.

At the same time she was highly aware of it all, her limbs numb but her mind still very much alive. With great effort she lifted her head and looked in the mirror again, somehow fascinated by its presence, unable to find a reason for this attraction.

She saw the woman sprawled over the man's body, her face almost hidden behind the curtain of her own hair, her smile still betraying her pleasure. At the same time she felt the thick prick stir between her breasts. Now it was time to reward the man.

First she rolled onto her side, sliding off him. Then she stood up next to the bed, the cold floor assaulting her naked feet. She stared at the body that lay on the white sheets, once again wanting to force it into submission.

She walked over to the other side and opened the door of the bed-side cupboard. Fumbling in the dark she managed to locate the leather restraints.

There was a chance he might object to what she had in mind but she remembered the procedure she had been taught at nursing school: first she had to grab the wrists quickly and secure the strap around them, then use her own weight if necessary to pull the other extremity and tie it to the head of the bed.

She acted swiftly and precisely, and by the time he realised what she was up to it was already too late. He whined in complaint but she ignored him, quickly picking her bra off the floor and gagging him with it. She thought of tying his feet as well but it was not really necessary, once she sat on him he wouldn't be in any position to go anywhere.

She climbed back on the bed and knelt next to him again, amused by the worried expression in his eyes. This time he was all hers. Once again she straddled him, this time setting her knees on either side of him, her inner thighs rubbing against his hips, and she bent down until she came to completely lie on top of him. She gently nibbled at his chin whilst her hands caressed the strong muscles of his biceps.

She could feel his heart heavily pounding in his chest. What was he feeling? Fear? Arousal? Anticipation? A strange mixture of all three? At least she knew he wasn't indifferent.

Her foot grazed the side of his cast and a series of weird associations sprung in her mind. When the cast would come off he would most certainly need extensive physiotherapy . . . With Desmond.

In a flash she imagined them together, the tanned athlete and the black therapist, their contrasting flesh melting together. Maybe she would get to see it for real, one of these days. But she got him first; right now he was hers, and hers alone.

She caressed his chest and his stomach lovingly, using only her fingertips, surveying every inch of his smooth skin. He was hot under her, and seemingly still getting hotter, his skin now exuding a moist, fresh aroma.

Against her belly his prick pressed harder and harder, trying to throb its way inside her. The engorged head seeped at the mouth. He was more than ready. But it was still too early for Judith, he would have to wait.

She could see his eyes sparkle in the dark, at times worried, at times lustful, and she took a wicked pleasure out of torturing him like this.

Her hands increased the intensity of their caresses on his skin, and little by little she began using her whole body to discover his, stroking the entire length of her arms against his, rubbing and pressing her erect nipples across his chest.

Her tongue also danced along his neck, travelling from one ear to the other, gently sucking on his earlobes for a moment before continuing its journey. She bathed him thus, remembering how she had felt when Edouard had done it to her, hoping it would have the same effect.

After a while her mouth worked its way down his chest, nibbling at his pectoral muscles in a succession of

690

wet kisses until she came to suck on his nipples. They were already stiff and engorged, but grew even bigger in Judith's mouth. She sucked on them greedily, flicking the tip of her tongue over them at a maddening speed, teasing them incessantly whilst her hands massaged his hard muscles.

He began to writhe under her, moaning loudly despite his gag, as if surprised at his own reaction. He lifted his head briefly. Judith stopped her ministrations and looked up at him.

His eyes were begging her to untie him, his maleness now growing impatient on her belly. She smiled wickedly.

'You asked for it,' she whispered. 'Now let me have my way.'

She went back to concentrate on his nipples, satisfied that he was getting impatient, quite determined not to let him loose for a while still. Yet at the same time the engorged cock that throbbed against her chest was calling to her. It wanted her, and she decided she wanted it too.

Putting her hands flat on his stomach to support herself, she sat up and rocked her pelvis back and forth a few times, feeling his thickness brush her moist vulva, covering him with her dew. She heard him moan again. Now she was happy to have tied him up, she could take him on her own terms.

Soon her clitoris quivered against his hardness and she longed to feel him inside her. She grabbed hold of his shaft and presented the swollen head to her entrance.

She lowered herself upon him, slowly, feeling him stretch her gradually, but not letting him enter her completely, before lifting herself up again. Her entrance teased his rigid member, never giving it the satisfaction of total penetration.

His hips jerked up in a vain effort to impale her but she lifted herself up even more, pressing hard on his stomach to prevent him from moving again. This was an uneven fight however, his range of movements limited by the weight of the plaster cast around his leg. Yet Judith still wanted to show him she had the upper hand.

'Stop this,' she warned, 'it's no use.'

But as she glided up and down upon his length she gradually conceded. Soon she began to ride him, at first by simply rocking back and forth, then increasing the movement of her hips as she felt him growing bigger inside her, her arousal now mounting quickly. She was becoming a victim to her own game, having meant to hold out as long as possible to torture him, but realising she was the one who could no longer wait.

But by now she was acting solely with the intention of reaching her own climax. It didn't really matter if he came as well in the process, he had earned this reward. She heard herself panting, the muscles of her thighs soon tied in a burning knot as she rapidly moved up and down upon his shaft, her knees locking under the strain.

Her vulva was melting onto his member and quivering with delight, as Judith willed herself to continue her assault despite the pain in her exhausted legs. The swollen head stroked her inside, up and down the smooth walls of her tunnel, triggering that sensation which would soon take her to the point of no return. Her stiff clitoris rubbed itself on the hard shaft as well, only enhancing the pleasure she could already feel was about to explode.

She was breathless, highly aware of the pressure building up within her, yet her climax almost took her by surprise. Her head jerked back and forth a few times as successive sobs escaped from her mouth.

Her vulva contracted around his member and provoked his own climax. She hardly felt him quiver inside her, but she recognised the spasm that shook him, as if escaping from her own body to transport him right after.

She let herself collapse on top of him once more, this time recoiling on his chest and nestling her face in the groove of his neck. She listened to his heartbeat slowly returning to its normal rate, as was hers.

Although she would have liked to stay a little longer,

she knew she had to shake herself from the cloud that now surrounded her, and fight the temptation to stay with him any longer.

His regular breathing told her he was completely relaxed now, and probably falling asleep. She rose with difficulty and felt his limp phallus slide out of her, falling back with a fat flop on his stomach.

Her patient was now in bed, she had done her duty. She undid the restraints and stored them back in the bedside cupboard, then took her bra from his mouth and began to dress.

The back panel was soaked with his saliva and felt cold against her warm skin, right between her shoulder blades; a silent reminder of the daring way she had treated him. She laughed softly. She wasn't sorry for what she had done.

She finished dressing and pulled the blanket on top of him, looking at him one more time, still bathed by the blue light coming from the window, before making her way to the bathroom. Her hair needed to be tamed before she returned to her nursing station.

In the bath tub the wet towel still lay in a bundle, and its sight gave a smile to Judith's lips. This was something she wasn't going to forget for some time. She quickly gathered her hair up and checked her image in the mirror one more time: prim and proper, who would have thought? Glancing at her watch she suddenly realised she had been gone for over an hour.

She turned off the light and almost ran out of the room, desperately trying to think of a good excuse in case her colleague started asking questions. The best she could do was to tell the truth: she had to assist a patient out of the bath tub and help him settle for the night. The rest didn't matter.

Once she got to the station, however, the other nurse was busy preparing an injection. Judith quickly grabbed the order chart and pretended to absorb herself in it. For a second she felt this crazy urge to turn to her colleague and tell her all about what she had just been up to.

She could still smell him, feel him inside her, and her sore knees were still complaining about the way she had abused them.

It wasn't easy keeping a straight face.

Chapter Eleven

'**G** ood evening, my sweet . . .'
Judith's neck stiffened and her heart quickened.
Jo's voice in her ear was unmistakable. Its hissing sound
sent a shiver through her limbs. It was reminiscent of a
rattle-snake, but just as sickly sweet as the morning she
and Tania had cornered Judith in the shower room. That
morning was over five weeks ago already, but suddenly
it seemed like it was only yesterday. She clutched her
pen to prevent her hand from shaking, but released her
grip when she felt the plastic crack under her fingers.

'So, we'll be spending the night together,' Jo continued.
'I'm sure we'll have a nice time.' Her voice shook slightly
and it was clear she was fighting a giggle. Yet Judith
wasn't in a laughing mood. What was Jo planning to do
to her this time?

There were only two nurses at each station during the
night shift. This was the second time Judith had been
assigned to do a series of night shifts, but so far she had
worked with a different nurse each night. Luckily, she
hadn't been assigned to work with either Tania or Jo,
who worked regular night shifts, but it was too good to
last.

This was her last night before going back to day shifts,
and her worse nightmare was about to come alive. Yet at

the same time a strange sensation seized her, her body cruelly reminding her what the girls had done to her that morning, and despite her fears she felt a weird antici- pation, some wicked desire to somehow fall into their clutches again.

Her mind racing, she stood up and walked toward the filing cabinet. She had to buy some time, calm her nerves and think of a way to stay outside of Jo's reach for the next eight hours. When she turned around again Jo was standing by the desk and still staring at her, smiling sweetly. For a moment she almost seemed friendly.

Judith looked straight into the blue eyes, trying to see in them what made her so afraid of the blond doll. But in fact, Jo didn't look threatening at all. She was shorter than Judith, and a bit plumper. The body was voluptu- ous, the breasts and the hips generous, the stomach nicely rounded.

Her blond hair was only loosely tied up, something that would perhaps make the directors frown, and her earrings were definitely too big. The make-up was over- done, too. Large patches of blue powder weighed on the eyelids, and a red blotch covered each cheek. The pouting lips were red as well, dark as blood and shimmering. The nails were painted a matching red, something else that wasn't in line with the regulations of the Clinic.

A doll, that's what she was. Something to cuddle softly, to play with, and then put aside in a corner when playtime was over.

In Judith's mind a wicked thought arose: the best way to fight her fears would be to tackle them head on, to turn the tables on the naughty nurse. All she had to do was to corner her colleague and frighten her the way she and Tania had frightened Judith, so the victim would become the attacker. But how? She was never keen on practical jokes, she never had the wicked imagination needed to be really successful. However, given enough time she would perhaps come up with something good.

The phone rang and interrupted her thoughts. Jo picked it up and Judith returned to the filing cabinet. She fished out the procedure sheet and rapidly glanced through it.

There were rounds to be made at 2 o'clock, and after that the nurses had to go to the stock room to do a brief inventory and order missing supplies for the next morning. The store room was right behind the station, and quite a distance from the patients' rooms. The two nurses would be alone in there, no-one could hear them.

Judith smiled and bit her lip. That would be the perfect moment. She had to attack first and surprise the girl, scare her as much as possible. But how? She had about three hours to think of something, something good. If she was alone with her she knew she was strong enough to have the upper hand.

She turned around to face Jo, determined to be just as sweet and show her she wasn't at all afraid of her. But instead she came face to face with Carol Martin, the night supervisor.

'I've been looking for you,' Carol said. 'We have a problem on the fourth floor. One of the nurses is ill and the other has just called in to say she would be late. Problems with her car, I think. I need you to go down there and mind the desk until she gets here, then help her with the rounds.'

Judith glanced at her watch, suddenly disappointed. It was already a few minutes past midnight, there was no way of knowing how long she would be away from her own desk, and away from Jo. But she had no option. Besides, being away would certainly buy her time and Jo would not become suspicious. It didn't really matter if she was away for the next couple of hours anyhow; she could set her plan in motion anytime after that.

She grabbed her handbag and made her way down to the fourth floor.

Judith paused in the stairwell and glanced at her watch. She had chosen to walk up the stairs to get back to her own station. This way, there wouldn't be any noises from the lift to betray her arrival. It was almost 3 o'clock; if Jo had worked fast and if there hadn't been any problems, she could very well be doing the inventory already.

Judith walked towards the desk quickly but silently, almost clinging to the wall, carefully passing each room. She briefly pressed her ear to each door, trying to figure out where Jo could be at this hour.

The nursing station was deserted and Judith slipped her handbag under the desk. She quickly glanced at the order chart and saw a long row of check marks, along with Jo's initials. The rounds had been done.

She tiptoed to the stock room and carefully pushed the door open, peering inside. Jo was standing near a stack of bed sheets, her back turned, holding her clipboard in one hand and using the other to toss the sheets whilst counting them aloud.

Judith slowly entered the room and silently shut the door behind her, her heart beating fast, desperately trying to pace her breath, lest it became so loud it would betray her presence.

She had decided to quickly pounce on the girl and take her by surprise, to simply grab her forcefully and perhaps even grope her a little. After that, she would have to improvise.

Of course Jo wouldn't know what hit her. Hopefully she would be scared out of her wits. Already Judith felt a warm flow collecting at her crotch, the excitement of the attack strangely fuelling some sort of arousal. This peculiar desire wasn't really directed at Jo, but rather at the concept of surprising and frightening the girl. Tonight Judith was in charge.

Her hands pushed at the door behind her to make sure it was completely shut. Rapidly she estimated the other nurse's position and distance. In her mind the plan was already in motion.

Reaching up along the wall she turned off the light and waited a second, wanting to make her attack even more startling. Then she stepped forward and almost immediately felt Jo's plump body stopping her advance.

Obviously the other girl hadn't realised what was

going on for she hadn't even turned around yet. In the dark, Judith pushed her forward, slipping one arm around the curvy waist and pressing her other hand against her victim's mouth.

'Not a word,' she muttered in the girl's ear, trying to change her voice and fighting a giggle. Already she felt elated and now she wished she could see Jo's face. But attacking like this in the complete darkness was even better than she would have expected.

She heard the clipboard falling to the floor and felt the tiny panic-stricken hands trying to pry hers off the painted mouth.

Judith pinned her victim face down against the stack of sheets, preventing her from going anywhere, not even giving her any room to move. She felt the thick lips protesting under her hand, and the heat of Jo's frightened body piercing through her uniform.

As she felt Jo writhing in her embrace, she suddenly became excited, now wanting to impress not only fear upon her victim, but arousal as well. Under her hand squealing sounds were trying to escape and she increased the strength of her grasp. At the same time she let her other hand roughly brush the rounded breasts, surprised to notice the nipples immediately growing hard under her fingertips.

Yet she could still feel Jo trembling against her and at this moment estimated victory was hers. She had succeeded in both frightening and arousing the girl.

Judith resisted the urge to laugh out loud, satisfied and almost surprised by the immediate success of her revenge. The joke was over, and she had vanquished her own fears. From now on she knew there was nothing Jo could ever do to frighten her.

And now all she had to do was to wait a little while without releasing the girl – just to make her worry a bit, wondering who this attacker was and what she wanted – and then she would let her go.

Yet at the same time Judith felt a strange desire to continue, to discover the rounded body that kept on writhing in a more and more sensual manner, the hips gyrating lasciviously, the buttocks pushing against Judith's thighs. For a minute she wondered what it would be like to caress the girl as she had herself been caressed.

She moved back slightly, hoping Jo would take this opportunity to escape. But instead she felt a tiny hand grab hers and bring it back to caress the engorged nipples. The soft buttocks continued pushing back against Judith's thighs and the body grew limp in surrender. Jo had stopped fighting. Judith's heart began beating faster.

Things were getting out of hand. She hadn't expected Jo to react like this ... Now she felt like she was falling into her own trap, being both aroused by the close contact with this plump body, and frightened by the way her own body now craved to caress the blond girl.

What was she to do? Her mind was telling her to stop right there, but her body was eager for her to go on, as if she would then miss out on something. If she kept going she would likely discover another source of pleasure and this notion quickly made her hesitation vanish.

She couldn't stop, not just yet. She decided to keep up the game just a little bit longer, just to see how Jo would react. Possibly the girl would soon begin to yearn for pleasure, and right at that point Judith would stop. That was the easiest option; some sort of compromise in reply to the dilemma between her reason and her senses. Just a little longer ...

She brought both her hands to the girl's breasts and gently cupped them, curious yet shy, no longer thinking but rather letting her body dictate her behaviour. Instinctively she knew Jo probably wore the same kind of underwear as she did, a lacy bra and matching panties, and the thought excited her even more.

Guided by Jo's hands, she fumbled to undo the buttons at the front of the girl's uniform, then slowly slipped her hands inside, her fingers instantly melting onto the warm skin.

Jo moaned gently and tilted her head back against Judith's shoulder, turning her face sideways to kiss her attacker's neck.

At that point Judith wondered if Jo knew who was caressing her like this, but immediately she realised that not knowing was probably even more exciting for a girl like Jo. The thrill of an unknown attacker, albeit female, probably added to the excitement she might have experienced through the attack itself.

Judith let her fingertips glide over the lacy cups of the bra, her nails gently scratching the erect nipples. Her own nipples grew stiff as well, her breasts swelling in arousal. She was holding a woman in her arms. How strange, how pleasant.

The need to possess the body she held in her grasp soon became overwhelming, yet Judith thought she could never bring herself to inflict on Jo the same treatment the two naughty nurses had submitted her to in the shower room.

The heat of the body pushing against hers was inviting; the rounded curves begged to be caressed. Judith suddenly wished she was a man, wanting to survey those curves with larger hands, and possess the girl with a strong, virile passion.

She heard Jo moan gently and felt tiny hands straying, fingers slowly pulling up her own dress to get at her thighs. Still holding the breasts in her cupped hands, she stopped thinking and abandoned herself to fully enjoy this new sensation. In her mind she saw the red fingernails slowly tracing the path of her thighs; she saw the breasts she held in her hands swelling under the soft caress. She moaned in reply and instinctively started to cover the girl's neck with gentle kisses.

Jo's aroma was sweetly perfumed with cinnamon undertones. A fine layer of sweat covered the offered cheek and Judith quickly brushed it with her chin. She was amazed by its softness; how different it was from a man's rough skin.

The hands once again grabbed hold of Judith's to guide

701

them under Jo's dress. At that moment Judith understood that although she had meant for Jo to be her victim, they were now equals.

Still standing behind the plump body that continued to press itself against hers, Judith began to caress it, marvelling at the softness of the skin her fingers had found.

Jo brought her hands up above and behind her head and gently encircled Judith's neck, abandoning herself. In the dark she put one foot up on a step stool in front of her, effectively parting her legs for the benefit of her attacker.

Judith saw her own image rising in her mind; how she had herself offered her body to her previous lovers, and what a sweet invitation it was indeed. Her hands glided up the girl's thighs, feeling their hot, fluid plumpness. She shuddered as her fingertips finally reached the lacy fabric of Jo's panties, hesitating a moment.

Once again she felt she shouldn't go on. But the warmth that had taken over and stunned her senses only urged her to keep going. In her arms the girl moaned again, as if inviting her to continue her search. This intoxicating feeling rendered Judith's mind numb. Only her senses were now guiding her on this unusual road to pleasure.

She placed the whole of her hand on the girl's crotch, letting its feminine wetness pierce through and bathe the palm of her hand. At the same time a familiar smell rose to her nostrils, the smell of lust, similar to the aroma of her own excitement.

The girl that writhed in her embrace was wanton, and her excitement was inevitably contagious. As Judith let herself be invaded by this voluptuous aroma she felt her own arousal bloom and at this instant decided that she wanted to feel Jo's naked skin. After all, Jo had herself boldly caressed Judith once, it was only natural to return the favour . . .

She undertook to undress her victim quickly. The uniforms they were wearing were similar, both fastening through a long row of buttons at the front. Strangely, Judith felt like she was undressing herself. Jo didn't display any resistance but didn't try to help her either, as if she had accepted she was a victim tonight.

Judith's excitement gave her fingers an unusual precision and even in the dark she was able to remove everything Jo wore without even seeing it. And again she wondered whether the blond girl knew the identity of her seducer.

Her hands worked fast and in a matter of seconds Jo stood completely naked. Being unable to see the naked body only made Judith more eager to discover it. She ran her hands all over it, delicately feeling the whole surface, endlessly marvelling at its warm softness.

Jo stood passively, moaning gently every time Judith's hands brushed her breasts or the inside of her legs. By now she had to brace herself by putting both hands on the pile of sheets in front of her, her legs parted wide in anticipation, in invitation.

Where Judith's hands went her mouth would soon follow, but not just yet. She pressed her clothed body against the naked back, cupping both breasts and worrying the puckered nipples whilst her lips lightly brushed Jo's neck and shoulders. She continued her discovery in this fashion for a while, her hands surveying the front of the plump body and her mouth caressing its back.

She worked her way down gradually, letting her tongue run down each bump of Jo's spine, sucking at them briefly. Her hands on the girl's breasts became a little rougher and grasped the rounded globes in a tighter grip, pinching and pulling at the nipples between her thumb and forefinger.

Soon Judith ended up on her knees, her hands now holding the girl's thighs and her face resting on the rounded buttocks. She had ceased to think a long time ago, yet she was still highly aware of what she was doing. Her caresses were not automatic but carefully planned, blindly obeying the orders dictated by her own desire.

She could also feel her own body alight, consumed by the desire to caress the girl in ways she wouldn't have dared only a few weeks ago. But now she was ready, she wanted to know a female body. She stood up and grabbed Jo by the shoulders, forcing her to turn around. Still pushing her against the stack of sheets she bent down and quickly took hold of a nipple in her mouth.

Jo let out a small cry of joy, tentatively putting her hands around Judith's neck and shyly pulling it even tighter to her generous bosom.

Judith took a demure lick at the puckered bud she now held in her mouth. It seemed to grow bigger, to swell as she teased it gently, its smokey taste pleasantly strange.

Her nose gently brushed Jo's cushiony breast, resting against the soft skin and caressing it with each breath. At the same time her hands wandered along the girl's thighs, stroking them endlessly in an up and down motion.

Jo's knees seemed to buckle under her, and Judith suddenly felt powerful, encouraged by the way she could get the girl to react to her caresses. She was still pinning the girl to the stack of sheets even though Jo wasn't showing any resistance. Yet Judith felt she was in charge, calling the shots, and Jo would have no option but to obey anyway.

Sensuously, wickedly, she let her fingers glide up the inside of her victim's thigh and only briefly brush the moist vulva. She heard Jo moan and felt her tremble, but Judith's own flesh reacted even more strongly.

She began to pant and engulfed Jo's breast deep in her mouth, locking her lips around the tender skin in a strong suction. She sucked at it as if it were the very air she breathed, the effect of her caresses somehow transferring onto her own body. She was feeling what she was doing, as if she were caressing herself. Her own vulva clenched violently as she touched Jo's again, ever so lightly, her fingers teasing the wet folds only in passing before continuing to caress the warm flesh of the rounded thighs.

Yet her fingers began spending more and more time brushing the wet bush, their eagerness continually increasing, discovering a treasure that was different, yet so similar, to her own.

She realised she probably knew what to do to make the girl climax, but she didn't want to make her reach her peak just yet. First Jo had to be deliciously tortured, perhaps even kept waiting forever without ever receiving the pleasure of release . . .

Tonight Judith was determined to be cruel. She remembered that fateful morning in the shower, and she also remembered the girls hadn't kept their promise to make her come. Now it would be her revenge.

Her mouth then turned to the other breast, bathing it with the warmth of her tongue, and began gently teasing the erect nipple with tiny butterfly licks, the tip of her tongue only darting at it lightly but rhythmically.

This role reversal wasn't only surprising for Judith but also terribly arousing. Once again, she curiously wished she were a man right now, to be able to possess the girl with all her might, to impale her and fill her passionately.

Her hands became frantic, kneading the soft skin of Jo's thighs with both hands whilst her mouth decidedly began its descent along the girl's belly. She felt Jo's warmth against her cheek as she glided down in a soft caress, and only stopped when she felt the downy mound tickle her chin.

By now she was kneeling in front of the girl. Jo still hadn't moved, content to be caressed. Judith could smell the musky dew, quite similar to her own. She remembered Edouard's words when he had cornered her in the corridor a few weeks ago: 'I can smell your desire . . .' Now she knew what he meant. The musky smell of a woman's arousal, its sweet and heady fragrance, could only serve to enhance a man's own desire.

And right now Judith's mouth was just a few inches away from this wet treasure, so compelling, so inviting. She buried her lips in the soft curls, her tongue shyly yet eagerly searching for the tiny shaft she now longed to taste.

It seemed to be waiting for her and throbbed with delight when she found it. She gently suckled its hardening bud, letting her tongue slide along its length, and brought her hand up to discover more of what lay amidst this soft bush.

Her fingers lost themselves along the wet folds, feeling their watery softness before being sucked in the silken cavern, the smooth walls of the vagina closing around them in a delightful grip.

Her mouth soon followed them, her tongue digging deep inside the girl whilst her other hand reached up and her thumb came flickering over the swollen clitoris. She tasted the girl's sweet dew, her taste buds awakening to this new nectar that now seemed to flow into her mouth.

Judith felt her own vulva react violently, demanding to be caressed as well. By now she was teasing the girl exactly the way she liked to be teased herself. And somehow she could feel it in her loins, her body alight with a fire on the verge of explosion.

She let go of the treasure she was holding in her mouth and stood up again. Without a word she took Jo's tiny hand and guided it to her own flesh, under her dress and inside her soaked panties.

Jo followed the silent instructions obediently, and her hand mimicked Judith's, both women caressing each other's silken flesh in a smooth, back and forth motion.

Only Judith bent forward slightly, eager to grab hold of the girl's pulpous breasts and again taste their smokiness. Jo's fingers on her vulva followed the tempo set by Judith's hand, and soon both women began moaning in pleasure as they kindled each other's arousal.

Judith forwent her previous intention not to let the girl reach her peak. By now it seemed they had entered some sort of silent pact, whereby giving and receiving pleasure could not be dissociated.

Judith's hips began swaying violently, as if desperately

706

trying to extract pleasure out of Jo's hand. Judith's hand on Jo's vulva also became frantic, torturing the stiff clitoris hard and fast. Judith was still pressing her clothed body against Jo's naked skin, moans of pleasure escaping from her throat with each breath. Both women reached their climax almost simultaneously, Jo sighing loudly, Judith almost grunting, her mouth still gripping the girl's breasts.

They had to lean against each other for a while, Judith's pleasure subsiding quickly, but Jo weakly holding on to her.

A second later Judith's brain began functioning again, suddenly realising she couldn't afford to abandon herself completely, she had to get out of there. With her foot she quickly scattered Jo's clothing around the room. She had to buy time and make sure the girl wouldn't get out of the stock room too soon lest she discovered who her attacker was, if she didn't know already.

Next she took some of the sheets from the stack and tossed them aside, reducing the height to make the limp body lean against it instead. She forced Jo to turn around, making her bend over the diminished stack, face down, and then covered her entirely with a couple of sheets. By the time Jo regained her senses, got out from under the sheets, retrieved her clothes and finally exited the room, Judith would have disappeared from the station, only to come back some time later.

For a second she was tempted to lock the door on her way out, but decided against it. Instead she left the room without turning on the lights, grabbed her handbag, and once again made her way to another floor using the stairs.

The door of the lift closed in front of her and Judith checked her watch: 5 o'clock. She had waited in the nurses' lounge for almost thirty minutes, just as if she had been on her break. Her timing was perfect and she smiled to herself, rather content that Jo would probably never find out who her attacker was.

The lift stopped with a squeaky hiss, sounding louder than usual in the silence of the early morning. With any chance Jo would hear her arriving this time.

She walked to the station decidedly, almost giggling, yet still trying to keep a straight face. Jo was sitting behind the desk, filling forms in for the morning shift.

'I hope you don't mind,' Judith said, 'but I decided to take my break before coming back up. Did you have time to do the inventory or do you need me to help you with it?' She tried to sound casual, a bit uncertain, trying to recapture the impression she must have given Jo when they first started their shift.

Jo didn't even look up, seemingly fascinated by the forms she had to complete for the laboratory tests.

'It's all done, I'll be going on my break now.'

Judith let out a small sigh, trying to sound relieved at the thought of not having to spend much time alone with her colleague. After all, Judith was supposed to be Jo's prey, wasn't she?

Chapter Twelve

The paper seemed to burn in her hands. Judith sat down in an armchair in the nurses' lounge adjacent to the locker room and read the letter over again, trying to make some sense out of the words that were now dancing in front of her and losing their shape as tears filled her eyes. All around her nurses were coming in and out of the room, laughing loudly, not paying attention to her. Many were on their way home and often slammed the metal doors of the lockers, only adding to the noisy confusion.

But Judith couldn't hear any of this anymore. Her mind was completely absorbed by the letter she had just received.

The envelope was included with her pay packet, marked 'personal and confidential'. At first she had thought it was probably something insignificant to do with her salary or taxes, but the first line of text had sent a bolt of sorrow through her heart and tears to her eyes.

NOTICE OF CONVOCATION TO A DISCIPLINARY HEARING
FOR: *Miss Judith Stanton*
REGARDING THE EVENT THAT TOOK PLACE:
the 17th of this month

709

She was required to attend the meeting which would take place the next morning in the Board Room. The 17th was two weeks ago already, but Judith had not forgotten that night: it was the night she had been with Mike Randall.

Obviously somebody had seen them and reported her. Probably the other nurse who was on duty that night, or maybe even Mike himself! But why had the directors waited so long before taking action? After that night each passing day had given Judith a sense of security, she was sure no-one would ever find out. Until now . . .

A disciplinary hearing for a nurse who had not completed her probation could only mean instant dismissal.

The offence was serious. Back in nursing school she had been told several times that physical relations with patients were regarded as highly unethical. Some hospitals even considered it as some kind of abuse since it was often implied the patient was under medication and therefore not really aware of what was happening.

It was her fault, there was no doubt about it, and the blame would be on her. She should have walked away that night, she should have been strong and resisted temptation. Now it was too late.

She tilted her head back against the wall and took a deep breath. She remembered every second of the time she had spent in Mike Randall's room; how his skin looked under the blue rays of the floodlight; how hot his flesh had felt under her touch . . .

Her sorrow quickly turned to anger. She folded the letter and put it back in the envelope, wishing she knew who had squealed on her. Somehow she doubted it could be Mike himself, what would he have to gain? Her colleague? That was a strong possibility; she could have been motivated by jealousy.

At that moment Judith realised she hadn't seen her

since that night. Now what was her name? ... Mary ... Mary Jenkins.

She stood up and went back into the locker room, reading the name tags on each of the narrow doors until she found the name: C. Jackson ... J. James ... M. Jenkins. The door was locked, of course, but the nurse who occupied the next locker was sitting on the long bench, tying up her shoelaces.

'Excuse me,' Judith inquired, 'have you seen Mary recently?'

'Mary Jenkins? No, not for a while. She hasn't been in for over a week now. Nobody knows why, maybe she's been ill or something. Why? Does she owe you money as well?'

Judith gave a faint smile. 'No, nothing like that. I was just wondering, that's all. Thank you.'

She turned around and went back to her own locker, in the next row. Time to go home. Thankfully she hadn't received the letter earlier during the day; she wouldn't have been able to carry on. She opened the narrow door and stared at the three uniforms quietly hanging in the locker. She had bought them only two days ago and still hadn't worn them. Her trembling fingers caressed the smooth fabric, wondering whether her short career could already be coming to an end. If she were dismissed it would make it even more difficult to find a job elsewhere.

She grabbed her coat and her bag and quickly closed the door with a bang, then made her way out of the locker room, desperately trying to hold back her tears, at least until she was out of the building.

Why had she bothered to wear her uniform this morning? After the hearing there was no doubt in Judith's mind she would be out of a job. She sat still, her limbs strangely steady, waiting to be called into the Board Room.

When she had arrived she had seen Mary Jenkins go in. At this very moment her colleague was probably still describing what she had witnessed that night, giving them all the details of how Judith had pulled the curtain around the bed, how she had undressed and wilfully hopped into bed with her patient. They would then quickly build up a case against Judith and just present her with the fact once she was called in.

Judith shuddered. She wanted to scream her pain, protesting she hadn't done anything wrong. But, of course, she had known all along that it wasn't really right either.

The clock ticked slowly, each second increasing the feeling of impending doom that hung about her. Last night she had thought about it for what seemed hours. There was always a slight chance she might just be reprimanded, in which case she would gladly accept any kind of punishment if in turn they would let her keep her job.

At that moment she had promised herself she would never again let her lustful desires get the best of her. She would restrain herself. She would pick up guys in bars to satisfy her needs if she had to. But not at work, never again.

She was startled when the door opened and Mr Armstrong, the personnel manager, came out.

'We're ready for you, Miss Stanton.'

She stood up quietly, feeling strangely calm, and followed him into the large room where she was invited to take a seat at the large oval, mahogany table. On the other side sat Doctor Marshall and Mrs Cox. Judith couldn't stand to look at them. This wasn't fair, she thought. They had been so blunt with her that day in Mrs Cox's office, making her take her clothes off and masturbate in front of them. And now they were about to fire her for giving free reign to her passion.

Mr Armstrong sat next to her. Judith furtively glanced around the table to see who else was there. She felt a cold chill as she noticed Robert Harvey sitting at the far end. What was he doing here? Then she remembered he was chief surgeon, and as such would be involved in administrative matters.

So there was only the four of them. However, three of

these people knew something about her, something very personal. The three of them had seen her naked body writhing with pleasure, they had all heard her cries as she had climaxed.

Again today she felt as if she was naked before them. Only this time it wasn't nice at all. Turning her head slightly, she saw Mary Jenkins sitting in a far corner, like a witness. Judith instantly felt betrayed and couldn't stand to look at her either. What was about to happen was not only very embarrassing, it was also very personal. How could they let Mary stay and watch?

'Miss Stanton,' Mr Armstrong began, 'I need to ask you a few questions about the night of the 17th. Now, it is very important that you answer in all honesty, do you understand?'

'Yes.'

'That night, you were working the night shift on the sixth floor, right? Which rooms were you responsible for?'

'616 to 630.'

'And Miss Jenkins here, which rooms was she looking after?'

'601 to 615.'

He paused and glanced at the table. Only then did Judith notice the small tape recorder and a feeling of panic seized her. They were recording her every word! How could they?!

She felt her face flush in outrage but before she could say anything Mr Armstrong had turned to her again. 'During your shift that night, did you at any time go into room 612?'

Judith felt surprised and her anger vanished for a moment. Room 612? What did this have to do with her?

'No . . . No . . .'

'Did you see Miss Jenkins go into that room during the shift?'

Judith's hands began to tremble. Why was he asking her this? His question took her aback, she had to make an effort to remember. That night her mind had worked on automatic pilot, completely dazed after what had

713

happened in Mike Randall's room. Room 612? Wasn't that Mrs Gibson's room, the one who was in for a facelift? Yes, now she remembered Mary having to tend to her quite often; the patient had spent an agitated night.

'Yes. She went in there quite a few times . . .'

'Now,' he said slowly, 'this is very important. When she came out of the room after checking on the patient, did you ever notice Miss Jenkins taking something out of the room?'

Judith began breathing fast, getting suddenly excited. Obviously there was something else going on today, maybe this hearing wasn't about her . . . She forced herself to concentrate, to recapture the images that were now so vague in her mind.

'Yes, I saw her taking something.'

'What?'

'I don't know . . .'

'Try to remember. Was it sheets? Clothes? A tray?'

'I'm . . . I'm not sure. It was something small . . . In her hand . . . Black . . '

'Miss Stanton, this is very important. Please make an effort.'

'It was like a purse, a black leather purse . . .'

'Are you sure?'

Judith breathed a smile. So this is what it was all about. Did her colleague take something from the patient's room? Then she remembered the words of the nurse in the locker room: 'does she owe you money as well?' Mary had been off work for a couple of weeks and nobody knew why. Could she have been suspended pending the hearing because she had stolen money from a patient?

'Quite sure,' Judith announced, suddenly relieved. And indeed she was sure. Now she distinctly remembered Mary going to check on Mrs Gibson towards the end of their shift, even though the patient had finally fallen asleep some time earlier. She had something with her when she had come out of the room, and she had put it in her handbag.

714

And now Mary's job was in Judith's hands.

'Did you see what she did with it? Did she ever bring it back to the patient's room?'

'I don't know.' Now she felt sorry for her colleague, and quite ashamed to have thought Mary had squealed on her. However the administration seemed to have pretty strong evidence against Mary already, and nothing Judith could say at this point would make a difference.

'Do you know whether it could have been her own purse? Is it possible she could have taken it to the patient's room for some reason, without you seeing her, and brought it back again later?'

'I don't know.'

'But you are sure she did take something that looked like a purse out of the patient's room?'

'Yes, I'm absolutely sure about that. But I wouldn't know whose purse it was.'

Mr Armstrong turned to Doctor Marshall. The men stared at each other for a few seconds until Doctor Marshall silently nodded. Mr Armstrong turned to Judith agam.

'Thank you,' he said with a smile. 'You may go back to your station now.'

Judith smiled in turn and stood up, her eyes quickly looking for some sign of acknowledgement from those seated on the other side of the table. But no-one was looking at her, they seemed to be busy exchanging glances between themselves.

At that moment Judith really felt that her own job was secure, for now. Before leaving the room she also looked at Mary, still sitting in the corner. The tear-stained face looked up at her with a faint smile.

Judith felt sorry for her colleague, but there was nothing she could do. She had to tell the truth otherwise she would have risked her own job. And after this she knew she would never do anything to risk that again.

Chapter Thirteen

The bell rang on the station board and Nurse Hard-castle sighed in exasperation.

'Lisa Baxter! Again!' She turned to Judith. 'Would you be an angel and go see what she wants this time? She's such a pest this morning! I've been to her room four times already. I'm just about to kill her. I have better things to do than help her put nail varnish on her toes!'

Judith laughed and made her way to room 218. One of the drawbacks of caring for rich people was that the nurses were often mistaken for servants, and the patients failed to realise the staff had more important things to do than cater to their every whim.

At the Dorchester Clinic, it seemed to be even worse on the second floor, where the patients were younger and the atmosphere was not unlike a wild party at times. From starlets who thought spending thousands of pounds just to get rid of a few tiny lines around their eyes would open the doors to fame, to affluent young men whose egos needed a little boost in the form of well-placed pectoral implants, the whole second floor looked more like a university college than a private clinic. And the patients all had one thing in common: they had a tendency to believe the staff had nothing to do but to wait on them.

Nevertheless, Judith felt more comfortable around this younger crowd and since she had started to work at the Clinic she had often wished she could be assigned to this floor more often.

The first thing she did as she entered the room was to turn down the radio, blasting so loud she could hear it all the way down the corridor. There hadn't been any complaints, but there were rules to be observed otherwise things would rapidly get out of control.

Lisa's room, like most rooms on the second floor, was decorated differently from the rooms on the upper floors: still luxurious and comfortable, but with a more youthful look. The small leather sofa in the corner was a deep red instead of pale orange. The bedcover also looked younger, featuring a rather psychedelic pattern in red and green instead of the usual, more subdued mint and peach print. In a corner sat an enormous panda bear, adding a black and white note.

Lisa was sitting on her bed, knees apart, brushing her long hair with one hand, the other still paused on the call button. She turned to the nurse.

'It's about time,' she whined in a comical voice, her nose still covered in bandages and forcing her to breathe through her mouth. Her blonde hair fell in straight strands, untamed, over her shoulders. The thick fringe on her forehead made her look even younger than she was.

She was wearing white satin pyjamas through which the twin peaks of her nipples were plainly visible. Judith remembered the sight of her naked body, the nipples the same colour as coffee, the way they had puckered when she had touched them . . .

That was already more than two weeks ago but Lisa was still here. Something had gone wrong in the operating theatre that morning and the procedure had to be rescheduled. As a result, Lisa had been sent home and had to come back a couple of weeks later.

Needless to say, from the moment she had set foot in the Clinic the second time around she had been very demanding, constantly throwing tantrums to members of the staff who had been advised to humour her. There were fears that if Lisa Baxter wasn't entirely happy with her stay, she might in turn complain to her friends who would otherwise someday become patients of the Clinic themselves. Since word of mouth was the only form of publicity for the Dorchester Clinic, it was important to avoid ending up with dissatisfied patients .

'What can I do for you, Lisa?' Judith asked as she turned towards the bed. She stopped about three feet away, somewhat intimidated by the girl's impatient tone, unwilling to irritate her any further.

'I want you to open the window; it's too hot in here!'

'We've told you before, we can't open the windows just now. It's too cold outside, you can't afford to catch a cold as long as your nose is still covered in bandages.'

'Then take the bloody bandages off!'

Judith bit her lips in an effort to kill the smile that rose to her lips. Lisa was fuming with anger, almost screaming, but the snuffling voice coming out of her mouth was incredibly out of place and made her sound like a cartoon character.

'Two more days, dear,' Judith replied, coming closer to the bed. 'And you'll be allowed to go home right after. Just be patient and bear with us.' She tried to remain calm and talk in a reassuring tone, having been warned by her colleagues to always remain polite and kind even if this particular patient became difficult. If Lisa started to complain to the directors, at least she wouldn't have anything to say against Judith.

In an effort to pacify the girl she approached the bed and gently took the hairbrush from her. Standing behind Lisa, she quietly ran her fingers through the girl's hair, draping the light mane over the back of her hands.

'You're becoming quite impatient,' she stated, trying to sound friendly. 'I bet you can't wait to get out of here. Has your boyfriend been to visit?'

'No,' Lisa replied, gradually calming down. 'He's such a wimp, he's afraid of hospitals!'

718

'Somehow I can't imagine you going out with a wimp!' Judith laughed.

'We're not really together. He's hardly my type, but he's such a good fuck.'

Judith gasped and almost dropped the hairbrush, although she knew she shouldn't be surprised to hear such a sophisticated girl using that kind of language. Nowadays, even rich, spoilt girls weren't immune to dirty words.

She tried to think of something to say, to change the subject, sensing that if Lisa wasn't entirely happy with her boyfriend she might start getting angry again. But before she could come up with another topic, Lisa spoke again.

'Do you have a boyfriend?' she asked.

'No, not really,' Judith replied

'I bet you're having it with the doctors here then, right? They're all so luscious! What do you think my chances would be? I have a friend who was in here a couple of months ago and she told me she had it with this doctor called Harvey. She said he was really something else! Do you know him?'

Judith pretended not to hear her and gave her back the hairbrush with trembling fingers. Lisa continued talking, as if she didn't really care whether the nurse was listening, but by now Judith couldn't hear her anymore.

Slowly she walked away from the bed, like an automaton, her mind completely absorbed by what Lisa had just said.

Robert Harvey had been to bed with one of his patients? That couldn't possibly be. How could he? A doctor with one of his patients ... Of course, that wasn't really surprising. He was good-looking, therefore probably popular with his patients. And Judith had no right to point the finger at anyone, considering what she had done with Mike Randall ...

And then there was also Edouard, with Lady Austin ... That wasn't surprising either, but now this was becoming a little too much for Judith to take. 'I have to go back to

719

the nursing station,' she breathed before opening the door and walking out.

In the corridor she had to lean against the wall. The mention of Robert Harvey was once again having a powerful effect on her, bringing back memories so powerful she could feel her skin react, and she shivered despite the comfortable temperature. She also remembered Edouard, the moment they had spent in his office, the way he had caressed her with his tongue . . .

The images were still vivid, bringing back this longing she had tried to quieten after the disciplinary hearing. On the whole she had been rather successful, having avoided being alone with her colleagues as well as the patients. She had also managed to keep her lust under control, concentrating on her duties and remembering the dread she had felt at the disciplinary hearing whenever she saw an attractive body. She had vowed to fight her lust, but her body was now seized with desire, her arousal stronger than ever, all those suppressed feelings surfacing again, coming back with a vengeance.

She slowly walked back to the station, her knees buckling under her, her steps uncertain. Hopefully, once she got back to work, there would be things to do, something to keep her mind occupied. As she turned the corner she bumped into Ray, the attendant who was responsible for her ending up in bed with Mike Randall.

'Hi there!' he chirped, grabbing her by the shoulders to stop her from falling. 'You don't look so hot. Are you all right?'

Judith felt her face flush. She was unable to think any longer. A sensation that was only too familiar had seized her, her flesh suddenly set alight and throbbing. She put her hand flat on his chest to retrieve her balance and raised the other on her forehead.

Ray took her arm and opened the door to a nearby utility room, ushering her in. 'What's the matter? Seen something you weren't supposed to?'

'No, I'll be fine,' Judith replied with a faint smile. 'I just felt faint for a moment, but I'm better now.'

'Your face is all red,' he said, making her lean against a sink and caressing her cheek with his finger. 'You're all warm. Do you want to go outside for a moment?'

'No, I'll be fine,' she repeated.

He took a towel from the stack next to the sink and wet it with cold water. Then he neatly folded the towel and delicately wiped her face, tenderly patting her red cheeks. 'Listen,' he said, 'I'm really grateful for your help the other night. I've been looking for you to say thanks. Did everything go OK? I hope you didn't get into any trouble because of me . . .'

Judith looked up at him. Why did he have to mention that night? If he had done his job she never would have ended up in Mike Randall's bed. The best way to fight temptation was to avoid it altogether. But now it was too late. Yet deep within herself she had to admit it wasn't really Ray's fault; she was the one who couldn't resist the sweet temptation.

And even now the mention of that evening only served to trigger her arousal, and that was the last thing Judith needed right now. She looked up at Ray, feeling her vulva clench, wondering if he knew the storm that was raging through her at that very moment.

He took her chin with his fingers and gently brushed her lips with his. 'Thanks again,' he whispered. 'You've been really sweet.'

His kiss took away the last remnant of the wall of defence she had tried to build up around her. Instinctively she pressed her body against his, oblivious to the look of surprise she read on his face. She demurely slid her arms around his neck, returning his kiss, sighing as she felt his arms encircling her waist.

Their lips barely touched but sensually brushed again and again. She closed her eyes and dissolved in his embrace, slightly opening her mouth in an invitation for him to discover its smoothness. She heard him laugh a few times, as if he was both amused and happy by her behaviour. Still he kept on kissing her, his lips growing insistent on hers.

721

Soon she felt his tongue searching hers, its caress rapidly increasing her arousal. Involuntarily her legs parted and her hips pressed against his thigh. He seemed to immediately guess what she wanted, for his hand wandered down the side of her leg to slide back up under her skirt. His hand felt hot and dry, soft yet scratchy like wool. His fingers travelled up her thigh in large, tantalising circles.

Judith rapidly grew impatient, enjoying his caresses but not wanting to be merely teased much longer. She seized his hand and brought it to her crotch, quickly guiding his fingers inside her panties, moving back slightly to allow him better access, her mouth never letting go of his.

As he softly caressed her silken mound she tossed her head forward and grabbed hold of his arm, forcing his hand to rub back and forth along her wet slit. She held on tight, clutching his biceps with both hands and resting her cheek against his shoulder, her mouth now gasping for air.

He let her move on his hand, standing motionless as she began to frantically ride his wrist, using his arm as a rigid pole against which she pressed her clothed body, his fingers sucked into her wet tunnel. As she opened her eyes she was almost surprised to him standing there. For a moment she had thought that once again she was with her imaginary lover, and all that mattered was her own pleasure.

In this respect, Ray was perfect. He anticipated her needs, clenching his hand into a fist and using his edge of his wrist to tease her tiny, swollen shaft in an up and down motion. He seemed amused by this little wanton that writhed in the palm of his hand, abusing his arm to attain her pleasure, almost bouncing up and down on his fist. Yet he didn't move, did absolutely nothing to stop her.

'Are you always like this?' he whispered in her ear. 'Maybe I should ask to work day shifts more often . . .'

Judith moaned in reply. If he was making fun of her,

722

so be it. Right now she needed him to fulfil the needs of her body, no matter what he might think of her.

There were voices coming from the other side of the door. Judith knew only too well that anybody could walk in on them at any second. Yet the danger of being discovered was only more exciting for her.

Her nipples pushed hard against the lacy fabric that held them prisoner, but Judith had no time for them. Right now the centre of her universe was between her legs; her slick and tender flesh was begging to be tortured, to submit in pleasure.

The whole of her body was also ablaze. She pressed herself against his arm, brushing the swollen breasts against the bulge of his biceps. Her hips continued to swing up and down, faster, harder.

She sealed her lips on his shoulder, gagging herself to smother the cry of joy that rose in her throat. She didn't care where she was, who she was. Her body was asking and she had to give.

Her climax came and went like an arrow through her loins, piercing her violently and suddenly. She whined loudly, collapsing against Ray's arms. Her heart seemed about to leap out of her chest, pounding furiously. Each beat sent a pulse throbbing through her vulva, like aftershocks of the quake still rumbling through her.

She gasped for air a few times and gave a long, final moan.

Ray just had time to catch her before she fell, guiding her limp body to a broken swivelling armchair near the large sink. The chair had a broken wheel and had been left there to be taken away and repaired. Despite its wobbly balance it did the job, giving Judith a chance to rest until her senses came back.

'You're really something else,' Ray laughed softly, crouching next to her.

Still panting, Judith looked at him and smiled. 'I'm sorry, I don't know what got into me.' He smiled in reply and let his eyes travel over her body. Judith looked at him as well.

Although he no longer seemed surprised by what she had done, she sensed he didn't want to touch her; his eyes rested on her in a way that was merely curious and not lustful.

Judith laughed in turn. 'I really needed that,' she said. 'My life has been hell since I started working here.' His smile changed to a confused expression but he didn't say anything. And she kept on talking, the words came out of her mouth naturally, as if he had been a dear friend and confidante. 'It seems everywhere I look people are trying to seduce me,' she explained. 'Their looks, their touch, even their words excite me. I don't know how to handle this anymore. It's got to the point where I'm afraid of losing my job.' A sob rose in her throat and she stopped talking.

For once it felt good to be able to express her feelings, to tell of the effort she had to make to keep her passion under control. Instinctively she knew she could trust Ray even though she didn't know him very well. She could still get him into trouble for having left her to help Mike Randall out of the bath tub the other night. He had asked her to do his job and so Judith had readily assumed he wouldn't betray her secret. In fact Ray wasn't surprised at all, and once again she saw an amused sparkle in his eyes.

'You just started working here then,' he said. 'You haven't been told, have you?'

'Told what?'

'This is all happening on purpose. It's supposed to be that way.'

Judith still couldn't make sense of what he was saying, and it occurred to her that he was trying to make fun of her.

'What are you talking about?'

'The Special Care Programme, have you heard about it?'

She vaguely shook her head. Indeed she had heard it mentioned a few times, but she hadn't figured out what it was all about, and had never even thought of asking.

724

'This clinic offers more than medical care, Judith,' Ray slowly said, emphasising each word. 'We are here to care for the patients, to do everything they want us to, *everything*.'

This still didn't make sense to Judith. What exactly did he mean? Before she could ask him he stood up and started to walk towards the door, looking at her one more time before stepping out.

'Don't fight it,' he said. 'Just let it happen. Enjoy it.' The door closed behind him.

His words prompted her memory, and were reminiscent of what Edouard had told her in his office. If her body craved to be pleasured she should just give in. Ray had just told her something similar. Yet somehow Judith doubted they were talking about the same thing.

She slowly stood up and flattened the front of her uniform with the palm of her hand. Once again she had to get back to the station before they came looking for her. This feeling was becoming only too familiar.

Her head sunk into her pillow. Judith opened her eyes and blinked several times, examining the ceiling to see if the images would appear again.

And still they danced in front of her; places, faces. If she closed her eyes the images would disappear, only to be replaced by words in her ears. She turned around and pulled the duvet over her head, trying to escape. But they wouldn't leave her alone, wouldn't let her sleep peacefully.

First it was Edouard's shadow on the curtain around Lady Austin's bed. The way he had kissed and touched the patient whilst Judith silently stood on the other side of the curtain, watching them. She should have known right then and there that something was up.

Later on, Lady Austin's words had also added to the puzzle by mentioning Robert Harvey: 'He can't keep his hands off me when I come here now.' And she had asked Judith to touch her, even to the point of complaining when Judith had refused!

725

And now the nurse's mind was in a daze. Just like that other morning, when she had come to the stupid conclusion that she had been hypnotised, to serve as some sort of sex slave to the directors of the Clinic. It was actually the other way around, if she could believe Ray. No wonder Edouard had found her accusations so hilarious!

She had been seeing those around her as sources of pleasure, most probably because they were probably feeding on her sensuality, as if she was an involuntary bird of prey.

Now she also understood what Mrs Cox meant: 'After you've been here a few weeks, you will have a different perspective on such situations.' Of course. She was blossoming, the force of her desire only barely awake back then.

But what exactly was going on at the clinic? Ray had mentioned the Special Care Programme, something she had first heard Doctor Marshall talk about at the monthly staff meeting ... 'Because Miss Stanton has not finished her probationary period with us I shall not discuss in detail the issue of our Special Care Programme which she doesn't know about yet ...' She hadn't paid any attention to it back then, but now she realised she should have asked about it.

There was also the cryptic message Mike Randall had given her, although at the time she had thought he was only joking: 'Aren't you supposed to do everything your patients ask you?'

Finally, she now understood the meaning of Jo's words in the shower, speaking about Tania: 'Not a man on this planet can tease a woman the way she does. That's why she got her job here, by the way ...' That morning, Judith had vaguely understood this as meaning that Tania had slept with someone as a favour in order to get her job. But in fact it was the other way around! She had been hired precisely *because* of her skills ...

But where did Judith fit in? Nobody had told her that contact between patients and staff was allowed. Or was

726

it just her imagination running wild again? The more she thought about it, the more improbable it seemed. Yet at the same time it would make things much simpler if it were true. Or was that only wishful thinking on her part?

She sat up in her bed. Of course, it wasn't just her imagination. Now she had something tangible on which to base her assumptions. She had to find out. And this time she wouldn't be stupid enough to confront anybody armed with foolish accusations. She would find out for herself.

Without asking any questions, all she had to do was to keep her ears and eyes open, even snoop around if she had to, but she would keep her mouth shut at all costs.

Strangely, this time she didn't feel any fear at having figured out the truth, if indeed she had. The thought of having been hypnotised and acting against her own will had confused and scared her. Now her excitement was fuelled by a feeling of sudden reassurance.

She turned onto her back once again, now hoping to see something on the ceiling, the solution to this enigma. She needed more clues, more information. Everything had to come to her; she couldn't find out the details by coincidence.

Surely there was a way of finding out where the truth lay. There had to be.

Chapter Fourteen

As the doors of the lift opened onto the corridor of the basement, Judith thought she could see a book opening instead; a book in which everything was written, all the answers to her questions.

She slowly walked the length of the corridor, the soles of her shoes making a funny, squeaky sound on the bare tile floor. She didn't know what had prompted her to come downstairs and see Desmond, but somehow she knew he could help her in her quest.

The man was mysterious, in his own way, and this made him strangely attractive. Would he talk to her? He hadn't uttered a word last time . . .

Judith knew she would find a way to get him to talk. If she put together all the information she had so far, she could only come to one conclusion: what Ray had said was true, and as a member of staff Desmond would also be expected to provide physical pleasure to the patients, which is probably what had happened when she had left him alone with the Major.

But how could she be sure? She would have to bluff, to pretend she already knew, and that she was coming to the physiotherapy room to learn more. That was a bit weak, but quite believable.

She turned the corner and immediately stopped in her

steps. Next to the door of the physiotherapy room, on the floor, lay a large spool of chains. Thick, coldly shining links, wound around a metal cylinder that was about waist high. Her heart began to beat fast. What could the clinic possibly need those chains for? Were they just meant as replacements for the chains already hanging in the treatment room? Or were there plans to extend the facilities and build another treatment room? In either case, Judith still didn't know the purpose of using chains in physiotherapy in the first place, but she knew she would find out soon enough.

They seemed to glare back at her, defiantly, reflecting the crude light of the ceiling fixtures, gleaming cruelly, yet invitingly. There was something both threatening and beckoning about them, as if they were instruments for both torture and pleasure. She walked past quickly, seeing her tiny reflection mirrored thousands of times and almost ran until she entered the lobby of the physiotherapy department.

Desmond didn't see her come in. He was in the adjoining treatment room, helping a patient back in her wheelchair, his large back to the door. Just like the other day he was wearing a white polo shirt and track suit trousers. And just like before his movements were gentle and caressing as he delicately deposited the body that seemed ever so frail compared to him.

Judith waited silently, not really knowing how to make her presence known. She glanced around furtively, trying to see whether anybody else was around. This late in the afternoon most of the patients had usually been given their treatment and returned to their room.

'Hello, Judith. Can I help you?'

Judith turned around and recognised Vicky, a short, dark physiotherapist who often had her lunch at the canteen at the same time as her. Vicky was fumbling with her coat, trying to put it on whilst still holding her handbag in one hand.

'I'm waiting for Desmond, I need a word with him . . .'

Vicky smiled. 'Don't keep him here too long, it's after

four. We're supposed to be closed by now.' She walked past Judith and left.

As the door closed Judith ventured another look in the treatment room. Desmond now was kneeling next to the wheelchair, trying to adjust the leg support but obviously experiencing some difficulties.

The mechanism was jammed for some reason, and he had to pry it forcefully. From where she was standing Judith could see the muscles of his shoulder and upper arm playing under his skin, his fingers clutched around a large knob which stubbornly refused to budge.

The patient was a middle-aged woman who winced every minute or so. Both her legs were neatly covered in bandages but still she seemed rather uncomfortable and was probably growing impatient, needing the leg support to be fixed as soon as possible to relieve her pain.

Judith was about to enter the treatment room and ask Desmond if he needed help when the main door opened behind her and another nurse walked in, pushing a wheelchair. She walked past as if Judith wasn't there and headed straight for the treatment room.

'Here,' she told Desmond and the patient. 'I think we'd better use this one. The other should be sent to be repaired instead.' She pushed the wheelchair next to the other one and gestured to Desmond to transfer the patient.

He stood up, unrolling his heavy body, and bent down to pick the patient up in his big arms. The lady demurely slipped her arms around his neck and he lifted her as if she had been a mere twig. The nurse pushed away the defective wheelchair and pulled the other one closer. Desmond bent down, gently deposited the patient once again and watched silently as the nurse rolled the chair and the patient out of the room.

Judith held the door open and both the nurse and the patient thanked her with a smile. As the door closed behind them, she now knew she was alone with Desmond. She made her way into the treatment room.

Desmond was busy tidying up the place, putting the

730

jars back on the shelf, discarding the dirty towels into the large laundry basket. If he saw Judith come in, he didn't acknowledge her presence.

Once again she realised she hadn't heard him speak a single word and started to wonder if he was mute. She came near the treatment table and hoisted herself onto its smooth leather surface. Legs dangling over the side, she began staring at Desmond, trying to figure out what she would say to him once he decided to stop ignoring her.

As he turned to face her a large smile appeared on his face, his white teeth making his skin look even darker. 'How can I help?' he asked.

She was so surprised by his baritone voice that it took her a few seconds to react. Yes, Desmond could talk, and each of his words was a velvet caress, as if flowing from a cavern, deep and warm.

He came closer and stood right in front of her, tilting his head slightly, like a intrigued child. Obviously he had no idea what she had come for; how could he? Judith tried to think of what to say, of asking the question that abounded in her mind but without actually saying it. She decided to bluff it.

'I've been told,' she began, 'about the Special Care Programme, about the staff and the patients. I know everything . . .'

His smile shifted to the corner of his mouth and Judith thought perhaps he could tell she was lying. Or maybe she was completely off the track . . . No, if he didn't know about the Special Care Programme he would look puzzled, not amused.

'But there are still things that intrigue me,' she continued, 'and I want to know more.'

His eyes looked down, glancing towards her legs, and the smile disappeared from his face, but he didn't reply. Judith knew she was on to something, otherwise it would show in his face. He knew, he could confirm her doubts. But instead he turned away and went back to the shelves, placing the pots and jars in order, his indifference telling Judith he had nothing to say to her.

731

'I want to know, 'she insisted.

'What does it matter what you know,' he finally replied. 'What is important is what you feel . . .'

She wished he had stayed and stared at her some more. Perhaps she could have smiled and tried to charm him somehow. But now her mind was working on finding words instead, something to say that would make him a little more talkative.

She looked up in exasperation; this was tougher than she would have thought. Above her head the chains were still attached to the ceiling, quietly hanging in bundles, the leather cuffs relaxed and yawning. The chains . . . What were the chains for? Treatment or pleasure? She had to find out.

Desmond still had his back turned. Judith reached up above her head and grabbed one of the cuffs, pulling hard. The thin piece of string that held the bundle together gave easily and the chain unrolled, coming down in a loud, rattling cascade.

He turned around suddenly and looked at Judith. In his eyes she read both surprise and admiration, and immediately knew she had done the right thing. But now that she had his attention, what else was she to do?

The leather piece was lightly resting on her lap, the chain released to its complete length. Delicately seizing the cuff between her fingers, Judith held out her hand and presented it to Desmond.

'I want to know,' she repeated. The tone of her own voice surprised her, halfway between a plea and an order. It must have had some sort of effect on Desmond for he silently walked back towards her. This time he wasn't smiling but had a rather severe expression.

He came so close that she instinctively parted her legs. Their bodies touched and she felt his hard stomach press against her breasts, thinking – and hoping – he was going to touch her with his hands as well. Instead he slowly reached up and pulled on a chain next to the one she had unwound.

It came down with the same clinking noise and the

cuff brushed her shoulder before landing on the treatment table. Desmond then pulled on another chain, and so on, until six chains came hanging around Judith, two at the head of the table, two at the foot, and two in the middle. For a few seconds the noise was deafening, then there was utter silence.

He looked down and peered into her eyes, silently asking her if she wanted him to continue. She tried to read his eyes but failed. What could he be thinking? A minute ago he seemed totally disinterested, and now he was doing exactly what she was wishing him to do . . .

His hands fell on her thighs and she felt the warmth of his large hands through her dress. Despite his impressive size his hips were incredibly narrow and Judith could let him come close enough for their bodies to touch without having to part her legs very wide.

He just stared at her, as if waiting for her to tell him to continue. In reply she squeezed her thighs against his hips and almost immediately felt the snake uncoil at his crotch.

At that moment she realised what Desmond did in addition to giving massages to injured patients: he was also a slave to their desires. She didn't have to utter a word, and he would understand what she wanted him to do, in fact he probably took his own pleasure out of silent obedience.

His big hands rose to her chest and his thick fingers started to unbutton the front of her uniform. Another man undressing her, this was something she was beginning to get used to . . . Only this time the man wasn't trying to seduce her. He was undressing her simply because he could feel that was what she wanted.

The buttons looked incredibly small in his big fingers, yet he never fumbled, slowly undoing them one after the other. His dark fingers contrasted with the whiteness of her uniform, his skin leathery against the crisp cotton.

As he worked his way down, the cool air of the room flowed inside her dress and strangely mixed with the heat of her body. He undid the last button and slid the dress off her shoulders, using only his fingers to gently grip the fabric, never touching her skin.

He brought his hands to her chest once more, taking hold of the clasp that held her bra fastened at the front. Judith looked down at his hands, fascinated to see his blackness so close to her own white skin, but still not touching it. He undid her bra and took it off her, gently folding it and placing on the small table nearby.

His hands then glided under her armpits and he gently lifted her off the table and onto her feet. Judith felt like a small child being undressed by an adult. His touch was just as gentle as if she were a baby, his movements just as loving.

Once she stood up her dress fell to the floor and he bent down to pick it up, folding it neatly and placing it next to her bra. Then he knelt next to her and lifted her feet one after the other, taking her shoes off. Her panties quickly followed, his thumbs grasping the elastic waistband to pull it down.

As she stood completely naked and barefoot on the cold floor he stood up and lifted her by the armpits once again to make her lie on the table, her calves and feet sticking out at one end. Moving to the end of the table and standing between her parted knees he then got to work, placing both hands on her right thigh.

Judith shivered as she finally felt his hands on her. Propping herself up on her elbows, she lifted her head and looked at his hands, now gently massaging her legs, black velvet on white silk. A heat wave travelled from his hands to her skin, and then all the way up her body to her breasts.

Her nipples contracted readily, her arousal coming to life. His hands were capable of holding the whole of her thigh in their grasp, enveloping it like a thick, soft stocking. She felt them move up and down both legs, massaging her tired muscles, kneading and awakening them.

Although strong and expert, his touch was also sensuous, his fingertips at times barely touching the tender

734

skin on the inside of Judith's legs, slowly snaking up, stopping a mere moment from her soft vulva before changing direction and sliding back down again towards her naked feet.

After a while he concentrated on her feet alone, pinching her toes and pulling on them one after the other, inserting his large finger between them and prying them apart.

Judith now felt relaxed and let her head fall back, enjoying his treatment. The last things she saw before closing her eyes were the chains. She remembered that was what she had really come for, but right now she didn't care much for them. It could wait.

Desmond seized her ankles, one in each hand, and lifted her feet up, pulling them towards his face. Before Judith could realise what he was doing, she felt his lips close around her big toe and his tongue twirl around it.

A bolt of excitement flashed up her leg and through her loins, and she moaned loudly. His mouth then slowly travelled from one foot to the other, licking and sucking each toe in turn.

The feeling was incredibly powerful, his tongue silken and moist, bathing her feet in soft warmth. She felt a rush of dew collect at the junction of her legs, and her arousal mounted. So far he had only touched her legs and her feet, but she felt more excited than ever before in her life.

She wanted him to come closer, to work on the whole of her body, but she decided to wait before asking him. She knew he would get to it eventually. And her guess was soon proven right.

Putting her feet down, his hands slowly caressed her thighs in an upward move, his thumbs brushing the inside of her legs, his other fingers the outside. When he got to the soft junction his hands parted either way and his thumbs completely forwent her downy mound, his fingers merely tracing the sides of her buttocks.

His thumbs came together again over her belly-button and his fingers continued gliding upwards, covering the whole of her abdomen, his fingertips slightly brushing the underside of her breasts. She moaned again. Under his touch her skin kept growing hotter until it was almost burning.

By now he was bending over her, just a few inches above her limp body. For Judith was now so relaxed she could no longer move. She opened her eyes and looked at him, but he wasn't looking at her.

At the end of the table, between her parted feet, she could see the bulge of his erection pushing at the nylon of his white track suit. Did he want her? Most probably. And, of course, Judith wanted him as well. But not just yet.

His hands then moved to her arms and gently settled on her wrists. She liked the way he towered above her, she liked to think that once he held her hands she couldn't escape from his grasp, that she wouldn't want to anyway.

Slowly, his hands glided up, fingertips first, along the length of her arms. His thumbs lightly brushed the sides of her breasts and she shuddered. She liked the way he proceeded, slowly, inch by inch, covering areas of her body which weren't usually so sensitive whilst completely forgoing her breasts and her vulva. But by now Judith was also growing impatient. How long would he keep on teasing her like this? She parted her legs slightly, hoping he would get her message.

But he didn't seem to. His hands briefly paused on her shoulders and cupped them, closing around them in a snug fit, his thumbs pointing down on the edge of her breasts. His wrists were just an inch above her erect nipples, all he had to do was to bend his elbows and he would touch them.

Instead, his hands continued their discovery, his fingertips following the slow curve of her shoulders and gently closing around her throat. Judith's heart began pounding fast when she realised he could very well strangle her at this moment. Putting his thumbs together at the front and his fingertips touching at the back, he

736

could encircle her neck completely. She stopped breathing for a moment, suddenly worried.

But he soon let go, his fingers running up along her scalp, burying themselves into the soft mass of her hair. He now held her head in both hands, the thickness of his large fingers pulling at the clip that held her hair up and quickly forcing it to slip off.

Then he let go to put his hands flat on either side of her head, and she finally felt his face descending towards hers. Soon his lips were on hers, thick, soft and cushiony, gently capturing her mouth. Still, only his lips touched her. The rest of his body was hovering above her, large and domineering, ever so close but not touching her, his elbows locked to stop him from crushing her.

But by then she wanted to feel his body on hers, even if it meant being smothered by this mass of muscles. Her hands refused to move when she tried lifting them off the table to touch him, as if she had been paralysed. Her mind and her body were no longer connected, her limbs refused to do what her brain asked. However, she knew there was no need to move. Soon, Desmond would take care of everything.

And even though his body had no contact with hers, Judith could feel his heat radiating through his clothes and enveloping her. She was ever so small underneath him, a frail and pale figure at the mercy of a dark giant.

His lips soon grew moist as his kisses became more and more passionate, gripping hers in a tight embrace, toying with them with his tongue.

Judith felt hot against the thin leather covering of the treatment table, sandwiched between two black entities, both soft and caressing, only one of them alive.

His lips let go of her mouth and gently slid down along her jaw to nestle in her neck. As she opened her eyes Judith could see nothing but the muscles of his shoulder playing under his skin, his big arms still locked to keep his body from touching hers.

Yet down there, at the junction of her legs, every now and again, she could feel his erect phallus brush her

737

thigh through the nylon fabric of his trousers, the throbbing shaft quickly growing impatient. Obviously, Desmond had to make a tremendous effort, both physically and mentally, not to fall on her and possess her. But Judith instinctively sensed that, for this man, his own pleasure didn't matter. He was there to serve her.

She felt his ear brush against her cheek and was surprised by its leathery hotness. The whole of Desmond seemed to be made of fabric, at times velvet, at times leather. Always smooth, always dark, always warm.

She was tempted to stick out a timid tongue and caress his earlobe but, just before she could move, Desmond's head had already resumed its journey, now slowly following the sinewy path of her shoulder, covering her warm skin with even warmer kisses, his chin at times brushing against her swollen breasts.

Judith began panting. His lips seemed to trigger something every time they touched her skin, like a series of live wires directly connected to her loins. Never before had she been so aroused, his teasing seemingly not progressing beyond smooth kisses on parts of her body that weren't usually so sensitive. She could only guess what would happen if he eventually dared touch her breasts . . .

A second later she found out. He took his time, of course, his lips merely touching her skin, progressing at a snail's pace towards her erect nipple, pausing, coming back up towards her shoulder, then resuming their descent.

Judith shuddered and moaned at the same time, feeling an incredible, overwhelming desire to simply wrap herself around this taut body. She also wanted to grab his head with both hands and direct his mouth onto her swollen breasts. Yet despite this powerful storm raging within her, she was enjoying his deliberately slow method, each of his kisses, no matter where he lay them.

She writhed on the table, her body now coming out of its slumber, alight with a fire that seemed to extend all the way down to her toes. At the same time her hands

738

recovered their strength and she took hold of Desmond's narrow hips, pulling them towards her crotch, wanting to feel his throbbing maleness against her own flesh.

But he immediately pulled away before she could feel no more than a mere brush of his erect phallus. Judith was somewhat disappointed, and rather puzzled. She was more than ready for him, and his desire was also obvious, so why wouldn't he want her to touch him?

He walked around the table and stood behind her head. In a couple of swift moves he caught each of her wrists and neatly wrapped them with the leather cuffs that were attached to the chains. He then pulled on the free end of each chain, adjusting its length so that Judith's arms were pulled up and she could no longer move them.

He then walked back down to the foot of the table and captured her ankles the same way. By then only Judith's back barely touched the table; her arms and legs were now prisoner's of the chains. Her head hung back, her blond tresses now set free brushed the table.

Her heart began to beat fast, both in apprehension and excitement. In her mind her doubts were now in the process of being confirmed. Soon she would know exactly what the chains were for. Although she had planned on receiving a verbal explanation, a demonstration would now be deliciously appropriate.

However her position soon grew uncomfortable. The joints of her shoulders and her hips were stretched to their limit and already felt slightly painful. Yet being restrained like this was a novelty, and the way her parted legs displayed her moist flesh in a sexy, wicked way aroused her even more.

Slowly progressing around the table, Desmond continued adjusting the chains, constantly forcing her legs to open wider. The air stream of the ventilation system descended straight unto Judith's exposed vulva, a soothing caress, yet not sufficiently cool to ease the fire that bathed her moist flesh.

Finally Desmond bent down and opened a drawer in

739

the large cabinet by the door, taking out a large piece of leather and bringing it to the table. He unfolded it slowly, and Judith was able to figure out it was some kind of corset, with about half a dozen straps and buckles making clinking sounds as he laid it flat on the table.

Supporting her back with one hand, he slid the corset underneath her, then brought the sides up and proceeded to fasten it around her waist. The piece of leather snugly covered her abdomen from the underswell of her breasts to the edge of her downy mound. On either side a thick metal hook was also fastened to the corset.

Desmond slid one arm under her back and lifted her clear off the table, seizing the hooks with his free hand, one after the other, and hooking her up to the last two chains that still hung at her midriff.

By now Judith hung in a horizontal position high up above the table, her arms and legs restrained and held apart, her waist harnessed to support the rest of her body.

Desmond came to stand behind her and took her head up in his hands to bring it to his level. He would no longer have to bend down to touch her, she had been brought up to his level.

A wicked smile played on his face as his lips came to touch hers, upside down. This time his kisses were nothing like what they had been before. His tongue went searching for hers immediately, caressing the inside of her mouth, at times also venturing outside and gently licking her chin.

Soon he held her head with only one hand and the other went where it had not dared before. Judith could see nothing but the blackness of his neck, but she could feel his hand now drawing closer to her swollen breasts. She moaned against his mouth. At last.

His fingers cupped them each in turn, the large hand able to cover the whole of the milky skin, the nipple growing harder in his palm. Soon he let go of her head completely and let it dangle backwards, then moved to the side of the table again.

Judith's body hung level with his chest. He quickly let

his hands run all over her, grabbing and releasing both her breasts, caressing her waist through the thin leather of the harness, then moving down to follow the curve of her hips.

She couldn't see anything but the shelf on the wall behind her, and upside down at that. Yet the touch of his hands on her naked skin felt even warmer than before and the image of his black fingers on her pale skin once again appeared in her mind.

One of his hands was on her legs, caressing the sensitive part behind her knees, then moving to the inside where the skin became baby-soft. Suddenly she felt the tip of his thick finger lightly rubbing the swollen bud of her clitoris.

Judith let out a faint scream, the muscles of her stomach contracting violently as she felt a bolt of lightning pierce her from deep within her loins to the very tip of her nipples, as if his finger was electrified.

Then it glided down her slippery folds, following the deep valley until it disappeared inside her slick vagina. She could feel it within her, searching her very core, triggering her pleasure from the inside. She moaned again.

He withdrew and slowly drew his hand up over her mound, his wet finger hovering above her curly bush and slicking the hairs. For a while his hand remained there and worked back and forth, spreading her love-juices from her wet folds to her bush, combing it with soaked fingers.

Each time he glided over her stiff clitoris Judith gasped, each passage seemingly briefer than the previous one, her bud now aching to feel his hand rubbing it instead of merely teasing it.

After a while she lifted her head up, laboriously, and looked at Desmond. He turned and looked at her in turn, as if sensing her eyes on him. For a while they held each other's stare, Judith trying to read intentions in his eyes, Desmond not letting anything show.

But she let her head fall back. Then she immediately

felt him raise one knee onto the table for support and his face swiftly dropped onto her chest. His hit was direct, his lips landing directly on her nipple and gently grabbing it.

The centre of her arousal shifted, her breasts quivering under the assault of his mouth, sending delicious waves down her abdomen. He laid one hand on her chest whilst the other supported her back, tilting her body this way and that, to provide better access for his mouth.

Judith's breasts were wickedly tossed from one side to the other, the tender skin on the underswell brushing against the edge of the leather corset time and time again. He devastated them with his mouth, his dark lips pinching her skin into tiny folds, his tongue circling around the erect nipple and flickering over it at a dizzying speed.

Judith rapidly grew even more excited and began writhing uncontrollably, adding to the motion Desmond had imparted to her body, tugging at the chains that supported her ankles.

This was more than she had ever thought she would be able to take; her arousal was extremely intense but her mind was unable to foresee the moment when her pleasure would finally release her. She could sense Desmond getting excited as well, but his behaviour never let anything show, his mouth and his hands still delicately caressing her.

At one point his hand strayed again, quickly hovering over the leather corset and once again seeking her wet vulva. His index finger slid over her slippery folds, back and forth, gently teasing her stiff clitoris and gradually increasing the pressure of his touch. His tongue continued to worry her nipple, and the line of contact between her breasts and her loins soon became overloaded.

Her pleasure pierced her and she bucked violently, tensing every muscle of her limbs and sending the chains rattling loudly a couple of times. Through her half-shut eyes she saw Desmond grin, amused by the results of his ministrations.

742

Judith's head fell back and her mind went numb. As usual, she felt as if she was floating on air, as she often did when she was swept by pleasure. Only this time she really was hanging in mid-air, yet her wrists and ankles no longer felt the restraint of the leather cuffs. She sighed and smiled, still reeling from her climax.

She felt Desmond getting busy around the table, going to each chain in turn and gradually lowering her until her back almost touched the table. Yet he never touched the cuffs, obviously not planning on releasing her just yet. Once all the chains were adjusted and Judith hung level with his hips, he slipped an arm under her back, lifting her in his arms to unhook the harness.

Judith was puzzled by his procedure. Why wasn't he undoing the buckles on her ankles and wrists? How long did he plan to keep her hanging like this?

He went to the foot of the table and reached up to the ceiling, unfastening some sort of mechanism that prevented the chains from sliding along the rails, and then did the same thing with the chains that held Judith's arms.

The noise overwhelmed her dozy mind, and she ceased trying to figure out what he was planning to do. All she knew was that the strain on her hips and shoulders eased up when he pushed her ankles and her wrists together and she felt relieved.

His hands took hold of her tiny waist, one on each side, almost encircling it completely with his large fingers, and he rolled her onto her stomach. He rapidly crossed her legs and uncrossed them the other way, the chains swapping places, and did the same with her arms.

Judith now lay flat on her stomach, her legs and arms spread out once again. And the strain returned to her shoulders and hips, at least until Desmond lifted her off the table and hooked the harness onto the chains.

And Judith finally understood what he was up to. Desmond wasn't planning on releasing her at all. All he had done was to turn her over and re-arrange the chains

743

so that she now hung face down, her arms and legs still wide apart.

Her hair fell all around her face like a curtain, and if she peered down she could see her breasts dangling with the pull of gravity, her nipples slightly rubbing on the surface of the table. Although initially they puckered further from the leathery caress, this soon grew somewhat uncomfortable, the skin not really gliding but dragging along painfully as her body swayed in mid-air.

She was just about to protest when she felt Desmond's hands lifting both her breasts up with his hand. In his other hand he held a bottle of talcum powder, which he sprinkled on the table and then spread evenly in a large circle. Putting the bottle aside, he then ran his powdered hand across Judith's breasts.

Her body swayed slightly and she immediately felt the soft caress of the powdered leather on her nipples. This unexpected change sent a sigh of appreciation to her lips. Then she felt Desmond's hands give a slight push on her hips, and her body began swinging from side to side.

She watched her nipples brushing on the table, left to right and back again, the twin peaks seemingly growing stiffer and longer in an attempt to increase the intensity of the caress. The minty scent of the powder rose to her flaring nostrils and warmed her mind.

Despite the restraints of her wrists her hands were warm, and now itching to move, to caress, to tease. But she knew it was impossible. The black giant's mission was to take Judith to the height of pleasure, he would probably never let her touch him.

Yet she longed to feel him, to caress every inch of this mass of flesh, to lose herself in the embrace of his big arms, to discover the black rod that palpitated under the thin fabric of his trousers. But right now it was out of the question. She had wanted to know, and she had to remain a docile pupil until his explanation was complete.

As her body continued swaying, thoughts began racing through her mind and she gradually understood the real nature of this unusual situation. Although at first it seemed he was a slave to her desires, that he would want nothing but to give her pleasure, at this point it appeared there was a role reversal in progress. Judith was no longer in control, she hadn't asked for what Desmond was doing. She had, in turn, become his submitted slave.

The tables had been turned, once again. Just like when she had pounced on Jo in the stock room, the victim had become the attacker. It had been the same pattern with Mike Randall: he had asked her to pleasure him but in the end she had been in control of both her desire and his.

All this had happened, not by accident, but through the force of her own will. Even now, with Desmond, she had silently agreed to be hung like this, she could have backed out. Yet her instincts had told her that obedience was the key to sweet pleasure.

And indeed it was. Her nipples were on fire, the dry caress of the powdered leather now generating a strange heat that radiated throughout her body. Then she felt Desmond's hand on the side of her buttocks stopping the swaying movement. What else lay ahead?

Her body stopped moving, and Judith didn't have the strength to generate any sort of movement either. Once again her vulva was screaming to be pleased and she wondered how long it would take for pleasure to sweep her again.

She heard Desmond move, the rustling sound of the nylon trousers louder than before. Gathering some strength, she lifted her head and managed to turn it slightly in his direction.

Her neck quickly grew sore and she had to drop her head again, but not without having had time to notice that he was now naked. She sighed. He was there, just a few inches from her, yet she couldn't touch him. She lifted her head again, desperately trying to catch his eyes. But then she remembered he was there for her own pleasure as well, all she had to do was ask . . .

'Come here!' she said in a loud voice.

She sensed him obediently walking to the head of the

table. Through the tangled mass of her hair she could see his phallus, long and thick and dark as coal, the tiny opening in the black head silently gaping at the ceiling. She licked her lips, now wanting to taste him.

As if reading her mind he gently lifted her chin in one hand and brushed the hair from her face with the other, then slowly thrust his throbbing member into her waiting mouth.

Judith was elated. He knew what she wanted, he had obeyed her command. And now he pulsed on her tongue, slowly sliding back and forth, in and out of the wet embrace of her lips. She moaned loudly. Despite her precarious position, she was still in charge, her submission wasn't complete.

He supported her head in both hands now, standing immobile, letting Judith thrust with her head. However, she soon grew tired and slackened her rhythm. She thought he would take over by moving his hips, but instead, he gave a gentle push on her shoulder and Judith's body began swaying again, this time from head to foot instead of sideways.

Her nipples rediscovered the soft caress of the powdered table and her arousal mounted again, resurrected with a fury. Her mouth grew impatient, sucking and licking the hard rod that stiffened with delight, the tip of her tongue pushing at the tiny mouth that seeped in anticipation. She could feel him hardening still under this assault, yet the rest of his body never even twitched.

Obviously his erection was for her own benefit, as if she could continue her caresses forever and never feel the jutting of his pleasure. He was there for her to enjoy, he was completely hers.

She relished him as if he were the first and last man, tasting him with all her senses, at times letting go of him completely and feeling him brush back and forth along her cheek, nudging him with her nose. Her whole face toyed with him, like a kitten with a rubber mouse, moving on him back and forth and sideways, caressing him with her mouth, her tongue, her lips, her chin, her cheeks, even her nose.

All the while his fingertips on her jaw helped her keep her head up, supporting it but without guiding it. After a while however she was tempted to try his obedience again.

'Enough,' she said. 'Now go on with what you were doing before.'

He went away silently, and Judith's heart started to pound in anticipation. What would he do next? Obviously he couldn't guess what she wanted, for she didn't even know herself. But he must have some idea in his mind . . .

She soon found out when she felt him kneel on the table, between her parted legs. His hips caressed the inside of her legs and she felt his thick shaft nudge at her entrance. Immediately she wanted him inside.

'Fuck me!' she heard herself whine. 'What are you waiting for?'

He entered her and she screamed with joy. And again the swinging motion resumed, back and forth, his hands on her buttocks pushing her away and letting her swing back, her wet tunnel thrusting on him.

She felt him fill her and then escape repeatedly, the dark shaft possessing her through her own motion, its swollen head inserting itself and stretching the slick walls of her vagina in a delicious assault.

His hips brushed against the side of her legs, his smooth skin caressing hers. By then he was holding her by the knees, pushing her away and letting her slide back onto him. He didn't move this time either, letting only the swinging motion of her body do the work.

Her nipples were happy again, running back and forth on the table, connecting with her loins in a long, tickled line inside her abdomen. She moaned again, twisting her wrists in an effort to grab hold of the chain.

The metal felt cold in her palm but she grasped it with all her strength, bending her elbows and pulling herself even further up. Her level of energy amazed her. The swinging motion imparted by Desmond's hands on her wasn't enough anymore, she needed to increase the speed, the range, the intensity. She pulled hard, her biceps burning under her own weight, trying to increase the momentum of her body. She swung up and she let herself fall back down again, impaling herself onto Desmond's thick rod, feeling him penetrate her even further.

He laughed loudly, his deep voice reverberating around the room. His hand then landed on her behind in a sharp slap and sent needles through her loins, followed by a hot wave of pleasure. The dark giant seemed amused by this little wanton that now desperately pulled on her chains, sending them rattling frantically, using them to wriggle her hips onto his shaft.

She needed to move on him, no longer content to just swing back and forth passively. But the harness around her waist and the complicated position of her ankles were playing against her. All she could control was her arms, all she could do was to laboriously lift herself up and fall back down freely.

Her vulva impaled itself again and again, the thick rod filling her more and more each time, to the limit, in a somewhat painful but pleasant fit. The strain on her breasts was also considerable. They hung freely and bobbed slightly as she let herself fall back down, hitting the table with a sharp flap, sending bolts of pleasure-pain through the whole of her body.

Desmond didn't need to move, she could take care of her own pleasure. Already she could feel it mounting, burning inside her, along the line that connected her breasts with her tiny, swollen shaft.

Her climax was like dropping a large stone in a pond, sending one major impulse through her loins, followed by ripples upon ripples of smaller waves, all starting from the same point, all radiating through her body in circles of decreasing intensity.

She let go with an ultimate sob, her head dropping forward one last time. The sweat of her effort trickled down her back and underneath the leather harness, collecting in a wet line between her buttocks. She panted, exhausted but happy.

Yet it wasn't over. Desmond was still inside her, throbbing under the clenching seizures of her slick vagina. Just as she stopped feeling the reeling waves of pleasure subsiding into oblivion, he began to move.

His hand grabbed one of the straps of the harness to stop her from swaying, and his hips began thrusting. Judith screamed with joy, her tiny bud still sensitive yet ready to be awakened again. His free hand landed on her behind repeatedly, smarting the sensitive skin, making her moan each time. His momentum soon grew frantic, his hips thrusting forcefully inside her and out again, his thick shaft hardening still.

By now he moved so fast that she could feel his balls hitting her mound, his hips forcing hers apart even wider, each jab sending a wave through her body that once again made her breasts wobble.

She heard him grunt behind her, his voice echoing hers as she felt her pleasure mounting for the third time, insidious, slowly bubbling to the surface and growing thick at the same time. She was too exhausted even to moan, her limp body barely feeling anything but the pleasure that swept her.

At the same time she felt Desmond pull her against his hips and keep her there, the shaft inside her jerking violently and a strangled sob coming out of his mouth. A second later she felt him fall on top of her, his hands landing flat on the table on either side of her breasts, his face descending upon her back.

His member was still inside her, its size diminishing quickly, his honey oozing out slowly, its acrid smell filling the room. She recognised the scent, the same aroma she had noted after she had left him alone with Major Johnson: the scent of male pleasure. Now she knew.

But what Desmond had told her was also still present in her mind. It wasn't important what she knew, what really mattered was what she felt. And she felt good.

His arm slid across her chest and lifted her up, his other hand fumbling at the hook to release the harness. The man was obviously weaker by now, as was Judith, drunk with pleasure, still reeling from its effect.

The chains were released one after the other, her hands first and then her feet. Now she lay flat on the table, her ankles and wrists still prisoners of the cuffs, but the strain of the chains now neutralised.

Desmond hovered on top of her for a while, licking the sweat off her back with the tip of his tongue. After a moment he undid the buckles that held the cuffs around her wrists and gently massaged her tender skin.

Judith looked up and was almost surprised by the sight of his thick, black fingers on her thin, pale wrist. The soft leather hadn't left any marks, which was rather amazing considering the weight her arms had to support.

Desmond's large hand slowly brushed her hair off her face and his lips deposited a faint kiss on her cheek. She closed her eyes and smiled. He lay on top of her for a while, supporting himself on his elbows, his cheek softly settling on hers, the heat of his body a comforting embrace in which Judith forgot herself.

Chapter Fifteen

*E*lizabeth Mason's perfume was nice, but after a while could become somewhat nauseating. She was sitting next to the patient on the leather, looking as comfortable as if she were having tea instead of removing Lisa's bandages.

Judith was standing by her side, bending down towards her and holding a metal tray. This proximity, although necessary, was quickly growing tiresome for the nurse, her back now sorely complaining.

On top of that, Judith hated the way the doctor kept talking all the time, seemingly not needing to stop and breathe every now and then. Everything Doctor Mason said sounded childish, especially the way in which she described to Lisa every step of the bandage removal.

'Now all I need is to take these tiny scissors here,' she said, like a mother talking to a small child, 'and make just a little bit of a cut on the fabric. You be a good girl and don't move. All right, sweetheart?'

Lisa didn't reply, but then again she didn't need to. She looked at Judith and then rolled her eyes up in exasperation.

Yet the doctor's hands were quick and expert, removing each layer of bandage and discarding it into a small container that Judith was holding for her.

751

Judith couldn't understand why they hadn't brought a rolling table or some other kind of mobile tray. It would surely look out of place in the bedroom but would be much more useful. Or else it might have been more convenient to bring the patient to a treatment room.

Instead, doctor and patient both sat on the dark red leather couch, like two friends having a chat. Meanwhile Judith's back was slowly dying in pain, although all she had to hold was a small tray with a few pairs of scissors and a small bowl to receive the soiled gauze.

To her right the sun shone through the window at such an angle that it only hit Judith's arm. She felt it burning her, yet because of this unconventional set-up it was impossible for Judith to change places.

Layer after layer came off and the procedure was soon over. Lisa immediately reached to the side table to pick up a hand mirror and hold it up to her face. Her nose was a bit swollen and showed a few, tiny red marks, and two large purple blotches hung under her eyes. However, this was entirely normal and nothing would show after a few days. The nose itself didn't look very different, albeit slightly shorter.

Doctor Mason smiled contentedly, obviously pleased at having done a good job, but Lisa's mouth twitched a few times and a sob escaped from her lips.

'It's . . . It's horrible!' she whined nervously.

Doctor Mason continued smiling sweetly. 'Not to worry,' she said. 'Once the swelling's gone it will be just perfect.'

'No!' Lisa cried. 'It's horrible! I hate it!'

Her smile quickly disappearing, Doctor Mason sighed and stood up. 'Just give it a few days. Once it's all healed, once you're back home, everybody will tell you how nice it looks . . .'

'I can't face anybody with a nose like this!' Lisa screamed. 'How can I ever go home? I could never dare show my face!'

'You'll have to,' Doctor Mason added with a sigh of impatience. 'Mrs Cox will be here in just a few minutes

752

to make you sign the release papers. You'll be going home tomorrow.'

'Tomorrow? But I don't want to! Not looking like this!'

Doctor Mason sighed again and stood up, looking at Judith. 'You deal with her,' she ordered. 'I have better things to do.' She walked out of the room and slammed the door behind her.

Judith bit her lower lip. She felt resentful, knowing that it wasn't ethical to leave a patient in such a distressed state. Now it was up to her to calm Lisa down, something that Doctor Mason should have done herself. This was especially tricky considering how difficult Lisa had been over the last few days. She deposited the tray and the bowl on the side table and sat next to Lisa.

'She's right, you know,' she told the girl. 'In a couple of days the marks will be all gone and you'll have the prettiest nose.'

'Really?' Lisa sobbed. 'I hate it, it's too short.'

'I think it's very nice. You just need a bit of time to get accustomed to it, that's all.'

In reply the girl tilted her head onto Judith's shoulders, letting her tears roll down the nurse's uniform. Judith didn't know what else to say. All she could think about is that she had to be very careful around Lisa, and that because her probation period wasn't over, any complaint from her patient would look bad and perhaps even compromise her future. She couldn't risk that, not now that she had come so close to finding out the truth about the Special Care Programme.

In addition, she knew that Mrs Cox was supposed to be coming to Lisa's room to make her sign the release papers, and she felt it was important that the girl calmed down beforehand.

She looked at her from the corner of her eye. Lisa's head was still gently resting on the nurse's shoulder, and she did seem to have calmed down already. Quite relieved, Judith encircled the girl's waist with one arm and gently caressed the silken hair with the other hand.

Lisa was sweet after all, a grown woman still not ready

to let go of her spoilt childhood. After a few seconds she snuggled up to the nurse, writhing against the white cotton of the uniform, and Judith felt the warmth of her young skin seeping through the silk pyjamas.

The small hand landed on Judith's thigh, hot and slightly moist. Lisa looked up at her.

'Do you think I'm pretty?' she asked, a tear still pearling in the corner of her right eye.

'Of course,' Judith replied. 'I think you're very pretty.'

'I think you're pretty too . . .'

The pale lips touched Judith's cheek and took some time before pulling away. Judith looked at her patient and smiled in turn. She was happy to have succeeded in changing the girl's frame of mind and pleased by Lisa's friendliness

'You're very sweet,' Judith said.

But just as she spoke, Lisa's eyes turned dry and lit up in a weird sparkle 'Am I really?' she asked in a rather sarcastic tone.

Judith was surprised by this sudden change and didn't reply.

'I like to think that I'm a bitch,' Lisa continued. 'People often tell me that I am. I don't know if it's true, but I'd like to be a bitch. That way I can get everything I want, and I can also get everybody to do whatever I want . . .'

Her hand slid up Judith's thigh, snake-like under her dress, and her index finger came poking at the nurse's crotch.

Judith shuddered, both in amazement and, curiously, in fear. At that moment she understood there was a difference between the girl she had met in the operating room a couple of days ago and had again seen sitting next to her just a few minutes ago, and the other Lisa who was demanding and spoilt. This was like a double personality, and Judith didn't quite know how to deal with it. But above all she could only think of how she had to do her best to avoid making Lisa angry.

'I was told the staff here are supposed to do everything the patients ask them,' the girl continued. 'Is that true?'

Judith breathed deeply. What was Lisa up to? What did she know? Obviously, this idea that the staff was supposed to yield to the desires of the patients had to come from someone . . . But who had told her? And why was she bringing it up now?

Did she only want confirmation from her nurse, or would she have the nerve to ask her to engage in some sort of sexy role-playing game?

Looking down, Judith saw Lisa's nipples growing stiff under the white pyjamas, and she felt her own nipples replying in turn. The girl noticed them as well and burst out laughing.

'You're just as horny as I am, aren't you? I should have known . . . Come on then, be a good nurse and do as I please. If I can't get the nose I wanted at least I'll have something to remember.'

She smiled wickedly and covered the whole of Judith's crotch with her hand, making the nurse shiver despite herself. Lisa laughed again, obviously amused by the way she could get the young nurse to react, as if it was just a game to her.

Yet in Judith's mind there was nothing to laugh about. Once again she was about to become a victim to her own lust, even though this time she was highly aware of it and she was still able to fight it. But she could sense she had to obey, being somewhat afraid of Lisa, knowing she couldn't refuse to do what the girl would ask without running the risk of making her angry.

And just as before she hesitated, also knowing that she couldn't comply to the girl's demands because Lisa was her patient. She had promised herself she would never again be weak . . .

And on top of it all, she also knew Mrs Cox could walk into the room at any moment. Curiously, this last thought only served to fuel her desires. If she were to be an obedient slave to her patient, and be caught in the act by her supervisor, maybe Mrs Cox would come to her rescue once again, release the nurse from the girl's hold and take care of Judith herself.

755

This was only a remote possibility, but it was worth trying. This would be a decisive moment. If what Ray had told her was true, if indeed she was expected to comply to special requests from her patients, then she didn't have anything to fear from having Mrs Cox walk in on them. This was perhaps the greatest gamble of her life, and suddenly made the situation much more exciting.

She tightened her embrace around the girl and let her fingers glide under the pyjama top, touching the soft skin of the waist, remembering the sight of the tanned flesh she had marvelled at just a few weeks ago in the operating theatre.

Lisa cooed and pressed herself against the nurse. 'Undress me,' she said. 'Now.'

From this moment Judith knew there would be no going back. The last flicker of hesitation disappeared from her mind but her free hand trembled as it undid the four buttons of the pyjama, the silk now feeling strangely cold under her fingertips. She wanted to abandon herself, to wantonly rediscover the naked body she knew was hiding under this thin layer of silk. How good it would feel to press her mouth against all this gorgeous skin. She had thought of Lisa often, but never actually thought this moment would ever come. And now it was all happening . . .

Against her neck the girl's mouth was already searching a sensitive point, the lips hovering and lightly brushing the underside of the earlobe. Judith closed her eyes for a moment, letting the heat of their bodies merge and awaken her senses.

Lisa smelled nice, a rich, probably expensive perfume that also emanated from her hair. Once Judith finished undoing the buttons she looked at Lisa again, as if trying to guess what would be asked of her next. In reply Lisa wriggled out of her top, the silk sliding off her shoulders and exposing her breasts.

The nipples seemed darker and smaller than before, but the skin was just as Judith had remembered, a tanned, light brown, the tiny hairs on her abdomen sunbleached to a soft gold.

Lisa let go of Judith's leg and brought her hand up to her own breasts, caressing them with the palm of her hand. At the same time she looked at Judith wickedly. 'Touch me.' Her voice was harsh now, an unmistakable order.

Just like the other morning Judith pressed the underswell of the girl's left breast and pushed it up slightly, then let it fall back again, but without taking her fingers away. And just as before she saw the nipple contract and shrink slightly, becoming even darker. Her fingers followed the contour of the smooth globe, gliding around the nipple but without really touching it.

'Suck it. Now.'

Judith didn't mind Lisa's tone. In fact, she felt her desire increase at the thought of becoming her slave, of having no option but to obey. She silently bowed her head and let her mouth slide down from the girl's shoulder all the way to the pointed nipple, gently sticking out her tongue to flick over its stiffness.

Almost immediately Lisa's body went limp against her, and she felt the pounding of the girl's heart against her cheek. Letting go of the tiny waist, she pushed her back on the sofa, in a half-reclining position.

Lisa grabbed Judith's hands and brought them both to her naked breasts, guiding them and pressing them into kneading her warm skin. Judith silently followed the instructions and after a while Lisa let go of the nurse's hands to take hold of her head instead, immediately pulling it towards her cleavage. And again Judith obeyed the silent command. Whatever Lisa would want, Judith would do.

She sucked at the nipples greedily, surprised by her own eagerness, finding pleasure in licking the stiff buttons that seemed to grow bigger in her mouth. Soon she heard Lisa moan, and that aroused her even more.

Her own breasts seemed to throb in tempo with her heartbeat and the folds of her vulva, her dew now quickly gathering at the junction of her legs. Her clitoris also ached with stiffness, yet curiously Judith didn't want to be touched. All she wanted was to caress the lovely body she had desired from the very first time she had seen it, but not been able to touch until now.

By now Lisa held Judith's head against her chest with both arms, guiding the nurse's face from one nipple to the other, writhing under the soft assault of Judith's mouth.

Judith felt elated, wanting to swallow the whole of the girl's breasts, her tongue animated with a life of its own, darting at the erect nipples and worrying them incessantly. Her hands also kept busy, gliding all over the smooth flesh, gently at first but also getting rough at times, kneading the smooth globes in a tight caress, pinching the nipples and the sensitive skin around them.

After a while however Lisa pushed her away, grabbing the nurse's shoulders.

'Get down,' she said. 'On your knees. Now.'

Lisa parted her legs and Judith obeyed without protesting, now a willing slave, her heart pounding in anticipation of what would be asked of her next.

The wooden floor was hard under her bare knees but the sensation soon turned to some kind of numbness, her whole body alight with a passion that made her forget everything else. Once again she pressed her face against Lisa's breasts, her arms now encircling the girl's waist, her hands quickly surveying the softness of her back, using her lower arms to caress all of this warm, smooth skin offered so invitingly.

Lisa threw her arms up and stopped trying to guide Judith's caresses, satisfied that the young nurse no longer needed instructions. She continued moaning loudly, her body writhing slightly under the heat of their combined passion.

Judith was pleased that her caresses had such an effect on Lisa, but she suddenly wondered if somebody passing in the corridor would hear them. She had this vision of several people gathered in the corridor, their ears glued

758

to the door, getting intrigued and excited by what they were hearing. The thought of being heard and attracting attention to what was going on in the room was exciting; the thought of somebody actually walking in on them even more so.

Through the window the rays of the sun now burnt her back and the top of her head, but that was also soon forgotten. Right now she cared about nothing but the desire to please her patient, to arouse the luscious body and be an obedient slave.

She held Lisa tight, burying her face in the soft cleavage, feeling the fluid heat of the young woman's breasts against her cheeks. Her own arousal grew and translated into a strong impulse to discover more velvet skin, more smooth curves. But she couldn't do anything about it. She had to wait for Lisa to ask.

By now Lisa was holding on to Judith's head, her fingers lost in the nurse's golden hair, her lips at times gently caressing the top of Judith's head. Soon her hips began to jerk slightly, and after a while Lisa let go of Judith's head to wriggle out of her pyjama trousers.

Judith didn't need to be told what to do then. She gripped the elastic band of the silk trousers with her fingers and pulled it down, helping Lisa lift her hips from the sofa to get rid of the garment.

The fabric glided down along the girl's tanned legs and Judith tossed it aside before going back to settle between the girl's parted legs. She could smell her desire, not unlike her own, sweet and heady. Judith continued kissing Lisa's breasts for a while and then slowly traced a long path of kisses down her abdomen, on her way to the soft treasure.

Finally her buttocks came resting on her heels and her lips began to gently hover above the curly bush. The fleece was also golden, sun-bleached, and neatly trimmed. It was quite thick but soft as baby hair, shining in the sunlight and fragrant with Lisa's dew.

Judith let her bare arms hang over the naked thighs for a moment, caressing the inside with her cheeks, turning her head this way and that to let her lips caress the soft skin as well. Just moments away from her mouth the wet vulva gaped and glistened, the tiny clitoris barely visible amidst the parted lips, but nevertheless throbbing with excitement, in sequence with the wet vagina that clenched sporadically.

She felt Lisa push her legs together, almost forcing her mouth towards the waiting flesh. 'Suck me!' she girl moaned loudly. 'Suck me now!'

Judith stuck out a timid tongue and tasted the soft folds, at first lightly, barely touching them, but soon covering the whole area with longer, deliberately slow licks.

Lisa moaned loudly and her hips jerked up towards Judith's face. It seemed she was already on the verge of climaxing, her legs shaking as her muscles tensed and relaxed in turn. Judith slid her hands under the girl's thighs and hoisted them unto her shoulders, bringing the writhing pelvis even closer to her face.

Her mouth took hold of the tiny clitoris and sucked it gently, her tongue flickering over it at the same time. Lisa screamed and Judith felt the legs on her shoulders grow heavy, the knees straightening and the toes pointing towards the opposite wall. At the same time Lisa ceased to breathe for a few seconds, only to expel a loud scream as Judith felt the vulva contract violently against her mouth.

The whole body then went limp again, and Judith sensed the wave that swept through the patient's loins, almost echoing against her own mouth. She turned her head slightly and continued to caress the soft thighs with her face.

Opening her eyes for a moment, she recognised a figure standing by the half-opened door. Mrs Cox.

The woman stared at them with a blank expression, but Judith immediately noticed the fingers clenched around the sheets of papers she was holding, the knuckles white and the grip so strong the paper seemed ready to rip.

Silently the supervisor walked to the bed, her gate somewhat unsteady, and simply dropped the papers on the bedside table. All the while she kept staring at Judith, the expression on her face never betraying her feelings; no anger, no surprise.

Still kneeling, fully clothed, between Lisa's parted legs, Judith continued caressing the soft skin, suddenly happy that her improvised plan had worked. She stared back at the woman through half-shut eyes and smiled smugly. There was nothing Mrs Cox could say or do, or else she would have intervened already.

At that moment Judith had the confirmation that what Ray had told her was true. There could no longer be any doubt about it. And Mrs Cox knew that Judith knew. What would happen next? It didn't really matter. All that mattered was that Judith was no longer afraid of losing her job. In her mind she knew they wouldn't let go of her now.

Mrs Cox turned around and left. Judith looked up at Lisa. The girl was looking at her with a wicked smile, her eyes half-shut as well, seemingly drunk with pleasure. Both women had managed to get what they had sought. Lisa to have someone to pleasure her, Judith to be caught in the act by her supervisor.

Yet she was still disappointed because she hadn't counted on Mrs Cox leaving the room like this. She wanted the woman to come to her rescue, in a funny sort of way, to be taken in by the scene Judith and Lisa offered. But instead she had walked out, completely disinterested, and now Judith would have to find another way to get Mrs Cox to come to her, to totally seduce her.

As she knelt between Lisa's parted legs, Judith wished for a moment that the roles could be reversed, that she would be the one sitting there, and have Mrs Cox torturing her tender flesh like an obedient slave.

At the same time her thoughts scared her. This was the second time she had had intimate contact with a woman, and her own desire was somewhat new to her. All her life she had only ever fantasised about men, but now her

761

lust knew no bounds. And her behaviour had changed, too. Whereas up until quite recently she had been rather inexperienced and somewhat passive, now she craved contact in an almost aggressive way; these were uncontrollable impulses.

She wanted to pleasure and be pleasured, again and again, to be both slave and master, in turn, to others as well as to her own lust. And again today the way Mrs Cox had reacted wasn't what Judith had expected. Perhaps something didn't ring true, as Judith had not really been forced into anything she didn't want to do and the supervisor had instinctively felt it.

Against her face she felt Lisa's legs stir a few times. She sighed and looked up at her. Lisa winked, obviously happy to have received satisfaction. Judith was happy, too, but in her mind nothing was settled.

She was so close to her goal she felt she could almost touch it. She wanted Mrs Cox to come back and pleasure her, and she knew that eventually she would get her. But when?

Chapter Sixteen

A ll that was missing this morning was the red carpet, Judith thought. She stood quietly by the nurses' desk, filling out her reports, immune to the feverish excitement around her.

The other nurses were running all over the place, chuckling loudly. Marina Stone was expected any minute, and her imminent arrival sent a tension through the air that was like a storm about to break, electrical and stimulating.

The great Marina, the actress who could hold audiences on the edge of their seats, make them cry just by snapping her fingers, stir in them emotions that would linger long after they had left the cinema or turned off the television set. She would be here any minute.

Judith couldn't help feeling that everybody was overreacting. After all, this was probably a woman just like any other once the cameras stopped rolling. And from the moment she would set foot in the Dorchester Clinic, she would be a patient, just like all the others.

Apparently, she had been here as a patient a couple of years ago, and on that occasion she had practically never set foot outside her room and those who hadn't actually seen her doubted she had been here at all.

Yet around the nurses' station and in the corridor,

763

nobody but Judith could keep calm. As of yet no-one knew the real reason why Marina had decided to check into the Clinic. The odds were in favour of another face-lift, although liposuction on her chin was a strong second. But did it really matter?

One of the attendants had his head out of a window overlooking the street, although it was always strictly forbidden to open the windows on that side of the building because of the traffic noises and the fumes.

'Here they come!' he screamed before shutting the window. Silence fell for a second, yet the tension continued to mount. The staff members all looked at each other, their faces stretched by large grins, and a minute later the noises resumed.

'How long do you think it will take her to get up here?'

'Is the room ready?'

'What about the flowers? Where did you put the flowers?'

'Has the phone been installed in her temporary office?'

Judging from all this commotion, Judith figured that even a member of the royal family could never generate such excitement. And there was more to come, of course. The Great One hadn't even made it up to the floor yet.

Right now she was probably being greeted by Doctor Marshall, and maybe another doctor, the one who would be operating on her, and perhaps even Mrs Cox as well. Of course this would all be done discretely, with taste; there would be no bouquets changing hands, no flashes from cameras.

If she was satisfied with her stay at the Clinic then Marina would perhaps tell some of her prestigious friends and this could only be good publicity. Therefore everything had to be perfect.

'They're on their way up,' Nurse Parsons announced, hanging up the phone. 'Look busy.'

Suddenly, life went back to normal, or at least something that looked like normal. Everyone was still very excited but no-one could let anything show. The instructions had been very detailed. There would be no requests for autographs, no going into the actress's room without a good reason, and, naturally, no leaks to the Press. Marina would be given the best room, the one that had a small adjoining office, for her personal assistant and other members of her entourage. Everything would be controlled from there, for Marina would not do something so mundane as to press the call button if she needed anything; she had people who were paid to do that for her.

But of course Marina Stone would be treated just like all the other patients, with class and professionalism, but still keeping in mind she was indeed somebody special.

The doors of the lift opened and she stepped out, flanked by Doctor Marshall and Mrs Cox, looking glamorous, as always. Although she was shorter than she seemed to be on screen, Marina Stone had a certain panache that commanded admiration. Her dark green coat looked simple yet expensive, the style and colour perfectly suited to her brown hair which was held up in a complicated chignon. The position of her gloved hand on her handbag seemed calculated and her make-up was discreet but impeccable. She exuded class, and just stepping out of the lift looked like a grandiose entrance, a well-rehearsed scene straight from one of her films.

Doctor Rogers followed, one step behind like a faithful puppy. Judith thought it was quite unusual to see him without Doctor Mason for a change. He looked pale and even more frail behind Marina, his boyish looks giving him the allure of a bell boy and not a doctor. But if he was with them it could only mean he would be the one to operate on her, therefore the great Marina was coming in for liposuction, as that was Doctor Rogers's speciality.

Three people also came out of the lift; Marina's staff. The first one behind Doctor Rogers was a tall woman, probably her secretary, carrying a briefcase in one hand and a wad of papers in the other. She immediately looked around with sharp, inquisitive eyes, casting a brief but thorough glance all around, inspecting even the ceiling.

The other woman was shorter and her opened coat

revealed a pink uniform. She was carrying a large, shiny plastic bag and a vanity case. Although Marina was coming in for surgery there was no reason why she shouldn't look her best; taking along her hairdresser wasn't such a farfetched notion to people like her.

The last one out of the lift was a tall and burly man, with very short hair and broad shoulders. Judith couldn't decide whether he was Marina's chauffeur or bodyguard or possibly a combination of both. Nevertheless he looked very impressive and almost frightening. He was also carrying a bag: an enormous, black leather satchel that was obviously filled to capacity, bulging from all sides. In his big hand, however, it seemed almost weightless.

Such was the star's retinue, the few people she couldn't manage without, even whilst in hospital. At first the staff had been told she would bring along her own nurse as well, but Marina had changed her mind at the last minute and it was announced that a few chosen nurses would take turns caring for her exclusively. The names of those nurses had not yet been announced and wild rumours were fuelled by the anticipation.

At first it was supposed that Miss Stone would choose for herself, then it was said it would be exclusively male nurses. But in the end the decision was up to Doctor Marshall, upon recommendations from Mrs Cox and the attending surgeon.

Judith doubted she would be chosen, mainly because she had only recently joined the staff. However, when the star stopped at the nurses' station en route to her bedroom, Mrs Cox took her apart and put her hand on Judith's shoulder.

Judith kept looking at Marina, now standing by the station desk and chatting with the nurse in charge, but all her attention was focused on Mrs Cox, and how warm the woman's breath felt on her neck. At the same time her heart began to pound furiously. The last time she had seen Mrs Cox was in Lisa Baxter's room, the previous morning. She hadn't heard anything since, hadn't been

766

called to the office, and still didn't know if being caught in such a compromising position would mean instant dismissal.

She dreaded what she was about to hear, yet at the same time felt a weird excitement at being touched by this woman who impressed her so much. The object of her recent fantasies was just a few inches from her, a hand on the nurse's shoulder and her mouth sensually close to her ear.

'Doctor Rogers has asked that you be assigned to his team for the operation,' Mrs Cox whispered confidentially. 'It would be in your best interest to accept . . .' She didn't give Judith the opportunity to reply and turned around to join Marina as the star continued her tour on her way to her room.

Judith felt a sob rise in her throat and tears to her eyes. That could only mean one thing: despite what had happened with Lisa Baxter yesterday she wasn't about to get fired. At least not just yet. She was elated, once again seized with a feeling of victory. Things were working out just fine, but she still didn't have the final confirmation of what Ray had told her. How long would she have to wait for that?

Marina finally entered her room, the last one at the end of the corridor, followed by her staff, and the door closed behind them. Simultaneously several sighs were heard, a combination of admiration, relief, and envy. From then on it seemed to be business as usual, but it was all a pretence, and would likely remain so at least whilst the star was in residence.

Judith's mind was working frantically. For the past three days she had been going through her plan time and time again. Normally she would have been happy to get three consecutive days off work – her reward for having assisted Doctor Rogers in surgery – but since she had felt Mrs Cox's breath on her neck she had been unable to quell the hunger she was feeling deep within her, the warm desire to be near the woman again.

The lift opened onto the top floor of the building, where all the directors and doctors' offices were located, and Judith stepped out decidedly. She walked along the silent corridor and looked at her watch: 10 o'clock. Everyone was gone at this hour, but Mrs Cox's car was still in the car park so she was probably working late.

This time Judith would not let her supervisor have the upper hand. In the same way she had managed to get what she had wanted out of Desmond, she was planning to make Mrs Cox reveal what she knew, to confirm what Ray had said. After that, all she would have to do was to find a weak point in the armour the woman seemed to wear. She would make Mrs Cox yield, make her pleasure her tender flesh once again. This time Judith wouldn't step out of that office until she had got what she had come for.

The harsh light coming from the ceiling gave the corridor a strange aspect, too bright, surreal. It was just like being enveloped in that light, like a bright cloud, hot and blinding, almost lifting her off the ground and making her walk straight into the light.

She passed a series of doors, each adorned by a shining brass sign with a name on it. All the doctors and directors had their offices on this floor. All of them were identical, except for the name on the door. And to Judith each name had come to mean something very specific.

Elizabeth Mason's office was, naturally, right next to Tom Rogers's. There was surely some kind of link between them, other than being colleagues. It was more than friendship but Judith still hadn't been able to figure out their relationship. It didn't really matter, it had nothing to do with her. However this unusual couple were also strange because they hadn't shown any interest in Judith, other than as a capable nurse. They had stared at her in a strange way the very first day in the operating theatre, but after that they had never given that bewildering look of barely disguised interest she had noticed from so many of her colleagues. As if they had sensed just by looking at her that she was too different from them, that the new nurse would fit into this special world of theirs.

Suddenly Judith remembered that she had seen Doctor Mason's red Mazda in the car park, so there was a chance she was still in her office, probably working late as well. Judith hastened her step, not wanting to see her and eager to get to the other wing, the older part of the Clinic where Mrs Cox had her office.

She trembled, shaken by a delicious shiver, as she read Edouard Laurin's name before turning the corner, remembering the time she had come up to confront him with what she thought was a conspiracy to hypnotise the staff and turn them into sex slaves. The time she had spent in there was unforgettable.

As it turned out, if indeed Mrs Cox could confirm it, it wasn't so far from the truth. Yes, there were slaves at the Dorchester Clinic, but they were willing servants, slaves to their own desires.

She turned the corner and pushed open the fire door separating the old part of the building from the new one. The only people who had their offices in this wing, next to each other's, were Mrs Cox and Doctor Marshall. Judith remembered one of her colleagues telling somebody that Doctor Marshall had left early today. That would mean only Mrs Cox remained in this part of the building, isolated from everyone else. No-one was to know Judith was here, especially at this hour; no-one was to hear them.

She had planned to enter Mrs Cox's office without knocking and lock the door behind her. The surprise was on her, however, when she discovered the door was locked. She tried the doorknob a few times, gripping it tightly, her hands moist with anticipation, desperately trying to make it turn and wondering if it was just that she had no strength left in her hands.

But the door was locked, there was no doubt about it. And Judith couldn't bring herself to knock. In her mind, she felt so sure everything would go according to her plan that this setback looked more like a failure. Right now everything was working against her. She pressed her ear to the door, hoping in vain to hear even the slightest noise that would tell her if indeed there was somebody in there. But there was no sound to be heard. Either the door was too thick or there was nobody in the office. So where could Mrs Cox be?

With a sigh of resignation she let go of the doorknob and turned around, frustrated and angry. Perhaps the supervisor had gone home already. She could have been making her way down one of the lifts whilst Judith was coming up in the other. The timing was all wrong and Judith realised she wouldn't find anything out today.

As she slowly made her way back towards the lift her hand strayed and she mechanically, almost by reflex, grabbed hold of the doorknob to Doctor Marshall's office. She froze in her steps when she realised this door wasn't locked, and that only a slight twist of her wrist would make it turn with a faint click. She let it go suddenly, as if it had been burning, and waited, her heart pounding.

She was expecting to hear a voice inside asking who was there, or at least some sign that there was someone in there. Surprisingly there was nothing but silence. She pushed the door with her fingertips, her lips going dry and her cheeks heating up in excitement.

The door opened silently onto a dark room, the brightness of the corridor offsetting the faint light coming from a small lamp that was lit on the desk. Still not a sound. Judith breathed deeply and ventured into the room hesitantly. As her eyes became accustomed to the semi-darkness she cast a look around.

Doctor Marshall's office was not unlike that of Mrs Cox, albeit a bit larger. The desk took pride of place and was almost identical to Mrs Cox's, as was the large wall unit behind it, and this one was loaded with books. Judith got bolder and walked across to take a look at the series of photos on a shelf alongside the far wall; Doctor Marshall and Mrs Cox, looking much younger, a photo probably taken quite a few years ago; the opening of the Clinic, a beaming doctor cutting a red ribbon; a collage of Doctor Marshall with a number of famous personalities, possibly all former patients of the Clinic; framed press cuttings, all relating to the Clinic.

Obviously, this man was proud of what he had built, and for very good reasons. But how could he leave his office without locking the door? This was quite worrisome for Judith; she would have to come up with a very good explanation if he were to show up behind her and demand to know what she was doing in his office . . .

As she continued to look around she suddenly noticed something familiar on the floor between the desk and side-door. The satchel she had seen Marina Stone's escort bring in just a few days ago blatantly lay wide open. Only this time it was no longer bulging and on the brink of bursting open. Yet it wasn't empty either.

She crouched down and peered in. Her heart began to pound again and she reached in with a trembling hand. Wads of bank notes, from 5 to 20, crisp and new, freshly minted and neatly stacked. Her fingers shuffled them about quickly and she realised there was a small fortune in there. However, this wasn't anywhere near the amount the satchel had contained when Marina had checked in if in fact it had contained nothing but money.

Judith vaguely knew the costs of surgery and a four-day stay at the Clinic. At least she knew there was more than enough in the bag as it stood. Marina had brought in way too much money, but why? And where did the rest of it go? And how could Doctor Marshall leave his office with so much money quietly sitting on the floor?

Anybody could walk in and whisk it away, and no-one would ever find out about it. This was more than carelessness on Doctor Marshall's part, it was downright stupid.

A wicked thought crossed Judith's mind. There was more in there than she could earn in a year. How tempting it was to just grab the bag and leave . . . but at the same time she was somewhat indifferent to the idea of sudden riches. She had come here for another purpose, and she wasn't ready to leave without having found out what she had been waiting to learn.

As she slowly stood up a faint voice rose to her ears, noises coming from the other side of a door near to the desk, a door she noticed was slightly ajar. She tilted her head slightly to peek in and realised this was actually a way into Mrs Cox's office. Her fingers now numb, she opened the door slightly and tried to figure out where the noises and voices were coming from.

Mrs Cox's office was completely dark, and there was nobody in there either, but what Judith had heard was without a doubt coming from inside. She glided into the room and closed the door behind her. At first, all she could see was the light coming through the window, directly above a lamppost, casting an upward orange glow.

Then she noticed a tiny yellow light, a slim line at the bottom of the far wall which rose at a right angle before thinning out and disappearing. It took her a few seconds to figure out it was coming from under another door, a door she hadn't noticed on her previous visits to the office.

She walked through the darkness towards this source of light, unsure of what she would find on the other side. Yet she knew it was too late to go back, and at this point she was so intrigued she could only go on and try to find out more.

When she got to the wall she encountered a major hurdle: there didn't seem to be any kind of doorknob, how could she open the door? Her fingers frantically followed the crack in the wall, feeling it getting thinner and disappearing, and she soon felt like giving up. A wave of despair seized her. She knew she was close, how could this happen to her now?

Then, on the other side, she heard a loud moan. At first she felt her blood freeze in her veins. The cry was deep, the voice female. But an instant later Judith was swept with a strange heat, her loins realising that this wasn't a moan of pain but one of pleasure. Simultaneously, her nipples grew stiff and her breath shallow. Her brain ceased to think and her instincts took over.

Whatever was going on behind that wall, it was exciting, in more ways than one. Her hands then started to work frantically, feeling up and down the wall, desperately looking for some kind of handle, some way of opening the door.

When she got to the top she inadvertently pushed the corner in. It gave a click and sprung out unexpectedly. Immediately the yellow line grew thicker and the door opened slightly. Judith managed to venture a look inside and nervously licked her dry lips.

The first time Judith had been in this part of the Clinic she had wondered what else could be on this floor, for it had seemed quite unusual that there would only be two offices occupying such a large amount of floor space. But now she knew.

This room was bigger than both offices put together, only it seemed to be accessible solely through this secret door. At first Judith had the impression it was some kind of museum. The set-up was most obviously antique.

From what she could see it seemed the room was rather narrow but quite long, with a row of brass beds neatly lined up along the wall, flanked on either side by ancient, metal utility cabinets. Peering in, Judith could only see six beds but that was enough to make out that there was nothing posh about this room, unlike the rest of the Clinic. In fact, it looked rather gloomy.

The beds were old, the paint on several of the metal cabinets was chipped. On the ceiling old lead pipes were clearly visible, as were the bars in the windows. On the whole it looked much like a Victorian hospital ward, probably what the Clinic might have looked like at the turn of the century.

The yellow light was coming from several candles. Sorry curtains hung at the windows, tattered and turned grey with age. For a minute Judith wondered if she could come in, for there didn't seem to be anybody in there either. But at that very moment she heard yet another

773

moan, stronger, betraying sensations she could almost feel herself, and that exerted such a pull on her loins that she just had to open the door and face whatever she would find on the other side.

She proceeded slowly, gradually stepping into another age, another world. There were about 15 beds in all lined up along the wall, and beyond them the rest of the room was set up to look like an operating theatre.

The smell of starch assaulted her nostrils as she walked past the first bed. The mattress was about waist high, the sheets crisp and neatly tucked. Looking down to the far end of the room she realised there were in fact several people there, two couples she couldn't recognise from where she was standing. She was obviously walking in on some secret get-together, now boldly inviting herself in. Nevertheless she kept on walking, as if in a dream, towards the unreal scene that was starting to reveal itself to her.

The first couple was a patient and a surgeon. The patient was lying on an old, narrow operating table, in a set-up very different from anything Judith had ever seen.

The patient was lying on his back, covered in bandages from head to toe, and the surgeon was standing next to him, with his back turned to Judith. Instead of the modern, green cotton garment, this doctor was completely naked under a large, dark rubber apron. All that was visible was a pair of rounded, smooth buttocks, topped by the apron strings neatly fastened around the waist.

The surgeon was quite obviously a shapely female, but there was no way of knowing who could be hiding under the worn, dark cotton hood; a gloomy head garment doctors used to wear a few hundred years ago, during the first years of modern medicine before surgical masks were invented.

As she walked closer, however, Judith noticed a few unmistakeable brown locks sticking out from under the hood. Her guess was proven correct when she got close enough to take a look at this doctor's hands: hands that belonged to Elizabeth Mason.

Doctor Mason turned around and looked at Judith, only her emerald eyes could be seen in this unusual head gear. She stopped for a second, one hand still clasped around her patient's ankle, the other holding a length of cotton gauze. Nothing in her eyes betrayed her emotions. If she was surprised to see Judith there, it never showed.

Her apron was fastened so tight it revealed the rounded contours of her breasts, the peaks of her large, erect nipples. Further down the small hole of her belly button was also emphasised by the tight rubber layer, which then fell straight down, almost touching the floor. Judith then ventured a look towards the patient who lay on the table, his arms and legs wide apart.

This silhouette was unmistakably male, but the identity of the patient would likely remain a mystery, for his head was completely covered in bandages. All that was uncovered was the underside of his nose, which showed the nostrils flaring sporadically.

His hands were thickly bandaged, looking like oversized bundles, and were both tied to a set of handles at the head of the table. The whole body was neatly wrapped in several layers of cotton gauze from head to toe, like a mummy, except for the most important part: his erect phallus, which reared, purplish and stiff, looking dark and mysterious in the midst of all these layers of white gauze.

The patient's thin frame made it easy for Judith to guess his identity. She also noticed that a lock of his pale hair had managed to escape through the bandages around his head. Such was the revelation of the real nature of that special relationship between Elizabeth Mason and Tom Rogers . . .

And right at this moment, Doctor Mason was busy tying up his legs at the foot of the table. The patient was now ready for the operation . . . What would she do with him? It was easy to imagine, at least for Judith. Yet to see these two prestigious doctors, surgeons she had assisted

775

in the operating theatre, in such a set-up was unbeliev-able, almost fantastic, and the scene was even more surreal in the yellow glow from the candles dripping on the windowsill.

She could hear them both breathing loudly, Doctor Mason through the strange mask she was wearing, Doctor Rogers with great difficulty because of the ban-dages around his face. It seemed Doctor Mason didn't mind having a spectator, and although Judith was more than willing to stay and watch, she was too intrigued by what the rest of this strange room contained to stop exploring it so soon. She continued walking around, like a visitor to some live exhibit, her brain quickly processing every detail of the dim room her eyes could survey.

A little further away was another couple in another kind of set up Judith was eager to investigate. She immediately recognised Doctor Marshall, although the sight of his naked body wasn't anything like she could ever have imagined. She was startled and stopped in her steps, wondering how daring she could be, if she could make her presence known and move closer. For a while she watched from afar, not knowing how he would react if he saw her there.

His arms and torso were pale but muscular and covered in a lush carpet of silver hairs, tiny drops of sweat pearling on his chest and glistening in the candle-light. At this moment Judith realised that his hair was probably not a good indication of his age, for his body was that of a much younger man, chiselled and taut. She saw he was holding something in his hand, some kind of slim, metallic instrument that faintly reflected the yellow flames of the candles.

He looked up and saw her, but remained silent. For a moment Judith boldly held his gaze, expecting him to tell her to get out, almost surprised that he didn't. As he diverted his eyes Judith understood he didn't mind her presence and she approached him, fascinated by the way his cock pointed up and twitched sporadically, and how the delicate metal ring piercing his foreskin shook as the purplish head of his phallus bobbed up and down.

Gazing towards his partner, she concluded that the woman who was bending backwards over the wooden trestle, her wrists and ankles bound by leather restraints, her back supported by a black leather saddle, could only be Mrs Cox.

Hesitantly, Judith continued coming closer, unable to control her own feet anymore. She had to get close, to see more. As she approached them Doctor Marshall looked up at her again and this time a wicked smile appeared at the corner of his mouth.

His erect phallus stood up, pointing towards Mrs Cox's parted legs, but was nowhere near to entering the gaping vulva just yet. There again Judith was astonished to see him in such an unusual situation, but she knew this was only the beginning of her discoveries. There was more to come.

She stopped looking at him to quickly glance at Mrs Cox. The woman's breasts also pointed towards the ceiling, the nipples stiff and long. And Judith finally saw how foolish she had been that morning in the supervisor's office, when she had wondered why the nipples pointing through the woman's uniform had such a distorted shape. Of course, there was nothing unusual about the nipples themselves, other than the fact that they were both pierced by large metal rings. These also dangled and shone in the candlelight, and the slight pull they seemed to effect on the erect nipples was sufficient to trigger Judith's arousal.

There she lay, right in front of her, exposed and defenceless, the woman Judith had been waiting for. Yet this wasn't like any of the many scenarios she had been fantasising about!

On a small table next to the trestle were a series of instruments Judith couldn't identify, ancient surgical tools, also museum pieces. Next to them was an old, worn leather case, spread open and holding even more tools.

777

What Doctor Marshall held in his hand was also mysterious, a slightly curved metal rod about eight inches long, with a brown wooden handle and a stumpy, rounded tip the size of a large grape. There was no way of knowing the original purpose of this instrument, but it was easy to guess what he was about to do with it.

Judith walked around the trestle slowly, oblivious to the sighs that rose from the opposite corner of the room where Doctor Mason and her 'patient' were. Rather, she was mesmerised by the sight of Mrs Cox's precarious position, and even more so when she realised the woman was also gagged, her mouth held open by a leather strap with a knot in it.

This was something Judith had heard of before, the way loud or violent patients were kept from screaming, back in the days, many years ago, when such practices were considered the norm.

The look she saw in Mrs Cox's half-shut eyes had nothing to do with pain or distress, however. It was one of sheer pleasure.

To see her like this rekindled Judith's arousal and her heart began to pound in anticipation once again. She looked up to Doctor Marshall and couldn't contain a triumphant smile, somehow wickedly happy to see Mrs Cox displayed like this. Of course, this meant the woman wouldn't be able to walk out on Judith, and although the nurse wasn't responsible for this awkward situation, she couldn't help being pleased with it. She didn't know what else Doctor Marshall intended to do to the supervisor, but she already knew she now had a powerful weapon in knowledge.

By now the man was also holding something in his other hand, some kind of leather strap, worn and slightly fraying. Judith closed her eyes for a second, desperately trying to capture this scene in her memory, almost afraid of opening her eyes again lest it be just a dream, yet compelled to look on as the rush of dew between her legs grew insistent and she demanded more of the bizarre, exciting vision.

This vision was enhanced by the flickering light of the candles, each flame differing in intensity, in height, in projection, and casting hundreds of different shadows on the naked body that was arched over the trestle. In effect, the skin looked like it had been painted on, brightly lit patches contrasting with the other parts of the body where little or no light fell.

Doctor Marshall took one step closer towards his victim, and raised his hand to gently rub the protruding clitoris with the tip of the metal rod. The woman moaned loudly.

Judith couldn't imagine what had taken place earlier, but the sounds she had heard from the other room had indeed come from Mrs Cox's gagged mouth. There could be no doubt about that, judging from the glistening patches of dew that had trickled down on the inside of her thighs and glistened in the yellow light.

Loud moans were also coming from the other corner of the room. Judith turned her head only briefly, yet long enough to see that Elizabeth Mason was now up on the table, straddling her man, and just about to impale herself upon his thick member. In a sudden flash Judith understood the reason for such an elaborate set up: Tom Rogers, all covered in bandages, was totally isolated in his own world and his skin was unable to sense anything; only his erect prick was susceptible to sensation from contact with the outside.

Turning her eyes back towards Mrs Cox and Doctor Marshall, she could see that what was going on here was quite different. It was some kind of multi-faceted torture, where everything lay in the fact that the treatment had to be slow to be efficient. She had known that herself, when she had been tied up by Desmond. Soon Mrs Cox's arousal would reach such a point that her whole body would seem about to explode, yet she would still be denied the final release, the ultimate point where everything began, where everything ended.

Judith looked around once again, unable to see all of the room but subjugated by what her eyes could make out. One of the beds had restraints already secured to the brass bars at either end. Some beds had thick mattresses with starched sheets, others bare, rough straw mattresses.

All the windows were blacked out. Obviously it was not really necessary as this was the seventh floor and it would be difficult to peep in from the outside, but it did add something frightening to the already gloomy atmosphere that reigned in the room.

Judith was walking as if in a dream, both couples unconcerned by her presence in this secret chamber. They didn't even seem at all curious about how she found the room either. Both Doctor Marshall and Elizabeth Mason looked at her with an amused smile, and then at each other. No-one had uttered a word since she had walked in. Doctor Marshall was the first one to speak.

'Take your clothes off, nurse,' he ordered. 'Your uniform is not in line with the regulations of this room.'

Judith was about to retort that she didn't know any of these rules, but managed to hold back her words just before they crossed her lips. She was in no position to protest, all she could do was obey.

On the operating table, Tom Rogers's bandaged body began to writhe, his arms tugging at the thick lengths of gauze that held him down, his slim hips pushing up to enter the woman who was straddling him. Elizabeth didn't move much, content to let him exert himself for her own benefit. Her behind swayed gently, slowly, back and forth and sideways, seemingly trying to direct his thrusting prick within her tunnel.

She began tossing her head back and forth as well, at first in a slow, gyrating motion, but her movements became swifter and soon turned into a series of jerks so violent that her black hood slipped off her head and her dark, curly mane bounced all around her face, strands sweeping over her eyes and into her mouth.

Judith could almost feel the woman's pleasure, and her loins were seized in a strong, hot grip. Despite its nightmarish set-up, this room was made for pleasure, different, old-fashioned, forbidden.

Her eyes constantly travelled from one couple to the other as she took her clothes off, her burning feet finding relief on the cold tiles, her bare skin taking on a smooth, evenly velvety look in the candlelight. Once she stood naked Doctor Marshall beckoned for her to join him. She approached hesitantly.

Instinctively she knew very few words were ever spoken in this place. This was the realm of sighs and moans. Yet she would have liked to be told, she needed to know in no uncertain terms. But again Desmond's words echoed in her mind. It did not matter what she knew, all that was important was how she felt.

And right now she felt good, walking around naked, her body bathed in the yellow light, the scent of the burning wax invading her brain. In front of her was a woman, a woman she had wanted to submit to. This wasn't at all what she had planned. In fact, it was the other way around. But this was better than nothing, more than she could ever have hoped for. It was up to her to make it what she wanted. At last, here was her chance.

Doctor Marshall handed her the metal instrument and stood back, a silent invitation for her to proceed. In her hand the wooden handle was smooth and warm, obviously old and often used. She took a closer look at it, wondering what it could be. Perhaps it wasn't even a surgical tool at all, but somehow she doubted that. Everything in this room was genuine, it couldn't be otherwise.

As she approached the parted legs she saw the woman's knees tremble. At that moment Judith's loins went ablaze, her own vulva yearning to feel the exquisite torture of this unknown tool. She reached out.

At first she let the rounded tip slide up on the inside of the woman's right leg, feeling it glide smoothly over a few inches, its progression somewhat impaired once it began to tread over the wetter area. Amidst dark, wet pubic hairs, she saw the tiny bud of the clitoris gleam faintly, the rest of the vulva barely visible as the parted legs shielded it from the light. She directed the instrument towards it, wickedly letting it slide up ever so slowly, feeling the metal dig a slight furrow against the tensed muscle.

At last the metal tip came to touch the stiff bud. Judith held back, letting it brush only lightly at first, then redirecting it towards the dark, secret entrance that hid in the shadows. She felt elated and her own arousal grew as she heard the first moan coming from the woman's throat. Victory was hers.

How long would she wait before granting the woman the pleasure she would silently beg for? She didn't know just yet, but she definitely was in no hurry. She would savour her triumph, watch the woman writhe endlessly under the cold metal caress, bring her just moments away from her climax but deny it to her at the very last minute.

Judith felt naughty, finally allowed to release all her frustrations and tease the woman for as long as she would please. She inserted the tip of the rod into the slick vagina once again, then took the handle with both hands to make the rod rotate quickly.

The hips jerked in a spasm as the bulbous tip spun within it. Judith tried to imagine what this could feel like, to have this cold metal ball spinning inside of her, rotating on itself and caressing the smooth walls of her tunnel. She shuddered at the thought, her imagination so powerful she could almost feel the metal ball inside her as well. Would it be painful or pleasant? Probably a strange mix of both sensations in more or less equal proportions.

She slowly pushed the rod as far as she could inside the woman's tunnel and pulled it back out before reinserting it again, repeating this motion time and time again, gradually increasing in speed.

Each time the rounded tip nudged at her entrance the woman moaned, and soon the insertions changed to rapid pokings. Judith slowly directed it towards the gaping vulva, then jerked her arm to thrust in forcefully, each insertion brief but forceful.

By now her victim was panting loudly, her breath escaping in tempo with each jab of the rod. Judith threw her head back and laughed loudly, wickedly happy with the woman's reaction. This was more than she had hoped for, and she knew there was still more to come.

She took the rod out and returned to caressing the thighs again, making the tip switch from one leg to the other with sharp twists of her wrist. As Judith gently hit the smooth flesh it responded with a faint wet slapping sound. She let the metal instrument slowly glide along the parted thighs and lightly brush the swollen clitoris now and again. Over the trestle, Mrs Cox seemed to relax and Judith thought the torture she would put her through would be like a roller coaster ride with intensely pleasurable episodes interspersed by more quiet, gentle teasing.

After a while, however, she was almost disappointed when she saw Doctor Marshall stepping forward to join her. He walked around slowly, looking at Mrs Cox's body but never at her face, his mouth now tightly shut in a severe, cruel expression. His gleeful eyes betrayed his lust, and Judith noticed several small drops pearling from the nether mouth of his erect phallus which was still pointing at the ceiling. He had been watching them silently, and was obviously excited by the spectacle of his woman being teased by a young, inexperienced nurse.

Judith pulled away for a minute, not really sure of his intentions. He looked at her and smiled complacently.

'Look at her,' he said cynically. 'When I met her a few years back she was just like you, sweet and innocent. Now, see what she's become ... A wanton creature, tortured yet beautiful in her quest for pleasure. I must admit she never ceases to amaze me.'

He stopped between the woman's parted legs and slowly ran the tip of the leather strap over the white flesh, its frayed edge making a slightly scratchy sound. He caressed her thus for a little while, then began to flick the strap from one thigh to the other. At first he just let it swing under the pull of its own weight, but gradually imparted some force to it, until it began to slap the smooth flesh which slowly grew red and raised.

The woman's hips jerked up a few times and her legs bucked. The slender muscles played under the skin, contracting forcefully against the restraints and as her vulva appeared in the pale light, Judith could see the entrance of her vagina clench violently. She was finding pleasure in pain, and at that moment Judith understood the woman's reaction when the nurse had confessed to being hit with a set of keys and having found it pleasurable.

So, in this respect Doctor Marshall was right. Judith had a lot in common with the woman who lay with her back arched and her extremities tied up. Their paths had crossed in their respective quests for pleasure and were now merging in an unexpected way. Judith was merely a novice compared to Mrs Cox, however. She still had a lot to learn, but the prospect of being guided through this realm of pleasure-pain was appealing.

The man moved back for a few seconds and the woman ceased moaning. Suddenly, Judith realised all was now silent in the large room. A powerful, eerie sensation seized her and, as she looked around, she was surprised to see that Doctor Mason and Doctor Rogers were gone. The only witness to their unusual encounter was a thick pile of gauze strips, scattered on the floor around the operating table. They had kept to themselves, enclosed in their own private world of pleasure, respectful yet oblivious of the others around them.

For such was this room, as far as Judith could make out. This was a place where people came to live out their fantasies, but without imposing on others. Everything had been carefully planned to offer a wide array of set-ups, all in respect to the old tradition of medical care, all imaginative and intriguing, all wickedly exciting and sexy.

Judith had found out more in one evening than she ever could have imagined. And she hadn't had to ask a single question. Now, more than ever, she understood

784

the meaning of Desmond's words, for knowing the truth was one thing, but discovering it with her body was much better.

She began to relax her mind and let her senses take over. This room, with its appearance, the faint yellow flickering lights, and smell of burning wax, all merged into a powerful, arousing mental caress which she could feel through her loins. This was more intense than anything she had ever experienced in her life. Now, she became impatient to see what else there was to this unusual encounter.

However, she was puzzled to see Doctor Marshall go down on his knees behind Mrs Cox's arched back and take away the piece of leather that gagged her. He looked up at Judith and smiled cruelly.

'Since you managed to find us,' he said, 'would you please be the one to give Mrs Cox the *coup de grâce?* You may use your hand, or your tongue, as you please.'

At first Judith couldn't quite figure out what he meant but she understood immediately once she saw him insert the tip of his erect phallus into the woman's mouth.

Judith wasn't ready for this. Things were not turning out as she had hoped. It was too soon to bring the woman to pleasure, at least from her point of view. There was more to come, that's how she wanted it. She needed to torture her victim endlessly, and then get the woman to return the favour. She had only just begun teasing her. This was way too soon!

Yet she also remembered that this session had probably started quite a while before she had joined in, and, of course, there was a limit to the amount of time anybody could remain in such an awkward position. Doctor Marshall was right, everything had to come to an end sooner or later, and there probably wasn't anything Judith could say or do to change the situation.

Her heart pounding, she came to stand next to the arched body. She saw Doctor Marshall grab Mrs Cox's full breasts with both hands and hold them tightly, inserting his thumbs inside the metal rings and gently tugging on them. At the same time, Mrs Cox's mouth, albeit upside down, also closed tightly around his erect member.

The scene was surreal and exciting. Judith reached down and timidly lay her hand on the tortured vulva. She felt it melt under her touch, soft and fluid, the sinewy folds throbbing slightly. Even before she moved her hand she felt the clitoris grow stiff under her fingertips and begin to pulsate. Judith rubbed it slightly, almost lovingly, feeling the woman's dew soak her hand almost immediately. Its sweet, heady scent rose in the room and numbed Judith's will. The momentum of her hand grew in tempo with Doctor Marshall's thrusting hips. She heard the woman moan and saw her red lips contracting around the thick rod that now entered and withdrew from her mouth at a frantic speed.

Yet Judith stood immobile, her hand moving from the elbow only. She closed her eyes and listened to this symphony of moans, sighs and grunts. The unusual music rocked her, soft and lascivious, and she barely felt the hand snaking up her naked thigh.

At first she thought it was only her imagination, but as she opened her eyes she saw that one of Mrs Cox's hands had been released and it was she who had reached out to touch the nurse's vulva.

By now Judith's arousal was so intense that the mere contact of the woman's slim fingers on her stiff bud was enough to trigger her climax. She moaned gently, her voice joining the others, as she felt pleasure sweep her. How ironic that she should be the one to climax first, since she had barely been touched. However, as sweet as her climax was, it was rather swift and faint. She didn't feel the series of recessing waves transport her again and again, like she usually did. And although she had felt pleasure, she also felt cheated.

It seemed there was a hierarchy even in sensual delight, for by now Doctor Marshall and Mrs Cox were both panting loudly, seized by the first pangs of their climax, which would no doubt be powerful.

He came first and let out a loud scream that travelled around the room and startled Judith. She saw his face contract in a pained expression, yet there was no doubt that he was being swept by pleasure. His hips jerked and he pushed his phallus deep inside the woman's mouth, to the hilt, his muscular thighs seemingly trying to thrust in further still. Mesmerised, Judith witnessed the contraction of his scrotum as his seed was released between the woman's tightened lips. He withdrew almost immediately and fell back onto his heels, almost collapsing on the cold tile floor.

Then she noticed a faint tremor shake the body she had been caressing. Against her own thigh she then sensed the muscles of the parted leg contract in turn, gradually, from the foot up to the upper part of the thigh. Then the wave transferred onto the woman's abdomen, the smooth belly growing rock hard under Judith's very eyes. She saw the thick veins of the neck bulge out against the distended skin and the mouth contract in an ultimate twist before the cry of joy came out, loud and sensual, tearing at Judith's loins.

The body shook several times, first in a rapid succession of spasms, then progressively subsiding as she took her hand away from the retracted clitoris. Without a word, Doctor Marshall stood up and untied the limp body before taking the woman in his arms to then gently deposit her on the floor. He turned to Judith.

'Get dressed and go home,' his tone turned authoritative and almost cruel. 'I want to see you in my office first thing tomorrow morning. In the meantime, not a word to anyone.'

Judith began to tremble uncontrollably, suddenly worried by the change in his attitude. Had she gone too far? She picked her clothes off the floor and ran out of the room, her naked feet barely touching the ground as she passed the endless row of beds.

Chapter Seventeen

Judith took a deep breath, trying to slow the pounding beat of her heart. She had been impatiently waiting in Doctor Marshall's office for over 20 minutes now, even though he had made a point of saying he would be back shortly.

All this time her nerves had been constantly on edge, the anticipation growing more intense with every passing moment. She was eager to talk to him, to finally have confirmation of what kind of treatment the Clinic also offered in addition to medical care.

It was just a formality at this stage, for she already knew what he was probably going to say, yet she needed to finally hear it from him, to clear up all the confusion in her mind. But she had been waiting for what seemed hours now, and she wasn't any closer to finding out the truth. Besides, she was late for her shift now.

She could hear him speak in the other room, Mrs Cox's office. However she couldn't identify the voice of the person he was talking to. Now and again there were loud bursts of laughter, with a predominant woman's voice, but on the whole it was all reduced to a confused rumbling of conversations and it was impossible to make out more than an occasional word. She knew Mrs Cox

788

wasn't in today, it was her day off. So who was in her office with Doctor Marshall?

Sitting legs crossed in a swivelling armchair, Judith fidgeted and pushed against the floor with her foot to make the chair turn. She quickly examined the room as it revolved around her. In the bright light the director's office looked different, the contrast between the black furniture and the white walls much more pronounced than what she had seen the previous evening.

In a corner stood a large television set, high up on a support cabinet, with a video recorder underneath. Strangely enough, there weren't any videocassettes to be seen anywhere in the office, so presumably the video recorder was hardly ever used.

She heard a door close in the next offfice and a third voice joined the first two. She expected Doctor Marshall would now come back, but each passing second made her realise she would still have to wait a little while longer. This only added to her curiosity. Who was this woman he had been talking to? And who had just walked in to join them?

Although she still couldn't make out their words, it was clear there were now three different voices, three people engaged in a lively conversation, but their words were inaudible. One of the voices belonged to Doctor Marshall; that was easy to figure out. As for the others, there seemed to be one male and one female voice, but Judith definitely couldn't tell who they were.

The voices died suddenly and she heard the sound of another door closing. A second later, the adjoining door to Mrs Cox's office opened and Doctor Marshall returned.

'Sorry to have kept you waiting,' he announced as he came to sit behind his desk. 'I had some rather important matters to attend to.' He pulled out a thin file from one of the drawers of his desk and opened it, taking out a few sheets of papers through which he quickly browsed.

'Miss Judith Stanton . . .' he said, as if speaking to himself. His eyes moved fast, seemingly taking in all the information they glanced over but without really pausing to read every detail.

Superficially, it almost looked like they were about to discuss some business matter, and Judith was stunned by his attitude. Considering what had happened the previous evening, he should have looked embarrassed right now, yet he didn't seem to be. His face was relaxed, his hands steady. He sat back in his chair and picked up a sheet of paper. Every now and again he would quickly glance at Judith then resume his reading again.

She was starting to get nervous. She knew she had nothing to fear, yet she had hoped he would have been a little more friendly and welcoming. She still hadn't forgotten the tone of his voice the previous night when he had told her to go home. And right now his attitude was similar. He was utterly cold, obviously not the least bit embarrassed by what she knew, just as if last night had never happened.

'You've been with us for nearly three months now,' he said after a while. 'Usually, this is Mrs Cox's domain, but in view of what happened yesterday we felt we had no option than to have this conversation with you as soon as possible . . .'

This sounded bad. Was it his way of telling her she was about to get fired? Judith's mind worked fast, her thoughts connecting and all ending up at the same result. She shouldn't have been in that room yesterday. They had not protested when she had come in, but obviously they were not happy with her crashing their private party.

She had felt the same way when she had been summoned to the disciplinary hearing. When she had seen them in the Board Room, she had thought they were about to fire her because she had given in to her desires and she had felt betrayed because they had encouraged her to express her sensuality just a few days beforehand.

Of course, she had been wrong that day, the disciplinary hearing had nothing to do with her, but her frame of

790

mind had been similar. Would she be wrong this time again?

He pulled up a pale pink sheet from the thin pile, which Judith recognised as her work contract. She closed her eyes for a few seconds and took a deep breath. The last image on her mind was that of his fingers holding the thin piece of paper as if he were about to tear it up. A sob rose in her throat but she managed to swallow it.

'You have not yet completed your probation,' he stated, 'you still have about two weeks to go. So far we are very pleased with your work. However, what I am about to reveal to you is usually not discussed until after at least three months have been completed ...' He stopped and cleared his throat several times, his eyes quickly travelling over the sheet of paper he held in his hands and never quite looking at Judith.

The young nurse suddenly felt strangely calm. Her palms were slightly moist and gently cupped the edge of the armrests. Judith was more curious than worried by now. If they were happy with her performance, there might still be hope. Perhaps her discovery of the previous night would only result in suspension or some other minor disciplinary action ...

'As you may already know,' Doctor Marshall began, 'I founded this clinic almost 12 years ago. At first I set out to offer mainly cosmetic and orthopaedic surgery, but soon it became clear that ...' He stopped abruptly and looked up at Judith, his eyes suddenly alight with an inquisitive sparkle. 'Have you heard about the Special Care Programme? Has anybody discussed it with you?'

Judith was taken aback by his question and took a few seconds to reply. 'N ... No ...' she stammered. She didn't dare confess that Ray had already told her, feeling it could only make matters worse. However, should he ask her how she found the secret room, she would have to think fast. She remained silent and forced herself to concentrate, to come up with a credible explanation should the need arise. Silence and obedience were probably the best strategy right now.

791

Doctor Marshall cleared his throat once again. 'I was hoping you would have,' he stated. 'This would have made things much easier for me.' He paused for what seemed to be an eternity and just strangely stared at her.

Staring back, Judith started to wonder if this was the same man she had seen the previous night, standing completely naked before her, engaged in such naughty activities that now seemed unreal in the light of day. Maybe she had imagined everything, maybe that secret room only existed in her mind.

She couldn't help thinking how cold he was, and she also remembered how cruel he had been just a few hours ago when he had submitted Mrs Cox to that wicked ordeal.

But now that he was sitting behind his desk, with his clothes and his white coat on, he seemed even worse. The whole office seemed cold and impersonal as well. This man had power, and she couldn't help feeling that he was in fact dangerous. She felt an icy chill pierce her and her heart began pounding furiously, this time in apprehension.

'As I was saying,' he continued, 'we have been pleased with your performance as far as your professional duties are concerned. But now the time has come to reveal what else our patients can expect when they come here. I suspect you might have a pretty good idea by now. Oh, it is not something we advertise. Most people only find out through word of mouth. But it is a fact that we do require our staff to dispense special care if such is the patients' desire.'

He continued to talk but Judith wasn't listening anymore. Although he was merely confirming what Ray had already told her, she couldn't help being surprised. Happily surprised, in fact. It was all true, and this realisation sent a shiver down her spine, a delicious thrill that coupled with her imagination to form a vivid image of what her life would be like now that she didn't have to fear her patients' unusual requests.

Judith felt immense relief. Once again she had overreacted. Chances were he wouldn't even mention the previous evening, or else he would already have done so. Now she could concentrate on what he had to say. Now that she had officially been told, things would be much easier. She wouldn't have to fight her impulses anymore, there would be no hesitation, no remorse ...

'I must admit you gave us a bit of a scare when you went to see Edouard with your story about being hypnotised,' Doctor Marshall continued. 'We knew you were having difficulties accepting this sudden blossoming of your desires but were still unable to resist advances. But I can assure you, everything you did was solely through your own will, although I must confess we did help matters a bit ...'

The last trace of worry and fear vanished to leave Judith feeling angry instead. What exactly did he mean by that? What did he know about what she had been doing? She shifted in her chair uneasily but continued to stare at him defiantly. This time, it was too much for her to take without protesting. She didn't mind him discussing what had happened the previous night, but the rest didn't concern him, that was personal.

'What gives you the right to bring this up?' she finally asked. 'What I have done, even if it was my choice, is not something open to discussion.'

Doctor Marshall stood up and looked at her. 'As Director of this Clinic, anything that goes on between these walls becomes my business.' This time his tone had turned arrogant, almost dictatorial. He walked around the desk slowly, never taking his eyes off her.

Judith held his gaze and kept staring at him. For a moment she thought he was coming towards her but instead he continued to walk to the far end of the room. He stopped by the large black filing cabinet which he unlocked with a key he pulled from the pocket of his white coat. 'I see you might still have some problems coming to terms with the unusual nature of our clinic,' he said, turning his back to Judith. 'But I can assure you we'd be quite happy if you accepted to join our staff permanently.'

'I do not wish to be employed in a place where my every move becomes common knowledge,' Judith replied. She knew that opposing him like this might have severe repercussions, but she really meant what she had said. Maybe working at the Dorchester Clinic wasn't such an enviable job after all. Not if it meant that people would be watching and squealing on her all the time!

'Don't spoil everything, Judith,' Doctor Marshall said placatingly, as if talking to a difficult child. 'We have invested a lot of time and effort in you. We sincerely believed you would enjoy working here.' As he spoke he casually rummaged through the drawer, pulling out a series of videocassettes and looking at their tags before replacing them.

Finally he picked one out, closed the drawer and locked it again. Then he silently walked to the opposite corner of the room and switched on the television set and the video recorder. 'We screen our new members of staff very carefully,' he explained whilst inserting the cassette in the video. 'I must confess that from the start you have given us nothing but hope ...' He turned around and smiled complacently at a fuming Judith, then used the remote control to dim the lights and start the cassette.

Judith turned her chair around to look at the television set. But as her anger grew she decided she wanted to leave instead. She wanted to leave not only this office but the Clinic altogether. It wasn't worth staying anymore. From the very start her time here had been a whirl of confusion. She had spent the best part of her days wondering what would happen next, in addition to having to cope with the stress of her first job.

The rare nights she had managed to find some sleep had been haunted by strange dreams. This suspense had been eating at her long enough. What else lay ahead for her? Somehow she sensed it could only be more confusion and more troubles. Just like it was right now.

She made a move to get up and leave but Doctor

Marshall, now standing behind her, put a firm hand on her shoulder and indicated that she remain seated. She elected to stay just a little longer, her curiosity slowly erasing her fear. What was she about to see? Some informative programme about the services offered by the clinic? She wrung her fingers nervously, her eyes quickly glancing at the door, which she knew wasn't locked. If this video turned out to be some form of brainwashing exercise, she would make a dash for the door so quickly that Marshall wouldn't have time to stop her. She forced herself to remain calm and looked at the screen.

At first she couldn't make out the image, some kind of recording from a security camera, black and white and rather blurred. Then she recognised a naked figure, the back of a woman with a blonde head, standing in the middle of what looked like an office. Then she noticed a man kneeling at the woman's feet. This office looked familiar, but all she could see was the back of those two people and she couldn't make out who they were.

Then there was a switch to a second camera, showing the same scene but from another angle. A similar image appeared, the same man, the same woman, but this time the woman's face was plainly visible. Judith almost choked and stopped breathing, feeling her blood freezing in horror and her life draining out of her when she recognised herself on the video.

Yes, it was her who was standing naked in the middle of the office, with Edouard crawling on the floor around her, covering her thighs with long licks. She saw her own face twisted in a grin of pleasure, her head tilted back and her lips slightly parted.

Judith breathed deeply, trying to calm the disturbing feeling that was slowly creeping up within her. To see herself like this was horrifying, yet fascinating, and although she clearly recognised herself, somehow she also felt she couldn't be this woman, this sensuous creature that stood on her feet whilst being pleasured.

She felt curiously aroused at the sight of herself,

especially by the expression of delight she could read on her face. Of course, she could still remember how good she had felt that morning, but seeing herself being bathed by Edouard's tongue was even better.

'I'm sorry about the poor quality of the image,' Doctor Marshall announced from behind her, 'but I'm afraid the cameras in Edouard's office are getting a bit old.'

But just as he spoke the image changed and turned dark. For a second Judith thought there was nothing else to be seen, but then some adjustment took place and the picture suddenly appeared clearer. She held her breath once again as the same blond woman appeared, standing next to a bed on which lay a naked man.

The first thing she recognised this time was the white patch of the plaster cast over the man's left leg. Then she saw his thick cock, stiff and upright. Suddenly it all fitted in her mind. That blond woman was also her, and although she couldn't see his face, she immediately knew the man on the bed could only be Mike Randall.

She watched silently as the blond woman slowly walked around the bed whilst pulling on the curtain, each of her steps sending her hips swaying lasciviously, and then climb on the bed before falling all over the luscious reclining body. Then the image cut and she saw herself at the head of the bed, straddling his face, her hips sensually gyrating onto his mouth, her hands clasped over her own breasts.

She saw her head was also tilted back in this scene, but then it came up and she looked straight at the camera.

Judith shifted again in her chair. The memory of this evening, coupled with the weird thrill of seeing herself naked and moving so sensuously on the video sent a heat wave building up between her legs, her dew gathering and wetting her panties.

Yet she couldn't understand how she could have looked straight at the camera and not remember anything about it. All she did remember was looking at herself in a large mirror, a rather common-looking mirror . . .

'The mirror . . .' she whispered. Doctor Marshall's

796

hands rested on her shoulders and she felt his head descending towards hers to speak in her ear.

'It was only a mirror from where you were,' he said smugly. 'We could see you from the other side . . .'

Judith kept watching the television set, mesmerised by this vision of herself, this luscious creature now bending down towards the erect phallus to take it in her mouth.

'Look at yourself,' Doctor Marshall continued. 'You enjoyed every moment of it. You still do, even now.'

Judith remained silent. On the television set she could see her own face now looking up and her mouth contracting in an expression of utter delight; she could almost hear her own screams of pleasure. She saw her body tense under the strength of her orgasm then fall, lifeless, over the taut body.

She remembered she had watched herself in the mirror that night, but to see it on video was perhaps even more arousing. Her hand dropped on her knee and she felt its heat through the cotton of her uniform. It didn't take much to trigger her arousal nowadays . . .

But at the same time she felt Doctor Marshall's hands getting heavy on her shoulders. What had he just said? That 'they' had been watching from the other side of the mirror . . . Who were 'they'? And what right did they have to watch her? Even worse, how dare they film her on video?

Before she could ask he let go of her shoulders and seized the remote control. In a matter of seconds the television set was switched off and the bright light came back. Judith blinked a few times, as if awakening from a dream.

'I could show you more,' he said walking back to sit behind his desk. 'But not right now. Suffice to say we know what you've been doing, and that's exactly what we were hoping for. Now all we need is to confirm that you agree to become a permanent member of our staff and then we can fill you in on all the details . . .'

'I don't know,' Judith interrupted. 'I need to think about this.' She felt weak and baffled once again. But this time at least she was thinking clearly. They had watched her, they had filmed her, been with her in her most intimate moments . . .

Curiously, although she was angry she couldn't help a strange feeling of satisfaction emerging slowly in her mind. If she had known she was being watched, perhaps her pleasure would have been even more intense . . .

Yet at the same time she didn't agree to this, and she couldn't let them get away with it.

Doctor Marshall looked up, slightly irritated. 'Think about it?' he said. 'What is there to think about? From what I can see, you have already agreed.'

'I have never agreed to anything,' she protested angrily. 'What happened with Edouard and Mike Randall was a private matter, you have no right to blackmail me like this.'

Doctor Marshall sighed and closed the folder. 'My dear,' he said in his regular business-like tone. 'It is not our intent to blackmail you. All we have done was give you the opportunity to express your sensuality, and it is clear to us that you enjoy physical pleasure tremendously.'

'Give me the opportunity?' she interrupted. 'What do you mean?'

He looked at her in disbelief. 'I thought you understood,' he replied slowly, resting his elbows on his desk. 'Surely, now that you know what we expect from our staff you cannot continue to think that all the encounters you have had in this clinic were fortuitous? It was all meant to happen.'

Judith was baffled, not really knowing what to make of his words. 'It was all planned?' she asked in a whisper. 'What do you mean?'

'From the first day you worked here, we tested your sensuality. Didn't you ever wonder why Robert Harvey had been so, shall we say, "familiar" with you? It was no coincidence. He was instructed to try seducing you, to test your sensuality and your experience with sexual matters. Then you came to us, or rather to Mrs Cox, to

798

seek advice on how to deal with your lustful impulses. We were very proud of you that day; the way you obeyed and displayed yourself for us. I must admit that this wasn't planned at all; you were the one who, voluntarily or not, gave us the opportunity to learn more about your sensuality.'

He paused for a second, his fingers now casually shuffling through the papers on his desk, then resumed his talk without looking at Judith, as if he were talking to himself once again.

'Of course, there were set-backs,' he continued. 'Lady Austin was rather disappointed with you, but since she's a regular patient she was also very understanding. Yet we knew it was only a matter of time before you came to give in to your desires. You did yourself an enormous favour when you went to Edouard's office with your wild accusations about being hypnotised. Thankfully, he was able to make you see that you were wrong and there was nothing to worry about. That's when we decided to set up some sort of "test" for you, to see how far you were ready to go.'

Judith looked up at him in amazement. 'A test?' she asked. 'What sort of test?'

Doctor Marshall took a while before answering her question. He looked at her and shook his head. 'I didn't think I'd have to spell it out for you . . .' he said. 'After what I've just told you I thought you'd be able to figure it out for yourself.'

He stood up again and walked towards her. By now Judith was beyond fear, anger or even surprise. All she knew was that she despised him, she despised the whole lot of them.

'If you must know,' he began, 'we arranged for you to find yourself alone with Mike Randall. We knew he would probably proposition you and we wanted to know if you would give in. Mrs Cox and I were in the next room, watching you through a one-way mirror.'

Judith was filled with dread. Her encounter with Mike Randall had all been staged, she had been set up. Now it all made sense: Ray's story about having to leave, it was all a lie! It had all been planned, a neatly set trap for her to fall into! Until now, Ray was about the only person she had thought she could trust in this place, yet he had betrayed her from the start.

She looked up at Doctor Marshall again.

'So the attendant lied to me?' she asked in a trembling voice. 'You had instructed him to con me into taking the patient out of the bath tub . . .'

Marshall looked surprised. 'The attendant?' he interrupted. 'No, you're wrong there. He was merely a pawn in our plan. We just made sure he would be kept busy on another floor so that he would ask you for your help. We knew he had a tendency to ask nurses for similar favours and we assumed he would ask you that evening. We were lucky it worked on the first attempt.'

'What about Mike Randall?' she asked. 'How much did he know about what was going on.'

'Mister Randall has a friend who had been a patient of ours some time ago. He already knew the staff were allowed to comply as per the patients' requests and when he mentioned it to us we assumed he would probably try something with you that evening. That is when we made sure to discontinue his daily dose of Desquel . . .'

Judith remained silent. She had to admit they were clever, very clever. Doctor Marshall rested his buttocks against his desk and bent down slightly towards her.

'There is no reason for you to be upset,' he said. 'You may feel that we set you up, which we did, in a way, but everything you did was entirely up to you.' His tone became harder, his voice cruel.

'Do you think we were unfair to you? We didn't arrange for you to seduce Nurse Stevens in the store room on the night you were working with her . . . Nor did we arrange for you to pay a visit to Desmond in Physiotherapy . . . And what can I say about young Lisa Baxter? That wasn't planned either, you know . . .'

He bent down further until his hands came resting on

her shoulders and forcefully gripped them, forcing her head up to look at him.

'All we did was wake your senses,' he said slowly. 'And judging from your reaction on these videos we can only assume that you enjoyed every moment of it. Now, you can hardly blame us for that, can you?' He let go of her and sighed.

'Obviously, it's up to you if you wish to remain part of our staff. If you don't, we'll even help you find work elsewhere. But I will ask you to consider this very carefully. You would have nothing to lose, and everything to gain, by staying here.'

He went back to sit behind his desk one more time. Judith didn't have the strength to reply. He was right, of course, but she was so confused by now that she didn't really know what to say.

'I want to think about it,' she whispered. 'I need time.'

Doctor Marshall lay both his hands flat on the desk and looked at her. 'Very well,' he said. 'Mrs Cox will be back tomorrow, she can answer any questions you may have. You'll be dealing with her from now on.'

Judith stood up slowly, feeling this was his way of telling her that he had said all he had to stay and that the matter was closed. 'Thank you,' she whispered one more time before turning around to leave his office.

As she opened the door she heard him get up behind her but she wasn't paying any attention to him anymore. She took only a few steps in the corridor before stopping to lean against the wall.

She was still shaking from what she had just been told, and her flesh was still throbbing from having watched herself on the video. His words were still haunting her as well ... Nothing to lose, everything to gain ... She would be dealing with Mrs Cox from now on ... Indeed there were many advantages to staying here permanently, many wickedly sweet reasons. There was endless pleasure to be discovered, experienced. And there was also Mrs Cox ...

Although Doctor Marshall hadn't mentioned the previous night, Judith was now keenly aware of what to do to get to the woman. She was so close to her goal, how could she give up now? All she had to do was to accept their conditions, which was not so bad in itself, was it?

She pondered it for a few minutes. What did she have to lose? Surely, signing a contract didn't mean she would have to remain here forever, did it? The least she could do was to give it a try. There would always be time to back out, right?

She resolutely walked back to Doctor Marshall's office. He was right: what was there to think about? All that mattered was how she felt. How true. She laughed.

She barged into his office. 'I've decided to . . .' she began. Her words echoed into the empty room and she stopped talking as she realised he was gone. But where could he be? Thinking fast, she knew he hadn't followed her into the corridor, so there was only one way he could have gone.

She opened the door to Mrs Cox's office and let herself in. Her eyes immediately searched the wall where she had found the door to the secret room the previous night. A thin crack was all that betrayed the existence of the secret panel. She walked toward it and pressed her ear against the white surface.

All she could hear were faint noises, objects being shuffled, furniture being moved. To her surprise and disappointment, there were no moans or sighs. If Doctor Marshall was in there, chances were he was alone.

She stood back a few feet and looked at the wall again. For anyone who didn't already know, there was nothing to reveal that the wall was in fact a secret panel, not even now in broad daylight. Judith could barely see the thin crack from where she was standing. Otherwise, it was just a blank wall like any other.

Then she heard sounds, loud laughter, but as she returned to press her ear to the door again she was surprised to realise that those sounds were not coming from there at all. She looked around. The office was the same as it had always been, of course, except for one small detail: a large crack in the wall on the other side of Mrs Cox's desk.

Judith nervously walked across the room towards it. She never would have seen this door if it hadn't been left slightly ajar. Obviously, it could only lead to yet another secret room. But just how many of those secret panels were there? And what did this one conceal?

As she approached, she heard noises coming from the other side. So, this was the place where all the laughter was coming from! Coming closer, she tilted her head slightly and was about to peep through the crack when she felt a presence behind her. A hand came pressing against her mouth and a familiar voice whispered in her ear.

'Do not make any noise,' Doctor Marshall warned. 'These people wouldn't appreciate having spectators.' His other hand came resting on the back of her head and pushed it forward slightly, as if he was forcing her to look inside this secret room.

First she heard another loud laugh and she finally realised this was the voice of the woman to whom Doctor Marshall had been talking earlier. She carefully looked in the room and saw part of a woman's face, and she recognised Marina Stone. Other then that, all she could see was part of the wall hehind the actress, which was covered in red, thick velvet-like wallpaper.

Silently, Doctor Marshall reached forward and grabbed the door to open it a little more. At that moment Judith was grateful that he still had his hand on her mouth, for nothing else could have muffled the cry of surprise that rose in her throat.

It was but a small room, not much bigger than a large closet and without any windows, but with one amazing peculiarity: the floor was completely buried under a thick pile of bank notes, forming a mattress about waist high. There was an incredible amount in there, layers upon layers of freshly minted notes.

Judith then remembered the satchel full of money that

803

Marina had brought with her. No doubt this was meant as the actress's personal contribution to this set-up.

The woman was laying completely naked on top of the notes, the weight of her body causing the thick pile to sink in like a soft cushion. Laying on her back, her hips were writhing sensually and her arms endlessly digging and disappearing underneath the crisp layers of money. Soon she began grabbing handfuls of notes and covering her body with them. Then she parted and closed her legs a few times until they disappeared under the money as well.

Judith watched silently, suddenly feeling a warm sensation invading her loins. The sight of Marina's white naked flesh moving amidst this sea of money was compelling, as was the expression of pleasure on the woman's face. She tried to imagine what it would feel like to simply lay on top of this fortune, to feel the rough paper brush against her naked flesh, to slowly be engulfed by thousands of bank notes. Yet even her wild imagination couldn't conceive of such a thing. She would have to experience it for herself.

At this moment she realised that Marina wasn't alone in there. Next to the actress an enormous pile started to move. The woman turned onto her side to face it, bank notes sensually slipping off her naked body. She laughed again and her hands dug deep into the pile, as if frantically searching for something.

Soon an arm appeared, then a leg, and finally a head. A man slowly came out from underneath the bank notes, a man Judith immediately recognised as Robert Harvey. He laughed in turn and his naked body emerged some more. Soon he shook himself out completely and came to cover Marina.

Together they writhed in this sea of money, their limbs tangling and their hips pressing against the other's. They laughed endlessly, kissing and caressing each other, their hands still gathering bundles of notes and digging until they both disappeared.

At that moment Doctor Marshall reached out once

again and closed the door in front of Judith's face. She turned to look at him, aroused and puzzled. He smiled smugly.

'As I already told you,' he whispered, 'you have nothing to lose and everything to gain.'

He put one hand on her back and swiftly ushered her back towards his office. As they reached the door Judith stopped and turned around one more time, staring at the empty wall, unable to erase from her mind the image of what she knew it concealed. She turned to Doctor Marshall once again.

'We have to cater to every taste,' he said simply.

Chapter Eighteen

*T*he squeaky noise from the door of Judith's locker seemed louder than usual this morning. Since there wasn't anybody else in the room at this early hour, it sounded even worse. Judith opened and closed the door a few times, examining the hinges and trying to figure out which one needed to be oiled. This noise had been getting on her nerves for a little while now, but there wasn't anything she could do about it, was there? She opened the door one more time and shrugged as she sat on the long bench in front of her locker.

She was alone in the large room, alone with her thoughts. She had to see Mrs Cox before starting her shift, and she still didn't know what she was going to say to the woman.

When she had left to go home the previous night she had already decided that she wanted to stay on at the Dorchester Clinic permanently. But now, deep within her, something was holding her back; some nagging doubt persisting in her mind.

What would Mrs Cox say to her? Yesterday, Doctor Marshall had said that the supervisor would answer any questions Judith might have, and in the young nurse's mind there were hundreds of questions still without answers. And she felt she needed to know more before she could reach a final decision.

It was now clear to her that intimate contact between the staff and the patients was definitely not frowned upon; it was quite the opposite, really. The same was true of members of staff themselves. But how were the patients told about this particular aspect of the Clinic's care? And how did they go about asking for it? Did they simply have to ask for a nurse to pleasure them, the same way others would ask for a sleeping pill?

And so far Judith knew about the unusual set-up down in physiotherapy, and the two secret rooms adjoining Mrs Cox's office. But were there other rooms that also served similar purposes? Rooms made especially for the pursuit of pleasure? If so, where were they, and what were they like? Perhaps she would be told this very morning? The thought of finding out more sent a thrilling shiver down her spine.

When Doctor Marshall had finally confirmed the true nature of the Special Care Programme, Judith had thought she knew everything. But now she realised she hardly knew anything! Surely there was more to learn about, to experience; other sources of sweet pleasure to discover . . .

And soon she would find herself in Mrs Cox's office again. The last time she had seen her superior was in the secret room, a couple of nights ago. The woman had been in a rather embarrassing position. Would she mention it to Judith today or act like it had never happened? Would she be embarrassed? Maybe; maybe not. Doctor Marshall hadn't been embarrassed at all . . .

Yet Judith was herself somewhat embarrassed, although she was also eager to talk about it. What she wanted especially was to return to the secret room and possibly get to see what else there was that she might not have noticed the other night; perhaps even convince Mrs Cox to give her some kind of demonstration. This time Judith knew exactly what to do to get to the woman. This time she wouldn't let her walk out.

She finished doing up her shoelaces and checked her watch. Another forty-five minutes before going on duty. She decided to go up to the seventh floor and wait by Mrs Cox's office if the woman wasn't in already.

'Good morning!' said a cheerful voice behind her. 'Are you just coming in or are you finishing?'

Judith looked at her colleague. 'Just coming in,' she said. This was a girl she had never seen before, a pretty nurse with shoulder-length brown locks, a round face and a broad smile.

'I'm on my way home myself!' the girl continued in a loud voice, holding out her hand. 'I'm Susan. I just started working here. Last night was my first shift. Fancy starting a new job and being assigned to a night shift right away! Mind you, I don't think it can get any worse than that!'

She shook Judith's hand enthusiastically, her head shaking as well and sending her brown locks bouncing up and down at the same time. Then she opened a locker diagonally opposite from Judith's and sat on the bench to untie her shoes.

'We were ever so busy last night!' she continued. 'I couldn't leave the station to go for my break so my colleague said I could go home early this morning instead. Isn't that nice of her? Everybody here is very nice, I find. Anyway, we had this patient in room 427, right? She had an operation yesterday and initially she was fine, but then something went wrong and we ended up having to send her back for surgery in the middle of the night! Poor darling! Do you help out in the operating theatre? I used to, a long time ago, but I haven't done it in a couple of years now. What's it like in this place? Are the surgeons nice or are they rude bastards like the ones I used to work with? Mind you, at the end of the day all that really matters is that they do good work, right? Doesn't really make a difference how they treat the nurses . . .'

The girl talked constantly, asking questions and answering them right away without even looking at

Judith, seemingly never having to stop to catch her breath.

Still sitting on the other side of the bench, Judith just stared at her without really paying attention to what she was saying, but feeling out of breath just listening to her!

Susan was extremely friendly, perhaps even too friendly. She spoke in a loud voice, grinning all the time and giggling at everything she said. As she kept on speaking she stood up and began to undress, quickly rolling her white uniform into a ball and carelessly stuffing it into a large canvas bag.

She went on and on as she peeled her panties off, babbling about the place she used to work, her car, her family, and all sorts of other things Judith didn't really want to hear about. Yet there was something about this new nurse that compelled her to keep listening and looking at her; something about this mindless chatter that was strangely appealing.

As Susan took off her bra, Judith noticed her breasts were rather small but very round and firm, the nipples small and pink and looking delicious. In fact, the slender silhouette was quite attractive. The limbs were sinewy and slightly more muscular than average, but the skin was very pale and dotted with freckles. Indeed there was something youthful and rather refreshing about this new member of staff.

At this moment Judith began to wonder whether Susan knew about the Special Care Programme yet. That was unlikely. If indeed she had only started work the previous night, chances were she hadn't even had her "test" yet.

Judith's imagination started running wild once again and she wondered who would be assigned to try seducing Susan. Robert Harvey? That was unlikely. Somehow Judith could sense he would not be her type. She couldn't picture them together.

Obviously, the directors would choose carefully and decide what type of person a girl like Susan would preferably fancy before assigning anyone to this delicate

809

task. Perhaps their plan was already in motion . . . Someone who had worked with her during the night shift might have tried to make a pass at her or began to flirt. Maybe nothing had happened yet, especially if they had been very busy through the night. However, sooner or later, Susan would be in for a rude, albeit delicious, awakening.

And in light of what she knew, Judith couldn't help being amused at the thought that the poor girl probably didn't have a clue as to what was expected of her now that she was working at the Dorchester Clinic. She was an attractive nurse, very friendly, even if a bit loud, and Judith couldn't help but think that the Clinic had made a good choice. This was a nice addition to the staff. Certain people might be put off by her constant chatter, but as Doctor Marshall had said, they needed to cater to every taste and some people might find her mindless talk quite attractive.

Right now the new nurse was standing naked just a few feet from Judith; having fished a bath towel out of a large plastic bag she was now searching for something in yet another bag.

'Now where's my soap?' she asked aloud. 'Ah! Here it is . . . Well, as I was saying, the salary they offered here was much better and I was looking forward to moving to London . . .'

As she kept on talking, a wicked thought rose in Judith's mind. In a way, Susan was not unlike herself when she had started to work at the Dorchester Clinic: trusting and innocent and probably not suspecting anything. And right now, Judith could remember a certain morning when she had been cornered by Tania and Jo in the very same shower room Susan was about to enter . . .

The memory of that morning almost made her laugh. She remembered how scared she had been, but now that she knew better, things looked very different indeed. She could even understand why Tania and Jo had set out to seduce her that morning.

Susan continued her mindless babble as she pushed

810

the last strands of her untamed hair underneath a shocking pink shower cap. She didn't seem shy at all, standing completely naked and talking to Judith as if they were long-time friends. The monologue continued for a while, then her naked figure slowly made its way to the shower room.

Judith stood up and followed a few paces behind her, pretending to be interested in everything the new girl had to say, when in fact her attention was focused on something completely different.

Her heartbeat accelerated with the excitement of what she was about to do. She felt a weird exhilaration, unlike how she had felt the night she had pounced on Jo in the store room. Today she meant to seduce, to give the new recruit a taste of what was yet to come but without necessarily scaring her. She wasn't seeking revenge this time.

Or was she? Was this her way of getting back at everyone for everything they had put her through? Did she want to inflict on poor Susan the same ordeal she had lived? Not really. All she knew was that there was a weird satisfaction to be gained out of giving the new nurse a taste of things to come. She didn't mean any harm, she just wanted to get to know her new colleague a little better. Who knew, maybe Susan would enjoy it?

Right now Susan had stopped talking whilst she adjusted the temperature of the water, seemingly unaware that Judith wasn't very far behind her. Soon the shower room was filled with steam and Judith stood immobile by the entrance, wondering if the girl knew she was being watched.

The constant chatter had changed to loud, grossly out-of-tune singing, slaughtering a song Judith couldn't recognise. Already the fruity aroma of Susan's soap floated in the air. This scene wasn't very different from that fateful morning.

That's when Judith decided to step forward. She walked up to Susan and stood by her for a few seconds before the new nurse even noticed her presence.

'Oh! You're here!' the girl said loudly. 'Be careful, you might get wet!'

Judith sensed Susan was just about to resume her tedious monologue and immediately pressed her hand against the girl's mouth. Her other arm snaked around the naked waist and grabbed it tightly.

In Susan's eyes she read surprise but didn't feel the wet body trying to wriggle out of her grasp. This disconcerted her somewhat. She would have expected her victim to protest violently but it seemed Susan was too surprised to even think of it.

She let her hand slip and uncovered a gaping mouth. The lips twitched a few times but no sound came out. Her other hand simultaneously slid along the rounded buttocks and caressed them lightly.

'What are you doing?' Susan asked after a while. 'This is a bit cheeky . . .'

Judith put her hand back on the girl's mouth. 'Shut up!' she ordered. 'Enough with all this nonsense!' She pushed the girl back against the wall and pressed her clothed body against her, placing both hands flat on either side of the girl's waist to stop her from going anywhere.

This time Susan didn't say anything, but Judith could see that the look of surprise had been replaced by one of fear. She burst out laughing. This was wickedly exciting.

'What's wrong, love? You're not used to sharing a shower with somebody else?' But before Susan could reply Judith had taken hold of her mouth and invaded it with her tongue.

She tried to imagine what could be going through the new nurse's head at that very moment, thinking it would most probably be worry or even fear. Yet she knew it wouldn't be entirely fair to scare the poor girl unduly so she let her hands wander over the wet skin to see how Susan would react.

Cupping the small breasts with both hands, she caressed them gently, toying with the nipples which readily grew stiff between her thumb and forefinger.

812

Susan let out a small cry and looked down at her breasts as if surprised to see that they would react to Judith's touch.

'What are you doing?' she asked again, her voice now a trembling whisper.

'What does it look like I'm doing?' Judith replied softly. She bowed her head and took one of the nipples in her mouth, sucking it greedily.

Susan started trembling and sobbed loudly. 'I'm not sure I like this,' she said as Judith switched to the other nipple. 'This isn't very proper, you know . . . Are you one of those lesbians? I don't know any lesbians . . . What are you going to do to me? Why won't you let me go? I promise I won't tell anybody! I really don't like this . . .'

'Shut up!' Judith repeated wearily. 'Just shut that big mouth of yours OK?' She was getting somewhat angry that Susan wasn't struggling but didn't seem to be aroused either. And most of all, she didn't want her to start talking again!

Her hand strayed and came down to fondle the girl's thighs. She heard Susan gasp a few times but she didn't say anything. By now the terrorised nurse was pushing back against the wall, her hands flat against the ceramic tiles, seemingly trying to push back further still in a vain effort to escape.

Judith was rapidly growing excited, her mouth discovering the slightly bitter taste of the warm, wet skin, her hands and her cheeks smoothly gliding along each slender curve. She lightly brushed the soft vulva and felt it getting hot and moist under her fingertips. Soon its heady aroma floated to her nostrils and only served to enhance her desire.

'Oh!' Susan whined. 'Why are you doing this! Please stop!' Judith slowly slid down until her knees came to touch the wet ceramic floor. By now her uniform was soaked but she didn't mind. Above her, Susan was shaking with fear, yet Judith knew this would change soon. Once she began toying with the tiny bud that was still hiding among the sinewy folds, once she took it in

813

her mouth and gently sucked on it, then Susan wouldn't mind so much anymore . . .

Already she could feel the little shaft rearing under her fingers, growing stiff and swollen, and she let her mouth slide towards it, her tongue coming out in anticipation of the moment . . .

'Get up! Now!' a voice shouted behind her.

Judith froze and slowly turned her head towards the entrance of the shower room. A feeling of panic seized her as she recognised Mrs Cox. Curiously, she also felt like laughing at the irony of the situation, thinking how amazing it was that the same scene should repeat itself almost identically. Yet at the same time she knew she would be in big trouble.

She felt tempted to continue what she was doing, just to see what the supervisor would do, but she decided it was too risky at this point and slowly stood up. Once again she felt shameful, keenly aware that she had stepped over the line. Quickly glancing towards Susan, she still read the same surprised look in the brown eyes. Then she turned towards Mrs Cox.

'Dry yourself and meet me in my office right away!' the supervisor ordered dryly, handing her a towel.

Judith swiftly made her way out of the shower room, her uniform soaking. She felt betrayed by Mrs Cox who had walked in on her just as she was about to get Susan to react to her caresses. Although she had been looking forward to seeing her again, this wasn't exactly what she had in mind. And, of course, she knew Mrs Cox would now probably go to the new nurse and offer to release her . . .

This wasn't fair at all. She should be the one about to be pleasured right now, she had earned it. How much longer would she have to wait for her reward, how many schemes would she have to come up with to finally be allowed feel her supervisor's slim fingers torturing her tender flesh into submission?

She held on to the frame around the entrance of the shower room before stepping out, afraid of slipping once her wet shoe touched the tile floor. This was yet another set back, she would probably have to wait even longer now.

But then she heard Mrs Cox talking to Susan.

'I'm really sorry about this,' the woman said to the new girl. 'She will be severely punished . . .'

Judith smiled, knowing she had already won.